# DANGEROUS VISIONS

Lucian of Samosah - Trip to moon w/ water spout.
Gulliver's Travels - 1726 - Anti scientific - Landmark
Frankenstein - 1818 - Anti-Scientific - Landmark

Edgar Allen Poe → Jules Verne (1828-1905)    H.G. Wells (1866-1946)

DATE important to Science Fiction -      Name where Hugo Award came from
   1926 - Hugo Gernsback - Amazing Stories - 1st entire Sci-fi Series - schlock
   1938 - John W. Campbell Jr. - Astounding Stories - socially effective
   1945 - 1st Atomic Bomb - An influence                              Sci-fo.
"New wave of Science Fiction during 1960's.

William Gibson - Neuromancer -.
Women Sci-Fi writers on the increase - 40+
            3 ways sci-fi poses possibilities to us.
               1. Straight forward extrapolation
               2. Sheer speculation
               3. Alternative models

Books by Harlan Ellison

- ■ Web of the City (1958)
- ■ The Deadly Streets (1958)
  The Sound of a Scythe (1960)
  A Touch of Infinity (1960)
  Children of the Streets (1961)
- ■ Gentleman Junkie *and other stories of the hung-up generation* (1961)
- ● Memos from Purgatory (1961)
- ■ Spider Kiss (1961)
  Ellison Wonderland (1962)
- ● Paingod *and other delusions* (1965)
- ■ I Have No Mouth & I Must Scream (1967)
  Doomsman (1967)
- ▲ Dangerous Visions [Editor] (1967)
  From the Land of Fear (1967)
  Nightshade & Damnations: *the finest stories of Gerald Kersh* [Editor] (1968)
- ■ Love Ain't Nothing but Sex Misspelled (1968)
  The Beast that Shouted Love at the Heart of the World (1969)
- ■ The Glass Teat *essays of opinion on television* (1970)
  Over the Edge (1970)
- ■ Partners in Wonder *sf collaborations with 14 other wild talents* (1971)
  Alone Against Tomorrow *stories of alienation in speculative fiction* (1971)
- ▼ Again, Dangerous Visions [Editor] (1972)
  All the Sounds of Fear [British publication only] (1973)
  The Time of the Eye [British publication only] (1974)
  Approaching Oblivion (1974)
  The Starlost #1: Phoenix Without Ashes [with Edward Bryant] (1975)
  Deathbird Stories (1975)
- ■ The Other Glass Teat *further essays of opinion on television* (1975)
- ■ No Doors, No Windows (1975)
  Strange Wine (1978)
  The Book of Ellison [Edited by Andrew Porter] (1978)
  The Illustrated Harlan Ellison [Edited by Byron Preiss] (1978)
  The Fantasies of Harlan Ellison (1979)
  All the Lies That Are My Life (1980)
- ▲ Shatterday (1980)
  Stalking the Nightmare (1982)


- ▲ Available in Berkley Books editions.
- ▼ Forthcoming in Berkley Books editions.
- ■ Available in Ace Books editions.
- ● Forthcoming in Ace Books editions.

# DANGEROUS VISIONS

33 ORIGINAL STORIES EDITED
WITH INTRODUCTIONS BY

# HARLAN ELLISON

Illustrations by Leo and Diane Dillon

BERKLEY BOOKS, NEW YORK

*All of the characters in this book
are fictitious, and any resemblance
to actual persons, living or dead,
is purely coincidental.*

This Berkley book contains the complete text of the
original hardcover edition.

DANGEROUS VISIONS

A Berkley Book / published by arrangement with
Doubleday & Company, Inc.

PRINTING HISTORY
Doubleday edition published 1967
Berkley trade paperback edition / September 1983

ISBN: 0-425-06176-0

A BERKLEY BOOK ® TM 757,375
Berkley Books are published by The Berkley Publishing Group,
200 Madison Avenue, New York, New York 10016.
The name "BERKLEY" and the stylized "B" with design are trademarks
belonging to Berkley Publishing Corporation.
PRINTED IN THE UNITED STATES OF AMERICA

Men learn from other men what they know of themselves, of the world in which they *must* live, and of the world in which they would *like* to live.

This book is dedicated with love, respect and admiration
to LEO & DIANE DILLON

who painstakingly, out of friendship, showed the Editor that black is black, white is white, and that goodness can come from either; but never from gray.

And to their son, LIONEL III
with a silent prayer that *his* world will not resemble *our* world.

# FOREWORD 1—THE SECOND REVOLUTION

## by Isaac Asimov

Today—on the very day that I write this—I received a phone call from the New York *Times*. They are taking an article I mailed them three days ago. Subject: the colonization of the Moon.

And they *thanked* me!

Leaping Luna, how times have changed!

Thirty years ago, when I started writing science fiction (I was very young at the time), the colonization of the Moon was strictly a subject for pulp magazines with garish covers. It was don't-tell-me-you-believe-all-that-junk literature. It was don't-fill-your-mind-with-all-that-mush literature. Most of all, it was escape literature!

Sometimes I think about that with a kind of disbelief. Science fiction was escape literature. We were *escaping*. We were turning from such practical problems as stickball and homework and fist fights in order to enter a never-never land of population explosions, rocket ships, lunar exploration, atomic bombs, radiation sickness and polluted atmosphere.

Wasn't that great? Isn't it delightful the way we young escapers received our just reward? All the great, mind-cracking, hopeless problems of today, we worried about twenty full years before anyone else did. How's *that* for escaping?

But now you can colonize the Moon inside the good, gray pages of the New York *Times;* and not as a piece of science fiction at all, but as a sober analysis of a hardheaded situation.

This represents an important change, and one which has an immediate relationship to the book you now hold in your hand. Let me explain!

I became a science fiction writer in 1938 just at the time John W. Campbell, Jr., was revolutionizing the field with the simple requirement that science fiction writers stand firmly on the borderline between science and literature.

Pre-Campbell science fiction all too often fell into one of two classes. They were either no-science or they were all-science. The no-science stories were adventure stories in which a periodic word of Western jargon was erased and replaced with an equivalent word of space jargon. The writer could be innocent of scientific knowledge, for all he needed was a vocabulary of technical jargon which he could throw in indiscriminately.

The all-science stories were, on the other hand, populated exclusively by scientist-caricatures. Some were mad scientists, some were absent-minded scientists, some were noble scientists. The only thing they had in common was their penchant for expounding their theories. The mad ones screeched them, the absent-minded ones mumbled them, the noble ones declaimed them, but all lectured at insufferable length. The story was a thin cement caked about the long monologues in an attempt to give the illusion that those long monologues had some point.

To be sure, there were exceptions. Let me mention, for instance, "A Martian Odyssey" by Stanley G. Weinbaum (who, tragically, died of cancer at the age of thirty-six). It appeared in the July 1934 issue of *Wonder Stories*—a perfect Campbellesque story four years before Campbell introduced his revolution.

Campbell's contribution was that he insisted that the exception become the rule. There had to be real science *and* real story, with neither one dominating the other. He didn't always get what he wanted, but he got it often enough to initiate what old-timers think of as the Golden Age of Science Fiction.

To be sure, each generation has its own Golden Age—but the Campbellesque Golden Age happens to be mine, and when *I* say "Golden Age" I mean that one. Thank goodness, I managed to get into the field just in time to have my stories contribute in their way (and a pretty good way it was too, and the heck with false modesty) to that Golden Age.

Yet all Golden Ages carry within themselves the seeds of their own destruction and after it is over you can look back and unerringly locate those seeds. (Lovely, lovely hindsight! How sweet it is to prophesy what has already happened. You're never wrong!)

In this case, Campbell's requirement for real science *and* real stories invited a double nemesis, one for the real science and one for the real stories.

With *real* science, stories came to sound more and more plausible and, indeed, *were* more and more plausible. Authors, striving for realism, described computers and rockets and nuclear weapons that were very like what computers and rockets and nuclear weapons came to be in a matter of a single decade. As a result, the real life of the Fifties and Sixties is very much like the Campbellesque science fiction of the Forties.

Yes, the science fiction writer of the Forties went far beyond anything we have in real life today. We writers did not merely aim for the Moon or send unmanned rockets toward Mars; we streaked through the Galaxy in faster-than-light drives. However, all our far-space adventures were based on the way of thought that today permeates NASA.

And because today's real life so resembles day-before-yesterday's fantasy, the old-time fans are restless. Deep within, whether they admit it or not, is a feeling of disappointment and even outrage that the outer world has invaded their private domain. They feel the loss of a "sense of wonder" because what was once truly confined to "wonder" has now become prosaic and mundane.

Furthermore, the hope that Campbellesque science fiction would storm upward in an increasingly lofty spiral of readership and respectability somehow was not fulfilled. Indeed, an effect rather unforeseen made itself evident. The new generation of potential science fiction readers found all the science fiction they needed in the newspapers and general magazines and many no longer experienced an irresistible urge to turn to the specialized science fiction magazines.

It happened, therefore, that after a short-lived spurt in the first half of the 1950s, when all the golden dreams seemed to be coming true for the science fiction writer and publisher, there was a recession and the magazines are not more prosperous now than they were in the 1940s. Not even the launching of Sputnik I could stay that recession; rather it accelerated it.

So much for the nemesis brought on by real science. And real story?

As long as science fiction was the creaky medium it was in the

Twenties and Thirties, good writing was not required. The science fiction writers of the time were safe, reliable sources; while they lived, they would write science fiction, since anything else required better technique and was beyond them. (I hasten to say there were exceptions and Murray Leinster springs to the mind as one of them.)

The authors developed by Campbell, however, had to write reasonably well or Campbell turned them down. Under the lash of their own eagerness they grew to write better and better. Eventually and inevitably, they found they had become good enough to earn more money elsewhere and their science fiction output declined.

Indeed, the two dooms of the Golden Age worked hand in hand to a certain extent. A considerable number of the Golden Age authors followed the essence of science fiction in its journey from fiction into fact. Men such as Poul Anderson, Arthur C. Clarke, Lester del Rey, and Clifford D. Simak took to writing science fact.

*They* didn't change, really; it was the medium that changed. The subjects they had once dealt with in fiction (rocketry, space travel, life on other worlds, etc.) shifted from fiction to fact, and the authors were carried along in the shift. Naturally, every page of non-science fiction written by these authors meant one page less of science fiction.

Lest some knowledgeable reader begin, at this point, to mutter sarcastic comments under his breath, I had better admit, at once and quite openly, that of all the Campbellesque crew, I possibly made the change most extremely. Since Sputnik I went up and America's attitude toward science was (at least temporarily) revolutionized, I have, as of this moment, published fifty-eight books, of which only nine could be classified as fiction.

Truly, I am ashamed, embarrassed and guilt-ridden, for no matter where I go and what I do, I shall always consider myself as a science fiction writer *first*. Yet if the New York *Times* asks me to colonize the Moon and if *Harper's* asks me to explore the edge of the Universe, how can I possibly refuse? These topics are the essence of my lifework.

And in my own defense, let me say that I have not entirely abandoned science fiction in its strictest sense either. The March 1967 issue of *Worlds of If* (on the stands as I write) contains a novelette of mine entitled "Billiard Ball."

But never mind me, back to science fiction itself. . . .

What was science fiction's response to this double doom? Clearly the field had to adjust, and it did. Straight Campbellesque material could still be written, but it could no longer form the backbone of the field. Reality encroached too closely upon it.

Again there was a science-fictional revolution in the early Sixties, marked most clearly perhaps in the magazine *Galaxy* under the guidance of its editor, Frederik Pohl. Science receded and modern fictional technique came to the fore.

The accent moved very heavily toward style. When Campbell started his revolution, the new writers who came into the field carried with them the aura of the university, of science and engineering, of slide rule and test tube. Now the new authors who enter the field bear the mark of the poet and the artist, and somehow carry with them the aura of Greenwich Village and the Left Bank.

Naturally, no evolutionary cataclysm can be carried through without some pretty widespread extinctions. The upheaval that ended the Cretaceous Era wiped out the dinosaurs, and the change-over from silent movies to talkies eliminated a horde of posturing mountebanks.

So it was with science fiction revolutions.

Read through the list of authors in any science fiction magazine of the early Thirties, then read through the list in a science fiction magazine of the early Forties. There is an almost complete change-over, for a vast extinction had taken place and few could make the transition. (Among the few who could were Edmond Hamilton and Jack Williamson.)

Between the Forties and the Fifties there was little change. The Campbellesque period was still running its course and this shows that the mere lapse of ten years is not in itself necessarily crucial.

But now compare the authors of a magazine in the early Fifties with a magazine today. There has been another change-over. Again some have survived, but a whole flood of bright young authors of the new school has entered.

This Second Revolution is not as clean-cut and obvious as the First Revolution had been. One thing present now that was not present then is the science fiction anthology, and the presence of the anthology blurs the transition.

Each year sees a considerable number of anthologies published, and always they draw their stories from the past. In the anthologies of the Sixties there is always a heavy representation of the stories of the Forties and Fifties, so that in these anthologies the Second Revolution has not yet taken place.

That is the reason for the anthology you now hold in your hands. It is not made up of stories of the past. It consists of stories written *now,* under the influence of the Second Revolution. It was precisely Harlan Ellison's intention to make this anthology represent the field as it now is, rather than as it then was.

If you look at the table of contents you will find a number of authors who were prominent in the Campbellesque period—Lester del Rey, Poul Anderson, Theodore Sturgeon, and so on. They are writers who are skillful enough and imaginative enough to survive the Second Revolution. You will also find, however, authors who are the products of the Sixties and who know only the new era. They include Larry Niven, Norman Spinrad, Roger Zelazny and so on.

It is idle to suppose that the new will meet universal approval. Those who remember the old, and who find this memory inextricably intertwined with their own youths, will mourn the past, of course.

I will not hide from you the fact that *I* mourn the past. (I am being given full leeway to say what I want, and I intend to be frank.) It is the First Revolution that produced me and it is the First Revolution that I keep in my heart.

That is why, when Harlan asked me to write a story for this anthology, I backed away. I felt that any story I wrote would strike a false note. It would be too sober, too respectable, and, to put it bluntly, too darned *square*. So I have agreed to write a foreword instead; a sober, respectable and utterly square foreword.

And I invite those of you who are not square, and who feel the Second Revolution to be *your* revolution, to meet examples of the new science fiction as produced by the new (and some of the old) masters. You will find here the field at its most daring and experimental; may you therefore be appropriately stimulated and affected!

*Isaac Asimov*
February 1967

# FOREWORD 2—HARLAN AND I

## by Isaac Asimov

This book is Harlan Ellison. It is Ellison-drenched and Ellison-permeated. I admit that thirty-two other authors (including myself in a way) have contributed, but Harlan's introduction and his thirty-two prefaces surround the stories and embrace them and soak them through with the rich flavor of his personality.

So it is only fitting that I tell the story of how I came to meet Harlan.

The scene is a World Science Fiction Convention a little over a decade ago. I had just arrived at the hotel and I made for the bar at once. I don't drink, but I knew that the bar would be where everybody was. They were indeed all there, so I yelled a greeting and everyone yelled back at me.

Among them, however, was a youngster I had never seen before: a little fellow with sharp features and the livest eyes I ever saw. Those live eyes were now focused on me with something that I can only describe as worship.

He said, "Are you Isaac Asimov?" And in his voice was awe and wonder and amazement.

I was rather pleased, but I struggled hard to retain a modest demeanor. "Yes, I am," I said.

"You're not kidding? You're *really* Isaac Asimov?" The words have not yet been invented that would describe the ardor and reverence with which his tongue caressed the syllables of my name.

I felt as though the least I could do would be to rest my hand upon his head and bless him, but I controlled myself. "Yes, I am," I said, and by now my smile was a fatuous thing, nauseating to behold. *"Really, I am."*

"Well, I think you're—" he began, still in the same tone of voice, and for a split second he paused, while I listened and the audience held its breath. The youngster's face shifted in that split second into an expression of utter contempt and he finished the sentence with supreme indifference, "—a *nothing!*"

The effect, for me, was that of tumbling over a cliff I had not known was there, and landing flat on my back. I could only blink foolishly while everyone present roared with laughter.

The youngster was Harlan Ellison, you see, and I had never met him before and didn't know his utter irreverence. But everyone else there knew him and they had waited for innocent me to be neatly poniarded—and I had been.

By the time I struggled back to something like equilibrium, it was long past time for any possible retort. I could only carry on as best I might, limping and bleeding, and grieving that I had been hit when I wasn't looking and that not a man in the room had had the self-denial to warn me and give up the delight of watching me get mine.

Fortunately, I believe in forgiveness, and I made up my mind to forgive Harlan completely—just as soon as I had paid him back with interest.

Now you must understand that Harlan is a giant among men in courage, pugnacity, loquacity, wit, charm, intelligence—indeed, in everything but height.

He is not actually extremely tall. In fact, not to put too fine a point on it, he is quite short; shorter, even, than Napoleon. And instinct told me, as I struggled up from disaster, that this young man, who was now introduced to me as the well-known fan, Harlan Ellison, was a trifle sensitive on that subject. I made a mental note of that.

The next day at this convention I was on the platform, introducing notables and addressing a word of kindly love to each as I did so. I kept my eye on Harlan all this time, however, for he was sitting right up front (where else?).

As soon as his attention wandered, I called out his name suddenly. He stood up, quite surprised and totally unprepared, and I leaned forward and said, as sweetly as I could:

"Harlan, stand on the fellow next to you, so that people can see you."

And while the audience (a much larger one this time) laughed fiendishly, I forgave Harlan and we have been good friends ever since.*

Isaac Asimov
February 1967

* IMPERTINENT EDITORIAL FOOTNOTE: While I am fully aware it is unbecoming for a young man to disagree publicly with his elders, my unbounded admiration and unflagging friendship for the Good Doctor, Asimov, compels me to add this footnote to his second Foreword—strictly in the interests of historically accurate reportage, an end to which he has been determinedly devoted for at least twice as long as I've been living. There is an unsavory tone inherent in the remark I am alleged to have made to Dr. Asimov, noted above. This tone of contempt was by no means present at the time, nor at any time before or since. Any man who would speak *to* Asimov or *about* Asimov with contempt is, himself, *beneath* contempt. My recollection of the incident, however, is perhaps a bit fresher. (Only a cad would remark on the faulty memories and colored nostalgia of our aging Giants In The Field.) I didn't say, "—you're a—*nothing!*" I said, "You aren't so much." I grant you, the difference is a subtle one; I was being an adolescent snot; but after reading all those Galaxy-spanning novels about heroic men of heroic proportions, I had been expecting a living computer, mightily thewed, something of a Conan with the cunning of Lije Bailey. Instead, here was this perfectly wonderful, robust, Skylark-shaped Jew with a Mel Brooks delivery and a Wally Cox bowtie. I have never been disappointed by an Asimov story, and I have never been disappointed by Asimov the man. But on that initial occasion, my dreams were somewhat greater than the reality, and the remark was more reflex than malice. Incidentally, Napoleon was 5'2". I am 5'5". This is the first time, I believe, that Dr. Asimov's facts have been in error. I hope he will be able to live with this; I'm able to live with my height.

—*Harlan Ellison*

# TABLE OF CONTENTS

# THIRTY-TWO SOOTHSAYERS

What you hold in your hands is more than a book. If we are lucky, it is a revolution.

This book, all two hundred and thirty-nine thousand words of it, the largest anthology of speculative fiction ever published of *all original* stories, and easily one of the largest of *any* kind, was constructed along specific lines of revolution. It was intended to shake things up. It was conceived out of a need for new horizons, new forms, new styles, new challenges in the literature of our times. If it was done properly, it will provide these new horizons and styles and forms and challenges. If not, it is still one helluva good book full of entertaining stories.

There is a coterie of critics, analysts and readers who contend that "mere entertainment" is not enough, that there must be pith and substance to a story, a far-reaching message or philosophy or superabundance of superscience. While there is certainly merit in their contentions, it has all too often become the *raison d'être* of the fiction, this sententious preoccupation with *saying things*. While we can no more suggest that fairy tales are the loftiest level to which modern fiction should attain than that the theory should dwarf the plot, we would be forced to opt for the former rather than the latter, were we chained down with the threat of bamboo shoots under the fingernails.

Happily, this book seems to hit directly in the mid-target area. Each story is almost obstinately entertaining. But each one is filled with ideas as well. Not merely run-of-the-pulps ideas you've read a hundred times before, but fresh and daring ideas; in their way, dangerous visions.

Why all this chatter about entertainment versus ideas? In an introduction of some length, to a book of even greater length? Why not let the stories speak for themselves? Because . . . though it may waddle like a duck, quack like a duck, look like a duck and go steady with ducks, it need not necessarily be a duck. This is a collection of ducks that will turn into swans before your very eyes. These are stories so purely entertaining that it seems inconceivable the impetus for their being written was an appeal for ideas. But such was the case, and as you wonderingly witness these ducks of entertainment change into swans of ideas, you will be treated to a thirty-three-story demonstration of "the new thing"—the *nouvelle vague,* if you will, of speculative writing.

And therein, gentle readers, lies the revolution.

There are those who say speculative fiction began with Lucian of Samosata or Aesop. Sprague de Camp, in his excellent *Science Fiction Handbook* (Hermitage House, 1953) offers Lucian, Virgil, Homer, Heliodoros, Apuleius, Aristophanes, Thucydides, and calls Plato "the second Greek 'father of science fiction.'" Groff Conklin, in *The Best of Science Fiction* (Crown, 1946), suggests the historical origins can be traced without difficulty from Dean Swift's Gulliver, from Frank R. Stockton's "The Great War Syndicate," from Richard Adams Locke's "The Moon Hoax," from Edward Bellamy's "Looking Backward," from Verne, from Arthur Conan Doyle, from H. G. Wells and Edgar Allan Poe. In the classic anthology *Adventures in Time and Space* (Random House, 1946), Healy and McComas opt for the great astronomer Johannes Kepler. My own personal seminal influence for the fantasy that is the basis of all great speculative fiction is the Bible. (Let us all pause for a microsecond in prayer that God does not strike me with a bolt of lightning in the spleen.)

But before I am accused of trying to wrest notoriety from the established historians of speculative fiction, let me assure you I offer these establishments of roots only to indicate I have done my homework and am thus entitled to make the impertinent remarks that follow.

Speculative fiction in modern times *really* got born with Walt Disney in his classic animated film, *Steamboat Willie,* in 1928. Sure it did. I mean: a mouse that can operate a paddle-wheeler?

It's as sensible a starting place as Lucian, after all, because when we get right down to the old nitty-gritty, the beginning of speculative fiction was the first Cro-Magnon who imagined what it was out there snuffling around in the darkness just beyond his fire. If he envisioned it as having nine heads, bee-faceted eyes, fire-breathing jaws, sneakers and a tattersall vest, he was creating speculative fiction. If he saw it as a mountain lion, he was probably just *au courant,* and he doesn't count. Besides, he was chicken.

No one can sanely deny that Gernsback's *Amazing Stories* in 1926 was the most obvious ancestor of what today, in this volume, we call "speculative fiction." And if this be accepted, then obeisances must be offered in the direction of Edgar Rice Burroughs, E. E. Smith, H. P. Lovecraft, Ed Earl Repp, Ralph Milne Farley, Captain S. P. Meek, USA (Ret.) . . . that whole crowd. And of course, to John W. Campbell, Jr., who used to edit a magazine that ran science fiction, called *Astounding,* and who now edits a magazine that runs a lot of schematic drawings, called *Analog.* Mr. Campbell is generally conceded to be the "fourth father of modern speculative fiction" or somesuch, because it was he who suggested the writers try putting characters inside their machines. Which brings you and me up to about the Forties, with the gadget stories.

But it doesn't say much about the Sixties.

After Campbell, there were Horace Gold and Tony Boucher and Mick McComas, who pioneered the radical concept that science fiction should be judged by the same high standards as all literary forms. It came as one whale of a shock to most of the poor devils who had been writing and selling in the field. It meant they had to learn to write well, not merely think cute.

With which background we now come trudging knee-deep through awful stories into the Swinging Sixties. Which has not really begun to swing. But the revolution is at hand. Bear with me.

For twenty-odd years the staunch fan of speculative fiction has been beating his chest and wailing that the mainstream of fiction does not recognize imaginative writing. He has lamented the fact that books like *1984* and *Brave New World* and *Limbo* and *On the Beach* have received critical acclaim but have never been labeled "science fiction." In point of fact, he contended, they were automatically excluded on the simplistic theory that "They're *good* books, they *can't* be that crazy fictional-science crap." He seized upon every borderline effort, no matter how dismal (e.g.: Wouk's "The Lomokome Papers," Ayn Rand's *Anthem,* Hersey's *White Lotus,* Boulle's *Planet of the Apes*), just to reassure himself and strengthen his argument that the mainstream was pilfering from the genre, and that there was much wealth to be divvied in the *ouvrage de longue haleine* that was science fiction.

That rabid fan is now out-of-date. He is twenty years behind the times. He can still be heard gibbering paranoiacally in the background, but he's now more a fossil than a force. Speculative fiction has been found, has been turned to good use by the mainstream, and is now in the process of being assimilated. Burgess' *A Clockwork Orange,* Vonnegut's *God Bless You, Mr. Rosewater,* and *Cat's Cradle,* Hersey's *The Child Buyer,* Wallis' *Only Lovers Left Alive* and Vercors' *You Shall Know Them* (to name only a recent scattering) are top-flight speculative novels, employing many of the tools honed by science fiction writers in their own little backwash eddy of a genre. Not an issue of a major slick magazine passes without some recognition of speculative fiction, either by reference to its having foretold some now commonplace item of scientific curiosity, or by openly currying favor with the leading names in the field via the inclusion of their work alongside the John Cheevers, the John Updikes, the Bernard Malamuds, the Saul Bellows.

We have arrived, is the inescapable conclusion.

And yet that highly vocal fan, and all the myriad writers, critics and editors who have developed tunnel vision through years of feeling themselves ghettoized, persist in their antediluvian lament, holding back the very recognition for which they weep and moan. This is what Charles Fort called "steam engine time." When it is time for the steam engine to be invented, even if James Watt doesn't do it, someone will.

It is "steam engine time" for the writers of speculative fiction. The millennium is at hand. *We* are what's happening.

And most of those wailing-wall aficionados of fantasy fiction hate it a lot. Because allofasudden even the bus driver and the dental technician and the beach bum and the grocery bag-boy are reading *his* stories; and what's worse, those johnny-come-latelies may not show the proper deference to the Grand Old Masters of the field, they may not think the Skylark stories are brilliant and mature and compelling;

they may not care to be confused by terminology that has been accepted in s-f for thirty years, they may want to understand what's going on; they may not fall in line with the old order. They may prefer *Star Trek* and Kubrick to Barsoom and Ray Cummings. And thus they are the recipients of the fan-sneer, a curling of the lips that closely resembles the crumbling of an old pulp edition of *Famous Fantastic Mysteries*.

But even *more* heinous is the entrance on the scene of writers who won't accept the old ways. The smartass kids who write "all that literary stuff," who take the accepted and hoary ideas of the speculative arena and stand them right on their noses. Them guys are blasphemers. God will send down lightning to strike *them* in their spleens.

Yet speculative fiction (notice how I cleverly avoid using the misnomer "science fiction"? getting the message, friends? you've bought one of those s—e f—n anthologies and didn't even know it! well, you've blown your bread, so you might as well hang around and get educated) is the most fertile ground for the growth of a writing talent without boundaries, with horizons that seem never to get any closer. And all them smartass punks keep emerging, driving the old guard out of their jugs with frenzy. And lord! how the mighty have fallen; for most of the "big names" in the field, who dominated the covers and top rates of the magazines for more years than they deserved, can no longer cut it, they no longer produce. Or they have moved on to other fields. Leaving it to the newer, brighter ones, and the ones who were new and bright once, and were passed by because they weren't "big names."

But despite the new interest in speculative fiction by the mainstream, despite the enlarged and variant styles of the new writers, despite the enormity and expansion of topics open to these writers, despite what is outwardly a booming, healthy market . . . there is a constricting narrowness of mind on the part of many editors in the field. Because many of the editors were once simply fans, and they retain that specialized prejudice for the s-f of their youth. Writer after writer is finding his work precensored even before he writes it, because he knows this editor won't allow discussions of politics in his pages, and that one shies away from stories exploring sex in the future, and this one down here in the baseboard doesn't pay except in red beans and rice, so why bother burning up all those gray cells on a daring concept when the louse-bug will buy the old madman-in-the-time-machine *shtick*.

This is called a taboo. And there isn't an editor in the field who won't swear under threat of the water torture that he hasn't got them, that he even sprays the office with insecticide on the off-chance there's a taboo nesting in the files like a silverfish. They've said it at conventions, they've said it in print, but there are over a dozen writers in this book alone who will, upon slight nudging, relate stories of horror and censorship that include every editor in the field, even the one who lives in the baseboard.

Oh, there are challenges in the field, and truly controversial, eye-opening pieces get published; but there are so many more that go a-begging.

And no one has ever told the speculative writer, "Pull out all the stops, no holds barred, get it said!" Until this book came along.

Don't look now, you're on the firing line in the big revolution.

In 1961 this editor . . .

. . . hold it a second. I just thought of something that had better get said. You may have noticed a lack of solemnity and reserve on the part of the editorial I. It stems not so much from youthful exuberance —though there are legions who will swear I've been fourteen years old for the past seventeen—as from a reluctance on the I's part to accept the harsh reality that the I who is all writer has abrogated a wee portion of the auctorial gestalt to become An Editor. It strikes me as odd that of all the wiser heads in the field, all the men who are so much more eminently suited to bring forth a book as important as I like to think this one is, that it fell to me. But then, on reflection, it seems inevitable; not so much from talent as from a sense of urgency and a dogged determination that it should be done. Had I known at the outset that it would take over two years to assemble this book, and the heartache and expense involved—I'd have done it anyhow.

So in exchange for all the goodies herein, you will have to put up with the intrusion of the editor, who is a writer like all the other writers here, and who is delighted to be able to play God just this once.

Where was I?

Ah. In 1961 this editor was engaged in putting together a line of paperbacks for a small house in Evanston, Illinois. Among the projects I wanted to put on the assembly line was a collection of stories of speculative fiction, by top writers, all original, and all highly controversial in nature. I hired a well-known anthologist, who did what many might have called a good job. I didn't happen to think so. The stories seemed to me either silly or pointless or crude or dull. There were some that have since been published elsewhere, even a few "best" stories among them. By Leiber, and Bretnor, and Heinlein, to remember just three. But the book did not excite me the way I felt a collection of this sort should. When I left the firm, another editor tried it with a second anthologist. They got no further. The project died a-borning. I have no idea what happened to the stories these anthologists gathered together.

In 1965, I was entertaining author Norman Spinrad in my itty-bitty Los Angeles tree-house, coyly called "Ellison Wonderland," from the book of the same title. We were sitting around talking about this and that, when Norman began bitching about anthologists, for one reason or another that now escapes memory. He said he thought I should implement some of the rabble-rousing ideas I had been spreading about "the new thing" in speculative fiction, with an anthology of same. I hasten to point out *my* "new thing" is neither Judith Merril's "new thing" nor Michael Moorcock's "new thing." Ask for us by our brand names.

I smiled inanely. I'd never edited an anthology, what the hell did *I* know about it? (An attitude many critics of this book may voice when they finish. But onward . . .)

I had, shortly prior to this, sold Robert Silverberg a short story for a forthcoming anthology he was assembling. I had beefed about some minor matter or other, and received a reply, part of which follows in Silverbob's own inimitable style.

Oct 2 65. Dear Harlan: You'll be glad to know that in the course of a long and wearying dream last night I watched you win *two* Hugos at last year's Worldcon. You acted pretty smug about it, too. I'm not sure which categories you led, but one of them was probably Unfounded Bitching. Permit me a brief and fatherly lecture in response to your letter of permission on the anthology (which I'm sure will startle the sweet ladies at Duell, Sloan & Pearce.) . . .

At which point he launched into a scathing denunciation of my attitudes toward accepting some piddling amount for anthology reprinting of a second-rate story he should have known better than to include to begin with. There then followed several paragraphs of chitchat intended (unsuccessfully, I might add) to mollify me; paragraphs which are hilarious, but which bear little import for here and now, and so you'll have to read them in the Syracuse University archives sometime in the future. But now we come down to the pee and the ess, which read thus and so:

> "Why *don't* you do an anthology? HARLAN ELLISON PICKS OFF-BEAT CLASSICS OF SF, or something. . . ."

He signed the letter "Ivar Jorgensen." But that's *another* story.

Spinrad *nuhdged* me. Edit, edit, *mein kind.* So I got on the phone longdistance (this is one word, I learned it from my Yiddish grandmother, who blanched every time you suggested making one). To Lawrence Ashmead, at Doubleday. He had never spoken to me before. Had he but known what new horrors! new horrors! awaited him because of his common civility, he would have dropped the offensive instrument out the eighth-story window of the Ministry of Truth-style building on Park Avenue where Doubleday keeps its Manhattan offices.

But he listened. I wove golden magic threads of spidery illusion. A big anthology, all new stories, controversial, too fierce for magazines to buy, top writers, headliners from the mainstream, action, adventure, pathos, a cast of thousands, a parsnip in a pear tree.

Hooked. On the spot, hooked. The silver-tongued orator had struck again. Oh, was he bagged on the idea. On October 18, I received the following letter:

> Dear Harlan: The consensus of the editors who have looked at your prospectus for DANGEROUS VISIONS is that we need something more definite to go on. . . . Unless you can find out exactly what is available in original stories and can supply me with a fairly definite table of contents, I don't stand a chance of getting approval on this project from our Publishing Committee. Anthologies are a dime a dozen these days and unless they are special, they just don't justify a large advance. In fact, it is my policy to limit anthologies (unless they are "special")

to authors who regularly contribute novels to the Doubleday list. So, if you can insure most of the contents of DANGEROUS VISIONS with some definite commitments . . . and I know this is tantamount to the situation of the Butterscotch Man who can't run until he is warm and can't get warm until he runs, but . . .

Now a piece of historical information. Traditionally, anthologies have been composed of stories already first published in serial, or magazine, form. They can be purchased for hardcover anthologization for a fraction of their original cost. The profit for a writer is made from subsequent sales, paperback reprint, foreign rights, etc. And since he has been paid once for the piece already, it is gravy. Thus, a fifteen-hundred-dollar advance against royalties paid to an anthologist means the editor can cop half the bread for himself and stretch the seven hundred and fifty dollars remaining over eleven or twelve authors, and have a pretty good-sized book. *This* book, however, was conceived as an all-original collection, which meant the stories would have to be written specifically *for* the book (or, in rare cases, be those stories already long since written and rejected by all the available markets on grounds of taboo, of one sort or another; these latter possibilities were, obviously, far less appealing, for usually, unless a story is exceeding hot, it can be sold *somewhere;* if no one had bought them, there was a better chance that they were simply gawdawful, rather than too controversial; I was to find out all too soon that my thinking was correct; stories of a controversial nature are often bought by editors not so much because they shock and startle, as because they are by "name authors" who can get away with it; the less well known writers have a *much* harder time of it; and unless they develop a more prominent name later, and go back to dig these "hot" stories out of their trunk, the stories never get seen).

But for a writer to do a story for the book, my price on acceptance would have to be competitive with the magazines that would offer him first sale. This meant the standard fifteen-hundred-dollar advance would not be enough. Not if this was to be a big, wide-ranging and representative project.

The extra three cents a word for magazine publication looms large to the free-lancer making his living strictly from the genre magazines.

So I needed at least three thousand dollars, double the advance. Ashmead, who is not allowed by Nelson Doubleday to dole out more that fifteen hundred dollars, would have to go to his Publishing Committee and he didn't think they would be too keen at this stage of the game. They didn't want to spring for the *first* fifteen hundred.

So the cadmium-throated orator once again took to the telephone lines. "Hi, Larry sweetheart pussycat!"

What emerged finally was the greatest boondoggle since the Teapot Dome scandal. Ashmead was to give me the first fifteen hundred dollars advance, out of which I would only buy, say, thirty thousand words of the proposed sixty thousand. Then I would send the stories in to him and say I needed another fifteen hundred to complete the project, and if things shaped up as well as we anticipated, there would be little difficulty going to the Committee and asking for the balance.

Now, two hundred and thirty-nine thousand words and nineteen months later, DANGEROUS VISIONS has cost Doubleday three thousand dollars, myself twenty-seven hundred dollars out of pocket (and no anthologist's fee), and author Larry Niven seven hundred and fifty dollars, which he put into the project to see it done properly. Additionally, four of the authors herein have not yet been paid. Their stories came in late, when the book was ostensibly closed; but having heard about the project, and being fired with it, they wanted to be included, and have agreed to delayed payment, which comes out of Ellison's share of the profits, not the author's royalties.

This introduction has almost run its course. Thank the stars. Many of the incredible incidents that happened in the course of its birthing will have to go untold here. The Thomas Pynchon story. The Heinlein anecdote. The Laumer Affair. The Incident of the Three Brunner stories. The last-minute flight to New York to insure the Dillon illustrations. The Kingsley Amis afterword. The poverty, the sickness, the hate!

Just a few last words on the nature of this book. First, it was intended as a canvas for new writing styles, bold departures, unpopular thoughts. I think with only one or two exceptions each of the stories included fits that intention. Expect nothing, remain wide open to what the authors are trying to do, and be delighted.

There are many authors familiar to readers of speculative fiction whose work is not included here. This was not intended as an all-inclusive anthology. By the very nature of what they write, many authors were excluded because they had said what they had to say years ago. Others found they had nothing controversial or daring to contribute. Some expressed lack of interest in the project. But with one exception this book was never closed to a writer owing to editorial prejudice. Thus, you will find new young writers like Samuel Delany side by side with established craftsmen such as Damon Knight. You will find visitors from other fields such as TV's Howard Rodman beside veterans of the s-f wars such as the charming (and in this instance frightening) Miriam Allen deFord. You will find traditionalists such as Poul Anderson chockablock with wildly experimental writers like Philip José Farmer. Only the new and the different was sought, but in some cases a story was so . . . so *story* (as a chair is very much *chair*), it forced itself to be included.

And last, it has been a privilege to do this book. After the assault of bombast, that may strike the reader as aw-shucks Jack Paar-style phony humbleness. All that can be offered is the editor's assurance that the word "privilege" is mild. To have seen the growth of this very lively and arresting volume was to have a peephole not only to the future but to the future of the field of speculative writing.

From which peeping, as these thirty-two soothsayers told their tales of tomorrow, this editor was able to conclude that the wonders and riches he saw in the form, when he was first starting to learn his craft, are truly there. If there be any doubt, move on to the stories themselves. None of them has seen print anywhere before, and for the next year at least, none of them will appear anywhere else, so you have bought wisely; and have rewarded the men who had these dangerous visions.

Thank you for your attention.

HARLAN ELLISON
Hollywood
January 1967

The Editor wishes to express his gratitude to, and acknowledges the assistance of, the following individuals, without whose contributions of time, money, suggestions and empathy this book might not have been impossible, but certainly would have come a helluva lot closer to sending the editor to a home for Tired Old Men:

Mr. Kingsley Amis
Mr. and Mrs. Terry Carr
Mr. Joseph Elder
Mr. Robert P. Mills
Mr. Robert Silverberg
Mr. Norman Spinrad
Miss Sherri Townsend
Mr. and Mrs. Ted White

If the editor has overlooked anyone deserving of note herein, apologies are offered in advance, entering a plea of temporary exhaustion, but *very* special thanks for service *way* above and beyond are herewith tendered to Messrs. Larry Niven and Lawrence P. Ashmead, and Mr. and Mrs. Leo Dillon—without whose strong backs this book *literally* would never have become a reality. God bless all.

Harlan Ellison
Hollywood
14 February 1967

## Introduction to EVENSONG:

I have chosen Lester del Rey to lead off the distinguished parade of authors in this anthology for several reasons. First, because . . . no, let me give the second reason first, because the first reason is strictly personal. Second, because the Guest of Honor at the 25th Annual World Science Fiction Convention, being held in New York City as this book is published, is Lester del Rey. The Convention's honoring of Lester, and the smaller honor of starting this book, are only piddles among the glory owing Lester, a debt long in arrears. Lester is one of the few "giants" of the field whose reputation rests not merely on one or two brilliant stories written twenty-five years ago, but on a massive body of work that has grown in versatility and originality with every new addition. Few men in the genre can be considered as seminal an influence as del Rey. Thus, the honors are tiny indeed.

But the first reason is a purely personal one. Lester was responsible for my becoming a professional writer, in many ways (an act that has left him open to unnecessary vilification; I assure you there was no kindness involved; that it would work out this way Lester could never have known). When I arrived in New York in 1955, fresh from having been ejected by Ohio State University, he and his lovely wife Evvie took me into their home in Red Bank, New Jersey, and under the sadistic lash of Lester's seemingly untiring tutelage (a kind of educational death-of-a-thousand-unkind-cuts Lester assured me would ripen my talent, strengthen my character and tone up my complexion), I began to understand the rudiments of my craft. For it seems to me, even now, on reflection of over ten years, that of all the writers in this field only a few—and Lester the most prominent of that few—can *explain* what makes good writing. He is the living, snarling refutation of the canard that those who can't do, teach. His skill as an editor, anthologist, critic and teacher stems directly from his muscularity as a writer.

It has been harshly said of Lester that, once planted, he will argue with the worms for possession of his carcass. Anyone who has ever been ranked across from del Rey in an argument will nod understandingly. And I submit *ranked*, for Lester is the fairest of men: he will not go for top-point efficiency in a discussion unless the odds are equal: about seven to one. I have never seen him lose an argument. No matter what your subject, no matter if you are the world's *only* authority on the topic, del Rey will command an arsenal of facts and theories so inexhaustible and formidable, defeat is assured you. I have seen strong men wither before del Rey. Harridans and shrikes he literally strips naked and sends squalling into toilets. He ranges somewhere around five and a half feet tall, has wispy "baby hair" he finds difficult to comb, wears glasses only slightly thicker than the bottom of a Dr. Pepper bottle, and is powered by some supernatural force the manufacturers of the Pacemaker ought to consider for their machines.

Lester del Rey was born R. Alvarez del Rey, on a tenant farm in Minnesota, in 1915. He has spent most of his life in Eastern cities though close acquaintances occasionally hear him murmur about his father, who was a devoted evolutionist in the boondocks. He has acted as an agent, writing teacher and plot doctor, and is circumspect about the (obviously) endless string of odd jobs he held before becoming a full-time writer thirty years ago. Lester is one of the few writers who can talk incessantly and not let it become a block to his writing the stories he tells. He has talked almost steadily for the past thirty years in bull sessions, lectures, pulpits, writers' conferences, television and over two thousand hours on Manhattan's Long John Nebel show, where he has consistently played the role of the Voice of Sanity. His first story was "The Faithful," sold to *Astounding Science Fiction* in 1937. His books are much too numerous to catalogue, chiefly because he has ten thousand pseudonyms and pantherishly clevers the bad ones under phony names.

Peculiarly, this first story in the book was the last one received. Among the first ten writers I contacted for this project, Lester was quick to assure me he would send along a story in the next few weeks. One year later, almost to the day, I met him at the Cleveland Science Fiction Convention and accused him of flummery. He assured me the story had gone out months before, that he had heard nothing about it and so had assumed I didn't want it. *This* from a professional whose attitude on stories—as imparted to me a decade ago—is to keep the manuscripts in motion till they are bought. Writing for the trunk is masturbation, so saith del Rey. After I returned to Los Angeles from the Convention, "Evensong" came in, with a whey-faced note from del Rey saying he was sending it along just to prove it had been written all the time. He also included an afterword, at my request. One of the fillips I intended to include in this anthology was a few post-fiction comments by the authors, anent their feelings about the story, or their view of why it was a "dangerous" vision, or how they felt about speculative writing, or their audience, or their place in the Universe . . . in other words, anything they felt they might want to say, to establish that rare writer-to-reader liaison. You will find one each of these afterwords following each story, but Lester's comments *about* the afterword seem apropos at the outset, for they reflect, in fact, the attitude of *many* of the authors here, about the act of afterwording. He said:

"The afterword isn't very bright or amusing, I'm afraid. But I'd pretty much wrapped up what I wanted to say in the story itself. So I simply gave the so-called critics a few words to look up in the dictionary and gnaw over learnedly. I felt that they should at least be told that there is such a form as allegory, even though they may not understand the difference between that and simple fantasy. I've always thought a story must stand by itself, and that the writer behind it is of no consequence to its merits. (And I did *so* have a carbon from which to send this copy of the story I already sent, I did, Idid, idid, ididid. . . .)"

# ● EVENSONG

## by Lester del Rey

By the time he reached the surface of the little planet, even the dregs of his power were drained. Now he rested, drawing reluctant strength slowly from the yellow sun that shone on the greensward around him. His senses were dim with an ultimate fatigue, but the fear he had learned from the Usurpers drove them outward, seeking a further hint of sanctuary.

It was a peaceful world, he realized, and the fear thickened in him at the discovery. In his younger days, he had cherished a multitude of worlds where the game of life's ebb and flow could be played to the hilt. It had been a lusty universe to roam then. But the Usurpers could brook no rivals to their own outreaching lust. The very peace and order here meant that this world had once been theirs.

He tested for them gingerly while the merest whisper of strength poured into him. None were here now. He could have sensed the pressure of their close presence at once, and there was no trace of that. The even grassland swept in rolling meadows and swales to the distant hills. There were marble structures in the distance, sparkling whitely in the late sunlight, but they were empty, their unknown purpose altered to no more than decoration now upon this abandoned planet. His attention swept back, across a stream to the other side of the wide valley.

There he found the garden. Within low walls, its miles of expanse were a tree-crowded and apparently untended preserve. He could sense the stirring of larger animal life among the branches and along the winding paths. The brawling vigor of all proper life was missing, but its abundance might be enough to mask his own vestige of living force from more than careful search.

It was at least a better refuge than this open greensward and he longed toward it, but the danger of betraying motion held him still where he was. He had thought his previous escape to be assured, but he was learning that even he could err. Now he waited while he tested once more for evidence of Usurper trap.

He had mastered patience in the confinement the Usurpers had designed at the center of the galaxy. He had gathered his power furtively while he designed escape around their reluctance to make final disposition. Then he had burst outward in a drive that should have thrust him far beyond the limits of their hold on the universe. And he had found failure before he could span even the distance to the end of this spiral arm of one galactic fastness.

Their webs of detection were everywhere, seemingly. Their great power-robbing lines made a net too fine to pass. Stars and worlds were linked, until only a series of miracles had carried him this far. And now the waste of power for such miracles was no longer within his reach. Since their near failure in entrapping and sequestering him, they had learned too much.

Now he searched delicately, afraid to trip some alarm, but more afraid to miss its existence. From space, this world had offered the only hope in its seeming freedom from their webs. But only microseconds had been available to him for his testing then.

At last he drew his perceptions back. He could find no slightest evidence of their lures and detectors here. He had begun to suspect that even his best efforts might not be enough now, but he could do no more. Slowly at first, and then in a sudden rush, he hurled himself into the maze of the garden.

Nothing struck from the skies. Nothing leaped upwards from the planet core to halt him. There was no interruption in the rustling of the leaves and the chirping bird songs. The animal sounds went on unhindered. Nothing seemed aware of his presence in the garden. Once that would have been unthinkable in itself, but now he drew comfort from it. He must be only a shadow self now, unknown and unknowable in his passing.

Something came down the path where he rested, pattering along on hoofs that touched lightly on the spoilage of fallen leaves. Something else leaped quickly through the light underbrush beside the path.

He let his attention rest on them as they both emerged onto the near pathway at once. And cold horror curled thickly around him.

One was a rabbit, nibbling now at the leaves of clover and twitching long ears as its pink nose stretched out for more. The other was a young deer, still bearing the spots of its fawnhood. Either or both might have seemingly been found on any of a thousand worlds. But neither would have been precisely of the type before him.

This was the Meeting World—the planet where he had first found the ancestors of the Usurpers. Of all worlds in the pested galaxy, it had to be *this* world he sought for refuge!

They were savages back in the days of his full glory, confined to this single world, rutting and driving their way to the lawful self-destruction of all such savages. And yet there had been something odd about them, something that then drew his attention and even his vagrant pity.

Out of that pity, he had taught a few of them, and led them upwards. He had even nursed poetic fancies of making them his companions and his equals as the life span of their sun should near its ending. He had answered their cries for help and given them at least some of what they needed to set their steps toward power over even space and energy. And they had rewarded him by overweening pride that denied even a trace of gratitude. He had abandoned them finally to their own savage ends and gone on to other worlds, to play out the purposes of a wider range.

It was his second folly. They were too far along the path toward unlocking the laws behind the universe. Somehow, they even avoided their own destruction from themselves. They took the worlds of their sun and drove outwards, until they could even vie with him for the worlds he had made particularly his own. And now they owned them all, and he had only a tiny spot here on their world—for a time at least.

The horror of the realization that this was the Meeting World abated a little as he remembered now how readily their spawning hordes possessed and abandoned worlds without seeming end. And again the tests he could make showed no evidence of them here. He began to relax again, feeling a sudden hope from what had been temporary despair. Surely they might also believe this was the one planet where he would never seek sanctuary.

Now he set his fears aside and began to force his thoughts toward the only pattern that could offer hope. He needed power, and power was available in any area untouched by the webs of the Usurpers. It had drained into space itself throughout the aeons, a waste of energy that could blast suns or build them in legions. It was power to escape, perhaps even to prepare himself eventually to meet them with at least a chance to force truce, if not victory. Given even a few hours free of their notice, he could draw and hold that power for his needs.

He was just reaching for it when the sky thundered and the sun seemed to darken for a moment!

The fear in him gibbered to the surface and sent him huddling from sight of the sky before he could control it. But for a brief moment there was still a trace of hope in him. It could have been a phenomenon caused by his own need for power; he might have begun drawing too heavily, too eager for strength.

Then the earth shook, and he knew.

The Usurpers were not fooled. They knew he was here—had never lost him. And now they had followed in all their massive lack of subtlety. One of their scout ships had landed, and the scout would come seeking him.

He fought for control of himself, and found it long enough to drive his fear back down within himself. Now, with a care that disturbed not even a blade of grass or leaf on a twig, he began retreating, seeking the denser undergrowth at the center of the garden where all life was thickest. With that to screen him, he might at least draw a faint trickle of power, a strength to build a subtle brute aura around himself and let him hide among the beasts. Some Usurper scouts were young and immature. Such a one might be fooled into leaving. Then, before his report could be acted on by others, there might still be a chance. . . .

He knew the thought was only a wish, not a plan, but he clung to it as he huddled in the thicket at the center of the garden. And then even the fantasy was stripped from him.

The sound of footsteps was firm and sure. Branches broke as the steps came forward, not deviating from a straight line. Inexorably, each firm stride brought the Usurper nearer to his huddling place. Now there was a faint glow in the air, and the animals were scampering away in terror.

He felt the eyes of the Usurper on him, and he forced himself away from that awareness. And, like fear, he found that he had learned prayer from the Usurpers; he prayed now desperately to a nothingness he knew, and there was no answer.

"Come forth! This earth is a holy place and you cannot remain upon it. Our judgment is done and a place is prepared for you. Come forth and let me take you there!" The voice was soft, but it carried a power that stilled even the rustling of the leaves.

He let the gaze of the Usurper reach him now, and the prayer in him was mute and directed outward—and hopeless, as he knew it must be.

"But—" Words were useless, but the bitterness inside him forced the words to come from him. "But why? I am God!"

For a moment, something akin to sadness and pity was in the eyes of the Usurper. Then it passed as the answer came. "I know. But I am Man. Come!"

He bowed at last, silently, and followed slowly as the yellow sun sank behind the walls of the garden.

And the evening and the morning were the eighth day.

## Afterword:

A writer who thinks seriously about his craft must surely find himself more and more engaged with the ancient problems of philosophy—good and evil, and causality—since these lie deep within every plot and character. As a science fiction writer, trying to scan the patterns of the future, I find myself also inevitably concerned with the question of teleology: is there a purpose and design to the universe and to man? It may not matter. If so, must we follow it blindly? If blind chance rules, can we not shape our own purpose, suitable to our ultimate possibilities? Personally, I take my *Invictus* straight, with just a dash of bitters. But I take it very seriously. And because I do, "Evensong" is not fiction, but allegory.

## Introduction to FLIES:

Robert Silverberg is one of my oldest friends. He is an excellent writer. Additionally, he is the compleat professional, which is unfortunately interpreted by the yahoos as meaning he is a story factory. They're wrong, but that's beside the point. More on Silverberg the Writer in a moment.

Silverberg the Fellah goes like so: he is from Brooklyn and he doesn't want any applause. He used to edit a fan magazine called *Spaceship* which was extremely literate. He graduated from Columbia University. He is married to Bobbie, who is a lovely research physicist, and they live in a stately manse that at one time belonged to Fiorello La Guardia. He has had somewhere between fifty and sixty hardcover books published on topics ranging from zoology to archaeology and back again. His first published story was in 1953, "Gorgon Plant," which appeared in the Scottish science fiction magazine, *Nebula*. He won a Hugo in 1956 as Most Promising New Writer, beating out (of all people) the author of this introduction.

Like many writers in the field of speculative fiction, the author of this introduction envies Silverberg's ability to *get the job done*. The delusion that genius and madness are but opposing faces of the same rare coin is one to which most writers subscribe, as a cop-out. It allows them to be erratic, beat their wives, demand fresh coffee at six ayem, come in late with manuscripts, default on their obligations, laze around reading paperback novels on the pretext that they are "researching," pick up stakes and move when things get too regimented, snarl and snap at fans, be tendentious or supercilious. It is safe for all of us to goof off as long as we can bilk the Average Man into believing it is necessary for the creative process. Silverberg does not operate on this principle. He works a steady schedule. He practices his craft five days a week, six hours a day. Writing is what he does, and not to do it means not to be functioning.

Unlike writers who find intricate and brilliant ways to send themselves into slumps, blocks, pressures, binds and hideous life-situations, Silverberg's orderly work-habits mean he can be relied upon. He has thus produced a large body of work of substantial merit, all the more impressive when one considers how many really *memorable* novels and stories and non-fiction works he has had published while in his twenties. Now, in his early thirties, Bob Silverberg writes books like *Man Before Adam, Lost Cities and Vanished Civilizations, Home of the Red Man: Indian North America Before Columbus, Needle in a Timestack, The Time-Hoppers,* and the marvelous book of living fossils, *Forgotten by Time*. His interests and authority have long since moved out of the realms of fiction, as a casual listing of only a few of his books demonstrates.

Yet Silverberg is a product of the field of science fiction. He is one of the last of the fans-turned-professional, and though the bulk of his income and assignments comes from other kinds of writing, he returns with pleasing regularity to speculative fiction, to re-establish his reputation, to reinforce his roots, to pleasure himself with the kind of stories he can only write in this form. Of these, his latest is presented here. Perhaps it is because of my decade-long friendship with Bob, and my acquaintance with much of what he has written, but I submit "Flies" is one of the most penetrating, most originally-written stories he has ever attempted. And the attempt is a success.

# ● FLIES

## by Robert Silverberg

Here is Cassiday:
  *transfixed on a table.*


There wasn't much left of him. A brain-box; a few ropes of nerves;
a limb. The sudden implosion had taken care of the rest. There was
enough, though. The golden ones didn't need much to go by. They had
found him in the wreckage of the drifting ship as it passed through their
zone, back of Iapetus. He was alive. He could be repaired. The others
on the ship were beyond hope.

Repair him? Of course. Did one need to be human in order to be
humanitarian? Repair, yes. By all means. And change. The golden
ones were creative.

What was left of Cassiday lay in dry dock on a somewhere table in
a golden sphere of force. There was no change of season here; only
the sheen of the walls, the unvarying warmth. Neither day nor night,
neither yesterday nor tomorrow. Shapes came and went about him.
They were regenerating him, stage by stage, as he lay in complete
mindless tranquillity. The brain was intact but not functioning. The
rest of the man was growing back: tendon and ligament, bone and
blood, heart and elbows. Elongated mounds of tissue sprouted tiny buds
that enlarged into blobs of flesh. Paste cell to cell together, build a
man from his own wreckage—that was no great chore for the golden
ones. They had their skills. But they had much to learn, too, and this
Cassiday could help them learn it.

Day by day Cassiday grew toward wholeness. They did not awaken
him. He lay cradled in warmth, unmoving, unthinking, drifting on the
tide. His new flesh was pink and smooth, like a baby's. The epithelial
thickening came a little later. Cassiday served as his own blueprint. The
golden ones replicated him from a shred of himself, built him back
from his own polynucleotide chains, decoded the proteins and reas-
sembled him from the template. An easy task, for them. Why not?

Any blob of protoplasm could do it—for itself. The golden ones, who were not protoplasm, could do it for others.

They made some changes in the template. Of course. They were craftsmen. And there was a good deal they wanted to learn.

Look at Cassiday:
*the dossier.*

BORN 1 August 2316
PLACE Nyack, New York
PARENTS Various
ECONOMIC LEVEL Low
EDUCATIONAL LEVEL Middle
OCCUPATION Fuel technician
MARITAL STATUS Three legal liaisons, duration eight months,
    sixteen months, and two months
HEIGHT Two meters
WEIGHT 96 kg
HAIR COLOR Yellow
EYES Blue
BLOOD TYPE A+
INTELLIGENCE LEVEL High
SEXUAL INCLINATIONS Normal

Watch them now:
*changing him.*

The complete man lay before them, newly minted, ready for re-birth. Now come the final adjustments. They sought the gray brain within its pink wrapper, and entered it, and traveled through the bays and inlets of the mind, pausing now at this quiet cove, dropping anchor now at the base of that slab-sided cliff. They were operating, but doing it neatly. Here were no submucous resections, no glittering blades carving through gristle and bone, no sizzling lasers at work, no clumsy hammering at the tender meninges. Cold steel did not slash the synapses. The golden ones were subtler; they tuned the circuit that was Cassiday, boosted the gain, damped out the noise, and they did it very gently.

When they were finished with him, he was much more sensitive. He had several new hungers. They had granted him certain abilities. Now they awakened him.

"You are alive, Cassiday," a feathery voice said. "Your ship was destroyed. Your companions were killed. You alone survived."

"Which hospital is this?"

"Not on Earth. You'll be going back soon. Stand up, Cassiday. Move your right hand. Your left. Flex your knees. Inflate your lungs. Open and close your eyes several times. What's your name, Cassiday?"

"Richard Henry Cassiday."

"How old?"

"Forty-one."

"Look at this reflection. Who do you see?"

"Myself."

"Do you have any further questions?"

"What did you do to me?"

"Repaired you, Cassiday. You were almost entirely destroyed."

"Did you change me any?"

"We made you more sensitive to the feelings of your fellow man."

"Oh," said Cassiday.

Follow Cassiday as he journeys:
   *back to Earth.*

He arrived on a day that had been programed for snow. Light snow, quickly melting, an aesthetic treat rather than a true manifestation of weather. It was good to touch foot on the homeworld again. The golden ones had deftly arranged his return, putting him back aboard his wrecked ship and giving him enough of a push to get him within range of a distress sweep. The monitors had detected him and picked him up. How was it you survived the disaster unscathed, Spaceman Cassiday? Very simple, sir, I was outside the ship when it happened. It just went swoosh and everybody was killed. And I only am escaped alone to tell thee.

They routed him to Mars and checked him out, and held him awhile in a decontamination lock on Luna, and finally sent him back to Earth. He stepped into the snowstorm, a big man with a rolling gait and careful calluses in all the right places. He had few friends, no relatives, enough cash units to see him through for a while, and a couple of ex-wives he could look up. Under the rules, he was entitled to a year off with full pay as his disaster allotment. He intended to accept the furlough.

He had not yet begun to make use of his new sensitivity. The golden ones had planned it so that his abilities would remain inoperative until he reached the homeworld. Now he had arrived, and it was time to begin using them, and the endlessly curious creatures who lived back at Iapetus waited patiently while Cassiday sought out those who had once loved him.

He began his quest in Chicago Urban District, because that was where the spaceport was, just outside of Rockford. The slidewalk took him quickly to a travertine tower, festooned with radiant inlays of ebony and violet-hued metal, and there, at the local Televector Central, Cassiday checked out the present whereabouts of his former wives. He was patient about it, a bland-faced, mild-eyed mass of flesh, pushing the right buttons and waiting placidly for the silken contacts to close somewhere in the depths of the earth. Cassiday had never been a violent man. He was calm. He knew how to wait.

The machine told him that Beryl Fraser Cassiday Mellon lived in Boston Urban District. The machine told him that Lureen Holstein Cassiday lived in New York Urban District. The machine told him that Mirabel Gunryk Cassiday Milman Reed lived in San Francisco Urban District.

The names awakened memories: warmth of flesh, scent of hair, touch of hand, sound of voice. Whispers of passion. Snarls of contempt. Gasps of love.

Cassiday, restored to life, went to see his ex-wives.

We find one now:
*safe and sound.*

Beryl Fraser Cassiday Mellon's eyes were milky in the pupil, greenish where they should have been white. She had lost weight in the last ten years, and now her face was parchment stretched over bone, an eroded face, the cheekbones pressing from within against the taut skin and likely to snap through at any moment. Cassiday had been married to her for sixteen months when he was twenty-four. They had separated after she insisted on taking the Sterility Pledge. He had not particularly wanted children, but he was offended by her maneuver all the same. Now she lay in a soothing cradle of webfoam, trying to smile at him without cracking her lips.

"They said you'd been killed," she told him.

"I escaped. How have you been, Beryl?"

"You can see that. I'm taking the cure."

"Cure?"

"I was a triline addict. Can't you see? My eyes, my face? It melted me away. But it was peaceful. Like disconnecting your soul. Only it would have killed me, another year of it. Now I'm on the cure. They tapered me off last month. They're building up my system with prosthetics. I'm full of plastic now. But I'll live."

"You've remarried?" Cassiday asked.

"He split long ago. I've been alone five years. Just me and the triline. But now I'm off that stuff." Beryl blinked, laboriously. "You look so relaxed, Dick. But you always were. So calm, so sure of yourself. *You'd* never get yourself hooked on triline. Hold my hand, will you?"

He touched the withered claw. He felt the warmth coming from her, the need for love. Great throbbing waves came lalloping into him, low-frequency pulses of yearning that filtered through him and went booming onward to the watchers far away.

"You once loved me," Beryl said. "Then we were both silly. Love me again. Help me get back on my feet. I need your strength."

"Of course I'll help you," Cassidy said.

He left her apartment and purchased three cubes of triline. Returning, he activated one of them and pressed it into Beryl's hand. The green-and-milky eyes roiled in terror.

"No," she whimpered.

The pain flooding from her shattered soul was exquisite in its intensity. Cassiday accepted the full flood of it. Then she clenched her fist, and the drug entered her metabolism, and she grew peaceful once more.

Observe the next one:
  *with a friend.*

The annunciator said, "Mr. Cassiday is here."

"Let him enter," replied Mirabel Gunryk Cassiday Milman Reed.

The door-sphincter irised open and Cassiday stepped through, into onyx and marble splendor. Beams of auburn palisander formed a polished wooden framework on which Mirabel lay, and it was obvious that she reveled in the sensation of hard wood against plump flesh. A cascade of crystal-colored hair tumbled to her shoulders. She had been Cassiday's for eight months in 2346, and she had been a slender, timid girl then, but now he could barely detect the outlines of that girl in this pampered mound.

"You've married well," he observed.

"Third time lucky," Mirabel said. "Sit down? Drink? Shall I adjust the environment?"

"It's fine." He remained standing. "You always wanted a mansion, Mirabel. My most intellectual wife, you were, but you had this love of comfort. You're comfortable now."

"Very."

"Happy?"

"I'm comfortable," Mirabel said. "I don't read much any more, but I'm comfortable."

Cassiday noticed what seemed to be a blanket crumpled in her lap —purple with golden threads, soft, idle, clinging close. It had several eyes. Mirabel kept her hands spread out over it.

"From Ganymede?" he asked. "A pet?"

"Yes. My husband bought it for me last year. It's very precious to me."

"Very precious to anybody. I understand they're expensive."

"But lovable," said Mirabel. "Almost human. Quite devoted. I suppose you'll think I'm silly, but it's the most important thing in my life now. More than my husband, even. I love it, you see. I'm accustomed to having others love me, but there aren't many things that I've been able to love."

"May I see it?" Cassiday said mildly.

"Be careful."

"Certainly." He gathered up the Ganymedean creature. Its texture was extraordinary, the softest he had ever encountered. Something fluttered apprehensively within the flat body of the animal. Cassiday detected a parallel wariness coming from Mirabel as he handled her pet. He stroked the creature. It throbbed appreciatively. Bands of iridescence shimmered as it contracted in his hands.

She said, "What are you doing now, Dick? Still working for the spaceline?"

He ignored the question. "Tell me the line from Shakespeare, Mirabel. About the flies. The flies and wanton boys."

Furrows sprouted in her pale brow. "It's from *Lear*," she said. "Wait. Yes. '*As flies to wanton boys are we to the gods. They kill us for their sport.*'"

"That's the one," Cassiday said. His big hands knotted quickly about the blanket-like being from Ganymede. It turned a dull gray, and reedy fibers popped from its ruptured surface. Cassiday dropped it to the floor. The surge of horror and pain and loss that welled from Mirabel nearly stunned him, but he accepted it and transmitted it.

"Flies," he explained. "Wanton boys. My sport, Mirabel. I'm a god now, did you know that?" His voice was calm and cheerful. "Goodby. Thank you."

One more awaits the visit:
*swelling with new life.*

Lureen Holstein Cassiday, who was thirty-one years old, dark-haired, large-eyed, and seven months pregnant, was the only one of his wives who had not remarried. Her room in New York was small and austere. She had been a chubby girl when she had been Cassiday's two-month wife five years ago, and she was even more chubby now, but how much of the access of new meat was the result of the pregnancy Cassiday did not know.

"Will you marry now?" he asked.

Smiling, she shook her head. "I've got money, and I value my independence. I wouldn't let myself get into another deal like the one we had. Not with anyone."

"And the baby? You'll have it?"

She nodded savagely. "I worked hard to get it! You think it's easy? Two years of inseminations! A fortune in fees! Machines poking around in me—all the fertility boosters—oh no, you've got the picture wrong. This isn't an unwanted baby. This is a baby I sweated to have."

"That's interesting," said Cassiday. "I visited Mirabel and Beryl, too, and they each had their babies, too. Of sorts. Mirabel had a little beast from Ganymede. Beryl had a triline addiction that she was very proud of shaking. And you've had a baby put into you, without any help from a man. All three of you seeking something. Interesting."

"Are you all right, Dick?"

"Fine."

"Your voice is so flat. You're just unrolling a lot of words. It's a little frightening."

"Mmm. Yes. Do you know the kind thing I did for Beryl? I bought her some triline cubes. And I took Mirabel's pet and wrung its—well, not its neck. I did it very calmly. I was never a passionate man."

"I think you've gone crazy, Dick."

"I feel your fear. You think I'm going to do something to your baby. Fear is of no interest, Lureen. But sorrow—yes, that's worth analyzing. Desolation. I want to study it. I want to help *them* study it. I think it's what they want to know about. Don't run from me, Lureen. I don't want to hurt you, not that way."

She was small-bodied and not very strong, and unwieldy in her pregnancy. Cassiday seized her gently by both wrists and drew her toward him. Already he could feel the new emotions coming from her, the self-pity behind the terror, and he had not even done anything to her.

How did you abort a fetus two months from term?

A swift kick in the belly might do it. Too crude, too crude. Yet Cassiday had not come armed with abortifacients, a handy ergot pill, a quick-acting spasmic inducer. So he brought his knee up sharply deploring the crudity of it. Lureen sagged. He kicked her a second time. He remained completely tranquil as he did it, for it would be wrong to take joy in violence. A third kick seemed desirable. Then he released her.

She was still conscious, but she was writhing. Cassiday made himself receptive to the outflow. The child, he realized, was not yet dead within her. Perhaps it might not die at all. But it would certainly be crippled in some way. What he drained from Lureen was the awareness that she might bring forth a defective. The fetus would have to be destroyed. She would have to begin again. It was all quite sad.

"Why?" she muttered. ". . . why?"

Among the watchers:
*the equivalent of dismay.*

Somehow it had not developed as the golden ones had anticipated. Even they could miscalculate, it appeared, and they found that a rewarding insight. Still, something had to be done about Cassiday.

They had given him powers. He could detect and transmit to them the raw emotions of others. That was useful to them, for from the data they could perhaps construct an understanding of human beings. But in rendering him a switching center for the emotions of others they had unavoidably been forced to blank out his own. And that was distorting the data.

He was too destructive now, in his joyless way. That had to be corrected. For now he partook too deeply of the nature of the golden ones themselves. *They* might have their sport with Cassiday, for he owed them a life. But he might not have his sport with others.

They reached down the line of communication to him and gave him his instructions.

"No," Cassiday said. "You're done with me now. There's no need to come back."

"Further adjustments are necessary."

"I disagree."

"You will not disagree for long."

Still disagreeing, Cassiday took ship for Mars, unable to stand aside from their command. On Mars he chartered a vessel that regularly made the Saturn run and persuaded it to come in by way of Iapetus. The golden ones took possession of him once he was within their immediate reach.

"What will you do to me?" Cassiday asked.

"Reverse the flow. You will no longer be sensitive to others. You will report to us on your own emotions. We will restore your conscience, Cassiday."

He protested. It was useless.

Within the glowing sphere of golden light they made their adjustments on him. They entered him and altered him, and turned his perceptions inward, so that he might feed on his own misery like a vulture tearing at its entrails. That would be informative. Cassiday objected until he no longer had the power to object, and when his awareness returned it was too late to object.

"No," he murmured. In the yellow gleam he saw the faces of Beryl and Mirabel and Lureen. "You shouldn't have done this to me. You're torturing me . . . like you would a fly. . . ."

There was no response. They sent him away, back to Earth. They returned him to the travertine towers and the rumbling slidewalks, to the house of pleasure on 485th Street, to the islands of light that blazed in the sky, to the eleven billion people. They turned him loose to go among them, and suffer, and report on his sufferings. And a time would come when they would release him, but not yet.

Here is Cassiday:
 *nailed to his cross.*

## Afterword:

One of the first science fiction stories I wrote was a deadly grim portrayal of a New York compelled into cannibalism. It was sufficiently realistic so that no one would buy it for four years, and only an inspired promotion job by the editor of this present anthology got it into print at all.

Now, twelve or thirteen years later, I've turned from the literal depiction of cannibalism to the symbolic presentation of vampirism, which I suppose indicates a healthy progression of morbidity. Every writer returns to his own obsessions when given a free hand, and every situation he invents, no matter how grotesque, says something about the nature of human relationships. If I seem to be saying that we devour each other, literally or figuratively, that we drain substance from one another, that we practice vampirism and cannibalism, so be it. Beneath any grotesquerie lies its opposite; behind the grimness of cannibalism lies the video sentimentality, "People need people." To devour, if nothing else.

No apologies offered. No excuses. Just a story, a made-up fiction, a fantasy about future times and other worlds. Nothing more than that.

## Introduction to THE DAY AFTER THE DAY THE MARTIANS CAME:

There is very little that can be said about Frederik Pohl, except everything. He is the editor of *Galaxy Magazine;* he was the man who, in 1953, conceived and edited the justly famous series of original anthologies called *Star Science Fiction Stories;* he was the co-author, with Cyril Kornbluth, of *The Space Merchants;* he was the anthologist who saved Cordwainer Smith's "Scanners Live in Vain" from obscurity in his 1952 collection, *Beyond the End of Time;* he was the bloodhound who tracked down Dr. Linebarger, who was Cordwainer Smith, and brought him back to the field of speculative fiction; he is the talent scout who set the tone for all of Ballantine Books' science fiction; he is the lecturer who roams the United States promulgating the latest in science and incidentally serving as good-will ambassador for the field of speculative fiction; he is the editor who ruthlessly blue-penciled a recent, brilliant story of mine on the grounds the words "douche bag" and "privates" were offensive. Well, no one's perfect.

Fred Pohl is an extremely tall man in his middle forties, who commutes between the Hudson Street offices of *Galaxy* and the Red Bank, New Jersey, home of his family. In the former he considers the possibilities of the world we are making for ourselves, and in the latter he studies television programs that carry the seeds of that world. He is obviously disturbed by what he sees. As the story that follows will attest.

Just a phrase or two about this story. It handles a terribly complex problem in the most basic, nitty-gritty terms: reducing irrational human reactions to their lowest possible common denominator, in order that they may be seen for the insensibilities they truly are. It is almost a journalistic story, but do not be fooled by its apparent simplicity; Pohl has gone for the jugular.

# ● THE DAY AFTER THE DAY THE MARTIANS CAME

### by Frederik Pohl

There were two cots in every room of the motel, besides the usual number of beds, and Mr. Mandala, the manager, had converted the rear section of the lobby into a men's dormitory. Nevertheless he was not satisfied and was trying to persuade his colored bellmen to clean out the trunk room and put cots in that too. "Now, please, Mr. Mandala," the bell captain said, speaking loudly over the noise in the lounge, "you know we'd do it for you if we could. But it cannot be, because, first, we don't have any other place to put those old TV sets you want to save and because, second, we don't *have* any more cots."

"You're arguing with me, Ernest. I told you to quit arguing with me," said Mr. Mandala. He drummed his fingers on the registration desk and looked angrily around the lobby. There were at least forty people in it, talking, playing cards and dozing. The television set was mumbling away in a recap of the NASA releases, and on the screen Mr. Mandala could see a picture of one of the Martians, gazing into the camera and weeping large, gelatinous tears.

"Quit that," ordered Mr. Mandala, turning in time to catch his bell-men looking at the screen. "I don't pay you to watch TV. Go see if you can help out in the kitchen."

"We been in the kitchen, Mr. Mandala. They don't need us."

"Go when I tell you to go, Ernest! You too, Berzie." He watched them go through the service hall and wished he could get rid of some of the crowd in the lounge as easily. They filled every seat and the over-flow sat on the arms of the chairs, leaned against the walls and filled the booths in the bar, which had been closed for the past two hours be-cause of the law. According to the registration slips, they were nearly all from newspapers, wire services, radio and television networks and so on, waiting to go to the morning briefing at Cape Kennedy. Mr. Mandala wished morning would come. He didn't like so many of them cluttering up his lounge, especially since he was pretty sure a lot of them were not even registered guests.

On the television screen a hastily edited tape was now showing the return of the Algonquin Nine space probe to Mars, but no one was watching it. It was the third time that particular tape had been repeated since midnight and everybody had seen it at least once; but when it changed to another shot of one of the Martians, looking like a sad dachshund with elongated seal flippers for limbs, one of the poker players stirred and cried: "I got a Martian joke! Why doesn't a Martian swim in the Atlantic Ocean?"

"It's your bet," said the dealer.

"Because he'd leave a ring around it," said the reporter, folding his cards. No one laughed, not even Mr. Mandala, although some of the jokes had been pretty good. Everybody was beginning to get tired of them, or perhaps just tired.

Mr. Mandala had missed the first excitement about the Martians, be-cause he had been asleep. When the day manager phoned him, waking him up, Mr. Mandala had thought, first, that it was a joke and, second, that the day man was out of his mind; after all, who would care if the Mars probe had come back with some kind of animals? Or even if they weren't animals, exactly. When he found out how many reservations were coming in over the teletype he realized that some people did in fact care. However, Mr. Mandala didn't take much interest in things like that. It was nice the Martians had come, since they had filled his motel, and every other motel within a hundred miles

of Cape Kennedy, but when you had said that you had said everything
about the Martians that mattered to Mr. Mandala.

On the television screen the picture went to black and was replaced
by the legend *Bulletin from NBC News.* The poker game paused
momentarily.

The lounge was almost quiet as an invisible announcer read a new
release from NASA. "Dr. Hugo Bache, the Fort Worth, Texas,
veterinarian who arrived late this evening to examine the Martians at
the Patrick Air Force Base reception center, has issued a preliminary
report which has just been released by Colonel Eric T. 'Happy' Wingerter, speaking for the National Aeronautics and Space Administration."

A wire-service man yelled, "Turn it up!" There was a convulsive
movement around the set. The sound vanished entirely for a moment,
then blasted out:

"—Martians are vertebrate, warm-blooded and apparently mam-
malian. A superficial examination indicates a generally low level of
metabolism, although Dr. Bache states that it is possible that this is in
some measure the result of their difficult and confined voyage through
137,000,000 miles of space in the specimen chamber of the Algonquin
Nine spacecraft. There is no, repeat no, evidence of communicable
disease, although standing sterilization precautions are—"

"Hell he says," cried somebody, probably a stringer from CBS.
"Walter Cronkite had an interview with the Mayo Clinic that—"

"Shut up!" bellowed a dozen voices, and the TV became audible
again:

"—completes the full text of the report from Dr. Hugo Bache as
released at this hour by Colonel Happy Wingerter." There was a pause;
then the announcer's voice, weary but game, found its place and went
on with a recap of the previous half dozen stories. The poker game
began again as the announcer was describing the news conference with
Dr. Sam Sullivan of the Linguistic Institute of the University of Indiana,
and his conclusions that the sounds made by the Martians were indeed
some sort of a language.

What nonsense, thought Mr. Mandala, drugged and drowsy. He
pulled a stool over and sat down, half asleep.

Then the noise of laughter woke him and he straightened up

belligerently. He tapped his call bell for attention. "Gentlemen! Ladies! Please!" he cried. "It's four o'clock in the morning. Our other guests are trying to sleep."

"Yeah, sure," said the CBS man, holding up one hand impatiently, "but wait a minute. I got one. What's a Martian high-rise? You give up?"

"Go ahead," said a red-haired girl, a staffer from *Life*.

"Twenty-seven floors of basement apartments!"

The girl said, "All right, I got one too. What is a Martian female's religious injunction requiring her to keep her eyes closed during intercourse?" She waited a beat. "God forbid she should see her husband having a good time!"

"Are we playing poker or not?" groaned one of the players, but they were too many for him. "Who won the Martian beauty contest? . . . Nobody won!" "How do you get a Martian female to give up sex? . . . Marry her!" Mr. Mandala laughed out loud at that one, and when one of the reporters came to him and asked for a book of matches he gave it to him. "Ta," said the man, puffing his pipe alight. "Long night, eh?"

"You bet," said Mr. Mandala genially. On the television screen the tape was running again, for the fourth time. Mr. Mandala yawned, staring vacantly at it; it was not much to see but, really, it was all that anyone had seen or was likely to see of the Martians. All these reporters and cameramen and columnists and sound men, thought Mr. Mandala with pleasure, all of them waiting here for the 10:00 A.M. briefing at the Cape would have a forty-mile drive through the palmetto swamps for nothing. Because what they would see when they got there would be just about what they were seeing now.

One of the poker players was telling a long, involved joke about Martians wearing fur coats at Miami Beach. Mr. Mandala looked at them with dislike. If only some of them would go to their rooms and go to sleep he might try asking the others if they were registered in the motel. Although actually he couldn't squeeze anyone else in anyway, with all the rooms doubly occupied already. He gave up the thought and stared vacantly at the Martians on the screen, trying to imagine people all over the world looking at that picture on their television sets, reading about them in their newspapers, *caring* about them. They did not look worth caring about as they sluggishly crawled about on their long,

weak limbs, like a stretched seal's flippers, gasping heavily in the
drag of Earth's gravity, their great long eyes dull.

"Stupid-looking little bastards," one of the reporters said to the pipe
smoker. "You know what I heard? I heard the reason the astronauts
kept them locked in the back was the stink."

"They probably don't notice it on Mars," said the pipe smoker
judiciously. "Thin air."

"Notice it? They love it." He dropped a dollar bill on the desk in
front of Mr. Mandala. "Can I have change for the Coke machine?"
Mr. Mandala counted out dimes silently. It had not occurred to him that
the Martians would smell, but that was only because he hadn't given
it much of a thought. If he had thought about it at all, that was what
he would have thought.

Mr. Mandala fished out a dime for himself and followed the two men
over to the Coke machine. The picture on the TV changed to some
rather poorly photographed shots brought back by the astronauts, of
low, irregular sand-colored buildings on a bright sand floor. These were
what NASA was calling "the largest Martian city," altogether about a
hundred of the flat, windowless structures.

"I dunno," said the second reporter at last, tilting his Coke bottle.
"You think they're what you'd call intelligent?"

"Difficult to say, exactly," said the pipe smoker. He was from Reuter's and looked it, with a red, broad English squire's face. "They
do build houses," he pointed out.

"So does a bull gorilla."

"No doubt. No doubt." The Reuter's man brightened. "Oh, just a
moment. That makes me think of one. There once was—let me see,
at home we tell it about the Irish—yes, I have it. The next spaceship
goes to Mars, you see, and they find that some dread terrestrial disease
has wiped out the whole race, all but one female. These fellows too,
gone. All gone except this one she. Well, they're terribly upset, and
they debate it at the UN and start an anti-genocide pact and America
votes two hundred million dollars for reparations and, well, the long
and short of it is, in order to keep the race from dying out entirely they
decide to breed a human man to this one surviving Martian female."

"Cripes!"

"Yes, exactly. Well, then they find Paddy O'Shaughnessy, down on
his luck, and they say to him, 'See here, just go in that cage there,

Paddy, and you'll find this female. And all you've got to do is render her pregnant, do you see?' And O'Shaughnessy says, 'What's in it for me?' and they offer him, oh, thousands of pounds. And of course he agrees. But then he opens the door of the cage and he sees what the female looks like. And he backs out." The Reuter's man replaced his empty Coke bottle in the rack and grimaced, showing Paddy's expression of revulsion. " 'Holy saints,' he says, 'I never counted on anything like this.' 'Thousands of pounds, Paddy!' they say to him, urging him on. 'Oh, very well then,' he says, 'but on one condition.' 'And what may that be?' they ask him. 'You've got to promise me,' he says, 'that the children'll be raised in the Church.' ' "

"Yeah, I heard that," said the other reporter. And he moved to put his bottle back, and as he did his foot caught in the rack and four cases of empty Coke bottles bounced and clattered across the floor.

Well, that was just about more than Mr. Mandala could stand and he gasped, stuttered, dinged his bell and shouted, "Ernest! Berzie! On the double!" And when Ernest showed up, poking his dark plum-colored head out of the service door with an expression that revealed an anticipation of disaster, Mr. Mandala shouted: "Oh, curse your thick heads, I told you a hundred times, keep those racks cleaned out." And he stood over the two bellmen, fuming, as they bent to the litter of whole bottles and broken glass, their faces glancing up at him sidewise, worried, dark plum and Arabian sand. He knew that all the reporters were looking at him and that they disapproved.

And then he went out into the late night to cool off, because he was sorry and knew he might make himself still sorrier.

The grass was wet. Condensing dew was dripping from the fittings of the diving board into the pool. The motel was not as quiet as it should be so close to dawn, but it was quiet enough. There was only an occasional distant laugh, and the noise from the lounge. To Mr. Mandala it was reassuring. He replenished his soul by walking all the galleries around the room, checking the ice makers and the cigarette machines, and finding that all was well.

A military jet from McCoy was screaming overhead. Beyond it the stars were still bright, in spite of the beginnings of dawn in the east. Mr. Mandala yawned, glanced mildly up and wondered which of them was Mars, and returned to his desk; and shortly he was too busy with

the long, exhausting round of room calls and checkouts to think about
Martians. Then, when most of the guests were getting nosily into their
cars and limo-buses and the day men were coming on, Mr. Mandala
uncapped two cold Cokes and carried one back through the service
door to Ernest.

"Rough night," he said, and Ernest, accepting both the Coke and the
intention, nodded and drank it down. They leaned against the wall that
screened the pool from the access road and watched the newsmen and
newsgirls taking off down the road toward the highway and the ten
o'clock briefing. Most of them had had no sleep. Mr. Mandala shook
his head, disapproving so much commotion for so little cause.

And Ernest snapped his fingers, grinned and said, "I got a Martian
joke, Mr. Mandala. What do you call a seven-foot Martian when he's
comin' at you with a spear?"

"Oh, hell, Ernest," said Mr. Mandala, "you call him sir. Everybody
knows that one." He yawned and stretched and said reflectively, "You'd
think there'd be some new jokes. All I heard was the old ones, only
instead of picking on the Jews and the Catholics and—and everybody,
they were telling them about the Martians."

"Yeah, I noticed that, Mr. Mandala," said Ernest.

Mr. Mandala stood up. "Better get some sleep," he advised, "because they might all be back again tonight. I don't know what for. . . .
Know what I think, Ernest? Outside of the jokes, I don't think that six
months from now anybody's going to remember there ever were such
things as Martians. I don't believe their coming here is going to make a
nickel's worth of difference to anybody."

"Hate to disagree with you, Mr. Mandala," said Ernest mildly, "but
I don't think so. Going to make a difference to some people. Going to
make a *damn* big difference to me."


**Afterword:**

It is and remains my conviction that a story has to speak for itself and
that any words a writer adds to it after he has finished telling it are a
cop-out, a lie or a mistake. But there is one thing that I would like to
say about the reason this story was written. Not to persuade you that it
is a good reason, or that the story accomplishes its purpose—you have

already made your mind up on those things, as indeed you should have. But to tell you how faithfully nature holds the mirror up to art.

Between the time I wrote "The Day After the Day the Martians Came" and now, I met a minister from a small town in Alabama. Like many churches, not only in Alabama, his is torn on the question of integration. He has found a way, he thinks, to solve it—or at least to ameliorate it—among the white teen-agers in his congregation: he is encouraging them to read science fiction, in the hope that they may learn, first, to worry about green-skinned Martians instead of black-skinned Americans and, second, that all men are brothers . . . at least in the face of a very large universe which is very likely to contain creatures who are not men at all.

I like the way this man serves his God. It's a good scheme. It ought to work. It *better* work, or God help all of us.

## Introduction to RIDERS OF THE PURPLE WAGE:

Philip José Farmer is one of the few truly *good* people I have ever met. He is a kind man, with the intonations of that word that connote strength and judiciousness and humanity. He is also indestructible. He has been stomped by masters and somehow managed to come away from the imbroglios undefeated. He has been cheated by *schlock* publishers, criminally mismanaged by inept agents, shamefully ignored by sententious critics, assaulted by the Furies of Chance and Bad Luck, and still, *still* managed to produce fifteen books of such singular eminence that he is considered a "writer's writer" in a field where jealousy and the snide kris in the ribs is s.o.p.

Phil Farmer is in his late forties, a soft-spoken man whose wealth of information on everything from archaeology to the nocturnal habits of Sir Richard Burton (not the actor) is formidable. He is a walker of streets, a drinker of coffee, a smoker of cigarettes, a lover of grandchildren. But most of all, he is a writer of stories. Stories like "The

Lovers" that burst on the science fiction field in a 1952 issue of *Startling Stories* like an explosion in a fresh-air factory. Until Phil Farmer took a long look at the subject, sex was something confined to Bergey covers involving heavily thighed young ladies in brass brassieres. He has examined every facet of abnormal psychology—it seems —in an adult and extrapolative manner most editors would have denied was possible, in 1951. Anyone who cares to deprecate this achievement, in a field where Kimball Kinnison's lack of genitalia never seemed to bother editors or aficionados, need only consider that, until Farmer and the vigor of his work, the closest thing the genre had to psychological explorations were the stories of Dr. David H. Keller, which fall somewhat short of the levels attained by, say, Dostoevsky or Kafka.

An editor should never show favoritism. Yet I am compelled by my awe of the story you are about to read, by my incredulity at the pyrotechnic writing, by my jealousy at the richness of thought and excellence of structure, to say simply that this is not merely the longest story in the book—something over 30,000 words—it is easily the best. No, make that the *finest*. It is a jewel of such brilliance that re-examination and rereading will reveal facet after facet, ramification after ramification, joy after delight that were only partially glimpsed first time around. The explanation of the bases of this story is fully detailed in Phil Farmer's excellent Afterword, and to attempt an original and pithy comment about what he is saying here would be ludicrous. The man speaks for himself more than well enough. I should like to take a moment, however, to address myself to three elements of Farmer's work that I think need explication.

The first is his courage. In the face of rejections from editors who are not fit to carry his pencil case, he has persisted in writing stories that demanded considerable cerebration and the knocking down of previous ways of thinking. Though his work has been met with the blank stares of readers accustomed to soft pink and white bunny rabbit stories, he has doggedly gone after one dangerous vision after another. Knowing he could make a substantial living writing pap, knowing the deeper and more unnerving topics would be met by animosity and stupidity, he still held firm to his styles, his concepts, his muse, if you will.

Second is his inability to let go of an idea. The smallest scintilla of a concept leads him outward and ever outward to extrapolations and consequences lesser writers would milk for a tetralogy. He is in the great tradition of all original thinkers. There is no mystery too complex for Farmer to unravel. No line of thought too bizarre for him to attempt a re-evaluation with the tools of logic. No story too big for him to write, no character too obscure for him to incorporate, no universe too distant for him to explore. Tragically, while Farmer writes immense orbits around lesser talents who endlessly examine the nits in their bearded reputations, the field on which he has chosen to shower his gifts largely ignores him.

Third is his style. Which is never the same twice. Which grows geometrically with each new story. Which demands of the reader a kind of intellectual mastication reserved for the best in literature. His work is steak, to be chewed thoroughly and digested; not tapioca pudding that can be gummed without effort.

I have gone on, I realize, at somewhat greater length than I had intended. The reader may chalk this up to the editor's enthusiasm for the story that follows. It was submitted upon commission, of course, as were all the pieces herein presented. But when it was completed, at 15,000 words, Farmer came to the editor and asked if he might rewrite it, expand it, without payment, for the ideas in it needed room to breathe. Farmer was paid, naturally, and the rewrite was done. But he was not paid nearly enough. Quote an estimate on originality and verve and an unflinching look at tomorrow. Further residuals are due Phil Farmer in the form of comment by the readers. Not to mention a Hugo or six, which would look remarkably as though they had been cast specifically to sit on the mantel of his Beverly Hills apartment. A word to the wise.

# ● RIDERS OF THE PURPLE WAGE
## or
## The Great Gavage

### by Philip José Farmer

> If Jules Verne could really have looked into the future, say
> 1966 A.D., he would have crapped in his pants. And 2166, oh,
> my!
>
> —from Grandpa Winnegan's unpublished Ms. *How I
> Screwed Uncle Sam & Other Private Ejaculations.*

## THE COCK THAT CROWED BACKWARDS

Un and Sub, the giants, are grinding him for bread.

Broken pieces float up through the wine of sleep. Vast treadings crush abysmal grapes for the incubus sacrament.

He as Simple Simon fishes in his soul as pail for the leviathan.

He groans, half-wakes, turns over, sweating dark oceans, and groans again. Un and Sub, putting their backs to their work, turn the stone wheels of the sunken mill, muttering Fie, fye, fo, fum. Eyes glittering orange-red as a cat's in a cubbyhole, teeth dull white digits in the murky arithmetic.

Un and Sub, Simple Simons themselves, busily mix metaphors non-self-consciously.

Dunghill and cock's egg: up rises the cockatrice and gives first crow, two more to come, in the flushrush of blood of dawn of I-am-the erection-and-the-strife.

It grows out and out until weight and length merge to curve it over, a not-yet weeping willow or broken reed. The one-eyed red head peeks over the edge of bed. It rests its chinless jaw, then, as body swells, slides over and down. Looking monocularly this way and those, it sniffs archaically across the floor and heads for the door, left open by the lapsus linguae of malingering sentinels.

A loud braying from the center of the room makes it turn back.

The three-legged ass, Baalim's easel, is heehawing. On the easel is the "canvas," an oval shallow pan of irradiated plastic, specially treated. The canvas is seven feet high and eighteen inches deep. Within the painting is a scene that must be finished by tomorrow.

As much sculpture as painting, the figures are in alto-relief, rounded, some nearer the back of the pan than others. They glow with light from outside and also from the self-luminous plastic of the "canvas." The light seems to enter the figures, soak awhile, then break loose. The light is pale red, the red of dawn, of blood watered with tears, of anger, of ink on the debit side of the ledger.

This is one of his Dog Series: *Dogmas from a Dog, The Aerial Dogfight, Dog Days, The Sundog, Dog Reversed, The Dog of Flinders, Dog Berries, Dog Catcher, Lying Doggo, The Dog of the Right Angle,* and *Improvisations on a Dog.*

Socrates, Ben Jonson, Cellini, Swedenborg, Li Po, and Hiawatha are roistering in the Mermaid Tavern. Through a window, Daedalus is seen on top of the battlements of Cnossus, shoving a rocket up the ass of his son, Icarus, to give him a jet-assisted takeoff for his famous flight. In one corner crouches Og, Son of Fire. He gnaws on a sabertooth bone and paints bison and mammoths on the mildewed plaster. The barmaid, Athena, is bending over the table where she is serving nectar and pretzels to her distinguished customers. Aristotle, wearing goat's horns, is behind her. He has lifted her skirt and is tupping her from behind. The ashes from the cigarette dangling from his smirking lips have fallen onto her skirt, which is beginning to smoke. In the doorway of the men's room, a drunken Batman succumbs to a long-repressed desire and attempts to bugger the Boy Wonder. Through another window is a lake on the surface of which a man is walking, a green-tarnished halo hovering over his head. Behind him a periscope sticks out of the water.

Prehensile, the penisnake wraps itself around the brush and begins to paint. The brush is a small cylinder attached at one end to a hose which runs to a dome-shaped machine. From the other end of the cylinder extends a nozzle. The aperture of this can be decreased or increased by rotation of a thumb-dial on the cylinder. The paint which the nozzle deposits in a fine spray or in a thick stream or in whatever color or hue desired is controlled by several dials on the cylinder.

Furiously, proboscisean, it builds up another figure layer by layer.

Then, it sniffs a musty odor of must and drops the brush and slides out the door and down the bend of wall of oval hall, describing the scrawl of legless creatures, a writing in the sand which all may read but few understand. Blood pumppumps in rhythm with the mills of Un and Sub to feed and swill the hot-blooded reptile. But the walls, detecting intrusive mass and extrusive desire, glow.

He groans, and the glandular cobra rises and sways to the fluting of his wish for cuntcealment. Let there not be light! The nights must be his cloaka. Speed past mother's room, nearest the exit. Ah! Sighs softly in relief but air whistles through the vertical and tight mouth, announcing the departure of the exsupress for Desideratum.

The door has become archaic; it has a keyhole. Quick! Up the ramp and out of the house through the keyhole and out onto the street. One person abroad a broad, a young woman with phosphorescent silver hair and snatch to match.

Out and down the street and coiling around her ankle. She looks down with surprise and then fear. He likes this; too willing were too many. He's found a diamond in the ruff.

Up around her kitten-ear-soft leg, around and around, and sliding across the dale of groin. Nuzzling the tender corkscrewed hairs and then, self-Tantalus, detouring up the slight convex of belly, saying hello to the bellybutton, pressing on it to ring upstairs, around and around the narrow waist and shyly and quickling snatching a kiss from each nipple. Then back down to form an expedition for climbing the mons veneris and planting the flag thereon.

Oh, delectation tabu and sickersacrosanct! There's a baby in there, ectoplasm beginning to form in eager preanticipation of actuality. Drop, egg, and shoot the chutychutes of flesh, hastening to gulp the lucky Micromoby Dick, outwriggling its million million brothers, survival of the fightingest.

A vast croaking fills the hall. The hot breath chills the skin. He sweats. Icicles coat the tumorous fuselage, and it sags under the weight of ice, and fog rolls around, whistling past the struts, and the ailerons and elevators are locked in ice, and he's losing altiattitude fast. Get up, get up! Venusberg somewhere ahead in the mists; Tannhäuser, blow your strumpets, send up your flares, I'm in a nosedive.

Mother's door has opened. A toad squatfills the ovoid doorway. Its dewlap rises and falls bellows-like; its toothless mouth gawps. Ginun-gagap. Forked tongue shoots out and curls around the boar cuntstrictor. He cries out with both mouths and jerks this way and those. The waves of denial run through. Two webbed paws bend and tie the flopping body into a knot—a runny shapeshank, of course.

The woman strolls on. Wait for me! Out the flood roars, crashes into the knot, roars back, ebb clashing with flood. Too much and only one way to go. He jerkspurts, the firmament of waters falling, no Noah's ark or arc; he novas, a shatter of millions of glowing wriggling meteors, flashes in the pan of existence.

Thigh kingdom come. Groin and belly encased in musty armor, and he cold, wet, and trembling.

## GOD'S PATENT ON DAWN EXPIRES

. . . the following spoken by Alfred Melophon Voxpopper, of the Aurora Pushups and Coffee Hour, Channel 69B. Lines taped during the 50th Folk Art Center Annual Demonstration and Competition, Beverly Hills, level 14. Spoken by Omar Bacchylides Runic, extemporaneously if you discount some forethought during the previous evening at the nonpublic tavern The Private Universe, and you may because Runic did not remember a thing about that evening. Despite which he won First Laurel Wreath A, there being no Second, Third, etc., wreaths classified as A through Z, God bless our democracy.

> A gray-pink salmon leaping up the falls of night
> Into the spawning pool of another day.
>
> Dawn—the red roar of the heliac bull
> Charging over the horizon.
>
> The photonic blood of bleeding night,
> Stabbed by the assassin sun.

and so on for fifty lines punctuated and fractured by cheers, hand-claps, boos, hisses, and yelps.

Chib is half-awake. He peeps down into the narrowing dark as the dream roars off into the subway tunnel. He peeps through barely opened lids at the other reality: consciousness.

"Let my peeper go!" he groans with Moses and so, thinking of long beards and horns (courtesy of Michelangelo), he thinks of his great-great-grandfather.

The will, a crowbar, forces his eyelids open. He sees the fido which spans the wall opposite him and curves up over half the ceiling. Dawn, the paladin of the sun, is flinging its gray gauntlet down.

Channel 69B, YOUR FAVORITE CHANNEL, LA's own, brings you dawn. (Deception in depth. Nature's false dawn shadowed forth with electrons shaped by devices shaped by man.)

Wake up with the sun in your heart and a song on your lips! Thrill to the stirring lines of Omar Runic! See dawn as the birds in the trees, as God, see it!

Voxpopper chants the lines softly while Grieg's *Anitra* wells softly. The old Norwegian never dreamed of this audience and just as well. A young man, Chibiabos Elgreco Winnegan, has a sticky wick, courtesy of a late gusher in the oilfield of the unconscious.

"Off your ass and onto your steed," Chib says. "Pegasus runs today."

He speaks, thinks, lives in the present tensely.

Chib climbs out of bed and shoves it into the wall. To leave the bed sticking out, rumpled as an old drunkard's tongue, would fracture the aesthetics of his room, destroy that curve that is the reflection of the basic universe, and hinder him in his work.

The room is a huge ovoid and in a corner is a small ovoid, the toilet and shower. He comes out of it looking like one of Homer's god-like Achaeans, massively thighed, great-armed, golden-brown-skinned, blue-eyed, auburn-haired—although beardless. The phone is simulating the tocsin of a South American tree frog he once heard over Channel 122.

"Open O sesame!"


## INTER CAECOS REGNAT LUSCUS


The face of Rex Luscus spreads across the fido, the pores of skin like the cratered fields of a World War I battlefield. He wears a black monocle over the left eye, ripped out in a brawl among art critics during the *I Love Rembrandt Lecture Series,* Channel 109. Although he has enough pull to get a priority for eye-replacement, he has refused.

*"Inter caecos regnat luscus,"* he says when asked about it and quite often when not. "Translation: among the blind, the one-eyed man is king. That's why I renamed myself Rex Luscus, that is, King One-eyed."

There is a rumor, fostered by Luscus, that he will permit the bioboys to put in an artificial protein eye when he sees the works of an artist great enough to justify focal vision. It is also rumored that he may do so soon, because of his discovery of Chibiabos Elgreco Winnegan.

Luscus looks hungrily (he swears by adverbs) at Chib's tomentum and outlying regions. Chib swells, not with tumescence but with anger.

Luscus says, smoothly, "Honey, I just want to reassure myself that you're up and about the tremendously important business of this day. You must be ready for the showing, must! But now I see you, I'm reminded I've not eaten yet. What about breakfast with me?"

"What're we eating?" Chib says. He does not wait for a reply. "No. I've too much to do today. Close O sesame!"

Rex Luscus' face fades away, goatlike, or, as he prefers to describe it, the face of Pan, a Faunus of the arts. He has even had his ears trimmed to a point. Real cute.

"Baa-aa-aa!" Chib bleats at the phantom. "Ba! Humbuggery! I'll never kiss your ass, Luscus, or let you kiss mine. Even if I lose the grant!"

The phone bells again. The dark face of Rousseau Red Hawk appears. His nose is as the eagle's, and his eyes are broken black glass. His broad forehead is bound with a strip of red cloth, which circles the straight black hair that glides down to his shoulders. His shirt is buckskin; a necklace of beads hangs from his neck. He looks like a Plains Indian, although Sitting Bull, Crazy Horse, or the noblest Roman Nose of them all would have kicked him out of the tribe. Not that they were anti-Semitic, they just could not have respected a brave who broke out into hives when near a horse.

Born Julius Applebaum, he legally became Rousseau Red Hawk on his Naming Day. Just returned from the forest reprimevalized, he is now reveling in the accursed fleshpots of a decadent civilization.

"How're you, Chib? The gang's wondering how soon you'll get here?"

"Join you? I haven't had breakfast yet, and I've a thousand things to do to get ready for the showing. I'll see you at noon!"

"You missed out on the fun last night. Some goddam Egyptians tried to feel the girls up, but we salaamed them against the walls."

Rousseau vanished like the last of the red men.

Chib thinks of breakfast just as the intercom whistles. Open O sesame! He sees the living room. Smoke, too thick and furious for the air-conditioning to whisk away, roils. At the far end of the ovoid, his little half-brother and half-sister sleep on a flato. Playing Mama-and-friend, they fell asleep, their mouths open in blessed innocence, beautiful as only sleeping children can be. Opposite the closed eyes of each is an unwinking eye like that of a Mongolian Cyclops.

"Ain't they cute?" Mama says. "The darlings were just too tired to toddle off."

The table is round. The aged knights and ladies are gathered around it for the latest quest of the ace, king, queen, and jack. They are armored only in layer upon layer of fat. Mama's jowls hang down like banners on a windless day. Her breasts creep and quiver on the table, bulge, and ripple.

"A gam of gamblers," he says aloud, looking at the fat faces, the tremendous tits, the rampant rumps. They raise their eyebrows. What the hell's the mad genius talking about now?

"Is your kid really retarded?" says one of Mama's friends, and they laugh and drink some more beer. Angela Ninon, not wanting to miss out on this deal and figuring Mama will soon turn on the sprayers anyway, pisses down her leg. They laugh at this, and William Conqueror says, "I open."

"I'm always open," Mama says, and they shriek with laughter.

Chib would like to cry. He does not cry, although he has been encouraged from childhood to cry any time he feels like it.

—It makes you feel better and look at the Vikings, what men they were and they cried like babies whenever they felt like it
—Courtesy of Channel 202 on the popular program *What's A Mother Done?*

He does not cry because he feels like a man who thinks about the mother he loved and who is dead but who died a long time ago. His mother has been long buried under a landslide of flesh. When he was sixteen, he had had a lovely mother.

Then she cut him off.


## THE FAMILY THAT BLOWS IS THE FAMILY THAT GROWS
—from a poem by Edgar A. Grist, via Channel 88.


"Son, I don't get much out of this. I just do it because I love you."

Then, fat, fat, fat! Where did she go? Down into the adipose abyss. Disappearing as she grew larger.

"Sonny, you could at least wrestle with me a little now and then."

"You cut me off, Mama. That was all right. I'm a big boy now. But you haven't any right to expect me to want to take it up again."

"You don't love me any more!"


"What's for breakfast, Mama?" Chib says.

"I'm holding a good hand, Chibby," Mama says. "As you've told me so many times, you're a big boy. Just this once, get your own breakfast."

"What'd you call me for?"

"I forgot when your exhibition starts. I wanted to get some sleep before I went."

"14:30, Mama, but you don't have to go."

Rouged green lips part like a gangrened wound. She scratches one rouged nipple. "Oh, I want to be there. I don't want to miss my own son's artistic triumphs. Do you think you'll get the grant?"

"If I don't, it's Egypt for us," he says.

"Those stinking Arabs!" says William Conqueror.

"It's the Bureau that's doing it, not the Arabs," Chib says. "The Arabs moved for the same reason we may have to move."


*From Grandpa's unpublished Ms.:* Whoever would have thought that Beverly Hills would become anti-Semitic?

"I don't want to go to Egypt!" Mama wails. "You got to get that grant, Chibby. I don't want to leave the clutch. I was born and raised here, well, on the tenth level, anyway, and when I moved all my friends went along. I won't go!"

"Don't cry, Mama," Chib says, feeling distress despite himself. "Don't cry. The government can't force you to go, you know. You got your rights."

"If you want to keep on having goodies, you'll go," says Conqueror. "Unless Chib wins the grant, that is. And I wouldn't blame him if he didn't even try to win it. It ain't his fault you can't say no to Uncle Sam. You got your purple and the yap Chib makes from selling his paintings. Yet it ain't enough. You spend faster than you get it."

Mama screams with fury at William, and they're off. Chib cuts off fido. Hell with breakfast; he'll eat later. His final painting for the Festival must be finished by noon. He presses a plate, and the bare egg-shaped room opens here and there, and painting equipment comes out like a gift from the electronic gods. Zeuxis would flip and Van Gogh would get the shakes if they could see the canvas and palette and brush Chib uses.

The process of painting involves the individual bending and twisting of thousands of wires into different shapes at various depths. The wires are so thin they can be seen only with magnifiers and manipulated with exceedingly delicate pliers. Hence, the goggles he wears and the long almost-gossamer instrument in his hand when he is in the first stages of creating a painting. After hundreds of hours of slow and patient labor (of love), the wires are arranged.

Chib removes his goggles to perceive the overall effect. He then uses the paint-sprayer to cover the wires with the colors and hues he desires. The paint dries hard within a few minutes. Chib attaches electrical leads to the pan and presses a button to deliver a tiny voltage through the wires. These glow beneath the paint and, Lilliputian fuses, disappear in blue smoke.

The result is a three-dimensional work composed of hard shells of paint on several levels below the exterior shell. The shells are of varying thicknesses and all are so thin that light slips through the upper to the inner shell when the painting is turned at angles. Parts of the shells are simply reflectors to intensify the light so that the inner images may be more visible.

When being shown, the painting is on a self-moving pedestal which turns the painting 12 degrees to the left from the center and then 12 degrees to the right from the center.

The fido tocsins. Chib, cursing, thinks of disconnecting it. At least, it's not the intercom with his mother calling hysterically. Not yet, anyway. She'll call soon enough if she loses heavily at poker.

Open O sesame!


## SING, O MEWS, OF UNCLE SAM

Grandpa writes in his *Private Ejaculations:* Twenty-five years after I fled with twenty billion dollars and then supposedly died of a heart attack, Falco Accipiter is on my trail again. The IRB detective who named himself Falcon Hawk when he entered his profession. What an egotist! Yet, he is as sharp-eyed and relentless as a bird of prey, and I would shiver if I were not too old to be frightened by mere human beings. Who loosed the jesses and hood? How did he pick up the old and cold scent?

Accipiter's face is that of an overly suspicious peregrine that tries to look everywhere while it soars, that peers up its own anus to make sure that no duck has taken refuge there. The pale blue eyes fling glances like knives shot out of a shirtsleeve and hurled with a twist of the wrist. They scan all with sherlockian intake of minute and significant detail. His head turns back and forth, ears twitching, nostrils expanding and collapsing, all radar and sonar and odar.

"Mr. Winnegan, I'm sorry to call so early. Did I get you out of bed?"

"It's obvious you didn't!" Chib says. "Don't bother to introduce yourself. I know you. You've been shadowing me for three days."

Accipiter does not redden. Master of control, he does all his blushing in the depths of his bowels, where no one can see. "If you know me, perhaps you can tell me why I'm calling you?"

"Would I be dumbshit enough to tell you?"

"Mr. Winnegan, I'd like to talk to you about your great-great-grandfather."

"He's been dead for twenty-five years!" Chib cries. "Forget him. And don't bother me. Don't try for a search warrant. No judge would give you one. A man's home is his hassle . . . I mean castle."

He thinks of Mama and what the day is going to be like unless he gets out soon. But he has to finish the painting.

"Fade off, Accipiter," Chib says. "I think I'll report you to the BPHR. I'm sure you got a fido inside that silly-looking hat of yours."

Accipiter's face is as smooth and unmoving as an alabaster carving of the falcon-god Horus. He may have a little gas bulging his intestines. If so, he slips it out unnoticed.

"Very well, Mr. Winnegan. But you're not getting rid of me that easily. After all . . ."

"Fade out!"

The intercom whistles thrice. What I tell you three times is Grandpa. "I was eavesdropping," says the 120-year-old voice, hollow and deep as an echo from a Pharaoh's tomb. "I want to see you before you leave. That is, if you can spare the Ancient of Daze a few minutes."

"Always, Grandpa," Chib says, thinking of how much he loves the old man. "You need any food?"

"Yes, and for the mind, too."

*Der Tag. Dies Irae. Götterdammerung.* Armageddon. Things are closing in. Make-or-break day. Go-no-go time. All these calls and a feeling of more to come. What will the end of the day bring?


## THE TROCHE SUN SLIPS INTO THE SORE THROAT OF NIGHT

—from Omar Runic


Chib walks towards the convex door, which rolls into the interstices between the walls. The focus of the house is the oval family room. In the first quadrant, going clockwise, is the kitchen, separated from the family room by six-meter-high accordion screens, painted with scenes from Egyptian tombs by Chib, his too subtle comment on modern food. Seven slim pillars around the family room mark the borders of room and corridor. Between the pillars are more tall accordion screens, painted by Chib during his Amerind mythology phase.

The corridor is also oval-shaped; every room in the house opens onto it. There are seven rooms, six bedroom-workroom-study-toilet-shower combinations. The seventh is a storeroom.

Little eggs within bigger eggs within great eggs within a megamonolith on a planetary pear within an ovoid universe, the latest cosmogony indicating that infinity has the form of a hen's fruit. God broods over the abyss and cackles every trillion years or so.

Chib cuts across the hall, passes between two pillars, carved by him into nymphet caryatids, and enters the family room. His mother looks sidewise at her son, who she thinks is rapidly approaching insanity if he has not already overshot his mark. It's partly her fault; she shouldn't have gotten disgusted and in a moment of wackiness called It off. Now, she's fat and ugly, oh, God, so fat and ugly. She can't reasonably or even unreasonably hope to start up again.

It's only natural, she keeps telling herself, sighing, resentful, teary, that he's abandoned the love of his mother for the strange, firm, shapely delights of young women. But to give them up, too? He's not a fairy. He quit all that when he was thirteen. So what's the reason for his chastity? He isn't in love with the fornixator, either, which she would understand, even if she did not approve.

Oh, God, where did I go wrong? And then, There's nothing wrong with me. He's going crazy like his father—Raleigh Renaissance, I think his name was—and his aunt and his great-great-grandfather. It's all that painting and those radicals, the Young Radishes, he runs around with. He's too artistic, too sensitive. Oh, God, if something happens to my little boy, I'll have to go to Egypt.

Chib knows her thoughts since she's voiced them so many times and is not capable of having new ones. He passes the round table without a word. The knights and ladies of the canned Camelot see him through a beery veil.

In the kitchen, he opens an oval door in the wall. He removes a tray with food in covered dishes and cups, all wrapped in plastic.

"Aren't you going to eat with us?"

"Don't whine, Mama," he says and goes back to his room to pick up some cigars for his Grandpa. The door, detecting, amplifying, and transmitting the shifting but recognizable eidolon of epidermal electrical fields to the activating mechanism, balks. Chib is too upset. Magnetic maelstroms rage over his skin and distort the spectral configuration. The door half-rolls out, rolls in, changes its mind again, rolls out, rolls in.

Chib kicks the door and it becomes completely blocked. He decides he'll have a video or vocal sesame put in. Trouble is, he's short of units and coupons and can't buy the materials. He shrugs and walks along the curving, one-walled hall and stops in front of Grandpa's door, hidden from view of those in the living room by the kitchen screens.

> "For he sang of peace and freedom,
> Sang of beauty, love, and longing;
> Sang of death, and life undying
> In the Islands of the Blessed,
> In the kingdom of Ponemah,
> In the land of the Hereafter.
> Very dear to Hiawatha
> Was the gentle Chibiabos."

Chib chants the passwords; the door rolls back.

Light glares out, a yellowish red-tinged light that is Grandpa's own creation. Looking into the convex oval door is like looking into the lens of a madman's eyeball. Grandpa, in the middle of the room, has a white beard falling to midthigh and white hair cataracting to just below the back of his knees. Although beard and headhair conceal his nakedness, and he is not out in public, he wears a pair of shorts. Grandpa is somewhat old-fashioned, forgivable in a man of twelve decadencies.

Like Rex Luscus, he is one-eyed. He smiles with his own teeth, grown from buds transplanted thirty years ago. A big green cigar sticks out of one corner of his full red mouth. His nose is broad and smeared as if time had stepped upon it with a heavy foot. His forehead and cheeks are broad, perhaps due to a shot of Ojibway blood in his veins, though he was born Finnegan and even sweats celtically, giving off an aroma of whiskey. He holds his head high, and the blue-gray eye is like a pool at the bottom of a prediluvian pothole, remnant of a melted glacier.

All in all, Grandpa's face is Odin's as he returns from the Well of Mimir, wondering if he paid too great a price. Or it is the face of the windbeaten, sandblown Sphinx of Gizeh.

"Forty centuries of hysteria look down upon you, to paraphrase Napoleon," Grandpa says. "The rockhead of the ages. *What, then, is Man?* sayeth the New Sphinx, Edipus having resolved the question of the Old Sphinx and settling nothing because She had already delivered another of her kind, a smartass kid with a question nobody's been able to answer yet. And perhaps just as well it can't be."

"You talk funny," Chib says. "But I like it."

He grins at Grandpa, loving him.

"You sneak into here every day, not so much from love for me as to gain knowledge and insight. I have seen all, heard everything, and thought more than a little. I voyaged much before I took refuge in this room a quarter of a century ago. Yet confinement here has been the greatest Odyssey of all.

## THE ANCIENT MARINATOR

I call myself. A marinade of wisdom steeped in the brine of over-salted cynicism and too long a life."

"You smile so, you must have just had a woman," Chib teases.

"No, my boy. I lost the tension in my ramrod thirty years ago. And I thank God for that, since it removes from me the temptation of fornication, not to mention masturbation. However, I have other energies left, hence, scope for other sins, and these are even more serious.

"Aside from the sin of sexual commission, which paradoxically involves the sin of sexual emission, I had other reasons for not asking that Old Black Magician Science for shots to starch me out again. I was too old for young girls to be attracted to me for anything but money. And I was too much a poet, a lover of beauty, to take on the wrinkled blisters of my generation or several just before mine.

"So now you see, my son. My clapper swings limberly in the bell of my sex. Ding, dong, ding, dong. A lot of dong but not much ding."

Grandpa laughs deeply, a lion's roar with a spray of doves.

"I am but the mouthpiece of the ancients, a shyster pleading for long-dead clients. Come not to bury but to praise and forced by my sense of fairness to admit the faults of the past, too. I'm a queer crabbed old man, pent like Merlin in his tree trunk. Samolxis, the Thracian bear god, hibernating in his cave. The Last of the Seven Sleepers."

Grandpa goes to the slender plastic tube depending from the ceiling and pulls down the folding handles of the eyepiece.

"Accipiter is hovering outside our house. He smells something rotten in Beverly Hills, level 14. Could it be that Win-again Winnegan isn't dead? Uncle Sam is like a diplodocus kicked in the ass. It takes twenty-five years for the message to reach its brain."

Tears appear in Chib's eyes. He says, "Oh, God, Grandpa, I don't want anything to happen to you."

"What can happen to a 120-year-old man besides failure of brain or kidneys?"

"With all due respect, Grandpa," Chib says, "you do rattle on."

"Call me Id's mill," Grandpa says. "The flour it yields is baked in the strange oven of my ego—or half-baked, if you please."

Chib grins through his tears and says, "They taught me at school that puns are cheap and vulgar."

"What's good enough for Homer, Aristophanes, Rabelais, and Shakespeare is good enough for me. By the way, speaking of cheap and vulgar, I met your mother in the hall last night, before the poker party started. I was just leaving the kitchen with a bottle of booze. She almost fainted. But she recovered fast and pretended not to see me. Maybe she did think she'd seen a ghost. I doubt it. She'd have been blabbing all over town about it."

"She may have told her doctor," Chib says. "She saw you several weeks ago, remember? She may have mentioned it while she was bitching about her so-called dizzy spells and hallucinations."

"And the old sawbones, knowing the family history, called the IRB. Maybe."

Chib looks through the periscope's eyepiece. He rotates it and turns the knobs on the handle-ends to raise and lower the cyclops on the end of the tube outside. Accipiter is stalking around the aggregate of seven eggs, each on the end of a broad thin curved branchlike walk projecting from the central pedestal. Accipiter goes up the steps of a branch to the door of Mrs. Applebaum's. The door opens.

"He must have caught her away from the fornixator," Chib says. "And she must be lonely; she's not talking to him over fido. My God, she's fatter than Mama!"

"Why not?" Grandpa says. "Mr. and Mrs. Everyman sit on their asses all day, drink, eat, and watch fido, and their brains run to mud and their bodies to sludge. Caesar would have had no trouble surrounding himself with fat friends these days. You ate, too, Brutus?"

Grandpa's comment, however, should not apply to Mrs. Applebaum. She has a hole in her head, and people addicted to fornixation seldom get fat. They sit or lie all day and part of the night, the needle in the fornix area of the brain delivering a series of minute electrical jolts. Indescribable ecstasy floods through their bodies with every impulse, a delight far surpassing any of food, drink, or sex. It's illegal, but the government never bothers a user unless it wants to get him for something else, since a fornic rarely has children. Twenty per cent of LA have had holes drilled in their heads and tiny shafts inserted for access of the needle. Five per cent are addicted; they waste away, seldom eating, their distended bladders spilling poisons into the bloodstream.

Chib says, "My brother and sister must have seen you sometimes when you were sneaking out to mass. Could they . . . ?"

"They think I'm a ghost, too. In this day and age! Still, maybe it's a good sign that they can believe in something, even a spook."

"You better stop sneaking out to church."

"The Church, and you, are the only things that keep me going. It was a sad day, though, when you told me you couldn't believe. You would have made a good priest—with faults, of course—and I could have had private mass and confession in this room."

Chib says nothing. He's gone to instruction and observed services just to please Grandpa. The church was an egg-shaped seashell which, held to the ear, gave only the distant roar of God receding like an ebb tide.

### THERE ARE UNIVERSES BEGGING FOR GODS
yet He hangs around this one looking for work.

—from Grandpa's Ms.

Grandpa takes over the eyepiece. He laughs. "The Internal Revenue Bureau! I thought it'd been disbanded! Who the hell has an income big enough to report on any more? Do you suppose it's still active just because of me? Could be."

He calls Chib back to the scope, directed towards the center of Beverly Hills. Chib has a lane of vision between the seven-egged clutches on the branched pedestals. He can see part of the central plaza, the giant ovoids of the city hall, the federal bureaus, the Folk Center, part of the massive spiral on which set the houses of worship, and the dora (from pandora) where those on the purple wage get their goods and those with extra income get their goodies. One end of the big artificial lake is visible; boats and canoes sail on it and people fish.

The irradiated plastic dome that enfolds the clutches of Beverly Hills is sky-blue. The electronic sun climbs towards the zenith. There are a few white genuine-looking images of clouds and even a V of geese migrating south, their honks coming down faintly. Very nice for those who have never been outside the walls of LA. But Chib spent two years in the World Nature Rehabilitation and Conservation Corps—the WNRCC—and he knows the difference. Almost, he decided to desert with Rousseau Red Hawk and join the neo-Amerinds. Then, he was going to become a forest ranger. But this might mean he'd end up shooting or arresting Red Hawk. Besides, he didn't want to become a sammer. And he wanted more than anything to paint.

"There's Rex Luscus," Chib says. "He's being interviewed outside the Folk Center. Quite a crowd."


## THE PELLUCIDAR BREAKTHROUGH

Luscus' middle name should have been Upmanship. A man of great erudition, with privileged access to the Library of Greater LA computer, and of Ulyssean sneakiness, he is always scoring over his colleagues.

He it was who founded the Go-Go School of Criticism.

Primalux Ruskinson, his great competitor, did some extensive research when Luscus announced the title of his new philosophy. Ruskinson triumphantly announced that Luscus had taken the phrase from obsolete slang, current in the mid-twentieth century.

Luscus, in the fido interview next day, said that Ruskinson was a rather shallow scholar, which was to be expected.

*Go-go* was taken from the Hottentot language. In Hottentot, *go-go* meant to examine, that is, to keep looking until something about the object—in this case, the artist and his works—has been observed.

The critics got in line to sign up at the new school. Ruskinson thought of committing suicide, but instead accused Luscus of having blown his way up the ladder of success.

Luscus replied on fido that his personal life was his own, and Ruskinson was in danger of being sued for violation of privacy. However, he deserved no more effort than a man striking at a mosquito.

"What the hell's a mosquito?" say millions of viewers. "Wish the bighead would talk language we could understand."

Luscus' voice fades off for a minute while the interpreters explain, having just been slipped a note from a monitor who's run off the word through the station's encyclopedia.

Luscus rode on the novelty of the Go-Go School for two years.

Then he re-established his prestige, which had been slipping somewhat, with his philosophy of the Totipotent Man.

This was so popular that the Bureau of Cultural Development and Recreation requisitioned a daily one-hour slot for a year-and-a-half in the initial program of totipotentializing.

> Grandpa Winnegan's penned comment in his *Private Ejaculations:*
>
> What about The Totipotent Man, that apotheosis of individuality and complete psychosomatic development, the democratic Übermensch, as recommended by Rex Luscus, the sexually one-sided? Poor old Uncle Sam! Trying to force the proteus of his citizens into a single stabilized shape so he can control them. And at the same time trying to encourage each and every to bring to flower his inherent capabilities—if any! The poor old long-legged, chin-whiskered, milk-hearted, flint-brained schizophrenic! Verily, the left hand knows not what the right hand is doing. As a matter of fact, the right hand doesn't know what the right hand is doing.

"What about the totipotent man?" Luscus replied to the chairman during the fourth session of the *Luscan Lecture Series*. "How does he conflict with the contemporary Zeitgeist? He doesn't. The totipotent man is the imperative of our times. He must come into being before the Golden World can be realized. How can you have a Utopia without utopians, a Golden World with men of brass?"

It was during this Memorable Day that Luscus gave his talk on The Pellucidar Breakthrough and thereby made Chibiabos Winnegan famous. And more than incidentally gave Luscus his biggest score over his competitors.

"Pellucidar? Pellucidar?" Ruskinson mutters. "Oh, God, what's Tinker Bell doing now?"

"It'll take me some time to explain why I use this phrase to describe Winnegan's stroke of genius," Luscus continues. "First, let me seem to detour

## FROM THE ARCTIC TO ILLINOIS

"Now, Confucius once said that a bear could not fart at the North Pole without causing a big wind in Chicago.

"By this he meant that all events, therefore, all men, are interconnected in an unbreakable web. What one man does, no matter how seemingly insignificant, vibrates through the strands and affects every man."

Ho Chung Ko, before his fido on the 30th level of Lhasa, Tibet, says to his wife, "That white prick has got it all wrong. Confucius didn't say that. Lenin preserve us! I'm going to call him up and give him hell."

His wife says, "Let's change the channel. Pai Ting Place is on now, and . . ."

Ngombe, 10th level, Nairobi: "The critics here are a bunch of black bastards. Now you take Luscus; he could see my genius in a second. I'm going to apply for emigration in the morning."

Wife: "You might at least ask me if I want to go! What about the kids . . . mother . . . friends . . . dog . . . ?" and so on into the lionless night of self-luminous Africa.

". . . ex-president Radinoff," Luscus continues, "once said that this is the 'Age of the Plugged-In Man.' Some rather vulgar remarks have been made about this, to me, insighted phrase. But Radinoff did not mean that human society is a daisy chain. He meant that the current of modern society flows through the circuit of which we are all part. This is the Age of Complete Interconnection. No wires can hang loose; otherwise we all short-circuit. Yet, it is undeniable that life without individuality is not worth living. Every man must be a *hapax legomenon* . . ."

Ruskinson jumps up from his chair and screams, "I know that phrase! I got you this time, Luscus!

He is so excited he falls over in a faint, symptom of a widespread hereditary defect. When he recovers, the lecture is over. He springs to the recorder to run off what he missed. But Luscus has carefully avoided defining The Pellucidar Breakthrough. He will explain it at another lecture.

Grandpa, back at the scope, whistles. "I feel like an astronomer. The planets are in orbit around our house, the sun. There's Accipiter, the closest, Mercury, although he's not the god of thieves but their nemesis. Next, Benedictine, your sad-sack Venus. Hard, hard, hard! The sperm would batter their heads flat against that stony ovum. You sure she's pregnant?

"Your Mama's out there, dressed fit to kill and I wish someone would. Mother Earth headed for the perigee of the gummint store to waste your substance."

Grandpa braces himself as if on a rolling deck, the blue-black veins on his legs thick as strangling vines on an ancient oak. "Brief departure from the role of Herr Doktor Sternscheissdreckschnuppe, the great astronomer, to that of der Unterseeboot Kapitan von Schooten die Fischen in der Barrel. Ach! I zee yet das tramp Schteamer, Deine Mama, yawing, pitching, rolling in the seas of alcohol. Compass lost; rhumb dumb. Three sheets to the wind. Paddlewheels spinning in the air. The black gang sweating their balls off, stoking the furnaces of frustration. Propellers tangled in the nets of neurosis. And the Great White Whale a glimmer in the black depths but coming up fast, intent on broaching her bottom, too big to miss. Poor damned vessel, I weep for her. I also vomit with disgust.

"Fire one! Fire two! Baroom! Mama rolls over, a jagged hole in her hull but not the one you're thinking of. Down she goes, nose first, as befits a devoted fellationeer, her huge aft rising into the air. Blub, blub! Full fathom five!

"And so back from undersea to outer space. Your sylvan Mars, Red Hawk, has just stepped out of the tavern. And Luscus, Jupiter, the one-eyed All-Father of Art, if you'll pardon my mixing of Nordic and Latin mythologies, is surrounded by his swarm of satellites."

## EXCRETION IS THE BITTER PART OF VALOR

Luscus says to the fido interviewers. "By this I mean that Winnegan, like every artist, great or not, produces art that is, first, secretion, unique to himself, then excretion. Excretion in the original sense of 'sifting out.' Creative excretion or discrete excretion. I know that my distinguished colleagues will make fun of this analogy, so I hereby challenge them to a fido debate whenever it can be arranged.

"The valor comes from the courage of the artist in showing his inner products to the public. The bitter part comes from the fact that the artist may be rejected or misunderstood in his time. Also from the terrible war that takes place in the artist with the disconnected or chaotic elements, often contradictory, which he must unite and then mold into a unique entity. Hence my 'discrete excretion' phrase.

Fido interviewer: "Are we to understand that everything is a big pile of shit but that art makes a strange sea-change, forms it into something golden and illuminating?"

"Not exactly. But you're close. I'll elaborate and expound at a later date. At present, I want to talk about Winnegan. Now, the lesser artists give only the surface of things; they are photographers. But the great ones give the interiority of objects and beings. Winnegan, however, is the first to reveal more than one interiority in a single work of art. His invention of the alto-relief multilevel technique enables him to epiphanize—show forth—subterranean layer upon layer."

Primalux Ruskinson, loudly, "The Great Onion Peeler of Painting!"

Luscus, calmly after the laughter has died: "In one sense, that is well put. Great art, like an onion, brings tears to the eyes. However, the light on Winnegan's paintings is not just a reflection; it is sucked in, digested, and then fractured forth. Each of the broken beams makes visible, not various aspects of the figures beneath, but whole figures. Worlds, I might say.

"I call this The Pellucidar Breakthrough. Pellucidar is the hollow interior of our planet, as depicted in a now forgotten fantasy-romance of the twentieth-century writer, Edgar Rice Burroughs, creator of the immortal Tarzan."

Ruskinson moans and feels faint again. "Pellucid! Pellucidar! Luscus, you punning exhumist bastard!"

"Burroughs' hero penetrated the crust of Earth to discover another world inside. This was, in some ways, the reverse of the exterior, continents where the surface seas are, and vice versa. Just so, Winnegan has discovered an inner world, the obverse of the public image Everyman projects. And, like Burroughs' hero, he has returned with a stunning narrative of psychic dangers and exploration.

"And just as the fictional hero found his Pellucidar to be populated with stone-age men and dinosaurs, so Winnegan's world is, though absolutely modern in one sense, archaic in another. Abysmally pristine. Yet, in the illumination of Winnegan's world, there is an evil and inscrutable patch of blackness, and that is paralleled in Pellucidar by the tiny fixed moon which casts a chilling and unmoving shadow.

"Now, I did intend that the ordinary 'pellucid' should be part of Pellucidar. Yet 'pellucid' means 'reflecting light evenly from all surfaces' or 'admitting maximum passage of light without diffusion or distortion.' Winnegan's paintings do just the opposite. But—under the broken and twisted light, the acute observer can see a primeval luminosity, even and straight. This is the light that links all the fractures and multilevels, the light I was thinking of in my earlier discussion of the 'Age of the Plugged-In Man' and the polar bear.

"By intent scrutiny, a viewer may detect this, feel, as it were, the photonic fremitus of the heartbeat of Winnegan's world."

Ruskinson almost faints. Luscus' smile and black monocle make him look like a pirate who has just taken a Spanish galleon loaded with gold.

Grandpa, still at the scope, says, "And there's Maryam bint Yusuf, the Egyptian backwoodswoman you were telling me about. Your Saturn, aloof, regal, cold, and wearing one of those suspended whirling manycolored hats that're all the rage. Saturn's rings? Or a halo?"

"She's beautiful, and she'd make a wonderful mother for my children," Chib says.

"The chic of Araby. Your Saturn has two moons, mother and aunt. Chaperones! You say she'd make a good mother! How good a wife! Is she intelligent?"

"She's as smart as Benedictine."

"A dumbshit then. You sure can pick them. How do you know you're in love with her? You've been in love with twenty women in the last six months."

"I love her. This is it."

"Until the next one. Can you really love anything but your painting? Benedictine's going to have an abortion, right?"

"Not if I can talk her out of it," Chib says. "To tell the truth, I don't even like her any more. But she's carrying my child."

"Let me look at your pelvis. No, you're male. For a moment, I wasn't sure, you're so crazy to have a baby."

"A baby is a miracle to stagger sextillions of infidels."

"It beats a mouse. But don't you know that Uncle Sam has been propagandizing his heart out to cut down on propagation? Where've you been all your life?"

"I got to go, Grandpa."

Chib kisses the old man and returns to his room to finish his latest painting. The door still refuses to recognize him, and he calls the gummint repair shop, only to be told that all technicians are at the Folk Festival. He leaves the house in a red rage. The bunting and balloons are waving and bobbing in the artificial wind, increased for this occasion, and an orchestra is playing by the lake.

Through the scope, Grandpa watches him walk away.

"Poor devil! I ache for his ache. He wants a baby, and he is ripped up inside because that poor devil Benedictine is aborting their child. Part of his agony, though he doesn't know it, is identification with the doomed infant. His own mother has had innumerable—well, quite a few—abortions. But for the grace of God, he would have been one of them, another nothingness. He wants this baby to have a chance, too. But there is nothing he can do about it, nothing.

"And there is another feeling, one which he shares with most of humankind. He knows he's screwed up his life, or something has twisted it. Every thinking man and woman knows this. Even the smug and dimwitted realize this unconsciously. But a baby, that beautiful being, that unsmirched blank tablet, unformed angel, represents a new hope. Perhaps it won't screw up. Perhaps it'll grow up to be a healthy confident reasonable good-humored unselfish loving man or woman. 'It won't be like me or my next-door neighbor,' the proud, but apprehensive, parent swears.

"Chib thinks this and swears that his baby will be different. But, like everybody else, he's fooling himself. A child has one father and mother, but it has trillions of aunts and uncles. Not only those that are its contemporaries; the dead, too. Even if Chib fled into the wilderness and raised the infant himself, he'd be giving it his own unconscious assumptions. The baby would grow up with beliefs and attitudes that the father was not even aware of. Moreover, being raised in isolation, the baby would be a very peculiar human being indeed.

"And if Chib raises the child in this society, it's inevitable that it will accept at least part of the attitudes of its playmates, teachers, and so on ad nauseam.

"So, forget about making a new Adam out of your wonderful potential-teeming child, Chib. If it grows up to become at least half-sane, it's because you gave it love and discipline and it was lucky in its social contacts and it was also blessed at birth with the right combination of genes. That is, your son or daughter is now both a fighter and a lover.

## ONE MAN'S NIGHTMARE IS ANOTHER MAN'S WET DREAM

Grandpa says.

"I was talking to Dante Alighieri just the other day, and he was telling me what an inferno of stupidity, cruelty, perversity, atheism, and outright peril the sixteenth century was. The nineteenth left him gibbering, hopelessly searching for adequate enough invectives.

"As for this age, it gave him such high-blood pressure, I had to slip him a tranquilizer and ship him out via time machine with an attendant nurse. She looked much like Beatrice and so should have been just the medicine he needed—maybe."

Grandpa chuckles, remembering that Chib, as a child, took him seriously when he described his time-machine visitors, such notables as Nebuchadnezzar, King of the Grass-Eaters; Samson, Bronze Age Riddler and Scourge of the Philistines; Moses, who stole a god from his Kenite father-in-law and who fought against circumcision all his life; Buddha, the Original Beatnik; No-Moss Sisyphus, taking a vacation from his stone-rolling; Androcles and his buddy, the Cowardly Lion of Oz; Baron von Richthofen, the Red Knight of Germany; Beowulf; Al Capone; Hiawatha; Ivan the Terrible; and hundreds of others.

The time came when Grandpa became alarmed and decided that Chib was confusing fantasy with reality. He hated to tell the little boy that he had been making up all those wonderful stories, mostly to teach him history. It was like telling a kid there wasn't any Santa Claus.

And then, while he was reluctantly breaking the news to his grandson, he became aware of Chib's barely suppressed grin and knew that it was his turn to have his leg pulled. Chib had never been fooled or else had caught on without any shock. So, both had a big laugh and Grandpa continued to tell of his visitors.

"There are no time machines," Grandpa says. "Like it or not, Miniver Cheevy, you have to live in this your time.

"The machines work in the utility-factory levels in a silence broken only by the chatter of a few mahouts. The great pipes at the bottom of the seas suck up water and bottom sludge. The stuff is automatically carried through pipes to the ten production levels of LA. There the inorganic chemicals are converted into energy and then into the matter of food, drink, medicines, and artifacts. There is very little agriculture or animal husbandry outside the city walls, but there is superabundance for all. Artificial but exact duplication of organic stuff, so who knows the difference?

"There is no more starvation or want anywhere, except among the self-exiles wandering in the woods. And the food and goods are shipped to the pandoras and dispensed to the receivers of the purple wage. *The purple wage.* A madison-avenue euphemism with connotations of royalty and divine right. Earned by just being born.

"Other ages would regard ours as a delirium, yet ours has benefits others lacked. To combat transiency and rootlessness, the megalopolis is compartmented into small communities. A man can live all his life in one place without having to go elsewhere to get anything he needs. With this has come a provincialism, a small-town patriotism and hostility towards outsiders. Hence, the bloody juvenile gang-fights between towns. The intense and vicious gossip. The insistence on conformity to local mores.

"At the same time, the small-town citizen has fido, which enables him to see events anywhere in the world. Intermingled with the trash and the propaganda, which the government thinks is good for the people, is any amount of superb programs. A man may get the equivalent of a Ph.D. without stirring out of his house.

"Another Renaissance has come, a fruition of the arts comparable to that of Pericles' Athens and the city-states of Michelangelo's Italy or Shakespeare's England. Paradox. More illiterates than ever before in the world's history. But also more literates. Speakers of classical Latin outnumber those of Caesar's day. The world of aesthetics bears a fabulous fruit. And, of course, fruits.

"To dilute the provincialism and also to make international war even more unlikely, we have the world policy of *homogenization.* The voluntary exchange of a part of one nation's population with another's. Hostages to peace and brotherly love. Those citizens who can't get along on just the purple wage or who think they'll be happier elsewhere are induced to emigrate with bribes.

"A Golden World in some respects; a nightmare in others. So what's new with the world? It was always thus in every age. Ours has had to deal with overpopulation and automation. How else could the problem be solved? It's Buridan's ass (actually, the ass was a dog) all over again, as in every time. Buridan's ass, dying of hunger because it can't make up its mind which of two equal amounts of food to eat.

"History: a *pons asinorum* with men the asses on the bridge of time.

"No, those two comparisons are not fair or right. It's Hobson's horse, the only choice being the beast in the nearest stall. Zeitgeist rides tonight, and the devil take the hindmost!

"The mid-twentieth-century writers of the Triple Revolution document forecast accurately in some respects. But they de-emphasized what lack of work would do to Mr. Everyman. They believed that all men have equal potentialities in developing artistic tendencies, that all could busy themselves with arts, crafts, and hobbies or education for education's sake. They wouldn't face the 'undemocratic' reality that only about ten per cent of the population—if that—are inherently capable of producing anything worth while, or even mildly interesting, in the arts. Crafts, hobbies, and a lifelong academic education pale after a while, so back to the booze, fido, and adultery.

"Lacking self-respect, the fathers become free-floaters, nomads on the steppes of sex. Mother, with a capital M, becomes the dominant figure in the family. She may be playing around, too, but she's taking care of the kids; she's around most of the time. Thus, with father a lower-case figure, absent, weak, or indifferent, the children often become homosexual or ambisexual. The wonderland is also a fairyland.

"Some features of this time could have been predicted. Sexual permissiveness was one, although no one could have seen how far it would go. But then no one could have foreknown of the Panamorite sect, even if America has spawned lunatic-fringe cults as a frog spawns tadpoles. Yesterday's monomaniac is tomorrow's messiah, and so Sheltey and his disciples survived through years of persecution and today their precepts are embedded in our culture."

Grandpa again fixes the cross-reticules of the scope on Chib.

"There he goes, my beautiful grandson, bearing gifts to the Greeks. So far, that Hercules has failed to clean up his psychic Augean stable. Yet, he may succeed, that stumblebum Apollo, that Edipus Wrecked. He's luckier than most of his contemporaries. He's had a permanent father, even if a secret one, a zany old man hiding from so-called justice. He has gotten love, discipline, and a superb education in this starred chamber. He's also fortunate in having a profession.

"But Mama spends far too much and also is addicted to gambling, a vice which deprives her of her full guaranteed income. I'm supposed to be dead, so I don't get the purple wage. Chib has to make up for all this by selling or trading his paintings. Luscus has helped him by publicizing him, but at any moment Luscus may turn against him. The money from the paintings is still not enough. After all, money is not the basic of our economy; it's a scarce auxiliary. Chib needs the grant but won't get it unless he lets Luscus make love to him.

"It's not that Chib rejects homosexual relations. Like most of his contemporaries, he's sexually ambivalent. I think that he and Omar Runic still blow each other occasionally. And why not? They love each other. But Chib rejects Luscus as a matter of principle. He won't be a whore to advance his career. Moreover, Chib makes a distinction which is deeply embedded in this society. He thinks that uncompulsive homosexuality is natural (whatever that means?) but that compulsive homosexuality is, to use an old term, queer. Valid or not, the distinction is made.

"So, Chib may go to Egypt. But what happens to me then?

"Never mind me or your mother, Chib. No matter what. Don't give in to Luscus. Remember the dying words of Singleton, Bureau of Relocation and Rehabilitation Director, who shot himself because he couldn't adjust to the new times.

"'What if a man gain the world and lose his ass?'"

At this moment, Grandpa sees his grandson, who has been walking along with somewhat drooping shoulders, suddenly straighten them. And he sees Chib break into a dance, a little improvised shuffle followed by a series of whirls. It is evident that Chib is whooping. The pedestrians around him are grinning.

Grandpa groans and then laughs. "Oh, God, the goatish energy of youth, the unpredictable shift of spectrum from black sorrow to bright orange joy! Dance, Chib, dance your crazy head off! Be happy, if only for a moment! You're young yet, you've got the bubbling of unconquerable hope deep in your springs! Dance, Chib, dance!"

He laughs and wipes a tear away.

## SEXUAL IMPLICATIONS OF THE CHARGE OF THE LIGHT BRIGADE

is so fascinating a book that Doctor Jespersen Joyce Bathymens, psycholinguist for the federal Bureau of Group Reconfiguration and Intercommunicability, hates to stop reading. But duty beckons.

"A radish is not necessarily reddish," he says into the recorder. "The Young Radishes so named their group because a radish is a radicle, hence, radical. Also, there's a play on roots and on red-ass, a slang term for anger, and possibly on ruttish and rattish. And undoubtedly on rude-ickle, Beverly Hills dialectical term for a repulsive, unruly, and socially ungraceful person.

"Yet the Young Radishes are not what I would call Left Wing; they represent the current resentment against Life-In-General and advocate no radical policy of reconstruction. They howl against Things As They Are, like monkeys in a tree, but never give constructive criticism. They want to destroy without any thought of what to do after the destruction.

"In short, they represent the average citizen's grousing and bitching, being different in that they are more articulate. There are thousands of groups like them in LA and possibly millions all over the world. They had normal life as children. In fact, they were born and raised in the same clutch, which is one reason why they were chosen for this study. What phenomenon produced ten such creative persons, all mothered in the seven houses of Area 69-14, all about the same time, all practically raised together, since they were put together in the playpen on top of the pedestal while one mother took her turn baby-sitting and the others did whatever they had to do, which . . . where was I?

"Oh, yes, they had a normal life, went to the same school, palled around, enjoyed the usual sexual play among themselves, joined the juvenile gangs and engaged in some rather bloody warfare with the Westwood and other gangs. All were distinguished, however, by an intense intellectual curiosity and all become active in the creative arts.

"It has been suggested—and might be true—that that mysterious stranger, Raleigh Renaissance, was the father of all ten. This is possible but can't be proved. Raleigh Renaissance was living in the house of Mrs. Winnegan at the time, but he seems to have been unusually active in the clutch and, indeed, all over Beverly Hills. Where this man came from, who he was, and where he went are still unknown despite intensive search by various agencies. He had no ID or other cards of any kind, yet he went unchallenged for a long time. He seems to have had something on the Chief of Police of Beverly Hills and possibly on some of the Federal agents stationed in Beverly Hills.

"He lived for two years with Mrs. Winnegan, then dropped out of sight. It is rumored that he left LA to join a tribe of white neo-Amerinds, sometimes called the Seminal Indians.

"Anyway, back to the Young (pun on Jung?) Radishes. They are revolting against the Father Image of Uncle Sam, whom they both love and hate. Uncle is, of course, linked by their subconsciouses with *unco,* a Scottish word meaning strange, uncanny, weird, this indicating that their own fathers were strangers to them. All come from homes where the father was missing or weak, a phenomenon regrettably common in our culture.

"I never knew my own father . . . Tooney, wipe that out as irrelevant. *Unco* also means news or tidings, indicating that the unfortunate young men are eagerly awaiting news of the return of their fathers and perhaps secretly hoping for reconciliation with Uncle Sam, that is, their fathers.

"Uncle Sam. Sam is short for Samuel, from the Hebrew *Shemu'el,* meaning Name of God. All the Radishes are atheists, although some, notably Omar Runic and Chibiabos Winnegan, were given religious instruction as children (Panamorite and Roman Catholic, respectively).

"Young Winnegan's revolt against God, and against the Catholic Church, was undoubtedly reinforced by the fact that his mother forced strong *cath*artics upon him when he had a chronic constipation. He probably also resented having to learn his *cat*echism when he preferred to play. And there is the deeply significant and traumatic incident in which a *cath*eter was used on him. (This refusal to excrete when young will be analyzed in a later report.)

"Uncle Sam, the Father Figure. *Figure* is so obvious a play that I won't bother to point it out. Also perhaps on *figger,* in the sense of 'a fig on thee!'—look this up in Dante's *Inferno*, some Italian or other in Hell said, 'A fig on thee, God!' biting his thumb in the ancient gesture of defiance and disrespect. Hmm? Biting the thumb—an infantile characteristic?

"Sam is also a multileveled pun on phonetically, orthographically, and semisemantically linked words. It is significant that young Winnegan can't stand to be called *dear;* he claims that his mother called him that so many times it nauseates him. Yet the word has a deeper meaning to him. For instance, *sambar* is an Asiatic *deer* with *three-*pointed antlers. (Note the *sam,* also.) Obviously, the three points symbolize, to him, the Triple Revolution document, the historic dating point of the beginning of our era, which Chib claims to hate so. The three points are also archetypes of the Holy Trinity, which the Young Radishes frequently blaspheme against.

"I might point out that in this the group differs from others I've studied. The others expressed an infrequent and mild blasphemy in keeping with the mild, indeed pale, religious spirit prevalent nowadays. Strong blasphemers thrive only when strong believers thrive.

"Sam also stands for *same,* indicating the Radishes' subconscious desire to conform.

"Possibly, although this particular analysis may be invalid, Sam corresponds to Samekh, the fifteenth letter of the Hebrew alphabet. (Sam! Ech!?) In the old style of English spelling, which the Radishes learned in their childhood, the fifteenth letter of the Roman alphabet is O. In the Alphabet Table of my dictionary, Webster's 128th New Collegiate, the Roman O is in the same horizontal column as the Arabic Dad. Also with the Hebrew Mem. So we get a double connection with the missing and longed-for Father (or Dad) and with the overdominating Mother (or Mem).

"I can make nothing out of the Greek Omicron, also in the same horizontal column. But give me time; this takes study.

"Omicron. The little O! The lower-case omicron has an egg shape. The little egg is their father's sperm fertilized? The womb? The basic shape of modern architecture?

"Sam Hill, an archaic euphemism for Hell. Uncle Sam is a Sam Hill of a father? Better strike that out, Tooney. It's possible that these highly educated youths have read about this obsolete phrase, but it's not confirmable. I don't want to suggest any connections that might make me look ridiculous.

"Let's see. Samisen. A Japanese musical instrument with *three* strings. The Triple Revolution document and the Trinity again. Trinity? Father, Son, and Holy Ghost. Mother the thoroughly despised figure, hence, the Wholly Goose? Well, maybe not. Wipe that out, Tooney.

"Samisen. Son of Sam? Which leads naturally to Samson, who pulled down the temple of the Philistines on them and on himself. These boys talk of doing the same thing. Chuckle. Reminds me of myself when I was their age, before I matured. Strike out that last remark, Tooney.

"Samovar. The Russian word means, literally, self-boiler. There's no doubt the Radishes are boiling with revolutionary fervor. Yet their disturbed psyches know, deep down, that Uncle Sam is their ever-loving Father-Mother, that he has only their best interests at heart. But they force themselves to hate him, hence, they self-boil.

"A samlet is a young salmon. Cooked salmon is a yellowish pink or pale red, near to a radish in color, in their unconsciouses, anyway. Samlet equals Young Radish; they feel they're being cooked in the great pressure cooker of modern society.

"How's that for a trinely furned phase—I mean, finely turned phrase, Tooney? Run this off, edit as indicated, smooth it out, you know how, and send it off to the boss. I got to go. I'm late for lunch with Mother; she gets very upset if I'm not there on the dot.

"Oh, postscript! I recommend that the agents watch Winnegan more closely. His friends are blowing off psychic steam through talk and drink, but he has suddenly altered his behavior pattern. He has long periods of silence, he's given up smoking, drinking, and sex."

## A PROFIT IS NOT WITHOUT HONOR

even in this day. The gummint has no overt objection to privately owned taverns, run by citizens who have paid all license fees, passed all examinations, posted all bonds, and bribed the local politicians and police chief. Since there is no provision made for them, no large buildings available for rent, the taverns are in the homes of the owners themselves.

*The Private Universe* is Chib's favorite, partly because the proprietor is operating illegally. Dionysus Gobrinus, unable to hew his way through the roadblocks, prise-de-chevaux, barbed wire, and booby-traps of official procedure, has quit his efforts to get a license.

Openly, he paints the name of his establishment over the mathematical equations that once distinguished the exterior of the house. (Math prof at Beverly Hills U. 14, named Al-Khwarizmi Descartes Lobachevsky, he has resigned and changed his name again.) The atrium and several bedrooms have been converted for drinking and carousing. There are no Egyptian customers, probably because of their supersensitivity about the flowery sentiments painted by patrons on the inside walls.

À BAS, ABU
MOHAMMED WAS THE SON OF A VIRGIN DOG
THE SPHINX STINKS
REMEMBER THE RED SEA!
THE PROPHET HAS A CAMEL FETISH

Some of those who wrote the taunts have fathers, grandfathers, and great-grandfathers who were themselves the objects of similar insults. But their descendants are thoroughly assimilated, Beverly Hillsians to the core. Of such is the kingdom of men.

Gobrinus, a squat cube of a man, stands behind the bar, which is square as a protest against the ovoid. Above him is a big sign:

ONE MAN'S MEAD IS ANOTHER MAN'S POISSON

Gobrinus has explained this pun many times, not always to his listener's satisfaction. Suffice it that Poisson was a mathematician and that Poisson's frequency distribution is a good approximation to the binomial distribution as the number of trials increases and probability of success in a single trial is small.

When a customer gets too drunk to be permitted one more drink, he is hurled headlong from the tavern with furious combustion and utter ruin by Gobrinus, who cries, "Poisson! Poisson!"

Chib's friends, the Young Radishes, sitting at a hexagonal table, greet him, and their words unconsciously echo those of the Federal psycholinguist's estimate of his recent behavior.

"Chib, monk! Chibber as ever! Looking for a chibbie, no doubt! Take your pick!"

Madame Trismegista, sitting at a little table with a Seal-of-Solomon-shape top, greets him. She has been Gobrinus' wife for two years, a record, because she will knife him if he leaves her. Also, he believes that she can somehow juggle his destiny with the cards she deals. In this age of enlightenment, the soothsayer and astrologer flourish. As science pushes forward, ignorance and superstition gallop around the flanks and bite science in the rear with big dark teeth.

Gobrinus himself, a Ph.D., holder of the torch of knowledge (until lately, anyway), does not believe in God. But he is sure the stars are marching towards a baleful conjunction for him. With a strange logic, he thinks that his wife's cards control the stars; he is unaware that card-divination and astrology are entirely separate fields.

What can you expect of a man who claims that the universe is asymmetric?

Chib waves his hand at Madame Trismegista and walks to another table. Here sits

## A TYPICAL TEEMAGER

Benedictine Serinus Melba. She is tall and slim and has narrow lemurlike hips and slender legs but big breasts. Her hair, black as the pupils of her eyes, is parted in the middle, plastered with perfumed spray to the skull, and braided into two long pigtails. These are brought over her bare shoulders and held together with a golden brooch just below her throat. From the brooch, which is in the form of a musical note, the braids part again, one looping under each breast. Another brooch secures them, and they separate to circle around behind her back, are brooched again, and come back to meet on her belly. Another brooch holds them, and the twin waterfalls flow blackly over the front of her bell-shaped skirt.

Her face is thickly farded with green, aquamarine, a shamrock beauty mark, and topaz. She wears a yellow bra with artificial pink nipples; frilly lace ribbons hang from the bra. A demicorselet of bright green with black rosettes circles her waist. Over the corselet, half-concealing it, is a wire structure covered with a shimmering pink quilty material. It extends out in back to form a semifuselage or a bird's long tail, to which are attached long yellow and crimson artificial feathers.

An ankle-length diaphanous skirt billows out. It does not hide the yellow and dark-green striped lace-fringed garter-panties, white thighs, and black net stockings with green clocks in the shape of musical notes. Her shoes are bright blue with topaz high heels.

Benedictine is costumed to sing at the Folk Festival; the only thing missing is her singer's hat. Yet, she came to complain, among other things, that Chib has forced her to cancel her appearance and so lose her chance at a great career.

She is with five girls, all between sixteen and twenty-one, all drinking P (for popskull).

"Can't we talk in private, Benny?" Chib says.

"What for?" Her voice is a lovely contralto ugly with inflection.

"You got me down here to make a public scene," Chib says.

"For God's sake, what other kind of scene is there?" she shrills. "Look at him! He wants to talk to me alone!"

It is then that he realizes she is afraid to be alone with him. More than that, she is incapable of being alone. Now he knows why she insisted on leaving the bedroom door open with her girl-friend, Bela, within calling distance. And listening distance.

"You said you was just going to use your finger!" she shouts. She points at the slightly rounded belly. "I'm going to have a baby! You rotten smooth-talking sick bastard!"

"That isn't true at all," Chib says. "You told me it was all right, you loved me."

" 'Love! Love!' he says! What the hell do I know what I said, you got me so excited! Anyway, I didn't say you could stick it in! I'd never say that, never! And then what you *did! What* you did! My God, I could hardly walk for a week, you bastard, you!"

Chib sweats. Except for Beethoven's Pastoral welling from the fido, the room is silent. His friends grin. Gobrinus, his back turned, is drinking scotch. Madame Trismegista shuffles her cards, and she farts with a fiery conjunction of beer and onions. Benedictine's friends look at their Mandarin-long fluorescent fingernails or glare at him. Her hurt and indignity is theirs and vice versa.

"I can't take those pills. They make me break out and give me eye trouble and screw up my monthlies! You know that! And I can't stand those mechanical uteruses! And you lied to me, anyway! You said you took a pill!"

Chib realizes she's contradicting herself, but there's no use trying to be logical. She's furious because she's pregnant; she doesn't want to be inconvenienced with an abortion at this time, and she's out for revenge.

Now how, Chib wonders, how could she get pregnant *that* night? No woman, no matter how fertile, could have managed that. She must have been knocked up before or after. Yet she swears that it was that night, the night he was

### THE KNIGHT OF THE BURNING PESTLE
### or
### FOAM, FOAM ON THE RANGE

"No, no!" Benedictine cries.

"Why not? I love you," Chib says. "I want to marry you."

Benedictine screams, and her friend Bela, out in the hall, yells, "What's the matter? What happened?"

Benedictine does not reply. Raging, shaking as if in the grip of a fever, she scrambles out of bed, pushing Chib to one side. She runs to the small egg of the bathroom in the corner, and he follows her.

"I hope you're not going to do what I think . . . ?" he says.

Benedictine moans, "You sneaky no-good son of a bitch!"

In the bathroom, she pulls down a section of wall, which becomes a shelf. On its top, attached by magnetic bottoms to the shelf, are many containers. She seizes a long thin can of spermatocide, squats, and inserts it. She presses the button on its bottom, and it foams with a hissing sound even its cover of flesh cannot silence.

Chib is paralyzed for a moment. Then he roars.

Benedictine shouts, "Stay away from me, you rude-ickle!"

From the door to the bedroom comes Bela's timid, "Are you all right, Benny?"

"I'll all-right her!" Chib bellows.

He jumps forward and takes a can of tempoxy glue from the shelf. The glue is used by Benedictine to attach her wigs to her head and will hold anything forever unless softened by a specific defixative.

Benedictine and Bela both cry out as Chib lifts Benedictine up and then lowers her to the floor. She fights, but he manages to spray the glue over the can and the skin and hairs around it.

"What're you doing?" she screams.

He pushes the button on the bottom of the can to full-on position and then sprays the bottom with glue. While she struggles, he holds her arms tight against her body and keeps her from rolling over and so moving the can in or out. Silently, Chib counts to thirty, then to thirty more to make sure the glue is thoroughly dried. He releases her.

The foam is billowing out around her groin and down her legs and spreading out across the floor. The fluid in the can is under enormous pressure in the indestructible unpunchable can, and the foam expands vastly if exposed to open air.

Chib takes the can of defixative from the shelf and clutches it in his hand, determined that she will not have it. Benedictine jumps up and swings at him. Laughing like a hyena in a tentful of nitrous oxide, Chib blocks her fist and shoves her away. Slipping on the foam, which is ankle-keep by now, Benedictine falls and then slides backward out of the bedroom on her buttocks, the can clunking.

She gets to her feet and only then realizes fully what Chib has done. Her scream goes up, and she follows it. She dances around, yanking at the can, her screams intensifying with every tug and resultant pain. Then she turns and runs out of the room or tries to. She skids; Bela is in her way; they cling together and both ski out of the room, doing a half-turn while going through the door. The foam swirls out so that the two look like Venus and friend rising from the bubble-capped waves of the Cyprian Sea.

Benedictine shoves Bela away but not without losing some flesh to Bela's long sharp fingernails. Bela shoots backwards through the door toward Chib. She is like a novice ice skater trying to maintain her balance. She does not succeed and shoots by Chib, wailing, on her back, her feet up in the air.

Chib slides his bare feet across the floor gingerly, stops at the bed to pick up his clothes, but decides he'd be wiser to wait until he's outside before he puts them on. He gets to the circular hall just in time to see Benedictine crawling past one of the columns that divides the corridor from the atrium. Her parents, two middle-aged behemoths, are still sitting on a flato, beer cans in hand, eyes wide, mouths open, quivering.

Chib does not even say goodnight to them as he passes along the hall. But then he sees the fido and realizes that her parents had switched it from EXT. to INT. and then to Benedictine's room. Father and mother have been watching Chib and daughter, and it is evident from father's not-quite dwindled condition that father was very excited by this show, superior to anything seen on exterior fido.

"You peeping bastards!" Chib roars.

Benedictine has gotten to them and on her feet and she is stammering, weeping, indicating the can and then stabbing her finger at Chib. At Chib's roar, the parents heave up from the flato as two leviathans from the deep. Benedictine turns and starts to run towards him, her arms outstretched, her long-nailed fingers curved, her face a medusa's. Behind her streams the wake of the livid witch and father and mother on the foam.

Chib shoves up against a pillar and rebounds and skitters off, helpless to keep himself from turning sidewise during the maneuver. But he keeps his balance. Mama and Papa have gone down together with a crash that shakes even the solid house. They are up, eyes rolling and bellowing like hippos surfacing. They charge him but separate, Mama shrieking now, her face, despite the fat, Benedictine's. Papa goes around one side of the pillar; Mama, the other. Benedictine has rounded another pillar, holding to it with one hand to keep her from slipping. She is between Chib and the door to the outside.

Chib slams against the wall of the corridor, in an area free of foam. Benedictine runs towards him. He dives across the floor, hits it, and rolls between two pillars and out into the atrium.

Mama and Papa converge in a collision course. The Titanic meets the iceberg, and both plunge swiftly. They skid on their faces and bellies towards Benedictine. She leaps into the air, trailing foam on them as they pass beneath her.

By now it is evident that the government's claim that the can is good for 40,000 shots of death-to-sperm, or for 40,000 copulations, is justified. Foam is all over the place, ankle-deep—knee-high in some places—and still pouring out.

Bela is on her back now and on the atrium floor, her head driven into the soft folds of the flato.

Chib gets up slowly and stands for a moment, glaring around him, his knees bent, ready to jump from danger but hoping he won't have to since his feet will undoubtedly fly away from under him.

"Hold it, you rotten son of a bitch!" Papa roars. "I'm going to kill you! You can't do this to my daughter!"

Chib watches him turn over like a whale in a heavy sea and try to get to his feet. Down he goes again, grunting as if hit by a harpoon. Mama is no more successful than he.

Seeing that his way is unbarred—Benedictine having disappeared somewhere—Chib skis across the atrium until he reaches an unfoamed area near the exit. Clothes over his arm, still holding the defixative, he struts towards the door.

At this moment Benedictine calls his name. He turns to see her sliding from the kitchen at him. In her hand is a tall glass. He wonders what she intends to do with it. Certainly, she is not offering him the hospitality of a drink.

Then she scoots into the dry region of the floor and topples forward with a scream. Nevertheless, she throws the contents of the glass accurately.

Chib screams when he feels the boiling hot water, painful as if he had been circumcised unanesthetized.

Benedictine, on the floor, laughs. Chib, after jumping around and shrieking, the can and clothes dropped, his hands holding the scalded parts, manages to control himself. He stops his antics, seizes Benedictine's right hand, and drags her out into the streets of Beverly Hills. There are quite a few people out this night, and they follow the two. Not until Chib reaches the lake does he stop and there he goes into the water to cool off the burn, Benedictine with him.

The crowd has much to talk about later, after Benedictine and Chib have crawled out of the lake and then run home. The crowd talks and laughs quite a while as they watch the sanitation department people clean the foam off the lake surface and the streets.

"I was so sore I couldn't walk for a month!" Benedictine screams.

"You had it coming," Chib says. "You've got no complaints. You said you wanted my baby, and you talked as if you meant it."

"I must've been out of my mind!" Benedictine says. "No, I wasn't! I never said no such thing! You lied to me! You forced me!"

"I would never force anybody," Chib said. "You know that. Quit your bitching. You're a free agent, and you consented freely. You have free will."

Omar Runic, the poet, stands up from his chair. He is a tall thin red-bronze youth with an aquiline nose and very thick red lips. His kinky hair grows long and is cut into the shape of the *Pequod,* that fabled vessel which bore mad Captain Ahab and his mad crew and the sole survivor Ishmael after the white whale. The coiffure is formed with a bowsprit and hull and three masts and yardarms and even a boat hanging on davits.

Omar Runic claps his hands and shouts, "Bravo! A philosopher! Free will it is; free will to seek the Eternal Verities—if any—or Death and Damnation! I'll drink to free will! A toast, gentlemen! Stand up, Young Radishes, a toast to our leader!"

And so begins

## THE MAD P PARTY

Madame Trismegista calls, "Tell your fortune, Chib! See what the stars tell through the cards!"

He sits down at her table while his friends crowd around.

"O.K., Madame. How do I get out of this mess?"

She shuffles and turns over the top card.

"Jesus! The ace of spades!"

"You're going on a long journey!"

"Egypt!" Rousseau Red Hawk cries. "Oh, no, you don't want to go there, Chib! Come with me to where the buffalo roam and . . ."

Up comes another card.

"You will soon meet a beautiful dark lady."

"A goddam Arab! Oh, no, Chib, tell me it's not true!"

"You will win great honors soon."

"Chib's going to get the grant!"

"If I get the grant, I don't have to go to Egypt," Chib says. "Madame Trismegista, with all due respect, you're full of crap."

"Don't mock, young man. I'm not a computer. I'm tuned to the spectrum of psychic vibrations."

Flip. "You will be in great danger, physically and morally."

Chib says, "That happens at least once a day."

Flip. "A man very close to you will die twice."

Chib pales, rallies, and says, "A coward dies a thousand deaths."

"You will travel in time, return to the past."

"Zow!" Red Hawk says. "You're outdoing yourself, Madame. Careful! You'll get a psychic hernia, have to wear an ectoplasmic truss!"

"Scoff if you want to, you dumbshits," Madame says. "There are more worlds than one. The cards don't lie, not when I deal them."

"Gobrinus!" Chib calls. "Another pitcher of beer for the Madame."

The Young Radishes return to their table, a legless disc held up in the air by a graviton field. Benedictine glares at them and goes into a huddle with the other teemagers. At a table nearby sits Pinkerton Legrand, a gummint agent, facing them so that the fido under his one-way window of a jacket beams in on them. They know he's doing this. He knows they know and has reported so to his superior. He frowns when he sees Falco Accipiter enter. Legrand does not like an agent from another department messing around on his case. Accipiter does not even look at Legrand. He orders a pot of tea and then pretends to drop into the teapot a pill that combines with tannic acid to become P.

Rousseau Red Hawk winks at Chib and says, "Do you really think it's possible to paralyze all of LA with a single bomb?"

"Three bombs!" Chib says loudly so that Legrand's fido will pick up the words. "One for the control console of the desalinization plant, a second for the backup console, the third for the nexus of the big pipe that carries the water to the reservoir on the 20th level."

Pinkerton Legrand turns pale. He downs all the whiskey in his glass and orders another, although he has already had too many. He presses the plate on his fido to transmit a triple top-priority. Lights blink redly in HQ; a gong clangs repeatedly; the chief wakes up so suddenly he falls off his chair.

Accipiter also hears, but he sits stiff, dark, and brooding as the diorite image of a Pharaoh's falcon. Monomaniac, he is not to be diverted by talk of inundating all LA, even if it will lead to action. On Grandpa's trail, he is now here because he hopes to use Chib as the key to the house. One "mouse"—as he thinks of his criminals—one "mouse" will run to the hole of another.

"When do you think we can go into action?" Huga Wells-Erb Heinsturbury, the science-fiction authoress, says.

"In about three weeks," Chib says.

At HQ, the chief curses Legrand for disturbing him. There are thousands of young men and women blowing off steam with these plots of destruction, assassination, and revolt. He does not understand why the young punks talk like this, since they have everything handed them free. If he had his way, he'd throw them into jail and kick them around a little or more than.

"After we do it, we'll have to take off for the big outdoors," Red Hawk says. His eyes glisten. "I'm telling you, boys, being a free man in the forest is the greatest. You're a genuine individual, not just one of the faceless breed."

Red Hawk believes in this plot to destroy LA. He is happy because, though he hasn't said so, he has grieved while in Mother Nature's lap for intellectual companionship. The other savages can hear a deer at a hundred yards, detect a rattlesnake in the bushes, but they're deaf to the footfalls of philosophy, the neigh of Nietzsche, the rattle of Russell, the honkings of Hegel.

"The illiterate swine!" he says aloud. The others say, "What?"

"Nothing. Listen, you guys must know how wonderful it is. You were in the WNRCC."

"I was 4-F," Omar Runic says. "I got hay fever."

"I was working on my second M.A.," Gibbon Tacitus says.

"I was in the WNRCC band," Sibelius Amadeus Yehudi says. "We only got outside when we played the camps, and that wasn't often."

"Chib, you were in the Corps. You loved it, didn't you?"

Chib nods but says, "Being a neo-Amerind takes all your time just to survive. When could I paint? And who would see the paintings if I did get time? Anyway, that's no life for a woman or a baby."

Red Hawk looks hurt and orders a whiskey mixed with P.

Pinkerton Legrand doesn't want to interrupt his monitoring, yet he can't-stand the pressure in his bladder. He walks towards the room used as the customers' catch-all. Red Hawk, in a nasty mood caused by rejection, sticks his leg out. Legrand trips, catches himself, and stumbles forward. Benedictine puts out her leg. Legrand falls on his face. He no longer has any reason to go to the urinal except to wash himself off.

Everybody except Legrand and Accipiter laugh. Legrand jumps up, his fists doubled. Benedictine ignores him and walks over to Chib, her friends following. Chib stiffens. She says, "You perverted bastard! You told me you were just going to use your finger!"

"You're repeating yourself," Chib says. "The important thing is, what's going to happen to the baby?"

"What do you care?" Benedictine says. "For all you know, it might not even be yours!"

"That'd be a relief," Chib says, "if it weren't. Even so, the baby should have a say in this. He might want to live—even with you as his mother."

"In this miserable life!" she cries. "I'm going to do it a favor. I'm going to the hospital and get rid of it. Because of you, I have to miss out on my big chance at the Folk Festival! There'll be agents from all over there, and I won't get a chance to sing for them!"

"You're a liar," Chib says. "You're all dressed up to sing."

Benedictine's face is red; her eyes, wide; her nostrils, flaring.

"You spoiled my fun!"

She shouts, "Hey, everybody, want to hear a howler! This great artist, this big hunk of manhood, Chib the divine, he can't get a hardon unless he's gone down on!"

Chib's friends look at each other. What's the bitch screaming about? So what's new?

From Grandpa's *Private Ejaculations:* Some of the features of the Panamorite religion, so reviled and loathed in the 21st century, have become everyday facts in modern times. Love, love, love, physical and spiritual! It's not enough to just kiss your children and hug them. But oral stimulation of the genitals of infants by the parents and relatives has resulted in some curious conditioned reflexes. I could write a book about this aspect of mid-22nd century life and probably will.

Legrand comes out of the washroom. Benedictine slaps Chib's face. Chib slaps her back. Gobrinus lifts up a section of the bar and hurtles through the opening, crying, "Poisson! Poisson!"

He collides with Legrand, who lurches into Bela, who screams, whirls, and slaps Legrand, who slaps back. Benedictine empties a glass of P in Chib's face. Howling, he jumps up and swings his fist. Benedictine ducks, and the fist goes over her shoulder into a girl-friend's chest.

Red Hawk leaps up on the table and shouts, "I'm a regular bearcat, half-alligator, half . . ."

The table, held up in a graviton field, can't bear much weight. It tilts and catapults him into the girls, and all go down. They bite and scratch Red Hawk, and Benedictine squeezes his testicles. He screams, writhes, and hurls Benedictine with his feet onto the top of the table. It has regained its normal height and altitude, but now it flips over again, tossing her to the other side. Legrand, tippytoeing through the crowd on his way to the exit, is knocked down. He loses some front teeth against somebody's knee cap. Spitting blood and teeth, he jumps up and slugs a bystander.

Gobrinus fires off a gun that shoots a tiny Very light. It's supposed to blind the brawlers and so bring them to their senses while they're regaining their sight. It hangs in the air and shines like

## A STAR OVER BEDLAM

The Police Chief is talking via fido to a man in a public booth. The man has turned off the video and is disguising his voice.

"They're beating the shit out of each other in *The Private Universe.*"

The Chief groans. The Festival has just begun, and They are at it already.

"Thanks. The boys'll be on the way. What's your name? I'd like to recommend you for a Citizen's Medal."

"What! And get the shit knocked out of me, too! I ain't no stoolie; just doing my duty. Besides, I don't like Gobrinus or his customers. They're a bunch of snobs."

The Chief issues orders to the riot squad, leans back, and drinks a beer while he watches the operation on fido. What's the matter with these people, anyway? They're always mad about something.

The sirens scream. Although the bolgani ride electrically driven noiseless tricycles, they're still clinging to the centuries-old tradition of warning the criminals that they're coming. Five trikes pull up before the open door of The Private Universe. The police dismount and confer. Their two-storied cylindrical helmets are black and have scarlet roaches. They wear goggles for some reason although their vehicles can't go over 15 m.p.h. Their jackets are black and fuzzy, like a teddy bear's fur, and huge golden epaulets decorate their shoulders. The shorts are electric-blue and fuzzy; the jackboots, glossy black. They carry electric shock sticks and guns that fire chokegas pellets.

Gobrinus blocks the entrance. Sergeant O'Hara says, "Come on, let us in. No, I don't have a warrant of entry. But I'll get one."

"If you do, I'll sue," Gobrinus says. He smiles. While it is true that government red tape was so tangled he quit trying to acquire a tavern legally, it is also true that the government will protect him in this issue. Invasion of privacy is a tough rap for the police to break.

O'Hara looks inside the doorway at the two bodies on the floor, at those holding their heads and sides and wiping off blood, and at Accipiter, sitting like a vulture dreaming of carrion. One of the bodies gets up on all fours and crawls through between Gobrinus' legs out into the street.

"Sergeant, arrest that man!" Gobrinus says. "He's wearing an illegal fido. I accuse him of invasion of privacy."

O'Hara's face lights up. At least he'll get one arrest to his credit. Legrand is placed in the paddywagon, which arrives just after the ambulance. Red Hawk is carried out as far as the doorway by his friends. He opens his eyes just as he's being carried on a stretcher to the ambulance and he mutters.

O'Hara leans over him. "What?"

"I fought a bear once with only my knife, and I came out better than with those cunts. I charge them with assault and battery, murder and mayhem."

O'Hara's attempt to get Red Hawk to sign a warrant fails because Red Hawk is now unconscious. He curses. By the time Red Hawk begins feeling better, he'll refuse to sign the warrant. He won't want the girls and their boy friends laying for him, not if he has any sense at all.

Through the barred window of the paddywagon, Legrand screams, "I'm a gummint agent! You can't arrest me!"

The police get a hurry-up call to go to the front of the Folk Center, where a fight between local youths and Westwood invaders is threatening to become a riot. Benedictine leaves the tavern. Despite several blows in the shoulders and stomach, a kick in the buttocks, and a bang on the head, she shows no signs of losing the fetus.

Chib, half-sad, half-glad, watches her go. He feels a dull grief that the baby is to be denied life. By now he realizes that part of his objection to the abortion is identification with the fetus; he knows what Grandpa thinks he does not know. He realizes that his birth was an accident—lucky or unlucky. If things had gone otherwise, he would not have been born. The thought of his nonexistence—no painting, no friends, no laughter, no hope, no love—horrifies him. His mother, drunkenly negligent about contraception, has had any number of abortions, and he could have been one of them.

Watching Benedictine swagger away (despite her torn clothes), he wonders what he could ever have seen in her. Life with her, even with a child, would have been gritty.

> In the hope-lined nest of the mouth
> Love flies once more, nestles down,
> Coos, flashes feathered glory, dazzles,
> And then flies away, crapping,
> As is the wont of birds,
> To jet-assist the takeoff.
> —Omar Runic

Chib returns to his home, but he still can't get back into his room. He goes to the storeroom. The painting is seven-eighths finished but was not completed because he was dissatisfied with it. Now he takes it from the house and carries it to Runic's house, which is in the same clutch as his. Runic is at the Center, but he always leaves his doors open when he's gone. He has equipment which Chib uses to finish the painting, working with a sureness and intensity he lacked the first time he was creating it. He then leaves Runic's house with the huge oval canvas held above his head.

He strides past the pedestals and under their curving branches with the ovoids at their ends. He skirts several small grassy parks with trees, walks beneath more houses, and in ten minutes is nearing the heart of Beverly Hills. Here mercurial Chib sees

## ALL IN THE GOLDEN AFTERNOON, THREE LEADEN LADIES

drifting in a canoe on Lake Issus. Maryam bint Yusuf, her mother, and aunt listlessly hold fishing poles and look towards the gay colors, music, and the chattering crowd before the Folk Center. By now the police have broken up the juvenile fight and are standing around to make sure nobody else makes trouble.

The three women are dressed in the somber clothes, completely body-concealing, of the Mohammedan Wahhabi fundamentalist sect. They do not wear veils; not even the Wahhabi now insist on this. Their Egyptian brethren ashore are clad in modern garments, shameful and sinful. Despite which, the ladies stare at them.

Their menfolk are at the edge of the crowd. Bearded and costumed like sheiks in a Foreign Legion fido show, they mutter gargling oaths and hiss at the iniquitous display of female flesh. But they stare.

This small group has come from the zoological preserves of Abyssinia, where they were caught poaching. Their gummint gave them three choices. Imprisonment in a rehabilitation center, where they would be treated until they became good citizens if it took the rest of their lives. Emigration to the megalopolis of Haifa, Israel. Or emigration to Beverly Hills, LA.

What, dwell among the accursed Jews of Israel? They spat and chose Beverly Hills. Alas, Allah had mocked them! They were now surrounded by Finkelsteins, Applebaums, Siegels, Weintraubs, and others of the infidel tribes of Isaac. Even worse, Beverly Hills had no mosque. They either traveled forty kilometers every day to the 16th level, where a mosque was available, or used a private home.

Chib hastens to the edge of the plastic-edged lake and puts down his painting and bows low, whipping off his somewhat battered hat. Maryam smiles at him but loses the smile when the two chaperones reprimand her.

"*Ya kelb! Ya ibn kelb!*" the two shout at him.

Chib grins at them, waves his hat, and says, "Charmed, I'm sure, mesdames! Oh, you lovely ladies remind me of the Three Graces."

He then cries out, "I love you, Maryam! I love you! Thou art like the Rose of Sharon to me! Beautiful, doe-eyed, virginal! A fortress of innocence and strength, filled with a fierce motherhood and utter faithfulness to thy one true love! I love thee, thou art the only light in a black sky of dead stars! I cry to you across the void!"

Maryam understands World English, but the wind carries his words away from her. She simpers, and Chib cannot help feeling a momentary repulsion, a flash of anger as if she has somehow betrayed him. Nevertheless, he rallies and shouts, "I invite you to come with me to the showing! You and your mother and aunt will be my guests. You can see my paintings, my soul, and know what kind of man is going to carry you off on his Pegasus, my dove!"

> There is nothing as ridiculous as the verbal outpourings of a young poet in love. Outrageously exaggerated. I laugh. But I am also touched. Old as I am, I remember my first loves, the fire, the torrents of words, lightning-sheathed, ache-winged. Dear lasses, most of you are dead; the rest, withered. I blow you a kiss.
>
> —Grandpa

Maryam's mother stands up in the canoe. For a second, her profile is to Chib, and he sees intimations of the hawk that Maryam will be when she is her mother's age. Maryam now has a gently aquiline face—"the sweep of the sword of love"—Chib has called that nose. Bold but beautiful. However, her mother does look like a dirty old eagle. And her aunt—uneaglish but something of the camel in those features.

Chib suppresses these unfavorable, even treacherous, comparisons. But he cannot suppress the three bearded, robed, and unwashed men who gather around him.

Chib smiles but says, "I don't remember inviting you."

They look blank since rapidly spoken LA English is a huftymagufty to them. Abu—generic name for any Egyptian in Beverly Hills— rasps an oath so ancient even the pre-Mohammed Meccans knew it. He forms a fist. Another Arab steps towards the painting and draws back a foot as if to kick it.

At this moment, Maryam's mother discovers that it is as dangerous to stand in a canoe as on a camel. It is worse, because the three women cannot swim.

Neither can the middle-aged Arab who attacks Chib, only to find his victim sidestepping and then urging him on into the lake with a foot in the rear. One of the young men rushes Chib; the other starts to kick at the painting. Both halt on hearing the three women scream and on seeing them go over into the water.

Then the two run to the edge of the lake, where they also go into the water, propelled by one of Chib's hands in each of their backs. A bolgan hears the six of them screaming and thrashing around and runs over to Chib. Chib is becoming concerned because Maryam is having trouble staying above the water. Her terror is not faked.

What Chib does not understand is why they are all carrying on so. Their feet must be on the bottom; the surface is below their chins. Despite which, Maryam looks as if she is going to drown. So do the others, but he is not interested in them. He should go in after Maryam. However, if he does, he will have to get a change of clothes before going to the showing.

At this thought, he laughs loudly and then even more loudly as the bolgan goes in after the women. He picks up the painting and walks off laughing. Before he reaches the Center, he sobers.

"Now, how come Grandpa was so right? How does he read me so well? Am I fickle, too shallow? No, I have been too deeply in love too many times. Can I help it if I love Beauty, and the beauties I love do not have enough Beauty? My eye is too demanding; it cancels the urgings of my heart."

## THE MASSACRE OF THE INNER SENSE

The entrance hall (one of twelve) which Chib enters was designed by Grandpa Winnegan. The visitor comes into a long curving tube lined with mirrors at various angles. He sees a triangular door at the end of the corridor. The door seems to be too tiny for anybody over nine years old to enter. The illusion makes the visitor feel as if he's walking up the wall as he progresses towards the door. At the end of the tube, the visitor is convinced he's standing on the ceiling.

But the door gets larger as he approaches until it becomes huge. Commentators have guessed that this entrance is the architect's symbolic representation of the gateway to the world of art. One should stand on his head before entering the wonderland of aesthetics.

On going in, the visitor thinks at first that the tremendous room is inside out or reversed. He gets even dizzier. The far wall actually seems the near wall until the visitor gets reorientated. Some people can't adjust and have to get out before they faint or vomit.

On the right hand is a hatrack with a sign: HANG YOUR HEAD HERE. A double pun by Grandpa, who always carries a joke too far for most people. If Grandpa goes beyond the bounds of verbal good taste, his great-great-grandson has overshot the moon in his paintings. Thirty of his latest have been revealed, including the last three of his Dog Series: *Dog Star, Dog Would,* and *Dog Tiered.* Ruskinson and his disciples are threatening to throw up. Luscus and his flock praise, but they're restrained. Luscus has told them to wait until he talks to young Winnegan before they go all-out. The fido men are busy shooting and interviewing both and trying to provoke a quarrel.

The main room of the building is a huge hemisphere with a bright ceiling which runs through the complete spectrum every nine minutes. The floor is a giant chessboard, and in the center of each square is a face, each of a great in the various arts. Michelangelo, Mozart, Balzac, Zeuxis, Beethoven, Li Po, Twain, Dostoyevsky, Farmisto, Mbuzi, Cupel, Krishnagurti, etc. Ten squares are left faceless so that future generations may add their own nominees for immortality.

The lower part of the wall is painted with murals depicting significant events in the lives of the artists. Against the curving wall are nine stages, one for each of the Muses. On a console above each stage is a giant statue of the presiding goddess. They are naked and have overripe figures: huge-breasted, broad-hipped, sturdy-legged, as if the sculptor thought of them as Earth goddesses, not refined intellectual types.

The faces are basically structured like the smooth placid faces of classical Greek statues, but they have an unsettling expression around the mouths and eyes. The lips are smiling but seem ready to break into a snarl. The eyes are deep and menacing. DON'T SELL ME OUT, they say. IF YOU DO . . .

A transparent plastic hemisphere extends over each stage and has acoustic properties which keep people who are not beneath the shell from hearing the sounds emanating from the stage and vice versa.

Chib makes his way through the noisy crowd towards the stage of Polyhymnia, the Muse who includes painting in her province. He passes the stage on which Benedictine is standing and pouring her lead heart out in an alchemy of golden notes. She sees Chib and manages somehow to glare at him and at the same time to keep smiling at her audience. Chib ignores her but observes that she has replaced the dress ripped in the tavern. He sees also the many policemen stationed around the building. The crowd does not seem in an explosive mood. Indeed, it seems happy, if boisterous. But the police know how deceptive this can be. One spark . . .

Chib goes by the stage of Calliope, where Omar Runic is extemporizing. He comes to Polyhymnia's, nods at Rex Luscus, who waves at him, and sets his painting on the stage. It is titled *The Massacre of the Innocents* (subtitle: *Dog in the Manger*).

The painting depicts a stable.

The stable is a grotto with curiously shaped stalactites. The light that breaks—or fractures—through the cave is Chib's red. It penetrates every object, doubles its strength, and then rays out jaggedly. The viewer, moving from side to side to get a complete look, can actually see the many levels of light as he moves, and thus he catches glimpses of the figures under the exterior figures.

The cows, sheep, and horses are in stalls at the end of the cave. Some are looking with horror at Mary and the infant. Others have their mouths open, evidently trying to warn Mary. Chib has used the

legend that the animals in the manger were able to talk to each
other the night Christ was born.

Joseph, a tired old man, so slumped he seems backboneless, is in
a corner. He wears two horns, but each has a halo, so it's all right.

Mary's back is to the bed of straw on which the infant is supposed
to be. From a trapdoor in the floor of the cave, a man is reaching
to place a huge egg on the straw bed. He is in a cave beneath the
cave and is dressed in modern clothes, has a boozy expression, and,
like Joseph, slumps as if invertebrate. Behind him a grossly fat woman,
looking remarkably like Chib's mother, has the baby, which the man
passed on to her before putting the foundling egg on the straw bed.

The baby has an exquisitely beautiful face and is suffused with
a white glow from his halo. The woman has removed the halo from
his head and is using the sharp edge to butcher the baby.

Chib has a deep knowledge of anatomy, since he has dissected
many corpses while getting his Ph.D. in art at Beverly Hills U. The
body of the infant is not unnaturally elongated, as so many of
Chib's figures are. It is more than photographic; it seems to be an
actual baby. Its viscera is unraveled through a large bloody hole.

The onlookers are struck in their viscera as if this were not a
painting but a real infant, slashed and disemboweled, found on their
doorsteps as they left home.

The egg has a semitransparent shell. In its murky yolk floats a
hideous little devil, horns, hooves, tail. Its blurred features resemble
a combination of Henry Ford's and Uncle Sam's. When the viewers
shift to one side or the other, the faces of others appear: prominents
in the development of modern society.

The window is crowded with wild animals that have come to
adore but have stayed to scream soundlessly in horror. The beasts
in the foreground are those that have been exterminated by man
or survive only in zoos and natural preserves. The dodo, the blue
whale, the passenger pigeon, the quagga, the gorilla, orangutan, polar
bear, cougar, lion, tiger, grizzly bear, California condor, kangaroo,
wombat, rhinoceros, bald eagle.

Behind them are other animals and, on a hill, the dark crouching
shapes of the Tasmanian aborigine and Haitian Indian.

"What is your considered opinion of this rather remarkable painting,
Doctor Luscus?" a fido interviewer asks.

Luscus smiles and says, "I'll have a considered judgment in a few minutes. Perhaps you'd better talk to Doctor Ruskinson first. He seems to have made up his mind at once. Fools and angels, you know."

Ruskinson's red face and scream of fury are transmitted over the fido.

"The shit heard around the world!" Chib says loudly.

"INSULT! SPITTLE! PLASTIC DUNG! A BLOW IN THE FACE OF ART AND A KICK IN THE BUTT FOR HUMANITY! INSULT! INSULT!"

"Why is it such an insult, Doctor Ruskinson?" the fido man says. "Because it mocks the Christian faith, and also the Panamorite faith? It doesn't seem to me it does that. It seems to me that Winnegan is trying to say that men have perverted Christianity, maybe all religions, all ideals, for their own greedy self-destructive purposes, that man is basically a killer and a perverter. At least, that's what I get out of it, although of course I'm only a simple layman, and . . ."

"Let the critics make the analysis, young man!" Ruskinson snaps. "Do you have a double Ph.D., one in psychiatry and one in art? Have you been certified as a critic by the government?

"Winnegan, who has no talent whatsoever, let alone this genius that various self-deluded blowhards prate about, this abomination from Beverly Hills, presents his junk—actually a mishmash which has attracted attention solely because of a new technique that any electronic technician could invent—I am enraged that a mere gimmick, a trifling novelty, can not only fool certain sectors of the public but highly educated and federally certified critics such as Doctor Luscus here—although there will always be scholarly asses who bray so loudly, pompously, and obscurely that . . ."

"Isn't it true," the fido man says, "that many painters we now call great, Van Gogh for one, were condemned or ignored by their contemporary critics? And . . ."

The fido man, skilled in provoking anger for the benefit of his viewers, pauses. Ruskinson swells, his head a bloodvessel just before aneurysm.

"I'm no ignorant layman!" he screams. "I can't help it that there have been Luscuses in the past! I know what I'm talking about! Winnegan is only a micrometeorite in the heaven of Art, not fit to shine the shoes of the great luminaries of painting. His reputation has been pumped up by a certain clique so it can shine in the reflected glory, the hyenas, biting the hand that feeds them, like mad dogs . . ."

"Aren't you mixing your metaphors a little bit?" the fido man says.

Luscus takes Chib's hand tenderly and draws him to one side where they're out of fido range.

"Darling Chib," he coos, "now is the time to declare yourself. You know how vastly I love you, not only as an artist but for yourself. It must be impossible for you to resist any longer the deeply sympathetic vibrations that leap unhindered between us. God, if you only knew how I dreamed of you, my glorious godlike Chib, with . . ."

"If you think I'm going to say yes just because you have the power to make or break my reputation, to deny me the grant, you're wrong," Chib says. He jerks his hand away.

Luscus' good eye glares. He says, "Do you find me repulsive? Surely it can't be on moral grounds . . ."

"It's the principle of the thing," Chib says. "Even if I were in love with you, which I'm not, I wouldn't let you make love to me. I want to be judged on my merit alone, that only. Come to think of it, I don't give a damn about anybody's judgment. I don't want to hear praise or blame from you or anybody. Look at my paintings and talk to each other, you jackals. But don't try to make me agree with your little images of me."


## THE ONLY GOOD CRITIC IS A DEAD CRITIC

Omar Runic has left his dais and now stands before Chib's paintings. He places one hand on his naked left chest, on which is tattooed the face of Herman Melville, Homer occupying the other place of honor on his right breast. He shouts loudly, his black eyes like furnace doors blown out by explosion. As has happened before, he is seized with inspiration derived from Chib's paintings.

> "Call me Ahab, not Ishmael.
> For I have hooked the Leviathan.
> I am the wild ass's colt born to a man.
> Lo, my eye has seen it all!

My bosom is like wine that has no vent.
I am a sea with doors, but the doors are stuck.
Watch out! The skin will burst; the doors will break.


"You are Nimrod, I say to my friend, Chib.
And now is the hour when God says to his angels,
If this is what he can do as a beginning, then
Nothing is impossible for him.
He will be blowing his horn before
The ramparts of Heaven and shouting for
The Moon as hostage, the Virgin as wife,
And demanding a cut on the profits
From the Great Whore of Babylon."


"Stop that son of a bitch!" the Festival Director shouts. "He'll cause a riot like he did last year!"

The bolgani begin to move in. Chib watches Luscus, who is talking to the fido man. Chib can't hear Luscus, but he's sure Luscus is not saying complimentary things about him.


"Melville wrote of me long before I was born.
I'm the man who wants to comprehend
The Universe but comprehend on my terms.
I am Ahab whose hate must pierce, shatter,
All impediment of Time, Space, or Subject
Mortality and hurl my fierce
Incandescence into the Womb of Creation,
Disturbing in its Lair whatever Force or
Unknown Thing-in-Itself crouches there,
Remote, removed, unrevealed."


The Director gestures at the police to remove Runic. Ruskinson is still shouting, although the cameras are pointing at Runic or Luscus. One of the Young Radishes, Huga Wells-Erb Heinsturbury, the science-fiction authoress, is shaking with hysteria generated by Runic's voice and with a lust for revenge. She is sneaking up on a *Time* fido man. *Time* has long ago ceased to be a magazine, since there are no magazines, but became a government-supported communications bureau. *Time* is an example of Uncle Sam's left-hand, right-hand, hands-off policy of providing communications bureaus with all they need and at the same time permitting the bureau executives to determine the bureau policies. Thus, government provision and free speech are united. This is fine, in theory, anyway.

*Time* has preserved several of its original policies, that is, truth and objectivity must be sacrificed for the sake of a witticism and science-fiction must be put down. *Time* has sneered at every one of Heinsturbury's works, and so she is out to get some personal satisfaction for the hurt caused by the unfair reviews.

> *"Quid nunc? Cui bono?*
> Time? Space? Substance? Accident?
> When you die—Hell? Nirvana?
> Nothing is nothing to think about.
> The canons of philosophy boom.
> Their projectiles are duds.
> The ammo heaps of theology blow up,
> Set off by the saboteur Reason.

> "Call me Ephraim, for I was halted
> At the Ford of God and could not tongue
> The sibilance to let me pass.
> Well, I can't pronounce shibboleth,
> But I can say shit!"

Huga Wells-Erb Heinsturbury kicks the *Time* fido man in the balls. He throws up his hands, and the football-shaped, football-sized camera sails from his hands and strikes a youth on the head. The youth is a Young Radish, Ludwig Euterpe Mahlzart. He is smoldering with rage because of the damnation of his tone poem, *Jetting The Stuff Of Future Hells,* and the camera is the extra fuel needed to make him blaze up uncontrollably. He punches the chief musical critic in his fat belly.

Huga, not the *Time* man, is screaming with pain. Her bare toes have struck the hard plastic armor with which the *Time* man, recipient of many such a kick, protects his genitals. Huga hops around on one foot while holding the injured foot in her hands. She twirls into a girl, and there is a chain effect. A man falls against the *Time* man, who is stooping over to pick up his camera.

"Ahaaa!" Huga screams and tears off the *Time* man's helmet and
straddles him and beats him over the head with the optical end of
the camera. Since the solid-state camera is still working, it is sending
to billions of viewers some very intriguing, if dizzying, pictures. Blood
obscures one side of the picture, but not so much that the viewers are
wholly cheated. And then they get another novel shot as the camera
flies into the air again, turning over and over.

A bolgan has shoved his shock-stick against her back, causing her
to stiffen and propel the camera in a high arc behind her. Huga's
current lover grapples with the bolgan; they roll on the floor; a
Westwood juvenile picks up the shock-stick and has a fine time
goosing the adults around him until a local youth jumps him.

"Riots are the opium of the people," the police chief groans. He
calls in all units and puts in a call to the chief of police of Westwood, who is, however, having his own troubles.

Runic beats his breast and howls

> "Sir, I exist! And don't tell me,
> As you did Crane, that that creates
> No obligation in you towards me.
> I am a man; I am unique.
> I've thrown the Bread out the window,
> Pissed in the Wine, pulled the plug
> From the bottom of the Ark, cut the Tree
> For firewood, and if there were a Holy
> Ghost, I'd goose him.
> But I know that it all does not mean
> A God damned thing,
> That nothing means nothing,
> That is is is and not-is not is is-not
> That a rose is a rose is a
> That we are here and will not be
> And that is all we can know!"

Ruskinson sees Chib coming towards him, squawks, and tries to
escape. Chib seizes the canvas of *Dogmas from a Dog* and batters
Ruskinson over the head with it. Luscus protests in horror, not because
of the damage done to Ruskinson but because the painting might
be damaged. Chib turns around and batters Luscus in the stomach
with the oval's edge.

"The earth lurches like a ship going down,
Its back almost broken by the flood of
Excrement from the heavens and the deeps,
What God in His terrible munificence
Has granted on hearing Ahab cry,
Bullshit! Bullshit!

"I weep to think that this is Man
And this his end. But wait!
On the crest of the flood, a three-master
Of antique shape. The Flying Dutchman!
And Ahab is astride a ship's deck once more.
Laugh, you Fates, and mock, you Norns!
For I am Ahab and I am Man,
And though I cannot break a hole
Through the wall of What Seems
To grab a handful of What Is,
Yet, I will keep on punching.
And I and my crew will not give up,
Though the timbers split beneath our feet
And we sink to become indistinguishable
From the general excrement.

"For a moment that will burn on the
Eye of God forever, Ahab stands
Outlined against the blaze of Orion,
Fist clenched, a bloody phallus,
Like Zeus exhibiting the trophy of
The unmanning of his father Cronus.
And then he and his crew and ship
Dip and hurtle headlong over
The edge of the world.
And from what I hear, they are still
                    F
                    a
                    l
                    l
                    i
                    n
                    g

Chib is shocked into a quivering mass by a jolt from a bolgan's electrical riot stick. While he is recovering, he hears his Grandpa's voice issuing from the transceiver in his hat.

"Chib, come quick! Accipiter has broken in and is trying to get through the door of my room!"

Chib gets up and fights and shoves his way to the exit. When he arrives, panting, at his home he finds that the door to Grandpa's room has been opened. The IRB men and electronic technicians are standing in the hallway. Chib bursts into Grandpa's room. Accipiter is standing in its middle and is quivering and pale. Nervous stone. He sees Chib and shrinks back, saying, "It wasn't my fault. I had to break in. It was the only way I could find out for sure. It wasn't my fault; I didn't touch him."

Chib's throat is closing in on itself. He cannot speak. He kneels down and takes Grandpa's hand. Grandpa has a slight smile on his blue lips. Once and for all, he has eluded Accipiter. In his hand is the latest sheet of his Ms.

## THROUGH BALAKLAVAS OF HATE, THEY CHARGE TOWARDS GOD

For most of my life, I have seen only a truly devout few and a great majority of truly indifferent. But there is a new spirit abroad. So many young men and women have revived, not a love for God, but a violent antipathy towards Him. This excites and restores me. Youths like my grandson and Runic shout blasphemies and so worship Him. If they did not believe, they would never think about Him. I now have some confidence in the future.

## TO THE STICKS VIA THE STYX

Dressed in black, Chib and his mother go down the tube entrance to level 13B. It's luminous-walled, spacious, and the fare is free. Chib tells the ticket-fido his destination. Behind the wall, the protein computer, no larger than a human brain, calculates. A coded ticket slides out of a slot. Chib takes the ticket, and they go to the bay, a great incurve, where he sticks the ticket into a slot. Another ticket protrudes, and a mechanical voice repeats the information on the ticket in World and LA English, in case they can't read.

Gondolas shoot into the bay and decelerate to a stop. Wheelless, they float in a continually rebalancing graviton field. Sections of the bay slide back to make ports for the gondolas. Passengers step into the cages designated for them. The cages move forward; their doors open automatically. The passengers step into the gondolas. They sit down and wait while the safety meshmold closes over them. From the recesses of the chassis, transparent plastic curves rise and meet to form a dome.

Automatically timed, monitored by redundant protein computers for safety, the gondolas wait until the coast is clear. On receiving the go-ahead, they move slowly out of the bay to the tube. They pause while getting another affirmation, trebly checked in microseconds. Then they move swiftly into the tube.

Whoosh! Whoosh! Other gondolas pass them. The tube glows yellowly as if filled with electrified gas. The gondola accelerates rapidly. A few are still passing it, but Chib's speeds up and soon none can catch up with it. The round posterior of a gondola ahead is a glimmering quarry that will not be caught until it slows before mooring at its destined bay. There are not many gondolas in the tube. Despite a 100-million population, there is little traffic on the north-south route. Most LAers stay in the self-sufficient walls of their clutches. There is more traffic on the east-west tubes, since a small percentage prefer the public ocean beaches to the municipality swimming pools.

The vehicle screams southward. After a few minutes, the tube begins to slope down, and suddenly it is at a 45-degree angle to the horizontal. They flash by level after level.

Through the transparent walls, Chib glimpses the people and architecture of other cities. Level 8, Long Beach, is interesting. Its homes look like two cut-quartz pie plates, one on top of another, open end on open end, and the unit mounted on a column of carved figures, the exit-entrance ramp a flying buttress.

At level 3A, the tube straightens out. Now the gondola races past establishments the sight of which causes Mama to shut her eyes.

Chib squeezes his mother's hand and thinks of the half-brother and cousin who are behind the yellowish plastic. This level contains fifteen percent of the population, the retarded, the incurable insane, the too-ugly, the monstrous, the senile aged. They swarm here, the vacant or twisted faces pressed against the tube wall to watch the pretty cars float by.

"Humanitarian" medical science keeps alive the babies that *should* —by Nature's imperative—have died. Ever since the 20th century, humans with defective genes have been saved from death. Hence, the continual spread of these genes. The tragic thing is that science can now detect and correct defective genes in the ovum and sperm. Theoretically, all human beings could be blessed with totally healthy bodies and physically perfect brains. But the rub is that we don't have near enough doctors and facilities to keep up with the births. This despite the ever decreasing drop in the birth rate.

Medical science keeps people living so long that senility strikes. So, more and more slobbering mindless decrepits. And also an accelerating addition of the mentally addled. There are therapies and drugs to restore most of them to "normalcy," but not enough doctors and facilities. Some day there may be, but that doesn't help the contemporary unfortunate.

What to do now? The ancient Greeks placed defective babies in the fields to die. The Eskimos shipped out their old people on ice floes. Should we gas our abnormal infants and seniles? Sometimes, I think it's the merciful thing to do. But I can't ask somebody else to pull the switch when I won't.

I would shoot the first man to reach for it.
                              —from Grandpa's *Private Ejaculations*

The gondola approaches one of the rare intersections. Its passengers see down the broad-mouthed tube to their right. An express flies towards them; it looms. Collision course. They know better, but they can't keep from gripping the mesh, gritting their teeth, and bracing their legs. Mama gives a small shriek. The flier hurtles over them and disappears, the flapping scream of air a soul on its way to underworld judgment.

The tube dips again until it levels out on 1. They see the ground below and the massive self-adjusting pillars supporting the megapolis. They whiz by over a little town, quaint, early 21st century LA preserved as a museum, one of many beneath the cube.

Fifteen minutes after embarking, the Winnegans reach the end of the line. An elevator takes them to the ground, where they enter a big black limousine. This is furnished by a private-enterprise mortuary, since Uncle Sam or the LA government will pay for cremation but not for burial. The Church no longer insists on interment, leaving it to the religionists to choose between being wind-blown ashes or underground corpses.

The sun is halfway towards the zenith. Mama begins to have trouble breathing and her arms and neck redden and swell. The three times she's been outside the walls, she's been attacked with this allergy despite the air conditioning of the limousine. Chib pats her hand while they're riding over a roughly patched road. The archaic eighty-year-old, fuel-cell-powered, electric-motor-driven vehicle is, however, rough-riding only by comparison with the gondola. It covers the ten kilometers to the cemetery speedily, stopping once to let deer cross the road.

Father Fellini greets them. He is distressed because he is forced to tell them that the Church feels that Grandpa has committed sacrilege. To substitute another man's body for his corpse, to have mass said over it, to have it buried in sacred ground is to blaspheme. Moreover, Grandpa died an unrepentant criminal. At least, to the knowledge of the Church, he made no contrition just before he died.

Chib expects this refusal. St. Mary's of BH-14 has declined to perform services for Grandpa within its walls. But Grandpa has often told Chib that he wants to be buried beside his ancestors, and Chib is determined that Grandpa will get his wish.

Chib says, "I'll bury him myself! Right on the edge of the graveyard!"

"You can't do that!" the priest, mortuary officials, and a federal agent say simultaneously.

"The hell I can't! Where's the shovel?"

It is then that he sees the thin dark face and falciform nose of Accipiter. The agent is supervising the digging up of Grandpa's (first) coffin. Nearby are at least fifty fido men shooting with their minicameras, the transceivers floating a few decameters near them. Grandpa is getting full coverage, as befits the Last Of The Billionaires and The Greatest Criminal Of The Century.

Fido interviewer: "Mr. Accipiter, could we have a few words from you? I'm not exaggerating when I say that there are probably at least ten billion people watching this historic event. After all, even the grade-school kids know of Win-again Winnegan.

"How do you feel about this? You've been on the case for 26 years. The successful conclusion must give you great satisfaction."

Accipiter, unsmiling as the essence of diorite: "Well, actually, I've not devoted full time to this case. Only about three years of accumulative time. But since I've spent at least several days each month on it, you might say I've been on Winnegan's trail for 26 years."

Interviewer: "It's been said that the ending of this case also means the end of the IRB. If we've not been misinformed, the IRB was only kept functioning because of Winnegan. You had other business, of course, during this time, but the tracking down of counterfeiters and gamblers who don't report their income has been turned over to other bureaus. Is this true? If so, what do you plan to do?"

Accipiter, voice flashing a crystal of emotion: "Yes, the IRB is being disbanded. But not until after the case against Winnegan's grand-daughter and her son is finished. They harbored him and are, therefore, accessories after the fact.

"In fact, almost the entire population of Beverly Hills, level 14, should be on trial. I know, but can't prove it as yet, that everybody, including the municipal chief of police, was well aware that Winnegan was hiding in that house. Even Winnegan's priest knew it, since Winnegan frequently went to mass and to confession. His priest claims that he urged Winnegan to turn himself in and also refused to give him absolution unless he did so.

"But Winnegan, a hardened 'mouse'—I mean, criminal, if ever I saw one, refused to follow the priest's urgings. He claimed that he had not committed a crime, that, believe it or not, Uncle Sam was the criminal. Imagine the effrontery, the depravity, of the man!"

Interviewer: "Surely you don't plan to arrest the entire population of Beverly Hills 14?"

Accipiter: "I have been advised not to."

Interviewer: "Do you plan on retiring after this case is wound up?"

Accipiter: "No. I intend to transfer to the Greater LA Homicide Bureau. Murder for profit hardly exists any more, but there are still crimes of passion, thank God!"

Interviewer: "Of course, if young Winnegan should win his case against you—he has charged you with invasion of domestic privacy, illegal housebreaking, and directly causing his great-great-grandfather's death—then you won't be able to work for the Homicide Bureau or any police department."

Accipiter, flashing several crystals of emotion: "It's no wonder we law enforcers have such a hard time operating effectively! Sometimes, not only the majority of citizens seem to be on the law-breaker's side but my own employers . . ."

Interviewer: "Would you care to complete that statement? I'm sure your employers are watching this channel. No? I understand that Winnegan's trial and yours are, for some reason, scheduled to take place *at the same time*. How do you plan to be present at both trials? Heh, heh! Some fido-casters are calling you The Simultaneous Man!"

Accipiter: "Well, ah, as you know, fifty years ago all large private-responsible! He incorrectly fed the data into a legal computer. The confusion of dates is being straightened out now. I might mention that the clerk is suspected of deliberately making the error. There have been too many cases like this . . ."

Interviewer: "Would you mind summing up the course of this case for our viewers' benefit? Just the highlights, please."

Accipiter: "Well, ah, as you know, fifty years ago all large private-enterprise businesses had become government bureaus. All except the building construction firm, the Finnegan Fifty-three States Company, of which the president was Finn Finnegan. He was the father of the man who is to be buried—somewhere—today.

"Also, all unions except the largest, the construction union, were dissolved or were government unions. Actually, the company and its union were one, because all employees got ninety-five per cent of the money, distributed more or less equally among them. Old Finnegan was both the company president and union business agent-secretary.

"By hook or crook, mainly by crook, I believe, the firm-union had resisted the inevitable absorption. There were investigations into Finnegan's methods: coercion and blackmail of U. S. Senators and even U. S. Supreme Court Justices. Nothing was, however, proved."

Interviewer: "For the benefit of our viewers who may be a little hazy on their history, even fifty years ago money was used only for the purchase of nonguaranteed items. Its other use, as today, was as an index of prestige and social esteem. At one time, the government was thinking of getting rid of currency entirely, but a study revealed that it had great psychological value. The income tax was also kept, although the government had no use for money, because the size of a man's tax determined prestige and also because it enabled the government to remove a large amount of currency from circulation."

Accipiter: "Anyway, when old Finnegan died, the federal government renewed its pressure to incorporate the construction workers and the company officials as civil servants. But young Finnegan proved to be as foxy and vicious as his old man. I don't suggest, of course, that the fact that his uncle was President of the U.S. at that time had anything to do with young Finnegan's success."

Interviewer: "Young Finnegan was seventy years old when his father died."

Accipiter: "During this struggle, which went on for many years, Finnegan decided to rename himself Winnegan. It's a pun on Win Again. He seems to have had a childish, even imbecilic, delight in puns, which, frankly, I don't understand. Puns, I mean."

Interviewer: "For the benefit of our non-American viewers, who may not know of our national custom of Naming Day . . . this was originated by the Panamorites. When a citizen comes of age, he may at any time thereafter take a new name, one which he believes to be appropriate to his temperament or goal in life. I might point out that Uncle Sam, who's been unfairly accused of trying to impose conformity upon his citizens, encourages this individualistic approach to life. This despite the increased record-keeping required on the government's part.

"I might also point out something else of interest. The government claimed that Grandpa Winnegan was mentally incompetent. My listeners will pardon me, I hope, if I take up a moment of your time to explain the basis of Uncle Sam's assertion. Now, for the benefit of those among you who are unacquainted with an early 20th-century classic, *Finnegan's Wake,* despite your government's wish for you to have a free lifelong education, the author, James Joyce, derived the title from an old vaudeville song."

(Half-fadeout while a monitor briefly explains "vaudeville.")

"The song was about Tim Finnegan, an Irish hod carrier who fell off a ladder while drunk and was supposedly killed. During the Irish wake held for Finnegan, the corpse is accidentally splashed with whiskey. Finnegan, feeling the touch of the whiskey, the 'water of life,' sits up in his coffin and then climbs out to drink and dance with the mourners.

"Grandpa Winnegan always claimed that the vaudeville song was based on reality, you can't keep a good man down, and that the original Tim Finnegan was his ancestor. This preposterous statement was used by the government in its suit against Winnegan.

"However, Winnegan produced documents to substantiate his assertion. Later—too late—the documents were proved to be forgeries."

Accipiter: "The government's case against Winnegan was strengthened by the rank and file's sympathy with the government. Citizens were complaining that the business-union was undemocratic and discriminatory. The officials and workers were getting relatively high wages, but many citizens had to be contented with their guaranteed income. So, Winnegan was brought to trial and accused, justly, of course, of various crimes, among which were subversion of democracy.

"Seeing the inevitable, Winnegan capped his criminal career. He somehow managed to steal 20 billion dollars from the federal deposit vault. This sum, by the way, was equal to half the currency then existing in Greater LA. Winnegan disappeared with the money, which he had not only stolen but had not paid income tax on. Unforgivable. I don't know why so many people have glamorized this villain's feat. Why, I've even seen fido shows with him as the hero, thinly disguised under another name, of course."

Interviewer: "Yes, folks, Winnegan committed the Crime Of The Age. And, although he has finally been located, and is to be buried today—somewhere—the case is not completely closed. The Federal government says it is. But where is the money, the 20 billion dollars?"

Accipiter: "Actually, the money has no value now except as collector's items. Shortly after the theft, the government called in all currency and then issued new bills that could not be mistaken for the old. The government had been wanting to do something like this for a long time, anyway, because it believed that there was too much currency, and it only reissued half the amount taken in.

"I'd like very much to know where the money is. I won't rest until I do. I'll hunt it down if I have to do it on my own time."

Interviewer: "You may have plenty of time to do that if young Winnegan wins his case. Well, folks, as most of you may know, Winnegan was found dead in a lower level of San Francisco about a year after he disappeared. His grand-daughter identified the body, and the fingerprints, earprints, retinaprints, teethprints, blood-type, hair-type, and a dozen other identity prints matched out."

Chib, who has been listening, thinks that Grandpa must have spent several millions of the stolen money arranging this. He does not know, but he suspects that a research lab somewhere in the world grew the duplicate in a biotank.

This happened two years after Chib was born. When Chib was five, his grandpa showed up. Without letting Mama know he was back, he moved in. Only Chib was his confidant. It was, of course, impossible for Grandpa to go completely unnoticed by Mama, yet she now insisted that she had never seen him. Chib thought that this was to avoid prosecution for being an accessory after the crime. He was not sure. Perhaps she had blocked off his "visitations" from the rest of her mind. For her it would be easy, since she never knew whether today was Tuesday or Thursday and could not tell you what year it was.

Chib ignores the mortuarians, who want to know what to do with the body. He walks over to the grave. The top of the ovoid coffin is visible now, with the long elephantlike snout of the digging machine sonically crumbling the dirt and then sucking it up. Accipiter, breaking through his lifelong control, is smiling at the fidomen and rubbing his hands.

"Dance a little, you son of a bitch," Chib says, his anger the only block to the tears and the wail building up in him.

The area around the coffin is cleared to make room for the grappling arms of the machine. These descend, hook under, and lift the black, irradiated-plastic, mocksilver-arabesqued coffin up and out and onto the grass. Chib, seeing the IRB men begin to open the coffin, starts to say something but closes his mouth. He watches intently, his knees bent as if getting ready to jump. The fidomen close in, their eyeball-shaped cameras pointing at the group around the coffin.

Groaning, the lid rises. There is a big bang. Dense dark smoke billows. Accipiter and his men, blackened, eyes wide and white, coughing, stagger out of the cloud. The fidomen are running every-which way or stooping to pick up their cameras. Those who were standing far enough back can see that the explosion took place at the bottom of the grave. Only Chib knows that the raising of the coffin lid has activated the detonating device in the grave.

He is also the first to look up into the sky at the projectile soaring from the grave because only he expected it. The rocket climbs up to five hundred feet while the fidomen train their cameras on it. It bursts apart and from it a ribbon unfolds between two round objects. The objects expand to become balloons while the ribbon becomes a huge banner.

On it, in big black letters, are the words

### WINNEGAN'S FAKE!

Twenty billions of dollars buried beneath the supposed bottom of the grave burn furiously. Some bills, blown up in the geyser of fireworks, are carried by the wind while IRB men, fidomen, mortuary officials, and municipality officials chase them.

Mama is stunned.

Accipiter looks as if he is having a stroke.

Chib cries and then laughs and rolls on the ground.

Grandpa has again screwed Uncle Sam and has also pulled his greatest pun where all the world can see it.

"Oh, you old man!" Chib sobs between laughing fits. "Oh, you old man! How I love you!"

While he is rolling on the ground again, roaring so hard his ribs hurt, he feels a paper in his hand. He stops laughing and gets on his knees and calls after the man who gave it to him. The man says, "I was paid by your grandfather to hand it to you when he was buried."

Chib reads.

I hope nobody was hurt, not even the IRB men.

Final advice from the Wise Old Man In The Cave. Tear loose. Leave LA. Leave the country. Go to Egypt. Let your mother ride the purple wage on her own. She can do it if she practices thrift and self-denial. If she can't, that's not your fault.

You are fortunate indeed to have been born with talent, if not genius, and to be strong enough to want to rip out the umbilical cord. So do it. Go to Egypt. Steep yourself in the ancient culture. Stand before the Sphinx. Ask her (actually, it's a he) the Question.

Then visit one of the zoological preserves south of the Nile. Live for a while in a reasonable facsimile of Nature as she was before mankind dishonored and disfigured her. There, where Homo Sapiens(?) evolved from the killer ape, absorb the spirit of that ancient place and time.

You've been painting with your penis, which I'm afraid was more stiffened with bile than with passion for life. Learn to paint with your heart. Only thus will you become great and true.

Paint.

Then, go wherever you want to go. I'll be with you as long as you're alive to remember me. To quote Runic, "I'll be the Northern Lights of your soul."

Hold fast to the belief that there will be others to love you just as much as I did or even more. What is more important, you must love them as much as they love you.

Can you do this?

## Afterword:

I'm strangely indifferent about getting a man onto the Moon. I say *strangely* because I've been reading science fiction since 1928 and selling science fiction stories since 1952. Moreover, I fully expected, and

hoped and prayed, that we would be on Mars by 1940. About the time
I was eighteen, I gave up this early date but still knew that someday,
maybe 1970, we'd make it.

Also, I've been a military and commercial electronic technical writer
since 1957 and at present am working for a company which is intimately concerned with the Saturn and Apollo space programs. Ten years
ago, I would have been close to ecstasy if I could have worked on a
space project. Rockets, Moon landings, airlocks, and all that.

But in the past eight years I've been increasingly interested in, and
worried over, terrestrial problems. These are population explosion; birth
control; the rape of Mother Nature; human, and animal, "rights"; international conflicts; and especially mental health. I'd like to see us explore
space, but I don't think we have to. If the U.S. wants to spend its (my)
money on space rockets, fine. I realize full well that space projects are
more than going to pay their present expenses someday. Technological
discoveries made along the way, serendipitous findings, plus such things
as weather control, etc., will eventually make all this effort and expense
worth while. I like to think so.

But let's spend at least an equal amount of money and research on
trying to find out what makes people tick and mistick. If there has to be
a choice between the two different kinds of projects, get rid of the space
project. If this be treason, so be it. People are more important than
rockets; we'll never be in harmony with that Nature which exists outside
our atmosphere; we're doing an inept enough job of getting into harmony with sublunary Nature.

The idea for this story was sparked off when I attended a lecture at
the home of Tom and Terry Pinckard. Lou Barron spoke of the Triple
Revolution document, among other things. This publication contains a
letter sent on March 22, 1964, by the Ad Hoc Committee on the Triple
Revolution to President Lyndon B. Johnson, the politically safe reply
from the President's Assistant Special Counsel, and the Triple Revolution report itself. The writers of the document know that mankind is on
the threshold of an age which demands a fundamental re-examination
of existing values and institutions. The three separate and mutually rein-
forcing revolutions are (1) the Cybernation Revolution, (2) the
Weaponry Revolution, and (3) the Human Rights Revolution.

I will not outline this document; even this would take much space. But
for those interested in the crises of our times, in what must be planned
and done, and in the immediate and distant future, this document is vital. It may be acquired by writing to: The Ad Hoc Committee on the
Triple Revolution, P. O. Box 4068, Santa Barbara, California.

Lou Barron was the first to mention the Triple Revolution in my presence and the last since. Yet this document may be a dating point for historians, a convenient pinpointing to indicate when the new era of "planned societies" began. It may take a place alongside such important documents as the Magna Carta, Declaration of Independence, Communist Manifesto, etc. Since the lecture, I've come across references to it in two magazines, but there were no elucidations. And during the lecture, Lou Barron said that the TRD, despite its importance, was still unknown to some economists and political science professionals on the UCLA campus.

Barron's lecture gave me the glimmerings of a story based on a future society extrapolated from present trends. I probably would not have done anything about it if Harlan Ellison, some months later, had not asked me for a story for this anthology. As soon as I heard that there would be no tabus, my eye rolled in a frenzy which some people may think coarse instead of fine. Up from the unconscious came the paraphrase of the Zane Grey title, *Riders of the Purple Sage*. Other things clicked into place as extrapolations followed.

Several things I'd like to make clear. One, this story represents only one of a dozen, each with entirely different future worlds, that I could write. The implications of the Triple Revolution document are many.

Two, the story here shows only the bones of what I wanted to write. Theoretically, there was no word limit, but in practice there had to be a stopping point. The 30,000 words here passed this, but the editors were indulgent. Actually, I wrote 40,000 words but forced myself to cut out many chapters and then to reduce those chapters left in. This resulted in 20,000 words which I later built up to 30,000 again. I had a number of episodes and of letters from various U. S. Presidents to various bureaus. The letters and replies were to show how the Great Withdrawal was initiated and how the enclosed multileveled cities were begun. A more detailed description of the physical construction of a community, THE OOGENESIS OF BEVERLY HILLS, LEVEL 14, was cut out, with the municipally organized jousts between teen-age gangs during the Folk Festival, a scene between Chib and his mother which would have given their relationship in more depth, a scene from a fido play based on the early days of the Panamorite sect, and about a dozen other chapters.

Three, the Triple Revolution document writers, it seems to me, are looking ahead only to the next fifty years. I jumped to 2166 A.D. because I'm sure that energy-matter conversion and duplication of material objects will be available by then. Probably before then. This belief is based on present developments in physics. (The protein computers mentioned in the story have already been predicted in a recent *Science News Letter*. I anticipated this in a science fiction story in 1955. As far as I know, my prediction was the first mention of protein computers in literature of any kind, science fiction, scientific, or otherwise.) Mankind will no longer have to rely on agriculture, stock-raising, fishing, or mining. Moreover, the cities will tend to become completely independent of national governments except as they need them to avoid international war. The struggle between the city-states and federal government is only implied in this story.

Four, the Triple Revolution document writers showed humility and good sense when they stated that they did not know as yet how to plan our society. They insist that a study of great width and depth must be made first and then the carrying out of recommendations should be done cautiously.

Five, I doubt that this will be done with the depth and caution required. The times are too pressing; the hot breath of Need is on our necks. Besides, the proper study of mankind has always been too much entangled with politics, prejudice, bureaucracy, selfishness, stupidity, ultraconservatism, and one trait all of us share: downright ignorance.

Six, despite which, I understand that our world *must* be planned, and I wish the planners good luck in their dangerous course.

Seven, I could be wrong.

Eight, I hope I am.

This story was written primarily as a story, not as a sounding board for ideas or as a prophecy. I became too interested in my characters. And, although the basic idea came from Lou Barron, he is responsible for nothing in the story. In fact, I doubt very much that he will like it.

Whatever the reception to the story, I had fun writing it.

## Introduction to THE MALLEY SYSTEM:

In a context almost obstinately dedicated to new, young voices in spec-ulative fiction, it is bewildering to find a story by a woman who has been a professional longer than I've *lived!* It is either a testimonial to the in-vigorating qualities inherent in this kind of writing, or to the singular nature of the woman. I would opt for the latter, as would you, had you ever met Miriam deFord. She is the kind of person who would deliver you a glance to wither asparagus should you mention semantic nonsense like "senior citizen" or "sun city." She would then, most likely, level you with a scathing aphorism from Schopenhauer ("The first forty years of life give us the text: the next thirty supply the commentary") or pos-sibly Ortega y Gasset ("A girl of fifteen generally has a greater number of secrets than an old man, and a woman of thirty more arcana than a chief of state"). And if neither of those did it, then how about a fast *fumikomi* on the right instep?

Miriam Allen deFord, aside from being the auctorially renowned deFord who wrote *The Overbury Affair* and *Stone Walls*—semi-classic studies in crime and punishment—is the author of ten, no, make that eleven books of history or biography. She is a stellar light in the field of crime fact and fiction. She is a favorite of s-f and fantasy readers. She has published incredible amounts of Latin translations, literary biography and criticism, articles on political and sociological themes; she was for many years a labor journalist; she is a much-published poet, including a volume of collected verse, *Penultimates*. A Philadelphian by birth, she lives and has lived most of her life where her heart is, in San Francisco. In private life she is Mrs. Maynard Shipley, whose late husband (who died in 1934) was a well-known writer and lecturer on scientific subjects.

I won't mention Miss deFord's age but I feel that a miracle is being suppressed. In a time when Everyman questions the sanity of the Universe, every morsel of wonder must be heralded, to reassure us one and all that there is hope and harmony in the scheme of things. For let us face the sad but omnipresent fact: most people of maturity, of substantial age, in our culture, are crotchety hearkeners after their lost youth. But Miriam deFord defies convention. For charm, few can equal her. For persuasiveness, none can approach. (Proof of this last is that the editor of this book wanted to retitle her story "Cells of Memory," or somesuch silly nonsense thing. Miss deFord "persuaded" the editor that he was making an ass of himself. Her original title stands, and the editor, though defeated, was not made to feel demeaned by the lady's arguments. That, children, is known as class.) But none of these, and certainly not her age, are what draw our attention. The vigor of her writing, the originality and uncompromising view she brings to a perplexing, pressing contemporary problem is what arrests us here.

Miriam Allen deFord serves the invaluable purpose, in this anthology and in the field as a whole, of being an object lesson. It is not merely the tots who can think hard, new thoughts and set them down in a compelling manner. If the writer *be* a writer, to hell with chronological labels. Knowing her age or not, you would have been impressed with the story. It makes one pause to consider how valid are the claims of writers who beg off for wretched writing on the grounds of age. Miriam deFord has a swift kick for them, even as her story has a swift kick for us. *Hie!*

# ● THE MALLEY SYSTEM

## by Miriam Allen deFord

SHEP:

"Is it far?" she asked. "I have to get home for my school telecast; I just slipped out to buy a vita-sucker. I'm in cybernetics already, and I'm only seven," she added boastfully.

I forced my voice out of a croak.

"No, only a step, and it won't take you a minute. My little girl asked me to come and get you. She described you so I'd know you."

The child looked doubtful.

"You don't look old enough to have a little girl. And I don't know who she is."

"Right down here." I held her skinny shoulder firmly.

"Down these steps? I don't like—"

I glanced around quickly; nobody in sight. I pushed her through the dark doorway and fastened the bolt.

"Why, you're a bomb-sight squatter!" she cried in terror. "You couldn't have a—"

"Shut up!" I clamped my hand over her mouth and threw her on the pile of rags that served me for a bed. Her feeble struggle was only an incitation. I ripped her shorts from her shaking legs. Oh, God! Now, now, now! The blood tickled.

The child tore her head loose and screamed, just as I was sinking into blissful lassitude. Furious, I circled her thin neck and pounded her head against the cement floor until blood and brains leaked from the shattered skull.

Without moving further, I let myself fall asleep. I never heard the pounding on the door.

CARLO:

"There's one!" Ricky said, pointing down.

My eyes followed his finger. Huddled under the framework of the moving sidewalk was a dark inert bundle.

"Can we get down?"

"He did, and he's high on goofer-dust or something, or he wouldn't be there."

There was nobody in sight; it was nearly twenty-four o'clock, and people were either home or still in some joy-joint. We'd been roaming the streets for hours, looking for something to break the monotony.

We managed, hand over hand. Those things are electrified, but you learn how to avoid the hot spots.

Ricky pulled out his atom-flash. It was an old geezer—in his second century, looked like—and dead to the world. He ought to've had more sense, at his age. He deserved whatever we gave him.

We gave him plenty. Boy, he waked up right away and started screeching, but I fixed that with a heel on his face. You ought to've seen him when we got his clothes off—nasty gray hair on his chest, all his ribs showing, but a big potbelly, and withered where we started carving. It was disgusting; we marked him up but good. He might have seen us, so I pushed his eyes in. Then I gave him a boot in the throat to keep him quiet, we went through his pockets—he didn't have much left after all the goofer he'd bought, but we took his credit codes in case we could figure out a way to use them without being caught—and we left him there and started to climb back.

We were halfway up when we heard the damned cop-copter buzzing above us.

MIRIAMNI:

"You're crazy," he snarled at me. "What the hell do you think—that I married you by ancient rites and you have some kind of hold on me?"

I could scarcely talk for crying.

"Don't you owe me some consideration?" I managed to say. "After all, I gave up other men for you."

"Don't be so damned possessive. You sound like some throwback to the Darker Age. When I want you and you want me, oke. The rest of the time we're both free. And it was the other men that gave *you* up, wasn't it?"

That put the stop-off to it. I reached behind the video-wall, where I'd cached the old-fashioned laser gun Grandpa gave me when I was a kid—it still worked, and he'd shown me how to use it—and I let him have it. Phft-phft, right between his lying lips.

I couldn't stop till it was empty. I guess I kalumphed then. The next thing I knew my son Jon by my first man opened the door with his print-key and there we both were, flat on the floor, but I was the only one alive. Oh, curse Jon and his degree in humanistics and his sense of civic duty!

RICHIE B:

Utterly uncontempojust! He was only a lousy Extraterry, and I was only having some fun. This is 2083, isn't it, and the new rules were issued two years ago, and Extraterries are supposed to know their place and not bull in where they're not wanted. The play-park was posted "Humans Only," and there he was, standing right by the booth where I had a date to meet Marta. He had a tape in his paw, so I guess he was a tourist, but they ought to find out what's what before they buy their tickets. Oughtn't to be allowed on Earth at all, to my way of thinking.

Instead of running, he had the nerve to speak to me. "Can you tell me," he began in that silly wheezing voice they have, with the filthy accent.

I was early, so I thought I'd see what happened next. "Yee-oh, I can tell you," I mimicked him. "One thing I can tell you is, you've got too many fingers on those forepaws to suit my taste."

He looked bewildered and I could hardly keep from laughing. I looked all around—those booths are private and there was nobody near, and I could see clear to the helipark and Marta wasn't in sight yet. I reached under my wraparound and got out my little snickeree I carry to defend myself.

"And I hate prehensile tails," I added. "I hate 'em, but I collect 'em. Gimme yours."

I leaned down and grabbed it and began to saw at the base.

Then he did yell and try to run, but I held fast. I'd just meant to scare him a little, but he made me mad. And the violet-colored blood turned me sick, and that made me still madder. I was on guard for him to try to hit me, but damned if he didn't just flop in a faint. Hell, you can't tell about those Extraterries—for all I know, he might have been a she.

I got the tail off, and shook it to drain the blood, and I was all set to give him—it—one behind the ear and dump it down under the bushes, when I heard somebody coming up. I thought it was Marta, and she's always game for a kick, so I called, "Hey, saccharine, look at the souvenir I just got for you!"

But it wasn't Marta. It was one of those slimy Planet Fed snoopers.

BRATHMORE:

I am hungry again. I am a strong, vital person; I need real nourishment. Do those fools expect me to live on neutrosynthetics and predigestos forever? When I am hungry I must eat.

And this time I was lucky. My little notice brings them always, but not always just what I need; then I have to let them go and wait for the next one. Just the right age—juicy and tender, but not too young. Too young there is no meat on the bones.

I am methodical; I keep a record. This was Number 78. And all in four years, since I got the inspiration to put the notice in the public communitape. "Wanted: partner for dance act, man or girl, 16–23 years old." Because after that, if they really are dancers, their muscles get tough.

With the twenty-hour week, every other compute-tender and service trainee goes in for some Leisure Cult, and I had a hunch a lot of them want to be pro dancers. I didn't *say* I was on tridimens or sensalive or in a joy-joint, but where else could I be?

"How old are you? Where have you trained? How long? What can you do? I'll turn on the music, and you show me."

They didn't show me long—long enough for me to give them the full once-over. I have a real office, on the 270th floor of the Sky-High Rise, no less. All very respectable. My name—or a name I use—on the door. "Entertainment Business."

The satisfactory ones, I say, "Oke. Now we'll go to my practice hall, and we'll see how we do together."

We go up and copt over—but that's to my hide-out. Sometimes they get nervous, but I soothe them. If I can't, I land at the nearest port and just say, "All out, brother or sister as the case may be. I can't work with anyone who hasn't confidence in me."

Twice the fuzz has come to my office on some simpleton's complaint, but I've got that fixed. I wouldn't have thought of dancing if I didn't have my credentials. You'd have known me once—I was a pro myself for twenty years.

The ones that disappear, nobody ever bothers about. Usually they haven't told anybody where they were going. If they have, and I'm asked, I just say they never came, and nobody can prove they did.

So here's Number 78. Female, nineteen, nice and plump but not muscle-bound yet.

Once home, the rest's easy. "Get into your tutu, sister, and we'll go to the practice room. Dressing room right in there."

The dressing room's gassed when I press the button. It takes about six minutes. Then to my specially fitted kitchen. Clothes to the incinerator. Macerator and dissolver for metal and glass. Contact lenses, jewelry, money, all goes in: I'm no thief. Then into the oven, well greased and seasoned.

About half an hour, the way I like it. After dinner, when I clean up, the macerator will take care of the bones and teeth. (And gall-stones once, believe it or not.) I dial a few drinks to sharpen my appetite, and get out my knife and fork—genuine antiques, cost me a lot, from the days when people ate real meat.

Rich and steaming, brown on the outside and oozing juice. My stomach rumbles in delight. I take my first delicious bite.

Aagh! What in the name of all— What was wrong with her? She must have been in one of those far-out poison-fancier teenster gangs! An awful pain shot right through me. I doubled up. I don't remember screaming, but they tell me they heard me clear out on the speedway, and somebody finally broke in and found me.

They flew me to the hospital, and I had to have half my stomach replaced.

And of course they found her too.


"Extremely interesting," said the visiting criminologist from the African Union. He and the warden, sitting in the warden's office, watched on the wide screen as the techs removed the brain probes and, flanked by the roboguards, led out the four men and the woman —or was that last one a woman too? it was hard to tell—dazed and shuffling, to the rest cubicles. "You mean this is done every day?"

"Every single day of their term. Most of them have life sentences."

"And is it done with all prisoners? Or just all felons?"

The warden laughed.

"Not even all felons," he answered. "Only what we call Class 1 homicide, rape, and mayhem. It would hardly be advisable to let a pro burglar live daily through his latest burglary—he'd just note the weak points and educate himself to make a better job of the next one after he got out!"

"And does it act as a deterrent?"

"If it didn't, we couldn't use it. We have a provision, you know, in the Inter-American Union, against 'cruel and unusual punishment.' This is no longer unusual, and our Supreme Court and the Appeals Court of the Terrestrial Regions have both ruled that it is not cruel. It is therapeutic."

"I meant deterrent to other would-be criminals on the outside."

"All I can say is that every secondary school in the Union includes a course in elementary penology, with a dozen screen-viewings of this procedure. We've had a lot of publicity. I've been interviewed often. And out of two thousand inmates of this institution, which is of average size, those five are the only present subjects for this treatment. Our homicide rate in this Union has gone down from the highest to the lowest on Earth in the ten years since we began."

"Ah, yes, I was aware of that, of course. It is why I was delegated to investigate, to see whether it might be desirable for us too. I understand I am only the latest of such visitors."

"Quite true. The East Asian Union is considering it now, and several other Unions are hoping to put it on their agenda."

"But in the other sense of deterrence, as it affects the people themselves? How does that work out? Of course I know they couldn't continue their criminal careers at present, but what is the psychological effect on them here and now?"

"The principle," said the warden, "was defined by Lachim Malley, our noted penologist—"

"Indeed yes, one of the very great."

"We think so. His idea came originally from a very minor and banal bit of folk history. Back in the old days, when they had privately owned stores and people were paid wages to work in them, it used to be the custom, in shops that sold pastries and confectionery and such delicacies, which the young particularly crave—and also, I believe, in breweries and wineries—to allow new employees to eat or drink their fill. It was found that soon they became satiated, and then actually averse to the very thing they had so much craved—which of course saved a good deal of money in the long run.

"It occurred to Malley that if an atrocious criminal should be obliged to relive constantly the episode which led to his incarceration—have it stuffed into him daily, so to speak, the incessant repetition would have a similar effect on him. Since we can now activate any part of the brain painlessly by electric probes in exact areas, the experiment was feasible. We here in this prison were the first to put it into practice."

"And does it so affect them?"

"At first some of the most vicious—that mass cannibal you saw, or the child molester, for example—seem actually to revel in the reliving of their crimes. The less deteriorated dread and shrink from it from the beginning. And even the worst—those two are only at the beginning of their terms—gradually become first bored, then sated, and eventually, in time, completely alienated from their former impulses. Terribly remorseful, too, some of them; I've had hardened criminals get down on their knees and beg me to let them forget. But of course I can't."

"And after they have served their time? For I suppose, as in our Union, a life sentence really means not more than fifteen years."

"About twelve, with us, on the average. But some of these—that last case, for instance—can never be safely released. They become reconciled, on the whole. For, apart from that daily ordeal, their lives aren't bad here. They live comfortably, they have every opportunity for education and recreation, where possible we arrange for conjugal visits, and many of them pursue useful careers as if they were not imprisoned."

"But what of those who *are* freed? Have any of them reverted to crime? Have you had any recidivists among them?"

The warden looked embarrassed.

"No, we've never had any subject of the Malley System come back here," he said reluctantly. "In fact, I feel it my duty to tell you that there is one slight disadvantage in the System.

"So far, we've never had one subject who could be released to the general community when his term was over. Every one of them up to now has had to be transferred instead to a mental hospital."

The African criminologist was silent. Then his eyes strayed around the office in which he sat. For the first time he noticed the armor-plated walls, the shatterproof glass, the electronic weapons trained on the door and ready to be activated by pressure on a button on the warden's desk.

The warden followed his glance, and flushed.

"I'm afraid I'm just chicken," he said defensively. "Actually, the subjects are kept under strict surveillance and the roboguards have orders to shoot to kill. But I keep remembering my predecessor's experience, when he and Lachim Malley—"

"I know, naturally," said the African, "that Malley died suddenly while he was visiting this prison. A heart attack, I understand."

"My predecessor was a little too careless," remarked the warden with a grim smile. "He had complete faith in Malley's System, and he didn't even have roboguards to back up the techs, or have the subjects frisked for shivs before their daily recapitulation. There were more subjects then, too—at least fourteen that day. So when they simultaneously overpowered the techs, with the probes already in place, and broke for this office—

"Oh yes, Malley died of a heart attack. So did my predecessor. Right through the heart, in both cases."

## Afterword:

Since fact crime and mystery shorts make up a major part of my writing, it is natural that even in science fiction the subject should appeal to me. This particular extrapolation came to me suddenly out of the blue, as much of my science fiction does. Murders are committed by people in a highly emotional state, even if the emotion is only rabid thrill-seeking; and that being so, what worse punishment could be inflicted than to force a repetition of the experience until the murderer is either wildly remorseful or (as seems more likely, and as I indicated) reduced to complete psychic breakdown.

Granted that mankind *has* a future, and that we somehow catch up socially and psychologically with our technical achievements, some such penological gambit might well suggest itself to future criminologists. Whether it would be any more of a deterrent to others than the chance of execution is today, is another question. And despite my disclaimer, I am not at all sure that the highest court of appeals of the time would not decide that the punishment was even crueler than the crime.

## Introduction to A TOY FOR JULIETTE:

What follows is, in the purest sense, the end-result of literary feedback. Recently the story editor of a prime-time television series, pressed for a script to shoot, sat down and wrote one himself rather than wait for the vagaries of a free-lance scenarist's schedule and dalliance. When he had completed the script, which was to go before the cameras in a matter of days, he sent it as a matter of form to the legal department of the studio. For the clearance of names, etc. Later that day the legal department called him back in a frenzy. Almost scene-for-scene and word-for-word (including the title), the non-s-f story editor had copied a well-known science fiction short story. When it was pointed out to him, the story editor blanched and recalled he had indeed read that story, some fifteen years before. Hurriedly, the story rights were purchased from the well-known fantasy writer who had originally conceived the idea. I hasten to add that I accept the veracity of the story editor when he swears he had no conscious knowledge of imitating the story. I believe him because this sort of unconscious plagiarism is commonplace in the world of the writer. It is inevitable that much of the mass of reading a writer does will stick with him somehow, in vague concepts, snatches of scenes, snippets of characterization, and it will turn up later, in the writer's own work; altered, transmogrified, but still a direct result of another writer's work. It is by no means "plagiarism." It is part of the answer to the question asked by idiots of authors at cocktail parties: "Where do you get your ideas?"

Poul Anderson dropped me a note several months ago explaining that he had just written a story he was about to send out to market when he realized it paralleled the theme of a story he had read at a writers' conference we had both attended, just a month or so before. He added that his story was only vaguely similar to mine, but he wanted to apprise me of the resemblance so there would be no question later. It was a rhetorical letter: I'm arrogant, but not arrogant enough to think Poul Anderson needs to crib from me. Similarly, at the World Science Fiction Convention held last year in Cleveland, the well-known German fan Tom Schlück and I were introduced. (Tom had been brought over by the fans as Fan Guest of Honor, an exchange tradition in fandom perpetuated by the TransAtlantic Fan Fund.) The first thing he did after we shook hands was to hand me a German science fiction paperback. I had some difficulty understanding why he had given me the gift. Tom opened the book—a collection of stories pseudonymously written by top German s-f fan/pro Walter Ernsting. The flyleaf said: "To Harlan Ellison with thanks and compliments." I still didn't understand. Then Tom turned to the first story, which was titled *"Die Sonnenbombe."* Under the title it said: (*Nach einer Idee von Harlan Ellison*). I wrinkled my brow. I still didn't understand. I recognized my own name, which looks the same in all languages save Russian, Chinese, Hebrew or Sanskrit, but I don't read German, and I'm afraid I stood there like a clot. Tom explained that the basic idea of a story I had written in 1957—"Run for the Stars"—had inspired Ernsting to write *"Die Sonnenbombe."* It was the literary feedback, halfway across the world. I was deeply touched, and even more, it was a feeling of justification. Every writer save the meanest hack hopes his words will live after he goes down the hole, that his thoughts will influence people. It isn't the primary purpose of the writing, of course, but it's the sort of secret wish that parallels the Average Man having babies, so his name doesn't die with him. And here, in my hands, was the visible proof that something my mind had conjured up had reached out and ensnared another man's imagination. It was obviously the sincerest form of flattery, and by no means "plagiarism." It was the literary feedback. The instances of this action-reaction among writers are numberless, and some of them are legend. It is the reason for writers' seminars, workshops, conferences and the endless exchange of letters among writers. What has all of this—or any of it—to do with Robert Bloch, the author of the story that follows? Everything.

In 1943 Robert Bloch had published a story titled "Yours Truly, Jack the Ripper." The number of times it has been reprinted, anthologized, translated into radio and TV scripts, and most of all plagiarized, are staggering. I read it in 1953, and the story stuck with me always. When I *heard* its dramatization on the Molle Mystery Theater, it became a recurring favorite memory. The story idea was simply that Jack the Ripper, by killing at specific times, made his peace with the dark gods and was thus allowed to live forever. Jack was immortal, and Bloch traced with cold methodical logic a trail of similar Ripper-style murders in almost every major city of the world, over a period of fifty or sixty years. The concept of Jack—who was never apprehended— living on, from era to era, caught my imagination. When it came time to put this anthology together, I called Robert Bloch and suggested that if Jack were, in fact, immortal, why then he would have to go on into the future. The image of a creature of Whitechapel fog and filth, the dark figure of Leather Apron, skulking through a sterile and automated city of the future, was an anachronism that fascinated me. Bob agreed, and said he would set to work at once. When his story came in, it was (pardon the word) a delight, and I bought it at once. But the concept of Jack in the future would not release my thoughts. I dwelled on it with almost morbid fascination. Finally I asked Bob if he minded my doing a story for this book that took up where his left off. He said he thought it would be all right. It was, as I've said, in the purest sense, the act of literary feedback. And again, the sincerest form of flattery. Bloch had literally triggered the creative process in another writer.

The story that follows Robert Bloch's story is the product of that feedback. Mr. Bloch has kindly and graciously agreed to write the introduction to *my* story, in an effort to gain revenge for this introduction to *his* story. Tied in a knot, the two introductions, the two stories and the two afterwords seem to have melded into a unified whole that demonstrates more admirably than any million words of literary critiques what it is that one writer obtains from another.

What *this* particular editor has obtained from *that* particular writer named Robert Bloch is far more than a story idea. I first saw Bloch— tall, debonair, sharp-featured, bespectacled, smoking through a long cigarette holder reminiscent of Eric von Stroheim—at the Midwest Sci-

ence Fiction Convention at Beatley's-on-the-Lake Hotel in Belle-
fontaine, Ohio, in 1951. I was almost eighteen. I was obnoxious, wide-
eyed and hungry to know all there was about science fiction. Bloch was
at that time, and had been for many years, a living legend. Even though
a recognized professional with many books and stories to his credit, he
had always made himself available to even the grubbiest fan anxious to
cadge a story or article for some half-legible fan magazine. Gratis, of
course. He was the perennial toastmaster, his wit a combination of cornball and cutlass-incisive. He knew everyone, and everyone knew him.
Up to this pillar of fantasy walked the snot Ellison.

I do not recall what happened on that occasion, the mists of time and
the ravages of senility having already reached me at age thirty-three, but
it must have been memorable, because someone took our photograph,
and I still have a copy: myself looking smug as a potato bug and Bloch
staring down on me with a peculiar expression that says benevolence,
toleration, amused confusion and stark terror. I have been privileged to
call myself a friend of Robert Bloch's since that time.

One more small anecdote, then I'll let Bloch speak for himself on the
subjects of his career, his childhood and the nature of violence. When
I arrived in Hollywood in 1962, literally without a dollar in my pocket
(I had ten cents, a wife, a son, and we had been so broke driving cross-
country we had only eaten the contents of a box of pecan pralines for
the last three hundred miles), in a battered 1951 Ford, Robert Bloch—
who was not all that well off himself—loaned me enough money to get
a place to stay and food to eat. He waited three years to be repaid, and
never once asked for the considerable sum. He is one of God's Good
People, as anyone who has ever come anywhere near him can attest. It
is one of the giant dichotomies of our times that a man as gentle, amusing, empathic and peaceful as Bloch can write the gruesome and warped
stories he produces with alarming regularity. One can only offer by way
of amelioration Sturgeon's lament that after he had written one—and
one only—story about homosexuality, everyone accused him of being
a fag. Bloch is an entity quite apart and diametrically opposite from the
horrors he sets on paper. (I might suggest the reader remember this
writer's lament when he comes to the story *after* Bloch's.)

And now, beaming with memorabilia and *bonhomie,* here is Bloch:

"As a small child I skipped several grades of grammar school, thus
finding myself in the company of older and bigger youngsters who introduced me to the savage jungle of the playground, with its secret
pecking order and ceaseless torment of the weak by the strong. Fortu-

nately for myself, I never became a physical victim nor was I an over-compensating bully; in some strange fashion I found that I was able to lead my companions into various intricate imaginative games as a sub-stitute activity. We dug trenches in the back yard and played war; the open front porch became the deck of a pirate ship and captured victims walked the plank (a leaf from the dining-room table) to jump off into the ocean of the front lawn. But I dimly recognized that the shows and circuses I devised didn't hold the interest of my playmates nearly as well as the games which were surrogates for violence. And later on, as they were inevitably lured towards the venerated violences of boxing, wrestling, football and other adult-approved outlets for outrage on the human person, I retreated to reading, sketching, drama and the enjoy-ment of the theater and motion pictures.

"The silent version of *The Phantom of the Opera* scared the daylights out of me as an eight-year-old, but a part of me was objective enough to find a fascination in this demonstration of the power of make-believe. I began to read widely in the field of imaginary violence. When, at the age of fifteen, I began corresponding with the fantasy writer, H. P. Love-craft, he encouraged me to try my own hand at writing. As a high school comic I'd discovered that I could make audiences laugh; now I began to realize that I could move them emotionally in other directions.

"At seventeen, I sold my first story to *Weird Tales* magazine and thus found a lifelong vocation. Since then I've made magazine appearances with upwards of four hundred short stories, articles and novelettes. I've conducted magazine columns, seen stories reprinted in close to a hun-dred anthologies here and abroad; twenty-five books, novels and short-story collections have been published. In addition, I've ghost-written for politicians and spent a term writing almost every conceivable variety of advertising copy. I adapted thirty-nine of my own stories for a radio series, and in recent years have concentrated largely on scripts for tele-vision and motion pictures.

"In the beginning my work was almost entirely in the field of fantasy, where the violent element was openly and obviously a product of imagi-nation. The mass violence of World War II caused me to examine vio-lence at its source—on the individual level. Still unwilling or unable to cope with its present reality, I retreated into history and re-created, as a prototype of apparently senseless violence, the infamously famous mass murderer who styled himself 'Yours Truly, Jack the Ripper.' This short story was to see endless reprint and anthologization, plus frequent dramatizing on radio, and finally appeared on television; at latest report it popped up as a dramatic reading in Israel. For some reason the notion of Jack the Ripper's survival in the present day touched a sensitive spot in the audience psyche.

"I myself was far from insensitive to this incarnation of violence in our midst, and I beat a hasty retreat from further consideration. As the war continued and real-life violence came dangerously near, I concentrated for a time upon humor and science fiction. It wasn't until 1945, when my first short-story collection (*The Opener of the Way*) appeared, that I rounded out its contents with a new effort, 'One Way to Mars,' in which a pseudo-science-fictional form is employed to describe the psychotic fugue of a contemporary man of violence.

"A year later I wrote my first novel, *The Scarf*—the first-person account of a mass murderer. Since that time, while still employing fantasy and science fiction for satire and social criticism, I've devoted many of my subsequent short stories and almost all of my novels (*Spiderweb, Shooting Star, The Kidnaper, The Will to Kill, Psycho, The Dead Beat, Firebug, The Couch, Terror*) to a direct examination of violence in our society.

"*Psycho* was inspired by a somewhat guarded newspaper account of a mass murderer in a small town close to the one where I resided; I knew none of the intimate details of the crimes, but I wondered just what sort of individual could perpetrate them while living as an apparently normal citizen in a notoriously gossip-ridden and constrictedly conventional environment. I created my schizophrenic character out of what I thought was whole cloth, only to discover, some years later, that the rationale I evolved for him was frighteningly close to his aberrated reality.

"Some of my other characters have also proved to be a bit too real for comfort. When I wrote *The Scarf*, for example, the editors insisted on deleting a short section in which the protagonist indulges in a bit of sadistic fantasy. He imagines what it would be like to take a high-powered rifle up to the top of a tall building and start shooting people below at random. Farfetched, said the editors. Today, I have the last laugh—but it's not necessarily a laugh of amusement.

"*The Scarf*, incidentally, was just republished in paperback. After twenty years, I naturally went through the book to update a few slang phrases and topical references. But my protagonist didn't need any changing; the passage of time alone did the job for me. Twenty years ago I wrote him as a villain—today he emerges as an anti-hero.

"For the violence has come into its own now; the violence I examined,

and at times projected and predicted, has become today's commonplace
and accepted reality. This, to me, is far more terrifying than anything I
could possibly imagine."

Ellison again. In an attempt to unify the whole, and believing firmly
that Bloch's piece loses very little impact for the revelation, this section
of the book has been structured to be read all of a piece. I urge you to
go from Bloch to his afterword to his introduction to the Ellison to *his*
afterword. It is a case of age before beauty.

Or possibly Beauty before the Beast.

# ● A TOY FOR JULIETTE

## by Robert Bloch

Juliette entered her bedroom, smiling, and a thousand Juliettes smiled
back at her. For all the walls were paneled with mirrors, and the
ceiling was set with inlaid panes that reflected her image.

Wherever she glanced she could see the blonde curls framing the
sensitive features of a face that was a radiant amalgam of both
child and angel; a striking contrast to the rich, ripe revelation of
her body in the filmy robe.

But Juliette wasn't smiling at herself. She smiled because she knew
that Grandfather was back, and he'd brought her another toy. In
just a few moments it would be decontaminated and delivered, and
she wanted to be ready.

Juliette turned the ring on her finger and the mirrors dimmed. Another turn would darken the room entirely; a twist in the opposite direction would bring them blazing into brilliance. It was all a matter of
choice—but then, that was the secret of life. To choose, for pleasure.

And what was her pleasure tonight?

Juliette advanced to one of the mirror panels and passed her hand
before it. The glass slid to one side, revealing the niche behind it;
the coffin-shaped opening in the solid rock, with the boot and thumbscrews set at the proper heights.

For a moment she hesitated; she hadn't played *that* game in years.

Another time, perhaps. Juliette waved her hand and the mirror moved to cover the opening again.

She wandered along the row of panels, gesturing as she walked, pausing to inspect what was behind each mirror in turn. Here was the rack, there the stocks with the barbed whips resting against the dark-stained wood. And here was the dissecting table, hundreds of years old, with its quaint instruments; behind the next panel, the electrical prods and wires that produced such weird grimaces and contortions of agony, to say nothing of screams. Of course the screams didn't matter in a soundproofed room.

Juliette moved to the side wall and waved her hand again; the obedient glass slid away and she stared at a plaything she'd almost forgotten. It was one of the first things Grandfather had ever given her, and it was very old, almost like a mummy case. What had he called it? The Iron Maiden of Nuremberg, that was it—with the sharpened steel spikes set inside the lid. You chained a man inside, and you turned the little crank that closed the lid, ever so slowly, and the spikes pierced the wrists and the elbows, the ankles and the knees, the groin and the eyes. You had to be careful not to get excited and turn too quickly, or you'd spoil the fun.

Grandfather had shown her how it worked, the first time he brought her a real *live* toy. But then, Grandfather had shown her everything. He'd taught her all she knew, for he was very wise. He'd even given her her name—Juliette—from one of the old-fashioned printed books he'd discovered by the philosopher De Sade.

Grandfather had brought the books from the Past, just as he'd brought the playthings for her. He was the only one who had access to the Past, because he owned the Traveler.

The Traveler was a very ingenious mechanism, capable of attaining vibrational frequencies which freed it from the time-bind. At rest, it was just a big square boxlike shape, the size of a small room. But when Grandfather took over the controls and the oscillation started, the box would blur and disappear. It was still there, Grandfather said—at least, the *matrix* remained as a fixed point in space and time—but anything or anyone within the square could move freely into the Past to wherever the controls were programed. Of course they would be invisible when they arrived, but that was actually an advantage, particularly when it came to finding things and bringing them back. Grandfather had brought back some very interesting objects from almost mythical places—the great library of Alexandria, the Pyramid of Cheops, the Kremlin, the Vatican, Fort Knox—all the storehouses of treasure and knowledge which existed thousands of years ago. He liked to go to *that* part of the Past, the period before the thermonuclear wars and the robotic ages, and collect things. Of course books and jewels and metals were useless, except to an antiquarian, but Grandfather was a romanticist and loved the olden times.

It was strange to think of him owning the Traveler, but of course he hadn't actually created it. Juliette's father was really the one who built it, and Grandfather took possession of it after her father died. Juliette suspected Grandfather had killed her father and mother when she was just a baby, but she could never be sure. Not that it mattered; Grandfather was always very good to her, and besides, soon he would die and she'd own the Traveler herself.

They used to joke about it frequently. "I've made you into a monster," he'd say. "And someday you'll end up by destroying me. After which, of course, you'll go on to destroy the entire world—or what little remains of it."

"Aren't you afraid?" she'd tease.

"Certainly not. That's my dream—the destruction of everything. An end to all this sterile decadence. Do you realize that at one time there were more than three billion inhabitants on this planet? And now, less than three thousand! Less than three thousand, shut up inside these Domes, prisoners of themselves and sealed away forever, thanks to the sins of the fathers who poisoned not only the outside world but outer space by meddling with the atomic order of the universe. Humanity is virtually extinct already; you will merely hasten the finale."

"But couldn't we all go back to another time, in the Traveler?" she asked.

"Back to *what* time? The continuum is changeless; one event leads inexorably to another, all links in a chain which binds us to the present and its inevitable end in destruction. We'd have temporary individual survival, yes, but to no purpose. And none of us are fitted to survive in a more primitive environment. So let us stay here and take what pleasure we can from the moment. *My* pleasure is to be the sole user and possessor of the Traveler. And yours, Juliette—"

Grandfather laughed then. They both laughed, because they knew what *her* pleasure was.

Juliette killed her first toy when she was eleven—a little boy. It had been brought to her as a special gift from Grandfather, from somewhere in the Past, for elementary sex play. But it wouldn't co-operate, and she lost her temper and beat it to death with a steel rod. So Grandfather brought her an older toy, with brown skin, and it co-operated very well, but in the end she tired of it and one day when it was sleeping in her bed she tied it down and found a knife.

Experimenting a little before it died, Juliette discovered new sources of pleasure, and of course Grandfather found out. That's when he'd christened her "Juliette"; he seemed to approve most highly, and from then on he brought her the playthings she kept behind the mirrors in her bedroom. And on his restless rovings into the Past he brought her new toys.

Being invisible, he could find them for her almost anywhere on his travels—all he did was to use a stunner and transport them when he returned. Of course each toy had to be very carefully decontaminated; the Past was teeming with strange micro-organisms. But once the toys were properly antiseptic they were turned over to Juliette for her pleasure, and during the past seven years she had enjoyed herself.

It was always delicious, this moment of anticipation before a new toy arrived. What would it be like? Grandfather was most considerate; mainly, he made sure that the toys he brought her could speak and understand Anglish—or "English," as they used to call it in the Past. Verbal communication was often important, particularly if Juliette wanted to follow the precepts of the philosopher De Sade and enjoy some form of sex relation before going on to keener pleasures.

But there was still the guessing beforehand. Would this toy be young or old, wild or tame, male or female? She'd had all kinds, and every possible combination. Sometimes she kept them alive for days before tiring of them—or before the subtleties of which she was capable caused them to expire. At other times she wanted it to happen quickly; tonight, for example, she knew she could be soothed only by the most primitive and direct action.

Once Juliette realized this, she stopped playing with her mirror panels and went directly to the big bed. She pulled back the coverlet, groped under the pillow until she felt it. Yes, it was still there—the big knife with the long, cruel blade. She knew what she would do now: take the toy to bed with her and then, at precisely the proper moment, combine her pleasures. If she could time her knife thrust—

She shivered with anticipation, then with impatience.

What kind of toy would it be? She remembered the suave, cool one—Benjamin Bathurst was his name, an English diplomat from the time of what Grandfather called the Napoleonic Wars. Oh, he'd been suave and cool enough, until she beguiled him with her body, into the bed. And there'd been that American aviatrix from slightly later on in the Past, and once, as a very special treat, the entire crew of a sailing vessel called the *Marie Celeste*. They had lasted for *weeks!*

Strangely enough, she'd even read about some of her toys afterwards. Because when Grandfather approached them with his stunner and brought them here, they disappeared forever from the Past, and if they were in any way known or important in their time, such disappearances were noted. And some of Grandfather's books had accounts of the "mysterious vanishing" which took place and was, of course, never explained. How delicious it all was!

Juliette patted the pillow back into place and slid the knife under it. She couldn't wait, now; what was delaying things?

She forced herself to move to a vent and depress the sprayer, shedding her robe as the perfumed mist bathed her body. It was the final allurement—but why didn't her toy arrive?

Suddenly Grandfather's voice came over the auditor.

"I'm sending you a little surprise, dearest."

That's what he always said; it was part of the game.

Juliette depressed the communicator-toggle. "Don't tease," she begged. "Tell me what it's like."

"An Englishman. Late Victorian Era. Very prim and proper, by the looks of him."

"Young? Handsome?"

"Passable." Grandfather chuckled. "Your appetites betray you, dearest."

"Who is it—someone from the books?"

"I wouldn't know the name. We found no identification during the decontamination. But from his dress and manner, and the little black bag he carried when I discovered him so early in the morning, I'd judge him to be a physician returning from an emergency call."

Juliette knew about "physicians" from her reading, of course; just as she knew what "Victorian" meant. Somehow the combination seemed exactly right.

"Prim and proper?" She giggled. "Then I'm afraid it's due for a shock."

Grandfather laughed. "You have something in mind, I take it."

"Yes."

"Can I watch?"

"Please—not this time."

"Very well."

"Don't be mad, darling. I love you."

Juliette switched off. Just in time, too, because the door was opening and the toy came in.

She stared at it, realizing that Grandfather had told the truth. The toy was a male of thirty-odd years, attractive but by no means handsome. It couldn't be, in that dark garb and those ridiculous side whiskers. There was something almost depressingly refined and mannered about it, an air of embarrassed repression.

And of course, when it caught sight of Juliette in her revealing robe, and the bed surrounded by mirrors, it actually began to *blush*.

That reaction won Juliette completely. A blushing Victorian, with the build of a bull—and unaware that this was the slaughterhouse!

It was so amusing she couldn't restrain herself; she moved forward at once and put her arms around it.

"Who—who are you? Where am I?"

The usual questions, voiced in the usual way. Ordinarily, Juliette would have amused herself by parrying with answers designed to tantalize and titillate her victim. But tonight she felt an urgency which only increased as she embraced the toy and pressed it back toward the waiting bed.

The toy began to breathe heavily, responding. But it was still bewildered. "Tell me—I don't understand. Am I alive? Or is this heaven?"

Juliette's robe fell open as she lay back. "You're alive, darling," she murmured. "Wonderfully alive." She laughed as she began to prove the statement. "But closer to heaven than you think."

And to prove *that* statement, her free hand slid under the pillow and groped for the waiting knife.

But the knife wasn't there any more. Somehow it had already found its way into the toy's hand. And the toy wasn't prim and proper any longer, its face was something glimpsed in nightmare. Just a glimpse, before the blinding blur of the knife blade, as it came down, again and again and again—

The room, of course, was soundproof, and there was plenty of time. They didn't discover what was left of Juliette's body for several days.

Back in London, after the final mysterious murder in the early morning hours, they never did find Jack the Ripper. . . .

## Afterword:

A number of years have passed since I sat down at the typewriter one gloomy winter day and wrote "Yours Truly, Jack the Ripper" for magazine publication. The magazine in which it appeared gave up its ghost, and interest in ghosts, a long time ago. But somehow my little story seems to have survived. It has since pursued me in reprint, collections, anthologies, foreign translations, radio broadcasts and television.

So when the editor of this anthology proposed that I do a story and suggested, "What about Jack the Ripper in the future?" I was capable of only one response.

You've just read it.

## Introduction to THE PROWLER IN THE CITY AT THE EDGE OF THE WORLD:

This is Robert Bloch, writing about Harlan Ellison. And believe me, it isn't easy.

His contribution to this anthology happens to be a sequel to my own, so he asked me to write an introduction, purely as a matter of poetic injustice.

I am not about to do a biographical sketch of the man; surely he wouldn't need me for that. Ellison has told the story of his life so many times, you'd think he'd know it by heart.

So I'm forced to fall back upon the consideration of Ellison as a phenomenon—a most phenomenal phenomenon—which has impinged upon my awareness, and the awareness of everyone in the science fictional genre, for the past fifteen years.

When I first met him (the preceding May I'd *seen* him), at the World

Science Fiction Convention of 1952, Harlan Ellison was a promising young man of eighteen. Today he is a promising young man of thirty-three. That's not a put-down, nor is it meant to be.

At eighteen he gave promise of becoming an outstanding fan. At thirty-three he gives promise of becoming an outstanding writer. Not only promise, but evidence.

As a fan he was articulate, ambitious and aggressive. As a professional writer, these qualities are still very obvious in all his work, and added to them is yet another conveniently alliterative quality—artistry.

Read his short stories, novels, articles and criticism. You may not always agree with what he says or the way in which he says it, but the artistry is there; the blend of emotion and excitement delivered with deep conviction and commitment. No matter what the apparent grammatical form may be, one is conscious that Ellison is really always writing in first person.

I mentioned emotion. Ellison often operates out of extremes that range from compassionate empathy to righteous indignation. He writes what he feels—and you feel what he writes.

I mentioned excitement. This is an inner climate; a constant tornado in which a part of Ellison remains as the eye—and a most perceptive one. There is small tranquillity to be found in his life or in his work. Ellison is definitely not one of those writers who cultivate the serenity of Buddha as they sit around contemplating their novels.

I mentioned conviction. Since he's not an obscurantist, his convictions come through loud and clear—in prose and in personal address. Those convictions create both admirers and enemies. Part gadfly, part raw ego, Ellison has been criticized by those who persist in regarding these qualities as admirable in a soldier, a politician or a business executive but somehow degrading in a creative artist. Ellison survives the strife; he is the only living organism I know whose natural habitat is hot water.

I mentioned commitment. The purpose and tenacity have carried him through a wide range of experience; a hitch in the army, a liaison with teenage gangs in search of background material, an editorial stint, and the eternal gantlet run by every writer who must temper his work to the taste of other arbiters.

Ellison has often clashed with those who attempted to direct his writing. In his progress from Cleveland to New York to Chicago he has left in his wake a trail of editorial gray hairs, many of them torn out by the roots. In Hollywood he has played picador to producers, his barbs forever poised and ready to be placed when he became aware of the bull.

Some people admire his nerve. Others hate his guts. But he has a way of proving—and improving—himself.

This anthology is a case in point.

During the fifteen years in which Ellison moved from fandom to professional status, literally hundreds of science fiction readers, writers and editors have dreamed of the publication of an anthology of this sort.

They dreamed it.

Ellison made it a reality.

I am aware that I've said nothing about Ellison's wit, or the sensitivity embodied in his work which has won for him both the World Science Fiction Convention's *Hugo* and the Science Fiction Writers of America's *Nebula*. You can assess those qualities for yourself by reading the story which follows.

It is a tour de force, surely, in the grand tradition of the Grand Guignol; a lineal literary descendant of such fearsome father figures as the Marquis de Sade and Louis-Ferdinand Céline. On the blood-spattered surface it is an obscenity, a violent rape of the senses and sensibilities.

But beneath the crude and shocking allusions to Eros and Thanatos is the meaningful portrayal of the Man Obsessed—the Violent Man whose transition from the past to the future leaves us with a deeper insight into the Violent Man of *today*.

For Jack the Ripper is with us now. He prowls the night, shunning the sun in a search for the blazing incandescence of an inner reality— and we see him plain in Ellison's story, to the degree that we can see (and admit to) the violence which lurks within our own psyches. Here all that is normally forbidden is abnormally released and realized. Metaphysical maundering? Before you make up your mind, read the story and let the Ripper rip *you* into an awareness of the urges and forces most of us will neither admit nor submit to; forces which, withal, remain potent within ourselves and our society. And ponder, if you will, upon the parable of Jack's dilemma as he seeks—in a phrase we all use but seldom comprehend—to "carve out a career" for himself.

An obscenity, yes. But a morality, too; a terrible morality implicit in the knowledge that the Ripper's inevitable and ultimate victim is always himself.

Even as you and I.

—ROBERT BLOCH

# ● THE PROWLER IN THE CITY AT THE EDGE OF THE WORLD

**by Harlan Ellison**

First there was the city, never night. Tin and reflective, walls of antiseptic metal like an immense autoclave. Pure and dust-free, so silent that even the whirling innards of its heart and mind were sheathed from notice. The city was self-contained, and footfalls echoed up and around—flat slapped notes of an exotic leather-footed instrument. Sounds that reverberated back to the maker like yodels thrown out across mountain valleys. Sounds made by humbled inhabitants whose lives were as ordered, as sanitary, as metallic as the city they had caused to hold them bosom-tight against the years. The city was a complex artery, the people were the blood that flowed icily through the artery. They were a gestalt with one another, forming a unified whole. It was a city shining in permanence, eternal in concept, flinging itself up in a formed and molded statement of exaltation; most modern of all modern structures, conceived as the pluperfect residence for the perfect people. The final end-result of all sociological blueprints aimed at Utopia. Living space, it had been called, and so, doomed to *live* they were, in that Erewhon of graphed respectability and cleanliness.

Never night.

Never shadowed.

. . . a shadow. A blot moving against the aluminum cleanliness. The movement of rags and bits of clinging earth from graves sealed ages before. A shape.

He touched a gunmetal-gray wall in passing: the imprint of dusty fingers. A twisted shadow moving through antiseptically pure streets, and they become—with his passing—black alleys from another time.

Vaguely, he knew what had happened. Not specifically, not with particulars, but he was strong, and he was able to get away without the eggshell-thin walls of his mind caving in. There was no place

in this shining structure to secrete himself, a place to think, but he had
to have time. He slowed his walk, seeing no one. Somehow—inexplicably—he felt . . . safe? Yes, safe. For the first time in a very long
time.

A few minutes before he had been standing in the narrow passageway
outside No. 13 Miller's Court. It had been 6:15 in the morning. London
had been quiet as he paused in the passageway of M'Carthy's Rents,
in that fetid, urine-redolent corridor where the whores of Spitalfields
took their clients. A few minutes before, the foetus in its bath of
formaldehyde tightly-stoppered in a glass bottle inside his Gladstone
bag, he had paused to drink in the thick fog, before taking the
circuitous route back to Toynbee Hall. That had been a few minutes
before. Then, suddenly, he was in another place and it was no longer
6:15 of a chill November morning in 1888.

He looked up as light flooded him in that other place. It had been
soot silent in Spitalfields, but suddenly, without any sense of having
moved or having *been* moved, he was flooded with light. And when he
looked up he was in that other place. Paused now, only a few minutes
after the transfer, he leaned against the bright wall of the city, and recalled the light. From a thousand mirrors. In the walls, in the ceiling.
A bedroom with a girl in it. A lovely girl. Not like Black Mary Kelly
or Dark Annie Chapman or Kate Eddowes or any of the other
pathetic scum he had been forced to attend. . . .

A lovely girl. Blonde, wholesome, until she had opened her robe
and turned into the same sort of slut he had been compelled to use
in his work in Whitechapel . . .

A sybarite, a creature of pleasures, a Juliette she had said, before
he used the big-bladed knife on her. He had found the knife under
the pillow, on the bed where she had led him—how shameful, un-
resisting had he been, all confused, clutching his black bag with all
the tremors of a child, he who had moved through the London night
like oil, moved where he wished, accomplished his ends unchecked
eight times, now led toward sin by another, merely another of the
tarts, taking advantage of him while he tried to distinguish what had
happened to him and where he was, how shameful—and he had
used it on her.

That had only been minutes before, though he had worked very
efficiently on her.

The knife had been rather unusual. The blade had seemed to be two wafer-thin sheets of metal with a pulsing, glowing *something* between. A kind of sparking, such as might be produced by a Van de Graaf generator. But that was patently ridiculous. It had had no wires attached to it, no bus bars, nothing to produce even the crudest electrical discharge. He had thrust the knife into the Gladstone bag, where now it lay beside the scalpels and the spool of catgut and the racked vials in their leather cases, and the foetus in its bottle. Mary Jane Kelly's foetus.

He had worked efficiently, but swiftly, and had laid her out almost exactly in the same fashion as Kate Eddowes: the throat slashed completely through from ear-to-ear, the torso laid open down between the breasts to the vagina, the intestines pulled out and draped over the right shoulder, a piece of the intestines being detached and placed between the left arm and the body. The liver had been punctured with the point of the knife, with a vertical cut slitting the left lobe of the liver. (He had been surprised to find the liver showed none of the signs of cirrhosis so prevalent in these Spitalfields tarts, who drank incessantly to rid themselves of the burden of living the dreary lives they moved through, grotesquely. In fact, this one seemed totally unlike the others, even if she had been more brazen in her sexual overtures. And that knife under the bed pillow . . .) He had severed the vena cava leading to the heart. Then he had gone to work on the face.

He had thought of removing the left kidney again, as he had Kate Eddowes'. He smiled to himself as he conjured up the expression that must have been on the face of Mr. George Lusk, chairman of the Whitechapel Vigilance Committee, when he received the cardboard box in the mail. The box containing Miss Eddowes' kidney, and the letter, impiously misspelled:

> *From hell, Mr. Lusk, sir, I send you half the kidne I took from one woman, prasarved it for you, tother piece I fried and ate it; was very nice. I may send you the bloody knif that took it out if you only wate while longer. Catch me when you can, Mr. Lusk.*

He had wanted to sign *that* one "Yours Truly, Jack the Ripper" or even Spring-Heeled Jack or maybe Leather Apron, whichever had ticked his fancy, but a sense of style had stopped him. To go too far was to defeat his own purposes. It may even have been too much to suggest to Mr. Lusk that he had eaten the kidney. How hideous. True, he *had* smelled it. . . .

This blonde girl, this Juliette with the knife under her pillow. She was the ninth. He leaned against the smooth steel wall without break or seam, and he rubbed his eyes. When would he be able to stop? When would they realize, when would they get his message, a message so clear, written in blood, that only the blindness of their own cupidity forced them to misunderstand! Would he be compelled to decimate the endless regiments of Spitalfields sluts to make them understand? Would he be forced to run the cobbles ankle-deep in black blood before they sensed what he was saying, and were impelled to make reforms?

But as he took his blood-soaked hands from his eyes, he realized what he must have sensed all along: he was no longer in Whitechapel. This was not Miller's Court, nor anywhere in Spitalfields. It might not even be London. But how could *that* be?

Had God taken him?

Had he died, in a senseless instant between the anatomy lesson of Mary Jane Kelly (that filth, she had actually *kissed* him!) and the bedroom disembowelment of this Juliette? Had Heaven finally called him to his reward for the work he had done?

The Reverend Mr. Barnett would love to know about this. But then, he'd have loved to know about it *all*. But "Leather Apron" wasn't about to tell. Let the reforms come as the Reverend and his wife wished for them, and let them think their pamphleteering had done it, instead of the scalpels of Jack.

If he was dead, would his work be finished? He smiled to himself. If Heaven had taken him, then it must be that the work *was* finished. Successfully. But if *that* was so, then who was this Juliette who now lay spread out moist and cooling in the bedroom of a thousand mirrors? And in that instant he felt fear.

What if even God misinterpreted what he had done?

As the good folk of Queen Victoria's London had misinterpreted. As Sir Charles Warren had misinterpreted. What if God believed the superficial and ignored the *real* reason? But no! Ludicrous. If anyone would understand, it was the good God who had sent him the message that told him to set things a-right.

God loved him, as he loved God, and God would know.

But he felt fear, in that moment.

Because who was the girl he had just carved?

"She was my granddaughter, Juliette," said a voice immediately beside him.

His head refused to move, to turn that few inches to see who spoke. The Gladstone was beside him, resting on the smooth and reflective surface of the street. He could not get to a knife before he was taken. At last they had caught up with Jack. He began to shiver uncontrollably.

"No need to be afraid," the voice said. It was a warm and succoring voice. An older man. He shook as with an ague. But he turned to look. It was a kindly old man with a gentle smile. Who spoke again, without moving his lips. "No one can hurt you. How do you do?"

The man from 1888 sank slowly to his knees. "Forgive me. Dear God, I did not know." The old man's laughter rose inside the head of the man on his knees. It rose like a beam of sunlight moving across a Whitechapel alleyway, from noon to one o'clock, rising and illuminating the gray bricks of soot-coated walls. It rose, and illuminated his mind.

"I'm not God. Marvelous idea, but no, I'm not God. Would you like to meet God? I'm sure we can find one of the artists who would mold one for you. Is it important? No, I can see it isn't. What a strange mind you have. You neither believe nor doubt. How can you contain both concepts at once . . . would you like me to straighten some of your brain-patterns? No. I see, you're afraid. Well, let it be for the nonce. We'll do it another time."

He grabbed the kneeling man and drew him erect.

"You're covered with blood. Have to get you cleaned up. There's an ablute near here. Incidentally, I was very impressed with the way you handled Juliette. You're the first, you know. No, how could you know? In any case, you *are* the first to deal her as good as she gave. You would have been amused at what she did to Caspar Hauser. Squeezed part of his brain and then sent him back, let him live out part of his life and then—the little twit—she made me bring him back a second time and used a knife on him. Same knife you took, I believe. Then sent him back to his own time. Marvelous mystery. In all the tapes on unsolved phenomena. But she was much sloppier than you. She had a great verve in her amusements, but very little éclat. Except with Judge Crater; there she was—" He paused, and laughed lightly. "I'm an old man and I ramble on like a muskrat. You want to get cleaned up and shown around, I know. And *then* we can talk.

"I just wanted you to know I was satisfied with the way you disposed of her. In a way, I'll miss the little twit. She was such a good fuck."

The old man picked up the Gladstone bag and, holding the man spattered with blood, he moved off down the clean and shimmering street. "You *wanted* her killed?" the man from 1888 asked, unbelieving.

The old man nodded, but his lips never moved. "Of course. Otherwise why bring her Jack the Ripper?"

*Oh my dear God,* he thought, *I'm in hell. And I'm entered as Jack.*

"No, my boy, no no no. You're not in hell at all. You're in the future. For you the future, for me the world of now. You came from 1888 and you're now in—" he stopped, silently speaking for an instant, as though computing apples in terms of dollars, then resumed "—3077. It's a fine world, filled with happy times, and we're glad to have you with us. Come along now, and you'll wash."

In the ablutatorium, the late Juliette's grandfather changed his head.

"I really despise it," he informed the man from 1888, grabbing fingerfuls of his cheeks and stretching the flabby skin like elastic. "But Juliette insisted. I was willing to humor her, if indeed that was what it took to get her to lie down. But with toys from the past, and changing my head every time I wanted her to fuck me, it was trying; very trying."

He stepped into one of the many identically shaped booths set flush into the walls. The tambour door rolled down and there was a soft *chukk* sound, almost chitinous. The tambour door rolled up and the late Juliette's grandfather, now six years younger than the man from 1888, stepped out, stark naked and wearing a new head. "The body is fine, replaced last year," he said, examining the genitals and a mole on his right shoulder. The man from 1888 looked away. This was hell and God hated him.

"Well, don't just *stand* there, Jack." Juliette's grandfather smiled. "Hit one of those booths and get your ablutions."

"That isn't my name," said the man from 1888 very softly, as though he had been whipped.

"It'll do, it'll do . . . now go get washed."

Jack approached one of the booths. It was a light green in color, but changed to mauve as he stopped in front of it. "Will it—"

"It will only *clean* you, what are you afraid of?"

"I don't want to be changed."

Juliette's grandfather did not laugh. "That's a mistake," he said cryptically. He made a peremptory motion with his hand and the man from 1888 entered the booth, which promptly revolved in its niche, sank into the floor and made a hearty *zeeeezzzz* sound. When it rose and revolved and opened, Jack stumbled out, looking terribly confused. His long sideburns had been neatly trimmed, his beard stubble had been removed, his hair was three shades lighter and was now parted on the left side, rather than in the middle. He still wore the same long, dark coat trimmed with astrakhan, dark suit with white collar and black necktie (in which was fastened a horseshoe stickpin) but now the garments seemed new, unsoiled of course, possibly synthetics built to look like his former garments.

"Now!" Juliette's grandfather said. "Isn't that much better? A good cleansing always sets one's mind to rights." And he stepped into another booth from which he issued in a moment wearing a soft paper jumper that fitted from neck to feet without a break. He moved toward the door.

"Where are we going?" the man from 1888 asked the younger grandfather beside him. "I want you to meet someone," said Juliette's grandfather, and Jack realized that he was moving his lips now. He decided not to comment on it. There had to be a reason.

"I'll walk you there, if you promise not to make gurgling sounds at the city. It's a nice city, but I live here, and frankly, tourism is boring." Jack did not reply. Grandfather took it for acceptance of the terms.

They walked. Jack became overpowered by the sheer *weight* of the city. It was obviously extensive, massive, and terribly clean. It was his dream for Whitechapel come true. He asked about slums, about doss houses. The grandfather shook his head. "Long gone."

So it had come to pass. The reforms for which he had pledged his immortal soul, they had come to pass. He swung the Gladstone and walked jauntily. But after a few minutes his pace sagged once more: there was no one to be seen in the streets.

Just shining clean buildings and streets that ran off in aimless directions and came to unexpected stops as though the builders had decided people might vanish at one point and reappear someplace else, so why bother making a road from one point to the other.

The ground was metal, the sky seemed metallic, the buildings loomed on all sides, featureless explorations of planed space by insensitive metal. The man from 1888 felt terribly alone, as though every act he had performed had led inevitably to his alienation from the very people he had sought to aid.

When he had come to Toynbee Hall, and the Reverend Mr. Barnett had opened his eyes to the slum horrors of Spitalfields, he had vowed to help in any way he could. It had seemed as simple as faith in the Lord what to do, after a few months in the sinkholes of White-chapel. The sluts, of what use were they? No more use than the disease germs that had infected these very same whores. So he had set forth as Jack, to perform the will of God and raise the poor dregs who inhabited the East End of London. That Lord Warren, the Metropolitan Police Commissioner, and his Queen, and all the rest thought him a mad doctor, or an amok butcher, or a beast in human form did not distress him. He knew he would remain anonymous through all time, but that the good works he had set in motion would proceed to their wonderful conclusion.

The destruction of the most hideous slum area the country had ever known, and the opening of Victorian eyes. But all time *had* passed, and now he was here, in a world where slums apparently did not exist, a sterile Utopia that was the personification of the Reverend Mr. Barnett's dreams—but it didn't seem . . . *right*.

This grandfather, with his young head.

Silence in the empty streets.

The girl, Juliette, and her strange hobby.

The lack of concern at her death.

The grandfather's expectation that he, Jack, *would* kill her. And now his friendliness.

Where were they going?

[Around them, the City. As they walked, the grandfather paid no attention, and Jack watched but did not understand. But this was what they saw as they walked:

[Thirteen hundred beams of light, one foot wide and seven molecules thick, erupted from almost-invisible slits in the metal streets, fanned out and washed the surfaces of the buildings; they altered hue to a vague blue and washed down the surfaces of the buildings; they bent and covered all open surfaces, bent at right angles, then bent again, and again, like origami paper figures; they altered hue a second time, soft gold, and penetrated the surfaces of the buildings, expanding and contracting in solid waves, washing the inner surfaces; they withdrew rapidly into the sidewalks; the entire process had taken twelve seconds.

[Night fell over a sixteen block area of the City. It descended in a solid pillar and was quite sharp-edged, ending at the street corners. From within the area of darkness came the distinct sounds of crickets, marsh-frogs belching, night birds, soft breezes in trees, and faint music of unidentifiable instruments.

[Panes of frosted light appeared suspended freely in the air, overhead. A wavery insubstantial quality began to assault the topmost levels of a great structure directly in front of the light-panes. As the panes moved slowly down through the air, the building became indistinct, turned into motes of light, and floated upward. As the panes reached the pavement, the building had been completely dematerialized. The panes shifted color to a deep orange, and began moving upward again. As they moved, a new structure began to form where the previous building had stood, drawing—it seemed—motes of light from the air and forming them into a cohesive whole that became, as the panes ceased their upward movement, a new building. The light-panes winked out of existence.

[The sound of a bumblebee was heard for several seconds. Then it ceased.

[A crowd of people in rubber garments hurried out of a gray pulsing hole in the air, patted the pavement at their feet, then rushed off around a corner, from where emanated the sound of prolonged coughing. Then silence returned.

[A drop of water, thick as quicksilver, plummeted to the pavement, struck, bounded, rose several inches, then evaporated into a crimson smear in the shape of a whale's tooth, which settled to the pavement and lay still.

[Two blocks of buildings sank into the pavement and the metal covering was smooth and unbroken, save for a metal tree whose trunk was silver and slim, topped by a ball of foliage constructed of golden fibers that radiated brightly in a perfect circle. There was no sound.

[The late Juliette's grandfather and the man from 1888 continued walking.]

"Where are we going?"

"To Van Cleef's. We don't usually walk; oh, sometimes; but it isn't as much pleasure as it used to be. I'm doing this primarily for you. Are you enjoying yourself?"

"It's . . . unusual."

"Not much like Spitalfields, is it? But I rather like it back there, at that time. I have the only Traveler, did you know? The only one ever made. Juliette's father constructed it, my son. I had to kill him to get it. He was thoroughly unreasonable about it, really. It was a casual thing for him. He was the last of the tinkerers, and he might just as easily have given it to me. But I suppose he was being cranky. That was why I had you carve up my granddaughter. She would have gotten around to me almost any time now. Bored, just silly bored is what she was—"

The gardenia took shape in the air in front of them, and turned into the face of a woman with long white hair. "Hernon, we can't wait much longer!" She was annoyed.

Juliette's grandfather grew livid. "You scum bitch! I *told* you pace. But no, you just couldn't, could you? Jump jump jump, that's all you ever do. Well, now it'll only be feddels less, that's all. Feddels, damn you! I set it for pace, I was *working* pace, and you . . . !"

His hand came up and moss grew instantly toward the face. The face vanished, and a moment later the gardenia reappeared a few feet away. The moss shriveled and Hernon, Juliette's grandfather, dropped his hand, as though weary at the woman's stupidity. A rose, a water lily, a hyacinth, a pair of phlox, a wild celandine, and a bull thistle appeared near the gardenia. As each turned into the face of a different person, Jack stepped back, frightened.

All the faces turned to the one that had been the bull thistle. "Cheat! Rotten bastard!" they screamed at the thin white face that had been the bull thistle. The gardenia-woman's eyes bulged from her face, the deep purple eye-shadow that completely surrounded the eyeball making her look like a deranged animal peering out of a cave. "Turd!" she shrieked at the bull thistle-man. "We all agreed, we all said and agreed; you *had* to formz a thistle, didn't you, scut! Well, now you'll see . . ."

She addressed herself instantly to the others. "Formz now! To hell with waiting, pace fuck! Now!"

"No, dammit!" Hernon shouted. "We were going to *paaaaace!*" But it was too late. Centering in on the bull thistle-man, the air roiled thickly like silt at a river-bottom, and the air blackened as a spiral began with the now terrified face of the bull thistle-man and exploded whirling outward, enveloping Jack and Hernon and all the flower-people and the City and suddenly it was night in Spitalfields and the man from 1888 was *in* 1888, with his Gladstone bag in his hand, and a woman approaching down the street toward him, shrouded in the London fog.

(There were eight additional nodules in Jack's brain.)

The woman was about forty, weary and not too clean. She wore a dark dress of rough material that reached down to her boots. Over the skirt was fastened a white apron that was stained and wrinkled. The bulbed sleeves ended midway up her wrist and the bodice of the dress was buttoned close around her throat. She wore a kerchief tied at the neck, and a hat that looked like a wide-brimmed skimmer with a raised crown. There was a pathetic little flower of unidentifiable origin in the band of the hat. She carried a beaded handbag of capacious size, hanging from a wrist-loop.

Her step slowed as she saw him standing there, deep in the shadows. Saw him was hardly accurate: sensed him.

He stepped out and bowed slightly from the waist. "Fair evenin' to ye, Miss. Care for a pint?"

Her features—sunk in misery of a kind known only to women who have taken in numberless shafts of male blood-gorged flesh—rearranged themselves. "Coo, sir, I thought was 'im for true. Old Leather Apron hisself. Gawdamighty, you give me a scare." She tried to smile. It was a rictus. There were bright spots in her cheeks from sickness and too much gin. Her voice was ragged, a broken-edged instrument barely workable.

"Just a solicitor caught out without comp'ny," Jack assured her. "And pleased to buy a handsome lady a pint of stout for a few hours' companionship."

She stepped toward him and linked arms. "Emily Matthewes, sir, an' pleased to go with you. It's a fearsome chill night, and with Slippery Jack abroad not safe for a respectin' woman such's m'self."

They moved off down Thrawl Street, past the doss houses where this drab might flop later, if she could obtain a few coppers from this neat-dressed stranger with the dark eyes.

He turned right onto Commercial Street, and just abreast of a stinking alley almost to Flower & Dean Street, he nudged her sharply sidewise. She went into the alley, and thinking he meant to steal a smooth hand up under her petticoats, she settled back against the wall and opened her legs, starting to lift the skirt around her waist. But Jack had hold of the kerchief and, locking his fingers tightly, he twisted, cutting off her breath. Her cheeks ballooned, and by a vagary of light from a gas standard in the street he could see her eyes go from hazel to a dead-leaf brown in an instant. Her expression was one of terror, naturally, but commingled with it was a deep sadness, at having lost the pint, at having not been able to make her doss for the night, at having had the usual Emily Matthewes bad luck to run afoul this night of the one man who would ill-use her favors. It was a consummate sadness at the inevitability of her fate.

*I come to you out of the night. The night that sent me down all the minutes of our lives to this instant. From this time forward, men will wonder what happened at this instant. They will silently hunger to go back, to come to my instant with you and see my face and know my name and perhaps not even try to stop me, for then I would not be who I am, but only someone who tried and failed. Ah. For you and me it becomes history that will lure men always; but they will never understand why we both suffered, Emily; they will never truly understand why each of us died so terribly.*

A film came over her eyes, and as her breath husked out in wheezing, pleading tremors, his free hand went into the pocket of the greatcoat. He had known he would need it, when they were walking, and he had already invaded the Gladstone bag. Now his hand went into the pocket and came up with the scalpel.

"Emily . . ." softly.

Then he sliced her.

Neatly, angling the point of the scalpel into the soft flesh behind and under her left ear. *Sternocleidomastoideus.* Driving it in to the gentle crunch of cartilage giving way. Then, grasping the instrument tightly, tipping it down and drawing it across the width of the throat, following the line of the firm jaw. *Glandula submandibularis.* The blood poured out over his hands, ran thickly at first and then burst spattering past him, reaching the far wall of the alley. Up his sleeves, soaking his white cuffs. She made a watery rattle and sank limply in his grasp, his fingers still twisted tight in her kerchief; black abrasions where he had scored the flesh. He continued the cut up past the point of the jaw's end, and sliced into the lobe of the ear. He lowered her to the filthy paving. She lay crumpled, and he straightened her. Then he cut away the garments laying her naked belly open to the wan and flickering light of the gas standard in the street. Her belly was bloated. He started the primary cut in the hollow of her throat. *Glandula thyreoeidea.* His hand was sure as he drew a thin black line of blood down and down, between the breasts. *Sternum.* Cutting a deep cross in the hole of her navel. Something vaguely yellow oozed up. *Plica umbilicalis media.* Down over the rounded hump of the belly, biting more deeply, withdrawing for a neat incision. *Mesenterium dorsale commune.* Down to the matted-with-sweat roundness of her privates. Harder here. *Vesica urinaria.* And finally, to the end, *vagina.*

Filth hole.

Foul-smelling die red lust pit wet hole of sluts.

And in his head, succubi. And in his head eyes watching. And in his head minds impinging. And in his head titillation

**for a gardenia**
  **a water lily**
  **a rose**
  **a hyacinth**

a pair of phlox
a wild celandine
and a dark flower with petals of obsidian, a stamen of onyx, pistils of anthracite, and the mind of Hernon, who was the late Juliette's grandfather.

They watched the entire horror of the mad anatomy lesson. They watched him nick the eyelids. They watched him remove the heart. They watched him slice out the fallopian tubes. They watched him squeeze, till it ruptured, the "ginny" kidney. They watched him slice off the sections of breast till they were nothing but shapeless mounds of bloody meat, and arrange them, one mound each on a still-staring, wide-open, nicked-eyelid eye. They watched.

They watched and they drank from the deep troubled pool of his mind. They sucked deeply at the moist quivering core of his id. And they delighted:

**Oh God how Delicious look at that It looks like the uneaten rind of a Pizza or look at That It looks like** lumaconi **oh god IIIIIwonder what it would be like to Tasteit!**

See how smooth the steel.

**He hates them all, every one of them, something about a girl, a venereal disease, fear of his God, Christ, the Reverend Mr. Barnett, he . . . he wants to fuck the reverend's wife!**

Social reform can only be brought about by concerted effort of a devoted few. Social reform is a justifiable end, condoning any expedient short of decimation of over fifty per cent of the people who will be served by the reforms. The best social reformers are the most audacious. He believes it! How lovely!

**You pack of vampires, you filth, you scum, you . . .**

He senses us!

**Damn him! Damn you, Hernon, you drew off too deeply, he knows we're here, that's disgusting, what's the sense now? I'm withdrawing!**

Come back, you'll end the formz. . . .

. . . back they plunged in the spiral as it spiraled back in upon itself and the darkness of the night of 1888 withdrew. The spiral drew in and in and locked at its most infinitesimal point as the charred and blackened face of the man who had been the bull thistle. He was quite dead. His eyeholes had been burned out; charred wreckage lay where intelligence had lived. They had used him as a focus.

The man from 1888 came back to himself instantly, with a full and eidetic memory of what he had just experienced. It had not been a vision, nor a dream, nor a delusion, nor a product of his mind. It had happened. They had sent him back, erased his mind of the transfer into the future, of Juliette, of everything after the moment outside No. 13 Miller's Court. And they had set him to work pleasuring them, while they drained off his feelings, his emotions and his unconscious thoughts; while they battened and gorged themselves with the most private sensations. Most of which, till this moment—in a strange feedback—he had not even known he possessed. As his mind plunged on from one revelation to the next, he felt himself growing ill. At one concept his mind tried to pull back and plunge him into darkness rather than confront it. But the barriers were down, they had opened new patterns and he could read it all, remember it all. *Stinking sex hole, sluts, they have to die.* No, that wasn't the way he thought of women, any women, no matter how low or common. He was a gentleman, and women were to be respected. *She had given him the clap. He remembered.* The shame and the endless fear till he had gone to his physician father and confessed it. The look on the man's face. He remembered it all. The way his father had tended him, the way he would have tended a plague victim. It had never been the same between them again. He had tried for the cloth. *Social reform hahahaha.* All delusion. He had been a mountebank, a clown . . . and worse. He had slaughtered for something in which not even he believed. They left his mind wide open, and his thoughts stumbled . . . raced further and further toward the thought of EXPLOSION!IN!HIS!MIND!

He fell face forward on the smooth and polished metal pavement, but he never touched. Something arrested his fall, and he hung suspended, bent over at the waist like a ridiculous Punch divested of strings or manipulation from above. A whiff of something invisible, and he was in full possession of his senses almost before they had left him. His mind was forced to look at it:

*He wants to fuck the Reverend Mr. Barnett's wife.*

Henrietta, with her pious petition to Queen Victoria—"Madam, we, the women of East London, feel horror at the dreadful sins that have been lately committed in our midst . . ."—asking for the capture of himself, of Jack, whom she would never, not *ever* suspect was residing right there with her and the Reverend in Toynbee Hall. The thought was laid as naked as her body in the secret dreams he had never remembered upon awakening. All of it, they had left him with opened doors, with unbounded horizons, and he saw himself for what he was.

A psychopath, a butcher, a lecher, a hypocrite, a clown.

"You did this to me! Why did you do this?"

Frenzy cloaked his words. The flower-faces became the solidified hedonists who had taken him back to 1888 on that senseless voyage of slaughter.

Van Cleef, the gardenia-woman, sneered. "Why do you think, you ridiculous bumpkin? (Bumpkin, is that the right colloquialism, Hernon? I'm so uncertain in the mid-dialects.) When you'd done in Juliette, Hernon wanted to send you back. But why should he? He owed us at least three formz, and you did passing well for one of them."

Jack shouted at them till the cords stood out in his throat. "Was it necessary, this last one? Was it important to do it, to help my reforms . . . was it?"

Hernon laughed. "Of course not."

Jack sank to his knees. The City let him do it. "Oh God, oh God almighty, I've done what I've done . . . I'm covered with blood . . . and for *nothing,* for *nothing* . . ."

Cashio, who had been one of the phlox, seemed puzzled. "Why is he concerned about *this* one, if the others don't bother him?"

Nosy Verlag, who had been a wild celandine, said sharply, "They do, all of them do. Probe him, you'll see."

Cashio's eyes rolled up in his head an instant, then rolled down and refocused—Jack felt a quicksilver shudder in his mind and it was gone—and he said lackadaisically, "Mm-hmm."

Jack fumbled with the latch of the Gladstone. He opened the bag and pulled out the foetus in the bottle. Mary Jane Kelly's unborn child, from November 9th, 1888. He held it in front of his face a moment, then dashed it to the metal pavement. It never struck. It vanished a fraction of an inch from the clean, sterile surface of the City's street.

"What marvelous loathing!" exulted Rose, who had been a rose.

"Hernon," said Van Cleef, "he's centering on you. He begins to blame you for all of this."

Hernon was laughing (without moving his lips) as Jack pulled Juliette's electrical scalpel from the Gladstone, and lunged. Jack's words were incoherent, but what he was saying, as he struck, was: "I'll show you what filth you are! I'll show you you can't do this kind of thing! I'll teach you! You'll die, all of you!" This is what he was saying, but it came out as one long sustained bray of revenge, frustration, hatred and directed frenzy.

Hernon was still laughing as Jack drove the whisper-thin blade with its shimmering current into his chest. Almost without manipulation on Jack's part, the blade circumscribed a perfect 360° hole that charred and shriveled, exposing Hernon's pulsing heart and wet organs. He had time to shriek with confusion before he received Jack's second thrust, a direct lunge that severed the heart from its attachments. *Vena cava superior. Aorta. Arteria pulmonalis. Bronchus principalis.*

The heart flopped forward and a spreading wedge of blood under tremendous pressure ejaculated, spraying Jack with such force that it knocked his hat from his head and blinded him. His face was now a dripping black-red collage of features and blood.

Hernon followed his heart, and fell forward, into Jack's arms. Then the flower-people screamed as one, vanished, and Hernon's body slipped from Jack's hands to wink out of existence an instant before it struck at Jack's feet. The walls around him were clean, unspotted, sterile, metallic, uncaring.

He stood in the street, holding the bloody knife.

*"Now!"* he screamed, holding the knife aloft. "Now it begins!"

If the city heard, it made no indication, but

[Pressure accelerated in temporal linkages.]

[A section of shining wall on a building eighty miles away changed from silver to rust.]

[In the freezer chambers, two hundred gelatin caps were fed into a ready trough.]

[The weathermaker spoke softly to itself, accepted data and instantly constructed an intangible mnemonic circuit.]

and in the shining eternal city where night only fell when the inhabitants had need of night and called specifically for night . . .

Night fell. With no warning save: *"Now!"*

In the City of sterile loveliness a creature of filth and decaying flesh prowled. In the last City of the world, a City on the edge of the world, where the ones who had devised their own paradise lived, the prowler made his home in shadows. Slipping from darkness to darkness with eyes that saw only movement, he roamed in search of a partner to dance his deadly rigadoon.

He found the first woman as she materialized beside a small waterfall that flowed out of empty air and dropped its shimmering, tinkling moisture into an azure cube of nameless material. He found her and drove the living blade into the back of her neck. Then he sliced out the eyeballs and put them into her open hands.

He found the second woman in one of the towers, making love to a very old man who gasped and wheezed and clutched his heart as the young woman forced him to passion. She was killing him as Jack killed her. He drove the living blade into the lower rounded surface of her belly, piercing her sex organs as she rode astride the old man. She decamped blood and viscous fluids over the prostrate body of the old man, who also died, for Jack's blade had severed the penis within the young woman. She fell forward across the old man and Jack left them that way, joined in the final embrace.

He found a man and throttled him with his bare hands, even as the man tried to dematerialize. Then Jack recognized him as one of the phlox, and made neat incisions in the face, into which he inserted the man's genitals.

He found another woman as she was singing a gentle song about eggs to a group of children. He opened her throat and severed the strings hanging inside. He let the vocal cords drop onto her chest. But he did not touch the children, who watched it all avidly. He liked children.

He prowled through the unending night making a grotesque collection of hearts, which he cut out of one, three, nine people. And when he had a dozen, he took them and laid them as road markers on one of the wide boulevards that never were used by vehicles, for the people of this City had no need of vehicles.

Oddly, the City did not clean up the hearts. Nor were the people vanishing any longer. He was able to move with relative impunity, hiding only when he saw large groups that might be searching for him. But *something* was happening in the City. (Once, he heard the peculiar sound of metal grating on metal, the *skrikkk* of plastic cutting into plastic—though he could not have identified it as plastic—and he instinctively knew it was the sound of a machine malfunctioning.)

He found a woman bathing, and tied her up with strips of his own garments, and cut off her legs at the knees and left her still sitting up in the swirling crimson bath, screaming as she bled away her life. The legs he took with him.

When he found a man hurrying to get out of the night, he pounced on him, cut his throat and severed off the arms. He replaced the arms with the bath-woman's legs.

And it went on and on, for a time that had no measure. He was showing them what evil could produce. He was showing them their immorality was silly beside his own.

But one thing finally told him he was winning. As he lurked in an antiseptically pure space between two low aluminum-cubes, he heard a voice that came from above him and around him and even from inside him. It was a public announcement, broadcast by whatever mental communications system the people of the City on the edge of the World used.

OUR CITY IS PART OF US, WE ARE PART OF OUR CITY. IT RE-SPONDS TO OUR MINDS AND WE CONTROL IT. THE GESTALT THAT WE HAVE BECOME IS THREATENED. WE HAVE AN ALIEN FORCE WITHIN THE CITY AND WE ARE GEARING TO LOCATE IT. BUT THE MIND OF THIS MAN IS STRONG. IT IS BREAKING DOWN THE FUNCTIONS OF THE CITY. THIS ENDLESS NIGHT IS AN EX-AMPLE. WE MUST ALL CONCENTRATE. WE MUST ALL CON-SCIOUSLY FOCUS OUR THOUGHTS TO MAINTAINING THE CITY. THIS THREAT IS OF THE FIRST ORDER. IF OUR CITY DIES, WE DIE.

It was not an announcement in those terms, though that was how Jack interpreted it. The message was much longer and much more complex, but that was what it meant, and he knew he was winning. He was destroying them. Social reform was laughable, they had said. He would show them.

And so he continued with his lunatic pogrom. He butchered and slaughtered and carved them wherever he found them, and they could not vanish and they could not escape and they could not stop him. The collection of hearts grew to fifty and seventy and then a hundred.

He grew bored with hearts and began cutting out their brains. The collection grew.

For numberless days it went on, and from time to time in the clean, scented autoclave of the City, he could hear the sounds of screaming. His hands were always sticky.

Then he found Van Cleef, and leaped from hiding in the darkness to bring her down. He raised the living blade to drive it into her breast, but she

van      ished

He got to his feet and looked around. Van Cleef reappeared ten feet from him. He lunged for her and again she was gone. To reappear ten feet away. Finally, when he had struck at her half a dozen times and she had escaped him each time, he stood panting, arms at sides, looking at her.

And she looked back at him with disinterest.

"You no longer amuse us," she said, moving her lips.

*Amuse?* His mind whirled down into a place far darker than any he had known before, and through the murk of his blood-lust he began to realize. It had all been for their amusement. They had *let* him do it. They had given him the run of the City and he had capered and gibbered for them.

Evil? He had never even suspected the horizons of that word. He went for her, but she disappeared with finality.

He was left standing there as the daylight returned. As the City cleaned up the mess, took the butchered bodies and did with them what it had to do. In the freezer chambers the gelatin caps were returned to their niches, no more inhabitants of the City need be thawed to provide Jack the Ripper with utensils for his amusement of the sybarites. His work was truly finished.

He stood there in the empty street. A street that would *always* be empty to him. The people of the City had all along been able to escape him, and now they would. He was finally and completely the clown they had shown him to be. He was not evil, he was pathetic.

He tried to use the living blade on himself, but it dissolved into motes of light and wafted away on a breeze that had blown up for just that purpose.

Alone, he stood there staring at the victorious cleanliness of this Utopia. With their talents they would keep him alive, possibly alive forever, immortal in the possible expectation of needing him for amusement again someday. He was stripped to raw essentials in a mind that was no longer anything more than jelly matter. To go madder and madder, and never to know peace or end or sleep.

He stood there, a creature of dirt and alleys, in a world as pure as the first breath of a baby.

"My name isn't Jack," he said softly. But they would never know his real name. Nor would they care. *"My name isn't Jack!"* he said loudly. No one heard.

"MY NAME ISN'T JACK, AND I'VE BEEN BAD, VERY BAD, I'M AN EVIL PERSON BUT MY NAME ISN'T JACK!" he screamed, and screamed, and screamed again, walking aimlessly down an empty street, in plain view, no longer forced to prowl. A stranger in the City.

## Afterword:

The paths down which our minds entice us are often not the ones we thought we were taking. And the destinations frequently leave something to be desired in the area of hospitality. Such a case is the story you have just read.

It took me fifteen months—off and on—to write "The Prowler In The City At The Edge Of The World." As I indicated in my introduction to Bob Bloch's story, it was first a visual image without a plot—the creature of filth in the city of sterile purity. It seemed a fine illustration, but it was little more than that, I'm afraid. At best I thought it might provide a brief moment of horror in a book where realism (even couched in fantasy) was omnipresent.

I suggested the illustration to Bloch and he did his version of it. But the folly of trying to put one man's vision in another man's head (even when the vision was directly caused by the vision of the first man) was obvious.

So I decided to color my own illustration. With Bloch's permission. But what was my story? I was intrigued by the entire *concept* of a Ripper, a killer of obvious derangement who nonetheless worked in a craftsmanlike manner to such estimable ends that he was never apprehended. And the letters of braggadocio he had sent to the newspapers and the police and George Lusk of the East London vigilantes. The audacity of the man! The eternal horror of him! I was hooked.

But I still had no story.

Still, I tried to write it. I started it two dozen times—easily—in the fifteen months during which I edited this anthology. Started it and slumped to a stop after a page or two, surfeited with my own fustian. I had nothing but that simple drawing in my head. Jack in the auto-clave. The story languished while I wrote a film and a half-dozen TV scripts and two dozen stories and uncountable articles, reviews, criticisms, introductions, and edited this book. (For those who think a writer is someone who gets his name on books, let me assure you *that* is an "author." A "writer" is the hapless devil who cannot keep himself from putting every vagrant thought he has ever had down on paper. I am a writer. I write. That's what I do. I do a lot of it.) The story gathered dust.

But a writer I once admired very much had told me that a "writer's slump" might very well not be a slump at all, but a transitional period. A plateau period in which his style, his views and his interests might be altering. I've found this to be true. Story ideas I've gotten that have not been able to be written, I've let sit. For years. And then, one day, as if magically, I leap on the snippet of story and start over and it gets itself written in hours. Unconsciously I had been working and working that story in my mind during the years in which other work had claimed me consciously. In my Writer's Brain I knew I simply did not have the skill or insight to do the story I wanted to do, and had I bulled through (as I did when I was much younger and needed to *get it all said*), I would have produced a half-witted, half-codified story.

This was precisely the case with "The Prowler." As the months passed, I realized what I was trying to do was say something about the boundaries and dimensions of evil in a total society. It was not merely the story of Jack, it was the story of the effects on evil, *per se,* of an evil culture.

It was becoming heady stuff. So I realized I could not write it from just the scant information on Jack I could recall from Bloch's "Yours Truly, Jack The Ripper," or from an E. Haldeman-Julius "Little Blue Book" I had read in junior high school, or even from the passing references, by Alan Hynd and by Mrs. Belloc Lowndes in *The Lodger,* I had encountered. I suddenly had a project on my hands. The integrity of the story demanded I do my homework.

So I read everything I could lay my hands on. I scoured the bookstores and the libraries for source books on Jack. And in this respect, I must express my gratitude and pleasure for the books by Tom A. Cullen, Donald McCormick, Leonard P. Matters and *The Harlot Killer,* edited by Allan Barnard, which only served to fire my curiosity about this incredible creature known as Jack.

I was hooked. I read ceaselessly about the slayings. And without my even knowing it, I began to form my own conclusions as to who Jack might have been.

The concept of the "invisible killer"—an assassin who could be seen near the site of a crime and not be considered a suspect—stuck with me. The audacity of the crimes and their relatively open nature—in streets and courts and alleys—seemed to insist that an "invisible killer" was my man. Invisible? Why, consider, in Victorian London, a policeman would be invisible, a midwife would be invisible, and . . . a clergyman would be invisible.

The way in which the poor harlots were butchered indicated two things to me: a man obviously familiar with surgical technique, and a man addicted to the concept of femininity prevalent at the time.

But most of all, the pattern and manner of the crimes suggested to me —over and above the obvious derangement of the assassin—that the clergyman/butcher was trying to make a statement. A grisly and quite mad statement, to be sure. But a statement, nonetheless.

So I continued my reading with these related facts in mind. And everywhere I read, the name of the Reverend Samuel Barnett appeared with regularity. He was a socially conscious man who lived in the general area, at Toynbee Hall. And his wife had circulated the petition to Queen Victoria. He had the right kind of background, he certainly had the religious fervor to want to see the slums cleared at almost any cost.

My mind bridged the gap. If not Barnett—to which statement, even in fiction, about a man long since dead, would be attached the dangers of libel and slander—then someone close to Barnett. A younger man, perhaps. And from one concept to another the theory worked itself out, till I had in my Writer's Brain a portrait of exactly who Jack the Ripper was and what his motives had been.

(I was gratified personally to read Tom Cullen's book on the Ripper, after this theory had been established in my mind, and find that in many ways—though not as completely or to the same suspect—he had attached the same drives to *his* Ripper as I to mine.)

Now began a period of writing that stretched out over many weeks. This was one of the hardest stories I ever wrote. I was furious at the limitations of the printed page, the line-for-line rigidity of QWERTYUIOP. I wanted to break out, and the best I could do was use typographical tricks, which are in the final analysis little more than tricks. There must be some way a writer can write a book that has all the visual and sensory impact of a movie!

In any case, my story is now told.

The Jack I present is the Jack in all of us, of course. The Jack that tells us to stand and watch as a Catherine Genovese gets knifed, the Jack that condones Vietnam because we don't care to get involved, the Jack that we need. We are a culture that needs its monsters.

We have to deify our Al Capones, our Billy the Kids, our Jesse Jameses, and all the others including Jack Ruby, General Walker, Adolf Hitler and even Richard Speck, whose Ripper-like butchery of the Chicago nurses has already begun to be thought of as modern legend.

We are a culture that *creates* its killers and its monsters and then provides for them the one thing Jack was never able to have: reality. He was a doomed man who wanted desperately to be recognized for what he had done (as consider the notes he wrote), but could not come out in the open for fear of capture. The torn-in-two-directions of a man who senses that the mob will revere him, even as they kill him.

That is the message of the story. *You* are the monsters.

## Introduction to THE NIGHT THAT ALL TIME BROKE OUT:

Brian Aldiss is an English fellah who won a Hugo for his *Hothouse* series a few years back, and a Nebula last year for "The Saliva Tree" (in a tie) for best novella. He also did this novel called *The Dark Light-Years* which was all about shit. Now *that* is what I call a dangerous vision.

He lives in Oxford, England. He was born August 18, 1925, in East Dereham, Norfolk. He submits he has no religion, and he is divorced and now remarried to Margaret (I am told), a delightful and charming girl.

Aldiss books include *Starship, Hothouse, Greybeard, Who Can Replace a Man?, Earthworks* and he is co-editor (with Harry Harrison) of *Nebula Awards Two*. He is also, incidentally, literary editor of the Oxford *Mail*. He was Guest of Honor at the 23rd World Science Fiction Convention, held in London in August 1965.

As editor of this anthology, I knew very little about Aldiss save that I admired his writing and wanted a story by him within these covers.

Having received, read and purchased the off-center item that follows, I feel my responsibility in the matter is at an end. I will, therefore, allow Mr. Aldiss (pronounced *Old-iss*) to speak his piece unfootnoted:

"Born in 1925, I can recall being taken to school—kindergarten—past rows of unemployed waiting for the dole, my nurse being very scared of them. That would be the great depression.

"I began writing almost as soon as I could read and have really never stopped. Wrote science fiction at the age of six before I knew what it was all about; wrote pornography at boarding school before I knew what it was all about! Spent four years in the armed forces (1943–47), being just old enough to be sent out to Burma on active service and see a little of the Japanese war. These adolescent years made a great impression—I saw India, Burma, Assam, Ceylon, Sumatra, Malaya, Hong Kong.

"After all that, I didn't want to do anything; I never have, except live and write. I drifted into bookselling, thinking that at least it would give me a chance to read. After a while I stopped private writing and tried to write for a public. It worked. I threw up bookselling. My writing career has been happy and widened my horizons and brought me in touch with many pleasant and interesting people. In this respect, I have been tremendously fortunate. My ill-luck came in my marriage, a battle that lasted some fifteen years—but that's over now and I'm happily remarried.

"In England, I am very well known, billed on my latest paperback as 'Britain's Premier Science Fiction Author'—it may not be accurate but it certainly rattles the opposition! Within the small field, I am very versatile, writing novels and short stories of different kinds, producing anthologies (the three I did for Penguin Books are still selling like hot cakes), appearing at conventions and on literary panels and on TV and radio. I also edit with Harry Harrison, a magazine devoted purely to s-f lit crit: *SF Horizons*.

"In 1964, with my marriage at an impasse, I bought a secondhand Land Rover and drove off to Yugoslavia for six months, travelling round, especially down in the south, Macedonia and all that. A book has come out of the experience. In time, I hope to cover all the other ex-Byzantine states. And I like travelling in Communist countries—the fact that when the chips are down they are on the other side of the fence gives life a mild frisson. Not that the Yugoslavs weren't pleasant.

"I still am a man without ambition—except one; I know I am the world's best s-f writer; I want others to know it too!"

# ● THE NIGHT THAT ALL TIME BROKE OUT

## by Brian W. Aldiss

The dentist bowed her smiling to the door, dialling a cab for her as he went. It alighted on the balcony as she emerged.

It was a non-automatic type, old-fashioned enough to be considered chic. Fifi Fevertrees smiled dazzlingly at the driver and climbed in.

"Extra-city service," she said. "The village of Rouseville, off Route Z4."

"You live in the country, huh?" said the cab driver, sailing up into the pseudo-blue, and steering like a madman with one foot.

"The country's okay," Fifi said defensively. She hesitated and then decided she could allow herself to boast. "Besides, it's even better now they got the time mains out there. We're just being connected to the time main at our house—it should be finished when I get home."

"The cabby shrugged. "Reckon it's costly out in the country."

"Three payts a basic unit."

He whistled significantly.

She wanted to tell him more, wanted to tell him how excited she was, how she wished daddy was alive to experience the fun of being on the time main. But it was difficult to say anything with a thumb in her mouth, as she looked into her wrist mirror and probed to see what the dentist had done to her.

He'd done a good job. The new little pearly tooth was already growing firmly in the pink gum. Fifi decided she had a very sexy mouth, just as Tracey said. And the dentist had removed the old tooth by time gas. So simple. Just a whiff of it and she was back in the day before yesterday, reliving that peasant little interlude when she had taken coffee with Peggy Hackenson, with not a thought of any pain. Time gas was so smart these days. She positively glowed to think they would have it themselves, on tap all the while.

The bubble cab soared up and out of one of the dilating ports of the great dome that covered the city. Fifi felt a momentary sorrow at leaving. The cities were so pleasant nowadays that nobody wished to live outside them. Everything was double as expensive outside, too, but fortunately the government paid a hardship allowance for anyone like the Fevertrees, who had to live in the country.

In a couple of minutes they were sailing down to the ground again. Fifi pinpointed their dairy farm, and the cabby set them neatly down on their landing balcony before holding out his paw for an extortionate number of kilopayts. Only when he had the cash did he lean back and unlock Fifi's door with one foot. You couldn't put a thing over these chimp drivers.

She forgot all about him as she hurried down through the house. This was the day of days! It had taken the builders two months to install the central timing—two weeks longer than they had originally anticipated—and everywhen had been in an awful muddle all that time, as the men trundled their pipes and wires through every room. Now all was orderly once more. She positively danced down the stairs to find her husband.

Tracey Fevertrees was standing in the kitchen, talking to the builder. When his wife burst in, he turned and took her hand, smiling in a way that was merely soothing to her, though it disturbed the slumbers of many a local Rouseville maiden. But his good looks could hardly match her beauty when she was excited as she was at present.

"Is it all in working order?" she asked.

"There is just one last-minute snag," Mr. Archibald Smith said grudgingly.

"Oh, there's always a last-minute snag! We've had fifteen of them in the last week, Mr. Smith. What now?"

"It's nothing that should affect you here. It's just that, as you know, we had to pipe the time gas rather a long way to you from the main supply down at Rouseville works, and we seem to have a bit of trouble maintaining pressure. There's talk of a nasty leak at the main pit in the works, which they're having a job to plug. But that shouldn't worry you."

"We've tested it all out here and it seems to work fine," Tracey said to his wife. "Come on and I'll show you!"

They shook hands with Mr. Smith, who showed a traditional builderly reluctance to leave the site of his labours. Finally he moved off, promising to be back in the morning to pick up a last bag of tools, and Tracey and Fifi were left alone with their new toy.

Among all the other kitchen equipment, the time panel hardly stood out. It was situated next to the nuclear unit, a discreet little fixture with a dozen small dials and twice that number of toggle switches.

He pointed out to her how the time pressures had been set: low for corridors and offices, higher for bedrooms, variable for the living room. She rubbed herself against him and made an imitation purr.

"You are thrilled, aren't you, honey?" she asked.

"I keep thinking of the bills we have to pay. And the bills to come—three payts a basic unit—wow!" Then he saw her look of disappointment and added, "But of course I love it, darling. You know I'm going to be delighted."

Then they bustled through the house, with the controls on. In the kitchen itself, they set themselves back to a recent early midmorning. They floated in time past at the time of day Fifi favoured most for kitchen work, when the breakfast chores were over and it was long before the hour when lunch need be planned and dialled. Fifi and Tracey had selected a morning when she had been feeling particularly calm and well; the entire ambience of that period swept over them now.

"*Mar*vellous! Delicious! I can do anything, cook you anything, now!"

They kissed each other, and ran into the corridor, crying, "Isn't science wonderful!"

They stopped abruptly. "Oh no!" Fifi cried.

The corridor was in perfect order, the drapes in place and gleaming metallically by the two windows, controlling the amount of light that entered, storing the surplus for off-peak hours, the creep-carpet in place and resprayed, carrying them smoothly forward, the panelling all warm and soft to the touch. But they were time-controlled back to three o'clock of an afternoon a month ago, a peaceful time of day—except that a month ago the builders had been at work here.

"Honey, they'll ruin the carpet! And I just know the panelling will not go back properly! Oh, Tracey, look—they've disconnected the drapes, and Smithy promised not to!"

He clutched her shoulder. "Honey, everything's in order, honest!"

"It's not! It's not in order! Look at these dirty old time tubes everywhere, and all these cables hanging about! They've ruined our lovely dust-absorbent ceiling—look at the way it's leaking dirt over *every-thing!"*

"Honey, it's the time effect!" But he had to admit that he could not credit the perfect corridor his eyes registered; he was carried away like Fifi by his emotions of a month ago when he viewed the place as it had been then, in the hands of Smithy and his terrible men.

They reached the end of the passage and jumped into the bedroom, escaping into another time zone. Peeping back through the door, Fifi said tearfully, "Gosh, Trace, the power of time! I guess we just have to alter the controls for the corridor, eh?"

"Sure, we'll tune in to a year ago, say a nice summer's afternoon along the passage. You name it, we dial it! That's the motto of Central Time Board, isn't it? Anyhow, how do you like the time in here?"

After gazing round the bedroom, she lowered her long lashes at him. "Mm, sort of relaxed, isn't it?"

"Two o'clock in the morning, honey, early spring, and everyone in the whole zone sleeping tight. We aren't likely to suffer from insomnia now!"

She came and stood against him, leaning on his chest and looking up at him. "You don't think that maybe eleven at night would be a more—well, *bedroomy* time?"

"You know I prefer the sofa for that sort of thing, honey. Come and sit on it with me and see what you think about the living room."

The living room was one flight down, with only the garage and the dairy on the two floors below between them and the ground. It was a fine large room with fine large windows looking over the landscape to the distant dome of the city, and it had a fine large sofa standing in the middle of it.

They sat down on this voluptuous sofa and, past associations being what they were, commenced to cuddle. After a while Tracey reached down to the floor and pulled up a hand-switcher that was plugged into the wall.

"We can control our own time from here, without getting up, Fifi! You name the time and we flip back to it."

"If you're thinking of what I *think* you're thinking, then we'd better not go back more than ten months because we weren't married before that."

"Now, come on, Mrs. Fevertrees, are you getting old-fashioned or something? You never let that thought bother you before we were married."

"I did too!—Though maybe more *after* than at the time, when I was sort of carried away."

He stroked her pretty hair gently. "Tell you what I thought we could try sometime—dial back to when you were twelve. You must have been very sexy in your preteens, and I'd sure as hell love to find out. How about it?"

She was about to deliver some conventional female rebuke, but her imagination got the better of her. "We could work back to when we were tots!"

"Attaboy! You know I have a touch of the Lolita complex!"

"Trace—we must be careful unless in our excitement we shoot back past the day we were born, or we'll wind up little blobs of protoplasm or something."

"Honey, you read the brochures! When we get up enough pressure to go right past our birth dates, we simply enter the consciousness of our nearest predecessors of the same sex—you your mother, me my father, and then your grandmother and my grandfather. Farther back than that, time pressure in the Rouseville mains won't let us go."

Conversation languished under other interests until Fifi murmured dreamily, "What a heavenly invention time is! Know what, even when we're old and grey and impotent, we'll be able to come back and enjoy ourselves as we were when we were young. We'll dial back to this very instant, won't we?"

"Mmmm," he said. It was a universally shared sentiment.

That evening, they dined off a huge synthetic lobster. In her excitement over being on the time mains, Fifi had somehow dialled a slightly incorrect mixture—though she swore there was a misprint in the cookbook programming she had fed the kitchputer—and the dish was not all it should be. But they dialled themselves back to the time of one of the first and finest lobsters they had ever eaten together, shortly after their meeting two years before. The remembered taste took off the disappointment of the present taste.

While they were eating, the pressure went.

There was no sound. Externally, all was the same. But inside their heads, they felt themselves whirling through the days like leaves blown over a moor. Mealtimes came and went, and the lobster was sickening in their mouths as they seemed to chew in turn turkey, or cheese, or game, or trifle or sponge pudding or ice cream or breakfast cereal. For several mind-wrenching moments they sat there at table, petrified, while hundreds of assorted tastes chased themselves over their taste buds. Tracey jumped up gasping and cut off the time flow entirely at the switch by the door.

"Something's gone wrong!" he exclaimed. "It's that guy Smith. I'll dial him straightaway. I'll shoot him!"

But when Smith's face floated up in the vision tank, it was as bland as ever.

"The fault's not mine, Mr. Fevertrees. As a matter of fact, one of my men just dialled me to say that there's trouble at the Rouseville time works, where your pipe joins the main supply. Time gas is leaking out. I told you this morning they were having some bother there. Go to bed, Mr. Fevertrees—that's my suggestion. Go to bed, and in the morning all will probably be fixed again."

"Go to bed! How dare he tell us to go to bed!" Fifi exclaimed. "What an immoral suggestion! He's trying to hide something, that man. I'll bet this is some mistake of his and he's covering up with this story about a leak at the time works."

"We can soon check on that. Let's drive down there and see!"

They caught the elevator down to the ground floor and climbed into their land vehicle. City folk might laugh at these little wheeled hovercraft, so quaintly reminiscent of the automobiles of bygone days, but there was no doubt that they were indispensable in the country outside the domes, where free public transport did not reach.

The doors opened and they rolled out, taking off immediately and floating forward a couple of feet above the ground. Rouseville lay over a low hill, and the time works was just on the far fringe of it. But as they sighted the first houses, something strange happened.

Though all was quiet, the land vehicle began to jerk around wildly. Fifi was flung about, and the next moment they were stuck in a hedge.

"Heck, these things are heavy! I must learn to drive one sometime!" Tracey said, climbing out.

"Aren't you going to help me down, Tracey?"

"Aw, I'm too big to play with girls!"

"You gotta help me! I lost my dolly!"

"You never had no dolly! Nuts to you!"

He ran on across the field and she had to follow him, calling as she ran. It was just so difficult trying to control the clumsy heavy body of an adult with the mind of a child.

She found her husband sitting in the middle of the Rouseville road, kicking and waving his arms. He giggled at her. "Tace go walkey-walkey!" he said.

But in a few moments they were able to move along again on foot, though it was painful for Fifi, whose mother had been lame toward the end of her life. Together they hobbled forward, two young things in old postures. When they entered the little domeless village, it was to find most of the inhabitants about, and going through the whole spectrum of human age-characteristics, from burbling infancy to rattling senility. Obviously, something serious had happened at the time works.

Ten minutes and a few generations later, they arrived at the gates. Standing below the Central Time Board sign was Smith. They did not recognise him; he was wearing an anti-time gas mask, its exhaust spluttering as it spat out old moments.

"I thought you two might turn up!" he exclaimed. "Didn't believe me, eh? Well, you'd better come in with me and see for yourselves. They've struck a major gusher and the cocks couldn't stand the pressure and collapsed. My guess is they'll have to evacuate the whole area before they get this one fixed."

As he led them through the gates, Tracey said, "I just hope this isn't Ruskie sabotage!"

"Rusty what?"

"Ruskie sabotage. The work of the Russians. I presume this plant is secret?"

Smith stared at him in amazement. "You gone crazy, Mr. Fevertrees? The Russian nation got time mains just the same as us. You were on honeymoon in Odessa last year, weren't you?"

"Last year, I was on active service in Korea, thank you!"

"Korea?!"

With mighty siren noises, a black shape bearing red flashing lights above and below its bulk settled itself down in the Time Board yard. It was a robot-piloted fire engine from the city, but its human crew tumbled out in a weird confusion, and one young fellow lay yelling for his pants to be changed before the Time Board men could issue them with anti-time gas masks. And then there was no fire for them to extinguish, only the great gusher of invisible time that by now towered over the building and the whole village, and blew to the four corners, carrying unimagined or forgotten generations on its mothproof breath.

"Let's get forward and see what we can see," Smith said. "We might just as well go home and have a drink as stand here doing nothing."

"You are a very foolish young man if you mean what I suppose you to mean," Fifi said, in an ancient and severe voice. "Most of the liquor currently available is bootleg and unsafe to consume—but in any case, I believe we should support the President in his worthy attempt to stamp out alcoholism, don't you, Tracey darling?"

But Tracey was lost in an abstraction of strange memory, and whistling "La Paloma" under his breath to boot.

Stumbling after Smith, they got to the building, where two police officials stopped them. At that moment a plump man in a formal suit appeared and spoke to one of the police through his gas mask. Smith hailed him, and they greeted each other like brothers. It turned out they were brothers. Clayball Smith beckoned them all into the plant, gallantly taking Fifi's arm—which, to reveal his personal tragedy, was about as much as he ever got of any pretty girl.

"Shouldn't we have been properly introduced to this gentleman, Tracey?" Fifi whispered to her husband.

"Nonsense, my dear. Rules of etiquette have to go by the board when you enter one of the temples of industry." As he spoke, Tracey seemed to stroke an imaginary side whisker.

Inside the time plant chaos reigned. Now the full magnitude of the disaster was clear. They were pulling the first miners out of the hole where the time explosion had occurred; one of the poor fellows was cursing weakly and blaming George III for the whole terrible matter.

The whole time industry was still in its infancy. A bare ten years had elapsed since the first of the subterrenes, foraging far below the Earth's crust, had discovered the time pockets. The whole matter was still a cause for wonder, and investigations were as yet at a comparatively early stage.

But big business had stepped in and, with its usual bigheartedness, seen that everyone got his fair share of time, at a price. Now the time industry had more capital invested than any other industry in the world. Even in a tiny village like Rouseville, the plant was worth millions. But the plant had broken down right now.

"It's terrible dangerous here—you folks better not stay long," Clayball said. He was shouting through his gas mask. The noise here was terrible, especially since a news commentator had just started his spiel to the nation a yard away.

In answer to a shouted question from his brother, Clayball said, "No, it's more than a crack in the main supply. That was just the cover story we put out. Our brave boys down there struck a whole new time seam and it's leaking out all over the place. Can't plug it! Half our guys were back to the Norman Conquest before we guessed what was wrong." He pointed dramatically down through the tiles beneath their feet.

Fifi could not understand what on earth he was talking about. Ever since leaving Plymouth, she had been adrift, and that not entirely metaphorically. It was bad enough playing Pilgrim Mother to one of the Pilgrim Fathers, but she did not dig this New World at all. It was now beyond her comprehension to understand that the vast resources of modern technology were fouling up the whole time schedule of a planet.

In her present state, she could not know that already the illusions of the time gusher were spreading across the continent. Almost every communication satellite shuttling above the world was carrying more or less accurate accounts of the disaster and the events leading up to it, while their bemused audiences sank back through the generations like people plumbing bottomless snowdrifts.

From these deposits came the supply of time that was piped to the million million homes of the world. Experts had already computed that at present rates of consumption all the time deposits would be exhausted in two hundred years. Fortunately, other experts were already at work trying to develop synthetic substitutes for time. Only the previous month, the small research team of Time Pen Inc., of Ink, Penn, had announced the isolation of a molecule nine minutes slower than any other molecule known to science, and it was firmly expected that even more isolated molecules would follow.

Now an ambulance came skidding up, with another behind it. Archibald Smith tried to pull Tracey out of the way.

"Unhand me, varlet!" quoth Tracey, attempting to draw an imaginary sword. But the ambulance men were jumping out of their vehicles, and the police were cordoning off the area.

"They're going to bring up our brave terranauts!" Clayball shouted.

He could hardly be heard above the hubbub. Masked men were everywhere, with here and there the slender figure of a masked nurse. Supplies of oxygen and soup were being marshalled, searchlights swung overhead, blazing down into the square mouth of the inspection pit. The men in yellow overalls were lowering themselves into the pit, communicating to each other by wrist radio. They disappeared. For a moment a hush of awe fell over the building and seemed to spread to the crowds outside.

But the moment stretched into minutes, and the noise found its way back to its own level. More grim-faced men came forward, and the commentators were pushed out of the picture.

"It thinks me we should suffer ourselves to get gone from here, by God's breath!" Fifi whispered faintly, clutching at her homespun with a trembling hand. "This likes me not!"

At last there was activity at the head of the pit. Sweating men in overalls hauled on ropes. The first terranaut was pulled into view, wearing the characteristic black uniform of his kind. His head lolled back, his mask had been ripped away, but he was fighting bravely to retain consciousness. Indeed, a debonair smile crossed his pale lips, and he waved a hand at the cameras. A ragged cheer went up from the onlookers.

This was the intrepid breed of men that went down into the uncharted seas of time gas below the Earth's crust, risking their lives to bring back a nugget of knowledge from the unknown, pushing back still further the boundaries of science, unsung and unhonoured by all save the constant battery of world publicity.

The ace commentator had struggled through the crowd to reach the terranaut and was trying to question him, holding a microphone to his lips while the hero's tortured face swam before the unbelieving eyes of a billion viewers.

"Hell down there. . . . Dinosaurs and their young," he managed to gasp, before he was whisked into the first ambulance. "Right down deep in the gas. Packs of 'em, ravening. . . . Few more hundred feet lower and we'd have fetched . . . fetched up against the creation . . . of the world. . . ."

They could hear no more. Now fresh police reinforcements were clearing the building of all unauthorised persons before the other terranauts were returned to the surface, although of their earth capsule there was as yet no sign. As the armed cordon approached, Fifi and Tracey made a dash for it. They could stand no more, they could understand no more. They pelted for the door, oblivious to the cries of the two masked Smiths. As they ran out into the darkness, high above them towered the great invisible plume of the time gusher, still blowing, blowing its doom about the world.

For some while they lay gasping in the nearest hedge. Occasionally one of them would whimper like a tiny girl, or the other would groan like an old man. Between times, they breathed heavily.

Dawn was near to breaking when they pulled themselves up and made along the track toward Rouseville, keeping close to the fields. They were not alone. The inhabitants of the village were on the move, heading away from the homes that were now alien to them and beyond their limited understanding. Staring at them from under his lowering brow, Tracey stopped and fashioned himself a crude cudgel from the hedgerow.

Together, the man and his woman trudged over the hill, heading back for the wilds like most of the rest of humanity, their bent and uncouth forms silhouetted against the first ragged banners of light in the sky.

"Ugh glumph hum herm morm glug humk," the woman muttered.

Which means, roughly translated from the Old Stone, "Why the heck does this always have to happen to mankind just when he's on the goddam point of getting civilised again?"


## Afterword:

If ever a dangerous vision was rooted in real life, "The Night That All Time Broke Out" is. I should explain that I am at present living in a remote corner of Oxfordshire, England, where I have purchased a marvellous old sixteenth-century house, all stone and timber and thatch, and considerably slumped in disrepair. I said to my friend Jim Ballard, the s-f writer, "It looks as if it's some strange vegetable form that has grown out of the ground," and he replied, "Yes, and it looks as if it's now growing back in again."

In an effort to keep the house above ground, my wife and I decided to have it put on to main drainage and fill in the old cesspit.

Our builders immediately surrounded the place with gigantic ditching systems and enormous pipes. In the thick of it all, I wondered how future generations would cope with similar problems. The result you see here.

At a rough count, this is my one hundred and tenth published story. I gave up work ten years ago and took up writing instead. It was one of the best ideas I ever had. I believe my story presented here contains one of the whackiest ideas I ever had. (Let's hope there are a few more whacky ideas in my head—I'd hate to have to go back to work. . . .)

## Introduction to THE MAN WHO WENT TO THE MOON—
TWICE:

Originally, one of the lesser (but no less important) intents of this
anthology was to commission and bring to the attention of the readers
stories by writers well outside the field of speculative fiction. The names
William Burroughs, Thomas Pynchon, Alan Sillitoe, Terry Southern,
Thomas Berger and Kingsley Amis were listed in my preliminary table
of contents. The name Howard Rodman was also listed. Circumstances
almost Machiavellian in nature prevented the appearance here of the
former sextet. Howard Rodman is with us. I am honored.

You are a fan of Rodman's work if you watch television at all. Because, if you watch TV in even the most peripheral way, you do it to
catch the best programs, and if that is the case you have seen Rodman's work. (A comment: how odd it seems to me that science fiction
fans, the ones who choose to exist in dream worlds of flying skyways,
cities of wonder, marvelous inventions, dilating doors, tri-vid and

"feelies," are the ones who most vocally despise modern television. The bulk of the fans I have met, when they discover I spend part of my time writing for the visual media, rather superciliously tell me they seldom watch, as though watching *at all* might be considered gauche. How sad it must be for them, to see television, space travel and all the other predictions of Gernsbackian "scientifiction" turned over to the Philistines. I suppose, in a way, it's a small tragedy, like having been so hip for years that you knew Tolkien was great, and now suddenly finding every *shmendrick* in the world reading paperback editions of *Lord of the Rings* on the IRT. But it is a far, far better thing, I submit, to have TV as the mass media it is, even as gawdawful as it is ninety-six per cent of the time, than to relegate it to the hideously antiseptic fate intended for it by the s-f of 1928.)

Howard Rodman has been nominated for and won more awards for television drama than anyone currently working in the medium. His famous *Naked City* script, "Bringing Far Places Together," won Emmys and Writers' Guild awards not only for himself but for the series, the director and the stars. Students of exemplary teleplays will recall last season's *Bob Hope-Chrysler Theater* drama, "The Game with Glass Pieces." It was, in point of fact, Howard Rodman's style that set the tone for the best of both *Naked City* and *Route 66* during their auspicious tenures on the channelways.

Howard Rodman was born in the Bronx, and decided at the age of ten to be a writer. He took that decision seriously at age fifteen and from fifteen to sixteen read a minimum of one volume of short stories daily; from sixteen to seventeen read only plays, five or six a day; and from seventeen to twenty-one he wrote 3000 words a day: short stories, scenes from plays, poems, narrative sequences, etc. He graduated from Brooklyn College and later did his graduate work at Iowa University. At twenty-one he went into the army (where among his assignments he was required to inspect the brothels of Lille as a sergeant in counterintelligence). He has had over a hundred and fifty short stories published, several hundred poems, forty one-act plays, four three-act plays (and has been included in volumes of best plays of the year). For the past ten years he has been active in radio, television and motion pictures. At forty-seven, Howard Rodman—big, hearty, incredibly witty and erudite Howard Rodman—the film buff, has been married, divorced and remarried to the lovely and talented actress Norma Connolly. They have four children, several of whom can be ranked as geniuses by the most stringent criteria.

I am particularly pleased that Howard is able to appear in this anthology, not merely because his story is something very different and very special from the others in this book, but for a number of secondary reasons, herewith noted: Long before I came to Hollywood, I was an admirer of Rodman's scripts. They seemed to me to embody the ideals a scenarist should strive for in a medium dedicated to drumming stench-deterrents for the hair, mouth, underarms and spaces between the toes. I made it a point to meet Rodman, within the first few months in Clown Town, and from him I learned an important lesson. A lesson any writer can use. Don't be afraid. That simple; don't let them scare you. There's nothing they can do to you. If they kick you out of films, do TV. If they kick you out of TV, write novels. If they won't buy your novels, sell short stories. Can't do that, then take a job as a bricklayer. A writer always writes. That's what he's for. And if they won't let you write one kind of thing, if they chop you off at the pockets in the market place, then go to another market place. And if they close off all the bazaars, then by God go and work with your hands till you *can* write, because the talent is always there. But the first time you say, "Oh, Christ, they'll kill me!" then you're done. Because the chief commodity a writer has to sell is his courage. And if he has none, he is more than a coward. He is a sellout and a fink and a heretic, because writing is a holy chore. *That* is what I learned from Howard Rodman.

Another reason for my delight at Rodman's inclusion among these pages is the tenor of the story he has told. It is a gentle story, seemingly commonplace and not very "dangerous." Yet when I first read it, and these thoughts occurred to me, I paused with the warning *read it again* signaling me from inside. Rodman is devious. So I read it again, and aside from the understatement of the handling, the pain of the concept struck me. He has attempted something very difficult, and in its own way unsettling. He has made a sage comment on the same subject which *I* commented upon, in the second paragraph of this introduction. (The part in parentheses.) It is the kind of story Heinlein used to write, and which Vonnegut has done several times, but which *most* speculative writers would not even consider. They are too far away in space. Rodman still has substantial ties with the here and now. And it is this concern (and affection) for the tragedy of the here and now that has prompted the story of the man who went to the moon—twice.

One final reason why Rodman's appearance here is a delight. He is a fighter, not merely a parlor liberal. His admonition to me never to be afraid was capped with an order to fight for what I had written. I've tried to do it, sometimes successfully. It's difficult in Hollywood. But my mentor, Howard Rodman, is the man who once threw a heavy ashtray at a man who had aborted one of his scripts, and had to be restrained from tearing the man's head from his shoulders. On another occasion he sent a very powerful producer, who had butchered one of his shows, a large package wrapped in black crêpe. Inside was a pair of scissors with a note that said *Requiescat in Pace,* and the name of the teleplay. There is a legend around the studios: if you aren't getting enough of a headache from Ellison writing for you, call in Rodman and work with the original item.

It is visible testimony to the quality of his work that Howard Rodman is one of the busiest writers in Hollywood.

# ● THE MAN WHO WENT TO THE MOON—TWICE

## by Howard Rodman

The first time Marshall Kiss went to the moon, he was nine years old, and the trip was accidental. A captive balloon broke loose at the county fair, and away it went, with Marshall in it.

It never came down till twelve hours later.

"Where've you been?" Marshall's pa asked.

"Up to the moon," Marshall answered.

"You don't say," Pa said, with his mouth slightly open and hanging. And off he went to tell the neighbors.

Marshall's ma, being of a more practical turn of mind, just put a heaping bowl of good hot cereal on the table in front of Marshall. "You must be good and hungry after a trip like that. You better have some supper before you go to bed."

"I guess I will," said Marshall, setting to work to clear out the bowl. He was hard at work when the reporters came—a big man with a little mustache, and a dry young man working on the newspaper for his tuition at the Undertakers' College.

"Well," said the mustache, "so you've been to the moon."

Marshall got timid and nodded without speaking.

The undertaker smirked, but he stopped that when Marshall's ma threw him a hot glare.

"What was it like?" the mustache asked.

"Very nice," Marshall answered politely. "Cold and fresh and lots of singing."

"What sort of singing?"

"Just singing. Nice tunes."

The undertaker leered, but he stopped that when Marshall's ma set the glass of milk down on the table with a bang and a scowl.

"Nice tunes," Marshall repeated. "Just like church hymns."

Three neighbors came by to take a look at Marshall. They stood back from the table a ways, gaping a little at the boy who'd been to the moon. "Who'd believe it?" one of them whispered. "He looks so young."

Marshall blushed with pride and ducked his head down toward his bowl of cereal.

Just then four schoolmates sneaked through the kitchen door and pushed their faces into the spaces between the neighbors. "Ask him!" the smallest schoolmate demanded.

"Hey, Marsh," the bravest one called out, "you gonna play ball tomorrow?"

"Sure," Marshall answered.

"He's all right," the bravest one told the others. "It ain't changed him at all."

Marshall's pa came back with two more neighbors, and a woman brought her husband and eight children from two and a half miles down the road. A horse poked his head through the kitchen window, and a chicken hopped in and hid under the stove.

Marshall's teacher rang the front doorbell, marched through the house into the kitchen by herself, when no one answered her ring.

Everybody looked at Marshall in a joyful and prideful sort of way, but nobody seemed to be able to think of anything to say. Even when the mayor arrived, freshly shaven and bursting to make a speech, something happened to him, and he closed his mouth without a word.

The kitchen got warm with so many people pressing in together, but it was a pleasant sort of warmth—cheerful and happy, and nobody jostled anybody else. Marshall's ma just grinned and glowed, and his pa puffed up on a corncob pipe, setting himself on an upturned crate beside the stove.

The reporter who was studying for the profession of undertaking started to ask Marshall, "How do you know you been to the moon?" But that was as far as he got, and somehow he found himself at the back of the crowd, looking out over everybody's head by standing on tiptoe.

Finally the chicken *cut-cutted,* and everybody thought that was funny, so they all laughed out loud, and clear.

Marshall finished his cereal and his milk, and looked up to see, through the window, that the yard outside was packed with people too: from miles around, by horse and buckboard, on foot and otherwise. He could see that they were waiting for word from him, so he stood up and made a speech.

"I never intended deliberately to go to the moon," Marshall started. "It just happened that way. The balloon kept going up and I kept going up with it. Pretty soon I was looking down on the tops of mountains, and that was something. But I just kept on going up and up anyway. On the way I got an eagle mad. He was trying to fly as high as me, but he just couldn't do it. He was hopping mad, that eagle. Screamed his head off."

All the people in the kitchen, and outside in the yard too, nodded approval.

"In the end," Marshall went on, "I got to the moon. Like I said, it was pretty nice." He stopped speeching, because he'd said everything he had to.

"Was you scared?" somebody asked.

"Somewhat," Marshall answered. "But the air was bracing, and I got over it."

"Well," said the mayor, bound to say something, "we're glad to have you back." And he stuck out his hand to shake with Marshall.

After that, Marshall shook hands all around and everybody went back to his own home. The horse took his head out the window and went back to cropping grass in the yard. The hen hopped out the door again, leaving an egg behind under the stove. The house was empty but still cheerful. It was as if everybody had come and brought their happiness and left it behind as a present, the way the chicken left the egg.

"Been a big day for you," Marshall's pa said.

"I guess you'd better go to bed now," Marshall's ma said.

"Might be," Marshall's pa went on, talking his thinking out loud, "might be you'll turn out to be a big explorer, time to come."

Marshall looked at his ma, saw her fear that the boy would turn out to be a gadabout. He answered for his mother's benefit. "I'll tell you, Pa. Seems more likely I'd just settle down now and stay put." Of course he winked at his father to show him that maybe he was right at that.

"Good night, Pa. Good night, Ma."

"Good night, son."

His ma kissed him good night.

Then Marshall went into his room, closed the door, and undressed, and put on his pajamas. He knelt by the side of his bed and folded his fingers for prayer.

"Been a happy day, O Lord. Happy as I can remember. Thanks."

He climbed into bed and went to sleep.

Well, you know the way time goes on. Marshall came to be a man, married and settled. He had children, and his children had children. His children grew up and just naturally went off their own ways, and his wife died a natural death. And there was Marshall Kiss left alone in the world, living on his farm and doing as much or as little work as he felt like.

Sometimes he went into town and sat by the stove in the general store and talked, and sometimes he stayed home and listened to the rain talking to the windowpanes. There came to be a time when Marshall was pushing ninety pretty hard. Most everybody who'd been alive when he was a boy had passed on.

The people in town were a new generation, and while they weren't unkind, they weren't very friendly, either. That's the way it is with a new generation—it doesn't look back—it keeps looking forward.

The time came when Marshall could walk through the town from one end to the other and not see a face he knew or that knew him. He'd nod and get nodded back at, but it wasn't a real, close, human thing—it was just a polite thing to do. And you know what the end is, when a man has to live like that—he gets lonely.

That's just what Marshall did—he got lonely.

First he thought he could forget his loneliness by staying off by himself. And there was a whole month when Marshall never showed his face around at all, expecting that somebody might show some curiosity and maybe come by to see how he was. But nobody ever did. So Marshall went back into town.

The clerk at the store seemed to have some vague recollection about not having seen Marshall, but he wasn't too sure. "You haven't been around for a couple of days or so, have you?" he asked Marshall.

"More like a month," Marshall said.

"You don't say," the clerk remarked, as he toted up the figures on Marshall's bill.

"Been away," said Marshall.

"Seeing your relatives?" the clerk asked.

"Been to the moon," Marshall said.

The clerk looked a little bored, and not at all interested, and not at all impressed. In fact, he didn't look as if he believed Marshall to begin with. But he was a polite man, so he commented. "Must be a nice trip," he commented, never thinking any more about it than that.

Marshall went stomping out of the store and down to have his hair trimmed.

"Pretty heavy growth, Mr. Kiss," the barber said.

"Should be," Marshall answered. "There ain't no barbershops on the moon, you know."

"Expect not," the barber said, and went ahead, busily clicking his shears and making believe he was clipping a hair here and a hair there, but never saying another word about the moon, never even having the common decency to ask what it was like on the moon.

So Marshall fell asleep till the barber should be finished.

The mayor came in for his daily shave. He was a young man with a heavy beard, and he glanced casually at Marshall. "Old-timer," he said to the barber.

The barber nodded as he worked.

"Looks tuckered out," the mayor said.

"Should be," the barber told him. "He just got back from the moon." He snickered loud.

"You don't say," the mayor said.

"That's what he claims." The barber snickered again. "Just got back from the moon."

"Well, no wonder he's tired, then." But the way the mayor laughed and the way the barber laughed, Marshall could tell that they were just making fun of him. For Marshall wasn't really sleeping, of course.

It got Marshall mad, and he sprang up and threw the sheet off of him and stomped on down to the newspaper office.

"My name is Marshall Kiss," Marshall said to the fresh cub at the desk, "and I've just come back from a trip to the moon!"

"Thanks for the tip, Pop," the reporter said, smiling a little crookedly. "I'll look into it when I get the time." And, saying that, he planted his big feet plump on the desk and clasped his hands behind his head.

Tears sprang up in Marshall's eyes. "I been to the moon twice," he shouted. "Once when I was nine years old, and it's been printed in your paper, too, at the time. Why, people came from twelve miles around just to look at me. I went up there in an old balloon and busted an eagle's heart when he tried to get up as high as I was." He looked at the reporter hard, and he could see that the reporter didn't believe him and wasn't going to try. "There's no pity left in the world any more," said Marshall, "and no joy." And with that, he walked out.

The road home was mostly rocky and uphill, and it seemed to take Marshall a long time to walk a short distance. "Can't figure out how people changed so much," Marshall thought. "Grass is still green, and horses have tails, and hens lay eggs—" He was interrupted by a little boy who came running up from behind, pretending to gallop and hitting himself on the rump as if he were a horse.

"Hello," the little boy said, "where are you going?"

"Just up the hill a way, back to my farm," Marshall answered.

"Where've you been?" the little boy asked.

"Just to town," Marshall said.

"Is that all?" the little boy asked, disappointed. "Ain't you never been nowhere else?"

"I been to the moon," Marshall said, a little timidly.

The boy's eyes opened and shone brightly.

"Twice," Marshall added.

The boy's eyes opened even wide. "How do you like that!" the little boy shouted, excited. "H-h-how do you like that?" He was so excited, he stammered.

"Matter of fact," Marshall said, "I just come back from the moon."

The little boy was silent for a second. "Say, mister," he asked finally, "do you mind if I bring my friend to see you?"

"Not at all. I live right back there, in that house you see." Marshall turned off to get to his house.

"I'll be right back," the little boy promised and ran away as fast as he could to get his friend.

It must have been about a half hour later that the little boy and the little girl got to Marshall's house. They knocked on the door, but there wasn't any answer, so they just walked in. "It's all right," the little boy said, "he's very friendly."

The kitchen was empty, so they looked in the parlor, and that was empty too.

"Maybe he's gone back to the moon," the little girl whispered, awed.

"Maybe he has," the little boy admitted, but just the same they looked in the bedroom.

There was Marshall, lying on the bed, and at first they thought he was sleeping. But after a while, when he didn't move or breathe, the little boy and the little girl knew he was further away than that.

"Guess you were right," the little boy said.

He and the little girl just looked and looked with their eyes as wide as wide can be, at the man who had been to the moon twice.

"I guess this makes three times now," the little girl said.

And suddenly, without knowing why, they became frightened and ran off, leaving the door opened behind them. They ran silently, hand in hand, frightened, but happy too, as if something very wonderful had happened that they couldn't understand.

After a while, though it was the first time it had ever happened on that farm, the horse wandered into the house and stuck his head through the bedroom door and looked.

And then a chicken hopped in and hid under the bed.

And a long time later, a lot of people came to look at the contented smile on Marshall's face.

"That's him," the little boy said, pointing. "That's the man who's been to the moon twice."

And somehow, with Marshall's smile, and the horse standing there swishing his tail, and the sudden *cut-cutt* of the chicken under the bed— somehow, nobody corrected the little boy.

That was the day the Mars rocket went on a regular three-a-day schedule. Hardly anybody went to the moon at all, any more. There wasn't enough to see.

## Afterword:

This particular story came out of a sudden, strongly personal understanding of certain aspects of my father's life—the enormous changes which took place in the history of his time: technological developments beyond dreaming when he was a boy.

He had told me of sitting and listening to a phonograph which was carried on the back of a man who went from village to village in Poland, where my father was born. For a kopek the man wound the handle, the disc turned, the needle scratched, and if you put your ear close to the horn there was the miracle of a voice, a music, a recitation.

Now, in 1928 or '29, my father stepped into an airplane which landed in a cornfield in the Catskill Mountains. For five dollars my father flew for five minutes.

If this was my father's story, it was the story of his generation. Within what seems to me an incredibly short time, the mystery and the miracle were lost. There is small marvel to television, despite the fact that the extraordinary complexity of the sending and reception of a television signal is beyond the understanding and capability of the tens and hundred of millions of television watchers. The television set is successful *because* the marvel has been eliminated. *Because* the set is truly an idiot box; not so much in its content as in the manner in which the controls have been simplified, so that the viewing may be had by anyone with the sense to push a button and twist a dial. The dial itself, so devised that one has merely to twist it: not even to a specific number. But, ipso facto, if one wants to see the show on channel 8, all one has to do is keep twisting the dial until that show appears on the screen. Ergo, one has dialed to channel 8.

And the marvel is gone.

Because the sweep of modern history seems to me to have a feeling of wonder; because it has a sense of fairy tale and unbelievability to me; because the miracle of the changes wrought from the time of my father's boyhood to my own seemed to me to have been lost, I wrote this story.

It is simply a reminder that fantasy lies in the day-to-day of our lives as much as it lies in the wonder of the future. And it is a reminder that the best of our civilization goes far beyond the comprehension of the ordinary of our citizens. The wonder is that there is so much civilization when so few are civilized.

In another mood I might have written a sharper story. But this time I thought simply that form should follow content. Hence, a fairy tale; old-fashioned and sentimental, written on an electric typewriter.

## Introduction to FAITH OF OUR FATHERS:

There was no doubt about it. If the book was to approach new concepts and taboo subjects, stories that would be difficult to sell to mass market magazines or more particularly the insulated specialist magazines of the science fiction field, I had to get the writers who were not afraid to walk into the dark. Philip K. Dick has been lighting up his own landscape for years, casting illumination by the klieg lights of his imagination on a terra incognita of staggering dimensions. I asked for Phil Dick and got him. A story to be written about, and under the influence of (if possible), LSD. What follows, like his excellent offbeat novel, *The Three Stigmata of Palmer Eldritch,* is the result of such a hallucinogenic journey.

Dick has the uncomfortable habit of shaking up one's theories. For instance, mine own about the value of artificial stimuli to encourage the creative process. (It's a cop-out on my part, I suppose, because I am unable to write without music blasting away in the background. Matters not if it's Honegger or the Tijuana Brass or Archie Shepp or the New Vaudeville Band doing "Winchester Cathedral." I must have it.) When I was a tot younger, and was making the rounds of the various jazz clubs in New York, both as critic and reviewer and plain listener, I became tight with many musicians who swore they needed either weed or speed to get into the proper bag. Then, after fixing or getting high, they settled down to blow; what emerged was lunacy. I've known ballerinas who were grassheads because they couldn't get the "in the air" feeling without their nickel bag; psychiatrists who were able to support their own habits with self-signed narcotics prescriptions—habits they had built on the delusion that junk freed their minds for more penetrating analyses; artists who were on acid constantly, whose work under the "mind-expanding" influences were something you'd scour out with Comet if you found it at the bottom of your wading pool. My theory, developed over years of seeing people deluding themselves for the bounce they got, was that the creative process is at its most lively when it merges clean and unfogged from whatever wells exist within the minds of the creators. Philip K. Dick puts the lie to that theory.

His experiments with LSD and other hallucinogens, plus stimulants of the amphetamine class, have borne such fruit as the story you are about to read, in every way a "dangerous" vision. The question now poses itself: how valid is the totality for the exception of rare successes like the work of Phil Dick? I don't presume to know. All I can venture is that proper administration of mind-expanding drugs might open whole new areas to the creative intellect. Areas that have been, till now, the country of the blind.

For the record, Philip K. Dick attended the University of California, has kicked around in various jobs which included running a record shop (he is a Bach, Wagner and Buddy Greco buff), advertising copy writing and emceeing a classical music program on station KSMO in San Mateo, California. Among his books are *Solar Lottery, Eye in the Sky, Time Out of Joint, The Simulacra, The Penultimate Truth, Martian Time-Slip, Dr. Bloodmoney, Now Wait for Last Year* and the 1963 *Hugo* winner, *The Man in the High Castle*. Although portly, bearded and married, he is a confirmed girl-watcher.

He is with us today in his capacity of shaker-upper of theories. And if he doesn't nibble away at your sense of "reality" just a little bit in "Faith of Our Fathers," check your pulse. You may be dead.

# ● FAITH OF OUR FATHERS

**by Philip K. Dick**

On the streets of Hanoi he found himself facing a legless peddler who rode a little wooden cart and called shrilly to every passer-by. Chien slowed, listened, but did not stop; business at the Ministry of Cultural Artifacts cropped into his mind and deflected his attention: it was as if he were alone, and none of those on bicycles and scooters and jet-powered motorcycles remained. And likewise it was as if the legless peddler did not exist.

"Comrade," the peddler called however, and pursued him on his cart; a helium battery operated the drive and sent the cart scuttling expertly after Chien. "I possess a wide spectrum of time-tested herbal remedies complete with testimonials from thousands of loyal users; advise me of your malady and I can assist."

Chien, pausing, said, "Yes, but I have no malady." Except, he thought, for the chronic one of those employed by the Central Committee, that of career opportunism testing constantly the gates of each official position. Including mine.

"I can cure for example radiation sickness," the peddler chanted, still pursuing him. "Or expand, if necessary, the element of sexual prowess. I can reverse carcinomatous progressions, even the dreaded melanomae, what you would call black cancers." Lifting a tray of bottles, small aluminum cans and assorted powders in plastic jars, the peddler sang, "If a rival persists in trying to usurp your gainful bureaucratic position, I can purvey an ointment which, appearing as a dermal balm, is in actuality a desperately effective toxin. And my prices, comrade, are low. And as a special favor to one so distinguished in bearing as yourself I will accept the postwar inflationary paper dollars reputedly of international exchange but in reality damn near no better than bathroom tissue."

"Go to hell," Chien said, and signaled a passing hovercar taxi; he was already three and one half minutes late for his first appointment of the day, and his various fat-assed superiors at the Ministry would be making quick mental notations—as would, to an even greater degree, his subordinates.

The peddler said quietly, "But, comrade; you *must* buy from me."

"Why?" Chien demanded. Indignation.

"Because, comrade, I am a war veteran. I fought in the Colossal Final War of National Liberation with the People's Democratic United Front against the Imperialists; I lost my pedal extremities at the battle of San Francisco." His tone was triumphant, now, and sly. *"It is the law.* If you refuse to buy wares offered by a veteran you risk a fine and possible jail sentence—and in addition disgrace."

Wearily, Chien nodded the hovercab on. "Admittedly," he said. "Okay, I must buy from you." He glanced summarily over the meager display of herbal remedies, seeking one at random. "That," he decided, pointing to a paper-wrapped parcel in the rear row.

The peddler laughed. "That, comrade, is a spermatocide, bought by women who for political reasons cannot qualify for The Pill. It would be of shallow use to you, in fact none at all, since you are a gentleman."

"The law," Chien said bitingly, "does not require me to purchase anything useful from you; only that I purchase something. I'll take that." He reached into his padded coat for his billfold, huge with the postwar inflationary bills in which, four times a week, he as a government servant was paid.

"Tell me your problems," the peddler said.

Chien stared at him. Appalled by the invasion of privacy—and done by someone outside the government.

"All right, comrade," the peddler said, seeing his expression. "I will not probe; excuse me. But as a doctor—an herbal healer—it is fitting that I know as much as possible." He pondered, his gaunt features somber. "Do you watch television unusually much?" he asked abruptly.

Taken by surprise, Chien said, "Every evening. Except on Friday when I go to my club to practice the esoteric imported art from the defeated West of steer-roping." It was his only indulgence; other than that he had totally devoted himself to Party activities.

The peddler reached, selected a gray paper packet. "Sixty trade dollars," he stated. "With a full guarantee; if it does not do as promised, return the unused portion for a full and cheery refund."

"And what," Chien said cuttingly, "is it guaranteed to do?"

"It will rest eyes fatigued by the countenance of meaningless official monologues," the peddler said. "A soothing preparation; take it as soon as you find yourself exposed to the usual dry and lengthy sermons which—"

Chien paid the money, accepted the packet, and strode off. Balls, he said to himself. It's a racket, he decided, the ordinance setting up war vets as a privileged class. They prey off us—we, the younger ones—like raptors.

Forgotten, the gray packet remained deposited in his coat pocket, as he entered the imposing postwar Ministry of Cultural Artifacts building, and his own considerable stately office, to begin his workday.

A portly, middle-aged Caucasian male, wearing a brown Hong Kong silk suit, double-breasted with vest, waited in his office. With the unfamiliar Caucasian stood his own immediate superior, Ssu-Ma Tso-pin. Tso-pin introduced the two of them in Cantonese, a dialect which he used badly.

"Mr. Tung Chien, this is Mr. Darius Pethel. Mr. Pethel will be headmaster at the new ideological and cultural establishment of didactic character soon to open at San Fernando, California." He added, "Mr. Pethel has had a rich and full lifetime supporting the people's struggle to unseat imperialist-bloc countries via pedagogic media; therefore this high post."

They shook hands.

"Tea?" Chien asked the two of them; he pressed the switch of his infrared hibachi and in an instant the water in the highly ornamented ceramic pot—of Japanese origin—began to burble. As he seated himself at his desk he saw that trustworthy Miss Hsi had laid out the information poop-sheet (confidential) on Comrade Pethel; he glanced over it, meanwhile pretending to be doing nothing in particular.

"The Absolute Benefactor of the People," Tso-pin said, "has personally met Mr. Pethel and trusts him. This is rare. The school in San Fernando will appear to teach run-of-the-mill Taoist philosophies but will, of course, in actuality maintain for us a channel of communication to the liberal and intellectual youth segment of western U.S. There are many of them still alive, from San Diego to Sacramento;

we estimate at least ten thousand. The school will accept two thousand. Enrollment will be mandatory for those we select. Your relationship to Mr. Pethel's programing is grave. Ahem; your tea water is boiling."

"Thank you," Chien murmured, dropping in the bag of Lipton's tea.

Tso-pin continued, "Although Mr. Pethel will supervise the setting up of the courses of instruction presented by the school to its student body, all examination papers will oddly enough be relayed here to your office for your own expert, careful, ideological study. In other words, Mr. Chien, you will determine who among the two thousand students is reliable, which are truly responding to the programing and who is not."

"I will now pour my tea," Chien said, doing so ceremoniously.

"What we have to realize," Pethel rumbled in Cantonese even worse than that of Tso-pin, "is that, once having lost the global war to us, the American youth has developed a talent for dissembling." He spoke the last word in English; not understanding it, Chien turned inquiringly to his superior.

"Lying," Tso-pin explained.

Pethel said, "Mouthing the proper slogans for surface appearance, but on the inside believing them false. Test papers by this group will closely resemble those of genuine—"

"You mean that the test papers of *two thousand* students will be passing through my office?" Chien demanded. He could not believe it. "That's a full-time job in itself; I don't have time for anything remotely resembling that." He was appalled. "To give critical, official approval or denial of the astute variety which you're envisioning—" He gestured. "Screw that," he said, in English.

Blinking at the strong, Western vulgarity, Tso-pin said, "You have a staff. Plus also you can requisition several more from the pool; the Ministry's budget, augmented this year, will permit it. And remember: the Absolute Benefactor of the People has hand-picked Mr. Pethel." His tone, now, had become ominous, but only subtly so. Just enough to penetrate Chien's hysteria, and to wither it into submission. At least temporarily. To underline his point, Tso-pin walked to the far end of the office; he stood before the full-length 3-D portrait of the Absolute

Benefactor, and after an interval his proximity triggered the tape-transport mounted behind the portrait; the face of the Benefactor moved, and from it came a familiar homily, in more than familiar accents. "Fight for peace, my sons," it intoned gently, firmly.

"Ha," Chien said, still perturbed, but concealing it. Possibly one of the Ministry's computers could sort the examination papers; a yes-no-maybe structure could be employed, in conjunction with a pre-analysis of the pattern of ideological correctness—and incorrectness. The matter could be made routine. Probably.

Darius Pethel said, "I have with me certain material which I would like you to scrutinize, Mr. Chien." He unzipped an unsightly, old-fashioned, plastic briefcase. "Two examination essays," he said as he passed the documents to Chien. "This will tell us if you're qualified." He then glanced at Tso-pin; their gazes met. "I understand," Pethel said, "that if you are successful in this venture you will be made vice-councilor of the Ministry, and His Greatness the Absolute Benefactor of the People will personally confer Kisterigian's medal on you." Both he and Tso-pin smiled in wary unison.

"The Kisterigian medal," Chien echoed; he accepted the examination papers, glanced over them in a show of leisurely indifference. But within him his heart vibrated in ill-concealed tension. "Why these two? By that I mean, what am I looking for, sir?"

"One of them," Pethel said, "is the work of a dedicated progressive, a loyal Party member of thoroughly researched conviction. The other is by a young *stilyagi* whom we suspect of holding petit bourgeois imperialist degenerate crypto-ideas. It is up to you, sir, to determine which is which."

Thanks a lot, Chien thought. But, nodding, he read the title of the top paper.

DOCTRINES OF THE ABSOLUTE BENEFACTOR
ANTICIPATED IN THE POETRY OF BAHA
AD-DIN ZUHAYR, OF THIRTEENTH-CENTURY
ARABIA.

Glancing down the initial pages of the essay, Chien saw a quatrain familiar to him; it was called "Death" and he had known it most of his adult, educated life.

> Once he will miss, twice he will miss,
>     He only chooses one of many hours;
> For him nor deep nor hill there is,
>     But all's one level plain he hunts for flowers.

"Powerful," Chien said. "This poem."

"He makes use of the poem," Pethel said, observing Chien's lips moving as he reread the quatrain, "to indicate the age-old wisdom, displayed by the Absolute Benefactor in our current lives, that no individual is safe; everyone is mortal, and only the supra-personal, historically essential cause survives. As it should be. Would you agree with him? With this student, I mean? Or—" Pethel paused. "Is he in fact perhaps satirizing the Absolute Benefactor's promulgations?"

Cagily, Chien said, "Give me a chance to inspect the other paper."

"You need no further information; decide."

Haltingly, Chien said, "I—had never thought of this poem that way." He felt irritable. "Anyhow, it isn't by Baha ad-Din Zuhayr; it's part of the *Thousand and One Nights* anthology. It is, however, thirteenth century; I admit that." He quickly read over the text of the paper accompanying the poem. It appeared to be a routine, uninspired rehash of Party clichés, all of them familiar to him from birth. The blind, imperialist monster who mowed down and snuffed out (mixed metaphor) human aspiration, the calculations of the still extant anti-Party group in eastern United States . . . He felt dully bored, and as uninspired as the student's paper. We must persevere, the paper declared. Wipe out the Pentagon remnants in the Catskills, subdue Tennessee and most especially the pocket of die-hard reaction in the red hills of Oklahoma. He sighed.

"I think," Tso-pin said, "we should allow Mr. Chien the opportunity of observing this difficult material at his leisure." To Chien he said, "You have permission to take them home to your condominium, this evening, and adjudge them on your own time." He bowed, half mockingly, half solicitously. In any case, insult or not, he had gotten Chien off the hook, and for that Chien was grateful.

"You are most kind," he murmured, "to allow me to perform this new and highly stimulating labor on my own time. Mikoyan, were he alive today, would approve." You bastard, he said to himself. Meaning both his superior and the Caucasian Pethel. Handing me a hot potato like this, and on my own time. Obviously the CP USA is in trouble; its indoctrination academies aren't managing to do their job with the notoriously mulish, eccentric Yank youths. And you've passed that hot potato on and on until it reaches me.

Thanks for nothing, he thought acidly.

That evening in his small but well-appointed condominium apartment he read over the other of the two examination papers, this one by a Marion Culper, and discovered that it, too, dealt with poetry. Obviously this was speciously a poetry class, and he felt ill. It had always run against his grain, the use of poetry—of any art—for social purposes. Anyhow, comfortable in his special spine-straightening, simulated-leather easy chair, he lit a Cuesta Rey Number One English Market immense corona cigar and began to read.

The writer of the paper, Miss Culper, had selected as her text a portion of a poem of John Dryden, the seventeenth-century English poet, final lines from the well-known "A Song for St. Cecilia's Day."

> . . . So when the last and dreadful hour
> This crumbling pageant shall devour,
> The trumpet shall be heard on high,
> The dead shall live, the living die,
> And Music shall untune the sky.

Well, that's a hell of a thing, Chien thought to himself bitingly. Dryden, we're supposed to believe, anticipated the fall of capitalism? That's what he meant by the "crumbling pageant"? Christ. He leaned over to take hold of his cigar and found that it had gone out. Groping in his pockets for his Japanese-made lighter, he half rose to his feet. . . .

Tweeeeeee! the TV set at the far end of the living room said.

Aha, Chien said. We're about to be addressed by the Leader. By the Absolute Benefactor of the People, up there in Peking where he's lived for ninety years now; or is it one hundred? Or, as we sometimes like to think of him, the Ass—

"May the ten thousand blossoms of abject self-assumed poverty flower in your spiritual courtyard," the TV announcer said. With a groan, Chien rose to his feet, bowed the mandatory bow of response;

each TV set came equipped with monitoring devices to narrate to the Secpol, the Security Police, whether its owner was bowing and/or watching.

On the screen a clearly defined visage manifested itself, the wide, unlined, healthy features of the one-hundred-and-twenty-year-old leader of CP East, ruler of many—far too many, Chien reflected. Blah to you, he thought, and reseated himself in his simulated-leather easy chair, now facing the TV screen.

"My thoughts," the Absolute Benefactor said in his rich and slow tones, "are on you, my children. And especially on Mr. Tung Chien of Hanoi, who faces a difficult task ahead, a task to enrich the people of Democratic East, plus the American West Coast. We must think in unison about this noble, dedicated man and the chore which he faces, and I have chosen to take several moments of my time to honor him and encourage him. Are you listening, Mr. Chien?"

"Yes, Your Greatness," Chien said, and pondered to himself the odds against the Party Leader singling *him* out this particular evening. The odds caused him to feel uncomradely cynicism; it was unconvincing. Probably this transmission was being beamed to his apartment building alone—or at least this city. It might also be a lip-synch job, done at Hanoi TV, Incorporated. In any case he was required to listen and watch—and absorb. He did so, from a lifetime of practice. Outwardly he appeared to be rigidly attentive. Inwardly he was still mulling over the two test papers, wondering which was which; where did devout Party enthusiasm end and sardonic lampoonery begin? Hard to say . . . which of course explained why they had dumped the task in his lap.

Again he groped in his pockets for his lighter—and found the small gray envelope which the war-veteran peddler had sold him. Gawd, he thought, remembering what it had cost. Money down the drain and what did this herbal remedy do? Nothing. He turned the packet over and saw, on the back, small printed words. Well, he thought, and began to unfold the packet with care. The words had snared him— as of course they were meant to do.

> Failing as a Party member and human?
> Afraid of becoming obsolete and dis-
> carded on the ash heap of history by

He read rapidly through the text, ignoring its claims, seeking to find out what he had purchased.

Meanwhile, the Absolute Benefactor droned on.

Snuff. The package contained snuff. Countless tiny black grains, like gunpowder, which sent up an interesting aromatic to tickle his nose. The title of the particular blend was Princes Special, he discovered. And very pleasing, he decided. At one time he had taken snuff— smoked tobacco for a time having been illegal for reasons of health— back during his student days at Peking U; it had been the fad, especially the amatory mixes prepared in Chungking, made from god knew what. Was this that? Almost any aromatic could be added to snuff, from essence of orange to pulverized babycrap . . . or so some seemed, especially an English mixture called High Dry Toast which had in itself more or less put an end to his yearning for nasal, inhaled tobacco.

On the TV screen the Absolute Benefactor rumbled monotonously on as Chien sniffed cautiously at the powder, read the claims—it cured everything from being late to work to falling in love with a woman of dubious political background. Interesting. But typical of claims—

His doorbell rang.

Rising, he walked to the door, opened it with full knowledge of what he would find. There, sure enough, stood Mou Kuei, the Building Warden, small and hard-eyed and alert to his task; he had his armband and metal helmet on, showing that he meant business. "Mr. Chien, comrade Party worker. I received a call from the television authority. You are failing to watch your screen and are instead fiddling with a packet of doubtful content." He produced a clipboard and ballpoint pen. "Two red marks, and hithertonow you are summarily ordered to repose yourself in a comfortable, stress-free posture before your screen and give the Leader your unexcelled attention. His words, this evening, are directed particularly to you, sir; to you."

"I doubt that," Chien heard himself say.

Blinking, Kuei said, "What do you mean?"

"The Leader rules eight billion comrades. He isn't going to single me out." He felt wrathful; the punctuality of the warden's reprimand irked him.

Kuei said, "But I distinctly heard with my own ears. You were mentioned."

Going over to the TV set, Chien turned the volume up. "But now he's talking about crop failures in People's India; that's of no relevance to me."

"Whatever the Leader expostulates is relevant." Mou Kuei scratched a mark on his clipboard sheet, bowed formally, turned away. "My call to come up here to confront you with your slackness originated at Central. Obviously they regard your attention as important; I must order you to set in motion your automatic transmission recording circuit and replay the earlier portions of the Leader's speech."

Chien farted. And shut the door.

Back to the TV set, he said to himself. Where our leisure hours are spent. And there lay the two student examination papers; he had that weighing him down, too. And all on my own time, he thought savagely. The hell with them. Up theirs. He strode to the TV set, started to shut it off; at once a red warning light winked on, informing him that he did not have permission to shut off the set—could not in fact end its tirade and image even if he unplugged it. Mandatory speeches, he thought, will kill us all, bury us; if I could be free of the noise of speeches, free of the din of the Party baying as it hounds mankind . . .

There was no known ordinance, however, preventing him from taking snuff while he watched the Leader. So, opening the small gray packet, he shook out a mound of the black granules onto the back of his left hand. He then, professionally, raised his hand to his nostrils and deeply inhaled, drawing the snuff well up into his sinus cavities. Imagine the old superstition, he thought to himself. That the sinus cavities are connected to the brain, and hence an inhalation of snuff directly affects the cerebral cortex. He smiled, seated himself once more, fixed his gaze on the TV screen and the gesticulating individual known so utterly to them all.

The face dwindled away, disappeared. The sound ceased. He faced an emptiness, a vacuum. The screen, white and blank, confronted him and from the speaker a faint hiss sounded.

The frigging snuff, he said to himself. And inhaled greedily at the remainder of the powder on his hand, drawing it up avidly into his nose, his sinuses, and, or so it felt, into his brain; he plunged into the snuff, absorbing it elatedly.

The screen remained blank and then, by degrees, an image once more formed and established itself. It was not the Leader. Not the Absolute Benefactor of the People, in point of fact not a human figure at all.

He faced a dead mechanical construct, made of solid state circuits, of swiveling pseudopodia, lenses and a squawk-box. And the box began, in a droning din, to harangue him.

Staring fixedly, he thought, *What is this?* Reality? Hallucination, he thought. The peddler came across some of the psychedelic drugs used during the War of Liberation—he's selling the stuff and I've taken some, taken a whole lot!

Making his way unsteadily to the vidphone he dialed the Secpol station nearest his building. "I wish to report a pusher of hallucinogenic drugs," he said into the receiver.

"Your name, sir, and conapt location?" Efficient, brisk and impersonal bureaucrat of the police.

He gave them the information, then haltingly made it back to his simulated-leather easy chair, once again to witness the apparition on the TV screen. This is lethal, he said to himself. It must be some preparation developed in Washington, D.C., or London—stronger and stranger than the LSD-25 which they dumped so effectively into our reservoirs. And I thought it was going to relieve me of the burden of the Leader's speeches . . . this is far worse, this electronic, sputtering, swiveling, metal and plastic monstrosity yammering away—this is terrifying.

To have to face *this* the remainder of my life—

It took ten minutes for the Secpol two-man team to come rapping at his door. And by then, in a deteriorating set of stages, the familiar image of the Leader had seeped back into focus on the screen, had supplanted the horrible artificial construct which waved its 'podia and squalled on and on. He let the two cops in shakily, led them to the table on which he had left the remains of the snuff in its packet.

"Psychedelic toxin," he said thickly. "Of short duration. Absorbed into the blood stream directly, through nasal capillaries. I'll give you details as to where I got it, from whom, all that." He took a deep shaky breath; the presence of the police was comforting.

Ballpoint pens ready, the two officers waited. And all the time, in the background, the Leader rattled out his endless speech. As he had done a thousand evenings before in the life of Tung Chien. But, he thought, it'll never be the same again, at least not for me. Not after inhaling that near-toxic snuff.

He wondered, Is that what they intended?

It seemed odd to him, thinking of a *they*. Peculiar—but somehow correct. For an instant he hesitated, not giving out the details, not telling the police enough to find the man. A peddler, he started to say. I don't know where; can't remember. But he did; he remembered the exact street intersection. So, with unexplainable reluctance, he told them.

"Thank you, Comrade Chien." The boss of the team of police carefully gathered up the remaining snuff—most of it remained—and placed it in his uniform—smart, sharp uniform—pocket. "We'll have it analyzed at the first available moment," the cop said, "and inform you immediately in case counter medical measures are indicated for you. Some of the old wartime psychedelics were eventually fatal, as you have no doubt read."

"I've read," he agreed. That had been specifically what he had been thinking.

"Good luck and thanks for notifying us," both cops said, and departed. The affair, for all their efficiency, did not seem to shake them; obviously such a complaint was routine.

The lab report came swiftly—surprisingly so, in view of the vast state bureaucracy. It reached him by vidphone before the Leader had finished his TV speech.

"It's not a hallucinogen," the Secpol lab technician informed him.

"No?" he said, puzzled and, strangely, not relieved. Not at all.

"On the contrary. It's a phenothiazine, which as you doubtless know is anti-hallucinogenic. A strong dose per gram of admixture, but harmless. Might lower your blood pressure or make you sleepy. Probably stolen from a wartime cache of medical supplies. Left by the retreating barbarians. I wouldn't worry."

Pondering, Chien hung up the vidphone in slow motion. And then walked to the window of his conapt—the window with the fine view of other Hanoi high-rise conapts—to think.

The doorbell rang. Feeling as if he were in a trance, he crossed the carpeted living room to answer it.

The girl standing there, in a tan raincoat with a babushka over her dark, shiny, and very long hair, said in a timid little voice, "Um, Comrade Chien? Tung Chien? Of the Ministry of—"

He led her in, reflexively, and shut the door after her. "You've been monitoring my vidphone," he told her; it was a shot in darkness, but something in him, an unvoiced certitude, told him that she had.

"Did—they take the rest of the snuff?" She glanced about. "Oh, I hope not; it's so hard to get these days."

"Snuff," he said, "is easy to get. Phenothiazine isn't. Is that what you mean?"

The girl raised her head, studied him with large, moon-darkened eyes. "Yes. Mr. Chien—" She hesitated, obviously as uncertain as the Secpol cops had been assured. "Tell me what you saw; it's of great importance for us to be certain."

"I had a choice?" he said acutely.

"Y-yes, very much so. That's what confuses us; that's what is not as we planned. We don't understand; it fits nobody's theory." Her eyes even darker and deeper, she said, "Was it the aquatic horror shape? The thing with slime and teeth, the extraterrestrial life form? Please tell me; we have to know." She breathed irregularly, with effort, the tan raincoat rising and falling; he found himself watching its rhythm.

"A machine," he said.

"Oh!" She ducked her head, nodding vigorously. "Yes, I understand; a mechanical organism in no way resembling a human. Not a simulacrum, something constructed to resemble a man."

He said, "This did not look like a man." He added to himself, And it failed—did not try—to talk like a man.

"You understand that it was not a hallucination."

"I've been officially told that what I took was a phenothiazine. That's all I know." He said as little as possible; he did not want to talk but to hear. Hear what the girl had to say.

"Well, Mr. Chien—" She took a deep, unstable breath. "If it was not a hallucination, then what was it? What does that leave? What is called 'extra-consciousness'—could that be it?"

He did not answer; turning his back, he leisurely picked up the two student test papers, glanced over them, ignoring her. Waiting for her next attempt.

At his shoulder she appeared, smelling of spring rain, smelling of sweetness and agitation, beautiful in the way she smelled, and looked, and, he thought, speaks. So different from the harsh plateau speech patterns we hear on the TV—have heard since I was a baby.

"Some of them," she said huskily, "who take the stelazine—it was stelazine you got, Mr. Chien—see one apparition, some another. But distinct categories have emerged; there is not an infinite variety. Some see what you saw; we call it the Clanker. Some the aquatic horror; that's the Gulper. And then there's the Bird, and the Climbing Tube, and—" She broke off. "But other reactions tell you very little. Tell *us* very little." She hesitated, then plunged on. "Now that this has happened to you, Mr. Chien, we would like you to join our gathering. Join your particular group, those who see what you see. Group Red. We want to know what it *really* is, and—" She gestured with tapered, wax-smooth fingers. "It can't be *all* those manifestations." Her tone was poignant, naïvely so. He felt his caution relax—a trifle.

He said, "What do you see? You in particular?"

"I'm a part of Group Yellow. I see—a storm. A whining, vicious whirlwind. That roots everything up, crushes condominium apartments built to last a century." She smiled wanly. "The Crusher. Twelve groups in all, Mr. Chien. Twelve absolutely different experiences, all from the same phenothiazines, all of the Leader as he speaks over TV. As *it* speaks, rather." She smiled up at him, lashes long—probably protracted artificially—and gaze engaging, even trusting. As if she thought he knew something or could do something.

"I should make a citizen's arrest of you," he said presently.

"There is no law, not about this. We studied Soviet juridical writings before we—found people to distribute the stelazine. We don't have much of it; we have to be very careful whom we give it to. It seemed to us that you constituted a likely choice . . . a well-known, postwar, dedicated young career man on his way up." From his fingers she took the examination papers. "They're having you pol-read?" she asked.

" 'Pol-read'?" He did not know the term.

"Study something said or written to see if it fits the Party's current world view. You in the hierarchy merely call it 'read,' don't you?" Again she smiled. "When you rise one step higher, up with Mr. Tso-pin, you will know that expression." She added somberly, "And with Mr. Pethel. He's very far up. Mr. Chien, there is no ideological school in San Fernando; these are forged exam papers, designed to read back to them a thorough analysis of *your* political ideology. And have you been able to distinguish which paper is orthodox and which is heretical?" Her voice was pixie-like, taunting with amused malice. "Choose the wrong one and your budding career stops dead, cold, in its tracks. Choose the proper one—"

"Do you know which is which?" he demanded.

"Yes." She nodded soberly. "We have listening devices in Mr. Tsopin's inner offices; we monitored his conversation with Mr. Pethel— who is not Mr. Pethel but the Higher Secpol Inspector Judd Craine. You have possibly heard mention of him; he acted as chief assistant to Judge Vorlawsky at the '98 war crimes trial in Zurich."

With difficulty he said, "I—see." Well, that explained that.

The girl said, "My name is Tanya Lee."

He said nothing; he merely nodded, too stunned for any cerebration.

"Technically, I am a minor clerk," Miss Lee said, "at your Ministry. You have never run into me, however, that I can at least recall. We try to hold posts wherever we can. As far up as possible. My own boss—"

"Should you be telling me this?" He gestured at the TV set, which remained on. "Aren't they picking this up?"

Tanya Lee said, "We introduced a noise factor in the reception of both vid and aud material from this apartment building; it will take them almost an hour to locate the sheathing. So we have"—she examined the tiny wristwatch on her slender wrist—"fifteen more minutes. And still be safe."

"Tell me," he said, "which paper is orthodox."

"Is that what you care about? Really?"

"What," he said, "should I care about?"

"Don't you see, Mr. Chien? You've learned something. The Leader is not the Leader; he is something else, but we can't tell what. Not yet. Mr. Chien, with all due respect, have you ever had your drinking water analyzed? I know it sounds paranoiac, but have you?"

"No," he said. "Of course not." Knowing what she was going to say.

Miss Lee said briskly, "Our tests show that it's saturated with hallucinogens. It is, has been, will continue to be. Not the ones used during the war; not the disorienting ones, but a synthetic quasi-ergot derivative called Datrox-3. You drink it here in the building from the time you get up; you drink it in restaurants and other apartments that you visit.

You drink it at the Ministry; it's all piped from a central, common source." Her tone was bleak and ferocious. "We solved that problem; we knew, as soon as we discovered it, that any good phenothiazine would counter it. What we did not know, of course, was this—a *variety* of authentic experiences; that makes no sense, rationally. It's the hallucination which should differ from person to person, and the reality experience which should be ubiquitous—it's all turned around. We can't even construct an ad hoc theory which accounts for that, and god knows we've tried. Twelve mutually exclusive hallucinations—that would be easily understood. But not one hallucination and twelve realities." She ceased talking, then, and studied the two test papers, her forehead wrinkling. "The one with the Arabic poem is orthodox," she stated. "If you tell them that they'll trust you and give you a higher post. You'll be another notch up in the hierarchy of Party officialdom." Smiling—her teeth were perfect and lovely—she finished, "Look what you received back for your investment this morning. Your career is underwritten for a time. And by us."

He said, "I don't believe you." Instinctively, his caution operated within him, always, the caution of a lifetime lived among the hatchet men of the Hanoi branch of the CP East. They knew an infinitude of ways by which to ax a rival out of contention—some of which he himself had employed; some of which he had seen done to himself and to others. This could be a novel way, one unfamiliar to him. It could always be.

"Tonight," Miss Lee said, "in the speech the Leader singled you out. Didn't this strike you as strange? You, of all people? A minor officeholder in a meager ministry—"

"Admitted," he said. "It struck me that way; yes."

"That was legitimate. His Greatness is grooming an elite cadre of younger men, postwar men, he hopes will infuse new life into the hidebound, moribund hierarchy of old fogies and Party hacks. His Greatness singled you out for the same reason that we singled you out; if pursued properly, your career could lead you all the way to the top. At least for a time . . . as we know. That's how it goes."

He thought, So virtually everyone has faith in me. Except myself; and certainly not after this, the experience with the anti-hallucinatory snuff. It had shaken years of confidence, and no doubt rightly so. However, he was beginning to regain his poise; he felt it seeping back, a little at first, then with a rush.

Going to the vidphone, he lifted the receiver and began, for the second time that night, to dial the number of the Hanoi Security Police.

"Turning me in," Miss Lee said, "would be the second most regressive decision you could make. I'll tell them that you brought me here to bribe me; you thought, because of my job at the Ministry, I would know which examination paper to select."

He said, "And what would be my first most regressive decision?"

"Not taking a further dose of phenothiazine," Miss Lee said evenly.

Hanging up the phone, Tung Chien thought to himself, I don't understand what's happening to me. Two forces, the Party and His Greatness on one hand—this girl with her alleged group on the other. One wants me to rise as far as possible in the Party hierarchy; the other—*What did Tanya Lee want?* Underneath the words, inside the membrane of an almost trivial contempt for the Party, the Leader, the ethical standards of the People's Democratic United Front—what was she after in regard to him?

He said curiously, "Are you anti-Party?"

"No."

"But—" He gestured. "That's all there is; Party and anti-Party. You must be Party, then." Bewildered, he stared at her; with composure she returned the stare. "You have an organization," he said, "and you meet. What do you intend to destroy? The regular function of government? Are you like the treasonable college students of the United States during the Vietnam War who stopped troop trains, demonstrated—"

Wearily Miss Lee said, "It wasn't like that. But forget it; that's not the issue. What we want to know is this: who or what is leading us? We must penetrate far enough to enlist someone, some rising young Party theoretician, who could conceivably be invited to a tête-à-tête with the Leader—you see?" Her voice lifted; she consulted her watch, obviously anxious to get away: the fifteen minutes were almost up. "Very few persons actually see the Leader, as you know. I mean really see him."

"Seclusion," he said. "Due to his advanced age."

"We have hope," Miss Lee said, "that if you pass the phony test which they have arranged for you—and with my help you have—you will be invited to one of the stag parties which the Leader has from time to time, which of course the 'papes don't report. Now do you see?" Her voice rose shrilly, in a frenzy of despair. "Then we would know; if you could go in there under the influence of the anti-hallucinogenic drug, could see him face to face as he actually is—"

Thinking aloud, he said, "And end my career of public service. If not my life."

"You owe us something," Tanya Lee snapped, her cheeks white. "If I hadn't told you which exam paper to choose you would have picked the wrong one and your dedicated public service career would be over anyhow; you would have failed—failed at a test you didn't even realize you were taking!"

He said mildly, "I had a fifty-fifty chance."

"No." She shook her head fiercely. "The heretical one is faked up with a lot of Party jargon; they deliberately constructed the two texts to trap you. They *wanted* you to fail!"

Once more he examined the two papers, feeling confused. Was she right? Possibly. Probably. It rang true, knowing the Party functionaries as he did, and Tso-pin, his superior, in particular. He felt weary then. Defeated. After a time he said to the girl, "What you're trying to get out of me is a quid pro quo. You did something for me—you got, or claim you got—the answer to this Party inquiry. But you've already done your part. What's to keep me from tossing you out of here on your head? I don't have to do a goddam thing." He heard his voice, toneless, sounding the poverty of empathic emotionality so usual in Party circles.

Miss Lee said, "There will be other tests, as you continue to ascend. And we will monitor for you with them too." She was calm, at ease; obviously she had forseen his reaction.

"How long do I have to think it over?" he said.

"I'm leaving now. We're in no rush; you're not about to receive an invitation to the Leader's Yellow River villa in the next week or even month." Going to the door, opening it, she paused. "As you're given covert rating tests we'll be in contact, supplying the answers—so you'll see one or more of us on those occasions. Probably it won't be me; it'll be that disabled war veteran who'll sell you the correct response sheets as you leave the Ministry building." She smiled a brief, snuffed-out-candle smile. "But one of these days, no doubt unexpectedly, you'll get an ornate, official, very formal invitation to the villa, and when you go you'll be heavily sedated with stelazine . . . possibly our last dose of our dwindling supply. Good night." The door shut after her; she had gone.

My god, he thought. They can blackmail me. For what I've done. And she didn't even bother to mention it; in view of what they're involved with it was not worth mentioning.

But blackmail for what? He had already told the Secpol squad that he had been given a drug which had proved to be a phenothiazine. *Then they know,* he realized. They'll watch me; they're alert. Technically I haven't broken a law, but—they'll be watching, all right.

However, they always watched anyhow. He relaxed slightly, thinking that. He had, over the years, become virtually accustomed to it, as had everyone.

I will see the Absolute Benfactor of the People as he is, he said to himself. Which possibly no one else has done. What will it be? Which of the subclasses of non-hallucination? Classes which I do not even know about . . . a view which may totally overthrow me. How am I going to be able to get through the evening, to keep my poise, if it's like the shape I saw on the TV screen? The Crusher, the Clanker, the Bird, the Climbing Tube, the Gulper—or worse.

He wondered what some of the other views consisted of . . . and then gave up that line of speculation; it was unprofitable. And too anxiety-inducing.

The next morning Mr. Tso-pin and Mr. Darius Pethel met him in his office, both of them calm but expectant. Wordlessly, he handed them one of the two "exam papers." The orthodox one, with its short and heart-smothering Arabian poem.

"This one," Chien said tightly, "is the product of a dedicated Party member or candidate for membership. The other—" He slapped the remaining sheets. "Reactionary garbage." He felt anger. "In spite of a superficial—"

"All right, Mr. Chien," Pethel said, nodding. "We don't have to explore each and every ramification; your analysis is correct. You heard the mention regarding you in the Leader's speech last night on TV?"

"I certainly did," Chien said.

"So you have undoubtedly inferred," Pethel said, "that there is a good deal involved in what we are attempting, here. The Leader has his eye on you; that's clear. As a matter of fact, he has communicated to myself regarding you." He opened his bulging briefcase and rummaged. "Lost the goddam thing. Anyhow—" He glanced at Tso-pin, who nodded slightly. "His Greatness would like to have you appear for dinner at the Yangtze River Ranch next Thursday night. Mrs. Fletcher in particular appreciates—"

Chien said, " 'Mrs. Fletcher'? Who is 'Mrs. Fletcher'?"

After a pause Tso-pin said dryly, "The Absolute Benefactor's wife. His name—which you of course had never heard—is Thomas Fletcher."

"He's a Caucasian," Pethel explained. "Originally from the New Zealand Communist Party; he participated in the difficult take-over there. This news is not in the strict sense secret, but on the other hand it hasn't been noised about." He hesitated, toying with his watchchain. "Probably it would be better if you forgot about that. Of course, as soon as you meet him, see him face to face, you'll realize that, realize that he's a Cauc. As I am. As many of us are."

"Race," Tso-pin pointed out, "has nothing to do with loyalty to the Leader and the Party. As witness Mr. Pethel, here."

But His Greatness, Chien thought, jolted. He did not appear, on the TV screen, to be occidental. "On TV—" he began.

"The image," Tso-pin interrupted, "is subjected to a variegated assortment of skillful refinements. For ideological purposes. Most persons holding higher offices are aware of this." He eyed Chien with hard criticism.

So everyone agrees, Chien thought. What we see every night is not real. The question is, How unreal? Partially? Or—completely?

"I will be prepared," he said tautly. And he thought, There has been a slip-up. They weren't prepared for me—the people that Tanya Lee represents—to gain entry so soon. Where's the anti-hallucinogen? Can they get it to me or not? Probably not on such short notice.

He felt, strangely, relief. He would be going into the presence of His Greatness in a position to see him as a human being, see him as he —and everybody else—saw him on TV. It would be a most stimulating and cheerful dinner party, with some of the most influential Party members in Asia. I think we can do without the phenothiazines, he said to himself. And his sense of relief grew.

"Here it is, finally," Pethel said suddenly, producing a white envelope from his briefcase. "Your card of admission. You will be flown by Sino-rocket to the Leader's villa Thursday morning; there the protocol officer will brief you on your expected behavior. It will be formal dress, white tie and tails, but the atmosphere will be cordial. There are always a great number of toasts." He added, "I have attended two such stag gets-together. Mr. Tso-pin"—he smiled creakily —"has not been honored in such a fashion. But as they say, all things come to him who waits. Ben Franklin said that."

Tso-pin said, "It has come for Mr. Chien rather prematurely, I would say." He shrugged philosophically. "But my opinion has never at any time been asked."

"One thing," Pethel said to Chien. "It is possible that when you see His Greatness in person you will be in some regards disappointed. Be alert that you do not let this make itself apparent, if you should so feel. We have, always, tended—been trained—to regard him as more than a man. But at table he is"—he gestured—"a forked radish. In certain respects like ourselves. He may for instance indulge in moderately human oral-aggressive and -passive activity; he possibly may tell an off-color joke or drink too much. . . . To be candid, no one ever knows in advance how these things will work out, but they do generally hold forth until late the following morning. So it would be wise to accept the dosage of amphetamines which the protocol officer will offer you."

"Oh?" Chien said. This was news to him, and interesting.

"For stamina. And to balance the liquor. His Greatness has amazing staying power; he often is still on his feet and raring to go after everyone else has collapsed."

"A remarkable man," Tso-pin chimed in. "I think his—indulgences only show that he is a fine fellow. And fully in the round; he is like the ideal Renaissance man; as, for example, Lorenzo de' Medici."

"That does come to mind," Pethel said; he studied Chien with such intensity that some of last night's chill returned. Am I being led into one trap after another? Chien wondered. That girl—was she in fact an agent of the Secpol probing me, trying to ferret out a disloyal, anti-Party streak in me?

I think, he decided, I will make sure that the legless peddler of herbal remedies does not snare me when I leave work; I'll take a totally different route back to my conapt.

He was successful. That day he avoided the peddler and the same the next, and so on until Thursday.

On Thursday morning the peddler scooted from beneath a parked truck and blocked his way, confronting him.

"My medication?" the peddler demanded. "It helped? I know it did; the formula goes back to the Sung Dynasty—I can tell it did. Right?"

Chien said, "Let me go."

"Would you be kind enough to answer?" The tone was not the expected, customary whining of a street peddler operating in a marginal fashion, and that tone came across to Chien; he heard loud and clear . . . as the Imperialist puppet troops of long ago phrased it.

"I know what you gave me," Chien said. "And I don't want any more. If I change my mind I can pick it up at a pharmacy. Thanks." He started on, but the cart, with the legless occupant, pursued him.

"Miss Lee was talking to me," the peddler said loudly.

"Hmm," Chien said, and automatically increased his pace; he spotted a hovercab and began signaling for it.

"It's tonight you're going to the stag dinner at the Yangtze River villa," the peddler said, panting for breath in his effort to keep up. "Take the medication—now!" He held out a flat packet, imploringly. "Please, Party Member Chien; for your own sake, for all of us. So we can tell what it is we're up against. Good lord, it may be non-terran; that's our most basic fear. Don't you understand, Chien? What's your goddam career compared with that? If we can't find out—"

The cab bumped to a halt on the pavement; its door slid open. Chien started to board it.

The packet sailed past him, landed on the entrance sill of the cab, then slid into the gutter, damp from earlier rain.

"Please," the peddler said. "And it won't cost you anything; today it's free. Just take it, use it before the stag dinner. And don't use the amphetamines; they're a thalamic stimulant, contra-indicated whenever an adrenal suppressant such as a phenothiazine is—"

The door of the cab closed after Chien. He seated himself.

"Where to, comrade?" the robot drive-mechanism inquired.

He gave the ident tag number of his conapt.

"That half-wit of a peddler managed to infiltrate his seedy wares into my clean interior," the cab said. "Notice; it reposes by your foot."

He saw the packet—no more than an ordinary-looking envelope. I guess, he thought, this is how drugs come to you; all of a sudden they're lying there. For a moment he sat, and then he picked it up.

As before, there was a written enclosure above and beyond the medication, but this time, he saw, it was handwritten. A feminine script: from Miss Lee:

We were surprised at the suddenness. But thank heaven we were ready. Where were you Tuesday and Wednesday? Anyhow, here it is, and good luck. I will approach you later in the week; I don't want you to try to find me.

He ignited the note, burned it up in the cab's disposal ashtray.

And kept the dark granules.

All this time, he thought. Hallucinogens in our water supply. Year after year. Decades. And not in wartime but in peacetime. And not to the enemy camp but here in our own. The evil bastards, he said to himself. Maybe I ought to take this; maybe I ought to find out what he or it is and let Tanya's group know.

I will, he decided. And—he was curious.

A bad emotion, he knew. Curiosity was, especially in Party activities, often a terminal state careerwise.

A state which, at the moment, gripped him thoroughly. He wondered if it would last through the evening, if, when it came right down to it, he would actually take the inhalant.

Time would tell. Tell that and everything else. We are blooming flowers, he thought, on the plain, which he picks. As the Arabic poem had put it. He tried to remember the rest of the poem but could not.

That probably was just as well.

The villa protocol officer, a Japanese named Kimo Okubara, tall and husky, obviously a quondam wrestler, surveyed him with innate hostility, even after he presented his engraved invitation and had successfully managed to prove his identity.

"Surprise you bother to come," Okubara muttered. "Why not stay home and watch on TV? Nobody miss you. We got along fine without up to right now."

Chien said tightly, "I've already watched on TV." And anyhow the stag dinners were rarely televised; they were too bawdy.

Okubara's crew double-checked him for weapons, including the possibility of an anal suppository, and then gave him his clothes back. They did not find the phenothiazine, however. Because he had already taken it. The effects of such a drug, he knew, lasted approximately four hours; that would be more than enough. And, as Tanya had said, it was a major dose; he felt sluggish and inept and dizzy, and his tongue moved in spasms of pseudo Parkinsonism—an unpleasant side effect which he had failed to anticipate.

A girl, nude from the waist up, with long coppery hair down her shoulders and back, walked by. Interesting.

Coming the other way, a girl nude from the bottom up made her appearance. Interesting, too. Both girls looked vacant and bored, and totally self-possessed.

"You go in like that too," Okubara informed Chien.

Startled, Chien said, "I understood white tie and tails."

"Joke," Okubara said. "At your expense. Only girls wear nude; you even get so you enjoy, unless you homosexual."

Well, Chien thought, I guess I had better like it. He wandered on with the other guests—they, like him, wore white tie and tails or, if women, floor-length gowns—and felt ill at ease, despite the tranquilizing effect of the stelazine. Why am I here? he asked himself. The ambiguity of his situation did not escape him. He was here to advance his career in the Party apparatus, to obtain the intimate and personal nod of approval from His Greatness . . . and in addition he was here to decipher His Greatness as a fraud; he did not know what variety of fraud, but there it was: fraud against the Party, against all the peace-loving democratic peoples of Terra. Ironic, he thought. And continued to mingle.

A girl with small, bright, illuminated breasts approached him for a match; he absent-mindedly got out his lighter. "What makes your breasts glow?" he asked her. "Radioactive injections?"

She shrugged, said nothing, passed on, leaving him alone. Evidently he had responded in the incorrect way.

Maybe it's a wartime mutation, he pondered.

"Drink, sir." A servant graciously held out a tray; he accepted a martini—which was the current fad among the higher Party classes in People's China—and sipped the ice-cold dry flavor. Good English gin, he said to himself. Or possibly the original Holland compound; juniper or whatever they added. Not bad. He strolled on, feeling better; in actuality he found the atmosphere here a pleasant one. The people here were self-assured; they had been successful and now they could relax. It evidently was a myth that proximity to His Greatness produced neurotic anxiety: he saw no evidence here, at least, and felt little himself.

A heavy-set elderly man, bald, halted him by the simple means of holding his drink glass against Chien's chest. "That frably little one who asked you for a match," the elderly man said, and sniggered. "The quig with the Christmas-tree breasts—that was a boy, in drag." He giggled. "You have to be cautious around here."

"Where, if anywhere," Chien said, "do I find authentic women? In the white ties and tails?"

"Darn near," the elderly man said, and departed with a throng of hyperactive guests, leaving Chien alone with his martini.

A handsome, tall woman, well dressed, standing near Chien, suddenly put her hand on his arm; he felt her fingers tense and she said, "Here he comes. His Greatness. This is the first time for me; I'm a little scared. Does my hair look all right?"

"Fine," Chien said reflexively, and followed her gaze, seeking a glimpse—his first—of the Absolute Benefactor.

What crossed the room toward the table in the center was not a man.

And it was not, Chien realized, a mechanical construct either; it was not what he had seen on TV. That evidently was simply a device for speechmaking, as Mussolini had once used an artificial arm to salute long and tedious processions.

God, he thought, and felt ill. Was this what Tanya Lee had called the "aquatic horror" shape? It had no shape. Nor pseudopodia, either flesh or metal. It was, in a sense, not there at all; when he managed to look directly at it, the shape vanished; he saw through it, saw the people on the far side—but not it. Yet if he turned his head, caught it out of a sidelong glance, he could determine its boundaries.

It was terrible; it blasted him with its awfulness. As it moved it drained the life from each person in turn; it ate the people who had assembled, passed on, ate again, ate more with an endless appetite. It hated; he felt its hate. It loathed; he felt its loathing for everyone present—in fact he shared its loathing. All at once he and everyone else in the big villa were each a twisted slug, and over the fallen slug-carcasses the creature savored, lingered, but all the time coming directly toward him—or was that an illusion? If this is a hallucination, Chien thought, it is the worst I have ever had; if it is not, then it is evil reality; it's an evil thing that kills and injures. He saw the trail of stepped-on, mashed men and women remnants behind it; he saw them trying to reassemble, to operate their crippled bodies; he heard them attempting speech.

I know who you are, Tung Chien thought to himself. You, the supreme head of the world-wide Party structure. You, who destroy whatever living object you touch; I see that Arabic poem, the searching for the flowers of life to eat them—I see you astride the plain which to you is Earth, plain without hills, without valleys. You go anywhere, appear any time, devour anything; you engineer life and then guzzle it, and you enjoy that.

He thought, You are God.

"Mr. Chien," the voice said, but it came from inside his head, not from the mouthless spirit that fashioned itself directly before him. "It is good to meet you again. You know nothing. Go away. I have no interest in you. Why should I care about slime? Slime; I am mired in it, I must excrete it, and I choose to. I could break you; I can break even myself. Sharp stones are under me; I spread sharp pointed things upon the mire. I make the hiding places, the deep places, boil like a pot; to me the sea is like a pot of ointment. The flakes of my flesh are joined to everything. You are me. I am you. It makes no difference, just as it makes no difference whether the creature with ignited breasts is a girl or boy; you could learn to enjoy either." It laughed.

He could not believe it was speaking to him; he could not imagine —it was too terrible—that it had picked him out.

"I have picked everybody out," it said. "No one is too small; each falls and dies and I am there to watch. I don't need to do anything but watch; it is automatic; it was arranged that way." And then it ceased talking to him; it disjoined itself. But he still saw it; he felt its manifold presence. It was a globe which hung in the room, with fifty thousand eyes, with a million eyes—billions: an eye for each living thing as it waited for each thing to fall, and then stepped on the living thing as it lay in a broken state. Because of this it had created the things, and he knew; he understood. What had seemed in the Arabic poem to be death was not death but god; or rather God was death, it was one force, one hunter, one cannibal thing, and it missed again and again but, having all eternity, it could afford to miss. Both poems, he realized; the Dryden one too. The crumbling; that is our world and you are doing it. Warping it to come out that way; bending us.

But at least, he thought, I still have my dignity. With dignity he set down his drink glass, turned, walked toward the doors of the room. He passed through the doors. He walked down a long carpeted hall. A villa servant dressed in purple opened a door for him; he found himself standing out in the night darkness, on a veranda, alone.

Not alone.

It had followed after him. Or it had already been here before him; yes, it had been expecting. It was not really through with him.

"Here I go," he said, and made a dive for the railing; it was six stories down, and there below gleamed the river, and death, real death, not what the Arabic poem had seen.

As he tumbled over, it put an extension of itself on his shoulder. "Why?" he said. But, in fact, he paused. Wondering. Not understanding, not at all.

"Don't fall on my account," it said. He could not see it because it had moved behind him. But the piece of it on his shoulder—it had begun to look to him like a human hand.

And then it laughed.

"What's funny?" he demanded, as he teetered on the railing, held back by its pseudo-hand.

"You're doing my task for me," it said. "You aren't waiting; don't you have time to wait? I'll select you out from among the others; you don't need to speed the process up."

"What if I do?" he said. "Out of revulsion for you?"

It laughed. And didn't answer.

"You won't even say," he said.

Again no answer. He started to slide back, onto the veranda. And at once the pressure of its pseudo-hand lifted.

"You founded the Party?" he asked.

"I founded everything. I founded the anti-Party and the Party that isn't a Party, and those who are for it and those who are against, those that you call Yankee Imperialists, those in the camp of reaction, and so on endlessly. I founded it all. As if they were blades of grass."

"And you're here to enjoy it?" he said.

"What I want," it said, "is for you to see me, as I am, as you have seen me, and then trust me."

"What?" he said, quavering. "Trust you to what?"

It said, "Do you believe in me?"

"Yes," he said. "I can see you."

"Then go back to your job at the Ministry. Tell Tanya Lee that you saw an overworked, overweight, elderly man who drinks too much and likes to pinch girls' rear ends."

"Oh, Christ," he said.

"As you live on, unable to stop, I will torment you," it said. "I will deprive you, item by item, of everything you possess or want. And then when you are crushed to death I will unfold a mystery."

"What's the mystery?"

"The dead shall live, the living die. I kill what lives; I save what has died. And I will tell you this: *there are things worse than I.* But you won't meet them because by then I will have killed you. Now walk back into the dining room and prepare for dinner. Don't question what I'm doing; I did it long before there was a Tung Chien and I will do it long after."

He hit it as hard as he could.

And experienced violent pain in his head.

And darkness, with the sense of falling.

After that, darkness again. He thought, I will get you. I will see that you die too. That you suffer; you're going to suffer, just like us, exactly in every way we do. I'll dedicate my life to that; I'll confront you again, and I'll nail you; I swear to god I'll nail you up somewhere. And it will hurt. As much as I hurt now.

He shut his eyes.

Roughly, he was shaken. And heard Mr. Kimo Okubara's voice. "Get to your feet, common drunk. Come on!"

Without opening his eyes he said, "Get me a cab."

"Cab already waiting. You go home. Disgrace. Make a violent scene out of yourself."

Getting shakily to his feet, he opened his eyes, examined himself. Our Leader whom we follow, he thought, is the One True God. And the enemy whom we fight and have fought is God too. They are right; he is everywhere. But I didn't understand what that meant. Staring at the protocol officer, he thought, You are God too. So there is no getting away, probably not even by jumping. As I started, instinctively, to do. He shuddered.

"Mix drinks with drugs," Okubara said witheringly. "Ruin career. I see it happen many times. Get lost."

Unsteadily, he walked toward the great central door of the Yangtze River villa; two servants, dressed like medieval knights, with crested plumes, ceremoniously opened the door for him and one of them said, "Good night, sir."

"Up yours," Chien said, and passed out into the night.

At a quarter to three in the morning, as he sat sleepless in the living room of his conapt, smoking one Cuesta Rey Astoria after another, a knock sounded at the door.

When he opened it he found himself facing Tanya Lee in her trenchcoat, her face pinched with cold. Her eyes blazed, questioningly.

"Don't look at me like that," he said roughly. His cigar had gone out; he relit it. "I've been looked at enough," he said.

"You saw it," she said.

He nodded.

She seated herself on the arm of the couch and after a time she said, "Want to tell me about it?"

"Go as far from here as possible," he said. "Go a long way." And then he remembered; no way was long enough. He remembered reading that too. "Forget it," he said; rising to his feet, he walked clumsily into the kitchen to start up the coffee.

Following after him, Tanya said, "Was—it that bad?"

"We can't win," he said. "You can't win; I don't mean me. I'm not in this; I just want to do my job at the Ministry and forget about it. Forget the whole damned thing."

"Is it non-terrestrial?"

"Yes." He nodded.

"Is it hostile to us?"

"Yes," he said. "No. Both. Mostly hostile."

"Then we have to—"

"Go home," he said, "and go to bed." He looked her over carefully; he had sat a long time and he had done a great deal of thinking. About a lot of things. "Are you married?" he said.

"No. Not now. I used to be."

He said, "Stay with me tonight. The rest of tonight, anyhow. Until the sun comes up." He added, "The night part is awful."

"I'll stay," Tanya said, unbuckling the belt of her raincoat, "but I have to have some answers."

"What did Dryden mean," Chien said, "about music untuning the sky? I don't get that. What does music do to the sky?"

"All the celestial order of the universe ends," she said as she hung her raincoat up in the closet of the bedroom; under it she wore an orange striped sweater and stretchpants.

He said, "And that's bad."

Pausing, she reflected. "I don't know. I guess so."

"It's a lot of power," he said, "to assign to music."

"Well, you know that old Pythagorean business about the 'music of the spheres.'" Matter-of-factly she seated herself on the bed and removed her slipperlike shoes.

"Do you believe in that?" he said. "Or do you believe in God?"

"'God'!" She laughed. "That went out with the donkey steam engine. What are you talking about? God, or god?" She came over close beside him, peering into his face.

"Don't look at me so closely," he said sharply, drawing back. "I don't ever want to be looked at again." He moved away, irritably.

"I think," Tanya said, "that if there is a God He has very little interest in human affairs. That's my theory, anyhow. I mean, He doesn't seem to care if evil triumphs or people and animals get hurt and die. I frankly don't see Him anywhere around. And the Party has always denied any form of—"

"Did you ever see Him?" he asked. "When you were a child?"

"Oh, sure, as a child. But I also believed—"

"Did it ever occur to you," Chien said, "that good and evil are names for the same thing? That God could be both good and evil at the same time?"

"I'll fix you a drink," Tanya said, and padded barefoot into the kitchen.

Chien said, "The Crusher. The Clanker. The Gulper and the Bird and the Climbing Tube—plus other names, forms, I don't know. I had a hallucination. At the stag dinner. A big one. A terrible one."

"But the stelazine—"

"It brought on a worse one," he said.

"Is there any way," Tanya said somberly, "that we can fight this thing you saw? This apparition you call a hallucination but which very obviously was not?"

He said, "Believe in it."

"What will that do?"

"Nothing," he said wearily. "Nothing at all. I'm tired; I don't want a drink—let's just go to bed."

"Okay." She padded back into the bedroom, began pulling her striped sweater over her head. "We'll discuss it more thoroughly later."

"A hallucination," Chien said, "is merciful. I wish I had it; I want mine back. I want to be before your peddler got to me with that phenothiazine."

"Just come to bed. It'll be toasty. All warm and nice."

He removed his tie, his shirt—and saw, on his right shoulder, the mark, the stigma, which it had left when it stopped him from jumping. Livid marks which looked as if they would never go away. He put his pajama top on, then; it hid the marks.

"Anyhow," Tanya said as he got into the bed beside her, "your career is immeasurably advanced. Aren't you glad about that?"

"Sure," he said, nodding sightlessly in the darkness. "Very glad."

"Come over against me," Tanya said, putting her arms around him. "And forget everything else. At least for now."

He tugged her against him, then, doing what she asked and what he wanted to do. She was neat; she was swiftly active; she was successful and she did her part. They did not bother to speak until at last she said, "Oh!" And then she relaxed.

"I wish," he said, "that we could go on forever."

"We did," Tanya said. "It's outside of time; it's boundless, like an ocean. It's the way we were in Cambrian times, before we migrated up onto the land; it's the ancient primary waters. This is the only time we get to go back, when this is done. That's why it means so much. And in those days we weren't separate; it was like a big jelly, like those blobs that float up on the beach."

"Float up," he said, "and are left there to die."

"Could you get me a towel?" Tanya asked. "Or a washcloth? I need it."

He padded into the bathroom for a towel. There—he was naked, now—he once more saw his shoulder, saw where it had seized hold of him and held on, dragged him back, possibly to toy with him a little more.

The marks, unaccountably, were bleeding.

He sponged the blood away. More oozed forth at once and, seeing that, he wondered how much time he had left. Probably only hours.

Returning to bed, he said, "Could you continue?"

"Sure. If you have any energy left; it's up to you." She lay gazing up at him unwinkingly, barely visible in the dim nocturnal light.

"I have," he said. And hugged her to him.


**Afterword:**

I don't advocate any of the ideas in "Faith of Our Fathers"; I don't, for example, claim that the Iron Curtain countries will win the cold war— or morally ought to. One theme in the story, however, seems compelling to me, in view of recent experiments with hallucinogenic drugs: the theological experience, which so many who have taken LSD have reported. This appears to me to be a true new frontier; to a certain extent the religious experience can now be scientifically studied . . . and, what is more, may be viewed as part hallucination but containing other, real components. God, as a topic in science fiction, when it appeared at all, used to be treated polemically, as in "Out of the Silent Planet." But I prefer to treat it as intellectually exciting. What if, through psychedelic drugs, the religious experience becomes commonplace in the life of intellectuals? The old atheism, which seemed to many of us—including me—valid in terms of our experiences, or rather lack of experiences, would have to step momentarily aside. Science fiction, always probing what is about to be thought, become, must eventually tackle without pre-conceptions a future neo-mystical society in which theology constitutes as major a force as in the medieval period. This is not necessarily a backward step, because now these beliefs can be tested—forced to put up or shut up. I, myself, have no real beliefs about God; only my experience that He is present . . . subjectively, of course; but the inner realm is real too. And in a science fiction story one projects what has been a personal inner experience into a milieu; it becomes socially shared, hence discussable. The last word, however, on the subject of God may have already been said: in A.D. 840 by John Scotus Erigena at the court of the Frankish king Charles the Bald. "We do not know what God is. God Himself does not know what He is because He is not anything. Literally God *is not,* because He transcends being." Such a penetrating—and Zen—mystical view, arrived at so long ago, will be hard to top; in my own experiences with psychedelic drugs I have had precious tiny illumination compared with Erigena.

## Introduction to THE JIGSAW MAN:

It is generally agreed that, of the newer, younger writers in the speculative writing arena, one of the most promising challengers is Larry Niven. He has been writing for two years and has already found his own style, his own voice. He writes what is called "hard" science fiction—i.e., his scientific extrapolation is based solidly in what is known at the date of his writing; in a Niven story you will find no beer cans on Mars and no hidden planet circling around the other side of Sol on the same orbit as Earth. To the casual consideration, it might seem that this would limit the horizons of Niven's work. For a lesser imagination that might be true. But Larry Niven deals in minutiae; and in the tinier facts—very often overlooked by writers who mistakenly suppose exciting speculative fiction can only be built around huge, obvious subjects—he finds fascinating areas for development of very personal, very unconventional stories.

He has worked so hard, and so well, in these past two years, that his fifth published story, "Becalmed in Hell," was a runner-up in the short-story category of the 1965 Nebula Awards presented by the Science Fiction Writers of America. He has already been anthologized in a handful of "best" collections. And the end is nowhere in sight. He is, in point of fact, a formidable Great White Hope of this genre.

Larry is a millionaire. No, really. A genuine, authentic moneyed-type millionaire. It is a comment on his dedication to the science fiction he loves that he chooses to live solely off the money he makes writing. There aren't many of us hungry, pale, struggling hacks who can say the same.

Larry Niven was born in Los Angeles, scion of the Doheny family, and grew up in Beverly Hills. As a math major going for a BA at Cal-Tech, he flunked out after five terms—one and two thirds years. Eventually completed BA in math at Washburn University, Topeka, Kansas, after slowing the process by taking a lot of philosophy and English courses and a minor in psychology. UCLA for his graduate MA in math, and after one year he suddenly turned around and said to the world (which was not, at that point, particularly attentive), "I've decided I'd rather write science fiction. It is June 1963 and now I begin." He sold his first story, "The Coldest Place," exactly one year later, to Fred Pohl, editor of *Worlds of If*. Of this sale, Larry comments: "The story was made totally obsolete by Russian astronomical discoveries concerning Mercury, circa August 1964. I had already cashed the check. Fred Pohl was stuck with the damned thing. He published it in December 1964. My family, which had given me enough static to jam all of Earth's transmissions for the next century, when I informed them I was going to be a writer ('Get an *honest* job!'), stopped bugging me immediately. Now I get to sleep late, which is what being a writer is all about, anyhow."

Interesting sidelight on Niven *et famille*. Having two sets of parents after a 1953 divorce, he must supply each with a Larry Niven Five-Foot Shelf of s-f, so they can brag about him when he's within earshot. His brother and sister-in-law gave him a scrapbook for his birthday in 1965, so he is required to buy a third copy of everything to tear up for that, and a fourth set to keep for his files. Thus, he loses money every time he sells a story.

He is the author of an excellent Ballantine novel, *World of Ptavvs*, and the author of the story that follows, an incisive and frighteningly logical comment on future penology, based solidly in today, God forbid.

# ● THE JIGSAW MAN

## by Larry Niven

In A.D. 1900 Karl Landsteiner classified human blood into four types: A, B, AB, and O, according to incompatibilities. For the first time it became possible to give a shock patient a transfusion with some hope that it wouldn't kill him.

The movement to abolish the death penalty was barely getting started, and already it was doomed.

Vh83uOAGn7 was his telephone number and his driving license number and his social security number and the number of his draft card and his medical record. Two of these had been revoked, and the others had ceased to matter, except for his medical record. His name was Warren Lewis Knowles. He was going to die.

The trial was a day away, but the verdict was no less certain for that. Lew was guilty. If anyone had doubted it, the persecution had ironclad proof. By eighteen tomorrow Lew would be condemned to death. Broxton would appeal the case on some grounds or other. The appeal would be denied.

His cell was comfortable, small, and padded. This was no slur on the prisoner's sanity, though insanity was no longer an excuse for breaking the law. Three of the walls were mere bars. The fourth wall, the outside wall, was cement painted a restful shade of green. But the bars which separated him from the corridor, and from the morose old man on his left, and from the big, moronic-looking teenager on his right—the bars were four inches thick and eight inches apart, padded in silicone plastic. For the fourth time that day Lew took a clenched fistful of the plastic and tried to rip it away. It felt like a sponge rubber pillow, with a rigid core the thickness of a pencil, and it wouldn't rip. When he let go it snapped back to a perfect cylinder.

"It's not fair," he said.

The teenager didn't move. For all of the ten hours Lew had been in his cell, the kid had been sitting on the edge of his bunk with his lank black hair falling in his eyes and his five o'clock shadow getting gradually darker. He moved his long, hairy arms only at mealtimes, and the rest of him not at all.

The old man looked up at the sound of Lew's voice. He spoke with bitter sarcasm. "You framed?"

"No, I—"

"At least you're honest. What'd you do?"

Lew told him. He couldn't keep the hurt innocence out of his voice. The old man smiled derisively, nodding as if he'd expected just that.

"Stupidity. Stupidity's always been a capital crime. If you *had* to get yourself executed, why not for something important? See the kid on the other side of you?"

"Sure," Lew said without looking.

"He's an organlegger."

Lew felt the shock freezing in his face. He braced himself for another look into the next cell—and every nerve in his body jumped. The kid was looking at him. With his dull dark eyes barely visible under his mop of hair, he regarded Lew as a butcher might consider a badly aged side of beef.

Lew edged closer to the bars between his cell and the old man's. His voice was a hoarse whisper. "How many did he kill?"

"None."

"?"

"He was the snatch man. He'd find someone out alone at night, drug the prospect and take him home to the doc that ran the ring. It was the doc that did all the killing. If Bernie'd brought home a dead prospect, the doc would have skinned *him* down."

The old man sat with Lew almost directly behind him. He had twisted himself around to talk to Lew, but now he seemed to be losing interest. His hands, hidden from Lew by his bony back, were in constant nervous motion.

"How many did he snatch?"

"Four. Then he got caught. He's not very bright, Bernie."

"What did you do to get put here?"

The old man didn't answer. He ignored Lew completely, his shoulders twitching as he moved his hands. Lew shrugged and dropped back on his bunk.

It was nineteen o'clock of a Thursday night.

The ring had included three snatch men. Bernie had not yet been tried. Another was dead; he had escaped over the edge of a pedwalk when he felt the mercy bullet enter his arm. The third was being wheeled into the hospital next door to the courthouse.

Officially he was still alive. He had been sentenced; his appeal had been denied; but he was still alive as they moved him, drugged, into the operating room.

The interns lifted him from the table and inserted a mouthpiece so he could breathe when they dropped him into freezing liquid. They lowered him without a splash, and as his body temperature went down they dribbled something else into his veins. About half a pint of it. His temperature dropped toward freezing, his heartbeats were further and further apart. Finally his heart stopped. But it could have been started again. Men had been reprieved at this point. Officially the organlegger was still alive.

The doctor was a line of machines with a conveyor belt running through them. When the organlegger's body temperature reached a certain point, the belt started. The first machine made a series of incisions in his chest. Skillfully and mechanically, the doctor performed a cardiectomy.

The organlegger was officially dead. His heart went into storage immediately. His skin followed, most of it in one piece, all of it still living. The doctor took him apart with exquisite care, like disassembling a flexible, fragile, tremendously complex jigsaw puzzle. The brain was flashburned and the ashes saved for urn burial; but all the rest of the body, in slabs and small blobs and parchment-thin layers and lengths of tubing, went into storage in the hospital's organ banks. Any one of these units could be packed in a travel case at a moment's notice and flown to anywhere in the world in not much more than an hour. If the odds broke right, if the right people came down with the right diseases at the right time, the organlegger might save more lives than he had taken.

Which was the whole point.

Lying on his back, staring up at the ceiling television set, Lew suddenly began to shiver. He had not had the energy to put the sound plug in his ear, and the silent motion of the cartoon figures had suddenly become horrid. He turned the set off, and that didn't help either.

Bit by bit they would take him apart and store him away. He'd never seen an organ storage bank, but his uncle had owned a butcher-shop. . . .

"Hey!" he yelled.

The kid's eyes came up, the only living part of him. The old man twisted round to look over his shoulder. At the end of the hall the guard looked up once, then went back to reading.

The fear was in Lew's belly; it pounded in his throat. "How can you stand it?"

The kid's eyes dropped to the floor. The old man said, "Stand what?"

"Don't you know what they're going to *do* to us?"

"Not to me. They won't take me apart like a hog."

Instantly Lew was at the bars. "Why not?"

The old man's voice had become very low. "Because there's a bomb where my right thighbone used to be. I'm gonna blow myself up. What they find, they'll never use."

The hope the old man had raised washed away, leaving bitterness. "Nuts. How could you put a bomb in your leg?"

"Take the bone out, bore a hole in it, build the bomb in the hole, get all the organic material out of the bone so it won't rot, put the bone back in. 'Course your red corpuscle count goes down afterward. What I wanted to ask you. You want to join me?"

"Join you?"

"Hunch up against the bars. This thing'll take care of both of us."

Lew found himself backing away. "No. No, thanks."

"Your choice," said the old man. "I never told you what I was here for, did I? I was the doc. Bernie made his snatches for me."

Lew had backed up against the opposite set of bars. He felt them touch his shoulders and turned to find the kid looking dully into his eyes from two feet away. Organleggers! He was surrounded by professional killers!

"I know what it's like," the old man continued. "They won't do that to me. Well. If you're sure you don't want a clean death, go lie down behind your bunk. It's thick enough."

The bunk was a mattress and a set of springs mounted into a cement block which was an integral part of the cement floor. Lew curled himself into fetal position with his hands over his eyes.

He was sure he didn't want to die *now*.

Nothing happened.

After a while he opened his eyes, took his hands away and looked around.

The kid was looking at him. For the first time there was a sour grin plastered on his face. In the corridor the guard, who was always in a chair by the exit, was standing outside the bars looking down at him. He seemed concerned.

Lew felt the flush rising in his neck and nose and ears. The old man had been playing with him. He moved to get up . . .

And a hammer came down on the world.

The guard lay broken against the bars of the cell across the corridor. The lank-haired youngster was picking himself up from behind his bunk, shaking his head. Somebody groaned; and the groan rose to a scream. The air was full of cement dust.

Lew got up.

Blood lay like red oil on every surface that faced the explosion. Try as he might, and he didn't try very hard, Lew could find no other trace of the old man.

Except for the hole in the wall.

He must have been standing . . . right . . . there.

The hole would be big enough to crawl through, if Lew could reach it. But it was in the old man's cell. The silicone plastic sheathing on the bars between the cells had been ripped away, leaving only pencil-thick lengths of metal.

Lew tried to squeeze through.

The bars were humming, vibrating, though there was no sound. As Lew noticed the vibration he also found that he was becoming sleepy. He jammed his body between the bars, caught in a war between his rising panic and the sonic stunners which must have gone on automatically.

The bars wouldn't give. But his body did; and the bars were slippery with . . . He was through. He poked his head through the hole in the wall and looked down.

Way down. Far enough to make him dizzy.

The Topeka County courthouse was a small skyscraper, and Lew's cell must have been near the top. He looked down a smooth concrete slab studded with windows set flush with the sides. There would be no way to reach those windows, no way to open them, no way to break them.

The stunner was sapping his will. He would have been unconscious by now if his head had been in the cell with the rest of him. He had to force himself to turn and look up.

He was *at* the top. The edge of the roof was only a few feet above his eyes. He couldn't reach that far, not without . . .

He began to crawl out of the hole.

Win or lose, they wouldn't get him for the organ banks. The vehicular traffic level would smash every useful part of him. He sat on the lip of the hole, with his legs straight out inside the cell for balance, pushing his chest flat against the wall. When he had his balance he stretched his arms toward the roof. No good.

So he got one leg under him, keeping the other stiffly out, and *lunged*.

His hands closed over the edge as he started to fall back. He yelped with surprise, but it was too late. The top of the courthouse was moving! It had dragged him out of the hole before he could let go. He hung on, swinging slowly back and forth over empty space as the motion carried him away.

The top of the courthouse was a pedwalk.

He couldn't climb up, not without purchase for his feet. He didn't have the strength. The pedwalk was moving toward another building, about the same height. He could reach it if he only hung on.

And the windows in that building were different. They weren't made to open, not in these days of smog and air conditioning, but there were ledges. Perhaps the glass would break.

Perhaps it wouldn't.

The pull on his arms was agony. It would be so easy to let go. . . . No. He had committed no crime worth dying for. He refused to die.

Over the decades of the twentieth century the movement continued to gain momentum. Loosely organized, international in scope, its members had only one goal: to replace execution with imprisonment and rehabilitation in every state and nation they could reach. They argued that killing a man for his crime teaches him nothing; that it serves as no deterrent to others who might commit the same crime; that death is irreversible, whereas an innocent man might be released from prison once his innocence is belatedly proven. Killing a man serves no good purpose, they said, unless for society's vengeance. Vengeance, they said, is unworthy of an enlightened society.

Perhaps they were right.

In 1940 Karl Landsteiner and Alexander S. Wiener made public their report on the Rh factor in human blood.

By mid-century most convicted killers were getting life imprisonment or less. Many were later returned to society, some "rehabilitated," others not. The death penalty had been passed for kidnaping in some states, but it was hard to persuade a jury to enforce it. Similarly with murder charges. A man wanted for burglary in Canada and murder in California fought extradition to Canada; he had less chance of being convicted in California. Many states had abolished the death penalty. France had none.

Rehabilitation of criminals was a major goal of the science/art of psychology.

But—

Blood banks were world wide.

Already men and women with kidney diseases had been saved by a kidney transplanted from an identical twin. Not all kidney victims had identical twins. A doctor in Paris used transplants from close relatives, classifying up to a hundred points of incompatibility to judge in advance how successful the transplant would be.

Eye transplants were common. An eye donor could wait until he died before he saved another man's sight.

Human bone could *always* be transplanted, provided the bone was first cleaned of organic matter.

So matters stood at midcentury.

By 1990 it was possible to store any living human organ for any reasonable length of time. Transplants had become routine, helped along by the "scalpel of infinite thinness," the laser. The dying regularly willed their remains to the organ banks. The mortuary lobbies couldn't stop it. But such gifts from the dead were not always useful.

In 1993 Vermont passed the first of the organ bank laws. Vermont had always had the death penalty. Now a condemned man could know that his death would save lives. It was no longer true that an execution served no good purpose. Not in Vermont.

Nor, later, in California. Or Washington. Georgia. Pakistan, England, Switzerland, France, Rhodesia . . .

The pedwalk was moving at ten miles per hour. Below, unnoticed by pedestrians who had quit work late and night owls who were just beginning their rounds, Lewis Knowles hung from the moving strip and watched the ledge go by beneath his dangling feet. The ledge was no more than two feet wide, a good four feet beneath his stretching toes.

He dropped.

As his feet struck he caught the edge of a window casement. Momentum jerked at him, but he didn't fall. After a long moment he breathed again.

He couldn't know what building this was, but it was not deserted. At twenty-one hundred at night, all the windows were ablaze. He tried to stay back out of the light as he peered in.

This window was an office. Empty.

He'd need something to wrap around his hand to break that window. But all he was wearing was a pair of shoesocks and a prison jumper. Well, he couldn't be more conspicuous than he was now. He took off the jumper, wrapped part of it around his hand, and struck.

He almost broke his hand.

Well . . . they'd let him keep his jewelry, his wristwatch and diamond ring. He drew a circle on the glass with the ring, pushing down hard, and struck again with the other hand. It *had* to be glass; if it was plastic he was doomed. The glass popped out in a near-perfect circle.

He had to do it six times before the hole was big enough for him.

He smiled as he stepped inside, still holding his jumper. Now all he needed was an elevator. The cops would have picked him up in an instant if they'd caught him on the street in a prison jumper, but if he hid the jumper here he'd be safe. Who would suspect a licensed nudist?

Except that he didn't have a license. Or a nudist's shoulder pouch to put it in.

Or a shave.

That was very bad. Never had there been a nudist as hairy as this. Not just a five o'clock shadow, but a full beard all over, so to speak. Where could he get a razor?

He tried the desk drawers. Many businessmen kept spare razors. He stopped when he was halfway through. Not because he'd found a razor, but because he now knew where he was. The papers on his desk made it all too obvious.

A hospital.

He was still clutching the jumper. He dropped it in the wastebasket, covered it tidily with papers, and more or less collapsed into the chair behind the desk.

A hospital. He *would* pick a hospital. And *this* hospital, the one which had been built right next to the Topeka County courthouse, for good and sufficient reason.

But he hadn't picked it, not really. It had picked him. Had he ever in his life made a decision except on the prompting of others? No. Friends had borrowed his money for keeps, men had stolen his girls, he had avoided promotion by his knack for being ignored. Shirley had bullied him into marrying her, then left him four years later for a friend who wouldn't be bullied.

Even now, at the possible end of his life, it was the same. An aging body snatcher had given him his escape. An engineer had built the cell bars wide enough apart to let a small man squeeze between them. Another had put a pedwalk along two convenient roofs. And here he was.

The worst of it was that here he had no chance of masquerading as a nudist. Hospital gowns and masks would be the minimum. Even nudists had to wear clothing sometime.

The closet?

There was nothing in the closet but a spiffy green hat and a perfectly transparent rain poncho.

He could run for it. If he could find a razor he'd be safe once he reached the street. He bit at a knuckle, wishing he knew where the elevator was. Have to trust to luck. He began searching the drawers again.

He had his hand on a black leather razor case when the door opened. A beefy man in a hospital gown breezed in. The intern (there were no human doctors in hospitals) was halfway to the desk before he noticed Lew crouching over an open drawer. He stopped walking. His mouth fell open.

Lew closed it with the fist which still gripped the razor case. The man's teeth came together with a sharp click. His knees were buckling as Lew brushed past him and out the door.

The elevator was just down the hall, with the doors standing open. And nobody coming. Lew stepped in and punched O. He shaved as the elevator dropped. The razor cut fast and close, if a trifle noisily. He was working on his chest as the door opened.

A skinny technician stood directly in front of him, her mouth and eyes set in the utterly blank expression of those who wait for elevators. She brushed past him with a muttered apology, hardly noticing him. Lew stepped out fast. The doors were closing before he realized that he was on the wrong floor.

That damned tech! She'd stopped the elevator before it reached bottom.

He turned and stabbed the Down button. Then what he'd seen in that one cursory glance came back to him, and his head whipped around for another look.

The whole vast room was filled with glass tanks, ceiling height, arranged in a labyrinth like the bookcases in a library. In the tanks was a display more lewd than anything in Belsen. Why, those things had been *men!* and *women!* No, he wouldn't look. He refused to look at anything but the elevator door. *What was taking that elevator so long?*

He heard a siren.

The hard tile floor began to vibrate against his bare feet. He felt a numbness in his muscles, a lethargy in his soul.

The elevator arrived . . . too late. He blocked the doors open with a chair. Most buildings didn't have stairs; only alternate elevators. They'd have to use the alternate elevator to reach him now. Well, where was it? . . . He wouldn't have time to find it. He was beginning to feel really sleepy. They must have several sonic projectors focused on this one room. Where one beam passed the interns would feel mildly relaxed, a little clumsy. But where the beams intersected, *here,* there would be unconsciousness. But not yet.

He had something to do first.

By the time they broke in they'd have something to kill him for. The tanks were faced in plastic, not glass: a very special kind of plastic. To avoid provoking defense reactions in all the myriads of body parts which might be stored touching it, the plastic had to have unique characteristics. No engineer could have been expected to make it shatterproof too!

It shattered very satisfactorily.

Later, Lew wondered how he managed to stay up as long as he did. The soothing hypersonic murmur of the stun beams kept pulling at him, pulling him down to a floor which seemed softer every moment. The chair he wielded became heavier and heavier. But as long as he could lift it, he smashed. He was knee deep in nutritive storage fluid, and there were dying things brushing against his ankles with every move; but his work was barely a third done when the silent siren song became too much for him.

He fell.

And after all that they never even mentioned the smashed organ banks!

Sitting in the courtroom, listening to the drone of courtroom ritual, Lew sought Mr. Broxton's ear to ask the question. Mr. Broxton smiled at him. "Why should they want to bring that up? They think they've got enough on you as it is. If you beat *this* rap, then they'll persecute you for wanton destruction of valuable medical sources. But they're sure you won't."

"And you?"

"I'm afraid they're right. But we'll try. Now, Hennessey's about to read the charges. Can you manage to look hurt and indignant?"

"Sure."

"Good."

The persecution read the charges, his voice sounding like the voice of doom coming from under a thin blond mustache. Warren Lewis

Knowles looked hurt and indignant. But he no longer felt that way. He had done something worth dying for.

The cause of it all was the organ banks. With good doctors and a sufficient flow of material in the organ banks, any taxpayer could hope to live indefinitely. What voter would vote against eternal life? The death penalty was his immortality, and he would vote the death penalty for any crime at all.

Lewis Knowles had struck back.

"The state will prove that the said Warren Lewis Knowles did, in the space of two years, willfully drive through a total of six red traffic lights. During that same period the same Warren Knowles exceeded local speed limits no less than ten times, once by as much as fifteen miles per hour. His record has never been good. We will produce records of his arrest in 2082 on a charge of drunk driving, a charge of which he was acquitted only through—"

"Objection!"

"Sustained. If he was acquitted, Counselor, the Court must assume him not guilty."


## Afterword:

There's an organ bank in your future, or your grandchildren's. Nothing short of a world holocaust could stop it. The rapid advance in transplant techniques is common knowledge. Many of the greats of science fiction have written on the organ bank problem, because it is so inevitable and because it is so interesting.

The following should not provoke arguments, but it has, and will: Human technology can change human morals.

If you doubt it, consider: dynamite, gunpowder, the printing press, the cotton gin, modern advertising techniques, psychology. Consider the automobile: it is now immoral to go home at all after a New Years' Eve party. (Unless you take a cab, which cannot be done except at gunpoint.) Consider the cobalt bomb, which has made total war immoral. Was total war immoral before the cobalt bomb? In 1945 the Allies demanded nothing less than total defeat for Germany. Were they wrong? Did you say so at the time? *I* didn't (being seven years old) and don't (at twenty-eight).

What happens when the death of one genuine criminal can save the lives of twenty taxpayers? Morals change.

Much of the science/art of psychology has dealt with rehabilitation of criminals. These techniques will soon be forgotten lore, like alchemy.

But organ transplants are only half the story. Alloplasty, the science and empirical technique of putting foreign matter in the human body for medical purposes, is a combating influence. Thousands walk today's streets with metal pacemakers in their hearts, nylon tubing replacing sections of artery, plastic valves replacing the organic valves in the large veins, transparent insets in the lenses of their eyes. When alloplasty heals a man, nobody dies.

You may think of the next five hundred years as a footrace between two techniques, alloplasty and organ transplantation. But organ transplantation will win. It is a simpler set of techniques.

The good side of organ transplantation is very good indeed. As long as the organ banks don't run short of materials, any citizen can live as long as his central nervous system holds out, since the doctors can keep shoving spare parts into him as fast as the old ones wear out. How long can the brain live with a dependable, youthful blood supply? It's your guess. I say centuries.

But, with centuries of life at stake, what citizen will vote against the death penalty for: false advertising, habitual jaywalking, rudeness, cheating on income tax, having children without a license? Or (and here's the real danger) criticizing government policy? Given the organ banks, "The Jigsaw Man" is a glimpse into the best of possible futures. The worst is a never-ending dictatorship.

On Christmas Day 1965, Harlan told me he was collecting material for an anthology. I was halfway through a novel dealing with the organ bank problem on one of Earth's interstellar colonies (almost finished), and I took time out to demonstrate how the problem may affect Earth.

I think I could have sold the story anywhere. But it will cause arguments, thus fulfilling its purpose. Because someone has to start thinking about this. We haven't much time. It's only an accident of history that Red Cross blood banks aren't supplied by the death house. Think of the advantages—and worry.

## Introduction to GONNA ROLL THE BONES:

The field of speculative fiction, oddly enough, tends to make specialists of its writers. There are alien ecologists such as Hal Clement, and poetic imagists such as Ray Bradbury, and world-destroyers such as Edmond Hamilton and A. E. van Vogt. There are all too few "renaissance" writers who span the speculative gamut from gothic fantasy to grommet-and-nozzle stories of "hard" science. And among these few jacks-of-all-forms, there are only a handful who can handle the tale of terror in a context of modern society.

Fritz Leiber, who as a two-time Hugo winner truly needs no introduction, is certainly the most ambidextrous of that handful. Born in Chicago in 1910, son of Shakespearean actors Fritz and Virginia Bronson Leiber, he was educated at the University of Chicago emerging with a Bachelor's in psychology with honors and a third-year Phi Beta Kappa. He has been an Episcopalian lay reader and attended General Theological Seminary in New York, acted in his father's touring company in 1935, done editorial work from 1937 through 1956 with one year teaching dramatics at Occidental College in Los Angeles. He was associate editor of *Science Digest* from 1945 to 1956 and has been a free-lance writer since.

For the benefit of historians, Fritz Leiber's first accepted story was "The Automatic Pistol," which appeared in *Weird Tales* for May 1940. His first published (and paid for) story was "Two Sought Adventure," the first of his memorable sword-and-sorcery series of Fahfred and the Grey Mouser, which saw publication in the August 1939 issue of *Unknown*. Among his fourteen books Leiber fans will warmly remember *Conjure Wife, Gather, Darkness!*, the 1958 and 1964 Hugo winners, *The Big Time* and *The Wanderer, Night's Black Agents, A Pail of Air* and the recent *Tarzan and the Valley of Gold*.

It is, incidentally, fitting that, of all the possible choices for writers to pen a *new* adventure employing the world-famous Edgar Rice Burroughs character, the job should have fallen to Fritz Leiber. His ability to bring not merely expertise but genuine poetry to anything he writes has kept him in the forefront of imaginative writing for over two decades. As demonstrated in the Tarzan novel, his wild talent for fusing the imaginative with the realistic is nonpareil. And as his contribution to this anthology, nothing could be more appropriate than the story Fritz has chosen to tell. For it singlehandedly explains why lines of demarcation between fantasy and science fiction can seldom be drawn.

"Gonna Roll the Bones" is Fritz Leiber's first short story in two years, as this introduction is written. It shows the Leiberesque conception of the Universe being unified by magic and science and superstition, as well as blatantly displaying the man's love affair with the English language. It is uncategorizable though it bears traces of pure horror, science fiction, the psychological fantasy and the Jungian explanations for the personal madness of our times. Insofar as prerequisites were established for stories for this collection, it satisfies estimably: the authors were asked to present "dangerous" visions, and I submit there are few more petrifying concepts than the one Fritz Leiber here proffers in finally naming the name of the Prince of Darkness.

# ● GONNA ROLL THE BONES

## by Fritz Leiber

Suddenly Joe Slattermill knew for sure he'd have to get out quick or else blow his top and knock out with the shrapnel of his skull the props and patches holding up his decaying home, that was like a house of big wooden and plaster and wallpaper cards except for the huge fireplace and ovens and chimney across the kitchen from him.

Those were stone-solid enough, though. The fireplace was chin-high at least twice that long, and filled from end to end with roaring flames. Above were the square doors of the ovens in a row—his Wife baked for part of their living. Above the ovens was the wall-long mantelpiece, too high for his Mother to reach or Mr. Guts to jump any more, set with all sorts of ancestral curios, but any of them that weren't stone or glass or china had been so dried and darkened by decades of heat that they looked like nothing but shrunken human heads and black golf balls. At one end were clustered his Wife's square gin bottles. Above the mantelpiece hung one old chromo, so high and so darkened by soot and grease that you couldn't tell whether the swirls and fat cigar shape were a whaleback steamer plowing through a hurricane or a spaceship plunging through a storm of light-driven dust motes.

As soon as Joe curled his toes inside his boots, his Mother knew what he was up to. "Going bumming," she mumbled with conviction. "Pants pockets full of cartwheels of house money, too, to spend on sin." And she went back to munching the long shreds she stripped fumblingly with her right hand off the turkey carcass set close to the terrible heat, her left hand ready to fend off Mr. Guts, who stared at her yellow-eyed, gaunt-flanked, with long mangy tail a-twitch. In her dirty dress, streaky as the turkey's sides, Joe's Mother looked like a bent brown bag and her fingers were lumpy twigs.

Joe's Wife knew as soon or sooner, for she smiled thin-eyed at him over her shoulder from where she towered at the centermost oven. Before she closed its door, Joe glimpsed that she was baking two long, flat, narrow, fluted loaves and one high, round-domed one. She was thin as death and disease in her violet wrapper. Without looking, she reached out a yard-long, skinny arm for the nearest gin bottle and downed a warm slug and smiled again. And without word spoken, Joe knew she'd said, "You're going out and gamble and get drunk and lay a floozy and come home and beat me and go to jail for it," and he had a flash of the last time he'd been in the dark gritty cell and she'd come by moonlight, which showed the green and yellow lumps on her narrow skull where he'd hit her, to whisper to him through the tiny window in back and slip him a half pint through the bars.

And Joe knew for certain that this time it would be that bad and worse, but just the same he heaved up himself and his heavy, muffledly clanking pockets and shuffled straight to the door, muttering, "Guess I'll roll the bones, up the pike a stretch and back," swinging his bent, knobby-elbowed arms like paddlewheels to make a little joke about his words.

When he'd stepped outside, he held the door open a hand's breadth behind him for several seconds. When he finally closed it, a feeling of deep misery struck him. Earlier years, Mr. Guts would have come streaking along to seek fights and females on the roofs and fences, but now the big tom was content to stay home and hiss by the fire and snatch for turkey and dodge a broom, quarreling and comforting with two housebound women. Nothing had followed Joe to the door but his Mother's chomping and her gasping breaths and the clink of the gin bottle going back on the mantel and the creaking of the floor boards under his feet.

The night was up-side-down deep among the frosty stars. A few of them seemed to move, like the white-hot jets of spaceships. Down below it looked as if the whole town of Ironmine had blown or buttoned out the light and gone to sleep, leaving the streets and spaces to the equally unseen breezes and ghosts. But Joe was still in the hemisphere of the musty dry odor of the worm-eaten carpentry behind him, and as he felt and heard the dry grass of the lawn brush his calves, it occurred to him that something deep down inside him had for years been planning things so that he and the house and his Wife and Mother and Mr. Guts would all come to an end together. Why the kitchen heat hadn't touched off the tindery place ages ago was a physical miracle.

Hunching his shoulders, Joe stepped out, not up the pike, but down the dirt road that led past Cypress Hollow Cemetery to Night Town.

The breezes were gentle, but unusually restless and variable tonight, like leprechaun squalls. Beyond the drunken, whitewashed cemetery fence dim in the starlight, they rustled the scraggly trees of Cypress Hollow and made it seem they were stroking their beards of Spanish moss. Joe sensed that the ghosts were just as restless as the breezes, uncertain where and whom to haunt, or whether to take the night off, drifting together in sorrowfully lecherous companionship. While among the trees the red-green vampire lights pulsed faintly and irregularly, like sick fireflies or a plague-stricken space fleet. The feeling of deep misery stuck with Joe and deepened and he was tempted to turn aside and curl up in any convenient tomb or around some half-toppled head board and cheat his Wife and the other three behind him out of a shared doom. He thought: Gonna roll the bones, gonna roll 'em up and go to sleep. But while he was deciding, he got past the sagged-open gate and the rest of the delirious fence and Shantyville too.

At first Night Town seemed dead as the rest of Ironmine, but then he noticed a faint glow, sick as the vampire lights but more feverish, and with it a jumping music, tiny at first as a jazz for jitterbugging ants. He stepped along the springy sidewalk, wistfully remembering the days when the spring was all in his own legs and he'd bound into a fight like a bobcat or a Martian sand-spider. God, it had been years now since he had fought a real fight, or felt *the power*. Gradually the midget music got raucous as a bunnyhug for grizzly bears and loud as a polka for elephants, while the glow became a riot of gas flares and flambeaux and corpse-blue mercury tubes and jiggling pink neon ones that all jeered at the stars where the spaceships roved. Next thing, he was facing a three-storey false front flaring everywhere like a devil's rainbow, with a pale blue topping of St. Elmo's fire. There were wide swinging doors in the center of it, spilling light above and below. Above the doorway, golden calcium light scrawled over and over again, with wild curlicues and flourishes, "The Boneyard," while a fiendish red kept printing out, "Gambling."

So the new place they'd all been talking about for so long had opened at last! For the first time that night, Joe Slattermill felt a stirring of real life in him and the faintest caress of excitement.

Gonna roll the bones, he thought.

He dusted off his blue-green work clothes with big, careless swipes and slapped his pockets to hear the clank. Then he threw back his shoulders and grinned his lips sneeringly and pushed through the swinging doors as if giving a foe the straight-armed heel of his palm.

Inside, The Boneyard seemed to cover the area of a township and the bar looked as long as the railroad tracks. Round pools of light on the green poker tables alternated with hourglass shapes of exciting gloom, through which drink girls and change girls moved like white-legged witches. By the jazz-stand in the distance, belly dancers made *their* white hourglass shapes. The gamblers were thick and hunched down as mushrooms, all bald from agonizing over the fall of a card or a die or the dive of an ivory ball, while the Scarlet Women were like fields of poinsettia.

The calls of the croupiers and the slaps of dealt cards were as softly yet fatefully staccato as the rustle and beat of the jazz drums. Every tight-locked atom of the place was controlledly jumping. Even the dust motes jigged tensely in the cones of light.

Joe's excitement climbed and he felt sift through him, like a breeze that heralds a gale, the faintest breath of a confidence which he knew could become a tornado. All thoughts of his house and Wife and Mother dropped out of his mind, while Mr. Guts remained only as a crazy young tom walking stiff-legged around the rim of his consciousness. Joe's own leg muscles twitched in sympathy and he felt them grow supplely strong.

He coolly and searchingly looked the place over, his hand going out like it didn't belong to him to separate a drink from a passing, gently bobbing tray. Finally his gaze settled on what he judged to be the Number One Crap Table. All the Big Mushrooms seemed to be there, bald as the rest but standing tall as toadstools. Then through a gap in them Joe saw on the other side of the table a figure still taller, but dressed in a long dark coat with collar turned up and a dark slouch hat pulled low, so that only a triangle of white face showed. A suspicion and a hope rose in Joe and he headed straight for the gap in the Big Mushrooms.

As he got nearer, the white-legged and shiny-topped drifters eddying out of his way, his suspicion received confirmation after confirmation and his hope budded and swelled. Back from one end of the table was the fattest man he'd ever seen, with a long cigar and a silver vest and a gold tie clasp at least eight inches wide that just said in thick script, "Mr. Bones." Back a little from the other end was the nakedest change-girl yet and the only one he'd seen whose tray, slung from her bare shoulders and indenting her belly just below her breasts, was stacked with gold in gleaming little towers and with jet-black chips. While the dice-girl, skinnier and taller and longer armed than his Wife even, didn't seem to be wearing much but a pair of long white gloves. She was all right if you went for the type that isn't much more than pale skin over bones with breasts like china doorknobs.

Beside each gambler was a high round table for his chips. The one by the gap was empty. Snapping his fingers at the nearest silver change-girl, Joe traded all his greasy dollars for an equal number of pale chips and tweaked her left nipple for luck. She playfully snapped her teeth toward his fingers.

Not hurrying but not wasting any time, he advanced and carelessly dropped his modest stacks on the empty table and took his place in the gap. He noted that the second Big Mushroom on his right had the dice. His heart but no other part of him gave an extra jump. Then he steadily lifted his eyes and looked straight across the table.

The coat was a shimmering elegant pillar of black satin with jet buttons, the upturned collar of fine dull plush black as the darkest cellar, as was the slouch hat with down-turned brim and for band only a thin braid of black horsehair. The arms of the coat were long, lesser satin pillars, ending in slim, long-fingered hands that moved swiftly when they did, but held each position of rest with a statue's poise.

Joe still couldn't see much of the face except for smooth lower forehead with never a bead or trickle of sweat—the eyebrows were like straight snippets of the hat's braid—and gaunt, aristocratic cheeks and narrow but somewhat flat nose. The complexion of the face wasn't as white as Joe had first judged. There was a faint touch of brown in it, like ivory that's just begun to age, or Venusian soapstone. Another glance at the hands confirmed this.

Behind the man in black was a knot of just about the flashiest and nastiest customers, male or female, Joe had ever seen. He knew from one look that each bediamonded, pomaded bully had a belly gun beneath the flap of his flowered vest and a blackjack in his hip pocket, and each snake-eyed sporting girl a stiletto in her garter and a pearl-handed silver-plated derringer under the sequined silk in the hollow between her jutting breasts.

Yet at the same time Joe knew they were just trimmings. It was the man in black, their master, who was the deadly one, the kind of man you knew at a glance you couldn't touch and live. If without asking you merely laid a finger on his sleeve, no matter how lightly and respectfully, an ivory hand would move faster than thought and you'd be stabbed or shot. Or maybe just the touch would kill you, as if every black article of his clothing were charged from his ivory skin outward with a high-voltage, high-amperage ivory electricity. Joe looked at the shadowed face again and decided he wouldn't care to try it.

For it was the eyes that were the most impressive feature. All great gamblers have dark-shadowed deep-set eyes. But this one's eyes were sunk so deep you couldn't even be sure you were getting a gleam of them. They were inscrutability incarnate. They were unfathomable. They were like black holes.

But all this didn't disappoint Joe one bit, though it did terrify him considerably. On the contrary, it made him exult. His first suspicion was completely confirmed and his hope spread into full flower.

This must be one of those really big gamblers who hit Ironmine only once a decade at most, come from the Big City on one of the river boats that ranged the watery dark like luxurious comets, spouting long thick tails of sparks from their sequoia-tall stacks with top foliage of curvy-snipped sheet iron. Or like silver space-liners with dozens of jewel-flamed jets, their portholes a-twinkle like ranks of marshaled asteroids.

For that matter, maybe some of those really big gamblers actually came from other planets where the nighttime pace was hotter and the sporting life a delirium of risk and delight.

Yes, this was the kind of man Joe had always yearned to pit his skill against. He felt *the power* begin to tingle in his rock-still fingers, just a little.

Joe lowered his gaze to the crap table. It was almost as wide as a man is tall, at least twice as long, unusually deep, and lined with black, not green, felt, so that it looked like a giant's coffin. There was something familiar about its shape which he couldn't place. Its bottom, though not its sides or ends, had a twinkling iridescence, as if it had been lightly sprinkled with very tiny diamonds. As Joe lowered his gaze all the way and looked directly down, his eyes barely over the table, he got the crazy notion that it went down all the way through the world, so that the diamonds were the stars on the other side, visible despite the sunlight there, just as Joe was always able to see the stars by day up the shaft of the mine he worked in, and so that if a cleaned-out gambler, dizzy with defeat, toppled forward into it, he'd fall forever, toward the bottommost bottom, be it Hell or some black galaxy. Joe's thoughts swirled and he felt the cold, hard-fingered clutch of fear at his crotch. Someone was crooning beside him, "Come on, Big Dick."

Then the dice, which had meanwhile passed to the Big Mushroom immediately on his right, came to rest near the table's center, contradicting and wiping out Joe's vision. But instantly there was another oddity to absorb him. The ivory dice were large and unusually round-cornered with dark red spots that gleamed like real rubies, but the spots were arranged in such a way that each face looked like a miniature skull. For instance, the seven thrown just now, by which the Big Mushroom to his right had lost his point, which had been ten, consisted of a two with the spots evenly spaced toward one side, like eyes, instead of toward opposite corners, and of a five with the same red eye-spots but also a central red nose and two spots close together below that to make teeth.

The long, skinny, white-gloved arm of the dice-girl snaked out like an albino cobra and scooped up the dice and whisked them onto the rim of the table right in front of Joe. He inhaled silently, picked up a single chip from his table and started to lay it beside the dice, then realized that wasn't the way things were done here, and put it back. He would have liked to examine the chip more closely, though. It was curiously lightweight and pale tan, about the color of cream with a shot of coffee in it, and it had embossed on its surface a symbol he could feel, though not see. He didn't know what the symbol was, that would have taken more feeling. Yet its touch had been very good, setting the power tingling full blast in his shooting hand.

Joe looked casually yet swiftly at the faces around the table, not missing the Big Gambler across from him, and said quietly, "Roll a penny," meaning of course one pale chip, or a dollar.

There was a hiss of indignation from all the Big Mushrooms and the moonface of big-bellied Mr. Bones grew purple as he started forward to summon his bouncers.

The Big Gambler raised a black-satined forearm and sculptured hand, palm down. Instantly Mr. Bones froze and the hissing stopped faster than that of a meteor prick in self-sealing space steel. Then in a whispery, cultured voice, without the faintest hint of derision, the man in black said, "Get on him, gamblers."

Here, Joe thought, was a final confirmation of his suspicion, had it been needed. The really great gamblers were always perfect gentlemen and generous to the poor.

With only the tiny, respectful hint of a guffaw, one of the Big Mushrooms called to Joe, "You're faded."

Joe picked up the ruby-featured dice.

Now ever since he had first caught two eggs on one plate, won all the marbles in Ironmine, and juggled six alphabet blocks so they finally fell in a row on the rug spelling "Mother," Joe Slattermill had been almost incredibly deft at precision throwing. In the mine he could carom a rock off a wall of ore to crack a rat's skull fifty feet away in the dark and he sometimes amused himself by tossing little fragments of rock back into the holes from which they had fallen, so that they stuck there, perfectly fitted in, for at least a second. Sometimes, by fast tossing, he could fit seven or eight fragments into the hole from which they had fallen, like putting together a puzzle block. If he could ever have got into space, Joe would undoubtedly have been able to pilot six Moon-skimmers at once and do figure eights through Saturn's rings blindfold.

Now the only real difference between precision-tossing rocks or alphabet blocks and dice is that you have to bounce the latter off the end wall of a crap table, and that just made it a more interesting test of skill for Joe.

Rattling the dice now, he felt the power in his fingers and palm as never before.

He made a swift low roll, so that the bones ended up exactly in front of the white-gloved dice-girl. His natural seven was made up, as he'd intended, of a four and a three. In red-spot features they were like the five, except that both had only one tooth and the three no nose. Sort of baby-faced skulls. He had won a penny— that is, a dollar.

"Roll two cents," said Joe Slattermill.

This time, for variety, he made his natural with an eleven. The six was like the five, except it had three teeth, the best-looking skull of the lot.

"Roll a nickel less one."

Two Big Mushrooms divided that bet with a covert smirk at each other.

Now Joe rolled a three and an ace. His point was four. The ace, with its single spot off center toward a side, still somehow looked like a skull—maybe of a Lilliputian Cyclops.

He took a while making his point, once absent-mindedly rolling three successive tens the hard way. He wanted to watch the dice-girl scoop up the cubes. Each time it seemed to him that her snake-swift fingers went under the dice while they were still flat on the felt. Finally he decided it couldn't be an illusion. Although the dice couldn't penetrate the felt, her white-gloved fingers somehow could, dipping in a flash through the black, diamond-sparkling material as if it weren't there.

Right away the thought of a crap-table-size hole through the earth came back to Joe. This would mean that the dice were rolling and lying on a perfectly transparent flat surface, impenetrable for them but nothing else. Or maybe it was only the dice-girl's hands that could penetrate the surface, which would turn into a mere fantasy Joe's earlier vision of a cleaned-out gambler taking the Big Dive down that dreadful shaft, which made the deepest mine a mere pin dent.

Joe decided he had to know which was true. Unless absolutely unavoidable, he didn't want to take the chance of being troubled by vertigo at some crucial stage of the game.

He made a few more meaningless throws, from time to time crooning for realism, "Come on, Little Joe." Finally he settled on his plan. When he did at last make his point—the hard way, with two twos—he caromed the dice off the far corner so that they landed exactly in front of him. Then, after a minimum pause for his throw to be seen by the table, he shot his left hand down under the cubes, just a flicker ahead of the dice-girl's strike, and snatched them up.

Wow! Joe had never had a harder time in his life making his face and manner conceal what his body felt, not even when the wasp had stung him on the neck just as he had been for the first time putting his hand under the skirt of his prudish, fickle, demanding Wife-to-be. His fingers and the back of his hand were in as much agony as if he'd stuck them into a blast furnace. No wonder the dice-girl wore white gloves. They must be asbestos. And a good thing he hadn't used his shooting hand, he thought as he ruefully watched the blisters rise.

He remembered he'd been taught in school what Twenty-Mile Mine also demonstrated: that the earth was fearfully hot under its crust. The crap-table-size hole must pipe up that heat, so that any gambler taking the Big Dive would fry before he'd fallen a furlong and come out less than a cinder in China.

As if his blistered hand weren't bad enough, the Big Mushrooms were all hissing at him again and Mr. Bones had purpled once more and was opening his melon-size mouth to shout for his bouncers.

Once again a lift of the Big Gambler's hand saved Joe. The whispery, gentle voice called, "Tell him, Mr. Bones."

The latter roared toward Joe, "No gambler may pick up the dice he or any other gambler has shot. Only my dice-girl may do that. Rule of the house!"

Joe snapped Mr. Bones the barest nod. He said coolly, "Rolling a dime less two," and when that still peewee bet was covered, he shot Phoebe for his point and then fooled around for quite a while, throwing anything but a five or a seven, until the throbbing in his left hand should fade and all his nerves feel rock-solid again. There had never been the slightest alteration in the power in his right hand; he felt that strong as ever, or stronger.

Midway of this interlude, the Big Gambler bowed slightly but respectfully toward Joe, hooding those unfathomable eye sockets, before turning around to take a long black cigarette from his prettiest and evilest-looking sporting girl. Courtesy in the smallest matters, Joe thought, another mark of the master devotee of games of chance. The Big Gambler sure had himself a flash crew, all right, though in idly looking them over again as he rolled, Joe noted one bummer toward the back who didn't fit in—a raggedy-elegant chap with the elflocked hair and staring eyes and TB-spotted cheeks of a poet.

As he watched the smoke trickling up from under the black slouch hat, he decided that either the lights across the table had dimmed or else the Big Gambler's complexion was yet a shade darker than he'd thought at first. Or it might even be—wild fantasy—that the Big Gambler's skin was slowly darkening tonight, like a meerschaum pipe being smoked a mile a second. That was almost funny to think of—there was enough heat in this place, all right, to darken meerschaum, as Joe knew from sad experience, but so far as he was aware it was all under the table.

None of Joe's thoughts, either familiar or admiring, about the Big Gambler decreased in the slightest degree his certainty of the supreme menace of the man in black and his conviction that it would be death to touch him. And if any doubts had stirred in Joe's mind, they would have been squelched by the chilling incident which next occurred.

The Big Gambler had just taken into his arms his prettiest-evilest sporting girl and was running an aristocratic hand across her haunch with perfect gentility, when the poet chap, green-eyed from jealousy and lovesickness, came leaping forward like a wildcat and aimed a long gleaming dagger at the black satin back.

Joe couldn't see how the blow could miss, but without taking his genteel right hand off the sporting girl's plush rear end, the Big Gambler shot out his left arm like a steel spring straightening. Joe couldn't tell whether he stabbed the poet chap in the throat, or judo-chopped him there, or gave him the Martian double-finger, or just touched him, but anyhow the fellow stopped as dead as if he'd been shot by a silent elephant gun or an invisible ray pistol and he slammed down on the floor. A couple of darkies came running up to drag off the body and nobody paid the least attention, such episodes apparently being taken for granted at The Boneyard.

It gave Joe quite a turn and he almost shot Phoebe before he intended to.

But by now the waves of pain had stopped running up his left arm and his nerves were like metal-wrapped new guitar strings, so three rolls later he shot a five, making his point, and set in to clean out the table.

He rolled nine successive naturals, seven sevens and two elevens, pyramiding his first wager of a single chip to a stake of over four thousand dollars. None of the Big Mushrooms had dropped out yet, but some of them were beginning to look worried and a couple were sweating. The Big Gambler still hadn't covered any part of Joe's bets, but he seemed to be following the play with interest from the cavernous depths of his eye sockets.

Then Joe got a devilish thought. Nobody could beat him tonight, he knew, but if he held onto the dice until the table was cleaned out, he'd never get a chance to see the Big Gambler exercise *his* skill, and he was truly curious about that. Besides, he thought, he ought to return courtesy for courtesy and have a crack at being a gentleman himself.

"Pulling out forty-one dollars less a nickel," he announced. "Rolling a penny."

This time there wasn't any hissing and Mr. Bones's moonface didn't cloud over. But Joe was conscious that the Big Gambler was staring at him disappointedly, or sorrowfully, or maybe just speculatively.

Joe immediately crapped out by throwing boxcars, rather pleased to see the two best-looking tiny skulls grinning ruby-toothed side by side, and the dice passed to the Big Mushroom on his left.

"Knew when his streak was over," he heard another Big Mushroom mutter with grudging admiration.

The play worked rather rapidly around the table, nobody getting very hot and the stakes never more than medium high. "Shoot a fin." "Rolling a sawbuck." "An Andrew Jackson." "Rolling thirty bucks." Now and then Joe covered part of a bet, winning more than he lost. He had over seven thousand dollars, real money, before the bones got around to the Big Gambler.

That one held the dice for a long moment on his statue-steady palm while he looked at them reflectively, though not the hint of a furrow appeared in his almost brownish forehead down which never a bead of sweat trickled. He murmured, "Rolling a double sawbuck," and when he had been faded, he closed his fingers, lightly rattled the cubes—the sound was like big seeds inside a small gourd only half dry—and negligently cast the dice toward the end of the table.

It was a throw like none Joe had ever seen before at any crap table. The dice traveled flat through the air without turning over, struck the exact juncture of the table's end and bottom, and stopped there dead, showing a natural seven.

Joe was distinctly disappointed. On one of his own throws he was used to calculating something like, "Launch three-up, five north, two and a half rolls in the air, hit on the six-five-three corner, three-quarter roll and a one-quarter side-twist right, hit end on the one-two edge, one-half reverse role and three-quarter side-twist left, land on five face, roll over twice, come up two," and that would be for just one of the dice, and a really commonplace throw, without extra bounces.

By comparison, the technique of the Big Gambler had been ridiculously, abysmally, horrifyingly simple. Joe could have duplicated it with the greatest ease, of course. It was no more than an elementary form of his old pastime of throwing fallen rocks back into their holes. But Joe had never once thought of pulling such a babyish trick at the crap table. It would make the whole thing too easy and destroy the beauty of the game.

Another reason Joe had never used the trick was that he'd never dreamed he'd be able to get away with it. By all the rules he'd ever heard of, it was a most questionable throw. There was the possibility that one or the other die hadn't completely reached the end of the table, or lay a wee bit cocked against the end. Besides, he reminded himself, weren't both dice supposed to rebound off the end, if only for a fraction of an inch?

However, as far as Joe's very sharp eyes could see, both dice lay perfectly flat and sprang up against the end wall. Moreover, everyone else at the table seemed to accept the throw, the dice-girl had scooped up the cubes, and the Big Mushrooms who had faded the man in black were paying off. As far as the rebound business went, well, The

Boneyard appeared to put a slightly different interpretation on that rule, and Joe believed in never questioning House Rules except in dire extremity—both his Mother and Wife had long since taught him it was the least troublesome way.

Besides, there hadn't been any of his own money riding on that roll.

In a voice like wind through Cypress Hollow or on Mars, the Big Gambler announced, "Roll a century." It was the biggest bet yet tonight, ten thousand dollars, and the way the Big Gambler said it made it seem something more than that. A hush fell on The Boneyard, they put the mutes on the jazz horns, the croupiers' calls became more confidential, the cards fell softlier, even the roulette balls seemed to be trying to make less noise as they rattled into their cells. The crowd around the Number One Crap Table quietly thickened. The Big Gambler's flash boys and girls formed a double semicircle around him, ensuring him lots of elbow room.

That century bet, Joe realized, was thirty bucks more than his own entire pile. Three or four of the Big Mushrooms had to signal each other before they'd agreed how to fade it.

The Big Gambler shot another natural seven with exactly the same flat, stop-dead throw.

He bet another century and did it again.

And again.

And again.

Joe was getting mighty concerned and pretty indignant too. It seemed unjust that the Big Gambler should be winning such huge bets with such machinelike, utterly unromantic rolls. Why, you couldn't even call them rolls, the dice never turned over an iota, in the air or after. It was the sort of thing you'd expect from a robot, and a very dully programed robot at that. Joe hadn't risked any of his own chips fading the Big Gambler, of course, but if things went on like this he'd have to. Two of the Big Mushrooms had already retired sweatingly from the table, confessing defeat, and no one had taken their places. Pretty soon there'd be a bet the remaining Big Mushrooms couldn't entirely cover between them, and then he'd have to risk some of his own chips or else pull out of the game himself—and he couldn't do that, not with the power surging in his right hand like chained lightning.

Joe waited and waited for someone else to question one of the Big

Gambler's shots, but no one did. He realized that, despite his efforts to look imperturbable, his face was slowly reddening.

With a little lift of his left hand, the Big Gambler stopped the dice-girl as she was about to snatch at the cubes. The eyes that were like black wells directed themselves at Joe, who forced himself to look back into them steadily. He still couldn't catch the faintest gleam in them. All at once he felt the lightest touch-on-neck of a dreadful suspicion.

With the utmost civility and amiability, the Big Gambler whispered, "I believe that the fine shooter across from me has doubts about the validity of my last throw, though he is too much of a gentleman to voice them. Lottie, the card test."

The wraith-tall, ivory dice-girl plucked a playing card from below the table and with a venomous flash of her little white teeth spun it low across the table through the air at Joe. He caught the whirling pasteboard and examined it briefly. It was the thinnest, stiffest, flattest, shiniest playing card Joe had ever handled. It was also the Joker, if that meant anything. He spun it back lazily into her hand and she slid it very gently, letting it descend by its own weight, down the end wall against which the two dice lay. It came to rest in the tiny hollow their rounded edges made against the black felt. She deftly moved it about without force, demonstrating that there was no space between either of the cubes and the table's end at any point.

"Satisfied?" the Big Gambler asked. Rather against his will Joe nodded. The Big Gambler bowed to him. The dice-girl smirked her short, thin lips and drew herself up, flaunting her white-china-doorknob breasts at Joe.

Casually, almost with an air of boredom, the Big Gambler returned to his routine of shooting a century and making a natural seven. The Big Mushrooms wilted fast and one by one tottered away from the table. A particularly pink-faced Toadstool was brought extra cash by a gasping runner, but it was no help, he only lost the additional centuries. While the stacks of pale and black chips beside the Big Gambler grew skyscraper-tall.

Joe got more and more furious and frightened. He watched like a hawk or spy satellite the dice nesting against the end wall, but never could spot justification for calling for another card test, or nerve himself to question the House Rules at this late date. It was maddening, in fact insanitizing, to know that if only he could get the cubes once more he could shoot circles around that black pillar of sporting aristocracy. He damned himself a googelplex of ways for the idiotic, conceited, suicidal impulse that had led him to let go of the bones when he'd had them.

To make matters worse, the Big Gambler had taken to gazing steadily at Joe with those eyes like coal mines. Now he made three rolls running without even glancing at the dice or the end wall, as far as Joe could tell. Why, he was getting as bad as Joe's Wife or Mother—watching, watching, watching Joe.

But the constant staring of those eyes that were not eyes was mostly throwing a terrific scare into him. Supernatural terror added itself to his certainty of the deadliness of the Big Gambler, Just who, Joe kept asking himself, had he got into a game with tonight? There was curiosity and there was dread—a dreadful curiosity as strong as his desire to get the bones and win. His hair rose and he was all over goose bumps, though the power was still pulsing in his hand like a braked locomotive or a rocket wanting to lift from the pad.

At the same time the Big Gambler stayed just that—a black satin-coated, slouch-hatted elegance, suave, courtly, lethal. In fact, almost the worst thing about the spot Joe found himself in was that, after admiring the Big Gambler's perfect sportsmanship all night, he must now be disenchanted by his machinelike throwing and try to catch him out on any technicality he could.

The remorseless mowing down of the Big Mushrooms went on. The empty spaces outnumbered the Toadstools. Soon there were only three left.

The Boneyard had grown still as Cypress Hollow or the Moon. The jazz had stopped and the gay laughter and the shuffle of feet and the squeak of goosed girls and the clink of drinks and coins. Everybody seemed to be gathered around the Number One Crap Table, rank on silent rank.

Joe was racked by watchfulness, sense of injustice, self-contempt, wild hopes, curiosity and dread. Especially the last two.

The complexion of the Big Gambler, as much as you could see of it, continued to darken. For one wild moment Joe found himself wondering if he'd got into a game with a nigger, maybe a witchcraft-drenched Voodoo Man whose white make-up was wearing off.

Pretty soon there came a century wager which the two remaining

Big Mushrooms couldn't fade between them. Joe had to make up a sawbuck from his miserably tiny pile or get out of the game. After a moment's agonizing hesitation, he did the former.

And lost his ten.

The two Big Mushrooms reeled back into the hushed crowd.

Pit-black eyes bored into Joe. A whisper: "Rolling your pile."

Joe felt well up in him the shameful impulse to confess himself licked and run home. At least his six thousand dollars would make a hit with his Wife and Ma.

But he just couldn't bear to think of the crowd's laughter, or the thought of living with himself knowing that he'd had a final chance, however slim, to challenge the Big Gambler and passed it up.

He nodded.

The Big Gambler shot. Joe leaned out over and down the table, forgetting his vertigo, as he followed the throw with eagle or space-telescope eyes.

"Satisfied?"

Joe knew he ought to say, "Yes," and slink off with head held as high as he could manage. It was the gentlemanly thing to do. But then he reminded himself that he wasn't a gentleman, but just a dirty, working-stiff miner with a talent for precision hurling.

He also knew that it was probably very dangerous for him to say anything but, "Yes," surrounded as he was by enemies and strangers. But then he asked himself what right had he, a miserable, mortal, homebound failure, to worry about danger.

Besides, one of the ruby-grinning dice looked just the tiniest hair out of line with the other.

It was the biggest effort yet of Joe's life, but he swallowed and managed to say, "No. Lottie, the card test."

The dice-girl fairly snarled and reared up and back as if she were going to spit in his eyes, and Joe had a feeling her spit was cobra venom. But the Big Gambler lifted a finger at her in reproof and she skimmed the card at Joe, yet so low and viciously that it disappeared under the black felt for an instant before flying up into Joe's hand.

It was hot to the touch and singed a pale brown all over, though otherwise unimpaired. Joe gulped and spun it back high.

Sneering poisoned daggers at him, Lottie let it glide down the end wall . . . and after a moment's hesitation, it slithered behind the die Joe had suspected.

A bow and then the whisper: "You have sharp eyes, sir. Undoubtedly that die failed to reach the wall. My sincerest apologies and . . . your dice, sir."

Seeing the cubes sitting on the black rim in front of him almost gave Joe apoplexy. All the feelings racking him, including his curiosity, rose to an almost unbelievable pitch of intensity, and when he'd said, "Rolling my pile," and the Big Gambler had replied, "You're faded," he yielded to an uncontrollable impulse and cast the two dice straight at the Big Gambler's ungleaming, midnight eyes.

They went right through into the Big Gambler's skull and bounced around inside there, rattling like big seeds in a big gourd not quite yet dry.

Throwing out a hand, palm back, to either side, to indicate that none of his boys or girls or anyone else must make a reprisal on Joe, the Big Gambler dryly gargled the two cubical bones, then spat them out so that they landed in the center of the table, the one die flat, the other leaning against it.

"Cocked dice, sir," he whispered as graciously as if no indignity whatever had been done him. "Roll again."

Joe shook the dice reflectively, getting over the shock. After a little bit he decided that though he could now guess the Big Gambler's real name, he'd still give him a run for his money.

A little corner of Joe's mind wondered how a live skeleton hung together. Did the bones still have gristle and thews, were they wired, was it done with force-fields, or was each bone a calcium magnet clinging to the next?—this tying in somehow with the generation of the deadly ivory electricity.

In the great hush of The Boneyard, someone cleared his throat, a Scarlet Woman tittered hysterically, a coin fell from the nakedest change girl's tray with a golden clink and rolled musically across the floor.

"Silence," the Big Gambler commanded and in a movement almost too fast to follow whipped a hand inside the bosom of his coat and out to the crap table's rim in front of him. A short-barreled silver revolver lay softly gleaming there. "Next creature, from the humblest nigger night-girl to you, Mr. Bones, who utters a sound while my worthy opponent rolls, gets a bullet in the head."

Joe gave him a courtly bow back, it felt funny, and then decided to start his run with a natural seven made up of an ace and a six. He rolled and this time the Big Gambler, judging from the movements of his skull, closely followed the course of the cubes with his eyes that weren't there.

The dice landed, rolled over, and lay still. Incredulously, Joe realized that for the first time in his crap-shooting life he'd made a mistake. Or else there was a power in the Big Gambler's gaze greater than that in his own right hand. The six cube had come down okay, but the ace had taken an extra half roll and come down six too.

"End of the game," Mr. Bones boomed sepulchrally.

The Big Gambler raised a brown skeletal hand. "Not necessarily," he whispered. His black eyepits aimed themselves at Joe like the mouths of siege guns. "Joe Slattermill, you still have something of value to wager, if you wish. Your life."

At that a giggling and a hysterical tittering and a guffawing and a braying and a shrieking burst uncontrollably out of the whole Boneyard. Mr. Bones summed up the sentiments when he bellowed over the rest of the racket, "Now what use or value is there in the life of a bummer like Joe Slattermill? Not two cents, ordinary money."

The Big Gambler laid a hand on the revolver gleaming before him and all the laughter died.

"I have a use for it," the Big Gambler whispered. "Joe Slattermill, on my part I will venture all my winnings of tonight, and throw in the world and everything in it for a side bet. You will wager your life, and on the side your soul. You to roll the dice. What's your pleasure?"

Joe Slattermill quailed, but then the drama of the situation took hold of him. He thought it over and realized he certainly wasn't going to give up being stage center in a spectacle like this to go home broke to his Wife and Mother and decaying house and the dispirited Mr. Guts. Maybe, he told himself encouragingly, there wasn't a power in the Big Gambler's gaze, maybe Joe had just made his one and only crap-shooting error. Besides, he was more inclined to accept Mr. Bones's assessment of the value of his life than the Big Gambler's.

"It's a bet," he said.

"Lottie, give him the dice."

Joe concentrated his mind as never before, the power tingled triumphantly in his hand, and he made his throw.

The dice never hit the felt. They went swooping down, then up, in a crazy curve far out over the end of the table, and then came streaking back like tiny red-glinting meteors toward the face of the Big Gambler, where they suddenly nested and hung in his black eye sockets, each with the single red gleam of an ace showing.

Snake eyes.

The whisper, as those red-glinting dice-eyes stared mockingly at him: "Joe Slattermill, you've crapped out."

Using thumb and middle finger—or bone rather—of either hand, the Big Gambler removed the dice from his eye sockets and dropped them in Lottie's white-gloved hand.

"Yes, you've crapped out, Joe Slattermill," he went on tranquilly. "And now you can shoot yourself"—he touched the silver gun— "or cut your throat"—he whipped a gold-handled bowie knife out of his coat and laid it beside the revolver—"or poison yourself"—the two weapons were joined by a small black bottle with white skull and crossbones on it—"or Miss Flossie here can kiss you to death." He drew forward beside him his prettiest, evilest-looking sporting girl. She preened herself and flounced her short violet skirt and gave Joe a provocative, hungry look, lifting her carmine upper lip to show her long white canines.

"Or else," the Big Gambler added, nodding significantly toward the black-bottomed crap table, "you can take the Big Dive."

Joe said evenly, "I'll take the Big Dive."

He put his right foot on his empty chip table, his left on the black rim, fell forward . . . and suddenly kicking off from the rim, launched himself in a tiger spring straight across the crap table at the Big Gambler's throat, solacing himself with the thought that certainly the poet chap hadn't seemed to suffer long.

As he flashed across the exact center of the table he got an instant photograph of what really lay below, but his brain had no time to develop that snapshot, for the next instant he was plowing into the Big Gambler.

Stiffened brown palm edge caught him in the temple with a light-ninglike judo chop . . . and the brown fingers or bones flew all apart like puff paste. Joe's left hand went through the Big Gambler's chest as if there were nothing there but black satin coat, while his right hand, straight-armedly clawing at the slouch-hatted skull, crunched it to pieces. Next instant Joe was sprawled on the floor with some black clothes and brown fragments.

He was on his feet in a flash and snatching at the Big Gambler's tall stacks. He had time for one left-handed grab. He couldn't see any gold or silver or any black chips, so he stuffed his left pants pocket with a handful of the pale chips and ran.

Then the whole population of The Boneyard was on him and after him. Teeth, knives and brass knuckles flashed. He was punched, clawed, kicked, tripped and stamped on with spike heels. A gold-plated trumpet with a bloodshot-eyed black face behind it bopped him on the head. He got a white flash of the golden dice-girl and made a grab for her, but she got away. Someone tried to mash a lighted cigar in his eye. Lottie, writhing and flailing like a white boa constrictor, almost got a simultaneous strangle hold and scissors on him. From a squat wide-mouth bottle Flossie, snarling like a feline fiend, threw what smelt like acid past his face. Mr. Bones peppered shots around him from the silver revolver. He was stabbed at, gouged, rabbit-punched, scragmauled, slugged, kneed, bitten, bearhugged, butted, beaten and had his toes trampled.

But somehow none of the blows or grabs had much real force. It was like fighting ghosts. In the end it turned out that the whole population of The Boneyard, working together, had just a little more strength than Joe. He felt himself being lifted by a multitude of hands and pitched out through the swinging doors so that he thudded down on his rear end on the board sidewalk. Even that didn't hurt much. It was more like a kick of encouragement.

He took a deep breath and felt himself over and worked his bones. He didn't seem to have suffered any serious damage. He stood up and looked around. The Boneyard was dark and silent as the grave, or the planet Pluto, or all the rest of Ironmine. As his eyes got accustomed to the starlight and occasional roving spaceship-gleam, he saw a padlocked sheet-iron door where the swinging ones had been.

He found he was chewing on something crusty that he'd somehow carried in his right hand all the way through the final fracas. Mighty tasty, like the bread his Wife baked for best customers. At that instant his brain developed the photograph it had taken when he had glanced down as he flashed across the center of the crap table. It was a thin wall of flames moving sideways across the table and just beyond the flames the faces of his Wife, Mother, and Mr. Guts, all looking very surprised. He realized that what he was chewing was a fragment of the Big Gambler's skull, and he remembered the shape of the three loaves his Wife had started to bake when he left the house. And he understood the magic she'd made to let him get a little ways away and feel half a man, and then come diving home with his fingers burned.

He spat out what was in his mouth and pegged the rest of the bit of giant-popover skull across the street.

He fished in his left pocket. Most of the pale poker chips had been mashed in the fight, but he found a whole one and explored its surface with his fingertips. The symbol embossed on it was a cross. He lifted it to his lips and took a bite. It tasted delicate, but delicious. He ate it and felt his strength revive. He patted his bulging left pocket. At least he'd start out well provisioned.

Then he turned and headed straight for home, but he took the long way, around the world.

## Afterword:

The story of the bogeyman is the oldest and best in the world, because it is the story of courage, of fear vanquished by knowledge gained by plunging into the unknown at risk or seeming risk: the discovery that the terrifying white figure is nothing but a man with a sheet over his head, or perhaps a black man smeared with white ashes. Primitive tribes such as the Australian aborigines ritualized the bogeyman story in their initiation ceremonies for boys and today we need it as much as ever. For the modern American male, as for Joe Slattermill, the ultimate bogey may turn out to be the Mom figure: domineering-dependent Wife or Mother, exaggerating their claims on him beyond all reason and bound. Science itself is a battle against such bogeys as Cancer Is Incurable, Sex Is Filthy, Backbreaking Toil Is Man's Lot Forever, People Can't Fly, the Stars Are Out of Reach, Man Was Not Meant to Know (or Do) This, That, or the Other. At least that was how I was feeling when I wrote "Gonna Roll the Bones."

I chose the American tall tale as a form (or it chose me) because the space age precision-fits the wild credulity-straining exploits of legendary figures such as Mike Fink, Pecos Pete, Tony Beaver, the steel-driving John Henry, and the space-striding though dubious Paul Bunyan, one quarter genuine north-woods article, three quarters twentieth century invention. I got a kick out of making a final story point out of the elementary proposition in solid geometry that between any two points on a sphere like Earth there are always two straight or direct great-circle routes, even if one is only a mile long and the other 24,000. A wild talent for crap shooting isn't just a gambler's dream; psycho-kinesis exercised on dice has long been a field of experimental inquiry among university researchers into extrasensory perception. I enjoyed pumping the lingo of dice for its poetry and mixing space flight with witchcraft, which is just another word for the powers of self-hypnotism, prayer, suggestion and the whole subconscious mind. It's a mistake to think that science fiction is an off-trail and posted literary area; it can be an ingredient of any sort of fiction, just as science and technology today enter into our lives at every point.

## Introduction to LORD RANDY, MY SON:

We were plunging *up* a dangerously twisting valley road in Madison, Indiana. The tires squealed like shoats and I cowered in a far-right corner of the front seat. It was a *big* car, and he continually executed four-wheel drifts around curves that sent the back wheels over the edge. I got one clear view down into the green and handsome valley in which Madison nestled as we tipped precariously, and he accelerated going into another turn. Behind us, I suddenly heard the growler of an Indiana State Trooper as his gumball machine flashed a warning red. He was coming up on us fast. The speed limit was twenty on these lunatic curves, but the lunatic behind the wheel was doing almost seventy. I was grateful for the fuzz coming up on us; I might spend the night in the slammer as unwilling accomplice to the driver, but by God I'd be alive to be arraigned. The driver could clearly see the fuzzmobile in his rear-view, but he didn't seem to give a damn. He floored the accelerator and the big sedan surged around another curve. I think I screamed.

(Most unusual for me. I used to drive a dynamite truck in North Carolina, than whose roads there are none twistier, and I'm not easily shook. But aside from Norman Spinrad's driving, I'm a good passenger, also having raced sports cars. But *this* time . . .)

Finally we mounted the crest of the hill and the big sedan let out full. Around 110 I yowled for the driver to stop before that bloody Indiana cop sailed right up our tailpipe. He grinned lopsidedly—which is the *only* way he can smile—and hit the brakes. We slewed to a stop, half into the oncoming lane, and I collapsed against the seat. The fuzzmobile jazzed in and around us, barely missing us, and locked brakes. The whipcord cop came on the run, his face spotted with fury. He took seven-league strides and was shrieking even before he got his head in the window. His gun was drawn. "You dumb sonofabitch!" he yelled, the throat cords standing out in cunning relief. "You know how fast you were goin', you ignorant goddam clown? You know you coulda killed me and you and everybody else on this goddam road, you goddam dumb . . . oh, hi, Joe."

He grinned and holstered the big-barreled weapon. "Sorry, Joe, didn't recognize you." He grinned hugely, shrugged his shoulders as if he knew it was the Natural Order, and walked away. He pulled out fast, Joe slipped it into drive and burned rubber following him. "Friend of mine," said Joe L. Hensley. Grinning lopsidedly. I think I fainted.

Carol Carr says Joe L. Hensley is a teddy bear. Sure he is.

Change of scene: Fort Knox, Kentucky, 1958. I am standing in front of the Captain, CO of my infantry company. He is very unhappy with me. I have hornswoggled him. I have been living out of the barracks in a trailer for the past six months though I'm no longer married, which he has only recently found out. He is furious with me. I have broken every rule imaginable in his company. He hates me a lot. He is yelling that he will see my ass in Leavenworth, and he means it. I suddenly break and run, dashing out of his office, through the orderly room, down the hall, and into the dayroom. I get into the phone booth and close the door, pulling the receiver with me. I dial long distance and ask for Madison, Indiana. They are looking for me. The slat-wood lower half of the booth hides me from sight. I get my number in Madison. "Joe!" I howl. "They're tryin' to railroad me. . . . HALP, JOE!" They have located me now, they are trying to get into the booth. I have my leg locked in position, holding it closed. They take a fire ax and break the glass. They drag me out; I'm still clutching the receiver screaming, "HALP, JOE!" They haul me back into the Captain's office. He puts me under armed guard until the court-martial papers can be drawn up.

"Your ass will die in Leavenworth!" shouts the Captain, becoming apoplectic.

Within two hours there are three, count 'em, *three* Congressional Inquiries on the Captain's desk. Why are you annoying Pfc Ellison? one of them says. Leave Pfc Ellison alone, a second one says. Pfc Ellison has *friends,* the third one warns. Then Stuart Symington's inquiry comes in, and the Captain knows he has been outgunned. He sentences me to one week washing barracks windows. My ass never sees the inside of Leavenworth. The Captain has a nervous breakdown and is sent to the Bahamas to recover, if possible. Joe L. Hensley is out there in Madison, Indiana, grinning lopsidedly.

Carol Carr says Joe L. Hensley is a pussycat. Better believe it.

Hensley is not to be believed. Legend-in-his-own-time kind of thing. He is one of the most gigantic men I've ever seen. Well over six foot six, he is solid meat from top to bottom, with a fuzzy crew cut that makes his head look like one of those plaster gimcracks you used to be able to buy in Woolworth's that you plant the grass seed in, and it grows out to look like Joe's crew cut. He has a face made of Silly Putty and he loves to twist it into imbecilic expressions, giving the impression he is a waterhead. It only serves to lull the opposition into a false sense of security. One night in a bar in Evansville, Indiana, Joe and I were braced by a pair of *lummoxen* who wanted to brawl. Joe got that cockeyed grin on his face, began making guttural sounds like Lenny in *Of Mice and Men* and burbled, "Sure I'd like t'fight, uh-huh, sure, sure I would," and he went over to a brick wall and started pounding it with his "dead" hand—the one with the nerve ends dulled from having been scorched in a fire—until the bricks shattered and his hand was ripped and torn and bits of bone were sticking out through the torn skin and blood was all over the place. The two bully boys suddenly went very green, one of them murmured, "This guy is a nut!" and they fled in horror. I think I vomited.

All of which only begins to shade in the incredible personality of Hensley the Runamuck. Despite the fact that he is the very incarnation of Morgan/McMurphy/Yossarian/Sebastian Dangerfield/Gully Jimson all hoisted up into one petard, Hensley is a pillar of the community, a highly respected attorney whose political record reads as follows:

County attorney for Jefferson County, Indiana, in 1960; attorney for the Madison City Plan Commission from 1959 to 1962; elected to Indiana General Assembly in 1960, serving in 1961–62; chairman of the Governor's Traffic Safety Advisory Commission from 1961 to 1965; member of the Criminal Code Commission of the state of Indiana;

elected prosecuting attorney of the Fifth Judicial Circuit of the state of Indiana. In 1966 he ran for the legislature again in a five-county area and was shabbily defeated by 70 votes. It was possibly his coming out in favor of smut and pornography that turned the tide. It was called Bluenose Backlash.

Joe was born in Bloomington, Indiana, in 1926 and grew up there, and grew up and up and up and up. He attended Indiana University for both undergrad and law school work. He served two years overseas during Nastiness No. 2 in the South Pacific, and was recalled for sixteen delightful months during WW II½, Korea. He is married to the lovely Charlotte (and she *gotta* be lovely for me to like her with a name like that, which was the name of my first wife, which is another story en*tire*ly) and has one child, Mike, age twelve.

I first met Hensley at a Midwestern Science Fiction Convention in the middle Fifties, and we have been chums ever since. There are those who contend we are the contemporary incarnation of the Rover Boys. Them as says it refuse to present themselves for personal attention by the deponents. Joe does not write nearly as much as he should. His talent is a natural, free-wheeling delight, kept in check chiefly by his analytical lawyer's mind. The emotional content of a Hensley story, however, is usually several points higher than most of the current scriveners' crop. I will let the madman speak in his own defense at this point:

"I began writing in 1951 and sold one of my early efforts to *Planet Stories*. Thereafter, I entered into an agreeable and interesting relationship with them. I would write a story, and *Planet* would buy it. I began selling to other magazines and have had sales to such magazines as *Swank* (with Harlan Ellison), *Rogue* (with Harlan Ellison), *Amazing Stories* (with Harlan Ellison), and to most of the science fiction and men's magazines, such as *Gent, Dapper* and others (without Harlan Ellison). A novel, *The Color of Hate,* was published in 1960; another, *Deliver Us to Evil,* is making the rounds; and a third, *Privileged Communication* (title suggested by Harlan Ellison), is under way and will be completed this year.

"The story that follows I consider to be the best short story that I have written, ever. *Other than that, deponent saith not.*"

## ● LORD RANDY, MY SON

### by Joe L. Hensley

*He rebelled on the night the call came to leave the warm and liquid place; but in that way he was weak and nature was strong. Outside, the rains came; a storm so formidable that forecasters referred to it for all of the time that was left. He fought to remain with the mother thing, but the mother thing expelled him and in fear and rage he hurt the mother thing subtly. Black clouds hid the stars and the trees bent only to the wind.*

The night before, Sam Moore had let his son Randall play late in the yard—if "play" it was. The boy had no formal games and the neighborhood children shunned the area of the Moore house. Sometimes a child would yell at the boy insultingly from some hidden place, but mostly now they stayed away.

Sam sat in the chaise longue and watched dully, trapped in the self-pity of writing his own obituary, asking the timeless questions: Who were you? What did you ever do? And why me? Why me now?

He watched the child with concealed revulsion. Randall moved quietly along the back line of hedges, his small boy eyes watchful of the other yards that bordered his own. There had been a time when it was a fetish with the neighbor children to fling a rock when passing, before the two Swihart boys, running away after disposing of their missiles, had fallen into a well no one had even known existed in the corner lot. Too bad about them, but Randall lived with the remembrance of the rocks and appeared to distrust the amnesty. Sam watched as the boy continued his patrol.

The pain within had been worse on that day and Sam longed for the forgetfulness of sleep.

Finally it was time.

*The first one came in silence and the memories of that night are lost in time. That one grew easily and alone, for only later life is chronicled. His people migrated and memory flickered into a mass of legends. But the blood was there.*

Item: The old man had gardened in the neighborhood for several years. He was a bent man with a soft, broken-toothed smile, bad English, and a remembrance of things past: swastikas, yellow stars, Buchenwald. Now and then he wrote simple poems and sent them to the local newspaper and once they had printed one. He was a friendly old man and he spoke to everyone, including one of the teenage, neighborhood queens. She chose to misunderstand him and reported his friendliness as something more.

On that day, a year gone now, the old man had been digging at rose-bushes in the front yard of the house across the street. Randall had watched, sucking at a peppermint stick the old man had given him, letting the juice run from the corners of his mouth.

The black car had squealed to a stop and the three purposeful boys gotten out. They wore yellow sweaters. On the back of each sweater an eagle had been cunningly worked into the material so that the woven wings seemed to take new flight as shoulders moved. Each boy carried a chain-saw band with a black taped handle. Randall watched them with growing interest, not really understanding yet.

They beat the old man with powerful, tackle-football arms and he had cowered away, crying out in a guttural, foreign tongue. It was over quickly. The old man lay crumpled and bleeding in the rich, dark dirt. The boys piled back into the black car and peeled away at high speed. Randall could hear the sounds of their laughter, like pennants fluttering after them.

Two blocks away the land was not suitable for building. There was a steep hill. The tire blew there and the black car went over the hill gaining speed. It cartwheeled down, spouting enormous geysers of flame, a miniature ferris wheel gone mad; and fire gushed out with an overpowering roaring sound that *almost* blocked out the screams.

In the morning Sam Moore awoke unrefreshed. On that Saturday the housekeeper-babysitter came on time for a change and he left them sitting in the family room. The television was blaring a bloody war movie, where men died in appalling numbers. Randall was seated, legs crossed, on the floor in front of the television, watching avidly. Mrs. Cable watched the screen and refused to meet Sam's glance, lost in her own bitter world. There'd been a time when Sam had issued instructions before leaving, but those days were gone. Not very many women would care for a retarded child. Now, enmeshed in his own problem, and really not caring much, he said little. If the watching was casual and the safety of the boy only probable . . . he had still carried out the formal, social necessities of child care.

He looked at the boy and something within him darkened. Ann had been brilliant and her pregnancy had been normal; but the birth had been difficult and the boy a monstrous problem. She had changed. The boy had not. Early tests on him had been negative, but physically there had always been a lack of interest, slow movement, eyes that could track and follow, but did not.

He could not force himself to approach the boy this morning.

"Good-by," he said, and received a brief look upward with minor recognition involved. A boy is only three once; but what happens when he is three and eight at the same time? When he will be three forever?

On the television screen a dark-skinned soldier dragged his white captain from the path of an onrushing tank. Sam remembered the script. It was one of Hollywood's message films. Comradeship would continue until the dark-skinned one needed another kind of help.

Outside, he failed to notice the loveliness of the day. He stood in front of the garage and considered. (With the rolling door down, the garage was tight. He could start the car and it would be easy. That was what Ann, his wife, had done, but for a different reason and in a different way. She'd swallowed a box of sleeping pills when he was out of town trying a case. That had been a long time ago after the hospitals and clinics, after the last of the faith healers with their larcenous, sickening morality, the confident, grasping herbalists, the slick charlatans and quacks to whom, in desperation, she'd taken the boy. Four years now. No one had examined Randall since.

(She'd never been really *there* after Randall was born. She'd wandered on for a while, large, sensitive eyes looking out from some faraway place, her mind a cluttered dustbin of what might have been.

("Just don't touch me," she had said. "I know they said we ought to have another, but don't. . . . Please, Sam." And that which was still partially alive in him had died. He knew it was the boy. Now . . . it wasn't that he'd not loved her, but he could recall her face only in the boy's face, in that small and hateful visage, that face that had killed the thing Sam loved.)

He rolled up the garage door with a clang, and drove to his law office. Another day, perhaps another dollar. There weren't many days left now. Dr. Yancey had said sixmonthstoayear and that had been more than four months ago; on the day they had opened Sam Moore and quickly sutured him again to hide the corrupt mass inside.

"Too far along," Yancey had said, and then added the old words of despair that many men finally hear: "Nothing we can do."

*Siddharta Gautama came easily in the park with the remembrance of elephants. Legends say that the trees bowed to him. His mother, Maya, felt sustained by an intense feeling of power. The blood was strong, but the child was slow and sheltered and the fulfillment never reached, the gift grown into vagueness, never fully used.*

Item: Randall sat under a tree in front of the Moore house. He watched the world around him with curious intensity. A honey bee flew near and he watched the creature with some concern, but it did not attack. They didn't bother him much since that one had stung him in the spring, and he'd destroyed them all for a ten-block radius.

He could hear the loud noise long before he could tell from where it came. A sound truck blared close by. In a few moments it came to Randall's corner and slowed. On its side there was a garish picture of a man in priestly robes holding a rifle in front of his chest, eyes flashing fire. The sign below said: "Father Tempest Fights Communism." Music boomed over the speakers, decibels above the permitted limits. Randall held his ears. The sound hurt.

The driver cut the music back and turned up the volume for his hand microphone. "Big rally tonight!" he called. "Hear Father Tempest save the world and tell YOU how to fight the infiltrators who would destroy us. High school gym, seven o'clock." The voice took on a threatening note. "Don't let your neighbors be there without you." In the other seat beside the driver, a man in priestly robes smiled and made beneficent gestures as people came to doors and windows.

Overhead there were sudden clouds and a few drops of rain fell. Lightning bolted from the sky, missed the tall trees, and made a direct hit on the sound truck. Silence came and Randall removed his hands from his ears. People ran into the street and, in a while, Randall could hear a siren.

He left the front yard and went to the window at the side. From there he could see Mrs. Cable. She had managed somehow to sleep through it all. Her mouth hung open and she snored with an easy rhythm. The television was still on, hot with a soap opera now.

Randall began to pace the back hedge fence, guarding it. There'd been one boy who appeared friendly and would smile at Randall and then slyly do little things of pinching and hitting when no one watched. That was the boy with the BB gun, who shot the squirrel that took the bits of food from Randall's hand, the boy who killed one of the fish in the fishpond. The squirrel still lived, but it was more cautious now. And there were still three fish in the pond. There had always been three, except for that one day. One of the fish now was not quite the same color and shape as the others.

The big dog came into the yard through the hedge and they frisked together.

Randall smiled at the dog. "Nice dog," he said. A stump of tail waved in adoration.

Sam spent a dreary day in the office, snapping at his secretary, being remote to clients. Now he was not as busy as he'd once been. He refused cases that might drag. Partly it was the alien thing that grew inside, but partly—and he had a sort of sullen pride about it—there was the matter of being too good at his job. He'd surrounded himself with that job when Ann had gone, merged into it. Now he refused the proffered retainers to defend or prosecute that which he knew he wouldn't live to see. It was a minor, ethical point, but a man takes greater cognizance of minor points when he begins to die.

His own decisions grew harder to make and clients read it in his eyes and voice. The motley mob that had once invaded his office fell to a whisper and soon, there was time.

He thought about the boy. He knew he'd ignored the child after Ann's death and, worse, he'd hated the boy, relating it back to Ann, knowing that her suicide was a product of what the boy was.

The newspaper offered escape. The world grew more sour daily and so seemed easier to leave. Today two more countries had quit the United Nations. Sweden reported increased fallout. There was indecisiveness over a new test ban. Two African nations announced the development of their own bombs. In Mississippi a member of a fanatical white organization had shot and killed a circuit judge who'd sentenced nine men accused and convicted of lynching a civil rights worker. In his own state an amendment to the state constitution outlawing the death penalty had lost by a wide margin.

On the way home there was an ache in his back that had never been there before.

*Ching-tsai dreamed deeply on the night of coming. The chi-lin appeared to her. She dreamed and missed the dragons that walked the quiet skies. Once again the child was slow and sheltered and kept apart.*

Item: Mrs. Cable slept on. Keeping away from prime time, which was reserved for westerns, giveaway shows, comedies and the like, the television presented a program on a housing development in New York. They showed the tenements that were being replaced; they showed the narrow streets and the tired and dirty people. Cameras cleverly watched as the buildings came down and high-rise, low-rent apartments were built. The reporter's voice was flat and laconic. Crime continued in the rebuilt area. The favorite now was to catch the rent collector in the elevator, strip him, and jam small change up his rectum. Rape increased, for the apartments were better soundproofed than the old tenements.

Randall watched. The people still looked tired and dirty.

After the documentary there was another soap opera. Mrs. Cable came awake and they watched together. This one was about a man and woman who were in love and who were married, but unfortunately not to each other.

The house was hot and empty. Sam went to the open window and saw them. Mrs. Cable was stretched out on the chaise longue, a paper held over her eyes to block the fierce sun. Randall was at the goldfish pond that Sam had constructed in a happier year. Three hardy goldfish had outlived the last harsh winter and the indifferent spring. What they subsisted on, Sam could not guess. He knew that *he* didn't feed them.

The boy held small hands over the pool and Sam watched covertly.

It was as if the child felt Sam's eyes on him, for he turned his head and smiled directly at the window. They he turned again to the pool, trailing quick hands in the water. The right one came up gently grasping a goldfish. The boy passed it from hand to hand, inspecting it as it wriggled, then dropped it into the water and the hand sought another.

It was something that Sam had never seen before, but the boy did it with an air, as if it were an often-repeated act.

Randall had an affinity for animals. Sam remembered the incident of the dog. The back neighbors owned a large and cantankerous German shepherd that had been a neighborhood terror since acquisition. Once, when Randall made one of his periodic runaways, Sam had come upon the boy huddled against the dog. Sam stood watching, half expecting the animal, which its owners normally kept carefully chained, to rend and tear. But the dog made no overt move and only whined when Sam took the boy away.

Lately the dog's conduct must have improved with age, for Sam had seen it playing happily about the neighborhood.

He made up a check and took it out to Mrs. Cable. It paid her for the week and she took it with good grace. Payday was the only time she unbent and showed any real desire to talk.

"Lots of excitement," she said. "Lightning hit a truck right down the street. I was asleep, but Mrs. Taldemp was telling me. Two men killed." She shook her head in wonder. "Right down the street and I missed it." She nodded at Randall. "He's coming along. He does things he didn't used to do. Those mean little ones that used to throw rocks don't come close any more. He used to try to run to them and give them his toys, but he just watches now if he sees one. They stay away when he's outside." She shook her head. "He still don't talk much, but sometimes he'll say something right out loud and clear when I ain't expecting it." She laughed her whinny laugh. "It's a shame nothing can be done for him. You still trying to get him in that state dumb school?"

Sam fought the pain inside. "Not much use," he said shortly. "They're full. He's way down the list to get in."

He escorted her to the front door. On most days she kept conversation to a minimum, but today she wouldn't run down.

"He's sure quick. There's a squirrel up in one of them trees. I turned my back and he was up there feeding it. I thought you said that old elm was rotten?"

Sam nodded. Every movement sent a wave of pain up his back.

"Well, he climbed up it and I had a dickens of a time getting him down. Don't seem rotten to me," she grumbled.

It was rotten. It had died this spring and never come out in leaves. Sam could see it vaguely out the back window. The other trees were in full leaf. He imagined that he could see buds and small leaves on the elm, but he knew he must be wrong.

He finally got Mrs. Cable out the door and called Doc Yancey. When that was done he eased gingerly into a chair. The pain receded slightly. The boy sat on the floor watching him with a child's curious intentness, head cocked slightly, completely without embarrassment. Sam admitted to himself that the boy was handsome. His features were regular, his body wiry and strong. Once Sam had visited the State Mentally Retarded Home and the eyes of the children there were what he most remembered. Most of those eyes had been dull and without luster. A few of the eyes had been foolers. Randall's eyes were foolers. They were bright with the brightness of cold snow, but they lacked involvement with the world around him.

"You hurt, Father?" Randall questioned. He made a tiny gesture with one hand, as if he were testifying and had found a sudden truth and was surprised by it. "You hurt, Father," he said again. He pointed out the window. "All hurt," he said.

"Yes," Sam said. "The whole world hurts."

The boy turned away as Sam heard the car in the drive. It was Dr. Yancey. The man came in with brisk steps and Sam had a moment of quick, consuming hatred for the other man; the solid, green envy of the sick for the well.

Dr. Yancey spoke first to the boy. "Hello, Randy. How are you to-day?"

For a moment Sam did not think the boy would answer.

Randall looked at the doctor without particular interest. "I am young," he said finally, in falsetto.

"He says that sometimes to people," Sam said. "I think he means he's all right."

Yancey went into the kitchen and brought back water and a yellow capsule. "This won't put you under." He handed the capsule and water to Sam and Sam downed them dutifully. He let Yancey help him from the chair to the couch. Expert fingers probed him. The boy watched with some interest.

"You're swollen, but there aren't any real signs of serious organ failure. You really ought to be in a hospital."

"Not yet," Sam said softly. "There's the boy." He looked up at Yancey. "How long, Doc?" He asked it not really wanting to know and yet wanting to know.

"Not very long now, Sam. I think the cancer's spread to the spine." He kept his voice low and turned to see if the boy was listening.

Randall got up from the floor. He moved quietly and gracefully out of the room and down the hall. A light clicked on in the study.

"He's sort of unnerving," Sam said. "He'll go back in the study and get down books and turn pages. I've got a good encyclopedia back there and some medical books I use in damage cases. I suppose he likes the pictures. Sometimes he spends hours back there."

*Some say Ubu'l Kassim destroyed his father two months before the coming. The shock of death and birth weakened the mother thing and she died a few years after. His life was confused, moving from relative to relative, slow maturation. Something within him hid from the world until early manhood.*

Item: The books were puzzling. There was so much in them that was so clearly wrong, but they were not cruel of themselves, only stupid and careless. He remembered the mother-thing and wondered why he had hurt her. The father-thing was hurt also, but he had not done that. There was no love in the father-thing, but the father-thing had never hurt him.

The books were no help.

Alone, unaided by what the world had become and what it meant to him, he made his decision. He made it for the one time and the one thing, putting the rest back, delaying.

The pill was effective for a few hours and then it began to wear off. He took another and checked the boy. Randall lay in his bed, small body lost in covers, breathing slowly, evenly, his eyes open.

"Where is the mother?" he asked.

There were two feelings. Sam had the desire to destroy the boy and an equal feeling to catch the child up and hold him close. He did neither. He rearranged the covers.

"She's gone far away," he said softly to the boy.

Randall nodded.

Sam straightened the study. The boy had been at his books again. He put them back on the shelves. He went to his own bed. Sleep came quickly.

Outside, in the neighborhood, most lights were still on. People stared uneasily at their television screens. There was another confrontation, this time in the Near East. Hands moved closer to the red button, the button that man had made. The President spoke and tensions eased, for some. The world, for what it was and what all men had made it, would remain for a while.

For Sam there was a dream.

The faces of a thousand clients came and blended into one sick and ignorant and prejudiced face, a "never-had" and "never-will" face that whined the injustice of life as it spawned children to be supported by the myriad public doles. It was a face that Sam knew well, a face that pleaded for divorce and demanded alimony and plotted rape and confessed murder. It was a face that hated all minorities and majorities of which it was not the leading member, that cursed fate and defrauded welfare. Partly the face was familiar and he knew it, for it was his own face.

It was a dream built of fifteen years of practice. It was not a nightmare, for it was far better than life.

The dream fit life though, and at the moment of dreaming, if he could have made a rational choice, if the instinct for life had not been so strong and inbred, he would have chosen death.

He came almost to wakefulness once, but he slid back into the well where there was only one tiny circle of light. Ann and the boy were there. They touched him with soft hands. He turned them into the circle of life and their faces could be seen and those faces bore the same marks as his client-self face, cruel, sick, angry, and in pain. Their hands still touched him and he writhed to escape, revolted at the touch. With horrible pain and with tearing and burning he retched the gorge within him away.

He awoke.

Only one pair of hands was real.

Randall stood by the bed. The boy's hands were laid lightly across the bed, resting and unmoving on Sam's chest. There was something in the boy's face, an awareness, a feeling. Sam could not read it all, but there was satisfaction and accomplishment and perhaps even love. Then expression wandered away. The boy yawned and removed his hands. He walked away and Sam soon heard the rustle of the silk comforter from the boy's bedroom.

A spasm of empty pain came. Sam got up weakly and made it to the kitchen and took another pill and sat for a while on the couch until it took effect. He came back past the boy's room and looked in. Randall lay straight in bed. There was a bright sheen of sweat on the child's forehead. His eyes were open, watching and waiting.

"I am young," the child said again, plaintively and to no one.

"Yes," Sam said softly. "So very young."

"There was a head thing," Randall said slowly, searching for words. "Hurt doggy." He reached a small finger out and laid it on Sam's wrist. "Fish always hungry. I gave to them." He shook his head. "See words. Can't say them." Confidence came in his voice. "I will grow more quickly now." He moved his hands off Sam's wrist and closer to the abdomen. "All gone now. All gone every place," he said, and the look of Sam's bedroom came fleetingly again.

Sam watched without comprehension.

The cold, lost eyes watched him and the next words turned Sam's blood cold. The boy's voice came up in volume and with a ferocity that Sam had never heard before. "See things on teevee, read them in the books and papers, so many bad things, all hate out there like others hate me." He touched his own small head. "So many things in here not ready yet." The eyelids closed tight and a tiny tear came at each corner. "Not sorry. I will grow older," Randall said, his voice a cruel, unhuman promise.

*There was Another who was born in a manger and died on a cross. That One was sheltered for a while and maturity was unforced.*

*But the new One, the One born for our times, would see man's consuming hate of all others, so consuming that the hate extends even to himself. See it in Alabama and Vietnam and even in the close world around Him. See it on television and read of it in the newspapers and then grow unsheltered in this world of mass and hysterical com-munication.*

*Then plan. Then decide.*

*This one would come to maturity and ripen angry.*

## Afterword:

As this story appears I will have passed my fortieth birthday, a danger-ous time in itself. I suppose that this is a story that I've wanted to do for a very long time, but the writing of it and particularly the finishing of it, the polishing that makes a told-tale into a story, had a depressing effect upon me. I was unable to shake the feeling that in some way I was flaunting God. There was a time when I seriously considered with-drawing the story, but I'm glad now that I didn't. In its way "Lord Randy, My Son" is a deeply religious story, combining that part of me which is best with that part of the world I recognize as worst, but then it's always been a bad but interesting world. I am a lawyer by profession and I will admit that parts of the dream sequence are intensely personal.

If a writer is ever happy with any story, except the "next" one that he's *going* to do, then I'm happy with this one.

## Introduction to EUTOPIA:

When it came time to write this introduction for Poul Anderson's story, I found—with panic rising—that somehow Poul had not been asked for biographical data to be worked into the piece. Each of the other writers had been asked and had sent in his background, as well as the afterword. I had an afterword for "Eutopia," but nothing on Anderson. For a moment I wondered why Poul and no one else had been overlooked. And then it became obvious to me. You would not have to threaten me with thumbscrews or the iron boot to get me to admit I am a sucker for Poul Anderson's work. Nor would it take pressure for me to confess I have read just about everything the man has written in the field of speculative fiction for the past sixteen years. Therefore, such familiarity bred an unconscious feeling in this editor that an introduction could be written with no facts at all. I would rather believe that than the alternative, which is that I'm a forgetful imbecile. One *must* cling to the cornerstones of one's personal religion.

I have my favorite Anderson stories, so do you. I have re-read "Un-

Man" and "Guardians of Time" and the Hoka stories (written with Gordy Dickson) and "The High Crusade" and "Three Hearts and Three Lions" at least three times each, and several of them half a dozen times. When it became clear that I would have to dredge up biographical facts from *somewhere,* I began scrounging my bookshelves for Anderson volumes: it was slim pickings, I was only able to pull down thirty-two books. The man is *incapable* of writing a dull word!

But aside from the obvious credentials, such as that he has won two Hugos, he is married and has a daughter named Astrid and lives in Orinda, California; he graduated from the University of Minnesota with a degree in physics; his *Perish by the Sword,* a mystery novel, won the first Macmillan Cock Robin Award; in 1959 he was Guest of Honor at the World Science Fiction Convention; he sold his first stories in 1947 (both were novelettes, "Tomorrow's Children" and "Logic") to *Astounding;* he was born in Bristol, Pennsylvania; aside from all of these rather mundane facts (and the singular one that *Esquire,* world-renowned for its depth of perceptivity and exhaustive research into anything it prints, cleverly managed—in its January 1966 issue—to label a full-page color photo of Poul with the name A. E. van Vogt, and Van's photo was slug-lined Poul Anderson), there are *secrets* so deeply buried that only personal acquaintance with the man's work can unearth them. So for the first time anywhere, in its own way a dangerous vision, the veil is ripped aside and the *truth* about Poul Anderson can be told:

Because of Anderson's extreme height and his penchant for writing stories about mightily thewed heroes, many of them either reincarnations or descendants of Viking conquerors, the rumor has persisted that Anderson is of Norse ancestry. This is sheer flummery. Poul Anderson (pronounced slightly softer than *pull*) is *actually* one meter tall in stockinged feet (and he wears those *odious* clocked lisle socks), tubby and golden-furred, with a round blunt-muzzled head and small black eyes. Except for his stubby-fingered hands, he resembles nothing so much as a giant teddy bear. It is a tribute to his powers of personal persuasion and the kindness of those around him that he is able to pass himself off as a gangling six-footer with a bushy head of hair and a raconteur's manner of speaking with wildly gesticulating hands the size of picnic hams.

Poul Anderson has never written one word of the stories credited to him. They have *all* been written by F. N. Waldrop, an asthmatic mail clerk in the rural free delivery office of Muscatine, Iowa. Anderson, by dint of threats and personal vilification, has kept Waldrop in thrall for better than twenty years. The fact that Anderson kidnaped Waldrop's three children in 1946 has not helped the situation much, either.

And as a last laughable untruth, Poul Anderson insists the story which follows is not "dangerous" and could have sold to any magazine. Tell that to *McCall's* or *Boy's Life* after you've read it. And please address all libel suits to F. N. Waldrop, RFD, Muscatine, Iowa.

# ● EUTOPIA

## by Poul Anderson

*"Gif thit nafn!"*

The Danska words barked from the car radio as a jet whine cut across the hum of motor and tires. "Identify yourself!" Iason Philippou cast a look skyward through the bubbletop. He saw a strip of blue between two ragged green walls where pine forest lined the road. Sunlight struck off the flanks of the killer machine up there. It wailed, came about, and made a circle over him.

Sweat started cold from his armpits and ran down his ribs. *I must not panic,* he thought in a corner of his brain. *May the God help me now.* But it was his training he invoked. Psychosomatics: control the symptoms, keep the breath steady, command the pulse to slow, and the fear of death becomes something you can handle. He was young, and thus had much to lose. But the philosophers of Eutopia schooled well the children given into their care. You will be a man, they had told him, and the pride of humanity is that we are not bound by instinct and reflex; we are free because we can master ourselves.

He couldn't pass as an ordinary citizen (no, they said mootman here) of Norland. If nothing else, his Hellenic accent was too strong. But he might fool yonder pilot, for just a few minutes, into believing he was from some other domain of this history. He roughened his tone, as a partial disguise, and assumed the expected arrogance.

"Who are you? What do you want?"

"Runolf Einarsson, captain in the hird of Ottar Thorkelsson, the Lawman of Norland. I pursue one who has brought feud on his own head. Give me your name."

*Runolf,* Iason thought. *Why, yes, I remember you well, dark and erect with the Tyrker side of your heritage, but you have blue eyes that came long ago from Thule.* In that detached part of him which stood aside watching: *No, here I scramble my histories. I would call the autochthons Erythrai, and you call the country of your European ancestors Danarik.*

"I hight Xipec, a trader from Meyaco," he said. He did not slow down. The border was not many stadia away, so furiously had he driven through the night since he escaped from the Lawman's castle. He had small hope of getting that far, but each turn of the wheels brought him nearer. The forest was blurred with his speed.

"If so be, of course I am sorry to halt you," Runolf's voice crackled. "Call the Lawman and he will send swift gild for the overtreading of your rights. Yet I must have you stop and leave your car, so I may turn the farseer on your face."

"Why?" Another second or two gained.

"There was a visitor from Homeland"—Europe—"who came to Ernvik. Ottar Thorkelsson guested him freely. In return, he did a thing that only his death can make clean again. Rather than meet Ottar on the Valfield, he stole a car, the same make as yours, and fled."

"Would it not serve to call him a nithing before the folk?" *I have learned this much of their barbaric customs, anyhow!*

"Now that is a strange thing for a Meyacan to say. Stop at once and get out, or I open fire."

Iason realized his teeth were clenched till they hurt. How in Hades could a man remember the hundreds of little regions, each with its own ways, into which the continent lay divided? Westfall was a more fantastic jumble than all Earth in that history where they called the place America. *Well,* he thought, *now we discover what the odds are of my hearing it named Eutopia again.*

"Very well," he said. "You leave me no choice. But I shall indeed want compensation for this insult."

He braked as slowly as he dared. The road was a hard black ribbon before him, slashed through an immensity of trees. He didn't know if these woods had ever been logged. Perhaps so, when white men first sailed through the Pentalimne (calling them the Five Seas) to found Ernvik where Duluth stood in America and Lykopolis in Eutopia. In those days Norland had spread mightily across the lake country. But then came wars with Dakotas and Magyars, to set a limit; and the development of trade—more recently of synthetics—enabled the people to use their hinterland for the hunting they so savagely loved. Three hundred years could re-establish a climax forest.

Sharply before him stood the vision of this area as he had known it at home: ordered groves and gardens, villages planned for beauty as well as use, lithe brown bodies on the athletic fields, music under moonlight . . . Even America the dreadful was more human than a wilderness.

They were gone, lost in the multiple dimensions of space-time, he was alone and death walked the sky. *And no self-pity, you idiot! Spend energy for survival.*

The car stopped, hard by the road edge. Iason gathered his thews, opened the door, and sprang.

Perhaps the radio behind him uttered a curse. The jet slewed around and swooped like a hawk. Bullets sleeted at his heels.

Then he was in among the trees. They roofed him with sun-speckled shadow. Their trunks stood in massive masculine strength, their branches breathed fragrance a woman might envy. Fallen needles softened his foot-thud, a thrush warbled, a light wind cooled his cheeks. He threw himself beneath the shelter of one bole and lay in a gasping and heartbeat which all but drowned the sinister whistle above.

Presently it went away. Runolf must have called back to his lord. Ottar would fly horses and hounds to this place, the only way of pursuit. But Iason had a few hours' grace.

After that—He rallied his training, sat up and thought. If Socrates, feeling the hemlock's chill, could speak wisdom to the young men of Athens, Iason Philippou could assess his own chances. For he wasn't dead yet.

He numbered his assets. A pistol of the local slug-throwing type; a compass; a pocketful of gold and silver coins; a cloak that might double as a blanket, above the tunic-trousers-boots costume of central Westfall. And himself, the ultimate instrument. His body was tall and broad—together with fair hair and short nose, an inheritance from Gallic ancestors—and had been trained by men who won wreaths at the Olympeion. His mind, his entire nervous system, counted for still more. The pedagogues of Eutopia had made logic, semantic consciousness, perspective as natural to him as breathing; his memory was under such control that he had no need of a map; despite one

calamitous mistake, he knew he was trained to deal with the most out-
landish manifestations of the human spirit.

And, yes, before all else, he had reason to live. It went beyond any
blind wish to continue an identity; that was only something the DNA
molecule had elaborated in order to make more DNA molecules. He
had his beloved to return to. He had his country: Eutopia, the Good
Land, which his people had founded two thousand years ago on a new
continent, leaving behind the hatreds and horrors of Europe, taking
along the work of Aristotle, and writing at last in their Syntagma, "The
national purpose is the attainment of universal sanity."

Iason Philippou was bound home.

He rose and started walking south.


That was on Tetrade, which his hunters called Onsdag. Some thirty-
six hours later, he knew he was not in Pentade but near sunset of
Thorsdag. For he lurched through the wood, mouth filled with mummy
dust, belly a cavern of emptiness, knees shaking beneath him, flies
a thundercloud about the sweat dried on his skin, and heard the distant
belling of hounds.

A horn responded, long brazen snarl through the leaf arches. They
had gotten his scent, he could not outrun horsemen and he would not
see the stars again.

One hand dropped to his gun. *I'll take a couple of them with me.*
. . . *No.* He was still a Hellene, who did not kill uselessly, not even
barbarians who meant to slay him because he had broken a taboo of
theirs. *I will stand under an open sky, take their bullets, and go down
into darkness remembering Eutopia and all my friends and Niki whom
I love.*

Realization came, dimly, that he had left the pine forest and was in
a second growth of beeches. Light gilded their leaves and caressed
the slim white trunks. And what was that growl up ahead?

He stopped. A portal might remain. He had driven himself near
collapse; but the organism has a reserve which the fully integrated man
may call upon. From consciousness he abolished the sound of dogs,
every ache and exhaustion. He drew breath after breath of air, noting
its calm and purity, visualizing the oxygen atoms that poured through
his starved tissues. He made the heartbeat quit racketing, go over to a
deep slow pulse; he tensed and relaxed muscles until each functioned

smoothly again; pain ceased to feed on itself and died away; despair gave place to calm and calculation. He trod forth.

Plowlands rolled southward before him, their young grain vivid in the light that slanted gold from the west. Not far off stood a cluster of farm buildings, long, low, and peak-roofed. Chimney smoke stained heaven. But his eyes went first to the man closer by. The fellow was cultivating with a tractor. Though the dielectric motor had been invented in this world, its use had not yet spread this far north, and gasoline fumes caught at Iason's nostrils. He had thought that stench one of the worst abominations in America—that hogpen they called Los Angeles!—but now it came to him clean and strong, for it was his hope.

The driver saw him, halted, and unshipped a rifle. Iason approached with palms held forward in token of peace. The driver relaxed. He was a typical Magyar: burly, high in the cheekbones, his beard braided, his tunic colorfully embroidered. *So I did cross the border!* Iason exulted. *I'm out of Norland and into the Voivodate of Dakoty.*

Before they sent him here, the anthropologists of the Parachronic Research Institute had of course given him an electrochemical inculcation in the principal languages of Westfall. (Pity they hadn't been more thorough about teaching him the mores. But then, he had been hastily recruited for the Norland post after Megasthenes' accidental death; and it was assumed that his experience in America gave him special qualifications for this history, which was also non-Alexandrine; and, to be sure, the whole object of missions like his was to learn just how societies on the different Earths did vary.) He formed the Ural-Altaic words with ease:

"Greeting to you. I come as a suppliant."

The farmer sat quiet, tense, looking down on him and listening to the dogs far off in the forest. His rifle stayed ready. "Are you an outlaw?" he asked.

"Not in this realm, freeman." (Still another name and concept for "citizen"!) "I was a peaceful trader from Homeland, visiting Lawman Ottar Thorkelsson in Ernvik. His anger fell upon me, so great that he broke sacred hospitality and sought the life of me, his guest. Now his hunters are on my trail. You hear them yonder."

"Norlanders? But this is Dakoty."

Iason nodded. He let his teeth show, in the grime and stubble of his face. "Right. They've entered your country without so much as a by-your-leave. If you stand idle, they'll ride onto your freehold and slay me, who asks your help."

The farmer hefted his gun. "How do I know you speak truth?"

"Take me to the Voivode," Iason said. "Thus you keep both the law and your honor." Very carefully, he unholstered his pistol and offered it butt foremost. "I am forever your debtor."

Doubt, fear and anger pursued each other across the face of the man on the tractor. He did not take the weapon. Iason waited. *If I've read him correctly, I've gained some hours of life. Perhaps more. That will depend on the Voivode. My whole chance lies in using their own barbarism—their division into petty states, their crazy idea of honor, their fetish of property and privacy—to harness them.*

*If I fail, then I shall die like a civilized man. That they cannot take away from me.*

"The hounds have winded you. They'll be here before we can escape," said the Magyar uneasily.

Relief made Iason dizzy. He fought down the reaction and said: "We can take care of them for a time. Let me have some gasoline."

"Ah . . . thus!" The other man chuckled and jumped to earth. "Good thinking, stranger. And thanks, by the way. Life has been dull hereabouts for too many years."

He had a spare can of fuel on his machine. They lugged it back along Iason's trail for a considerable distance, dousing soil and trees. If that didn't throw the pack off, nothing would.

"Now, hurry!" The Magyar led the way at a trot.

His farmstead was built around an open courtyard. Sweet scents of hay and livestock came from the barns. Several children ran forth to gape. The wife shooed them back inside, took her husband's rifle, and mounted guard at the door with small change of expression.

Their house was solid, roomy, aesthetically pleasing if you could accept the unrestrained tapestries and painted pillars. Above the fireplace was a niche for a family altar. Though most people in Westfall had left myth long behind them, these peasants still seemed to adore the Triple God Odin-Attila-Manitou. But the man went to a sophisticated radiophone. "I don't have an aircraft myself," he said, "but I can get one."

Iason sat down to wait. A girl neared him shyly with a beaker of beer and a slab of cheese on coarse dark bread. "Be you guest-holy," she said.

"May my blood be yours," Iason answered by rote. He managed to take the refreshment not quite like a wolf.

The farmer came back. "A few more minutes," he said. "I am Arpad, son of Kalman."

"Iason Philippou." It seemed wrong to give a false name. The hand he clasped was hard and warm.

"What made you fall afoul of old Ottar?" Arpad inquired.

"I was lured," Iason said bitterly. "Seeing how free the unwed women were—"

"Ah, indeed. They're a lickerish lot, those Danskar. Nigh as shameless as Tyrkers." Arpad got pipe and tobacco pouch off a shelf. "Smoke?"

"No, thank you." *We don't degrade ourselves with drugs in Eutopia.*

The hounds drew close. Their chant broke into confused yelps. Horns shrilled. Arpad stuffed his pipe as coolly as if this were a show. "How they must be swearing!" he grinned. "I'll give the Danskar credit for being poets, also in their oaths. And brave men, to be sure. I was up that way ten years back, when Voivode Bela sent people to help them after the floods they'd suffered. I saw them laugh as they fought the wild water. And then, their sort gave us a hard time in the old wars."

"Do you think there will ever be wars again?" Iason asked. Mostly he wanted to avoid speaking further of his troubles. He wasn't sure how his host might react.

"Not in Westfall. Too much work to do. If young blood isn't cooled enough by a duel now and then, why, there're wars to hire out for, among the barbarians overseas. Or else the planets. My oldest boy champs to go there."

Iason recalled that several realms further south were pooling their resources for astronautical work. Being approximately at the technological level of the American history, and not required to maintain huge military or social programs, they had put a base on the moon and sent expeditions to Ares. In time, he supposed, they would do what the Hellenes had done a thousand years ago, and make Aphrodite into a new Earth. But would they have a true civilization—be rational men in a rationally planned society—by then? Wearily, he doubted it.

A roar outside brought Arpad to his feet. "There's your wagon," he said. "Best you go. Red Horse will fly you to Varady."

"The Danskar will surely come here soon," Iason worried.

"Let them," Arpad shrugged. "I'll alert the neighborhood, and they're not so stupid that they won't know I have. We'll hold a slanging match, and then I'll order them off my land. Farewell, guest."

"I . . . I wish I could repay your kindness."

"Bah! Was fun. Also, a chance to be a man before my sons."

Iason went out. The aircraft was a helicopter—they hadn't discovered gravitics here—piloted by a taciturn young autochthon. He explained that he was a stockbreeder, and that he was conveying the stranger less as a favor to Arpad than as an answer to the Norlander impudence of entering Dakoty unbidden. Iason was just as happy to be free of conversation.

The machine whirred aloft. As it drove south he saw clustered hamlets, the occasional hall of some magnate, otherwise only rich undulant plains. They kept the population within bounds in Westfall as in Eutopia. But not because they knew that men need space and clean air, Iason thought. No, they acted from greed on behalf of the reified family. A father did not wish to divide his possessions among many children.

The sun went down and a nearly full moon climbed huge and pumpkin-colored over the eastern rim of the world. Iason sat back, feeling the engine's throb in his bones, almost savoring his fatigue, and watched. No sign of the lunar base was visible. He must return home before he could see the moon glitter with cities.

And home was more than infinitely remote. He could travel to the farthest of those stars which had begun twinkling forth against purple dusk—were it possible to exceed the speed of light—and not find Eutopia. It lay sundered from him by dimensions and destiny. Nothing but the warpfields of a parachronion might take him across the time lines to his own.

He wondered about the why. That was an empty speculation, but his tired brain found relief in childishness. Why had the God willed that time branch and rebranch, enormous, shadowy, bearing universes

like the Yggdrasil of Danskar legend? Was it so that man could realize
every potentiality there was in him?

Surely not. So many of them were utter horror.

Suppose Alexander the Conqueror had not recovered from the fever
that smote him in Babylon. Suppose, instead of being chastened thereby,
so that he spent the rest of a long life making firm the foundations of
his empire—suppose he had died?

Well, it *did* happen, and probably in more histories than not. There
the empire went down in mad-dog wars of succession. Hellas and the
Orient broke apart. Nascent science withered away into metaphysics,
eventually outright mysticism. A convulsed Mediterranean world was
swept up piecemeal by the Romans: cold, cruel, uncreative, claiming
to be the heirs of Hellas even as they destroyed Corinth. A heretical
Jewish prophet founded a mystery cult which took root everywhere,
for men despaired of this life. And that cult knew not the name of
tolerance. Its priests denied all but one of the manifold ways in which
the God is seen; they cut down the holy groves, took from the house
its humble idols, and martyred the last men whose souls were free.

*Oh yes,* Iason thought, *in time they lost their grip. Science could be
born, almost two millennia later than ours. But the poison remained:
the idea that men must conform not only in behavior but in belief.
Now, in America, they call it totalitarianism. And because of it, the
nuclear rockets have had their nightmare hatching.*

*I hated that history, its filth, its waste, its ugliness, its restriction,
its hypocrisy, its insanity. I will never have a harder task than when
I pretended to be an American that I might see from within how they
thought they were ordering their lives. But tonight . . . I pity you, poor
raped world. I do not know whether to wish you soon dead, as you
likeliest will be, or hope that one day your descendants can struggle to
what we achieved an age ago.*

*They were luckier here. I must admit that. Christendom fell before
the onslaught of Arab, Viking and Magyar. Afterward the Islamic
Empire killed itself in civil wars and the barbarians of Europe could
go their own way. When they crossed the Atlantic, a thousand years
back, they had not the power to commit genocide on the natives; they
must come to terms. They had not the industry, then, to gut the hemi-*

*sphere; perforce they grew into the land slowly, taking it as a man takes his bride.*

*But those vast dark forests, mournful plains, unpeopled deserts and mountains where the wild goats run . . . those entered their souls. They will always, inwardly, be savages.*

He sighed, settled down, and made himself sleep. Niki haunted his dreams.

Where a waterfall marked the head of navigation on that great river known variously as the Zeus, Mississippi and Longflood, a basically agricultural people who had not developed air transport as far as in Eutopia were sure to build a city. Trade and military power brought with them government, art, science and education. Varady housed a hundred thousand or so—they didn't take censuses in Westfall—whose inward-turning homes surrounded the castle towers of the Voivode. Waking, Iason walked out on his balcony and heard the traffic rumble. Beyond roofs lay the defensive outworks. He wondered if a peace founded on the balance of power between statelets could endure.

But the morning was too cool and bright for such musings. He was here, safe, cleansed and rested. There had been little talk when he arrived. Seeing the condition of the fugitive who sought him, Bela Zsolt's son had given him dinner and sent him to bed.

*Soon we'll confer,* Iason understood, *and I'll have to be most careful if I'm to live.* But the health which had been restored to him glowed so strong that he felt no need to suppress worry.

A bell chimed within. He re-entered the room, which was spacious and airy however overornamented. Recalling that custom disapproved of nudity, he threw on a robe, not without wincing at its zigzag pattern. "Be welcome," he called in Magyar.

The door opened and a young woman wheeled in his breakfast. "Good luck to you, guest," she said with an accent; she was a Tyrker, and even wore the beaded and fringed dress of her people. "Did you sleep well?"

"Like Coyote after a prank," he laughed.

She smiled back, pleased at his reference, and set a table. She joined him too. Guests did not eat alone. He found venison a rather strong dish this early in the day, but the coffee was delicious and the girl chattered charmingly. She was employed as a maid, she told him, and saving her money for a marriage portion when she returned to Cherokee land.

"Will the Voivode see me?" Iason asked after they had finished.

"He awaits your pleasure." Her lashes fluttered. "But we have no haste." She began to untie her belt.

Hospitality so lavish must be the result of customal superimposition, the easygoing Danskar and still freer Tyrker mores influencing the austere Magyars. Iason felt almost as if he were now home, in a world where individuals found delight in each other as they saw fit. He was tempted, too—that broad smooth brow reminded him of Niki. But no. He had little time. Unless he established his position unbreakably firm before Ottar thought to call Bela, he was trapped.

He leaned across the table and patted one small hand. "I thank you, lovely," he said, "but I am under vow."

She took the answer as naturally as she had posed the question. This world, which had the means to unify, chose as if deliberately to remain in shards of separate culture. Something of his alienation came back to him as he watched her sway out the door. For he had only glimpsed a small liberty. Life in Westfall remained a labyrinth of tradition, manner, law and taboo.

Which had well-nigh cost him his life, he reflected; and might yet. Best hurry!

He tumbled into the clothes laid out for him and made his way down long stone halls. Another servant directed him to the Voivode's seat. Several people waited outside to have complaints heard or disputes adjudicated. But when he announced himself, Iason was passed through immediately.

The room beyond was the most ancient part of the building. Age-cracked timber columns, grotesquely carved with gods and heroes, upheld a low roof. A fire pit in the floor curled smoke toward a hole; enough stayed behind for Iason's eyes to sting. They could easily have given their chief magistrate a modern office, he thought—but no, because his ancestors had judged in this kennel, so must he.

Light filtering through slit windows touched the craggy features of Bela and lost itself in shadow. The Voivode was thickset and gray-haired; his features bespoke a considerable admixture of Tyrker chromosomes. He sat a wooden throne, his body wrapped in a blanket, horns and feathers on his head. His left hand bore a horse-tailed staff and a drawn saber was laid across his lap.

"Greeting, Iason Philippou," he said gravely. He gestured at a stool. "Be seated."

"I thank my lord." The Eutopian remembered how his own people had outgrown titles.

"Are you prepared to speak truth?"

"Yes."

"Good." Abruptly the figure relaxed, crossed legs and extracted a cigar from beneath the blanket. "Smoke? No? Well, I will." A smile meshed the leathery face in wrinkles. "You being a foreigner, I needn't keep up this damned ceremony."

Iason tried to reply in kind. "That's a relief. We haven't much in the Peloponnesian Republic."

"Your home country, eh? I hear things aren't going so well there."

"No. Homeland grows old. We look to Westfall for our tomorrows."

"You said last night that you came to Norland as a trader."

"To negotiate a commercial agreement." Iason was staying as near his cover story as possible. You couldn't tell different histories that the Hellenes had invented the parachronion. Besides changing the very conditions that were being studied, it would be too cruel to let men know that other men lived in perfection. "My country is interested in buying lumber and furs."

"Hm. So Ottar invited you to stay with him. I can grasp why. We don't see many Homelanders. But one day he was after your blood. What happened?"

Iason might have claimed privacy, but that wouldn't have sat well. And an outright lie was dangerous; before this throne, one was automatically under oath. "To a degree, no doubt, the fault was mine," he said. "One of his family, almost grown, was attracted to me and —I had been long away from my wife, and everyone had told me the Danskar hold with freedom before marriage, and—well, I meant no harm. I merely encouraged—But Ottar found out, and challenged me."

"Why did you not meet him?"

No use to say that a civilized man did not engage in violence when any alternative existed. "Consider, my lord," Iason said. "If I lost, I'd be dead. If I won, that would be the end of my company's project. The Ottarssons would never have taken weregild, would they?

No, at the bare least they'd ban us all from their land. And Peloponnesus needs that timber. I thought I'd do best to escape. Later my associates could disown me before Norland."

"M-m . . . strange reasoning. But you're loyal, anyhow. What do you ask of me?"

"Only safe conduct to—Steinvik." Iason almost said "Neathenai." He checked his eagerness. "We have a factor there, and a ship."

Bela streamed smoke from his mouth and scowled at the glowing cigar end. "I'd like to know why Ottar grew wrathful. Doesn't sound like him. Though I suppose, when a man's daughter is involved, he doesn't feel so lenient." He hunched forward. "For me," he said harshly, "the important thing is that armed Norlanders crossed my border without asking."

"A grievous violation of your rights, true."

Bela uttered a horseman's obscenity. "You don't understand, you. Borders aren't sacred because Attila wills it, whatever the shamans prate. They're sacred because that's the only way to keep the peace. If I don't openly resent this crossing, and punish Ottar for it, some hothead might well someday be tempted; and now everyone has nuclear weapons."

"I don't want war on my account!" Iason exclaimed, appalled. "Send me back to him first!"

"Oh no, no such nonsense. Ottar's punishment shall be that I deny him his revenge, regardless of the rights and wrongs of your case. He'll swallow that."

Bela rose. He put his cigar in an ashtray, lifted the saber, and all at once he was transfigured. A heathen god might have spoken: "Henceforward, Iason Philippou, you are peace-holy in Dakoty. While you remain beneath our shield, ill done you is ill done me, my house and my people. So help me the Three!"

Self-command broke down. Iason went on his knees and gasped his thanks.

"Enough," Bela grunted. "Let's arrange for your transportation as fast as may be. I'll send you by air, with a military squadron. But of course I'll need permission from the realms you'll cross. That will take time. Go back, relax, I'll have you called when everything's ready."

Iason left, still shivering.

He spent a pleasant couple of hours adrift in the castle and its courtyards. The young men of Bela's retinue were eager to show off before a Homelander. He had to grant the picturesqueness of their riding, wrestling, shooting and riddling contests; something stirred in him as he listened to tales of faring over the plains and into the forests and by river to Unnborg's fabled metropolis; the chant of a bard awakened glories which went deeper than the history told, down to the instincts of man the killer ape.

*But these are precisely the bright temptations that we have turned our backs on in Eutopia. For we deny that we are apes. We are men who can reason. In that lies our manhood.*

*I am going home. I am going home. I am going home.*

A servant tapped his arm. "The Voivode wants you." It was a frightened voice.

Iason hastened back. What had gone wrong? He was not taken to the room of the high seat. Instead, Bela awaited him on a parapet. Two men-at-arms stood at attention behind, faces blank under the plumed helmets.

The day and the breeze were mocked by Bela's look. He spat on Iason's feet. "Ottar has called me," he said.

"I— Did he say—"

"And I thought you were only trying to bed a girl. Not seeking to destroy the house that befriended you!"

"My lord—"

"Have no fears. You sucked my oath out of me. Now I must spend years trying to make amends to Ottar for cheating him."

"But—" *Calm! Calm! You might have expected this.*

"You will not ride in a warcraft. You'll have your escort, yes. But the machine that carries you must be burned afterward. Now go wait by the stables, next to the dung heap, till we're ready."

"I meant no harm," Iason protested. "I did not know."

"Take him away before I kill him," Bela ordered.

Steinvik was old. These narrow cobbled streets, these gaunt houses, had seen dragon ships. But the same wind blew off the Atlantic, salt and fresh, to drive from Iason the last hurt of that sullenness which had ridden here with him. He pushed whistling through the crowds.

A man of Westfall, or America, would have slunk back. Had he not failed? Must he not be replaced by someone whose cover story bore no hint of Hellas? But they saw with clear eyes in Eutopia. His failure was due to an honest mistake: a mistake he would not have made had they taught him more carefully before sending him out. One learns by error.

The memory of people in Ernvik and Varady—gusty, generous people whose friendship he would have liked to keep—had nagged him awhile. But he put that aside too. There were other worlds, an endlessness of them.

A signboard creaked in the wind. The Brotherhood of Hunyadi and Ivar, Shipfolk. Good camouflage, that, in a town where every second enterprise was bent seaward. He ran to the second floor. The stairs clattered under his boots.

He spread his palm before a chart on the wall. A hidden scanner identified his fingerpatterns and a hidden door opened. The room beyond was wainscoted in local fashion. But its clean proportions spoke of home; and a Nike statuette spread wings on a shelf.

*Nike . . . Niki . . . I'm coming back to you!* The heart leaped in him.

Daimonax Aristides looked up from his desk. Iason sometimes wondered if anything could rock the calm of that man. "Rejoice!" the deep voice boomed. "What brings you here?"

"Bad news, I'm afraid."

"So? Your attitude suggests the matter isn't catastrophic." Daimonax's big frame left his chair, went to the wine cabinet, filled a pair of chaste and beautiful goblets, and relaxed on a couch. "Come, tell me."

Iason joined him. "Unknowingly," he said, "I violated what appears to be a prime taboo. I was lucky to get away alive."

"Eh." Daimonax stroked his iron-gray beard. "Not the first such turn, or the last. We fumble our way toward knowledge, but reality will always surprise us. . . . Well, congratulations on your whole skin. I'd have hated to mourn you."

Solemnly, they poured a libation before they drank. The rational man recognizes his own need for ceremony; and why not draw it from otherwise outgrown myth? Besides, the floor was stainproof.

"Do you feel ready to report?" Daimonax asked.

"Yes, I ordered the data in my head on the way here."

Daimonax switched on a recorder, spoke a few cataloguing words and said, "Proceed."

Iason flattered himself that his statement was well arranged: clear, frank and full. But as he spoke, against his will experience came back to him, not in the brain but in the guts. He saw waves sparkle on that greatest of the Pentalimne; he walked the halls of Ernvik castle with eager and wondering young Leif; he faced an Ottar become beast; he stole from the keep and overpowered a guard and by-passed the controls of a car with shaking fingers; he fled down an empty road and stumbled through an empty forest; Bela spat and his triumph was suddenly ashen. At the end, he could not refrain:

"Why wasn't I informed? I'd have taken care. But they said this was a free and healthy folk, before marriage anyway. How could I know?"

"An oversight," Daimonax agreed. "But we haven't been in this business so long that we don't still tend to take too much for granted."

"Why are we here? What have we to learn from these barbarians? With infinity to explore, why are we wasting ourselves on the second most ghastly world we've found?"

Daimonax turned off the recorder. For a time there was silence between the men. Wheels trundled outside, laughter and a snatch of song drifted through the window, the ocean blazed under a low sun.

"You do not know?" Daimonax asked at last, softly.

"Well . . . scientific interest, of course—" Iason swallowed. "I'm sorry. The Institute works for sound reasons. In the American history we're observing ways that man can go wrong. I suppose here also."

Daimonax shook his head. "No."

"What?"

"We are learning something far too precious to give up," Daimonax said. "The lesson is humbling, but our smug Eutopia will be the better for some humility. You weren't aware of it, because to date we haven't sufficient hard facts to publish any conclusions. And then, you are new in the profession, and your first assignment was elsewhen. But you see, we have excellent reason to believe that Westfall is also the Good Land."

"Impossible," Iason whispered.

Daimonax smiled and took a sip of wine. "Think," he said. "What does man require? First, the biological necessities, food, shelter, medicine, sex, a healthful and reasonably safe environment in which to raise his children. Second, the special human need to strive, learn, create. Well, don't they have these things here?"

"One could say the same for any Stone Age tribe. You can't equate contentment with happiness."

"Of course not. And if anything, is not ordered, unified, planned Eutopia the country of the cows? We have ended every conflict, to the very conflict of man with his own soul; we have mastered the planets; the stars are too distant; were the God not so good as to make possible the parachronion, what would be left for us?"

"Do you mean—" Iason groped after words. He reminded himself that it was not sane to take umbrage at any mere statement, however outrageous. "Without fighting, clannishness, superstition, ritual and taboo . . . man has nothing?"

"More or less that. Society must have structure and meaning. But nature does not dictate what structure or what meaning. Our rationalism is a non-rational choice. Our leashing of the purely animal within us is simply another taboo. We may love as we please, but not hate as we please. So are we more free than men in Westfall?"

"But surely some cultures are better than others!"

"I do not deny that," Daimonax said; "I only point out that each has its price. For what we enjoy at home, we pay dearly. We do not allow ourselves a single unthinking, merely felt impulse. By excluding danger and hardship, by eliminating distinctions between men, we leave no hopes of victory. Worst, perhaps, is this: that we have become pure individuals. We belong to no one. Our sole obligation is negative, not to compel any other individual. The state—an engineered organization, a faceless undemanding mechanism—takes care of each need and each hurt. Where is loyalty unto death? Where is the intimacy of an entire shared lifetime? We play at ceremonies, but because we know they are arbitrary gestures, what is their value? Because we have made our world one, where are color and contrast, where is pride in being peculiarly ourselves?

"Now these Westfall people, with all their faults, do know who they are, what they are, what they belong to and what belongs to them. Tradition is not buried in books but is part of life; and so their dead remain with them in loving memory. Their problems are real; hence their successes are real. They believe in their rites. The family, the kingdom, the race is something to live and die for. They use their brains less, perhaps—though even that I am not certain of—but they use nerves, glands, muscles more. So they know an aspect of being human which our careful world has denied itself.

"If they have kept this while creating science and machine technology, should we not try to learn from them?"

Iason had no answer.

Eventually Daimonax said he might as well return to Eutopia. After a vacation, he could be reassigned to some history he might find more congenial. They parted in friendly wise.

The parachronion hummed. Energies pulsed between the universes. The gate opened and Iason stepped through.

He entered a glazed colonnade. White Neathenai swept in grace and serenity down to the water. The man who received him was a philosopher. Decent tunic and sandals hung ready to be donned. From somewhere resounded a lyre.

Joy trembled in Iason. Leif Ottarsson fell out of memory. He had only been tempted in his loneliness by a chance resemblance to his beloved. Now he was home. And Niki waited for him, Nikias Demostheneou, most beautiful and enchanting of boys.


# Afterword:

Readers ought to know that writers are not responsible for the opinions and behavior of their characters. But many people don't. In consequence, I, for instance, have been called a fascist to my face. Doubtless the present story will get me accused of worse. And I only wanted to spin a yarn!

Well, perhaps a bit more. That can't be helped. Everybody views the world from his particular philosophical platform. Hence any writer who tries to report what he sees is, inevitably, propagandizing. But as a rule the propaganda lies below the surface. This is twice true of science fiction, which begins by transmuting reality to frank unreality.

So what have I been advocating here? Not any particular form of society. On the contrary, humankind seems to me so splendidly and ironically variable that there can be no perfect social order. I do suspect that few people are biologically adapted to civilization; consider its repeated collapses. This idea could be wrong, of course. Even if true, it may just be another factor which our planning should take into account. But the mutability of man is hardly open to question.

Thus each arrangement he makes will have its flaws, which in the end bring it to ruin; but each will also have its virtues. I myself don't think here-and-now is such a bad place to live. But others might. In fact, others do. At the same time, we cannot deny that *some* ways of life are, on balance, evil. The worst and most dangerous are those which cannot tolerate anything different from themselves.

So in an age of conflict we need a clear understanding of our own values—and the enemy's. Likewise we have to see with equal clarity the drawbacks of both cultures. This is less a moral than a strategic imperative. Only on such a basis can we know what we ought to do and what is possible for us to do.

For we are not caught in a meaningless nightmare. We are inhabiting a real world where events have understandable causes and causes have effects. We were never given any sacred mission, and it would be fatal to believe otherwise. We do, though, have the right of self-preservation. Let us know what it is we want to preserve. Then common sense and old-fashioned guts will probably get us through.

This is rather a heavy sermon to load on a story which was, after all, meant as entertainment. The point was made far better by Robinson Jeffers:

"Long live freedom and damn the ideologies."

**Introduction to A PAIR OF BUNCH:**

Only one writer has two stories in this anthology, and surprise! it ain't me. It is David R. Bunch, a writer whose work I admire vastly. And a writer who has, oddly enough, barely received the acclaim due him. The first time I read a Bunch story was in a handsome fan magazine called *Inside*, published by Ron Smith. He had come across Bunch (or vice versa) and had been intrigued by the man's unusual style, his sense of poetry, the almost Dada-like visions he was able to convey in the medium of fantasy and science fiction. Bunch was published regularly in *Inside*. His work drew mixed reactions. Some very perceptive critics (such as John Ciardi) commented knowledgeably. The *schmuck* fans scratched their heads and wondered why space was wasted on Bunch when they could be reading more and better analyses of the inertialess drive as utilized in the stories of Ed Earl Repp, or somedamnsuch. Half a dozen years ago the attractive and intelligent ex-editor of *Amazing Stories,* Cele Goldsmith Lalli, began publishing stories by Bunch. Once again the furor and the mixed reaction. But Bunch had found a home.

With considerable courage both Bunch and Cele began releasing stories about Moderan, a world of robots. They were frankly cautionary tales, the finger of warning jammed directly in the eye or up the nose of the reader. I have waited ten years to be able to publish Bunch myself. Therefore, *two* by Bunch, a tiny bunch of Bunch, maybe a nosegay.

Bunch is a native of Missouri. He has a wide educational background; class valedictorian in high school, he was awarded a scholarship to Central Missouri State College, where he majored in English with a double minor in physics and social science, graduating with a Bachelor of Science degree; he received a Master of Arts at Washington University, where he concentrated on English and American literature. At one point he had done the course work for the Ph.D. with admission to candidacy, but just before the last grind for the final grind he fled from the dissertation writing to the Writer's Workshop at the State University of Iowa. There he found surcease for a time, and finally left even that hallowed hall of ivy to write his own way, on his own time. He has never returned.

The flight has seemingly harmed him little. He has been published in over forty magazines, represented by poetry and short stories of a wide variety. Most of his work has seen publication in the "little" magazines or the science fiction magazines. Of the former he has been seen in *San Francisco Review, Southwest Review, New Mexico Quarterly, Chelsea, Perspective, Genesis West, The Smith, Shenandoah, New Frontiers, Simbolica, The Fiddlehead, Epos, The Galley Sail Review, Forum* and a host of others. He has been published in almost every s-f journal extant, and has outlived a score of others. He has been honored three times by Judith Merril in her *Year's Best SF* anthologies. A collection of his short stories has been accepted for hardcover publication this year. His verse has appeared in as many more magazines as those noted above, and a collection of poetry is scheduled for book publication.

Bunch is possibly the most dangerous visionary of all those represented here. He has been that way all through his speculative writing career, not merely stretched-out for this special occasion as are some of the men herein. He writes of the enigma, the conundrum, the query, the fable of futurity. He speaks in riddles. It is to the reader's advantage to try unraveling them.

# ● INCIDENT IN MODERAN

## by David R. Bunch

In Moderan we are not often between wars, but this was a truce time. A couple of Strongholds in the north had malfunctioned—some breakdown in their ammo-transport belts, I think—and we had all voted to hold up the war a day or so to give them a chance to get back in the blasting. Don't get me wrong—this was no lily-white flower-heart fairplay kind of thing or love-thy-neighbor-Stronghold sort of hypocrisy, like might have been in the Old Days. This was a hard-neck commonsense compromise with reality. The bigger and better the war, the bigger and better the chance to hate voluminously and win honors. It was as simple as that.

But at any rate, it was between wars that I was doing some odd-job things just outside the eleventh, outermost Wall of my Stronghold. To be right truthful, I was mostly just sitting out there in my hip-snuggie chair, enjoying the bleary summer sun through the red-brown vapor shield of July and telling my head weapons man what to do. He was, so it chanced, polishing an honors plaque that proclaimed on Wall 11 how our fort, Stronghold 10, was FIRST IN WAR, FIRST IN HATE, AND FIRST IN THE FEARS OF THE ENEMY.

Things were getting tedious. What I mean is, it was getting dull, this sitting around between wars, directing the polishing of plaques and dozing in the filtered summer sun. Out of sheer boredom, and for the amusement of it all, I suppose, I was just about ready to get up and start beating my weapons man with my new-metal swagger stick loaded with lead. Not that he wasn't doing an excellent job, you understand, but just to have something to do. I was saved this rather stupid and perhaps pointless, though not altogether unpleasant, expedient by a movement on the ninth hill to my left. Quickly I adjusted my wide-range Moderan vision to pinpoint look, threw my little pocko-scope viewer up to my eyes and caught a shape.

When it got there, it was a shape, all right! I immediately saw it was one of those pieces of movement—man? animal? walking vegetable?—well, what are we going to say for most of these mutant forms that roam the homeless plastic in Moderan? When he stood before me, I felt disturbed. Strangely I felt somehow guilty, and ashamed, that he was so bent and twisted and mushy-looking with flesh. Oh, why can't they all be hard and shining with metal, and clean, like we Stronghold masters are, with a very minimum of flesh-strip holding them in shape? It makes for such a well-ordered and hate-happy life, the way we masters are in Moderan, so shiny and steellike in our glory, with our flesh-strips few and played down and new-metal alloy the bulk of our bodily splendor. But I suppose there must always be lower forms, insects for us to stride on. . . . I decided to try speech, since I couldn't just sit there with him looking at me so. "We're between wars here," I said conversationally. "Two of the mighty Strongholds of the north broke down, so we decided to hold up."

He didn't say anything. He was looking at the honors plaque on Wall 11 and at the weapons man polishing the proud words. "It's just a kind of fill-in in-between job," I said. "Besides, it gives me a chance to doze out here in this filtered summer sun while the weapons man does the work. But it gets tedious. Before you came, I was right on the point of getting up to start beating him with my new-metal swagger stick loaded with lead, even if he is all-metal new-metal alloy, and doing an excellent job, and probably wouldn't have felt the beating anyway. But just to have something to do, you know. As you perhaps realize, a Stronghold master mustn't do any real work in Moderan. It's against the code." I laughed a little, but strangely I felt nervous in my flesh-strips and vague along the rims of my joins. Why did he look at me that way? Even so, why should the stares of such an insignificant piece of life affect me at all?

Could he talk? He could. Blue soft lips parted and a yellow-pink piece of gristly meat jigged up and down in wet slop in his mouth that was raw-flesh red. When this somewhat vulgar performance of meat and air was through, I realized he had said, "We had a little funeral for Son a while ago. We hacked away at the plastic with our poor makeshift grave kits and put him under the crust on time. We hurried. We knew you couldn't guarantee much truce. I come to thank you for what you did."

I shook a little at this strange speech and turn, then recovered myself quickly and waved a steel hand airily. "Consider that I'm thanked," I said. "If you'd wish a steel flower for a decoration, take one."

He shuddered in all his loose-flesh parts. "I came to thank you," he told me in what I supposed passed for blunt speech in his tribe, "not to be ridiculed." In his stare there was a look of puzzlement and doubt now.

Suddenly I found the whole thing growing quite ludicrous. Here I was, a Moderan man between wars, minding my own business, sitting outside the eleventh Wall of my Stronghhold, waiting for the war to resume, and some strange walking lump of sentimentality that I didn't even know existed hurries across from the ninth hill to my left to thank me for a funeral. "You had a good one?" I suggested. Frantically I tried to remember things from the Old Days. The mourners stretched down for a mile? Music—a lot? Flowers—banked all about?

"Just us," he said, "I and his mother. And Son. We hurried. We were sure you couldn't give much time from all the busy times. We thank you for what you did—for the decency."

Decency? Now, what an odd word! What could he mean by decency? "Decency?" I said.

"The rites. You know! We had time for a little prayer. We asked that Son be allowed to live forever in a happy home."

"Listen," I said, a little fed up already with all this, "I don't more than half remember from the Old Days enough about this to discuss it. But you poor flesh mutants bury your dead and then ask that they be allowed to rise and live again about twenty-five times lighter than a dehumidified air bubble. Isn't that about it? But isn't that taking quite a chance? Why don't you just get wise and do it like we Moderan masters do? Just have that operation while you're young and vigorous, throw away what flesh you don't need, 'replace' yourself with all-metal new-metal alloy 'replacements' and live forever. Feed yourself this pure honey-of-introven extract we've come up with and it's a cinch, you'll have it made. We know what we've got, and we know how to live. . . . And now, if you'll excuse me, according to that report arriving at this very moment over the Warner, those Strongholds that aborted the war seem to be fixed up again. We stopped the blasting because of them so we'll just have to really move now to make up hate-time. I would guess the firing may be a little heavier than you've ever seen it."

Through the last parts of this speech I watched what looked like puzzlement and doubt flicker strangely across his flesh-encumbered countenance. "You stopped the war because—because those two Strongholds aborted in the north? You—you didn't really do it then so we could bury Son and have the decency?!" A cold thought must have wrapped him round; he seemed to shrink and shrivel and go inches shorter right there on the plastic. I marveled anew at the great hard times these flesh things gave themselves with their emotions and their heart palpitations. I thumped my "replaced" chest in a kind of meditation and thanked the lucky iron stars in our splendid new-satellite heavens for my calm-cool condition. "In a little while," I said, "we'll open up this blasting. We're clearing the lines now for first countdown and a general resumption. You see, we try to start even. After that it's every Stronghold for itself to just blast away and make the most expeditious use of the ammo."

He looked at me a long time for some sign of joking. After a while he said in a tone that I supposed with the flesh things passed for great sadness and great resignation, "No, I guess you really didn't stop it so we could bury Son and have the decency. I guess it truly was the aborted Strongholds in the north. I see now I read something true and fine into it and that true and fine something wasn't there at all. And so I—I came across to thank you for a decency—for nothing—"

I probably nodded ever such a little, or possibly I didn't, because I was hearing the Voice now, hearing the Warner say that all was about in readiness for Great Blast to go and for the masters again to take their positions at the switch panels of War Rooms. "That's it!" I said to no one and nothing in particular. "It'll be double firing now and around-the-day launching of war heads until we make up our time in hate units."

Just as, bidding my weapons man not to forget the hip-snuggie, I was about to turn and go, hustle off to my War Room and resume Great Blast, a cold sound struck through my steel. What was that high whimpering along the plastic? Then I saw. It was the little flesh-bum. He had lost control of his emotions, had fallen down and was now blubbering real tears. "It's okay, don't be scared," I shouted at him as I turned to hurry. "Keep low in the draws, avoid even halfway up hills and travel swiftly. You'll make it. We fire only at peaks, first go."

But as I passed through the Wall and was bidding the weapons man make all secure, I noticed the little flesh-fellow remained prone, blubbering along the plastic. He was not making any effort to get clear and save himself! And suddenly old Neighboring Stronghold to the east let loose with such a cheating early burst that the little flesh-bum was quite pancaked down—indeed even far further than pancaked, as it got him with a deadly Zump bomb that I'm sure was capable of punching him to the center of the earth even as he was being vaporized to high sky and all winds, and I was ever so glad this had fallen just a little bit short of my complex. But as I glanced at the smoking havoc and a large patch of nothing now, where but a moment before had been the good plastic earth-cover, I could not help but rejoice that the war was certainly again GO. For the flesh-bum I didn't even try for tears, and nothing in my mind could bring my heart rain as I raced on to the War Room to punch my launch knobs down.

## ● THE ESCAPING

### by David R. Bunch

In my small room with the red-cover bed and the two gray shade-drawn windows I would see the Tower, not in the sundown of memory, for indeed I had never been there, but in the moonlight of thinking. And in my thinking it would be a glorious thing, if only four feet tall, with the moon striking down on the tank that would hold my chains, and the platform inviting, empty. A tall form would stand in the street, hale and straight for an instant, in the moonlight of thinking (although *I* am a good five inches less than a decent height), then turn and stride for the goal, in good tread, in good speed, the chains riding easy on two little carriers with wheels, silent and clear of the road. In a celebration of moonglow we would scale the Tower to its very top and easily sit on the platform over the metal tank. The chains would slip silently from the wheeled carriers, down through the slotted holes of the tank, pulling our feet after them, until we sat quite triumphantly in silence measuring the win we had done. Not ashamed of the small-ness of our victory, indeed quite not ashamed, we would pull out the gay flaunters we had saved, long and patiently saved, against this hour of our deed. Inflating the two small balloons, one red, one almost impossibly bright green, and tying one each to a wrist, we would sit there gay and victorious in the moonglow, our chains down in the tank, our head up in the stars, from a Tower but four feet tall. . . . So much for moonglow.

The mornings yawn, the sun comes real, cruel and bright, to magnify our chains. The moonglow is gone and the thinking. It is instinct now, pure instinct and fight, to face them where they snarl. Sure, we have dreamed of elephants, big brown elephants with gold houses on their backs and we in a house each morning, riding down in triumph, striding down on stately elephant strides to our tank and leaping off so fast onto the platform that no one would see our chains. A clink, a slip, a small tink-rattle and they're gone, down in the tank, the chains quite gone to all the world but us, and we sitting high on the platform, four feet high, blowing up the balloons and stone-facing to the crowd. And the crowd muttering, angry, disappointed, somehow debased, and refusing finally to believe that their victim is truly without his chains. I can see them now, bobbing their tonsured and greasy and bald and curled and shave-cut gray old heads together in small worry-clusters, pecking out their shame and their shameful need, wanting somehow to know, desperately needing to know, that though they may not be there now showing to the air, somehow the chains are still there. They must be! Oh yes, they'll circle the tank; they'll peer and thump and in small-childish spite kick at my elephant, and they'll hate me as I sit so gay with my celebration balloons whipping in a spanking cherry-apple wind on that bloom-filled rejoiceful fair spring day. And some one of them, some desperate bright spiteful one of them, will suddenly think all on a sorry debased instant, "They're in the tank! Probably. He's dropped them down through holes!" Then it will hit them all, like a big wave on a beach hit them, break across them and engulf them with the pleasant wetty thought, "We've got him again! They're in the tank. Probably! He's dropped them down through holes!"

Well!—then it will be just a short matter of bringing up the X-ray machines, taking pictures from all sides and all angles and confirming what is to be confirmed. They'll cut in after that, with their big acetylene torches, and some will be on the far side from the heat, with little can openers, busily working, making with the marks, so desperate will be their need to get in through the bottom, expose me and confirm that I still have my chains. The acetylene torches will get in; the can openers will not. But it will be all the same. They'll pull my chains out through the bottom of the tank, through the holes they've carved with the acetylene, and they'll pull my legs out too as far as it is reasonable to do it. And I know I'll make a sorry sight then, my celebration balloons whipping smartly and pertly above, green and red flashes in the apple-cherry-blossom air, my leg chains, feet and legs blooming small common unnecessary arcs, twin-pendulumlike down from the tank holes, and I in between the gaiety and the common shame, grim and exposed and determined. . . . So much for elephants. So much for Towers and tanks too, for that matter. But don't think we've been beaten. Defeated? *Oh no!* I've a trick for it; for just this kind of thing, I've a trick.

It is called mooning the sky egg and working up the air. What we do, we stick a structure such as an egg, one with smooth brown walls and little specky windows, up into the sky, up into the blue, high, high, impossibly, almost, high, high as we can go in thought, in any thought. Then we pick a task for the baser one of our selves—everyone being at least two selves as I guess is almost universally unarguably understood—and put him on the rock pile of his job. My self with leg chains, the self that longs to go up on a little Tower for a small victory and a concealment of chains, but never makes it, I have been putting here of late on a job that is called rolling the air, or on a job that is about the equivalent of rolling the air, this job being called unrolling the air. Either of these jobs requires very little or no physical labor, not a prohibitive amount of mental strength or mental health, and either of these jobs can keep a person's self well occupied for quite a long, long time. And sometimes in thinking of it I am at a loss to know why this type, or a closely related type, of work shouldn't just as well be all the people's tasks for a lifetime of achievement.

To roll the air, I first divide, mentally, all the air in my task block into neat, uniform strips, each strip being as wide and as thick as I want it to be for it to make the kind of roll I think will best fit in with the overall air-rolling mission for that day. And this stripping-the-air, as I speak of it, necessarily lends itself to almost, or quite, an infinite number of variations in strip width and strip thickness. I can have every other strip the same, every third strip the same, side-by-side strips the same, no two strips the same, all of the strips the same, five strips the same, then vary four or five or six and on and on. But I do always try to keep to some recognizable pattern, some sense, as it were, in my stripping. And I never start the actual roll part of the job until I have completed the entire stripping of the task block or, as you might say, my complete air area, and have tabbed it in my mind. Then, after stripping the complete air area and tabbing it firmly in my mind, it is just the jolly and diverting task of sitting there on my chains in the middle of the street on an edge of the task block and amidst the smirking, the coughing and the bright sayings of the crowd, starting my roll and winding in! Of course I have to be mentally sharp, up on my toes, as the saying is, to keep each strip stacked with its sister or brother size, which can have a very great bearing on the intensity of my task when it comes to the unrolling part of the job. Because I'm just doing this as a kind of exercise actually, or a diversion in achievement, we could say, and I have absolutely no intention or desire to permanently rearrange the air in the task block or, as we said, the air area. To leave it that way, permanently rearranged, indeed would make me feel unworthy, and from such an act very guilty of a violation of nature.

And up in the sky-high egg, high, high away from the chains, the tanks, the tasks, and all the tonsured, greasy, bald, curled or shave-cut peering heads—all, All! malicious watchers—how goes it? Well, it goes fine there. And how means it? Well, it means fine there. Ummm . . . mm . . . mmm . . . mmmm . . . Oh, the blisses of swaying in the sky-high egg . . .

## Afterword:

When I am not writing literary stories (and verse) that pay usually nothing or very close to that, or science-fiction-fantasy stories that pay usually closer to nothing than they should, I earn my living doing things (in a civilian capacity) for the U. S. Air Forces. Because I do not have to depend upon my writing for a livelihood, I wear no editor's and no publisher's collar when I sit down to that white paper. Which isn't to say that I wouldn't like to earn a living as a writer. But I should also like to keep my writer's soul intact. And since I'm no fool in such matters, I've accepted a compromise. It's a hard compromise really, because the other work takes considerable time and energy away from the writing. But then the whole bit is a bit of a compromise, I suppose, the whole little drama of the kicking and threshing around between the long sleep of the Before and the longer sleep of the After.

Except in Moderan! In Moderan there is no sleep of the After. Those chaps are designed for forever. And do they compromise? You'd better believe they do not! They just sit back at the switch panels of War Rooms for around-the-clock launching of war heads—*varoom varoom varoom*—in their main game of war. And when an uneasy truce flares up, they don't plant flowers or rush off to Sunday school. They are their true-bad selves. They know how to earn mean-points in peace as well as in war. And they don't bend or pretend. Hate is their main virtue, as war is their main play. And entirely admirable they, because they have no hypocrisy. They step right out there and say it in the daylight, speak of good launchings, of Strongholds honeycombed and of arms and legs of enemies stacked by the Wall.

So I've overdrawn it. But I'm saying something in both these stories about truth and untruth, as indeed what else does a serious writer ever have in mind? The I in both is true. In one the I suffers a great deal, being a dreamer, from the niggling nagging cares of the everyday world and its people. But he escapes to truth finally in his sky-high egg, after first confounding his tormentors and saying something to them in his own way (the absurd air-rolling and -unrolling tasks) which they no doubt do not understand. In the other story the I has arrived at truth a long time ago. Just by being a Moderan master, shiny and sure, he is at truth, the cold unarguable truth of the switch panels, the War Rooms, the "replacements" to live forever, the introven, as opposed to the absurd hopes and unsureties of the flabby flesh-bum and his talk of decency, whatever in the world such an alien word could mean! . . . In one story the I has to escape into fantasy for the world of truth he wants. In the other there is no escape required. He has the world he wants, the only world he knows really, and the only one he can see as possibly workable for a satisfying life forever. The world of the flesh-bum, replete with flesh-hopes and flesh-doubts, is merely an absurdity the Moderan people have left a long time ago and far back.

## Introduction to THE DOLL-HOUSE:

The act of compiling most anthologies (I observed, prior to starting work on the volume before you) is ludicrously easy. There are men and women who have made whole careers of the act. An act about as complicated as clearing one's throat. I will not for a moment minimize the distillation of taste and selectivity that must be present in the editor for an anthology to be enjoyable and well rounded; it is the sole quality a reader needs to make him an anthologist. (And when even that is absent, why, of course, the book that results is not fit to be purchased.) But essentially, even at its best, the assembling of other men's work into a coherent, or "themed," grouping is not a particularly laboring labor. It merely requires a complete backlog of old pulp magazines, a number of friends with eidetic memories, and a clear line to the copyright office to ascertain what is in the public domain.

The book in your hands is rather another matter. I don't intend to make any great claims for myself as an anthologist, or suggest that some special kind of bravery was necessary to take on the job (only a special

kind of stupidity). But this book entailed the actual prodding and pushing of specific writers to unleash themselves, to open up fully and write
stories they had perhaps always wanted to write, but had never felt they
could sell. It took the laborious months of sifting through manuscript
after manuscript to find stories that were offbeat and compelling enough
to live up to the advance publicity this book has received, and be as rich
and explosive as I felt they had to be to justify the existence of DAN-
GEROUS VISIONS. Not just "another anthology" was good enough. It was,
then, not simply the collecting of crumbling pulp-paper tearsheets or
mildewed carbons from scrivener's trunks, but the creation of almost an
entity, a living thing.

The initial list of contributors I hoped would appear in the final version to be published was constantly revised. One writer was desperately
ill, another was in a two-year slump, a third was so shackled by his
wife's doctor's bills he had contracted to do a garbage novel under another man's more famous by-line, and still another had left the country
on assignment from a major slick publication. Revise, revise, grope and
revise. And when it seemed impossible to build the meat of the book as
I wanted it—in the early stages I panicked more readily than now—I
contacted the literary agents and sent them the prospectus for the book,
asking them to select submissions carefully.

From one agent I received string-bundled stacks of refuse dredged
out of reject drawers. (One ms. in one batch had a reject note from
Dorothy McIlwraith, editor of the long-defunct *Weird Tales*, stuck inside. I hesitate to think how long *that* one had been kicking around.)
From another agent I received incredibly inferior work by a top-name
professional in the mainstream. From a third I received a story so blatantly licentious it must certainly have been written for one of those
"private printings" we hear about. That it was dreadfully bad must have
been the reason for its not having been sold, for the sexual explications
in it were sufficient to get it in print at least in *Eros*. But from my own
agent, Robert P. Mills (a very good agent indeed), I received only two
submissions. Both of which I bought. One was by John Sladek, elsewhere in this volume; the second was "The Doll-House" by James Cross.

I confess I had never heard of James Cross before receiving this story.
He was not known to me as a science fiction writer, which isn't odd because ordinarily he isn't one. In point of fact, there is no such person
as "James Cross." He is a pseudonym. He has asked that his true name
be kept privileged information, and so it shall be, here at least. Thus it
is no wonder I looked upon this manuscript as perhaps just another
quickie submission, one of the scatter-gun offerings I had been getting

from the agents. I should have known better. Bob Mills does not work that way. "The Doll-House" is a bravura effort. It is as singular and effective a story as John Collier's "Evening Primrose" or Richard Matheson's "Born of Man and Woman" or Charles Beaumont's "Miss Gentilbelle." It is a one-time happening. It is part science fiction and almost entirely fantasy and completely chilling.

Of "Cross," the author writes the following:

"For a year now I have been both professor of sociology at George Washington University and associate director of the university's Social Research Group, where my current assignment is directing a national study on the incidence of various psychosomatic symptoms and the use of psychotropic drugs among the adult population of the United States.

"Before that, for more than a decade, I was involved in specialized foreign research for the U. S. Information Agency and other branches of the government—work dealing with the collection of sociological and psychological intelligence and with the measurement of propaganda effectiveness. This particular type of research was my field since the beginning of World War II. Earlier, I was a newspaperman. I have degrees from Yale, Columbia and Southern California.

"I live in Chevy Chase, Maryland. I am happily married and have four interesting (if sometimes deplorable) children, ranging down from eighteen to two. My wife is a very good public relations consultant. In my spare time, when I am not writing, I am reading, sleeping, eating, traveling, playing golf or tennis, or watching ball games on TV. In the course of my life I have: been a theatrical press agent; taught at three universities; played semi-pro ball (left-handed knuckle ball and "junk" pitcher); been a naval officer and later a foreign service officer; written and acted in an abortive educational TV show.

" 'James Cross' is a pen name. I started using it because: (a) I publish articles in various professional journals under my given name, and I did not want to get the two entities mixed up or give reviewers a chance at the easy jibe that as a writer of suspense novels I was a good sociologist and as a sociologist a good writer of suspense novels; (b) most of my writing was done while I worked for the government and had to be cleared in advance—even fiction. 'James Cross' was a way of making me unofficial.

"I have had four novels published to date: *Root of Evil, The Dark Road, The Grave of Heroes,* and in February 1967 Random House brought out *To Hell for Half-a-Crown,* a suspense novel with an international setting. All have appeared in hardcover and paperback reprint and have been translated into such languages as French, Italian, Swedish, Dutch and Norwegian. *The Dark Road* was serialized in the *Saturday Evening Post*. I have had two book club sales, but since they were Swedish and Dutch, the circulation was relatively limited and did not make me rich. Pity."

Ellison again. Thus "James Cross" prepares us for that for which there is no preparation: a genuine experience. "The Doll-House" is a marvelous story.

Those of you with tiny daughters will never again, after reading this story, be able to watch them playing on the floor with their Barbie dolls in their playhouses, without a chill quiver of memory.

# • THE DOLL-HOUSE

## by James Cross

"Two hundred and fifty dollars for your lousy Alumnae Fund," Jim Eliot said, holding the canceled check in his hand. "What the hell do you think they're going to do with it—name some building after you, the Julia Wardell Eliot memorial gateway?"

His wife looked at him coldly.

"Just because you went to the sort of place that gets its money from the state legislature, and all the professors are under civil service . . ."

"All right, all right, knock it off—only next time try balancing the checkbook first; you're lucky it didn't bounce. How the hell much do you think we have in the account?"

"How do I know? You're the great brain, you check the balance."

"About twenty-five dollars, plus my pay check tomorrow—$461.29 exactly, after deductions. And next week the mortgage, and the gas and electricity, and oil, and the doctor and the dentist and the car payments, and any bills you've run up for clothes."

"I've run up! Like the $250 cashmere suit you had to have last month. And the new golf clubs, and the credit card lunches—why don't you get on an expense account like everyone else?"

"All right," Eliot said wearily, "just let me balance the goddam account. If something's going to bounce I want to know about it."

"You just do that, lover," Julia said. "I'm going to bed—and don't wake me when you come up."

She swung around toward the door, the silk taffeta of her red housecoat rustling like a swarm of cicada—$99.75, Eliot thought savagely, Saks-Fifth Avenue. But the anger left him slowly as he thought of the bills, his as much as Julia's, the children's, the American way of life. Mortgage; country club; schools; lessons—for Christ's sake, dancing, and swimming and golf and tennis and ballet and the slide trombone; Dr. Smedley, the orthodontist, twenty-five bucks every time he tightened a screw on Pamela's braces; Michael at prep school and his J. Press sport jackets that seemed to average four a year; Julia's charge accounts and Dr. Himmelfarb at thirty dollars an hour because she was bored and scared, and pretty soon he'd be a candidate for the good doctor's couch himself; and, he forced himself to admit, his own clothes, his bar bills, the golf clubs, the expensive women he took out from time to time when he called Julia and told her he'd have to stay over in town. And above all, he thought, above all, me, myself, for allowing any of us to live this way, when I make $15,000 a year. But what can I do? he thought. In a couple or three years there'll be the vice-presidency open when old Calder retires; and I have to live as if I already had it, and if I don't they won't consider me—"not real executive timber"—and I'll end up like Charlie Wainwright—good old Charlie—chief cashier, with the small gold watch and the smaller pension.

There was a storm blowing up, the wind was rising, he could feel the too large house, with its second mortgage, creaking in the wind and calling out for money and more money, not just the extra personal loan he was paying off at usurious rates, but big money, a bundle, the long green.

He sat down wearily at the desk and began to figure it out. But even with the hypothetical Christmas bonus, he would still be in the red. For a while he could juggle bills, forget the doctor and dentist, stave off creditors, but sooner or later they would get nasty (while the new bills kept pouring in) and garnishee his salary, and that would be the end of him at the bank. It was two before he crawled into bed.

The next day was Saturday and he was up early, still groggy with fatigue, while the rest of the house slept. He left a note for Julia, saying he would be back in the afternoon, and then he drove north, toward his last hope.

It was not much of a hope. John Wardell, Julia's uncle, had never liked him and had never hidden his feelings. He had always let Eliot know he considered him a provincial *arriviste* who had had the insolence to marry into a fine old New England family. With his endowed Harvard chair, with his world-wide reputation as an authority on classical civilization, he made Eliot feel like some sort of trousered and bearded Goth trespassing in the Roman Senate. But Uncle John was retired now; he lived well in an old farmhouse upstate; he traveled to Greece and Italy every summer; he wintered in the West Indies. He should have a lot to leave Julia, his only relative, and Jim Eliot wanted to get some of it now, when they needed it, not later when it would just be extra income.

The huge black dog who began barking at him savagely, straining at its chain-link leash, reminded Eliot of the Roman hound from the Pompeian mural. *Cave canem,* he thought, standing back nervously, stretching out a carefully placating hand and waiting for someone to call the beast off. In a minute or two the front door opened and John Wardell stood there in corduroys and a red flannel shirt.

"Down, Brennus," he said, "quiet, boy."

The hound sat back impassively and Eliot walked by him nervously, with his hand outstretched.

"Well, Jim," John Wardell said, giving him a perfunctory handshake, "I don't see you here often; you must be in trouble. Come in and have a drink."

It took a long time to get it out—three drinks, in fact—but in the end Eliot told it all to the old man who hated him.

"It's not for myself, it's for Julia and the kids. If I don't get some help, we're dead."

"Of course, of course, Jim," the old man said, "I know you're not thinking about yourself. But just the same," he said, smiling maliciously, "I don't see any way out of it—unless you start embezzling from the bank."

Eliot jerked his head nervously, as if the old man were reading his mind. Then he forced a smile.

"I was thinking you might be able to tide us over for a while . . . Uncle John," he added, gravely and sincerely.

John Wardell began to laugh.

"You think I have money, Jim? You think Julia has expectations? You're waiting for dead men's shoes? Good God, all I have is my pension, and not much of that, and the big annuity I bought years ago. That takes care of it all. There's enough for me to live on, and it ends when I die."

Eliot looked at him hopelessly and extended his glass for a refill. Oblivious of the old man's clinical, detached amusement.

"The hell of it is," he said loudly, "if I had a bit of money, I couldn't lose. I could spread the risks. The trend is up. I could be rich."

"But you have even less than nothing, Jim," the old man said, "you owe more than you possess. Even if you could know the future, you couldn't raise enough to make it worth while."

"If I knew the future," Eliot said, "I could get hold of the money somehow."

"Is that all you want, Jim? That's really pretty simple. All you need is an oracle to consult—or a sibyl, as the Romans called it. You ask the questions, and the god gives you the answer through his priestess. No house should be without one."

For a while Eliot had thought that the old man had softened to him. Now, looking at the over-red cynical lips below the hawk nose and the white halo of hair, he knew that the fires were only banked.

"How would you like your own oracle, Jim?"

"If you're not going to help, don't needle me."

"There's a story in Petronius about an oracle in a bottle in Cumae. You just feed her regularly and she lives forever. Could you use something like that?"

"I'm going," Eliot said, struggling to his feet unsteadily.

"This is no joke, Jim. I've owed you a wedding present for eighteen years, and now I think I'll give you one. Just sit down."

John Wardell left the room, and in two minutes returned carrying a small doll-house. He put it carefully on the table. Eliot looked at it curiously. It was not the standard Victorian-mansion doll-house but strangely reminiscent of something he had seen ten years ago, on his one trip to Europe, at Pompeii.

The old man looked at him carefully.

"You recognize it? The house of the Vettii at Pompeii. In perfect scale. Look at the atrium and the pool, the rooms to the sides. I bought it there."

Eliot lowered his head to gaze through the gate into the atrium and the pool. From that position he could see nothing else; but he remembered that with most doll-houses the roof was hinged and could be lifted so as to give a bird's-eye view of the interior. He fumbled around the side of the model looking for a hook to unfasten. For a moment he thought he heard a scurrying noise inside the doll-house. He drew back his hand sharply, brushing against the structure and almost knocking it off the table.

"Leave it alone," John Wardell said, suddenly and sharply. "Don't look at the Oracle, she doesn't like it. Never do it, on your life."

"Are you trying to say there's something inside?"

"I don't need to, you heard her move. But don't open it, ever."

"How does it operate, then?" Eliot asked, humoring the old man.

"Do you see that empty pool past the atrium? Well, write your question on a slip of paper, fold it up and put it in the pool. Get a tiny bowl and fill it with milk sweetened with honey and push it inside the gateway. Then go away and the next morning take the piece of paper from the pool. There will be an answer written on it."

"Can you make it work faster?"

"Sometimes it can be done, but I wouldn't advise you to try. It stirs things up."

"Can't you make it work right now? Show me."

John Wardell shrugged his shoulders. Then he went to the kitchen and returned with a dried bay leaf. He lit it, holding it until it smoked aromatically. Then he pushed it into the doll-house, watching the pungent vapor curl through it.

"Now," he said, "what you want to know. Anything. Write it down quickly."

Eliot tore off a slip of paper and wrote on one side of it, "Who will win the World Series?" Then he folded it and slipped it into the empty pool.

"All right," John Wardell said, "we have to leave. Bring the bottle."

When they returned in half an hour, the pungent bay-leaf vapor had died out. Wardell leaned down and reached into the doll-house. In his hand was a folded piece of paper which he handed to Eliot.

Eliot unfolded it and read it quickly. Then he read it more slowly. *"Fringillidae sunt,"* he quoted, "what kind of crap is that?"

"The second word is easy," John Wardell said. "It means 'they [the winners] are.' But *Fringillidae,* wait a minute."

He pulled out the third volume of a twenty-volume classical dictionary, thumbed through it for a minute or two, then shook his head.

"It's a new word to me. I've never seen it."

"Then what the hell good is it?"

"I should have told you, the Oracle uses several languages and she tends to be obscure. You know—'If King Croesus crosses the river Halys with his army, he will destroy a mighty empire'—which one? Well, as it turned out, his own. He just didn't read it right."

"Don't worry about me, I can figure it out."

"Well, in that case you have no troubles."

There was a tinge of unpleasant mockery in Uncle John's voice, as though he knew something very nasty about Eliot, something the younger man should also sense about himself, something, above all, at which he should bridle if he owned the sensitivity to understand or the touchy sense of personal honor to take offense.

Then, abruptly, Eliot caught himself. This was advanced senility talking. He wanted money, a life preserver, a hook to fasten into the mountain from which he was falling, and here this crazy and slightly malevolent old bastard was offering him dreams and fantasies.

"Look, I don't know how you worked this dime store Cassandra, but if it isn't too much bother, would you mind telling me how this—this *Oracle* happened? I mean, what the hell is she? Where did she come from?"

"You really don't know?" the old man asked him. "No, I forgot, you wouldn't, of course. I imagine you majored in business administration, or salesmanship, or art appreciation at that educational cafeteria you attended."

Like uncle, like niece, Eliot thought savagely, remembering Julia's taunts the night before. You'd think I was some kind of a savage because I didn't go to Harvard. For a moment he was tempted to walk out, but his need and desperation were too great; and, too, for the first time in their association, he told himself he could sense something different from the cold, mocking hostility with which the old man normally treated him, as if Eliot had advanced from the status of outsider to that of bungling, inferior relative, but none-theless relative. Or perhaps to the status of a large, stupid, clumsy dog with annoying habits, but still not completely outside.

"The Cumaean Sibyl," Uncle John went on, "as you would know if you had been given a decent education, was believed to be immortal. Originally, she was a young priestess of Apollo, and the god spoke through her lips when she was in a trance and foretold the future to those who asked. There were half a dozen such priestesses operating, but the one at Cumae took the fancy of the god Apollo and he gave her two presents—the gift of prophecy and immortality. Like any other mortal suitor, he was fatuously in love—but not completely so: when he caught his girl friend out on the grass one night with a local fisherman, he couldn't take away the gifts he had granted her, but he had wisely held back on giving her eternal youth to go along with immortality. And just to make sure there would be no more young fishermen, he reduced her to the size of a large mouse, shut her up in a box and turned her over to the priests of the temple to use for all eternity."

"You believe all this hogwash?"

Uncle John almost shrugged. There was too much uncertainty in the gesture for it to have been called a definite movement.

"I don't know really. There is a story in Livy that the second king of Rome talked with the immortal oracle at Cumae, and that was around 700 B.C. And then a contemporary reference in Petronius seven or eight hundred years after indicates that the same person, or maybe creature, was alive in his day, still functioning. I've tried to find out on several occasions, to go beyond the myths, but each time I get a reply that only confuses me more. Maybe she fell from the sky and couldn't get back. Maybe you'd feel more scientific and rational if I talked in terms of slipping over from another continuum, another frame of illusion, some other . . ."

"Oh, Christ, cut the crap," Eliot said under his breath. Then aloud, "What is it inside—a cockroach, a mouse, or what? How do you do the writing trick? Is it like the old money machine?"

"As long as you don't open the top and try to find out, and as long as it tells you what will be, what does it matter? If you find it more comforting to believe I'm a trainer of rodents or lice, or am lapsing into senility, then do so. Or if your conception of the universe is too limited to accept a miracle—from Mars or the Moon, or the past or the future, or *wherever*—then leave it by all means, and we'll both consider this visit fruitless. All I can tell you is that I bought it a few years ago somewhere between Cumae and the ruins of Pompeii, that I got it cheap, and that I've seen it work. *'La vecchia religione'*—the old religion, the man said, and he wanted a quick sale—probably dug it up illegally."

The old kook really believes it, Eliot thought. He found himself looking at the older man with growing disquiet. Not for a moment did he believe that within the doll-house was the Oracle of Pompeii or Cumae or wherever the hell it came from; but the old man seemed convinced of it, and he had learned not to underestimate the old man. Could it be? Had the night suddenly opened like a giant mouth, just beyond his peripheral range of understanding, and belched forth a genuine miracle? He decided to go along with the weird . . .

"Look," Eliot said suddenly. "I believe you about the money. You just have the pension and annuity. Otherwise you're broke; and so am I. But will you sell it to me? I can't pay now, but if this thing works, I'll have plenty, I've got some angles figured out already. Just put a price on it."

"No," the old man said. "Just take it as a delayed wedding present. You can have it. I know all I want about the future at my age. Like a fool, last year I asked it how long I would live—and it's not pleasant to know."

Uncle John Wardell paused and looked at Eliot with an odd expression. It was a very brief pause and a moment later the old man had resumed his normal controlled and guarded look; but in that transitory second Eliot, impervious as he usually was to other people's unexpressed feelings, had read the cold despairing hatred of someone who is going to die for someone who is going to live.

"Go on, take it," the old man continued. "Just remember to feed the Oracle every night, milk and honey. Don't open the top of the house. She doesn't like to be disturbed or looked at. Leave your question at night, but don't expect an answer until the morning. Don't try to rush her."

"I really appreciate this," Eliot said.

"Nothing at all," the old man replied, smiling oddly. "Don't thank me yet. You can show yourself out, I imagine."

When Eliot got home, he was surprised to find that Julia was rather touched that he had visited Uncle John on his own. She was warm and affectionate, and it was not until late at night that he was able to go quietly out to the car, while she slept, and take the doll-house down to the little plyboard room in the cellar that was his undisturbed private study.

On Monday he took the slip of paper to the public library and asked for a translation. In the ensuing days he made ten phone calls unavailingly, while the World Series became locked at three games apiece and the bookmakers' odds fluctuated wildly. Finally, two days after the end of the Series, the slip of paper got to a reference librarian who had majored in zoology as an undergraduate. *Fringillidae,* Eliot was told, was a genus of birds of which the North American cardinal was among the best known.

He stood there, scratching his head, two days too late to collect on the victory of the St. Louis Cardinals. It was then that he realized that the predictions of the Oracle were sometimes too obscure to be of value, sometimes too late to profit by.

In the next weeks he tested the Oracle, each night faithfully putting out the bowl of milk and honey, each morning, when he had left a question, patiently pulling out the answer. He was becoming satisfied with the tests.

In late October he asked the Oracle who would win the presidential election and got the answer: *filius Johanni victor est.* By that time he had invested in a Latin dictionary and had no difficulty in translating the less than elegant Latin (after all, the Oracle was Greek by birth), "The son of John is the victor," a day or so before he read the headlines, "Johnson Landslide."

But he was still cautious. The next week he asked the Oracle whether he should buy Space Industries, Ltd., of Canada, selling at two cents a share. The two words *"caveat emptor,"* warned him off, so that it was with little surprise that he read the next month that the shares had dropped to nothing and that the officers of the company had been indicted.

As a last test, he asked the Oracle when John Wardell would die. He was still looking at the reply, *"ille fuit,"* when the long-distance call for Julia told them that the old man had died that night in his sleep. Poor old boy, Eliot thought as he sat through the interminable funeral services. We had our quarrels, but at the end I guess he was coming around to like me after all. He wanted to do me a favor—at last.

One of the best clients of the bank, and a man whom Jim Eliot had dealt with for five years, was in the undyed cloth end of the textile business. To hear Max Siegal tell it, it seemed relatively simple: You bought up a lot of undyed cloth—often on credit—you figured what colors would be in fashion in the coming season, then you had your cloth dyed and resold at a profit. But it was a lot more complicated and dangerous than that. If you guessed wrong, you could be left with a few hundred thousand dollars' worth of cloth dyed the wrong colors. If that happened, you could hold it, paying storage costs, for years until the colors came in again; you could sell it at a loss; or you could have it redyed and hope to God that the cost of redying wouldn't put you out of business. Max Siegal had shown an uncanny knack of anticipating the fashionable colors, and the bank had been glad to give him short-term loans, since they had always been repaid before they became due.

"All right, Max," Jim Eliot said over the second luncheon martini, "there'll be no trouble over the loan. You know your credit's good. By the way, what's the color this year?"

"You thinking of taking a flyer, Jim? Forget it, you get paid regularly every two weeks. Bank your money."

"It's just so I can give Julia a little fashion preview."

"Well, I'm going forest green, one hundred per cent."

That night Eliot asked the Oracle the question and in the morning had the answer, *"ex Tyre ad Caesarem."* It was easy enough to read— "from Tyre to Caesar"—but it didn't make sense to him. He tried the library again, and this time learned in ten minutes that the city of Tyre manufactured a rare purple dye that was reserved for the Roman emperors.

Jim Eliot handled a few investment accounts, and the best of them was about $500,000 owned by an out-of-town spinster whom he rarely saw, an elderly woman who usually left matters entirely in the hands of the bank provided the returns remained at a level of better than five per cent. At any given time, about a tenth of the estate was in savings accounts waiting to be transferred into a more profitable investment; another tenth was in cash in a safe deposit box, as the old lady insisted. It was the first time for Eliot, and his hands were sweating as he took $10,000 from the safe deposit box.

With the cash, he bought $10,000 worth of undyed cloth and then arranged with a dyer for thirty days' credit. When he specified the color—royal purple—the man looked at him as if he wanted to cancel the agreement. But Eliot was beyond fear by now. "Purple," he said, "royal purple, all of it."

It was the next week when Max Siegal called him for lunch.

"Jim," he said, "I'm in real trouble. I've just seen the advances on *Vogue,* and this year it's purple, royal purple, and here I am stuck with forest green."

"You want another loan, Max?"

"It's too late. By the time I got the cloth dyed, the market would be flooded. Everybody would have switched. The green I could take a loss on and wait for next year; but if I could lay my hands on the purple, I could still break even."

"Suppose you could get your hands on about $10,000 worth of cloth that had been dyed royal purple?"

"I'd pay $25,000 and still make a good profit."

The next Monday, Jim Eliot cashed Siegal's check, paid the dyer, put the $10,000 back in the safe deposit box, beefed up his checking account with the balance. It was enough to pay off the more pressing debts, to retire much of the second mortgage, to pay up the loan at the personal finance company; but at the end of it he was still broke and the bills continued to roll in. One coup wasn't enough.

One of the most frequently traded stocks on the market was that of a gold mine in Asia, which fluctuated daily between a dollar and a dollar and a half. It was common knowledge on Wall Street that if ever the price of gold went up there would be a killing. Eliot asked the question of the Oracle and got the answer, this time in English, "The sea will be as full of gold as it is of fishes." There was something odd about the wording, and he waited. Next week he learned, knocking wood gratefully, of a new process of extracting gold from sea water which caused the price of gold to plummet all over the world.

He was not in a position where simply avoiding loss was enough. What he needed was a favorable answer, something he could act upon. The bills continued to pour in and the bank account was again down to about a hundred dollars. He was getting sick of obscure answers from the Oracle and answers in foreign languages. He wrote a note demanding clear messages in English. The next morning he got his reply: *"Vox dei multas linguas habet* [The voice of the god has many tongues]."

Very funny, Eliot thought; and that night he deliberately neglected the daily feeding. The bowl was put in its place, but he left it empty of milk and honey. He repeated his demand. He burned bay leaves. In the morning there was still no answer. It went on like that for a week. Occasionally, when he put his ear close to the doll-house, he could hear a scurrying around inside, and once, he thought, a small voice crying out. But there was no answer and he realized that something that could live two thousand years could fast for quite a long time.

Wednesday night was a bad one. He had forgotten to answer a letter from one of his accounts, and the indignant old gentleman had written directly to the president of the bank to complain. When he got home, there was a letter from Michael's school reminding him that tuition for the year was overdue. Then Julia, very handsome in new gold lamé stretch pants and leopard-skin pullover, looked up from the pitcher of martinis she was stirring, to tell him: that she had signed Pamela up for elocution lessons—"it's the braces, darling, they make her mumble"—and Charm School sessions; that the washing machine was broken down for good; that the Durkees next door had a new station wagon; that it was about time they got a full-time, live-in maid, even if they had to build a new room on the house; and, finally, that Pongo, the cat, needed a series of vitamin shots.

Eliot drank five martinis before dinner, and afterwards dozed in a chair. When he awoke, it was past one; Julia was already asleep. He ran cold water on his head and neck. Then he made himself a long scotch and sat thinking. After a while he headed for the cellar, with Pongo, the fat, sullen, castrated tomcat, under his arm, squirming and miaowing.

It was Julia's fancy occasionally to walk Pongo on a leash as if he were a dog. On his way to the cellar, Eliot rummaged in a kitchen drawer and found the ornate leash with its twisted silver wire threads, and attached it to the cat's rhinestone-studded collar. When he got close to the doll-house he tied the end of the leash securely to a pipe. Pongo sat there licking himself lazily.

Eliot went to the doll-house and reached along one side of the roof for the tiny catch that held it in place, and flipped it open. For a moment he remembered how old Wardell had warned him about looking inside the doll-house. Then he swung the roof over on its hinges. He pointed a standing lamp downward and peered carefully inside. In one of the small rooms off the atrium he could see what looked like a tiny old woman lying on a couch. She was about six inches long, and dressed in a dark robe. She turned her head and stared at Eliot, coldly and viciously.

He lifted her up, holding her firmly between curved middle finger and the two adjoining ones, as a fisherman holds an eel; but the wriggling was very feeble. Then he brought her close to the cat. For a moment he thought Pongo would break the leash. The cat strained forward, crying horribly with the need to put its teeth into the small, warm creature. Only a few inches separated the two. Eliot could see the frustrated cat's jaws move and hear the frenzied click-click-click of its teeth. He brought the doll-woman still closer, so close that he could feel the cat's breath and its sprayed spittle on the back of his hand. The little body held between his fingers was trembling weakly. Then Pongo began to howl. After a moment Eliot put the Oracle back on her couch and closed the roof of the doll-house. He left the message he had been leaving for many nights, but again he left the feeding bowl empty.

The next morning there was a message for him—"ask and it shall be answered."

That night he resumed feeding the Oracle.

The next day he borrowed $5000 from the same account he had used before, and that night he posed the question. There was no time now to wait for a stock to rise or a business opportunity; he was near bankruptcy; indeed, he would be bankrupt when all the bills came in. All he wanted was three winners; a three-horse parlay. Even if they were all the favorites, he would clear about $100,000, put back what he had borrowed, clean up the debts and be left with capital to use again.

In the morning the three names were there on the slip of paper.

He copied them down carefully into a notebook: Sun-Ray, Snake-killer, and Apollo: first, second, and third races at the local track.

At the $100 window, he bought fifty tickets on Sun-Ray, and a few minutes later in his seat by the finish line, watched the odds drop from 5–3 down to 3–2. Even so, he thought, that would be $12,500 to bet on the second race. He did not even wait to see the finish. In the stretch, Sun-Ray was seven lengths ahead and pulling away. He was close to the front of the line of winners, cashing in their tickets.

There was a little delay in cashing his tickets. He was forced to give his name and address, and back it up with his operator's license—"for the tax boys," the cashier told him apologetically, counting out $12,500. Oh, Christ, Eliot thought, I forgot Mr. Big, there won't be much left after he's taken it off the top. Next time, he thought, next time, I'll stick to capital gains, once I get out of this hole.

At the $100 window, he put it all on Snake-killer. For a moment he wondered whether it would be safer to keep out the original $5000 he'd have to replace the next day; but there was no use playing it safe now, he was in too deep. Snake-killer he didn't like. No better than even money on the board, once his bet was down; but he had Apollo in the third at 10–1, and even when he put $25,000 down, the odds would at least stay at 4–1 or 5–1.

He didn't leave his position early during the second race. It was too close. He stood there, cold with fear, while Snake-killer and an unknown filly battled it out nose and nose. Then he saw the number go up on the board and realized Snake-killer had won. His breath came very fast, his eyes were blurred with sweat and he slumped in his seat.

Then Eliot sprinted to the pay-off window, feeling his heart pounding. There was not much time until the third and, for him, final race. Again he was asked to identify himself and quickly gave his name and address.

In a couple of minutes he was on his way to the $100 window, with $25,000 to bet on Apollo, and was soon pushing a huge strip of tickets into his pockets. Again, for half a second, he kicked himself mentally for not holding out the original $5000 he had taken from the account. Tomorrow morning it goes back, he told himself, first thing tomorrow. He looked up at the odds on the board: even after his huge bet, still 5–1; $125,000 for him in about five minutes.

This time he didn't even go out to the track, but stood there by the cashiers watching the board and waiting for the number 11, Apollo, to go up. It was very fast. He heard the roar that greeted the start, then a rising uneven crescendo of sound as the horses disappeared around the turn; then the final roar as they came into the home-stretch; then something approaching silence as number 11 went up. Eliot turned from the board and walked rapidly to the cashier, holding out his tickets. Right at the track, he thought, there's a branch of my bank. I'll pay it right in, except for the $5000. But, by God, my own separate savings account. Nothing Julia can get at.

"Just a minute," the cashier said. "There's a foul claim against Apollo going up."

Eliot smiled confidently. The smile was still on his face when the cashier turned to him again.

"Your bad day, buddy. They just disqualified Apollo. Better tear up them tickets."

Eliot looked around and saw the 11 coming down, and number 4, the place-horse, going up in its stead.

"They can't," he said, "she told me . . ."

"Tough, buddy; come on; out of line; they're waiting."

He stumbled aside, looking for a long time at the board, hoping that in some impossible way there could be an appeal against the appeal. But nothing happened, and after a while he went home.

On the train he looked again at the whole message. "These will run the fastest tomorrow: Sun-Ray, Snake-killer, Apollo." Oh, Christ, he thought, the bitch tricked me again—"run the fastest," nothing about fouling. This time I'll let the cat play with her a little.

When he got home there was no one there. Only a note from Julia. "Pamela is at a pajama party at the Evans'. I'm going to the movies. Food in refrigerator. Pongo is in the cellar, be sure to put him out."

He sat drinking rapidly. Five thousand dollars short. There was no way to raise it. Two mortgages on the house; no equity in the cars; he had already borrowed on his life insurance. And one of these days old Miss Winston would suddenly turn up at the bank, as she always did, and count the money in the safe deposit box. Or the examiners would make their check. If only there were some way to be sure with that lousy Oracle. There's still a lot left in the safe deposit box. I could try it again. I won't get any longer sentence if they catch me. This time, he said, I'll really starve her out; this time I'll let the cat have her for a while till she calls out to me for help.

He was quite drunk when he remembered Julia's note and stumbled down to the cellar to let the cat out. At first he didn't really notice Pongo over in a corner of his study; he only took note that the cat was there, glancing rapidly out of one corner of his eye, as he went quickly to the doll-house, holding the cat's leash in one hand.

He looked at the doll-house. The entrance was a ruin. The thin wood and papier-mâché had been torn aside, and he could see deep scratch marks around the pool where claws had searched. He opened the catch quickly and swung back the roof. The couch on which the Oracle had rested was on its side in a corner of the little room, in pieces. There was no one inside the doll-house.

In the far corner Pongo purred ecstatically. Eliot came slowly toward the cat, as it crouched down defensively over something in its two paws that looked like a crumpled piece of dark cloth. Eliot brought the leash down on the cat's shoulders savagely, watching it scurry away, leaving whatever it had been playing with.

He picked it up. It was only a torn tube of black cloth with something crushed inside. If he had not felt the dark stains on the garment and held his finger up to the light to see the little smear of blood on it, he would have thought it was simply a headless doll.

Julia, among her other traits, suffered from an exaggerated fear of burglars; but once Eliot had bought the stubby .38 Bankers Special revolver, she had made him keep it, not in the night table by his bed —she was equally terrified of guns—but in a desk drawer in his cellar study, locked.

The key was on his key ring, and he opened the drawer quickly and took out the revolver, weighing it in his hand. He went over to the doll-house swinging the revolver. He looked inside once more on the wild, impossible chance that the Oracle was still there, that the old woman had somehow escaped the cat. But the doll-house was empty, or rather, almost empty; because there was a scrap of paper in one corner of the pool.

He picked it up. When shall I die, he thought, and read the last message he was to get—*"ille die* [today]."

When the revolver went off in the enclosed cellar, it was as loud as artillery.

The movie that Julia saw was a double feature. Neither picture was much good, but she was thrifty in small things and once she had paid for her ticket would sit through hours of clumsy triteness. When she got back to the house she parked the car and came in through the carport entrance to the kitchen. It looked as though a chef had gone crazy. On the shelves, boxes and bottles were knocked on their sides. The spice cabinet hanging on the wall was askew, and on the kitchen table an opened bottle of bay leaves spilled out its aromatic contents.

She cleaned them up mechanically, almost without thought, then she looked for her husband. He was not in the living room or the bedroom, so at last she looked for him in the cellar study. When she entered the cellar, the lights were off in the main section but she could see a faint yellow glow escaping under the study door. She switched on the overhead light.

Pongo the cat was on the floor, stiff and ungainly with a pool of blood around him. For a moment she wondered what had happened; then she saw the revolver tossed on the floor by the dead cat's ruined head. She went up to the door of the study. All she could hear was a low monotonous repetition of words she could not understand. She opened the door slowly and carefully.

The first thing that struck her was the harshly aromatic smell of burning bay leaves and the curl of blue-gray smoke from a little copper ash tray.

Her husband was kneeling in front of a large doll-house at one end of the room. His left hand held a small wooden bowl, and incongruously, in his right hand was a half-filled milk bottle that he was pouring into the bowl. She called to him sharply, but he did not answer. Then she went forward. The top of the doll-house was raised. She had never looked inside it before so she craned forward eagerly. All she could see was a courtyard with an empty pool, and several small rooms surrounding it. In one of them there seemed to be a little antique couch, with something lying on it. After a moment Eliot turned to look at her blindly. Then he reached into the doll-house and took from the couch what looked like a tiny rag doll. He began to talk to it, crooning in a language she did not know, ignoring her completely. He was still on his knees crooning when she went upstairs, and he had not moved much later when the ambulance arrived.

## Afterword:

To re-create the steps that lead to the writing of a short story normally requires something close to total recall, unless you are one of those very methodical writers who make a point of jotting story ideas, development and progress down in a notebook. In the case of "The Doll-House," however, I do have a pretty clear recollection of how it got started.

I was with my son Brian, then two years old, and we were looking at the fantastic doll-house in the old Smithsonian building here. Brian was fascinated by some of the puppets in the old doll-house, and asked whether they were "real people," did they move around, and so on. I thought of M. R. James's story of the eighteenth-century doll-house where the puppets did come alive after midnight, in a very gruesome way; but obviously I couldn't re-use that for an idea. For no particular reason, I then thought of the Palazzo Vettii at Pompeii, and how that handsome Roman summerhouse would make a wonderful doll-house. Then, being mentally in the Naples area, I remembered the story in Petronius about the Oracle who had been somehow captured and imprisoned in a bottle. Then I thought of my son's question again, and the various avenues of thought became enmeshed with each other and took on a rough shape and pattern. (All this took place in about thirty seconds.) On the way home I began thinking more deliberately and systematically; and by the time I got there I had a story idea pretty well roughed out in my head. This is the way that I find I have to work most stories out—using every stimulus and every scrap of time available; because I have always had a full-time job and have written for pleasure, relaxation, because I find it hard *not* to write.

The danger part of the "dangerous vision" in my story is really there from the beginning. Jim Eliot is a would-be *arriviste* who has not arrived, someone with a great future behind him. He would like to be "upwardly mobile," as the sociologists put it, in fact as well as in temperament. He has married upwardly, he is living in a very expensive exurb in the hopes that his income will someday reach his way of life—just as some primitive cultures believe that acting out the effects that follow a cause will actually bring about the cause: wet yourself and it will rain. He still has the dangerous vision that guides his life—the vision of the Land of Pelf, the long green, the crisp bills falling gently from the money trees like dead leaves; and meanwhile, even before he gets the doll-house, he is acting as though the vision were true. And what he himself fails to spend, his wife takes care of. He is extended; in debt; juggling creditors; stretched thin; on a tightrope; near a breakdown. This is why he is willing to believe the unbelievable. This is why he is avid to accept a dubious gift from a dying man who is obviously his enemy. And this is why even a setback or two—plain warnings—do not deter him: he still has that dangerous vision of the perfect gimmick that will open the doors to the U. S. Mint.

"It is the custom of the gods," Caesar said to King Ariovistus, "to raise men high, so that their fall will be all the greater." Jim Eliot doesn't even get all that high, except for a matter of minutes; but his fall is just as great.

Most of my novels and short stories, I find, revolve a great deal around money, sex and status. This particular one is about money and the various symbols that men exchange it for; about easy money and the eternally dangerous vision—that there is somewhere, just around the corner, in another country, another time, another dimension, a fool-proof way to get it.

## Introduction to SEX AND/OR MR. MORRISON:

No one writes like Carol Emshwiller. Absolutely no one. And no one ever *has*. She is her own woman, has her own voice, defies comparison, probes areas usually considered dangerous, and is as close to being the pure artist as any writer I have met.

It is difficult talking about Carol . . . even as it is difficult talking about her work. They don't align with the usual symbologies and standards. And Carol (to strangers) has trouble talking for herself. In sessions of critical analysis, she has a tendency to fall into gesticulation, murmurs, gropings for sound. This hesitancy does not show up in her stories. (It may be true that she must go through rewrites to find the language for a particular story, but that is *ex post facto*. The idea was there, it is merely the craft of the writer to accept and reject the various vibratory elements till the special harmony is achieved.) From this disparity, I draw a natural conclusion: Carol Emshwiller speaks most eloquently through her work. It is often so with the best writers. It is often so with the most special people.

As to her being a pure artist, she is the first writer I ever encountered who said she wrote to please herself whom I believed. The kinds of stories Carol brings forth are seldom commercial. They are quite frankly personal visions. (I have always contended that a writer must first learn the basics of his craft, the commercial manner of telling a story in its simplest, most direct ways, before attempting to break the rules and establish new approaches. Carol is, again, an exception to that rule. From the very first work of hers I read, she was an innovator, an experimenter. Either she knows the rules so well, inherently, that she can accept or reject them according to the needs of the project, or she is—as I suspect—a natural talent that is not governed by the same rules as the rest of us. It's academic, really, for the proof is in the reading. She gets away with it every time.) Her "visions" are never completely substantial. They shift and waver, like oil rainbows in a pool. It is almost as if Carol's stories turn a corner into another dimension. Only a portion of the whole, intended work is visible. What she may *really* be saying is half glimpsed, shadowy, alluring, a beckoning from the mist. It isn't like the visible part of an iceberg, or the hidden meaning of a *haiku* or anything encountered previously. Once again, it is singular. But for want of a handier explanation, I'll stick with the turning-the-corner-to-another-dimension.

But being a "pure" artist is not merely a product of the *kind* of work one does. It is a state of mind, from the outset. And it is infinitely harder, by far, to hoe *that* row than simply to aspire to sell what one writes. Carol seems unconcerned about selling her stories—at least in the way most writers are concerned. She naturally wants the reality of seeing her work in print, but if that entails writing what she does not wish to write, she will pass. She has set herself a lofty reach of quality and attack that almost verges on the impossible. And she writes the stories full well aware that they may never sell. She is by no means an ivory tower writer, one who writes strictly for the trunk, one who is too insecure to release the work for public criticism. There is none of that in Carol. But she is cognizant of the facts of publishing life. There are too few magazines and editors who care to risk the experimental, the far out, the individual, when they can continue to make their sales break-even point with the hand-me-downs of antediluvian fantasy. None of this daunts Carol. She continues her own way, writing magnificently.

The genius of the Emshwiller talent (and I use the word "genius" with full awareness of every implication of its definition) is not confined to Carol, incidentally. As most people know, she is the wife of talented artist and film maker Ed Emshwiller, whose avant-garde films many of us have enjoyed for far longer than the teenie-boppers and underground cinemaphiles who erroneously lump Ed in with Warhol and Brakhage and Anger and David Brooks. The Emshwiller genius—both husband and wife—is a combination of professional expertise sparingly employed in the forming of lean, moody and occasionally ominous art, both in fiction and in film. It would be a happy inevitability if Ed were to translate Carol's work for the screen.

In personally describing herself, Carol's image of the pertinent facts paint her as a Levittown housewife—three kids, bad housekeeper, can cook if she makes the effort and now and then she does—and I suspect the view is a cultivated one. Carol the housewife is someone Carol the writer is forced to keep split off. But beneath the superficialities there are some fascinating things to learn about the woman: "I once hated everything and anything to do with writing, though if I'd ever had anyone give me a little tiny hint as to what it was about, I think I'd have loved it as I do now. I nearly flunked freshman English in college and had to take an agonizing extra semester of English because of my bad grade. (I feel strongly about the lousy way things to do with literature are generally taught.) I started out in music school, playing the violin, and then switched to art school. I was a bad musician but a good artist. I met Ed in art school at the University of Michigan. I got a Fulbright to France. It wasn't until I'd met some writers, later, in New York, that I began to see what writing was all about. I see all the underground movies I can. I like interesting failures better than works where the artist always knows exactly what he's doing."

The story Carol tells here is by no means a failure. It is a complete success, easily the strangest sex story ever written, and functionally science fiction as well. It is considerably further out than the bulk of the stories Carol has had published in the commercial magazines, and is as close to being "the new thing" as anything in this book. I recommend it to younger writers breaking in, looking for new directions.

# ● SEX AND/OR MR. MORRISON

## by Carol Emshwiller

I can set my clock by Mr. Morrison's step upon the stairs, not that he is that accurate, but accurate enough for me. 8:30 thereabouts. (My clock runs fast anyway.) Each day he comes clumping down and I set it back ten minutes, or eight minutes or seven. I suppose I could just as well do it without him but it seems a shame to waste all that heavy treading and those puffs and sighs of expending energy on only getting downstairs, so I have timed my life to this morning beat. Funereal tempo, one might well call it, but it is funereal only because Mr. Morrison is fat and therefore slow. Actually he's a very nice man as men go. He always smiles.

I wait downstairs sometimes looking up and sometimes holding my alarm clock. I smile a smile I hope is not as wistful as his. Mr. Morrison's moonface has something of the Mona Lisa to it. Certainly he must have secrets.

"I'm setting my clock by you, Mr. M."

"Heh, heh . . . my, my," grunt, breath. "Well," heave the stomach to the right, "I hope . . ."

"Oh, you're on time enough for *me*."

"Heh, heh. Oh. Oh yes." The weight of the world is certainly upon him or perhaps he's crushed and flattened by a hundred miles of air. How many pounds per square inch weighing him down? He hasn't the inner energy to push back. All his muscles spread like jelly under his skin.

"No time to talk," he says. (He never has time.) Off he goes. I like him and his clipped little Boston accent, but I know he's too proud ever to be friendly. Proud is the wrong word, so is shy. Well, I'll leave it at that.

He turns back, pouting, and then winks at me as a kind of softening of it. Perhaps it's just a twitch. He thinks, if he thinks of me at all: What can she say and what can I say talking to her? What can she possibly know that I don't know already? And so he duck-walks, knock-kneed, out the door.

And now the day begins.

There are really quite a number of things that I can do. I often spend time in the park. Sometimes I rent a boat there and row myself about and feed the ducks. I love museums and there are all those free art galleries and there's window-shopping and, if I'm very careful with my budget, now and then I can squeeze in a matinee. But I don't like to be out after Mr. Morrison comes back. I wonder if he keeps his room locked while he's off at work?

His room is directly over mine and he's too big to be a quiet man.

The house groans with him and settles when he steps out of bed. The floor creaks under his feet. Even the walls rustle and the wallpaper clicks its dried paste. But don't think I'm complaining of the noise. I keep track of him this way. Sometimes, here underneath, I ape his movements, bed to dresser, step, clump, dresser to closet and back again. I imagine him there, flat-footed. Imagine him. Just imagine those great legs sliding into pants, their godlike width (for no mere man could have legs like that), those Thor-legs into pants holes wide as caves. Imagine those two landscapes, sparsely fuzzed in a faint, wheat-colored brush finding their way blindly into the waist-wide skirt-things of brown wool that are still damp from yesterday. Ooo. Ugh. Up go the suspenders. I think I can hear him breathe from here.

I can comb my hair three times to his once and I can be out and waiting at the bottom step by the time he opens his door.

"I'm setting my clock by you, Mr. M."

"No time. No time. I'm off. Well . . ." and he shuts the front door so gently one would think he is afraid of his own fat hands.

And so, as I said, the day begins.

The question is (and perhaps it is the question for today): Who is he really, one of the Normals or one of the Others? It's not going to be so easy to find out with someone so fat. I wonder if I'm up to it. Still, I'm willing to go to certain lengths and I'm nimble yet. All that rowing and all that walking up and down and then, recently, I've spent all night huddled under a bush in Central Park and twice I've crawled out on the fire escape and climbed to the roof and back again (but I haven't seen much and I can't be sure of the Others yet).

I don't think the closet will do because there's no keyhole, though I could open the door a crack and maybe wedge my shoe there. (It's double A.) He might not notice it. Or there's the bed to get under. While it's true that I am thin and small, almost child-sized, one might say, still it will not be so easy, but then neither has it been easy to look for lovers on the roof.

Sometimes I wish I were a little, fast-moving lizard, dull green or a yellowish brown. I could scamper in under his stomach when he opened the door and he'd never see me, though his eyes are as quick as his feet are clumsy. Still I would be quicker. I would skitter off behind the bookcase or back of his desk or maybe even just lie very still in a corner, for surely he does not see the floor so much. His room is no larger than mine and his presence must fill it, or rather his stomach fills it and his giant legs. He sees the ceiling and the pictures on the wall, the surfaces of night table, desk and bureau, but the floor and the lower halves of everything would be safe for me. No, I won't even have to regret not being a lizard, except for getting in. But if he doesn't lock his room it will be no problem and I can spend all day scouting out my hiding places. I'd best take a snack with me too if I decide this is the night for it. No crackers and no nuts, but noiseless things like cheese and fig newtons.

It seems to me, now that I think about it, that I was rather saving Mr. Morrison for last, as a child saves the frosting of the cake to eat after the cake part is finished. But I see that I have been foolish, for, since he is really one of the most likely prospects, he should have been first.

And so today the day begins with a gathering of supplies and an exploratory trip upstairs.

The room is cluttered. There is no bookcase but there are books and magazines by the hundreds. I check behind the piles. I check the closet, full of drooping, giant suit coats I can easily hide in. Just see how the shoulders extend over the ordinary hangers. I check under the bed and the kneehole of the desk. I squat under the night table. I nestle among the dirty shirts and socks tossed in the corner. Oh, it's better than Central Park for hiding places. I decide to use them all.

There's something very nice about being here, for I do like Mr. Morrison. Even just his size is comforting; he's big enough to be everybody's father. His room reassures with all his father-sized things in it. I feel lazy and young here.

I eat a few fig newtons while I sit on his shoes in the closet, soft, wide shoes with their edges all collapsed and all of them shaped more like cushions than shoes. Then I take a nap in the dirty shirts. It looks like fifteen or so but there are only seven and some socks. After that I hunch down in the kneehole of the desk, hugging my knees, and I wait and I begin to have doubts. That pendulous stomach, I can already tell, will be larger than all my expectations.

There will certainly be nothing it cannot overshadow or conceal, so why do I crouch here clicking my fingernails against the desk leg when I might be out feeding pigeons? Leave now, I tell myself. Are you actually going to spend the whole day, and maybe night too, cramped and confined in here? Yet haven't I done it plenty of times lately and always for nothing too? Why not one more try? For Mr. Morrison is surely the most promising of all. His eyes, the way the fat pushes up his cheeks under them, look almost Chinese. His nose is Roman and in an ordinary face it would be overpowering, but here it is lost. Dwarfed. "Save me," cries the nose, "I'm sinking." I would try, but I will have other more important duties, after Mr. Morrison comes back. Duty it is, too, for the good of all and I do mean *all,* but do not think that I am the least bit prejudiced in this.

You see, I did go to a matinee a few weeks ago. I saw the Royal Ballet dance "The Rites of Spring" and it occurred to me then . . . Well, what would *you* think if you saw them wearing their suits that were supposed to be bare skin? Naked suits, I called them. And all those well-dressed, cultured people clapping at them, accepting even though they knew perfectly well . . . like a sort of Emperor's New Clothes in reverse. Now just think, there are only two sexes and every one of us *is* one of those and certainly, presumably that is, knows something of the other. But then that may be where I have been making my mistake. You'd think . . . why, just what I *did* start thinking: that there must be Others among us.

But it is not out of fear or disgust that I am looking for them. I am open and unprejudiced. You can see that I am when I say that I've never seen (and doesn't this seem strange?) the very organs of my own conception, neither my father nor my mother. Goodness knows what *they* were and what this might make me?

So I wait here, tapping my toes inside my slippers and chewing hangnails off my fingers. I contemplate the unvarnished underside of the desk top. I ridge it with my thumbnail. I eat more cookies and think whether I should make his bed for him or not but decided not to. I suck my arm until it is red in the soft crook opposite the elbow. Time jerks ahead as slowly as a school clock, and I crawl across the floor and stretch out behind the books and magazines. I read first paragraphs of dozens of them. What with the dust back here and lying in the shirts and socks before, I'm getting a certain smell and a sort of gray, animal fuzz that makes me feel safer, as though I really did belong in this room and could actually creep around and not be noticed by Mr. Morrison at all except perhaps for a pat on the head as I pass him.

Thump . . . pause. Clump . . . pause. One can't miss his step. The house shouts his presence. The floors wake up squeeking and lean towards the stairway. The banister slides away from his slippery ham-hands. The wallpaper seems suddenly full of bugs. He must think: Well, this time she isn't peeking out of her doorway at me. A relief. I can concentrate completely on climbing up. Lift the legs against the pressure. Ooo. Ump. Pause and seem to be looking at the picture on the wall.

I skitter back under the desk.

It's strange that the first thing he does is to put his newspaper on the desk and sit down with his knees next to my nose, regular walls, furnaces of knees, exuding heat and dampness, throwing off a miasma delicately scented of wet wool and sweat. What a wide roundness they have to them, those knees. Mother's breasts pressing towards me. Probably as soft. Why can't I put my cheek against them? Observe how he can sit so still with no toe tapping, no rhythmic tensing of the thigh. He's not like the rest of us, but could a man like this do *little* things?

How the circumstantial evidence piles up, but that is all I've had so far and it is time for something concrete. One thing, just one fact, is all I need.

He reads and adjusts the clothing at his crotch and reads again. He breathes out winds of sausages and garlic and I remember that it is after supper and I take out my cheese and eat it as slowly as possible in little rabbit bites. I make a little piece last a half an hour.

At last he goes down the hall to the bathroom and I shift back under the shirts and socks and stretch my legs. What if he undresses like my grandmother did, under a nightgown? under, for him, some giant, double-bed-sized thing?

But he doesn't. He hangs his coat on the little hanger and his tie on the closet doorknob. I receive his shirt and have to make myself another spy hole. Then off with the shoes, then socks. Off come the huge pants with slow, unseeing effort (he stares out the window).

He begins on his yellowed undershorts, scratching himself first behind and starting earthquakes across his buttocks.

Where could he have bought those elephantine undershorts? In what store were they once folded on the shelf? In what factory did women sit at sewing machines and put out one after another after another of those other-worldly items? Mars? Venus? Saturn more likely. Or perhaps, instead, a tiny place, some moon of Jupiter with less air per square inch upon the skin and less gravity, where Mr. Morrison can take the stairs three at a time and jump the fences (for surely he's not particularly old) and dance all night with girls his own size.

He squints his oriental eyes towards the ceiling light and takes off the shorts, lets them fall loosely to the floor. I see Alleghenies of thigh and buttock. How does a man like that stand naked even before a small-sized mirror? I lose myself, hypnotized. Impossible to tell the color of his skin, just as it is with blue-gray eyes or the ocean. How tan, pink, olive and red and sometimes a bruised elephant-gray. His eyes must be used to multiplicities like this, and to plethoras, conglomerations, to an opulence of self, to an intemperant exuberance, to the universal, the astronomical.

I find myself completely tamed. I lie in my cocoon of shirts not even shivering. My eyes do not take in what they see. He is utterly beyond my comprehension. Can you imagine how thin my wrists must seem to him? He is thinking (if he thinks of me at all), he thinks: She might be from another world. How alien her ankles and leg bones. How her eyes do stand out. How green her complexion in the shadows at the edges of her face. (For I must admit that perhaps I may be as far along the scale at my end of humanity as he is at his.)

Suddenly I feel like singing. My breath purrs in my throat in hymns as slow as Mr. Morrison himself would sing. Can this be love, I wonder? My first *real* love? But haven't I always been passionately interested in people? Or rather in those who caught my fancy? But isn't this feeling different? Can love really have come to me this late in life? (La, la, lee la from whom all blessings flow.) I shut my eyes and duck my head into the shirts. I grin into the dirty socks. Can you imagine *him* making love to *me!*

Well below his abstracted, ceilingward gazes, I crawl on elbows and knees back behind the old books. A safer place to shake out the silliness. Why, I'm old enough for him to be (had I ever married) my youngest son of all. Yet if he were a son of mine, how he would have grown beyond me. I see that I cannot ever follow him (as with all sons). I must love him as a mouse might love the hand that cleans the cage, and as uncomprehendingly too, for surely I see only a part of him here. I sense more. I sense deeper largenesses. I sense excesses of bulk I cannot yet imagine. Rounded afterimages linger on my eyeballs. There seems to be a mysterious darkness in the corners of the room and his shadow covers, at the same time, the window on one wall and the mirror on the other. Certainly he is like an iceberg, seven eighths submerged.

But now he has turned towards me. I peep from the books holding a magazine over my head as one does when it rains. I do so more to shield myself from too much of him all at once than to hide.

And there we are, confronting each other eye to eye. We stare and he cannot seem to comprehend me any more than I can comprehend him, and yet usually his mind is ahead of mine, jumping away on unfinished phrases. His eyes are not even wistful and not yet surprised. But his belly button, that is another story. Here is the eye of God at last. It nestles in a vast, bland sky like a sun on the curve of the universe flashing me a wink of heat, a benign, fat wink. The stomach eye accepts and understands. The stomach eye recognizes me and looks at me as I've always wished to be looked at. (Yea, though I walk through the valley of the shadow of death.) I see you now.

But I see him now. The skin hangs in loose, plastic folds just there, and there is a little copper-colored circle like a fifty-cent piece made out of pennies. There's a hole in the center and it is corroded green at the edges. This must be a kind of "naked suit" and whatever the sex organs may be, they are hidden behind this hot, pocked and pitted imitation skin.

I look up into those girlish eyes of his and they are as blank as though the eyeballs were all whites, as blank as having no sex at all, eggs without yolks, like being built like a boy-doll with a round hole for the water to empty out.

God, I think. I am not religious but I think, My God, and then I stand up and somehow, in a limping run, I get out of there and down the stairs as though I fly. I slam the door of my room and slide in under my bed. The most obvious of hiding places, but after I am there I can't bear to move out. I lie and listen for his thunder on the stairs, the roar of his feet splintering the steps, his hand tossing away the banister.

I know what I'll say. "I accept. I accept," I'll say. "I will love, I love already, whatever you are."

I lie listening, watching the hanging edges of my bedspread in the absolute silence of the house. Can there be anyone here at all in such a strange quietness? Must I doubt even my own existence?

"Goodness knows," I'll say, "if I'm normal myself." (How is one to know such things when everything is hidden?) "Tell all of them that we accept. Tell them it's the naked suits that are ugly. Your dingles, your dangles, wrinkles, ruts, bumps and humps, we accept whatever there is. Your loops, strings, worms, buttons, figs, cherries, flower petals, your soft little toad-shapes, warty and greenish, your cat's tongues or rat's tails, your oysters, one-eyed between your legs, garter snakes, snails, we accept. We think the truth is lovable."

But what a long silence this is. Where is he? for he must (mustn't he?) come after me for what I saw. But where has he gone? Perhaps he thinks I've locked my door, but I haven't. I haven't.

Why doesn't he come?


### Afterword:

Blake wrote: "The head Sublime, the heart Pathos, the genitals Beauty, the hands & feet Proportion."

It would be nice to live in a society where the genitals were really considered Beauty. It seems to me any other way of seeing is obscene. After all, there they are. Why not like them? You can't have all this hiding and have people grow up not thinking there's a reason for hiding. (And when you think that every animal, or almost every animal, in the world has come into being from what we call a "dirty" word, it does seem a sick society.)

I wrote a series of stories on this theme. "Sex and/or Mr. Morrison" really did come into my head while I was attending "The Rites of Spring" ballet at the Metropolitan Opera House. Not the sort of thing I usually do, by the way, but the tickets were gifts. The dancers wore "naked suits," skin-colored leotards with hand prints and stripes in imitation body paint. Sitting there with all those mature-looking, married-looking people in the audience (each of them *was* one of the sexes and there are only two . . . for goodness' sake, only two!), I suddenly remembered that as a small child I really did feel that people must be hiding themselves so carefully because they were each entirely different from one another. I figured there may be a general male-female opposition, you know, males out, females in (though at that age I suppose I felt, males out, females nothing), but that was all the similarity there could be. And if people didn't wear clothes, I thought, what peculiar and wondrous things we'd see.

This all came back to me as I sat there at the ballet. It suddenly seemed very strange to have those naked suits onstage, as though what I thought as a child was the only possible, logical explanation for all the hiding. Why else should adults, especially this audience, educated-looking and rather elderly, each one sex and looking married to the other, why should they have to see a program with pretend skin on the dancers? Ludicrous!

So, this story. . . .

**Introduction to SHALL THE DUST PRAISE THEE?:**

Somehow, inexplicably, I have grown rather fond of Damon Knight, 1st president and founder of the Science Fiction Writers of America. After thought, I must chalk it up to the fact that he is married to Kate Wilhelm, who is a better writer than I am, which offends me, but is one of those truths one must finally face up to. She is also lots prettier. Ergo, because Kate is a better writer than I, I recognize that she is a better person than I, and being a better person, there must be *something* she sees in Damon that makes him lovable and worth while, and out of respect and admiration for Kate, I have let it slop over onto Damon. A sticky and entirely unseemly situation, at best.

Now there are those who contend Damon Knight is worth while in his own right. As author of *Hell's Pavement* and *The Analogs* and *Mind Switch*, which many contend are brilliant novels of pure speculative fiction. As editor of *A Century of Science Fiction* and *Cities of Wonder* and *13 French Science Fiction Stories* and eleven other anthologies, touted as the peak of literacy in the genre. As critic of the scene, epitomized by his collection of essays, *In Search of Wonder,* which helped win him a Hugo in 1956 as Best Science Fiction Book Reviewer. All this is said in defense of Damon Knight. There may even be merit in it.

Yet if this be so, if Knight is indeed the paragon his fans would have us believe, then explain the following:

> Knight, sitting in a restaurant with friends, watching James Blish and myself at another table, as Blish explained in pantomime a hilarious newspaper cartoon to me, totally bewildered and bursting into tears when Blish refused to explain the meaning of his bizarre hand movements. . . .

> Knight, having incurred the wrath of a host of writers in attendance at the Milford (Pa.) SF Writers Conference (of which he is the founder and director, since 1956), finding two fifteen-foot hardwood pilings inserted through front and back windows of his car, not uttering a word of anger or protest, but merely sulking for two days. . . .

> Knight, managing not only to *sell* "The Man in the Jar" to a leading magazine, but having the audacity to include it in his latest collection, *Turning On,* without cleaning up the specious logic of the denouement. . . .

> Knight, having a surfeit of brilliant Kate Wilhelm stories already bought up for his *Orbit* series of original science fiction anthologies, refusing to sell a perfect *gem* of a Kate story to this anthology, forcing the poor woman to sell it to *him* for some nebulous far-distant collection he is putting together. . . .

Each of these imponderables forces the conclusion that Damon Knight is a spoilsport. Now how's *that* for feet of clay!

Spoilsport was born in Baker, Oregon, in 1922. He was semi-educated in Hood River, Oregon, public schools. He spent a year after high school studying at the WPA Art Center in Salem, Oregon, then moved to New York and joined an early fraternity of science fiction buffs called The Futurians in 1941. He did some science fiction illustration (which he admits was bad), worked for Popular Publications as an assistant editor on their pulp magazines, and as a reader for the Scott Meredith Literary Agency. He has been a free-lance writer since 1950, pouting all the while.

His first story sale (a result of flagrant intimidation and temper tantrums) was to Donald Wollheim (now editor of Ace Books) at *Stirring Science Fiction* when he was eighteen; since then he has sold close to a hundred stories, five novels, four collections of stories and the previously noted anthologies, et al.

About this Damon Knight story: he sent it in despite the fact that I told him bluntly there was no place for *his* kind of fellow in such an august collection. I liked it well enough, but I was going to send it back, just to show him nobody likes a smartass, when I received a letter from Kate. She said he had been making her life a living hell. They live in "a large delicate Victorian mansion in Milford, with three active boys, three tomcats and an indeterminate number of tropical fish," and Damon was really taking it out on Kate because I'd asked *her* for a story, but not him, and he threatened her that if *his* story was rejected and *hers* sold, he would have her shanghaied onto a white slave boat sailing for Marrakech.

Needless to say, he got his way, as usual. Thus, you will find in this anthology one Damon Knight story, and none by Kate Wilhelm. We're taking this up at the next Inquisition of the Science Fiction Writers of America.

# ● SHALL THE DUST PRAISE THEE?

## by Damon Knight

The Day of Wrath arrived. The sky pealed with trumpets, agonized, summoning. Everywhere the dry rocks rose, groaning, and fell back in rubble. Then the sky split, and in the dazzle appeared a throne of white fire, in a rainbow that burned green.

Lightnings flickered away toward the horizons. Around the throne hovered seven majestic figures in white, with golden girdles across their paps; and each one carried in his gigantic hand a vial that smoked and fumed in the sky.

Out of the brightness in the throne came a voice: "Go your ways, and pour out the vials of the wrath of God upon the earth."

And the first angel swooped down, and emptied his vial in a torrent of darkness that smoked away across the bare earth. And there was silence.

Then the second angel flew down to earth, and darted this way and that, with his vial unemptied: and at last turned back to the throne, calling, "Lord, mine is to be poured out upon the sea. But where is the sea?"

And again there was silence. For the dry, dusty rocks of the earth stretched away limitless under the sky; and where the oceans had been, there were only runneled caverns in the stone, as dry and empty as the rest.

The third angel called, "Lord, mine is for the rivers and fountains of waters."

Then the fourth angel called, "Lord, let me empty mine." And he poured out his vial upon the sun: and in an instant grew hot with a terrible radiance: and he soared back and forth letting fall his light upon the earth. After some time he faltered and turned back to the throne. And again there was silence.

Then out of the throne came a voice saying, "Let be."

Under the wide dome of heaven, no bird flew. No creature crawled or crept on the face of the earth; there was no tree, and no blade of grass.

The voice said, "This is the day appointed. Let us go down."

Then God walked on the earth, as in the old time. His form was like a moving pillar of smoke. And after Him trooped the seven white angels with their vials, murmuring. They were alone under the yellow-gray sky.

"They who are dead have escaped our wrath," said the Lord God Jehovah. "Nevertheless they shall not escape judgment." The dry valley in which they stood was the Garden of Eden, where the first man and first woman had been given a fruit which they might not eat. To eastward was the pass through which the wretched pair had been driven into the wilderness. Some little distance to the west they saw the pitted crag of Mount Ararat, where the Ark had come to rest after a purifying Flood.

And God said in a great voice, "Let the book of life be opened; and let the dead rise up from their graves, and from the depths of the sea."

His voice echoed away under the sullen sky. And again the dry rocks heaved and fell back; but the dead did not appear. Only the dust swirled, as if it alone remained of all earth's billions, living and dead.

The first angel was holding a huge book open in his arms. When the silence had endured for some time, he shut the book, and in his face was fear; and the book vanished out of his hands.

The other angels were murmuring and sighing together. One said, "Lord, terrible is the sound of silence, when our ears should be filled with lamentations."

And God said, "This is the time appointed. Yet one day in heaven is as a thousand years on earth. Gabriel, tell me, as men reckoned time, how many days have passed since the Day?"

The first angel opened a book and said, "Lord, as men reckoned time, one day has passed since the Day."

A shocked murmur went through the angels.

And turning from them, God said, "Only one day: a moment. And yet they do not rise."

The fifth angel moistened his lips and said, "Lord, are You not God? Shall any secrets be hid from the Maker of all things?"

"Peace!" said Jehovah, and thunders rumbled off toward the gloomy horizon. "In good season, I will cause these stones to bear witness. Come, let us walk further."

They wandered over the dry mountains and through the empty canyons of the sea. And God said, "Michael, you were set to watch over these people. What was the manner of their last days?"

They paused near the fissured cone of Vesuvius, which in an aeon of heavenly inattention had twice erupted, burying thousands alive.

The second angel answered, "Lord, when last I saw them, they were preparing a great war."

"Their iniquities were past belief," said Jehovah. "Which were the nations of those that prepared the war?"

The second angel answered, "Lord, they were called England and Russia and China and America."

"Let us go then to England."

Across the dry valley that had been the Channel, the island was a tableland of stone, crumbling and desolate. Everywhere the stones were brittle and without strength. And God grew wroth, and cried out, "Let the stones speak!"

Then the gray rocks fountained up into dust, uncovering caverns and tunnels, like the chambers of an empty anthill. And in some places bright metal gleamed, lying in skeins that were graceful but without design, as if the metal had melted and run like water.

The angels murmured; but God said, "Wait. This is not all."

He commanded again, "Speak!" And the rocks rose up once more, to lay bare a chamber that was deeper still. And in silence, God and the angels stood in a circle around the pit, and leaned down to see what shapes glittered there.

In the wall of that lowest chamber, someone had chiseled a row of letters. And when the machine in that chamber had been destroyed, the fiery metal had sprayed out and filled the letters in the wall, so that they gleamed now like silver in the darkness.

And God read the words.

"WE WERE HERE. WHERE WERE YOU?"

## Afterword:

This story was written some years ago, and all I remember about it is that my then agent returned it with loathing, and told me I might possibly sell it to the *Atheist Journal* in Moscow, but nowhere else.

The question asked in the story is a frivolous one to me, because I do not believe in Jehovah, who strikes me as a most improbable person; but it seems to me that, for someone who does believe, it is an important question.

## Introduction to IF ALL MEN WERE BROTHERS, WOULD YOU LET ONE MARRY YOUR SISTER?:

This will be the shortest introduction in the book. Because, of all the writers in this anthology, the one who *truly* needs no introduction is Theodore Sturgeon? Well, there's that, certainly. Because nothing anyone could say would prepare the reader for what is to follow, the first Sturgeon story in over three years? It's a valid point. Because each Sturgeon story is a long-awaited experience, no two alike, so why bother gilding the caviar? Okay, I'll accept that.

But none of them happens to be the reason why I am unable to write as beefy an introduction as the others in this book. The reason is simply that Sturgeon saved my life recently. Literally.

In February of 1966 I committed one of those incredible life-blunders that defy explanation or analysis. I entered into a marriage with a woman . . . a person . . . a something whose mind was as alien to me as the mind of a Martian might be. The union was a disaster, a forty-five-day nightmare that left me closer to the edge of the cliff than I had ever been. At the precise moment I thought surely I couldn't retain my grip on the handle of—everything, I received a letter from Ted Sturgeon. It was part of the interchange of letters that resulted in obtaining this story for the anthology, but it was concerned entirely with what was happening to me. It pulled together the sprung wires of my life. It was one of those pieces of honest concern that (if lucky) everyone will clutch onto at a terrible time of helplessness and desperation. It demonstrates the most obvious characteristic of Sturgeon's work—love. (We once talked about that. It became clear to Sturgeon and myself that I knew virtually nothing about love but was totally familiar with hate, while Ted knew almost nothing about hate, yet was completely conversant with love in almost all its manifestations.) I would like, with Ted's permission, to quote from that letter. It will say infinitely more about his work and what motivates him than anything I could attempt. From here down, Sturgeon speaking:

"Dear Harlan: For two days I have not been able to get my mind off your predicament. Perhaps it would be more accurate to say that your predicament is on my mind, a sharp-edged crumb of discomfort which won't whisk away or dissolve or fall off, and when I move or think or swallow, it gigs me.

"I suppose the aspect that gigs me the most is 'injustice.' Injustice is not an isolated homogeneous area any more than justice is. A law is a law and is either breached or not, but justice is reciprocal. That such a thing should have happened to you is a greater injustice than if it happened to most representatives of this exploding population.

"I know exactly why, too. It is an injustice because you are on the side of the angels (who, by the way, stand a little silent for you just now). You are in the small company of Good Guys. You are that, not by any process of intellectualization and decision, but reflexively, instantly, from the glands, whether it shows at the checkout in a supermarket where you confront the Birchers, or in a poolroom facing down a famous bully, or in pulling out gut by the hank and reeling it up on the platen of your typewriter.

"There is no lack of love in the world, but there is a profound shortage in places to put it. I don't know why it is, but most people who, like yourself, have an inherent ability to claw their way up the sheerest rock faces around, have little of it or have so equipped themselves with spikes and steel hooks that you can't see it. When it shows in such a man—like it does in you—when it lights him up, it should be revered and cared for. This is the very nub of the injustice done you. It should not happen at all, but if it must happen, it should not happen to you.

"You have cause for many feelings, Harlan: anger, indignation, regret, grief. Theodor Reik, who has done some brilliant anatomizations of love, declares that its ending is in none of these things: if it is, there is a good possibility that some or one or all of them were there all along. It is ended with *indifference*—really ended with real indifference. This is one of the saddest things I know. And in all my life, I have found one writer, once, who was able to describe the exact moment when it came, and it is therefore the saddest writing I have ever read. I give it to you now in your sadness. The principle behind the gift is called 'counter-irritation.' Read it in good health—eventual. I would like you to know that if it helps and sustains you at all, you have my respect and affection. Yours, T. H. Sturgeon."

Thus ended the letter that helped and sustained me. Enclosed with the letter was №20 of "Twenty Love Poems based on the Spanish of Pablo Neruda," by Christofer Logue. From *Songs,* Hutchinson & Co., London, 1959. It is this freedom of giving, this ability and anxiousness to meet love and give it freely in all its forms, that makes Sturgeon the mythical creature that he is. Complex, tormented, struggling, blessed by incredible gentleness and, above all, enormously talented, what you have just read is the soul of Theodore Sturgeon. I pray you, go on now to the very best thing to be found in all writers: a sample of the work that motivates the life that is led. And thank you.

# ● IF ALL MEN WERE BROTHERS, WOULD YOU LET ONE MARRY YOUR SISTER?

## by Theodore Sturgeon

The Sun went Nova in the year 33 A.E. "A.E." means "After the Exodus." You might say the Exodus was a century and a half or so A.D. if "A.D." means "After the Drive." The Drive, to avoid technicalities, was a device somewhat simpler than Woman and considerably more complicated than sex, which caused its vessel to cease to exist *here* while simultaneously appearing *there,* by-passing the limitations imposed by the speed of light. One might compose a quite impressive account of astrogation involving the Drive, with all the details of orientation *here* and *there* and the somewhat philosophical difficulties of establishing the relationships between them, but this is not that kind of a science fiction story.

It suits our purposes rather to state that the Sun went Nova with plenty of warning, that the first fifty years A.D. were spent in improving the Drive and exploring with unmanned vehicles which located many planets suitable for human settlement, and that the next hundred years were spent in getting humanity ready to leave. Naturally there developed a number of ideological groups with a most interesting assortment of plans for one Perfect Culture or another, most of which were at bitter odds with all the rest. The Drive, however, had presented Earth with so copious a supply of new worlds, with insignificant subjective distances between them and the parent, that dissidents need not make much of their dissent, but need merely file for another world and they would get it. The comparisons between the various cultural theories are pretty fascinating, but this is not that kind of a science fiction story either. Not quite.

Anyway, what happened was that, with a margin of a little more than three decades, Terra depopulated itself by its many thousands of ships to its hundreds of worlds (leaving behind, of course, certain die-hards who died, of course, certainly) and the new worlds were established with varying degrees of bravery and a pretty wide representation across the success scale.

It happened, however (in ways much too recondite to be described in this kind of a science fiction story), that Drive Central on Earth, a computer central, was not only the sole means of keeping track of all the worlds; it was their only means of keeping track with one another; and when this installation added its bright brief speck to the ocean of Nova-glare, there simply was no way for all the worlds to find one another without the arduous process of unmanned Drive-ships and search. It took a long while for any of the new worlds to develop the necessary technology, and an even longer while for it to be productively operational, but at length, on a planet which called itself Terratu (the suffix meaning both "too" and "2") because it happened to be the third planet of a GO-type sun, there appeared something called the Archives, a sort of index and clearinghouse for all known inhabited worlds, which made this planet the communications central and general dispatcher for trade with them all and their trade with one another—a great convenience for everyone. A side result, of course, was the conviction on Terratu that, being a communications central, it was also central to the universe and therefore should control it, but then, that is the occupational hazard of all conscious entities.

We are now in a position to determine just what sort of a science fiction story this really is.


"Charli Bux," snapped Charli Bux, "to see the Archive Master."

"Certainly," said the pretty girl at the desk, in the cool tones reserved by pretty girls for use on hurried and indignant visitors who are clearly unaware, or uncaring, that the girl is pretty. "Have you an appointment?"

He seemed like such a nice young man in spite of his hurry and his indignation. The way, however, in which he concealed all his niceness by bringing his narrowed eyes finally to rest on her upturned face, and still showed no signs of appreciating her pretty-girlhood, made her quite as not-pretty as he was not-nice.

"Have you," he asked coldly, "an appointment book?"

She had no response to that, because she had such a book; it lay open in front of her. She put a golden and escalloped fingernail on his name therein inscribed, compared it and his face with negative enthusiasm, and ran the fingernail across to the time noted. She glanced at the clockface set into her desk, passed her hand over a stud, and said, "A Mr. Charli uh Bux to see you, Archive Master."

"Send him in," said the stud.

"You may go in now."

"I know," he said shortly.

"I don't like you."

"What?" he said; but he was thinking about something else, and before she could repeat the remark he had disappeared through the inner door.

The Archive Master had been around long enough to expect courtesy, respect, and submission, to get these things, and to like them. Charli Bux slammed into the room, banged a folio down on the desk, sat down uninvited, leaned forward and roared redly, "Goddamit—"

The Archive Master was not surprised because he had been warned. He had planned exactly what he would do to handle this brash young man, but faced with the size of the Bux temper, he found his plans somewhat less useful than worthless. Now he was surprised, because a single glance at his gaping mouth and feebly fluttering hands—a gesture he thought he had lost and forgotten long ago—accomplished what no amount of planning could have done.

"Oh-h-h . . . bitchballs," growled Bux, his anger visibly deflating. "Buggerly bangin' bumpin' *bitch*balls." He looked across at the old man's horrified eyebrows and grinned blindingly. "I guess it's not your fault." The grin disappeared. "But of all the hydrocephalous, drool-toothed, cretinoid runarounds I have ever seen, this was the stupidest. Do you know how many offices I've been into and out of with this"—he banged the heavy folio—"since I got back?"

The Archive Master did, but, "How many?" he asked.

"Too many, but only half as many as I went to before I went to Vexvelt." With which he shut his lips with a snap and leaned forward again, beaming his bright penetrating gaze at the old man like twin lasers. The Archive Master found himself striving not to be the first to turn away, but the effort made him lean slowly back and back, until he brought up against his chair cushions with his chin up a little high. He began to feel a little ridiculous, as if he had been bamboozled into Indian wrestling with some stranger's valet.

It was Charli Bux who turned away first, but it was not the old man's victory, for the gaze came off his eyes as tangibly as a pressing palm might have come off his chest, and he literally slumped forward as the pressure came off. Yet if it was Charli Bux's victory, he seemed utterly unaware of it. "I think," he said after his long, concentrated pause, "that I'm going to tell you about that—about how I happened to get to Vexvelt. I wasn't going to—or at least, I was ready to tell you only as much as I thought you needed to know. But I remember what I had to go through to get there, and I know what I've been going through since I got back, and it looks like the same thing. Well, it's not going to be the same thing. Here and now, the runaround stops. What takes its place I don't know, but by all the horns of all the owls in Hell's northeast, I have been pushed around my last push. All right?"

If this was a plea for agreement, the Archive Master did not know what he would be agreeing to. He said diplomatically, "I think you'd better begin *some*where." Then he added, not raising his voice, but with immense authority, "And quietly."

Charli Bux gave him a boom of laughter. "I never yet spent upwards of three minutes with anybody that they didn't shush me. Welcome to the Shush Charli Club, membership half the universe, potential membership, everybody else. And I'm sorry. I was born and brought up on Biluly where there's nothing but trade wind and split-rock ravines and surf, and the only way to whisper is to shout." He went on more quietly, "But what I'm talking about isn't that sort of shushing. I'm talking about a little thing here and a little thing there and adding them up and getting the idea that there's a planet nobody knows anything about."

"There are thousands—"

"I mean a planet nobody *wants* you to know anything about."

"I suppose you've heard of Magdilla."

"Yes, with fourteen kinds of hallucinogenic microspores spread through the atmosphere, and carcinogens in the water. Nobody wants to go there, nobody wants anybody to go—but nobody stops you from getting information about it. No, I mean a planet not 99 per cent Terran Optimum, or 99 point 99, but so many nines that you might just as well shift your base reference and call Terra about 97 per cent in comparison."

"That would be a little like saying '102 per cent normal,'" said the Master smugly.

"If you like statistical scales better than the truth," Bux growled. "Air, water, climate, indigenous flora and fauna, and natural resources six nines or better, just as easy to get to as any place else—and nobody knows anything about it. Or if they do, they pretend they don't. And if you pin them down, they send you to another department."

The Archive Master spread his hands. "I would say the circumstances prove themselves. If there is no trade with this, uh, remarkable place, it indicates that whatever it has is just as easily secured through established routes."

Bux shouted, "In a pig's bloody and protruding—" and then checked himself and wagged his head ruefully. "Sorry again, Archive Master, but I just been too mad about this for too long. What you just said is like a couple troglodytes sitting around saying there's no use building a house because everybody's living in caves." Seeing the closed eyes, the long white fingers tender on the white temples, Bux said, "I said I was sorry I yelled like that."

"In every city," said the Archive Master patiently, "on every settled human planet in all the known universe, there is a free public clinic where stress reactions of any sort may be diagnosed, treated or prescribed for, speedily, effectively, and with dignity. I trust you will not regard it as an intrusion on your privacy if I make the admittedly non-professional observation (you see, I do not pretend to be a therapist) that there are times when a citizen is not himself aware that he is under stress, even though it may be clearly, perhaps painfully obvious to others. It would not be a discourtesy, would it, or an unkindness, for some understanding stranger to suggest to such a citizen that—"

"What you're saying, all wrapped up in words, is I ought to go have my head candled."

"By no means. I am not qualified. I did, however, think that a visit to a clinic—there's one just a step away from here—might make—ah—communications between us more possible. I would be glad to arrange another appointment for you, when you're feeling better. That is to say, when you are . . . ah . . ." He finished with a bleak smile and reached toward the calling stud.

Moving almost like a Drive-ship, Bux seemed to cease to exist on the visitor's chair and reappeared instantaneously at the side of the desk, a long thick arm extended and a meaty hand blocking the way to the stud. "Hear me out first," he said, softly. Really softly. It was a much more astonishing thing than if the Archive Master had trumpeted like an elephant. "Hear me out. Please."

The old man withdrew his hand, but folded it with the other and set the neat stack of fingers on the edge of the desk. It looked like stubbornness. "I have a limited amount of time, and your folio is very large."

"It's large because I'm a bird dog for detail—that's not a brag, it's a defect: sometimes I just don't know when to quit. I can make the point quick enough—all that material just supports it. Maybe a tenth as much would do, but you see, I—well, I give a damn. I really give a high, wide, heavy damn about this. Anyway—you just pushed the right button in Charli Bux. 'Make communication between us more possible.' Well, all right. I won't cuss, I won't holler, and I won't take long."

"Can you do all these things?"

"You're goddam—whoa, Charli." He flashed the thirty-thousand-candlepower smile and then hung his head and took a deep breath. He looked up again and said quietly, "I certainly can, sir."

"Well, then." The Archive Master waved him back to the visitor's chair: Charli Bux, even a contrite Charli Bux, stood just too tall and too wide. But once seated, he sat silent for so long that the old man shifted impatiently. Charli Bux looked up alertly, and said, "Just getting it sorted out, sir. A good deal of it's going to sound as if you could diagnose me for a stun-shot and a good long stay at the funny farm, yeah, and that without being modest about your professional knowledge. I read a story once about a little girl was afraid of the dark because there was a little hairy purple man with poison fangs in the closet, and everybody kept telling her no, no, there's no such thing, be sensible, be brave. So they found her dead with like snakebite and her dog killed a little hairy purple and so on. Now if I told you there was some sort of a conspiracy to keep me from getting information about a planet, and I finally got mad enough to go there and see for myself, and 'They' did their best to stop me; 'They' won me a sweepstake prize trip to somewhere else that would use up my vacation time; when I turned that down 'They' told me there was no Drive Guide orbiting the place, and it was too far to reach in real space (and that's a God, uh, doggone *lie,* sir!) and when I found a way to get there by hops, 'They' tangled up my credit records so I couldn't buy passage; why, then I can't say I'd blame you for peggin' me paranoid and doing me the kindness of getting me cured. Only thing was, these things did happen and they were not delusions, no matter what everybody plus two thirds of Charli Bux (by the time 'They' were done with me) believed. I had an ounce of evidence and I believed it. I had a ton of opinion saying otherwise. I tell you, sir, I *had* to go. I had to stand knee-deep in Vexvelt sweet grass with the cedar smell of a campfire and a warm wind in my face," *and my hands in the hands of a girl called Tyng, along with my heart and my hope and a dazzling wonder colored like sunrise and tasting like tears,* "before I finally let myself believe I'd been right all along, and there is a planet called Vexvelt and it does have all the things I knew it had," *and more, more, oh, more than I'll ever tell you about, old man.* He fell silent, his gaze averted and luminous.

"What started you on this—this quest?"

Charli Bux threw up his big head and looked far away and back at some all-but-forgotten detail. "Huh! 'D almost lost that in the clutter. Workin' for Interworld Bank & Trust, feeding a computer in the clearin'house. Not as dull as you might think. Happens I was a mineralogist for a spell, and the cargoes meant something to me besides a name, a quantity and a price. Huh!" came the surprised I've-found-it! little explosion. "I can tell you the very item. Feldspar. It's used in porcelain and glass, antique style. I got a sticky mind, I guess. Long as I'd been there, feldspar ground and bagged went for about twenty-five credits a ton at the docks. But here was one of our customers bringing it in for eight and a half F.O.B. I called the firm just to check; mind, I didn't care much, but a figure like that could color a statistical summary of imports and exports for years. The bookkeeper there ran a check and found it was so: eight and a half a ton, high-grade feldspar, ground and bagged. Some broker on Lethe: they hadn't been able to contact him again.

"It wasn't worth remembering until I bumped into another one. Niobium this time. Some call it columbium. Helps make steel stainless, among other things. I'd never seen a quotation for rod stock at less than a hundred and thirty-seven, but here was some—not much, mind you—at ninety credits *delivered.* And some sheets too, about 30 per cent less than I'd ever seen it before, freight paid. I checked that one out too. It was correct. Well-smelted and pure, the man said. I forgot that one too, or I thought I had. Then there was that space-hand." *Moxie Magiddle—honest!—that was his name. Squint-eyed little fellow with a great big laugh bulging the walls of the honkytonk out at the spaceport. Drank only alcohol and never touched a needle. Told me the one about the fellow had a big golden screwhead in his belly button. Told me about times and places all over—full of yarns, a wonderful gift for yarning.* "Just mentioned in passing that Lethe was one place where the law was 'Have Fun' and nobody ever broke it. The whole place just one big transfer point and rest-and-rehab. A water world with only one speck of land in the tropics. Always warm, always easy. No industry, no agriculture, just—well, services. Thousands of men spent hundreds of thousands of credits, a few dozen pocketed millions. Everybody happy. I mentioned the feldspar, I guess just so I would sound as if I knew something about Lethe too." *And laid a big fat egg, too. Moxie looked at me as if he hadn't seen me before and didn't like what he saw. If it was a lie I was telling it was a stupid one.* "Y'don't dig feldspar out of a swamp, fella. You puttin' me on, or you kiddin' y'rself?" *And a perfectly good evening dried up and blew away.* "He said it couldn't possibly have come from Lethe—it's a water world. I guess I could have forgotten that too but for the coffee beans. Blue Mountain Coffee, it was called; the label claimed it descended in an unbroken line from Old Earth, on an island called Jamaica. It went on to say that it could be grown only in high cool land in the tropics—a real mountain plant. I liked it better than any coffee I ever tasted but when I went back for more they were sold out. I got the manager to look in the records and traced it back through the Terratu wholesaler to the broker and then to the importer—I mean, I *liked* that coffee!

"And according to him, it came from Lethe. High cool mountain land and all. The port at Lethe was tropical all right, but to be cool it would have to have mountains that were really mountains.

"The feldspar that did, but couldn't have, come from Lethe—and at those prices!—reminded me of the niobium, so I checked on that one too. Sure enough—Lethe again. You don't—you just do *not* get pure niobium rod and sheet without mines and smelters and mills.

"Next off-day I spent here at Archives and got the history of Lethe halfway back, I'll swear, to Ylem and the Big Bang. It was a swamp, it practically always has been a swamp, and something was wrong.

"Mind you, it was only a little something, and probably there was a good simple explanation. But little or not, it bothered me." *And besides, it had made me look like a horse's ass in front of a damn good man. Old man, if I told you how much time I hung around the spaceport looking for that bandy-legged little space-gnome, you'd stop me now and send for the stun-guns. Because I was obsessed—not a driving addiction kind of thing, but a very small deep splinter-in-the-toe kind of thing, that didn't hurt much but never failed to gig me every single step I took. And then one day—oh, months later—there was old Moxie Magiddle, and he took the splinter out. Hyuh! Ol' Moxie . . . he didn't know me at first, he really didn't. Funny little guy, he has his brains rigged to forget anything he doesn't like—honestly forget it. That feldspar thing, when a fella he liked to drink with and yarn to showed up to be a know-it-all kind of liar, and to boot, too dumb to know he couldn't get away with it—well, that qualified Charli for zero minus the price of five man-hours of drinking. Then when I got him cornered —I all but wrestled him—and told about the feldspar and the niobium and now the mountain-grown coffee, all of it checked and cross- checked, billed, laded, shipped, insured—all of it absolutely Lethe and here's the goddam proof, why, he began to laugh till he cried, a little at himself, a little at the situation, and a whole lot at me. Then we had a long night of it and I drank alcohol and you know what? I'll never in life find out how Moxie Magiddle can hold so much liquor. But he told me where those shipments came from, and gave me a vague idea why nobody wanted much to admit it. And the name they call all male Vexveltians.* "I mentioned it one day to a cargo handler," Bux told the Archive Master, "and he solved the mystery—the feldspar and niobium and coffee came from Vexvelt and had been transshipped at Lethe by local brokers, who, more often than not, get hold of some goods and turn them over to make a credit or so and dive back into the local forgetteries.

"But any planet which could make a profit on goods of this quality at such prices—transshipped, yet!—certainly could do much better direct. Also, niobium is Element 41, and Elkhart's Hypothesis has it that, on any planet where you find elements in Periods Three to Five, chances are you'll find 'em all. And that coffee! I used to lie awake at night wondering what they had on Vexvelt that they liked too much to ship, if they thought so little of their coffee that they'd let it out.

"Well, it was only natural that I came here to look up Vexvelt. Oh, it was listed at the bank, all right, but if there ever had been trade, it had been cleared out of the records long ago—we wipe the memory cells every fifty years on inactive items. I know at least that it's been wiped four times, but it could have been blank the last three.

"What do you think Archives has on Vexvelt?"

The Archive Master did not answer. He *knew* what Archives had on the subject of Vexvelt. He knew where it was, and where it was not. He knew how many times this stubborn young man had been back worrying at the mystery, how many ingenious approaches he had made to the problem, how little he had gotten, how much less he or anyone would get if they tried it today. He said nothing.

Charli Bux held up fingers to count. "Astronomical: no observations past two light-years. Nothing but sister planets (all dead) and satellites within two light-years. Cosmological: camera scan, if ever performed (but it must have been performed, or the damn thing wouldn't even be listed at all!), missing and never replaced. So there's no way of finding out where in real space it is, even. Geological: unreported. Anthropological: unreported. Then there's some stuff about local hydrogen tension and emission of the parent star, but they're not much help. And the summation in Trade Extrapolation: untraded. Reported undesirable. Not a word as to who reported it or why he said it.

"I tried to sidle into it by looking up manned exploration, but I could find only three astronauts' names in connection with Vexvelt. Troshan. He got into some sort of trouble when he came back and was executed—we used to kill certain criminals six, seven hundred years ago, did you know that?—but I don't know what for. Anyway, they apparently did it before he filed his report. Then Balrou. Oh—Balrou —he did report. I can tell you his whole report word for word: 'In view of conditions on Vexvelt contact is not recommended,' period. By the word, that must be the most expensive report ever filed."

It was, said the Archive Master, but he did not say it aloud.

"And then somebody called Allman explored Vexvelt but—how did the report put it—'it was found on his return that Allman was suffering from confinement fatigue and his judgment was so severely impaired that his report is discounted.' Does that mean it was destroyed, Archive Master?"

Yes, thought the old man, but he said, "I can't say."

"So there you are," said Charli Bux. "If I wanted to present a classic case of what the old books called persecution mania, I'd just have to report things exactly as they happened. Did I have a right to suspect, even, that 'They' had picked me as the perfect target and set up those hints—low-cost feldspar, high-quality coffee—bait I couldn't miss and couldn't resist. Did I have the right to wonder if a living caricature with a comedy name—Moxie for-god's-sake Magiddle—was working for Them? Then, what happened next, when I honestly and openly filed for Vexvelt as my next vacation destination? I was told there was no Drive Guide orbiting Vexvelt—it could only be reached through normal space. That happens to be a lie, but there's no way of checking on it here, or even on Lethe—Moxie never knew. Then I filed for Vexvelt via Lethe and a real-space transport, and was told that Lethe was not recommended as a tourist stop and there was no real-space service from there anyhow. So I filed for Botil, which I *know* is a tourist stop, and which I know has real-space shuttles and charter boats, and which the star charts call Kricker III while Lethe is Kricker IV, and that's when I won the God—uh, the sweepstakes and a free trip to beautiful, beautiful Zeenip, paradise of paradises with two indoor 36-hole golf courses and free milk baths. I gave it to some charity or other, I said to save on taxes, and went for my tickets to Botil, the way I'd planned. I had it all to do over because they'd wiped the whole transaction when they learned about the sweepstakes. It seemed reasonable but it took so long to set it all up again that I missed the scheduled transport and lost a week of my vacation. Then when I went to pay for the trip my credit showed up zero, and it took another week to straighten out that regrettable error. By that time the tour service had only one full passage open, and in view of the fact that the entire tour would outlast my vacation by two weeks, they wiped the whole deal again—they were quite sure I wouldn't want it."

Charli Bux looked down at his hands and squeezed them. The Archives Office was filled with a crunching sound. Bux did not seem to notice it. "I guess anybody in his right mind would have got the message by then, but 'They' had underestimated me. Let me tell you exactly what I mean by that. I *don't* mean that I am a man of steel and by the Lord when my mind is made up it stays made. And I'm not making brags about the courage of my convictions. I had very little to be convinced about, except that there was a whole chain of coincidences which nobody wanted to explain even though the explanation was probably foolishly simple. And I never thought I was specially courageous.

"I was just—scared. Oh, I was frustrated and I was mad, but mostly I was scared. If somebody had come along with a reasonable explanation I'd've forgotten the whole thing. If someone had come back from Vexvelt and it was a poison planet (with a pocket of good feldspar and one clean mountainside) I'd have laughed it off. But the whole sequence—especially the last part, trying to book passage—really scared me. I reached the point where the only thing that would satisfy me as to my own sanity was to stand and walk on Vexvelt and *know* what it was. And that was the one thing I wasn't being allowed to do. So I couldn't get my solid proof and who's to say I wouldn't spend the next couple hundred years wondering when I'd get the next little splinter down deep in my toe? A man can suffer from a thing, Master, but then he can also suffer for fear of suffering from a thing. No, I was scared and I was going to stay scared until I cleared it up."

"My." The old man had been silent, listening, for so long that his voice was new and arresting. "It seems to me that there was a much simpler way out. Every city on every human world has free clinics where—"

"That's twice you've said that," crackled Charli Bux. "I have something to say about that, but not now. As to my going to a patch-up parlor, you know as well as I do that they don't change a thing. They just make you feel good about being the way you are."

"I fail to see the distinction, or what is wrong if there is one."

"I had a friend come up to me and tell me he was going to die of cancer in the next eight weeks, 'just in time,' he says, and whacks me so hard I see red spots, 'just in time for my funeral,' and off he goes down the street whooping like a loon."

"Would it be better if he huddled in his bed terrified and in pain?"

"I can't answer that kind of a question, but I do know what I saw is just as wrong. Anyway—there was something out there called Vexvelt, and it wouldn't make me feel any better to get rolled through a machine and come out thinking there isn't something called Vexvelt, and don't tell me that's not what those friendly helpful spot removers would do to me."

"But don't you see, you'd no longer be—"

"Call me throwback. Call me radical if you want to, or ignorant." Charli Bux's big voice was up again and he seemed angry enough not to care. "Ever hear that old line about 'in every fat man there's a thin man screaming to get out'? I just can't shake the idea that if something is *so,* you can prick, poke and process me till I laugh and scratch and giggle and admit it ain't so after all, and even go out and make speeches and persuade other people, but away down deep there'll be a me with its mouth taped shut and its hands tied, bashing up against my guts trying to get out and say it is so after all. But what are we talking about me for? I came here to talk about Vexvelt."

"First tell me something—do you really think there was a 'They' who wanted to stop you?"

"*Hell* no. I think I'm up against some old-time stupidity that got itself established and habitual, and that's how come there's no information in the files. I don't think anybody today is all that stupid. I like to think people on this planet can look at the truth and not let it scare them. Even if it scares them they can think it through. As to that rat race with the vacation bookings, there seemed to be a good reason for each single thing that happened. Science and math have done a pretty good job of explaining the mechanics of 'the bad break' and 'a lucky run,' but neither one of them ever got repealed."

"So." The Master tented his fingers and looked down at the ridgepole. "And just how did you manage to get to Vexvelt after all?"

Bux flicked on his big bright grin. "I hear a lot about this free society, and how there's always someone out to trim an edge off here and a corner there. Maybe there's something in it, but so far they haven't got around to taking away a man's freedom to be a damn fool. Like, for example, his freedom to quit his job. I've said it was just a gruesome series of bad breaks, but bad breaks can be outwitted just as easily as a superpowerful masterminding 'They.' Seems to me most bad breaks happen inside a man's pattern. He gets out of phase with it and every step he takes is between the steppin'stones. If he can't phase in, and if he tries to maintain his pace, why there's a whole row of stones ahead of him laid just exactly where each and every one of them will crack his shins. What he should do is head upstream. It might be unknown territory, and there might be dangers, but one thing for sure, there's a whole row of absolutely certain, absolutely planned agonies he is just not going to have to suffer."

"How did you get to Vexvelt?"

"I told you." He waited, then smiled. "I'll tell you again. I quit my job. 'They,' or the 'losing streak,' or the stinking lousy Fates, or whatever had a bead on me—they could do it to me because they always knew where I was, when I'd be the next place, and what I wanted. So they were always waiting for me. So I headed upstream. I waited till my vacation was over and left the house without any luggage and went to my local bank and had all my credits before I could have any tough breaks. Then I took a Drive jumper to Lunatu, booked passage on a semi-freight to Lethe."

"You booked passage, but you never boarded the ship."

"You know?"

"I was asking."

"Oh," said Charli Bux. "Yeah, I never set foot in that cozy little cabin. What I did, I slid down the cargo chute and got buried in Hold #2 with a ton of oats. I was in an interesting position, Archive Master. In a way I'm sorry nobody dug me out to ask questions. You're not supposed to stow away but the law says—and I know exactly what it says—that a stowaway is someone who rides a vessel without booking passage. But I did book passage, and paid in full, and all my papers were in order for where I was going. What made things a lot easier, too, was that where I was going nobody gives much of a damn about papers."

"And you felt you could get to Vexvelt through Lethe."

"I felt I had a chance, and I knew of no other. Cargoes from Vexvelt *had* been put down on Lethe, or I wouldn't have been sucked into this thing in the first place. I didn't know if the carrier was Vexveltian or a tramp (if it was a liner I'd have known it) or when one might come or if it would be headed for Vexvelt when it departed. All I knew was that Vexvelt had shipped here for sure, and this was the only place where maybe they might be back. Do you know what goes on at Lethe?"

"It has a reputation."

"Do you *know?*"

The old man showed a twinge of irritation. Along with respect and obedience, he had become accustomed to catechizing and not to being catechized. "Everyone knows about Lethe."

Bux shook his head. "They don't, Master."

The old man lifted his hands and put them down. "That kind of thing has its function. Humanity will always—"

"You approve of Lethe and what goes on there."

"One neither approves nor disapproves," said the Archive Master stiffly. "One knows about it, recognizes that for some segments of the species such an outlet is necessary, realizes that Lethe makes no pretensions to being anything but what it is, and then—one accepts, one goes on to other things. How did you get to Vexvelt?"

"On Lethe," said Charli Bux implacably, "you can do anything you want to or with any kind of human being, or any number or combination of them, as long as you can pay for it."

"I wouldn't doubt it. Now, the next leg of your trip—"

"There are men," said Charli Bux, suddenly and shockingly quiet, "who can be attracted by disease—by sores, Archive Master, by the stumps of amputated limbs. There are people on Lethe who cultivate diseases to attract such men. Crones, Master, with dirty leather skin, and boys and little—"

"You will cease this nauseating—"

"In just a minute. One of the unwritten and unbreakable traditions of Lethe is that, what anyone pays to do, anyone else may pay to watch."

*"Are you finished?"* It was not Bux who shouted now.

"You accept Lethe. You condone Lethe."

"I have not said I approve."

"You trade with Lethe."

"Well, of course we do. That doesn't mean we—"

"The third day—night, rather, that I was there," said Bux, overriding what was surely about to turn into a helpless sputter, "I turned off one of the main streets into an alley. I knew this might be less than wise, but at the moment there was an ugly fight going on between me and the corner, and some wild gunning. I was going to turn right and go to the other avenue anyway, and I could see it clearly through the alley.

"I couldn't describe to you how fast this happened, or explain where they came from—eight of them, I think, in an alley, not quite dark and very narrow, when only a minute before I had been able to see it from end to end.

"I was grabbed from all sides all over my body, lifted, slammed down flat on my back and a bright light jammed in my face.

"A woman said, 'Aw shoot, 'tain't him.' A man's voice said to let me up. They picked me up. Somebody even started dusting me off. The woman who had held the light began to apologize. She did it quite nicely. She said they had heard that there was a—Master, I wonder if I should use the word."

"How necessary do you feel—"

"Oh, I guess I don't have to; you know it. On any ship, any construction gang, in any farm community—anywhere where men work or gather, it's the one verbal bullet which will and must start a fight.

If it doesn't, the victim will never regain face. The woman used it as casually as she would have said Terran or Lethean. She said there was one right here in town and they meant to get him. I said, 'Well, how about that.' It's the one phrase I know that can be said any time about anything. Another woman said I was a good big one and how would I like to tromp him. One of the men said all right, but he called for the head. Another began to fight him about it, and a third woman took off her shoe and slapped both their faces with one swing of the muddy sole. She said for them to button it up or next time she'd use the heel. The other woman, with the light, giggled and said Helen was Veddy Good Indeed that way. She spoke in a beautifully cultivated accent. She said Helen could hook out an eye neat as a croupier. The third woman suddenly cried out, 'Dog turds!' She asked for some light. The dog turds were very dry. One of the men offered to wet them down. The woman said no—they were her dog turds and she would do it herself. Then and there she squatted. She called for a light, said she couldn't see to aim. They turned the light on her. She was one of the most beautiful women I have ever seen. Is there something wrong, Master?"

"I would like you to tell me how you made contact with Vexvelt," said the old man a little breathlessly.

"But I am!" said Charli Bux. "One of the men pressed through, all grunting with eagerness, and began to mix the filth with his hands. And then, by a sort of sixth sense, the light was out and they were simply—gone! Disappeared. A hand came out of nowhere and pulled me back against a house wall. There wasn't a sound—not even breathing. And only then did the Vexveltian turn into the alley. How they knew he was coming is beyond me.

"The hand that had pulled me back belonged to the woman with the light, as I found out in a matter of seconds. I really didn't believe her hand meant to be where I found it. I took hold of it and held it, but she snatched it away and put it back. Then I felt the light bump my leg. And the man came along toward us. He was a big man, held himself straight, wore light-colored clothes, which I thought was more foolhardy than brave. He walked lightly and seemed to be looking everywhere—and still could not see us.

"If this all happened right this minute, after what I've learned about Vexvelt—about Lethe too—I wouldn't hesitate, I'd know exactly what to do. What you have to understand is that I didn't know anything at all at the time. Maybe it was the eight against one that annoyed me." He paused thoughtfully. "Maybe that coffee. What I'm trying to say is that I did the same thing then, in my ignorance, that I'd do now, knowing what I do.

"I snapped the flashlight out of the woman's hand and got about twenty feet away in two big bounds. I turned the light on and played it back where I'd come from. Two of the men had crawled up the sheer building face like insects and were ready to drop on the victim. The beautiful one was crouched on her toes and one hand; the other, full of filth, was ready to throw. She made an absolutely animal sound and slung her handful, quite uselessly. The others were flattened back against wall and fence, and in the light, for a long second, they flattened all the more, blinking. I said over my shoulder, 'Watch yourself, friend. You're the guest of honor, I think.'

"You know what he did? He laughed. I said. 'They won't get by me for a while. Take off.' 'What for?' says he, squeezing past me. 'There's only eight of them.' And he marches straight down on them.

"Something rolled under my foot and I picked it up—half a brick. What must have been the other half of it hit me right on the breastbone. It made me yelp, I couldn't help it. The tall man said to douse the light, I was a target. I did, and saw one of the men in silhouette against the street at the far end, standing up from behind a big garbage can. He was holding a knife half as long as his forearm, and he rose up as the big man passed him. I let fly with the brick and got him right back of the head. The tall man never so much as turned when he heard him fall and the knife go skittering. He passed one of the human flies as if he had forgotten he was there, but he hadn't forgotten. He reached up and got both the ankles and swung the whole man screaming off the wall like a flail, wiping the second one off and tumbling the both of them on top of the rest of the gang.

"He stood there with the back of his hands on his hips for a bit, not even breathing hard, watching the crying, cursing mix-up all over the alley pavement. I came up beside him. One, two got to their feet and ran limping. One of the women began to scream—curses, I suppose, but you couldn't hear the words. I turned the light on her face and she shut right up.

" 'You all right?' says the tall man.

"I told him, 'Caved in my chest is all, but that's all right, I can use it for a fruit bowl lying in bed.' He laughed and turned his back on the enemy and led me the way he had come. He said he was Vorhidin from Vexvelt. I told him who I was. I said I'd been looking for a Vexveltian, but before we could go on with that a black hole opened up to the left and somebody whispered, 'Quick, quick.' Vorhidin clapped a hand on my back and gave me a little shove. 'In you go, Charli Bux of Terratu.' And in we went, me stumbling all over my feet down some steps I didn't know were there, and then again because they weren't there. A big door boomed closed behind us. Dim yellow light came on. There was a little man with olive skin and shiny, oily mustachios. 'Vorhidin, for the love of God, I told you not to come into town, they'll kill you.' Vorhidin only said, 'This is Charli Bux, a friend.' The little man came forward anxiously and began to pat Vorhidin on the arms and ribs to see if he was all right.

"Vorhidin laughed and brushed him off. 'Poor Tretti! He's always afraid something is going to happen! Never mind me, you fusspot. See to Charli here. He took a shot in the bows that was meant for me.' The little one, Tretti, sort of squeaked and before I could stop him he had my shirt open and the light out of my hand switched on and trained on the bruise. 'Your next woman can admire a sunset,' says Vorhidin. Tretti's away and back before you can blink, and sprays on something cool and good and most of the pain vanished.

" 'What do you have for us?' and Tretti carries the light into another room. There's stacks of stuff, mostly manufactured goods, tools and instruments. There was a big pile of trideo cartridges, mostly music and new plays, but a novel or so too. Most of the other stuff was one of a kind. Vorhidin picked up a forty-pound crate and spun it twice by diagonal corners till it stopped where he could read the label. 'Molar spectroscope. Most of this stuff we don't really need but we like to see what's being done, how it's designed. Sometimes ours are better, sometimes not. We like to see, that's all.' He set it down gently and reached into his pocket and palmed out a dozen or more stones that flashed till it hurt. One of them, a blue one, made its own light. He took Tretti's hand and pulled it to him and poured it full of stones. 'That enough for this load?' I couldn't help it— I glanced around the place and totted it up and made a stab estimate—a hundred each of everything in the place wouldn't be worth that one blue stone. Tretti was goggle-eyed.

He couldn't speak. Vorhidin wagged his head and laughed and said, 'All right, then,' and reached into his pants pocket again and ladled out four or five more. I thought Tretti was going to cry. I was right. He cried.

"We had something to eat and I told Vorhidin how I happened to be here. He said he'd better take me along. I said where to? and he said Vexvelt. I began to laugh. I told him I was busting my brains trying to figure some way to make him say that, and he laughed too and said I'd found it, all right, twice over. 'Owe you a favor for that,' he says, dipping his head at the alley side of the room. 'Reason two, you wouldn't live out the night on Lethe if you stayed here.' I wanted to know why not, because from what I'd seen there were fights all the time, then you'd see the fighters an hour later drinking out of the same bowl. He says it's not the same thing. Nobody helps a Vexveltian but a Vexveltian. Help one, you are one, far as Lethe was concerned. So I wanted to know what Lethe had against Vexvelt, and he stopped chewing and looked at me a long time as if he didn't understand me. Then he said, 'You really don't know anything about us, do you?' I said, not much. 'Well,' he says, 'now there's three good reasons to bring you.'

"Tretti opened the double doors at the far end of the storeroom. There was a ground van in there, with another set of doors into the street. We loaded the crates into it and got in, Vorhidin at the tiller. Tretti climbed a ladder and put his eyes to something and spun a wheel. 'Periscope,' Vorhidin told me. 'Looks like a flagpole from outside.' Tretti waved his hand at us. He had tears running down his cheeks again. He hit a switch and the doors banged out of the way. The van screeched out of there as the doors bounced and started back. After that Vorhidin drove like a little old lady. One-way glass. Sometimes I wondered what those crowds of drunks and queers would do if they could see in. I asked him, 'What are they afraid of?' He didn't seem to understand the question. I said, 'Mostly when people gang up on somebody, it's because one way or another they're afraid. What do they think you're going to take away from them?'

"He laughed and said, 'Their decency.' And that's all the talk I got out of him all the way out to the spaceport.

"The Vexveltian ship was parked miles away from the terminal, way the hell and gone at the far end of the pavement near some trees.

There was a fire going near it. As we got closer I saw it wasn't near it, it was spang under it. There was a big crowd, maybe half a hundred, mostly women, mostly drunk. They were dancing and staggering around and dragging wood up under the ship. The ship stood up on its tail like the old chemical rockets in the fairy stories. Vorhidin grunted, 'Idiots,' and moved something on his wrist. The rocket began to rumble and everybody ran screaming. Then there was a big explosion of steam and the wood went every which way, and for a while the pavement was full of people running and falling and screaming, and cycles and ground cars milling around and bumping each other. After a while it was quiet and we pulled up close. The high hatch opened on the ship and a boom and frame came out and lowered. Vorhidin hooked on, threw the latches on the van bed, beckoned me back there with him, reached forward and set the controls of the van, and touched the thing on his wrist. The whole van cargo section started up complete with us, and the van started up and began to roll home by itself.

"The only crew he carried," said Charli Bux carefully, "was a young radio officer." *With long shining black wings for hair and bits of sky in her tilted eyes, and a full and asking kind of mouth. She held Vorhidin very close, very long, laughing the message that there could be no words for this: he was safe.* "Tamba, this is Charli. He's from Terratu and he fought for me." *Then she came and held him too, and she kissed him; that incredible mouth, that warm strong soft mouth, why, he and she shared it for an hour; for an hour he felt her lips on his, even though she had kissed him for only a second. For an hour her lips could hardly be closer to her than they were to his own astonished flesh.* "The ship blasted off and headed sunward and to the celestial north. It held this course for two days. Lethe has two moons, the smaller one just a rock, an asteroid. Vorhidin matched velocities with it and hung half a kilo away, drifting in."

*And the first night he had swung his bunk to the after bulkhead and had lain there heavily against the thrust of the jets, and against the thrust of his heart and his loins. Never had he seen such a woman—only just become woman, at that. So joyful, so utterly and so rightly herself. Half an hour after blastoff:* "Clothes are in the way on a ship, don't you think? But Vorhidin says I should ask you, because customs are different from one world to another, isn't that so?"

"Here we live by your customs, not mine," *Charli had been able to say, and she had thanked him, thanked him! and touched the bit of glitter at her throat, and her garment fell away. "There's much more privacy this way," she said, leaving him. "A closed door means more to the naked; it's closed for a real reason and not because one might be seen in one's petticoat." She took her garment into one of the staterooms. Vorhidin's. Charli leaned weakly against the bulkhead and shut his eyes. Her nipples were like her mouth, full and asking. Vorhidin was casually naked but Charli kept his clothes on, and the Vexveltians made no comment. The night was very long. For a while part of the weight on Charli turned to anger, which helped. Old bastard, silver-temples. Old enough to be her father. But that could not last, and he smiled at himself. He remembered the first time he had gone to a ski resort. There were all kinds of people there, young, old, wealthy, working, professionals; but there was a difference. The resort, because it was what it was, screened out the pasty-faced, the round-shouldered lungless sedentaries, the plumping sybarites. All about him had been clear eyes, straight backs, and skin with the cosmetics of frost and fun. Who walked idled not, but went somewhere. Who sat lay back joyfully in well-earned weariness. And this was the aura of Vorhidin—not a matter of carriage and clean color and clear eyes, though he certainly had all these, but the same qualities down to the bone and radiating from the mind. A difficult thing to express and a pleasure to be with. Early on the second day Vorhidin had leaned close when they were alone in the control room and asked him if he would like to sleep with Tamba tonight. Charli gasped as if he had been clapped on the navel with a handful of crushed ice. He also blushed, saying, "If she, if she—" wildly wondering how to ask her. He need not have wondered, for "He'd love to, honey," Vorhidin bellowed. Tamba popped her face into the corridor and smiled at Charli. "Thank you so much," she said. And then (after the long night) it was going to be the longest day he had ever lived through, but she let it happen within the hour instead, sweetly, strongly, unhurried. Afterward he lay looking at her with such total and long-lasting astonishment that she laughed at him. She flooded his face with her black hair and then with her kisses and then all of him with her supple strength; this time she was fierce and most demanding until with a shout he toppled from the very peak of joy straight and instantly down into the most total slumber he had ever known. In perhaps twenty minutes he opened his eyes and found his gaze plunged deep in a blue glory, her eyes so close their lashes meshed. Later, talking to her in the wardroom, holding both her hands, he turned to find Vorhidin standing in the doorway. He was on them in one long stride, and flung an arm around each. Nothing was said. What could be said?*

"I talked a lot with Vorhidin," Charli Bux said to the Archive Master. "I never met a man more sure of himself, what he wanted, what he liked, what he believed. The very first thing he said when I brought up the matter of trade was 'Why?' In all my waking life I never thought to ask that about trade. All I ever did, all anyone does, is to trade where he can and try to make it more. 'Why?' he wanted to know. I thought of the gemstones going for that production-line junk in the hold, and pure niobium at manganese prices. One trader would call that ignorance, another would call it good business and get all he could—glass beads for ivory. But cultures have been known to trade like that for religious or ethical reasons—always give more than you get in the other fellow's coin. Or maybe they were just—*rich*. Maybe there was so much on Vexvelt that the only thing they could use was—well, like he said: manufactures, so they could look at the design 'sometimes better than ours, sometimes not.' So—I asked him.

"He gave me a long look that was, at four feet, exactly like" *drowning in the impossibly blue lakes of Tamba's eyes, but watch yourself, don't think about that when you talk to this old man* "holding still for an X-ray continuity. Finally he said, 'Yes, I suppose we're rich. There's not much we need.'

"I told him, all the same, he could get a lot higher prices for the little he did trade. He just laughed a little and shook his head. 'You have to pay for what you get or it's no good. If you "trade well," as you call it, you finish with more than you started with; you didn't pay. That's as unnatural as energy levels going from lesser to greater, it's contrary to ecology and entropy.' Then he said, 'You don't understand that.' I didn't and I don't."

"Go on."

"They have their own Drive cradle back of Lethe's moon, and their own Guide orbiting Vexvelt. I told you—all the while I thought the planet was near Lethe; well, it isn't."

"Now, that I do *not* understand. Cradles and guides are public utilities. Two days, you say it took. Why didn't he use the one at the Lethe port?"

"I can't say, sir. Uh—"

"Well?"

"I was just thinking about that drunken mob building a fire under the ship."

"Ah yes. Perhaps the moon cradle is a wise precaution after all. I have always known, and you make it eminently clear, that these people are not popular. All right—you made a Drive jump."

"We made a Drive jump." Charli fell silent for a moment, reliving that breathless second of revelation as black, talc-dusted space and a lump moonlet winked away to be replaced by the great arch of a purple-haloed horizon, marbled green and gold and silver and polished blue, with a chromium glare coming from the sea on the planet's shoulder. "A tug was standing by and we got down without trouble." The spaceport was tiny compared even with Lethe—eight or ten docks, with the warehouse area under them and passenger and staff areas surrounding them under a deck. "There were no formalities—I suppose there's not enough space travel to merit them."

"Certainly no strangers, at any rate," said the old man smugly.

"We disembarked right on the deck and walked away." *Tamba had gone out first. It was sunny, with a warm wind, and if there was any significant difference between this gravity and that of Terratu, Charli's legs could not detect it. In the air, however, the difference was profound. Never before had he known air so clear, so winy, so clean— not unless it was bitter cold, and this was warm. Tamba stood by the silent, swiftly moving "up" ramp, looking out across the foothills to the most magnificent mountain range he had ever seen, for they had everything a picture-book mountain should have—smooth vivid high-range, shaggy forest, dramatic gray, brown, and ocher rock cliff, and a starched white cloth of snowcap tumbled on the peaks to dry in the sun. Behind them was a wide plain with a river for one margin and foothills for the other, and then the sea, with a wide golden beach curving a loving arm around the ocean's green shoulder. As he approached the pensive girl the warm wind curled and laughed down on them, and her short robe streamed from her shoulders like smoke, and fell about her again. It stopped his pace and his breath and his heart for a beat, it was so lovely a sight. And coming up beside her, watching the people below, the people rising on one ramp and sliding down the other, he realized that in this place clothing had but two conventions—ease and beauty. Man, woman and child, they wore what they chose, ribbon or robe, clogs, coronets, cummerbunds or kilts, or a ring, or a snood, or nothing at all. He remembered a wonderful line he had read by a pre-Nova sage called Rudofsky, and murmured it:* Modesty is not so simple a virtue as honesty. *She turned and smiled at him; she thought it was his line. He smiled back and let her think so. "You don't mind waiting a bit? My father will be along in a moment and then we'll go. You're to stay with us. Is that all right?"*

*Did he mind. Would he wait, bracketed by the thundering colors of that mountain, the adagio of the sea. Is that all right.*

*There was nothing, no way, no word to express his reponse but to raise his tense fists as high as he could and shout as loud as he could and then turn it into laughter and to tears.*

*Vorhidin, having checked out his manifests, joined them before Charli was finished. He had locked gazes with the girl, who smiled up at him and held his forearm in both her hands, stroking, and he laughed and laughed. "He drank too much Vexvelt all at once," she said to Vorhidin. Vorhidin put a big warm hand on Charli's shoulder and laughed with him until he was done. When he had his breath again, and the water-lenses out of his eyes, Tamba said, "That's where we're going."*

*"Where?"*

*She pointed, very carefully. Three slender dark trees like poplars came beseeching out of a glad tumble of luminous light willow-green. "Those three trees."*

*"I can't see a house . . ."*

*Vorhidin and Tamba laughed together: this pleased them. "Come."*

*"We were going to wait for—"*

*"No need to wait any longer. Come."*

Charli said, "The house was only a short walk from the port, but you couldn't see the one from the other. A big house, too, trees all around it and even growing up through it. I stayed with the family and worked." He slapped the heavy folio. "All this. I got all the help I needed."

*"Did* you indeed." The Archive Master seemed more interested in this than in anything else he had heard so far. Or perhaps it was a dif-

ferent kind of interest. "Helped you, did they? Would you say they're anxious to trade?"

The answer to this was clearly an important one. "All I can say," Charli Bux responded carefully, "is that I asked for this information—a catalogue of the trade resources of Vexvelt, and estimates of F.O.B. prices. None of them are very far off a practical, workable arrangement, and every single one undercuts the competition. There are a number of reasons. First of all, of course, is the resources themselves—almost right across the board, unbelievably rich. Then they have mining methods like nothing you've ever dreamed of, and harvesting, and preserving—there's no end to it. At first blush it looks like a pastoral planet—well, it's not. It's a natural treasure house that has been organized and worked and planned and understood like no other planet in the known universe. Those people have never had a war, they've never had to change their original cultural plan; it works, Master, it *works*. And it has produced a sane healthy people which, when it goes about a job, goes about it single-mindedly and with . . . well, it might sound like an odd term to use, but it's the only one that fits: with joy. . . . I can see you don't want to hear this."

The old man opened his eyes and looked directly at the visitor. At Bux's cascade of language he had averted his face, closed his eyes, curled his lip, let his hands stray over his temples and near his ears, as if it was taking a supreme effort to keep from clapping the palms over them.

"All I can hear is that a world which has been set aside by the whole species, and which has kept itself aloof, is using you to promote a contact which nobody wants. Do they want it? They won't get it, of course, but have they any idea of what their world would be like if this"—he waved at the folio—"is all true? How do they think they could control the exploiters? Have they got something special in defenses as well as all this other?"

"I really don't know."

"I know!" The old man was angrier than Bux had yet seen him. "What they are is their defense! No one will *ever* go near them, not *ever*. Not if they strip their whole planet of everything it has, and refine and process the lot, and haul it to their spaceport at their own expense, and give it away free."

"Not even if they can cure cancer?"

"Almost all cancer is curable."

"They can cure *all* cancer."

"New methods are discovered every—"

"They've had the methods for I don't know how many years. Centuries. *They have no cancer.*"

"Do you know what this cure is?"

"No, I don't. But it wouldn't take a clinical team a week to find out."

"The incurable cancers are not subject to clinical analysis. They are all deemed psychosomatic."

"I know. That is exactly what the clinical team would find out."

There was a long, pulsing silence. "You have not been completely frank with me, young man."

"That's right, sir."

Another silence. "The implication is that they are sane and cancer-free because of the kind of culture they have set up."

This time Bux did not respond, but let the old man's words hang there to be reheard, reread. At last the Archive Master spoke again in a near whisper, shaking and furious. "Abomination! Abomination!" Spittle appeared on his chin: he seemed not to know. "I—would—rather—die—eaten alive—with cancer—and raving *mad* than live with such sanity as that."

"Perhaps others would disagree."

"No one would disagree! Try it? Try it! They'll tear you to pieces! That's what they did to Allman. That's what they did to Balrou! We killed Troshan ourselves—he was the first and we didn't know then that the mob would do it for us. That was a thousand years ago, you understand that? And a thousand years from now the mob will still do it for us! And that—that *filth* will go to the locked files with the others, and someday another fool with too much curiosity and not enough decency and his mind rotten with perversion will sit here with another Archive Master, who will send him out as I'm sending you out, to shut his mouth and save his life or open it and be torn to pieces. Get *out!* Get *out!* Get *out!*" His voice had risen to a shriek and then a sort of keening, and had rasped itself against itself until it was a painful forced whisper and then nothing at all: the old eyes glared and the chin was wet.

Charli Bux rose slowly. He was white with shock. He said quietly,

"Vorhidin tried to tell me, and I wouldn't believe it. I couldn't believe it. I said to him, 'I know more about greed than you do; they will not be able to resist those prices.' I said, 'I know more about fear than you do; they will not be able to stand against the final cancer cure.' Vorhidin laughed at me and gave me all the help I needed.

"I started to tell him once that I knew more about the sanity that lives in all of us, and very much in some of us, and that it could prevail. But I knew while I was talking that I was wrong about that. Now I know that I was wrong in everything, even the greed, even the fear, and he was right. And he said Vexvelt has the most powerful and the least expensive defense ever devised—sanity. He was right."

Charli Bux realized then that the old man, madly locking gazes with him as he spoke, had in some way, inside his head, turned off his ears. He sat there with his old head cocked to one side, panting like a foundered dog in a dust bowl, until at last he thought he could shout again. He could not. He could only rasp, he could only whisper-squeak, "Get out! Get out!"

Charli Bux got out. He left the folio where it was; it, like Vexvelt, defended itself by being immiscible—in the language of chemistry, by being noble.

*It was not Tamba after all, but Tyng who captured Charli's heart.*

When they got to the beautiful house, so close to everything and yet so private, so secluded, he met the family. Breerho's radiant—almost heat-radiant—shining red hair, and Tyng's, showed them to be mother and daughter. Vorhid and Stren were the sons, one a child, the other in his mid-teens, were straight-backed, wide-shouldered like their father, and by the wonderful cut and tilt of their architectured eyes, were brothers to Tyng, and to Tamba.

There were two other youngsters, a lovely twelve-year-old girl called Fleet, who was singing when they came in, and for whose song they stopped and postponed the introductions, and a sturdy tumblebug of a boy they called Handr, possibly the happiest human being any of them would ever see. In time Charli met the parents of these two, and black-haired Tamba seemed much more kin to the mother than to flame-haired Breerho.

It was at first a cascade of names and faces, captured only partially, kaleidoscoping about in his head as they all did in the room, and making a shyness in him. But there was more love in the room than ever the peaks of his mind and heart had known before, and more care and caring.

Before the afternoon and evening were over, he was familiar and accepted and enchanted. And because Tamba had touched his heart and astonished his body, all his feelings rose within him and narrowed and aimed themselves on her, hot and breathless, and indeed she seemed to delight in him and kept close to him the whole time. But when the little ones went off yawning, and then others, and they were almost alone, he asked her, he begged her to come to his bed. She was kind as could be, and loving, but also completely firm in her refusal. "But, darling, I just can't now. I can't. I've been away to Lethe and now I'm back and I *promised*."

"Promised who?"

"Stren."

"But I thought . . ." He thought far too many things to sort out or even to isolate one from another. Well, maybe he hadn't understood the relationships here—after all, there were four adults and six children and he'd get it straight by tomorrow who was who, because otherwise she—oh. "You mean you promised Stren you wouldn't sleep with me."

"No, my silly old dear. I'll sleep with Stren tonight. Please, darling, don't be upset. There'll be other times. Tomorrow. Tomorrow morning?" She laughed and took his cheeks in her two hands and shook his whole head as if she could make the frown drop off. "Tomorrow morning *very* early?"

"I don't mean to be like this my very first night here, I'm sorry, I guess there's a lot I don't understand," he mumbled in his misery. And then anguish skyrocketed within him and he no longer cared about host and guest and new customs and all the rest of it. "I love you," he cried, "don't you know that?"

"Of course, of course I do. And I love you, and we will love one another for a long, long time. Didn't you think I knew that?" Her puzzlement was so genuine that even through pain-haze he could see it. He said, as close to tears as he felt a grown man should ever get, that he just guessed he didn't understand.

"You will, beloved, you will. We'll talk about it until you do, no matter how long it takes." Then she added, with absolutely guileless cruelty, "Starting tomorrow. But now I have to go, Stren's waiting. Good night, true love," and she kissed the top of his averted head and sprinted away lightly on bare tiptoe.

She had reached something in him that made it impossible for him to be angry at her. He could only hurt. He had not known until these past two days that he could feel so much or bear so much pain. He buried his face in the cushions of the long couch in the—living room? —anyway, the place where indoors and outdoors were as tangled as his heart, but more harmoniously—and gave himself up to sodden hurt.

In time, someone knelt beside him and touched him lightly on the neck. He twisted his head enough to be able to see. It was Tyng, her hair all but luminous in the dimness, and her face, what he could see of it, nothing but compassion. She said, "Would you like me to stay with you instead?" and with the absolute honesty of the stricken, he cried, "There couldn't be anyone else instead!"

Her sorrow, its genuineness, was unmistakable. She told him of it, touched him once more, and slipped away. Sometime during the night he twisted himself awake enough to find the room they had given him, and found surcease in utter black exhaustion.

Awake in daylight, he sought his other surcease, which was work, and began his catalogue of resources. Everyone tried at one time or another to communicate with him, but unless it was work he shut it off (except, of course, for the irresistible Handr, who became his fast and lifelong friend). He found Tyng near him more and more frequently, and usefully so; he had not become so surly that he would refuse a stylus or reference book (opened at the right place) when it was placed in his hand exactly at the moment he needed it. Tyng was with him for many hours, alert but absolutely silent, before he unbent enough to ask her for this or that bit of information, or wondered about weights and measures and man-hour calculations done in the Vexveltian way. If she did not know, she found out with a minimum of delay and absolute clarity. She knew, however, a very great deal more than he had suspected. So the time came when he was chattering like a macaw, eagerly planning the next day's work with her.

He never spoke to Tamba. He did not mean to hurt her, but he could sense her eagerness to respond to him and he could not bear it. She, out of consideration, just stopped trying.

One particularly knotty statistical sequence kept him going for two days and two nights without stopping. Tyng kept up with him all the way without complaint until, in the wee small hours of the third morning, she rolled up her eyes and collapsed. He staggered up on legs gone asleep with too much sitting, and shook the statistics out of his eyes to settle her on the thick fur rug, straighten the twisted knee. In what little light spilled from his abandoned hooded lamp, she was exquisite, especially because of his previous knowledge that she was exquisite in the most brilliant of glares. The shadows added something to the alabaster, and her unconscious pale lips were no longer darker than her face, and she seemed strangely statuesque and non-living. She was wearing a Cretan sort of dress, a tight stomacher holding the bare breasts cupped and supporting a diaphanous skirt. Troubled that the stomacher might impede her breathing, he unhooked it and put it back. The flesh of her midriff where it had been was, to the finger if not to the eye, pinched and ridged. He kneaded it gently and pursued indefinable thoughts through the haze of fatigue: pyrophyllite, Lethe, brother, recoverable vanadium salts, Vorhidin, precipitate, Tyng's watching me. Tyng in the almost dark was watching him. He took his eyes from her and looked down her body to his hand. It had stopped moving some vague time ago, slipped into slumber of its own accord. Were her eyes open now or closed? He leaned forward to see and overbalanced. They fell asleep with their lips touching, not yet having kissed at all.

The pre-Nova ancient Plato tells of the earliest human, a quadruped with two sexes. And one terrible night in a storm engendered by the forces of evil, all the humans were torn in two; and ever since, each has sought the other half of itself. Any two of opposite sexes can make something, but it is usually incomplete in some way. But when one part finds its true other half, no power on earth can keep them apart, nor drive them apart once they join. This happened that night, beginning at some moment so deep in sleep that neither could ever remember it. What happened to each was all the way into new places where nothing had ever been before, and it was forever. The essence of such a thing is acceptance, and lest he be judged, Charli Bux ceased to judge quite so much and began to learn something of the ways of life around him. Life around him certainly concealed very little. The children slept where they chose. Their sexual play was certainly no more enthusiastic or more frequent than any other kind of play—and no more concealed. There was very much less talk about sex than he had ever encountered in any group of any age. He kept on working hard, but no longer to conceal facts from himself. He saw a good many things he had not permitted himself to see before, and found to his surprise that they were not, after all, the end of the world.

He had one more very, very bad time coming to him. He sometimes slept in Tyng's room, she sometimes in his. Early one morning he awoke alone, recalling some elusive part of the work, and got up and padded down to her room. He realized when it was too late to ignore it what the soft singing sound meant; it was very much later that he was able to realize his fury at the discovery that this special song was not his alone to evoke. He was in her room before he could stop himself, and out again, shaking and blind.

He was sitting on the wet earth in the green hollow under a willow when Vorhidin found him. (He never knew how Vorhidin had accomplished this, nor for that matter how he had come there himself.) He was staring straight ahead and had been doing so for so long that his eyeballs were dry and the agony was enjoyable. He had forced his fingers so hard down into the ground that they were buried to the wrists. Three nails were bent and broken over backwards and he was still pushing.

Vorhidin did not speak at all at first, but merely sat down beside him. He waited what he felt was long enough and then softly called the young man's name. Charli did not move. Vorhidin then put a hand on his shoulder and the result was extraordinary. Charli Bux moved nothing visibly but the cords of his throat and his jaw, but at the first touch of the Vexveltian's hand he threw up. It was what is called clinically "projectile" vomiting. Soaked and spattered from hips to feet, dry-eyed and staring, Charli sat still. Vorhidin, who understood what had happened and may even have expected it, also remained just as he was, a hand on the young man's shoulder. "Say the words!" he snapped.

Charli Bux swiveled his head to look at the big man. He screwed up his eyes and blinked them, and blinked again. He spat sour out of his mouth, and his lips twisted and trembled. "Say the words," said Vorhidin quietly but forcefully, because he knew Charli could not contain them but had vomited rather than enunciate them. "Say the words."

"Y-y—" Charli had to spit again. "You," he croaked. "You—her *father!*" he screamed, and in a split second he became a dervish, a windmill, a double flail, a howling wolverine. The loamy hands, blood-muddy, so lacked control from the excess of fury that they never became fists. Vorhidin crouched where he was and took it all. He did not attempt to defend himself beyond an occasional small accurate movement of the head, to protect his eyes. He could heal from almost anything the blows might do, but unless the blows were spent, Charli Bux might never heal at all. It went on for a long time because something in Charli would not show, probably would not even feel, fatigue. When the last of the resources was gone, the collapse was sudden and total. Vorhidin knelt grunting, got painfully to his feet, bent dripping blood over the unconscious Terran, lifted him in his arms, and carried him gently into the house.

Vorhidin explained it all, in time. It took a great deal of time, because Charli could accept nothing at all from anyone at first, and then nothing from Vorhidin, and after that, only small doses. Summarized from half a hundred conversations, this is the gist:

"Some unknown ancient once wrote," said Vorhidin, " ' 'Tain't what you don't know that hurts you; it's what you do know that ain't so.' Answer me some questions. Don't stop to think. (Now that's silly. Nobody off Vexvelt ever stops to think about incest. They'll say a lot, mind you, and fast, but they don't think.) I'll ask, you answer. How many bisexual species—birds, beasts, fish and insects included— how many show any sign of the incest taboo?"

"I really couldn't say. I don't recall reading about it, but then, who'd write such a thing? I'd say—quite a few. It would be only natural."

"Wrong. Wrong twice, as a matter of fact. *Homo sapiens* has the patent, Charli—all over the wall-to-wall universe, only mankind. Wrong the second: it would *not* be natural. It never was, it isn't, and it never will be natural."

"Matter of terms, isn't it? I'd call it natural. I mean, it comes naturally. It doesn't have to be learned."

"Wrong. It does have to be learned. I can document that, but that'll wait—you can go through the library later. Accept the point for the argument."

"For the argument, then."

"Thanks. What percentage of people do you think have sexual feelings about their siblings—brothers and sisters?"

"What age are you talking about?"

"Doesn't matter."

"Sexual feelings don't begin until a certain age, do they?"

"Don't they? What would you say the age is, on the average?"

"Oh—depends on the indi—but you did say 'average,' didn't you? Let's put it around eight. Nine maybe."

"Wrong. Wait till you have some of your own, you'll find out. I'd put it at two or three minutes. I'd be willing to bet it existed a whole lot before that, too. By some weeks."

"I don't believe it!"

"I know you don't," said Vorhidin. " 'Strue all the same. What about the parent of the opposite sex?"

"Now, that would have to wait for a stage of consciousness capable of knowing the difference."

"Wel-l-l—you're not as wrong as usual," he said, but he said it kindly. "But you'd be amazed at how early that can be. They can smell the difference long before they can see it. A few days, a week."

"I never knew."

"I don't doubt that a bit. Now, let's forget everything you've seen here. Let's pretend you're back on Lethe and I ask you, what would be the effects on a culture if each individual had immediate and welcome access to all the others?"

"*Sexual* access?" Charli made a laugh, a nervous sort of sound. "Sexual excess, I'd call it."

"There's no such thing," said the big man flatly. "Depending on who you are and what sex, you can do it only until you can't do it any more, or you can keep on until finally nothing happens. One man might get along beautifully with some mild kind of sexual relief twice a month or less. Another might normally look for it eight, nine times a day."

"I'd hardly call that normal."

"I would. Unusual it might be, but it's 100 per cent normal for the guy who has it, long as it isn't pathological. By which I mean, capacity is capacity, by the cupful, by the horsepower, by the flight ceiling. Man or machine, you do no harm by operating within the parameters of design. What does do harm—lots of it, and some of the worst kind —is guilt and a sense of sin, where the sin turns out to be some sort of natural appetite. I've read case histories of boys who have suicided because of a nocturnal emission, or because they yielded to the temptation to masturbate after five, six weeks of self-denial—a denial, of course, that all by itself makes them preoccupied, absolutely obsessed by something that should have no more importance than clearing the throat. (I wish I could say that this kind of horror story lives only in the ancient scripts, but on many a world right this minute, it still goes on.)

"This guilt and sin thing is easier for some people to understand if you take it outside the area of sex. There are some religious orthodoxies which require a very specific diet, and the absolute exclusion of certain items. Given enough indoctrination for long enough, you can keep a man eating only (we'll say) 'flim' while 'flam' is forbidden. He'll get along on thin moldy flim and live half starved in a whole warehouse full of nice fresh flam. You can make him ill—even kill him, if you have the knack—just by convincing him that the flim he just ate was really flam in disguise. Or you can drive him psychotic by slipping him suggestions until he acquires a real taste for flam and gets a supply and hides it and nibbles at it secretly every time he fights temptation and loses.

"So imagine the power of guilt when it isn't a flim-and-flam kind of manufactured orthodoxy you're violating, but a deep pressure down in the cells somewhere. It's as mad, and as dangerous, as grafting in an ethical-guilt structure which forbids or inhibits yielding to the need for the B-vitamin complex or potassium."

"Oh, but," Charli interrupted, "now you're talking about vital necessities—survival factors."

"I sure as hell am," said Vorhidin in Charli's own idiom, and grinned a swift and hilarious—and very accurate—imitation of Charli's flash-beacon smile. "Now it's time to trot out some of the things I mentioned before, things that can hurt you much more than ignorance —the things you know that ain't so." He laughed suddenly. "This is kind of fun, you know? I've been to a lot of worlds, and some are miles and years different from others in a thousand ways: but this thing I'm about to demonstrate, this particular shut-the-eyes, shut-the-brains conversation you can get anywhere you go. Are you ready? Tell me, then: what's wrong with incest? I take it back—you know me. Don't tell me. Tell some stranger, some fume-sniffer or alcohol addict in a spaceport bar." He put out both hands, the fingers so shaped that one could all but see light glisten from the imaginary glass he held. He said in a slurred voice, "Shay, shtranger, whut's a-wrong wit' in-shest, hm?" He closed one eye and rolled the other toward Charli.

Charli stopped to think. "You mean, morally, or what?"

"Let's skip that whole segment. Right and wrong depend on too many things from one place to another, although I have some theories of my own. No—let's be sitting in this bar and agree that incest is just awful, and go on from there. What's really wrong with it?"

"You breed too close, you get faulty offspring. Idiots and dead babies without heads and all that."

"I knew it! I knew it!" crowed the big Vexveltian. "Isn't it wonderful? From the rocky depths of a Stone Age culture through the brocades and knee-breeches sort of grand opera civilizations all the way out to the computer technocracies, where they graft electrodes into their heads and shunt their thinking into a box—you ask that question and you get that answer. It's something everybody just *knows*. You don't have to look at the evidence."

"Where do you go for evidence?"

"To dinner, for one place, where you'll eat idiot pig or feeble-minded cow. Any livestock breeder will tell you that, once you have a strain you want to keep and develop, you breed father to daughter and to granddaughter, and then brother to sister. You keep that up indefinitely until the desirable trait shows up recessive, and you stop it there. But it might never show up recessive. In any case, it's rare indeed when anything goes wrong in the very first generation; but you in the bar, there, you're totally convinced that it will. And are you prepared to say that every mental retard is the product of an incestuous union? You'd better not, or you'll hurt the feelings of some pretty nice people. That's a tragedy that can happen to anybody, and I doubt there's any more chance of it between related parents than there is with anyone else.

"But you still don't see the funniest . . . or maybe it's just the oddest part of that thing you know that just ain't so. Sex is a pretty popular topic on most worlds. Almost every aspect of it that is ever mentioned has nothing to do with procreation. For every mention of pregnancy or childbirth, I'd say there are hundreds which deal only with the sex act itself. But mention incest, and the response always deals with offspring. Always! To consider and discuss a pleasure or love relationship between blood relatives, you've apparently got to make some sort of special mental effort that nobody, anywhere, seems able to do easily—some not at all."

"I have to admit I never made it. But then—what *is* wrong with incest, with or without pregnancy?"

"Aside from moral considerations, you mean. The moral consideration is that it's a horrifying thought, and it's a horrifying thought because it always has been. Biologically speaking, I'd say there's nothing wrong with it. Nothing. I'd go even further, with Dr. Phelvelt —ever hear of him?"

"I don't think so."

"He was a biological theorist who could get one of his books banned on worlds that had never censored anything before—even on worlds which had science and freedom of research and freedom of speech as the absolute keystones of their whole structure. Anyway, Phelvelt had a very special kind of mind, always ready to take the next step no matter where it is, without insisting that it's somewhere where it isn't. He thought well, he wrote well, and he had a vast amount of knowledge outside his specialty and a real knack for unearthing what he happened not to know. And he called that sexual tension between blood relatives a survival factor."

"How did he come to that?"

"By a lot of separate paths which came together in the same place. Everybody knows (this one *is* so!) that there are evolutionary pressures which make for changes in a species. Not much (before Phelvelt) had been written about stabilizing forces. But don't you see, inbreeding is one of them?"

"Not offhand, I don't."

"Well, look at it, man! Take a herd animal as a good example. The bull covers his cows, and when they deliver heifers and the heifers grow up, he covers them too. Sometimes there's a third and even a fourth generation of them before he gets displaced by a younger bull. And all that while, the herd characteristics are purified and reinforced. You don't easily get animals with slightly different metabolisms which might tend to wander away from the feeding ground the others were using. You won't get high-bottom cows which would necessitate Himself bringing something to stand on when he came courting." Through Charli's shout of laughter he continued, "So there you have it—stabilization, purification, greater survival value—all resulting from the pressure to breed in."

"I see, I see. And the same thing would be true of lions or fish or tree toads, or—"

"Or any animal. A lot of things have been said about Nature, that she's implacable, cruel, wasteful and so on. I like to think she's—reasonable. I concede that she reaches that state cruelly, at times, and wastefully and all the rest. But she has a way of coming up with the pragmatic solution, the one that works. To build in a pressure which tends to standardize and purify a successful stage, and to call in the exogene, the infusion of fresh blood, only once in several generations—that seems to me most reasonable."

"More so," Charli said, "than what we've always done, when you look at it that way. Every generation a new exogene, the blood kept churned up, each new organism full of pressures which haven't had a chance with the environment."

"I suppose," said Vorhidin, "you could argue that the incest taboo is responsible for the restlessness that pulled mankind out of the caves, but that's a little too simplistic for me. I'd have preferred a mankind that moved a little more slowly, a little more certainly, and never fell back. I think the ritual exogamy that made inbreeding a crime and 'deceased wife's sister' a law against incest is responsible for another kind of restlessness."

He grew very serious. "There's a theory that certain normal habit patterns should be allowed to run their course. Take the sucking reflex, for example. It has been said that infants who have been weaned too early plague themselves all their lives with oral activity—chewing on straws, smoking intoxicants in pipes, drinking out of bottle by preference, nervously manipulating the lips, and so on. With that as an analogy, you may look again at the restlessness of mankind all through his history. Who but a gaggle of frustrates, never in their lives permitted all the ways of love within the family, could coin such a concept as 'motherland' and give their lives to it and for it? There's a great urge to love Father, and another to topple him. Hasn't humanity set up its beloved Fathers, its Big Brothers, loved and worshiped and given and died for them, rebelled and killed and replaced them? A lot of them richly deserved it, I concede, but it would have been better to have done it on its own merits and not because they were nudged by a deep-down, absolutely sexual tide of which they could not speak because they had learned that it was unspeakable.

"The same sort of currents flow within the family unit. So-called 'sibling rivalry' is too well known to be described, and the frequency of bitter quarreling between siblings is, in most cultures and their literature, a sort of cliché. Only a very few psychologists have dared to put forward the obvious explanation that, more often than not, these frictions are inverted love feelings, well salted with horror and guilt. It's a pattern that makes conflict between siblings all but a certainty, and it's a problem which, once stated, describes its own solution. . . . Have you ever read Vexworth? No? You should—I think you'd find him fascinating. Ecologist; in his way quite as much of a giant as Phelvelt."

"Ecologist—that has something to do with life and environment, right?"

"Ecology has *everything* to do with life and environment; it studies them as reciprocals, as interacting and mutually controlling forces. It goes without saying that the main aim and purpose of any life form is optimum survival; but 'optimum survival' is a meaningless term without considering the environment in which it has to happen. As the environment changes, the organism has to change its ways and means, even its basic design. Human beings are notorious for changing their environment, and in most of our history in most places, we have made these changes without ecological considerations. This is disaster, every time. This is overpopulation, past the capabilities of producing food and shelter enough. This is the rape of irreplaceable natural resources. This is the contamination of water supplies. And it is also the twisting and thwarting of psychosexual needs in the emotional environment.

"Vexvelt was founded by those two, Charli—Phelvelt and Vexworth —and is named for them. As far as I know it is the only culture ever devised on ecological lines. Our sexual patterns derive from the ecological base and are really only a very small part of our structure. Yet for that one aspect of our lives, we are avoided and shunned and pretty much unmentionable."

It took a long time for Charli to be able to let these ideas in, and longer for him to winnow and absorb them. But all the while he lived surrounded by beauty and fulfillment, by people, young and old, who were capable of total concentration on art and learning and building and processing, people who gave to each other and to their land and air and water just a little more than they took. He finished his survey largely because he had started it; for a while he was uncertain of what he would do with it.

When at length he came to Vorhidin and said he wanted to stay on Vexvelt, the big man smiled, but he shook his head. "I know you want to, Charli—but do you?"

"I don't know what you mean." He looked out at the dark bole of one of the Vexveltian poplars; Tyng was there, like a flower, an orchid. "It's more than that," said Charli, "more than my wanting to be a Vexveltian. You need me."

"We love you," Vorhidin said simply. "But—need?"

"If I went back," said Charli Bux, "and Terratu got its hands on my survey, what do you think would become of Vexvelt?"

"You tell me."

"First Terratu would come to trade, and then others, and then others; and then they would fight each other, and fight you . . . you need someone here who knows this, really knows it, and who can deal with it when it starts. It will start, you know, even without my survey; sooner or later someone will be able to do what I did—a shipment of feldspar, a sheet of pure metal. They will destroy you."

"They will never come near us."

"You think not. Listen: no matter how the other worlds disapprove, there is one force greater: greed."

"Not in this case, Charli. And this is what I want you to be able to understand, all the way down to your cells. Unless you do, you can never live here. We are shunned, Charli. If you had been born here, that would not matter so much to you. If you throw in your lot with us, it would have to be a total commitment. But you should not make such a decision without understanding how completely you will be excluded from everything else you have ever known."

"What makes you think I don't know it now?"

"You say we need defending. You say other-world traders will exploit us. That only means you don't understand. Charli: listen to me. Go back to Terratu. Make the strongest presentation you can for trade with Vexvelt. See how they react. Then you'll know—then you can decide."

"And aren't you afraid I might be right, and because of me, Vexvelt will be robbed and murdered?"

And Vorhidin shook his big head, smiling, and said, "Not one bit, Charli Bux. Not one little bit."

So Charli went back, and saw (after a due delay) the Archive Master, and learned what he learned, and came out and looked about him at his home world and, through that, at all the worlds like it; and then he went to the secret place where the Vexveltian ship was moored, and it opened to him. Tyng was there, Tamba, and Vorhidin. Charli said, "Take me home."

In the last seconds before they took the Drive jump, and he could look through the port at the shining face of Terratu for the last time in his life, Charli said, "Why? Why? How did human beings come to hate this one thing so much that they would rather die insane and in agony than accept it? How did it happen, Vorhidin?"

"I don't know," said the Vexveltian.

## Afterword:

And now you know what sort of a science fiction story this is, and perhaps something about science fiction stories that you didn't know before.

I have always been fascinated by the human mind's ability to think itself to a truth, and then to take that one step more (truly the basic secret of all human progress) and the inability of so many people to learn the trick. Case in point: "We mean to get that filth off the newsstands and out of the bookstores." Ask why, and most such crusaders will simply point at the "filth" and wonder that you asked. But a few will take that one step more: "Because youngsters might get their hands on it." That satisfies most, but ask: "And suppose they do?" a still smaller minority will think it through to: "Because it's bad for them." Ask again: "In what way is it bad for them?" and a handful can reach this: "It will arouse them." By now you've probably run out of crusaders, but if there are a couple left, ask them, "How does being aroused harm a child?" and if you can get them to take that one more step, they will have to take it out of the area of emotional conviction and into the area of scientific research. Such studies are available, and invariably they show that such arousement is quite harmless—indeed, there is something abnormal about anyone who is not or cannot be so aroused. The only possible harm that can result comes not from the sexual response itself but from the guilt-making and punitive attitude of the social environment—most of all that part of it which is doing the crusading.

Casting about for some more or less untouched area in which to exercise this one-step-more technique, I hit on this one. That was at least twenty years ago, and I have had to wait until now to find a welcome for anything so unsettling. I am, of course, very grateful. I hope the yarn starts some fruitful argument.

What a torturous and plotful genesis! I think, over all, the haunt was my desperate desire to give you the very best I could, as close as possible to your purpose in the anthology, a feeling inflamed by the news I got from Mills at one point that you had been bitterly disappointed by some of the submissions you had received, hence my desire to make up to you other people's defalcations. All this overlaid on a series of shattering personal experiences which included a pretty complete breakdown on September 4 and a very difficult (though highly successful) rebuilding process afterward. Your story is the first in a long, long time, and as such is especially meaningful to me; I hope it is to you too.

Let's see, that Saturday, the twelfth, was the third day of three days and nights I had been slogging away at it, and at last I had it going the way I wanted to. And it seems I have these good kind friends whom we will call Joe and Selma (because I have the feeling—very strong—that you will meet them one day). And they are close and helpful and admiring (and admired) friends and they were with me all the way in my struggle, and they live in Kingston. When noon (Saturday) came and went they were here running coffee and more or less shouting encouragement, and they said never mind missing the last mail at Woodstock, they'd stick around until it was finished and run it into the central post office in Kingston where it would get off even late Saturday night. Betimes Selma had to leave but Joe stuck around. 'Long about six Selma called to find out how it was going because now their own affairs were pressing: Joe had to take a bus to Stroudsburg where he would spend a week. He said for her to pack for him, he'd be in in plenty of time. Finally I was done and he grabbed the envelopes (one to Ashmead and one to you) and jumped in his car and beat it. I was so bushed I couldn't sleep and spent almost the whole night glassy-eyed; when you called the next day I was something like delirious.

Comes—what was it, Thursday? I was more normal and biting nails over how much you might have liked or hated the story so called you, to find to my very real horror that you didn't have it. Events here had been sort of complex as well: my wife has gone to Mexico and I have the four kids to ride herd on. So anyway when I hung up on you I called Ashmead and found he hadn't gotten the ms. either, and sat there trying to find an alternative to going right out of my mind. I felt a little like the guy in the story talking about what "They" were doing to him. Then I called Selma and told her and she just didn't believe it. She said she'd call back. She phoned Stroudsburg and asked Joe and Joe was just as horrified. Seems he'd arrived home that Saturday just in time to throw on his traveling suit and be driven to the bus. He thought she mailed it and she thought he mailed it. So *where was it?*

I got into my car and drove to their house and she was in what I can euphemistically call a State. And thank the Lord for that because taking care of her State kept me from going into one of my own. It must have hit us both in the same instant because we practically cracked our heads together jumping up to look in their car, and there were the effing envelopes, with all the red and white hurry-up stickers all over them, slid down between the right front seat and seat back and thence under the seat. I can even reconstruct their exact trajectory. Joe's big and long-legged and Selma's a little bit of a thing, and that Saturday night he ran out of my house with the envelopes and put them on the seat beside him and they slid back. Then when she drove him to the bus she slid the seat forward and down they went underneath. Anyway I made her promise not to commit suicide until after she talked to me again and then maybe we'd do it together, and scooted back to Woodstock where I knew I'd catch an outgoing mail.

All of which, being the truth, is too incredible for anyone's fiction book, and is not intended for the uses you said you wanted to put some material to in the book. I'm a little hazy about what exactly it was you did say but it was something to the effect that you wanted a bio (oh yes, I recall saying that the very idea gives me amnesia) and some words about the circumstances that produced the story. All right, I'll try to do both: see attached.

Anyway, Harlan, whether or not you like the story I'm glad you asked me and I'm glad I did it. It broke a lot of kinds of ice. I'm back at my *Playboy* story and will at long last be firing yarns at them regularly. I've reread the story twice and once thought it was dreadful and once thought it was wonderful. It has a kind of structure I've never used before; usually I employ one "angle" character who alone thinks and feels and remembers, and with whom the reader identifies, while everyone else *acts* angry or *says* sorrowful things or has no memories unless he says them aloud. But in this one I (more or less) stayed in the minds of minor characters and watched the protagonist through their eyes. Also that trick of self-interruption in italics is one I shall polish and perfect and use again. . . . What I'm trying to say is that you put the tools back in my hands and they feel very good. So thanks. Even if you don't like it. If that's the case I'll give you back your advance. I'm working again and can say that and mean it.

**Introduction to WHAT HAPPENED TO AUGUSTE CLAROT?:**

I have nothing to say about Larry Eisenberg. Except that he ought to be put away. I have nothing to say about this *thing* that follows except for buying it *I* ought to be put away. And if you break up at it as much as I did when I read it, then *you* ought to be put away, because the damned thing makes no sense, and I don't care if I *did* try to reject it seventeen times, and I don't care if Larry Ashmead at Doubleday got the same reaction and said go ahead and buy it, because everyone knows Ashmead should have been put away years ago!

Of himself, Eisenberg has this to say: "I've been selling since 1958, first humor, then science fiction, then humorous science fiction. My 'Dr. Belzov's Kasha Oil Diet' (a guide for the fat) appeared in *Harper's*. 'The Pirokin Effect' (in which I prove there are Jews on Mars) is in Judith Merril's tenth annual of *The Year's Best SF*. Around July 1966, *Limericks for the Loo,* a collection of original bawdy limericks (co-authored by George Gordon), was published in England. *Games*

*People Shouldn't Play* (same co-author) was published in America in November 1966. To support my wife and two children, I do research in bio-medical electronics."

A likely story, indeed! And for those who may ask why such a piece of *dreck* as what follows should get into a book of "dangerous visions," let me assure you that its convincing *everyone* who's read it that it *should* be here makes it the most dangerous thing since Typhoid Mary. You hold him down—I'll call the fuzz.

# ● WHAT HAPPENED TO AUGUSTE CLAROT?

## by Larry Eisenberg

(Who among us has not speculated on the whereabouts of Judge Crater? In Paris, the disappearance of Auguste Clarot caused an equally large splash.)

When I was summoned posthaste to the topsy turvy office of Emile Becque, savage editor of *L'Expresse,* I knew in my bones that an assignment of extraordinary dimensions awaited me. Becque glared at me as I entered, his green-tinted eyeshade slanted forward like an enormous bill.

We sat there, neither of us saying a word, for Becque is a strong believer in mental telepathy. After several moments I had gathered nothing but waves of hatred for a padded expense account and then, all at once, I knew. It was *l'affaire Clarot.* I leaped to my feet crying out, "I will not let you down, Emile," and stumbled (almost blinded by tears) out of his office.

It was an intriguing assignment and I could hardly believe it had fallen to me. The disappearance of Auguste Clarot, Nobel-prize-winning chemist, some fifteen years earlier, had thrown all of Paris into a turmoil. Even my mother, a self-centered bourgeoise given to surreptitious squeezing of tomatoes to reduce their price, had remarked to me that the Earth could hardly have swallowed up so eminent a scientist.

On a hunch, I went to see his wife, Madame Ernestine Clarot, a formidable woman with a black mustache and pre-eminent bosom. She received me with dignity, camomile tea, and a crepe-fringed portrait of her husband. I tried to trick her into spilling the beans by alluding to rumors that Clarot had gone to Buenos Aires with a *poulet* from Montmartre. Although her eyes filled with tears at this egregious insult, Madame Ernestine quietly defended her husband's honor. I flushed to the roots, apologized a thousand times, and even offered to fight a duel with anyone she might choose, but she would not spare me the pain of my humiliation.

Later, at the Café Père-Mère, I discussed the matter with Marnay, charming, insouciant, but completely unreliable. He told me, on his honor, that he could find out for me (at a price) where Clarot was. I knew he was lying and he knew that I knew he was lying, but on sadistic impulse I accepted his offer. He blanched, drained his pernod at a gulp, and began to drum with furious fingers on the table top. It was evident that he now felt honor bound to find Clarot but did not know how to do it.

I bade Marnay a courteous adieu and left the Café Père-Mère. So distracted was Marnay that he did not notice that the check was unpaid until I was almost out of sight. I ignored his frenzied semaphoring and struck up a temporary acquaintance with a lovely young maiden who was patrolling the Boulevard Sans Honneur.

In the morning, when I awoke, she had fled with my wallet containing, among other things, five hundred new francs and a list of aphrodisiacs which I had purchased from a gypsy. I had the very devil of a time with the concierge, who did not entertain the truth of my story for a single moment. He broke into violent abuse as I delineated what had occurred and began to belabor me about the neck and arms with a chianti bottle from which, *hélas,* he had removed the straw covering.

I sat on the curb, black and blue, penniless and at my wit's end as to how I might proceed. I could not go back to Emile Becque and tell him how I had been duped. Honor forbade so humiliating a course. But Fate in the guise of an American tourist's lost credit card intervened. Within hours I had wined and dined sumptuously, having outfitted myself to the nines at Manchoulette's exclusive haberdashery.

I inhaled the bracing winelike air of Paris at twilight and stood there, surveying the twinkling buttocks of energetic women hastening to affairs of the heart. All at once I saw an enormous Chinese staggering under a terrible burden of laundry. He winked at me and thrust the bundle into my unsuspecting hands, toppling me to the ground. When I had arisen, kicking and struggling to free myself of the cloying cloth, he had vanished into a nearby kiosk.

I stared at the bundle, terrified at the prospect of what it might contain, but at last I summoned up my nerve and loosened the double knots. There was nothing within but four undershorts and eleven dirty shirts with two collars that needed turning. A written note within, almost painful in its intensity, implored the avoidance of starch in the undershorts.

As I mulled over the secret meaning of this event, Marnay appeared before me like a wraith materializing out of smoke. He glared at me, his eyes laced with the most curious red lines, held up a white embossed card and then fell forward, a victim (as I later learned) of an exploded bladder, a medical event last recorded over a century earlier.

I picked up the card and waved its dull white edge under my nose. There was at once a heady and yet repellent fragrance wafted toward me. The card itself bore the name A. Systole, 23 Rue de Daie. Easing the corpse under a bush of eglantine where some venturesome dog would surely discover it before morning, I made my way to the residence of Monsieur Systole. It was, I found, a dark structure of brownstone, no more than forty feet in height but still kept spick and span by a thorough and constant owner.

I stepped up to the gargoyle knocker just as a small poodle passing along the sidewalk turned and snarled at me in the most unfriendly manner. I have always prided myself on an uncanny rapport with poodles and I was quite taken aback by the sheer nastiness of this neurotic creature. I rapped the knocker once, twice, ever so gently but nonetheless firmly because the poodle's leash was frayed and might give way under his insistent tugging.

A florid face appeared behind a sliding mahogany panel, a face too well fed and too well lived. One of the enormous eyes winked at me and then the door swung wide and I was assisted in by means of strong fingers tugging at my elbow. Later, over a flaming anisette, Clarot, for it was indeed he, told me everything.

"You have seen my wife?" he said, nodding encouragingly at me.

"I certainly have," I said apologetically.

"Then you can see why I skipped the roost," said Clarot. "But how was I to live? To deliver myself to a chemist's shop would have meant certain exposure. I decided to turn my efforts toward a venture at once creative and lucrative, yet something not requiring an outlay of too many francs."

"You succeeded, of course," I cried, unable to contain myself.

"Handsomely," said Clarot. He rose to his feet and stretched his bloated frame like a monstrous cat. "Come after me and you shall see," he said boastfully.

I followed his limping form through room after room of Chinese modern, averting my eyes from some of the more extreme examples. Below, in the basement, was the most ramshackle of all laboratories with broken retorts strewn about, an idle Bunsen burner lying on its side, and a mortar of solidified chemicals with a pestle imbedded in the mass.

"It was within this hallowed dungeon that I discovered the aromatic which incenses all canines," said Clarot. "One whiff and the mildest of lap dogs becomes a raging monster, determined to attack me and tear me to bits."

"Of what earthly use could such an aromatic be?" I cried.

Clarot placed his finger to one side of his nose, sagely.

"It gets me bitten over and over again," he said, smiling crookedly.

"Bitten? Merciful God!"

"You forget the law, my good fellow. I am judicious, of course, and permit my permeated trouser leg within range of only the tiniest of dogs. Nevertheless, some of the little beggars bite like the very devil."

He leaned over and massaged a shinbone thoughtfully.

"But the owners," he resumed, "settle generously at the threat of a lawsuit. At least most of them do. I live quite handsomely on the proceeds as you can see."

"Then the odor on your card?"

"Was *aromatique Clarot.*"

"You won't mind if all this appears in *L'Expresse?*" I said, for every good reporter worth his salt wishes to protect his sources.

"Mind?" said Clarot airily. "Why on earth should I? As we chatted here, I liberally doused your trouser legs with my aromatic. When

I press the chartreuse button on this wall, it will release my hypertensive bloodhounds, who will proceed to tear you into very tiny bits."

It was a gross blunder on Clarot's part. Soft living had put him terribly out of condition and it took me but a short moment of struggling and kicking to divest him of his trousers and place my own pair on his naked legs. I then pressed the chartreuse button and stepped out of the room, ignoring Clarot's cries for mercy.

As I left the brownstone house I was struck at the base of the skull by a nearsighted *cocotte,* betrayed by Clarot and mistaking me for him because I wore his fawn-colored trousers. Her blow sent me to the curb where I narrowly averted being run over by a blue Funke, a British sports car.

I lay in the charity ward at L'Hopital des Trois Balles, amnesiac for over three months. My memory restored, I tottered over to the office of *L'Expresse* and discovered that Emile Becque had been garroted by the huge Chinese, who had misread his telepathic silence in the face of demands that he pay his delinquent laundry bill.

The new editor, a sullen Breton, listened to my halting explanation with unflagging attention. When I had finished, he escorted me to the door and placed his iron-tipped toe to my rump, enabling me to leave at an extraordinary burst of speed.

I had no choice but to seek out Madame Clarot once more. After a short but impassioned courtship, she joined me at my apartment over the Tavern of the Four Griffins. She no longer sips camomile tea and it is with considerable nostalgia that I look back upon the day when she greeted me with cold sobriety. But then, I owe *that* much to Clarot.


**Afterword:**

It may be that, unknown to myself, "Auguste Clarot" is riddled with displaced symbolism. Perhaps I can't cope with escalated brotherhood in Vietnam, equal but separate mistreatment for men of color, and bulging clichés mouthed in high and low places. "Auguste Clarot" was a joyful catharsis for me and, I hope, for the reader.

## Introduction to ERSATZ:

The act of collaboration, between writers as very definitely opposed to the act of collaboration between lovers, is only satisfying when it is ended, never while it is being performed. It has been my annoyance and pleasure to have collaborated with perhaps half a dozen writers in the eleven years I've been a professional. (I have never been a lover of any of them.) With Avram Davidson I wrote a Ring Lardneresque bit of tomfoolery so fraught with personal jokes and literary references that I was compelled to write a 10,000-word article explaining the story, to accompany the 7000-word fiction before it could be sold. Not unexpectedly, the story was called "Up Christopher to Madness" and the article was titled "Scherzo for Schizoids." With Huckleberry Barkin I wrote a *Playboy* story of humorous seduction (which I contend is a contradiction in terms) called "Would You Do It for A Penny?" and with Robert Silverberg a crime story called "Ship-Shape Pay-Off." I even wrote a story with Budrys once.

But collaborating is generally a dismal chore, fraught with such traps as conceptual disagreement, clash of styles, incipient laziness, verbosity, confusion and simple bad writing. How Pratt & De Camp or Nordhoff & Hall did it, I will never fully understand. Yet with two writers I have been able to collaborate easily, and the products have been something more than either of us might have attained singly. The first is Joe L. Hensley, who appears elsewhere in this book, and of whom there is much to say; but in another place. The second is Henry Slesar, of whom there is much to say here. I am delighted at the opportunity to say these things, for they have been in my mind many years, and since they verge on being a poem of love, they are obviously not the kind of thing one can say to a man's face.

(The concept of affection between men has been so emasculated—literally—that to display any sign of joy at the presence or companionship or understanding of another man is taken, by the yahoos, as a sure sign of faggotry. I choose not to dignify the implication, yet will state bluntly that I do not subscribe to the snide theory there is anything between Batman and Robin but big-brotherliness. Some folks just have a one-track gutter.)

I think the operable element in any successful collaboration is friendship. Based on respect and admiration and trust in the other man's morality, sense of craft and sense of fairness. To accept another writer's judgment on the form and direction of a story, one must first respect and admire what the other has done on his own. He must have paid his dues. Then, it must be unconsciously safe for one to go with the other man's instincts as to what the story is saying in larger terms, in terms of ethic and morality. Only then does one feel safe in allowing the unformed creation to be molded by other hands. And finally, by the extensions and implications of friendship, one knows the other man wants a unified whole, a product of *two* minds and individual talents, rather than one story that has been stolen from another man's store of minutiae. Yes, I think friendship must be present if the collaboration is to succeed. Henry Slesar and I have been friends for over ten years.

I first met Henry after a lecture I delivered at New York University in 1956. The presumption of me telling a class on creative writing how to function in the commercial arena, after only one year of professional work, was staggering. But apparently (Henry has told me many times) up till that time the class had been fed gross amounts of the usual literary horse manure, a great deal of theory culled from inept texts, but very little practical advice on how to sell what the class had written. Since I was a selling writer—for however short a time, at that time— I felt justified only in telling them where to get the best buck, and how to keep from being shafted, rather than how to pick up the mantle of Chekhov. (Comment: as demonstrated by the preponderance of writers in this volume *alone,* memorable writers are born, not trained. I believe this firmly. Oh, it's possible to learn how to handle the English language in a competent manner, it is even possible to learn how to plot like a computer. But that is something else: it is the difference between being an author and being a writer. The former get their names on books, the latter write. Of all the writing courses I have known—as class member, guest lecturer, auditor or interested listener—I have encountered only one that seemed to know where it was at. That was the series of classes given by Robert Kirsch at UCLA. He laid it on the line in the first ten minutes that, if they couldn't write already, they'd better sign up for another subject, because he was ready and able to teach them the superficialities, but the spark of creativity had to be there or they'd wind up merely masturbating. Born, not made, despite what the reading-fee agencies tell their poor befuddled victims.)

After the class, Henry and I got together many times. He was at that time creative director for the Robert W. Orr advertising agency. (Henry is the man who created the Life Saver advertisement that was merely a page of candies laid out in rows, with the inked-in words, "Don't lick this page." It was an award winner, and so is Henry.) But aside from Bix Beiderbecke records, Henry's driving urgency was for writing. I have never met a man who so wanted to set words on paper and who, from the very first, had such a sure, talented manner of so doing. Within the first year of his career he sold to *Ellery Queen's Mystery Magazine, Playboy* and over a dozen other top markets. We would get together of an evening, either in my tiny apartment on West Eighty-second Street off Amsterdam, or his sprawling residence overlooking West End Avenue, and after the usual few hours of chitchat between us and our wives (I was, at that juncture, married to Disaster Area #1), we would vanish into Henry's office and do a short story. Complete in one evening. Usually science fiction or detective stories: "The Kissing Dead," "Sob Story," "Mad Dog," "RFD #2," "The Man with the Green Nose." We worked well together, though not entirely rationally. Sometimes I would start with a title and a first paragraph, writing something so off-beat and peculiar that there was no place to go plot-wise. Or Henry would open the story and write a thousand words of devious plot threads, leaving off in mid-speech. Once in a while we plotted the whole thing out in advance. But whichever form or direction was used, we always got a salable story from the collaboration. We sold everything we ever wrote together. It was a parlor trick, a party game, a hobby that paid for itself in enjoyment and cigarette money.

Henry Slesar was born in 1927 in Brooklyn. He is the personification of quality and tact and honor in a field singularly spare in such qualities: he is an advertising man. He has been vice-president and creative director of three top New York agencies and is now president and CD of his own: Slesar & Kanzer, Inc., Founded 1965. As a writer he has published over 600 stories, novels, etc., to such markets as *Playboy, Cosmopolitan, Diners Club Magazine,* all of the men's magazines, mystery magazines and most of the science fiction magazines. He has been anthologized fifty-five times, has written three novels including *The Gray Flannel Shroud* (Random House), which won the 1959 Mystery Writers of America Edgar as Best First Mystery Novel. He has had two short-story collections published, both introduced by Alfred Hitchcock, who looks with great favor on our Henry, who has written over sixty television scripts, many of which were for the Hitchcock half-hour and hour series. He has also written for *77 Sunset Strip, The Man from U.N.C.L.E., Run for Your Life* and half a dozen of the coveted high-paying pilot film assignments. He has written four motion pictures for Warner Bros.

Henry is married to one of the loveliest women any writer possesses —the O. in his pen name O. H. Leslie—and has one daughter—the Leslie of the pseudonym. They all live together in New York City, which is a pleasant arrangement.

The Henry Slesar story in this anthology is only 1100 words long. About half the length of this introduction, I now realize. There are two comments to be made on this bizarre fact. First, my admiration and friendship for Slesar know no bounds—not even the simple bounds of conversation of verbiage. The second is more important. Henry Slesar is a master of the short-short story. He can kill you with a line. He takes 1100 words to do what lesser writers would milk for 10,000 words. If there is a better short-short writer working in America today, I can't think of his name, and I've got a helluva memory.

## ● ERSATZ

### by Henry Slesar

There were sixteen hundred Peace Stations erected in the eighth year of the conflict, the contribution of the few remaining civilians on the American continent; sixteen hundred atomproofed shelters where the itinerant fighting man could find food, drink, and rest. Yet Sergeant Tod Halstead, in five dreary months of wandering across the wastelands of Utah, Colorado, and New Mexico, had relinquished hope of finding even one. In his lead-lined aluminum armor he appeared to be a perfectly packaged war machine, but the flesh within the gleaming housing was weak and unwashed and weary of the lonely, monotonous task of seeking a friend to join or an enemy to kill.

He was a Rocket Carrier, Third Class, the rank signifying that it was his duty to be a human launching pad for the four hydrogen-headed rockets strapped to his back, their fuses to be ignited by a Rocket Carrier, Second Class, upon command and countdown by a Rocket Carrier, First Class. Tod had lost the other two thirds of his unit months before; one of them had giggled and slipped a bayonet in his throat; the other had been shot and killed by a sixty-year-old farm wife who was resisting his desperate, amorous advances.

Then early one morning, after he was certain that the burst of light in the east was the sun and not the enemy's atomic fire, he trudged along a dusty road and saw beyond the shimmering waves of heat a square white building set amid a grove of naked gray trees. He stumbled towards it, and knew it was no mirage of the man-created desert, but a Peace Station. In its doorway a white-haired man with a Father Christmas face beckoned and smiled and helped him inside.

"Thank God," Tod said, falling into a chair. "Thank God. I'd almost given up. . . ."

The jolly old man clapped his hands, and two young boys with hair like eagles' nests came running into the room. Like service station attendants, they set about him busily, removing his helmet, his boots, unhooking his weapons. They fanned him, chafed his wrists, put cool lotion on his forehead; a few minutes later, his eyes closed, and with sleep approaching, he was conscious of a gentle hand on his cheek, and woke to find his months-old beard gone.

"There now," the station manager said, rubbing his hands in satisfaction. "Feel better, soldier?"

"Much better," Tod said, looking about at the bare but comfortable room. "How does the war go with you, civilian?"

"Hard," the man said, no longer jolly. "But we do our best, serving the fighting men as we can. But relax, soldier; food and drink will be here soon. It won't be anything special; our ersatz supply is low. There's a new chemical beef we've been saving, you can have that. I believe it's made of wood bark, but it's not at all bad on the tongue."

"Do you have a cigarette?" Tod said.

He proffered a brown cylinder. "Ersatz, too, I'm afraid; treated wool fibers. But it burns, anyway."

Tod lit it. The acrid smoke seared his throat and lungs; he coughed, and put it out.

"I'm sorry," the station manager said sadly. "It's the best we have. Everything, everything is ersatz; our cigarettes, our food, our drink . . . the war goes hard with us all."

Tod sighed and leaned back. When the woman came out of the doorway, bearing a tray, he sat up and his eyes were first for the food. He didn't even notice how lovely she was, how her ragged, near-transparent gown hugged her rounded breasts and hips. When she bent towards him, handing him a steaming bowl of strange-smelling broth, her blonde hair tumbled forward and brushed his cheek. He looked up and caught her eyes; they dropped shyly.

"You'll feel better after this," she said huskily, and made a movement with her body that dulled his appetite for food, created a different kind of hunger. It was four years since he had seen a woman like this. The war had taken them first, with bombs and radioactive dust, all the young women who remained behind while the men escaped to the comparative safety of battle. He dipped into the broth and found it vile, but he downed every drop. The wood-based beef was tough and chewy, but it was better than the canned rations he had grown accustomed to. The bread tasted of seaweed, but he slathered it with an oily rancid oleo and chewed great mouthfuls.

"I'm tired," he said at last. "I'd like to sleep."

"Yes, of course," the Peace Station manager said. "This way, soldier, come this way."

He followed him into a small windowless room, its only furniture a rusty metal cot. The sergeant dropped across its canvas mattress wearily, and the station manager closed the door quietly behind him. But Tod knew he wouldn't sleep, despite his sated stomach. His mind was too full, and his blood was streaming too fast through his veins, and the ache for the woman was strong in his body.

Then the door opened and she came in.

She said nothing. She came to the bed and sat beside him. She leaned over and kissed his mouth. "My name is Eleanora," she whispered, and he seized her roughly. "No, wait," she said, wriggling coyly out of his grasp. She got off the cot and went to the corner of the room.

He watched her slither out of her clothing. The blonde hair slipped as she pulled the dress over her head, and the curls hung at a crazy angle over her brow. She giggled, and put the wig back into position. Then she reached behind her and unhooked the brassiere; it dropped to the floor, revealing the flat slope of the hairy chest. She was about to remove the rest of her undergarments when the sergeant started to scream and run for the door; she reached out and held his arm and crooned words of love and pleading. He struck the creature with all the strength in his fist, and it fell to the floor, weeping bitterly, its skirt hoisted high on the muscular, hairy legs. The sergeant didn't pause to retrieve his armor or his weapons; he went out of the Peace Station into the smoky wasteland, where death awaited the unarmed and despairing.

## Afterword:

"Ersatz" is a rejected story. It was returned to me by an editor who simply said, "Don't like future-war stuff." He isn't the only one with the attitude. Several editors feel that future wars don't really constitute a "dangerous vision," and prefer their authors to steer clear of the subject. Atomic conflicts are "trite." Postatomic holocausts are "cliché." Armageddon is "overdone." In the world of fiction, at least, there is some opinion that our case of atomic jitters has been cured, and that readers would rather do without reminders of ruin and radiation. But the playing field of science fiction is the future, and the future has to be extrapolated from the ingredients of the present. And if you don't think that those ingredients of doom are still with us, your radio needs tubes, your prescription needs changing, and you have wax in your ears. Personally, I hope our authors, particularly the science fiction writers who have special privileges and talents, continue to barrage the world with fresh words on the subject, to make us continually afraid of what might be, and continually concerned with prevention and cure. To me, the most dangerous vision of all is the one that's rose-colored, and I'm grateful that the editor of this volume has spectacles of clear glass.

## Introduction to GO, GO, GO, SAID THE BIRD:

To know Sonya Dorman is to love her, if you'll pardon the mickey-mouse on my part. Also, it might bug her husband Jerry, who has very powerful forearms, and with whom Sonya Dorman raises and shows Akitas (a kind of Japanese baby pony of a dog that looks as if it should want to tear out your jugular but generally only wants to slobber drool all over you in slaphappy friendliness) at their Parnassus Kennels in Stony Point, New York, which has got to be the most strictured syntax since Victor Hugo did a twenty-two-page sentence in *The Hunchback of Notre Dame,* which is the shape this sentence is in.

She writes, in reply to a request for autobiographical goodies: "My auto. story is so preposterous I hardly know what to tell you. I did not have a classical education. I went to private schools (progressive) in New England, with the result that I have very little education but am just crummy with culture. I grew up around horses but can't afford them now, which is why I raise and show Akitas—the perceptive dog for sensitive people—in between writing poems and stories. Have been a cook, receptionist, riding instructor, flamenco dancer and married. I like speculative fiction because I believe art and science should be lovers, not enemies or adversaries."

None of the foregoing, of course, will prepare you for the genuine horror and immediacy of the story kindly little Sonya has written. A story that can only be compared, and then only remotely, with the work of the late Shirley Jackson. It also says nothing about the substantial reputation she has acquired in the last few years as a contributor to magazines as various as *Cavalier, Galaxy, Redbook,* Damon Knight's excellent *Orbit 1* anthology of originals, *The Saturday Evening What-everitis* and *The Magazine of Fantasy & Science Fiction.*

You can read Leigh Brackett or Vin Packer or C. L. Moore and think jeezus, the muscularity of the writing, and when you find out they are women, you say, jeezus, they write like men, with strength. Or you can read Zenna Henderson and think, jeezus, she writes just like a woman, all pastels. Or you can read Ayn Rand and think jeezus!

But that's another line of criticism.

But when you read Sonya Dorman you don't think of the muscularity of male writing. You read it as written by a woman, but there is no pretense. There is no attempt to emulate the particular strengths of male writing. It is purely female reasoning and attack, but it is *strong.* A special kind of tensile strength. It is what is meant by something turned out by a potent woman. It is a kind of writing *only* a woman can do. Carol Emshwiller, who is elsewhere in this book, has something like this strength, but most perfectly germinated is S. Dorman's development. It deals with reality in the unflinching way women *will* deal with it, when they are no longer shucking themselves or those watching. And I submit it is all the more teeth-clenching for the relentless truth it proffers.

This is a memorable story, and provides merely one more facet of the talent that writes under the drab by-line S. Dorman. It's a by-line you might watch for.

# ● GO, GO, GO, SAID THE BIRD

## by Sonya Dorman

> *Go, go, go, said the bird: human kind*
> *Cannot bear very much reality.*
>
> T. S. Eliot

Seizing the shriek in her stained teeth, she ran away, in spite of the voices crying after her from every crevice and glittering façade. Faces at the broken windows became a collage of grins as she ran, still holding the shriek between her teeth, determined not to let it escape. Her heels ached from pounding down the concrete highways, leaping over cracks and gaps in what used to be the most traveled road in the country.

"Oh no, no," she sobbed as she ran.

Bindweed grasped her ankles and she tore it loose with frantic fingers and ran on.

Choices appeared at the roadside, the entrances to burrows, underground shanties. Once some thing flew down and landed near her, beckoning, but she shut her teeth on the writhing shriek and looked straight ahead, down the length of the cracked roadbed, with its overgrown promenades at each side. She would continue on the obvious path, for fear of being lost beyond help.

"Here, chickie, here, chickie," called an old woman, beckoning, grinning, offering her a hidey-hole, perhaps at the expense of her hide, for she was still young, and succulent.

"No, no, no," she panted as she ran. For she was only thirty, and was unique, and to be eaten was all right, for people must exist, but to die was terrible. Plain and simple, she did not want to die. Not now, running for her life, and not ever, when her inevitable time came, but she was immediately concerned with now, and later on would have to take care of itself. Even as she ran, she began to tremble for later on, as if now weren't severe enough.

Think of it, she conversed in great gasps with herself, leaping over a crevasse where a southbound lane had split off from the main runway. Think of it, she insisted, scarcely having breath left but unable to control her mind, which was galloping faster than her weary legs.

I'm only thirty, I'm unique, there's no one in this world, this universe, who is me, with my memories:

### SNAPSHOT ⚹1

It had snowed. She stood in the sagging doorway, bundled up for winter in her fur leggings, and waited for Marn. They would hunt some animal for the stewpot. She saw things in negative, according to the moonlight: white trees, dark snow pockets. A feather seemed to breathe near her.

"Hey, come on," Marn said, taking her by the shoulder, and they drifted like two dark flakes onto the powdered grass, toward the woods. "We'll smoke it," Marn said confidently, and the water ran into her mouth. The smokehouse was hot and dark, a womb out of which the good things were trundled for distribution. It was her good luck to be headman's woman. Her children were less cold and hungry. Still, she had a greasy feeling, somewhere, when she heard the cries of other children. Marn said it was because she was young.

Her furs had lateral stripes like those of a tiger. She was a headman's daughter, and wife of a headman. She was tall, educated, privileged, and at length on the sleeping skins she would burn like fat in Marn's fire.

"Come on, rest a wee," a young girl called to her, but she put on a burst of speed, for the girl's teeth were shining like daggers, and as she went, she sobbed to herself (saving her real breath for the running), No, I can't die, I'm not ready to. Oh no, no, and it was the same sound she had made that winter when:

### SNAPSHOT ⚹2

The orchards had borne no fruit and the deer were famished. Back into the mountains withdrew all animals except those that were slaughtered where open water ran. By solstice there was no open water left. The fish slept at the bottom of the lake. Smelts would not rise to the cold, blue holes cut by the fishers. The leathers cracked and split on their feet, the chimney of the smokehouse stopped breathing, most of the fires were silent.

Into this famine was born her third child, with a bad foot. Holding him up in the air, Marn said, "He is not good," and snapped his neck.

"Oh no," she cried, holding her swollen abdomen with both palms and feeling the blood run down her thighs. "No, no," she cried to the headman, her man, for nine months in the hot dark, waiting, only to come to this? We are all going to come to this?

Marn handed the dead baby to the old woman, who took him out to the smokehouse. She lay in her blood and tears, crying, for the sizzled fat on the baby. Then the eyes dried, hers, and the baby's, in the fire smoke, and she felt it was all more than could be asked of any woman.

Where the broken concrete split into a fork, one side going south, one west, she would have paused, to determine her advantage, but at the crotch of the fork two youngsters arrived with knives.

She wanted more than anything to stop and rest. There were no alternatives offered her; either she must run and run, or she must stop and be killed. She couldn't prevent her mind from balancing one against the other, even while she knew it was no choice to make.

"Catch your breath," the youngsters jeered at her, and she chose the west road without thinking. One of them hurled a chancy knife after her, which split open the skin of her shoulder. Ignoring the pale blood which poured down, she went on. I can't die now, she thought. I'm not ever going to die. I am the only I in this world. She knew there was too much of her to be lost, much which could never be anyone else, and it was all precious and irreplaceable. Why didn't they realize how important it was for her to survive? She contained:

## SNAPSHOT #3

After the hard winter, the iron world split open and flowers came up. It was so astonishing. She passed the place where Marn's last bone was buried (only a headman would have his skull buried, intact, the jaws still hinged as if speaking to his community) and went down to the riverbank where the children were bathing. Her Neely stood tall this spring. In spite of food shortages over the winter, he had filled out. At least Daddyporridge had helped to nourish him, and give him this spring strength.

"Ah, spring," said a lazy voice. There was Tichy, under the willow. He might have been next headman, but was too lazy, and more likely destined for the smokehouse if he didn't mind himself. Yet several community members had discovered he was quicker and livelier than predicted, and Marn himself had died under Tichy's hammer.

"Oh yes, it certainly is spring," she said, walking very slowly, approaching him with great care. For if he had disposed so quickly of her man, and was idling here, watching her son, what next?

Tichy put out an unclenched hand toward her, and she was surprised to take it and find it so warm. Then another surprise followed, for he gave a quick, skillful pull, and she fell full length on his body.

"Oh no," she said, half smothered in his chin whiskers. "No, Tichy," for his teeth were at her and she didn't know, caught in his arms and legs, whether she was going to be loved or eaten or one at a time, or why.

"Hell yes," Tichy said. "After all, why not?"

He was reasonable. He let her have the best blanket in his hardwood hut, and when she couldn't find enough flavoring for the stew in the pot, he ate it anyway, without beating her.

Desperately holding the shriek, that siren to call them all out after her, between her teeth, she went on and on, breath rasping in her worn throat.

She would get back to Tichy. She was not going to die. There couldn't be anything in the world that really demanded her death, could there? Neely had taken the daughter of Gancho, a dark, low-browed girl with a peculiar sense of rightness. Not bad, she thought. Very good for Neely. I must get back before she has the baby. Who else will help her? She mustn't have the first one alone, only I can help her. I am needed, really, truly, I am needed very much. She'll be all alone, because:

## SNAPSHOT #4

Toward fall, when not even the warmest rains brought up another spear of wild asparagus, Neely and Tichy had a fight on the north slope of the dead orchard. Tichy gave Neely a blow with his hammer which knocked the young one over and might have done for him. Yet Neely got up on his feet once more, with his lips writhen back from his dark gums, showing his five teeth. Watching from the roof of the hardhut, she saw Neely rise up on his toes and split open Tichy's skull.

"That's my son!" she cried at the top of her lungs.

Then Neely brought home the dark girl, who snorted when he made love to her, and never got tired, and kept the floor swept. It was all right to have another woman in the hut, and especially a woman who understood the right and traditional. She was, after all, a headman's daughter, and not to be displaced.

"Gotcha!" yelled a woman, almost falling on her as she swerved along an embankment. She kicked the woman in the belly and heard the anguished groan as she ran on.

"No, you haven't," she gasped, not just to the groaning woman, but to all of them, to the world. What made her think she would get back to Tichy, who was dead, skull and all? The grandchildren would welcome her. They were good children, lean and hard as nuts, the likeness of Neely. They'd be glad to see her, who would dandle them, feed them special treats, stir the stewpot for the dark girl while she and Neely went hunting. If the deer ever came back she would make them a roast. The drought had been so bad all summer the snakes had come. First the copperheads, with their smell of garlic in the mating season, like brown worms on the stones of the old world. Then the rattlers, with their hysterical warning which came too late. Poisoned flesh was worse than no flesh. Moreover, a snake-bitten person was generally dismembered before the poison had a chance to spread.

Now as she ran she saw landmarks of home which echoed in her mind. The country became happily familiar, for she had hunted here, with Marn, and then with Tichy. She wasn't going to die, not this time, not now, she would of course continue, for she was she, unique, full, splendid.

"I gotcha!" someone screamed in her ear, and she felt the blow, shattering her, and lay stunned by the side of the road, her muscles still running. The snapshots began to flicker in her mind; seasons of the year, people she had known, her sons, her daughters, herself above all, the only one, the only I am I in all the world of stars.

"No, no," she moaned as the man raised the ax over her forehead.

"Oh yes, yes," he said, grinning with pleasure. Behind him the rest of the hunting party appeared. It was Neely with the dark girl, and two lean children.

"Neely," she screamed. "Save me. I'm your mother."

Neely grinned too, and said, "We're all hungry."

The ax fell, breaking her pictures into pieces, and they fell like snowflakes to the ground, where a little dust rose up and began to slowly settle. The small children began to squabble over the thumb bones.

## Afterword:

Perhaps I wrote the story because sometimes that's the way the world seems, or perhaps I hope that when my daughter's generation grows up it won't need or want to run for its life, or perhaps because, in the seventeenth century, Jeremy Taylor wrote: ". . . when it is enquired whether such a person be a good man or no, the meaning is not what does he believe, or what does he hope, but what he loves." Amen.

## Introduction to THE HAPPY BREED:

This is the second of two stories I bought from writers whose work I did not know. It came in, one of a pair, from Robert Mills, my own agent. The note accompanying it said simply, "You'll like the way he thinks." That, in the trade, is called the undersell. When I was younger, when I worked in a bookstore on Times Square, an area where the hard sell was invented (or at least perfected), I used the undersell—or "mush" as it is called—with only two items. The first was with a book called *The Alcoholic Woman*. It was ostensibly a volume of case histories intended for medical students, dealing with psychiatric aberrations attendant on female alcoholism. But there was one passage, on page 73, if I recall properly, that was extremely steamy. Something about lesbianism, rather graphically reported by the lushed female herself. When we would get in one of the moist-palmed salesmen from Mashed Potato Falls, Wyoming, in search of "lively reading" (because he couldn't pick up some bimbo in a bar for the evening's release), we would conduct him to the rear of the shop and hold up the book. It invariably fell open to page 73. "Here, read anywhere," we would say, jamming his nose, like a lump of silly putty, right onto that paragraph. His eyes would water. A pair of poached eggs. He would always buy the book. We stiffed them fourteen bucks for the thing. (I think it's in paperback now, for about half a buck, but them was in the days before Fanny Hill.) Page 73 held the only really "lively" action in the book. The rest was a jungle of electroshock therapy and stomach pumping. But the mush worked marvelously.

The other item was a twelve-inch Italian stiletto in the knife case. When a customer asked for a blade, I would unlock the case and pull out all that steel. I would hold it up, closed, to show it had no switch button on it. Then I would carelessly flip my wrist in a hard, downward movement, and the blade would snap open, quivering. It would usually be about two inches under the customer's tie knot. Eyes bulge. Poached eggs. Et cetera. Seven-buck sale. Every time.

The only times you can use the mush with any degree of assurance are the times you know for damn dead certain you've got a winning item, something that won't let go of them. Bob Mills was smart to use the mush on me. He knew he had a winner. John T. Sladek's "The Happy Breed" is a helluva story.

Sladek was born in Iowa on 12/15/37, and attended the University of Minnesota 19 years later as student ⌗449731. He studied mechanical engineering, then English literature. He left school to work (Social Security ⌗475–38–5320) as a technical writer, bar waiter and for the Great Northern Railway as switchman ⌗17728. He thumbed through Europe with passport ⌗D776097 until he found himself standing in a soup line at Saint-Severin in Paris. He worked as a draftsman in New York, then returned to Europe. He is now living in England, registered as Alien ⌗E538368. He has been published in *New Worlds*, *Escapade*, *Ellery Queen's Mystery Magazine* and elsewhere. He has just finished his first novel of speculative fiction, *The Reproductive System*.

The only mushy thing about Sladek or his story is his lousy head for figures. Carry on.

# • THE HAPPY BREED

## by John T. Sladek

A.D. *1987*

"I don't know," said James, lifting himself from the cushions scattered like bright leaves on the floor. "I can't say that I'm really, you know, *happy*. Gin or something phony?"

"Aw, man, don't give me decisions, give me drink," said Porter. He lay across the black, tufted chaise that he called James's "shrink couch."

"Gin it is, then." James thumbed a button, and a martini glass, frosty and edible-looking, slid into the wall niche and filled. Holding it by the stem, he passed it to Porter, then raised his shaggy brows at Marya.

*"Nada,"* she said. She was sprawled in a "chair," really a piece of sculpture, and one of her bare feet had reached out to touch Porter's leg.

James made himself a martini and looked at it with distaste. If you broke this glass, he thought, it would not leave any sharp edges to, say, cut your wrists on.

"What was I saying? Oh—I can't say I'm really *happy,* but then I'm not—uh—"

"Sad?" volunteered Marya, peering from under the brim of her deerstalker.

"Depressed. I'm not depressed. So I must be happy," he finished, and hid his confusion behind the glass. As he sipped, he looked her over, from her shapely calves to her ugly brown deerstalker. Last year at this time she'd been wearing a baseball cap, blue with gold piping. It was easy to remember it, for this year all the girls in the Village were wearing baseball caps. Marya Katyovna was always ahead of the pack, in her dress as well as in her paintings.

"How do you know you're happy?" she said. "Last week I thought I was happy too. I'd just finished my best work, and I tried to drown myself. The Machine pulled the drain. Then I was sad."

"Why did you try to kill yourself?" James asked, trying to keep her in focus.

"I had this idea that after a perfect work the artist should be destroyed. Dürer used to destroy the plates of his engravings after a few impressions."

"He did it for money," muttered Porter.

"All right then, like that architect in Arabia. After he created his *magnum opus*, the Sultan had him blinded, so he couldn't do any cheap copies. See what I mean? An artist's life is supposed to lead toward his masterpiece, not away from it."

Porter opened his eyes and said, "Exist! The end of life is life. Exist, man, that's all you gotta do."

"That sounds like cheap existentialism," she snarled, withdrawing her foot. "Porter, you are getting more and more like those damned Mussulmen."

Porter smiled angrily and closed his eyes.

It was time to change the subject.

"Have you heard the one about the Martian who thought he was an Earthman?" James said, using his pleasant-professional tone. "Well, he went to his psychiatrist—"

As he went on with the joke, he studied the two of them. Marya was no worry, even with her dramatic suicide attempts. But Porter was a mess.

O. Henry Porter was his full adopted name, after some minor earlier writer. Porter was a writer, too, or had been. Up to a few months ago, he'd been considered a genius—one of the few of the twentieth century.

Something had happened. Perhaps it was the general decline in reading. Perhaps there was an element of self-defeat in him. For whatever reason, Porter had become little more than a vegetable. Even when he spoke, it was in the cheapest clichés of the old "hip" of twenty years ago. And he spoke less and less.

Vaguely, James tied it in with the Machines. Porter had been exposed to the Therapeutic Environment Machines longer than most, and perhaps his genius was entangled with whatever they were curing. James had been too long away from his practice to guess how this was, but he recalled similar baby/bathwater cases.

" 'So that's why it glows in the dark,' " James finished. As he'd expected, Marya laughed, but Porter only forced a smile, over and above his usual smirk of mystical bliss.

"It's an old joke," James apologized.

"You are an old joke," Porter enunciated. "A headshrinker without no heads to shrink. What the hell do you do all day?"

"What's eating you?" said Marya to the ex-writer. "What brought you up from the depths?"

James fetched another drink from the wall niche. Before bringing it to his lips, he said, "I think I need some new friends."

As soon as they were gone, he regretted his boorishness. Yet somehow there seemed to be no reason for acting human any more. He was no longer a psychiatrist, and they were not his patients. Any little trauma he might have wreaked would be quickly repaired by their Machines. Even so, he'd have made an extra effort to side-step the neuroses of his friends if he were not able to dial FRIENDS and get a new set.

Only a few years had passed since the Machines began seeing to the happiness, health and continuation of the human race, but he could barely remember life before Them. In the dusty mirror of his unused memory there remained but a few clear spots. He recalled his work as a psychiatrist on the Therapeutic Environment tests.

He recalled the argument with Brody.

"Sure, they work on a few test cases. But so far these gadgets haven't done anything a qualified psychiatrist couldn't do," said James.

"Agreed," said his superior. "But they haven't made any mistakes, either. Doctor, these people are cured. Moreover, they're happy!"

Frank envy was written all over Dr. Brody's heavy face. James knew his superior was having trouble with his wife again.

"But, Doctor," James began, "these people are *not* being taught to deal with their environment. Their environment is learning to deal with them. That isn't medicine, it's spoon-feeding!

"When someone is depressed, he gets a dose of ritalin, bouncy tunes on the Muzik, and some dear friend drops in on him un-expectedly. If he is manic or violent, he gets thorazine, sweet music, melancholy stories on TV, and maybe a cool bath. If he's bored, he gets excitement; if he's frustrated, he gets something to break; if—"

Brody interrupted. "All right," he said. "Let me ask you the sixty-four-dollar question: could you do better?"

No one could do better. The vast complex of Therapeutic Environment Machines which grew up advanced medicine a millennium in a year. The government took control, to ensure that anyone of however modest means could have at his disposal the top specialists in the country, with all the latest data and techniques. In effect, these specialists were on duty round the clock in each patient's home, keeping him alive, healthy and reasonably happy.

Nor were they limited to treatment. The Machines had extensions clawing through the jungles of the world, spying on witch doctors and learning new medicines. Drug and dietary research became their domain, as did scientific farming and birth control. By 1985, when it became manifest that Machines could and did run everything better, and that nearly everyone in the country wanted to be a patient, the U. S. Government capitulated. Other nations followed suit.

By now, no one worked at all, so far as James knew. They had one and only one duty—to be happy.

And happy they were. One's happiness was guaranteed, by every relay and transistor from those that ran one's air conditioner right up to those in the chief complex of computers called MEDCENTRAL in Washington—or was it The Hague now? James had not read a newspaper since people had stopped killing each other, since the news had dwindled to weather and sports. In fact, he'd stopped reading the newspaper when the M.D. Employment Wanted ads began to appear.

There were no jobs, only Happiness Jobs—make-work invented by the Machines. In such a job, one could never find an insoluble or even difficult problem. One finished one's daily quota without tiring one's mind or body. Work was no longer work, it was therapy, and as such it was constantly rewarding.

Happiness, normality. James saw the personalities of all people drifting downward, like so many different intricate snowflakes falling at last into the common, shapeless mound.

"I'm drunk, that's all," he said aloud. "Alcohol's a depressant. Need another drink."

He lurched slightly as he crossed the room to the niche. The floor must have detected it, for instead of a martini his pressing the button drew blood from his thumb. In a second the wall had analyzed his blood and presented him with a glass of liquid. A sign lit: "Drink this down at once. Replace glass on sink."

He drained the pleasant-tasting liquid and at once felt drowsy and warm. Somehow he found his way to the bedroom, the door moving to accommodate him, and he fell into bed.

As soon as James R. Fairchild, AAAAGTR-RHO1A, was asleep, mechanisms went into action to save his life. That is, he was in no immediate danger, but MED 8 reported his decrease in life expectancy by .00005 years as a result of overindulgence, and MED 19 evaluated his behavior, recorded on magetic tape, as increasing his suicide index by a dangerous fifteen points. A diagnostic unit detached itself from the bathroom wall and careened into the bedroom, halting silently and precisely by his side. It drew more blood, checked pulse, temp, resp, heart and brain-wave pattern, and X-rayed his abdomen. Not instructed to go on to patellar reflexes, it packed up and zoomed away.

In the living room, a housekeeper buzzed about its work, destroying the orange cushions, the sculpture, the couch and the carpet. The walls took on an almost imperceptibly warmer tone. The new carpet matched them.

The furniture—chosen and delivered without the sleeping man's knowledge—was Queen Anne, enough to crowd the room. Its polyethylene wraps were left on while the room was disinfected.

In the kitchen, PHARMO 9 ordered and received a new supply of anti-depressants.

It was always the sound of a tractor that awoke Lloyd Young, and though he knew it was an artificial sound, it cheered him all the same. Almost made his day start right. He lay and listened to it awhile before opening his eyes.

Hell, the real tractors didn't make no sound at all. They worked in the night, burrowing along and plowing a field in one hour that would take a man twelve. Machines pumped strange new chemicals into the soil, and applied heat, to force two full crops of corn in one short Minnesota summer.

There wasn't much use being a farmer, but he'd always wanted to have a farm, and the Machines said you could have what you wanted. Lloyd was about the only man in these parts still living in the country by now, just him and twelve cows and a half-blind dog, Joe. There wasn't much to do, with Them running it all. He could go watch his cows being milked, or walk down with Joe to fetch the mail, or watch TV. But it was quiet and peaceful, the way he liked it.

Except for Them and Their pesky ways. They'd wanted to give Joe a new set of machine eyes, but Lloyd said no, if the good Lord wanted him to see, He'd never have blinded him. That was just the way he'd answered Them about the heart operation, too. Seemed almost like They didn't have enough to keep 'em busy or something. They was always worrying about him, him who took real good care of himself all through M.I.T. and twenty years of engineering.

When They'd automated, he'd been done out of a job, but he couldn't hold that against Them. If Machines was better engineers than him, well, shoot!

He opened his eyes and saw he'd be late for milking if he didn't look sharp. Without even thinking, he chose the baby-blue overalls with pink piping from his wardrobe, jammed a blue straw hat on his head, and loped out to the kitchen.

His pail was by the door. It was a silver one today—yesterday it had been gold. He decided he liked the silver better, for it made the milk look cool and white.

The kitchen door wouldn't budge, and Lloyd realized it meant for him to put on his shoes. Dammit, he'd of liked to go barefoot. Dammit, he would of.

He would of liked to do his own milking, too, but They had explained how dangerous it was. Why, you could get kicked in the head before you knew it! Reluctantly, the Machines allowed him to milk, each morning, one cow that had been tranquilized and had all its legs fastened in a steel frame.

He slipped on his comfortable blue brogans and picked up his pail again. This time the kitchen door opened easily, and as it did, a rooster crowed in the distance.

Yes, there had been a lot of doors closed in Lloyd's face. Enough to have made a bitter man of him, but for Them. He knew They could be trusted, even if They had done him out of his job in nineteen and seventy. For ten years he had just bummed around, trying to get factory work, anything. At the end of his rope, until They saved him.

In the barn, Betsy, his favorite Jersey, had been knocked out and shackled by the time he arrived. The Muzik played a bouncy, lighthearted tune, perfect for milking.

No, it wasn't Machines that did you dirt, he knew. It was people. People and animals, live things always trying to kick you in the head. As much as he liked Joe and Betsy, which was more than he liked people, he didn't really trust 'em.

You could trust Machines. They took good care of you. The only trouble with Them was—well, They *knew* so much. They were always so damned smart and busy, They made you feel kind of useless. Almost like you were standing in Their light.

It was altogether an enjoyable ten minutes, and when he stepped into the cool milkhouse to empty the pail into a receptacle that led God knew where, Lloyd had a strange impulse. He wanted to taste the warm milk, something he'd promised not to do. They had warned him about diseases, but he just felt too good to worry this morning. He tilted the silver pail to his lips—

And a bolt of lightning knocked it away, slamming him to the floor. At least it felt like a bolt of lightning. He tried to get up and found he couldn't move. A green mist began spraying from the ceiling. Now what the hell was that? he wondered, and drifted off to sleep in the puddle of spilled milk.

The first MED unit reported no superficial injuries. Lloyd C. Young, AAAAMTL-RHO1AB, was resting well, pulse high, resp normal. MED 8 disinfected the area thoroughly and destroyed all traces of the raw milk. While MED 1 pumped his stomach and swabbed nose, throat, esophagus and trachea, MED 8 cut away and destroyed all his clothing. An emergency heating unit warmed him until fresh clothing could be constructed. Despite the cushioned floor, the patient had broken a toe in falling. It was decided not to move him but to erect bed and traction on the spot. MED 19 recommended therapeutic punishment.

When Lloyd awoke, the television came to life, showing an amiable-looking man with white hair.

"You have my sympathy," the man said. "You have just survived what we call a 'Number One Killer Accident,' a bad fall in your home. Our Machines were in part responsible for this, in the course of saving your life from—" The man hesitated, while a sign flashed behind him: "BACTERIAL POISONING." Then he went on, "—by physically removing you from the danger. Since this was the only course open to us, your injury could not have been avoided.

*"Except by you.* Only *you* can save your life, finally." The man pointed at Lloyd. "Only *you* can make all of modern science worth while. And only *you* can help lower our shocking death toll. You will co-operate, won't you? Thank you." The screen went dark, and the set dispensed a pamphlet.

It was a complete account of his accident, and a warning about unpasteurized milk. He would be in bed for a week, it said, and urged him to make use of his telephone and FRIENDS.

Professor David Wattleigh sat in the tepid water of his swimming pool in Southern California and longed to swim. But it was forbidden. The gadgets had some way of knowing what he was doing, he supposed, for every time he immersed himself deeper than his chest, the motor of the resuscitator clattered a warning from poolside. It sounded like the snarl of a sheepdog. Or perhaps, he reflected, a Hound of Heaven, an anti-Mephistopheles, come to tempt him into virtue.

Wattleigh sat perfectly still for a moment, then reluctantly he heaved his plump pink body out of the water. Ah, it was no better than a bath. As he passed into the house, he cast a glance of contempt and loathing at the squat Machine.

It seemed as if anything he wished to do was forbidden. Since the day he'd been forced to abandon nineteenth-century English literature, the constraints of *mechanica* had tightened about Wattleigh, closing him off from his old pleasures one by one. Gone were his pipe and port, his lavish luncheons, his morning swim. In place of his library, there now existed a kind of vending machine that each day "vended" him two pages of thoroughly bowdlerized Dickens. Gay, colorful, witty passages they were, too, set in large Schoolbook type. They depressed him thoroughly.

Yet he had not given up entirely. He pronounced anathema upon the Machines in every letter he wrote to Delphinia, an imaginary lady of his aquaintance, and he feuded with the dining room about his luncheons.

If the dining room did not actually withhold food from him, it did its best to take away his appetite. At various times it had painted itself bilious yellow, played loud and raucous music, and flashed portraits of naked fat people upon its walls. Each day it had some new trick to play, and each day Wattleigh outwitted it.

Now he girded on his academic gown and entered the dining room, prepared for battle. Today, he saw, the room was upholstered in green velvet and lit by a gold chandelier. The dining table was heavy, solid oak, unfinished. There was not a particle of food upon it.

Instead there was a blonde, comely woman.

"Hello," she said, jumping down from the table. "Are you Professor David Wattleigh? I'm Helena Hershee, from New York. I got your name through FRIENDS, and I just had to look you up."

"I—how do you do?" he stammered. By way of answer, she unzipped her dress.

MED 19 approved what followed as tending to weaken that harmful delusion, "Delphinia." MED 8 projected a year of treatment, and found the resultant weight loss could add as much as .12 years to patient Wattleigh's life.

After Helena had gone to sleep the professor played a few games with the Ideal Chessplayer. Wattleigh had once belonged to a chess club, and he did not want to lose touch with the game entirely. And one did get rusty. He was amazed at how many times the Ideal Chessplayer had to actually cheat to let him win.

But win he did, game after game, and the Ideal Chessplayer each time would wag its plastic head from side to side and chuckle, "Well, you really got me that time, Wattleigh. Care for another?"

"No," said Wattleigh, finally disgusted. Obediently the Machine folded its board into its chest and rolled off somewhere.

Wattleigh sat at his desk and started a letter to Delphinia.

"My Darling Delphinia," scratched his old steel pen on the fine, laid paper. "Today a thought occurred to me while I was ~~swimming~~ bathing at Brighton. I have often told you, and as often complained of the behavior of my servant, M———. It, for I cannot bring myself to call it "he" or "she," has been most distressing about my writing to you, even to the point of blunting my pens and hiding my paper. I have not discharged it for this disgraceful show, for I am bound to it—yes, *bound* to it by a strange ~~and terrible secret~~ fate that makes me doubt at times which is master and which man. It reminds one of several old comedies in which, man and master having changed roles, and maid and mistress likewise, they meet. I mean, of course, in the works of"

Here the letter proper ended, for the professor could think of no name to fit. After writing, and lining out, "Dickens, Dryden, Dostoyevsky, Racine, Rousseau, Camus," and a dozen more, his inkwell ran dry. He knew it would be no use to inquire after more ink, for the Machine was dead set against this letter—

Looking out the window, he saw a bright pink- and yellow-striped ambulance. So, the doctor next door was going off to zombie-land, was he? Or, correctly, to the Hospital for the Asocial. In the East, they called them "Mussulmen"; here, "zombies," but it all came to the same thing: the living dead who needed no elaborate houses, games, ink. They needed only intravenous nourishment, and little of that. The drapes drew themselves, so Wattleigh knew the doctor was being carried out then. He finished his interrupted thought.

—and in any case he was wholly dissatisfied with this letter. He had not mentioned Helena, luncheon, his resuscitator which growled at him, and so much more. Volumes more, if only he had the ink to write, if only his memory would not fail him when he sat down to write, if only—

James stood with his elbow on the marble mantelpiece of Marya's apartment, surveying the other guests and sizing them up. There was a farmer from Minnesota, incredibly dull, who claimed to have once been an engineer, but who hardly knew what a slide rule was. There was Marya in the company of some muscular young man James disliked at sight, an ex-mathematician named Dewes or Clewes. Marya was about to play chess with a slightly plump Californian, while his girl, a pretty little blonde thing called Helena Hershee, stood by to kibitz.

"I'm practically a champion," explained Wattleigh, setting up the pieces. "So perhaps I ought give you a rook or two."

"If you like," said Marya. "I haven't played in years. About all I remember is the Fool's Mate."

James drifted over to Helena's side and watched the game.

"I'm James Fairchild," he said, and added almost defiantly, "M.D."

Helena's lips, too bright with lipstick, parted. "I've heard of you," she murmured. "You're the aggressive Dr. Fairchild who runs through friends so fast, aren't you?"

Marya's eyes came up from the game. Seemingly her eyes had no pupils, and James guessed she was full of ritalin. "James is not in the least aggressive," she said. "But he gets mad when you won't let him psychoanalyze you."

"Don't disturb the game," said Wattleigh. He put both elbows on the table in an attitude of concentration.

Helena had not heard Marya's remark. She had turned to watch the muscular mathematician lecture Lloyd.

"Hell yes. The Machines got to do all the bearing and raising of children. Otherwise, we'd have a population explosion, you get me? I mean, we'd run out of food—"

"You really pick 'em, Marya," said James. He gestured at the young man. "Whatever became of that 'writer'? Porter, was it? Christ, I can still hear him saying, 'Exist, man!'" James snorted.

Marya's head came up once more, and tears stood in her pupil-less eyes. "Porter went to the hospital. He's a Mussulman now," she said brightly. "I wish I could feel something for him, but They won't let me."

"—it's like Malthus' law, or somebody's law. Animals grow faster than vegetables," the mathematician went on, speaking to the farmer.

"Checkmate," said Marya, and bounced to her feet. "James, have you a Sugarsmoke? Chocolate?"

He produced a bright orange cigar. "Only bitter orange, I'm afraid. Ask the Machine."

"I'm afraid to ask it for anything, today," she said. "It keeps drugging me—James, Porter was put away a month ago, and I haven't been able to paint since. Do you think I'm crazy? The Machine thinks so."

"The Machine," he said, tearing off the end of the cigar with his teeth, "is always right."

Seeing Helena had wandered away to sit on Marya's Chinese sofa, he excused himself with a nod and followed.

Wattleigh still sat brooding over the Fool's Mate. "I don't understand. I just can't understand," he said.

"—it's like the hare and the tortoise," boomed the mathematician. Lloyd nodded solemnly. "The slow one can't ever catch up, see?"

Lloyd spoke. "Well, you got a point. You got a point. Only I thought the slow one was the winner."

"Oh." Dewes (or Clewes) lapsed into thoughtful silence.

Marya wandered about the room, touching faces as if she were a blind person looking for someone she knew.

"But I don't understand!" said Wattleigh.

"I do," James mumbled about the cigar. The bittersweet smoke was thick as liquid in his mouth. He understood, all right. He looked at them, one by one: an ex-mathematician now having trouble with the difference between arithmetic and geometry; an ex-engineer, ditto; a painter not allowed to paint, not even to feel; a former chess "champion" who could not play. And that left Helena Hershee, mistress to poor, dumb Wattleigh.

"Before the Machines—?" he began.

"—I was a judge," she said, running her fingertips over the back of his neck provocatively. "And you? What kind of doctor were you?"

A.D. *1988*

"It was during the Second World War," Jim Fairchild said. He lay on his back on the long, tiger-striped sofa, with a copy of *Hot Rod Komiks* over his eyes.

"I thought it only started in the sixties," said Marya.

"Yeah, but the *name* 'Mussulman'—that started in the Nazi death camps. There were some people in them who couldn't—you know—get with it. They stopped eating and seeing and hearing. Everybody called them 'Mussulmen,' because they seemed like Moslems, mystics . . ."

His voice trailed off, for he was thinking of the Second World War. The good old days, when a man made his own rules. No Machines to tell you what to do.

He had been living with Marya for several months now. She was his girl, just as the other Marya, in *Hot Rod Komiks,* was the girl of the other Jim, Jim (Hell-on-Wheels) White. It was a funny thing about Komiks. They were real life, and at the same time they were better than life.

Marya—his Marya—was no intellectual. She didn't like to read and think, like Jim, but that was okay, because men were supposed to do all the reading and thinking and fighting and killing. Marya sat in a lavender bucket seat in the corner, drawing with her crayons. Easing his lanky, lean body up off the sofa, Jim walked around behind her and looked at the sketch.

"Her nose is crooked," he said.

"That doesn't matter, silly. This is a fashion design. It's only the dress that counts."

"Well, how come she's got yellow hair? People don't have yellow hair."

"Helena Hershee has."

"No, she hasn't!"

"She has so!"

"No, it ain't yellow, it's—it ain't yellow."

Then they both paused, because Muzik was playing their favorite song. Each had a favorite of his own—Jim's was "Blap," and Marya's was "Yes, I Know I Rilly Care for You"—but they had one favorite together. Called "Kustomized Tragedy," it was one of the songs in which the Muzik imitated their voices, singing close harmony:

> *Jim Gunn had a neat little kustom job,*
> *And Marya was his girl.*
> *They loved each other with a love so true,*
> *The truest in the worl'.*
> *But Jim weren't allowed to drive his kar,*
> *And Marya could not see;*
> *Kust'mized Traju-dee-ee-ee.*

The song went on to articulate how Jim Gunn wanted more than anything in the worl' to buy an eye operation for his girl, who wished to admire his kustom kar. So he drove to a store and held it up, but someone recognized his kar. The police shot him, but:

> He kissed his Marya one last time;
> The policeman shot her too.
> But she said, "I can see your kustom, Jim!
> It's pretty gold and bloo!"
> He smiled and died embracing her,
> Happy that she could see.
> Kust'mized Traju-dee.

Of course, in real life, Marya could see very well, Jim had no kar, and there were no policemen. But it was true for them, nevertheless. In some sense they could not express, they felt their love was a tragedy.

Knowing Jim felt lonesome and bloo, Marya walked over and kissed his ear. She lay down beside him, and at once they were asleep.

MEDCENTRAL's audit showed a population of 250,000,000 in NORTHAMER, stabilized. Other than a few incubator failures, and one vat of accidentally infected embryos, progress was as predicted, with birth and death rates equal. The norm had shifted once more toward the asocial, and UTERINE CONTROL showed 90.2 per cent adult admissions at both major hospitals.

Trenchant abnormals were being regressed through adolescence, there being no other completely satisfactory method of normalizing them without shock therapy, with its attendant contraindications.

Lloyd pulled his pocket watch from the bib of his plaid overalls. The hands of Chicken Licken pointed straight up, meaning there was just time to fetch the mail before Farm Kartoons on TV. On Impulse, Lloyd popped the watch into his mouth and chewed. It was delicious, but it gave him little pleasure. Everything was too easy, too soft. He wanted exciting things to happen to him, like the time on Farm

Kartoons when Black Angus tried to kill the hero, Lloyd White, by breaking up his Machine, and Lloyd White had stabbed him with a pitchfork syringe and sent him off to the hospital.

Mechanical Joe, knowing it was time to fetch the mail, came running out of the house. He wagged his tail and whined impatiently. It didn't make any difference that he wasn't a real dog, Lloyd thought as they strolled toward the mailbox. Joe still liked it when you scratched his ears. You could tell, just by the look in his eyes. He was livelier and a lot more fun than the first Joe.

Lloyd paused a moment, remembering how sad he'd been when Joe died. It was a pleasantly melancholy thought, but now mechanical Joe was dancing around him and barking anxiously. They continued.

The mailbox was chock-full of mail. There was a new komik, called *Lloyd Farmer and Joe,* and a whole big box of new toys.

Yet later, when Lloyd had read the komik and watched Farm Kartoon and played awhile with his building set, he still felt somehow heavy, depressed. It was no good being alone all the time, he decided. Maybe he should go to New York and see Jim and Marya. Maybe the Machines there were different, not so bossy.

For the first time another, stranger thought came to him. Maybe he should go *live* in New York.

> DEAR DELPHINIA, [Dave printed.] THIS IS GOING TO BE MY LAST LETTER TO YOU, AS I DONT LOVE YOU ANY MORE. I KNOW NOW WHAT HAS BEEN MAKING ME FEEL BAD, AND IT IS YOU. YOU ARE REALLY MY MASHINE, ARENT YOU HA HA I'LL BET YOU DIDNT THINK I NEW.
>
> NOW I LOVE HELENA MORE THAN YOU AND WE ARE GOING AWAY TO NEW YORK AND SEE LOTS OF FRIENDS AND GO TO LOTS OF PARTYS AND HAVE LOTS OF FUN AND I DONT CARE IF I DONT SEE YOU NO MORE.
>
> LOVE, AND BEST OF LUCK TO A SWELL KID,
>
> DAVE W.

After an earthquake destroyed seventeen million occupants of the Western hospital, MEDCENTRAL ordered the rest moved at once to the East. All abnormals not living near the East hospital were also persuaded to evacuate to New York. Persuasion was as follows:

Gradually, humidity and pressure were increased to .9 discomfort while, subliminally, pictures of New York were flashed on all surfaces around each patient.

Dave and Helena had come by subway from L.A., and they were tired and cross. The subway trip itself took only two or three hours, but they had spent an additional hour in the taxi to Jim's and Marya's.

"It's an electric taxi," Dave explained, "and it only goes about a mile an hour. I'll sure never make that trip again."

"I'm glad you came," said Marya. "We've been feeling terrible lonesome and bloo."

"Yes," Jim added, "and I got an idea. We can form a club, see, against the Machines. I got it all figured out. We—"

"Babay, tell them about the zombies—I mean, the Mussulmen," said Helena.

Dave spoke with an excited, wild look about him. "Jeez, yeah, they had about a million cars of them on the train, all packed in glass bottles. I wasn't sure what the hell they were at first, see, so I went up and looked at one. It was a skinny, hairless man, all folded up in a bottle inside another bottle. Weird-looking."

In honor of their arrival, the Muzik played the favorite songs of all four: "Zonk," "Yes, I Know I Rilly Care for You," "Blap," and "That's My Babay," while the walls went transparent for a moment, showing a breath-taking view of the gold towers of New York. Lloyd, who spoke to no one, sat in the corner keeping time to the music. He had no favorite song.

"I want to call this the Jim Fairchild Club," said Jim. "The purpose of this here club is to get rid of the Machines. Kick 'em out!"

Marya and Dave sat down to a game of chess.

"I know how we can do it, too," Jim went on. "Here's my plan: Who put the Machines in, in the first place? The U. S. Government. Well, there ain't any U. S. Government any more. So the Machines are illegal. Right?"

"Right," said Helena. Lloyd continued to tap his foot, though no Muzik was playing.

"They're outlaws," said Jim. "We oughta kill them!"

"But how?" asked Helena.

"I ain't got all the details worked out yet. Give me time. Because, you know, the Machines done us wrong."

"How's that?" asked Lloyd, as if from far away.

"We all had good jobs, and we were smart. A long time ago. Now we're all getting dumb. You know?"

"That's right," Helena agreed. She opened a tiny bottle and began painting her toenails.

"I think," said Jim, glaring about him, "the Machines are trying to make us all into Mussulmen. Any of you want to get stuffed into a bottle? Huh?"

"A bottle inside a bottle," Dave corrected, without looking up from his game.

Jim continued, "I think the Machines are drugging us into Mussulmen. Or else they got some kind of ray, maybe, that makes us stupider. An X ray, maybe."

"We gotta do something," said Helena, admiring her foot.

Marya and Dave began to quarrel about how the pawn moves. Lloyd continued to tap his foot, marking time.

A.D. *1989*

Jimmy had a good idea, but nobody wanted to listen. He remembered, once when he was an itsy boy, a Egg Machine that tooked the eggs out of their shells and putted them into plastic—things. It was funny, the way the Machine did that. Jimmy didn't know why it was so funny, but he laughed and laughed, just thinking about it. Silly, silly, silly eggs.

Mary had a idea, a real good one. Only she didn't know how to say it so she got a crayon and drew a great Big! picture of the Machines: Mommy Machine and Daddy Machine and all the little Tiny Tot Machines.

Loy-Loy was talking. He was building a block house. "Now I'm putting the door," he said. "Now I'm putting the lit-tle window. Now the—why is the window littler than the house? I don't know. This is the chimney and this is the stee-ple and open the door and where's all the peo-ple? I don't know."

Helena had a wooden hammer, and she was driving all the pegs. Bang! Bang! Bang! "One, two, three!" she said. "Banga-banga-bang!"

Davie had the chessmen out, lined up in rows, two by two. He wanted to line them all up three by three, only somehow he couldn't. It made him mad and he began to cry.

Then one of the Machines came and stuck something in his mouth, and everybody else wanted one and somebody was screaming and more Machines came and . . .

The coded message came to MEDCENTRAL. The last five abnormals had been cured, and all physical and mental functions reduced to the norm. All pertinent data on them were switched over to UTERINE SUPPLY, which clocked them in at 400 hrs GMT, day 1, yr 1989. MEDCENTRAL agreed on the time check, then switched itself off.

## Afterword:

"The Happy Breed" demonstrates one version of what I like to think of as the Horrible Utopia. Ionesco's play, *The Bald Soprano,* had already shown a world without evil. In a sense, this was my model; I tried to show a world without pain. In both instances, the same phenomena obtain: without evil or pain, preference and choice are meaningless; personality blurs; figures merge with their backgrounds, and thinking becomes superfluous and disappears. I believe these are the inevitable results of achieving Utopia, if we make the mistake of assuming that Utopia equals perfect happiness. There is, after all, a pleasure center in everyone's head. Plant an electrode there, and presumably we could be constantly, perfectly happy on a dime's worth of electricity a day.

If not of happiness, then, of what material do we construct our Utopia? The avoidance of pain, perhaps? Perfect security from disease, accident, natural disaster? We gain these only at the cost of contact with our environment—ultimately at the cost of our humanity. We become "etherized," in both of Eliot's senses of the word: numb and unreal.

To some, this story might seem itself unreal and hypothetical. I can only point out that dozens of electronic firms are now inventing and developing new diagnostic equipment; in a short time physicians will depend almost entirely upon machines for accurate diagnoses. There is no reason why it must stop there, or at any point short of mechanical doctors.

If we elect to build machines to heal us, we must be certain we know what power we are giving them and what it is we ask in return. In "The Happy Breed" the agency through which the anesthetic world comes to be is a kind of genie, the Slave of the Pushbutton. It is a peculiarly literal-minded genie, and it will give us *exactly* what we ask, no more and no less. Norbert Wiener noticed the similarity between the behavior of literal-minded machines and that of magical agents in fairy tales, myths, ghost stories and even modern jokes.

Semele thought she wanted Jove to make love to her exactly as he would to a goddess—but it turned out to be with lightning. The sorcerer's apprentice thought he'd give up his work to a magical helper. Wells wrote of a rather dull-witted clerk who stopped the rotation of the earth suddenly. At one end of the spectrum are horror stories like "The Dancing Partner" or "The Monkey's Paw," and at the other is Lennie Bruce's joke about the druggist who left a genie to mind his store. Said the genie's first customer, "Make me a chocolate malted."

If we decide we really want health, security, freedom from pain, we must be willing to exchange our individuality for it. The use of any tool implies a loss of freedom, as Freud pointed out in *Civilization and Its Discontents*. When man started using a hand ax he lost the freedom to climb or walk on four limbs, but more important, he lost the freedom not to use the hand ax. We have now lost the freedom to do without computers, and it is no longer a question of giving them power over us, but of how much power, of what kind, and of how fast we turn it over to them.

A professor at the University of Minnesota once told me of a term when he was late in making up grades. The department secretary kept calling him, asking if he were ready to turn in his grades yet. Finally a clerk from administration called him. On learning the grades were still not ready, the clerk said exasperatedly, "But, Professor, the machines are waiting!"

They are indeed.

## Introduction to ENCOUNTER WITH A HICK:

The first time I saw Jonathan Brand, he was lounging on a grassy knoll in Milford, Pennsylvania, wearing hiking boots on his feet, a knapsack on his back, a six-blade tracker's knife on his belt and a badge sewn on his blue shirt indicating he was a member of the American Forestry Association, or somesuch. He was lying there propped on his elbows, a blade of grass in his mouth, watching half a dozen of the older, more sophisticated giants of the science fiction field dousing each other with beer from quart bottles on the lawn of Damon Knight's home. Jonathan Brand was amused.

Kindness forbids my explaining why Jim Blish, Ted Thomas, Damon and Gordy Dickson were cavorting in such an unseemly manner. Kindness and a suspicion that it is this innocence of childhood or nature that supplies the *élan* for their excellent writings, God forbid.

Jon was in Milford for the 11th Annual Science Fiction Writers Conference, a week of discussions, seminars and workshops in which members of the craft exchanged ideas, market information and wet shirts in the pursuance of greater facility in their chosen profession.

He made quite an impression on attendees. His ready wit, his familiarity with the genre, and most of all the work he submitted for consideration in the workshops made him a new voice to be listened to. The story he had put in for comment—an act very close to hara-kiri—was ready by all the writers present, and the criticism was stiff. It always is. The naked ids and exposed predilections of a blue-ribbon gathering of fantasists is not guaranteed to balm one's creative soul or convince him he should be anything other than a hod carrier. But Jon and his story came off rather well. The praise was honest and with very few reservations. So well off did he appear that I asked Jon if I might buy the story for this anthology. He did a few minor editing flourishes, and the yarn appears here.

Jonathan Brand admits he has been a graduate student for altogether too long. Carnegie Tech. He lives alone, walks to school each weekday in semester, hibernates in the summer, has no telephone, cherishes trolley cars, hates to talk or listen, likes to read and write, refuses to state his age, condition of marital servitude, background or any other damned thing that would make this introduction something more meaningful than an announcement that Jonathan Brand has written a very funny, slightly whacky, irreverent and definitely dangerous story for this book.

# ● ENCOUNTER WITH A HICK

## by Jonathan Brand

How would I know what made the simple old hayseed flip his lid? He was old. He was simple. He was the final in hayseeds. Wouldn't you flip your lid? But nevertheless I will support my local police, I will testify to the conversation which preceded the dissolution of the cuddly patriarch. Who knows, *post hoc, ergo propter hoc?*

All right, all right, I *am* being serious. You think I'm not serious, you can look at my credit cards and diplomas. I got a Bachelor's, I got a Master's, I got about ten Doctorates, my dad operates a lot of planets, they gotta lotta universities. Which is incidentally how I came to attend this distinctly hip conference taking place right here in your picturesque old planet, namely the Colloquium of the Universe Academy of Sciences, North-West-Up Octant.

Myself, I would not say I was strictly an academic. I am more in the improvisation and drugs experience, but I am warm toward the academic milieu. Those eggs speak, I tell you, Your Honor, Officer, Sire, etc., it is all one sentence, they do not let themselves be trammeled, no punctuation or meaning, but oh the rhythm and structure and balance. Now those things constitute also judo, not to mention improvisation, not to mention sex, which are all key items in the life stream.

What do you mean—"stick to the point"? I am striving to give you the conspectus or overview of this egghead scene in which the whole interpersonal encounter was embedded, I mean me and my girl Patsy and this aged hick with his beard which is 100% human hair, I and she and he and it all having drinks in the Continuum Bar in the Trans-Port Hotel, which is where the above Colloquium is being held. Yes, I know you know, Your Reverence, Squire, and/or Justice of the Peace.

Now you have the need to know with respect to Patsy? The bit with Patsy is she has this father who is primarily a rich man, also he is in the construction business like my own dad, the two sires are anxious to unite the dynasties, they yearn to cuddle, dandle, and burp a curly-headed heir, so they send Patsy and me on this cruise together, it is all a transparent plot, our acquaintance is to ripen and mellow into love. The chick comes before the egg, ha-ha. Do not sweat it, Sheriff, Lawman, Gunslinger, do not wave and shake the long arm of the law, I am coming to the point. I shall be considerably grateful if and when *you* do not flip your noodle, one per day is sufficiently superfluous for me.

Okay, if you are truly all right, stop now twitching and I will proceed to recall at length and depth the precise conversation subsequent to which the loony old hayseed went critical, namely lay down upon the rug and chewed it, simultaneously foaming and weeping. As a start, he comes up to me in the bar, he introduces himself, I have a friendly face, I do not rebuff the humble. How would I remember the old peasant's name? It was Doctor something. This old guy, it seems he's the intellectual flower of his planet, absolutely the topmost blossom, I mean the apex in theology, music, surgery, politics, maybe improvisation and sex as well, I forget. He gives me the picture his planet is strictly bluegrass, I mean a net exporter of glass beads and rush mats, but all the same they pool their credits, the womenfolk melt down their golden earrings, they mail this old guy to the Colloquium. Heed me, I do not dump upon this laudable desire, namely for Podunk University to send a professor to the Colloquium, I dare say it does a lot for Podunk U.

So we were tossing the ball, we were pretty friendly, I am paying and seeing how he was partly in theology and I am not aloof from the folk scene I am saying, "Well, fill me in, move me with mingled pity and terror, recount to me one of your doubtless beautiful old myths." Now this is fine with the grizzled old musician/priest/surgeon he launches into a Creation Myth, than which I may say (having taken not a few courses in the past, courses in "The Past," ha-ha), than which there is nothing finer. But he is halfway through the noble recital, hallowed by centuries, handed down orally by dynasties of blind bards, the whole bit, when I suddenly receive the distinct impression that his planet is one of those built by my father's firm!

So this is quite a coincidence, and not stopping to think in my youthful enthusiasm, I pull out a pamphlet advertising my daddy's company which pioneered the Accelerated Photo-Synthetic Evolution process. To be sufficiently brief, this is a process for creating habitable planets from anything which swings in that right temperature zone where anthropoid types can walk around without any clothes on, which is a key experience, as I see it, I mean like drugs and sex and improvisation even. The actual process of creation is basically geared to planetary rotation, you have to get it spinning first, you work always on the sunside, seeing as the process requires two or three billion billion billion ergs, which is a measure of energy. There's really six complete phases, so you get the whole thing finished in time for the weekend, going once around the planet on each rotation, it's quite accelerated. Are you still with me? Actually *I* am not altogether with me, I have to confess the details are hazy to me, but it's all in our brochure. The first day you bring in your equipment, the second day you fix the rotation, the third day you consolidate the foundation, the fourth day you truck in soil and water and germ plasm, here's the gimmick now, you operate this Accelerated Photo-Synthetic Evolution deal, you breed accelerated cycles of life forms on the fourth day it's land plants, you stabilize the weather by the fifth day, on the sixth day you seed the oceans and fix up the animals.

No shit, it's an interesting routine, cheap and quick, here's the firm's card in case you ever want a job done, nothing to it, it leaves some pretty loamy foamy topsoil (which we throw in free), the only mess is from time to time you dig up by-products of this Accelerated Evolution, bits of petrified bone and stuff, but that's no sweat. Anyway, on the sixth day you're ready for colonization, you bring in a guy and a chick, there's a bit of a ceremony and they're on their own. And they get to work with the fecundity bit, I mean it springs eternal in the human breast.

Okay, okay, do not nag. Where was I? Yes, when I get through retailing this to the hoary old cracker-barrel philosopher/priest/surgeon he is conspicuously not so pleased as I hope. I suppose I had noticeably trampled on his priceless cultural heritage a bit, though I meant no harm, I trespassed anyways. To be frank, the salted old peanut is now definitely enraged, I mean much madder than you are now, he is purple in the face and quivering from top to bottom. Also, what with seven or eight steins of kumiss and V8 inside him which I have paid for, this pensive wrinkled doctor/philosopher/bard/okie is approximately as high as an elephant's eye. I seem to see on his forehead the blinking sign which says ON THE AIR, and he stands up and points a gnarled old calloused finger and he says—and I quote his noble old sincere approach:

"Gird up thy loins now like a man. I will demand of thee and declare thou unto me." (You see I aim to reproduce his colorful dead language right down to its woolen jerkin. I should have taken notes. What a thesis.) "By whom were all things created, that are in heaven? All the stars of light, the heavens of heavens, and the waters that be above the heavens—who commanded, and they were created? Who set the stars in the firmament of heaven, to give light over the earth? He that darkeneth counsel, let him answer it."

These words were inspiringly composed and declaimed (the old cornball lacked nothing in those departments, especially with that beard), but they were incidentally his last, for it was soon after this that the herbivore cuts his mustard.

Now relax, Gendarme, Polizei, Beefeater, do not fret, I am hiding not one jot and/or tittle, I truly do not know what precise thing bugged him, all I can do is relate what was the last thing I did before his spectacular and regrettable collapse.

"A very good and cogent question, Doc baby, which I am glad you raised," I say, and I turn away from the decrepit politician/priest/surgeon/subsistence-farmer and I begin to rummage in Patsy's little old bottomless purse which is lying on the bar.

"What are you seeking, you bustard?" whoops Patsy, successfully attempting to contuse my ankle with her left shoe.

Now I think I was already recounting how her daddy has money like other folk have troubles, namely in considerable amounts. My own dad is rich, he is in the subdivision business, he owns more than two hundred galaxies, he is chairman of the local Kiwanis, he is solid, but Patsy's dad, he is bigger than all of us, he operates this Continuous Creation process, which is his very own patented and money-spinning property, oh, a genuine something-for-nothing proposition. And now I am in a position to tell you word for word what all I said before the old wowser puts on his supreme performance, when he drums his heels, he topples from the bar stool, he immolates himself upon the floor in an armageddon of cocktail sticks.

I turn to Patsy, my hot cross bun, and I say: "Peace, eskimo pie. Let me look in your purse. Did you not hear our new friend ask to see a picture of your dad?"

## Afterword:

I believe in Jesus, Thoreau, and Mao Tse-tung—and not in God. However, I try to give as much serious thought to the last as to the first three. My story deals with the obvious fallacy in the argument from first cause, which assumes a connection between the creator of the universe and the source of ethics and salvation. To think that the creator of the universe is necessarily the moral superior of man is as naïve as to think that the builder of skyscrapers is greater than the carpenter just because his product is larger.

Back to earth: I must thank the Milford Science Fiction Writers Conference of 1966, but for which this story would not be where it is or quite what it is.

## Introduction to FROM THE GOVERNMENT PRINTING OFFICE:

No one who has encountered them will soon forget Kris Neville's marvelous stories, "Bettyann" or "Special Delivery." They were written over fifteen years ago, and even today continue to turn up in anthologies of the best-in-genre. Kris Neville is a hearty man with an unplaceable Southern accent. He says it's a Missouri accent, but damned if it don't sound Texas. Kris Neville is what the writers of book-jacket copy call a "hard-living man." That means he milks every minute. He talks endlessly on topics without number, can drink under the table any three science fiction writers going (with the possible exception of George O. Smith), and manages to come up with fresh angles on themes generally considered well plowed. One such is the story that follows, submitted upon this editor's comment that DANGEROUS VISIONS was lacking a good story on the theme of education.

Kris Neville (has there ever been a more perfect name for a writer? I mean, if you had your choice of being known as Bernard Malamud or

Louis Auchincloss, wouldn't *you* pick Kris Neville?) was born in Carthage, Missouri, in 1925, served in the U. S. Army during World War II, and received his degree in English from UCLA in 1950. His first science fiction story was published in 1949 ("The Hand from the Stars" in *Super Science Stories*), and since then he has sold some fifty-odd others. Some were *very* odd indeed.

For eleven years Kris was involved with research and development of epoxy resins. This is what is known in the trade as stick-to-it-iveness. Sorry.

In collaboration with Henry Lee, he has published two books on the subject from McGraw-Hill, one of which (selling for $32.50 in case you are in need) is a massive volume intended to be the definitive treatment of the subject. Additionally, with Drs. Lee and Stauffey, he has written a volume on new thermoplastic high polymers, to be published this year. He has been contributor to a number of symposiums and encyclopedias, and holds "a patent which has covered business into seven figures." His last industrial job was as program manager on research and development contracts, one of the more interesting involving work for the National Institutes of Health in the use of plastic materials for dental applications.

Kris is the author of one science fiction novel, *The Unearth People,* and since early in 1966 he has been a full-time writer. He lives in Los Angeles with wife and children.

# ● FROM THE GOVERNMENT PRINTING OFFICE

## by Kris Neville

At three and a half, it's logical for adults to wear eyeglasses to keep their eyeballs warm. Cold eyeballs is an adult affliction no different from many other adult afflictions equally as incomprehensible.

Adults talk always too loudly. A sonic boom for a whisper. Little ears hear the movement of air molecules in the quiet night, when listening for something else to happen.

Adults live too fast. What passes for thinking is habit. Press a button. Listen. Press a button. Listen. Open a drawer. One of the big bastards does it without thinking, doesn't really care what's in there, is looking for a special thing, and he closes the drawer and hasn't really seen anything in it. Tiny hands, eyes peering over the rim, sees a strange little world in the drawer. There isn't enough time made to know the contents. Stop the press. Here is a thing that looks like a key. See how big it is. Wow! What sort of wild surface bug goes with it? Enormous! Nobody has ever seen one that big. Where do they keep it?

Now here's something: a thing for which there is no conceivable use at all. It has moving parts but it doesn't do anything. There's no place to plug it in. I'll bet rabbits made it. Chickens make eggs.

"Get out of that drawer! Let that alone!"

*There she is.* I knew it. Too good to last. What was I hurting? Ask what that is, they just kiss the problem off. Push the button. Listen. Tell you nonsense. Maybe she'll go away. Now what's this thing? Looks interesting. What do you suppose—

"Get *out* of there!"

Aw, hell! I'll try to reason with her. Maybe get a conversation going.

"Candy in here."

"There's no candy in there."

How can she possibly know that? No candy in there, indeed! My God, look at all the things there are in there. How can she possibly tell there's no candy: she hasn't even looked. It's not even her drawer. It's Poppa's. "What's this for?"

"It's not candy. Put it down."

No luck. Sometimes, though, you can get to them by talking about candy. Most times, like now, they don't think at all. I'll cry. Start quiet: it may take a long time. First a little blob, blob, waa. Makes you feel bad, but don't get carried away, you burn out too soon. May have to keep it up for a long time, start slow and easy. She'll wait to see how serious I am. It's easy if you don't rush into it. Get going good, the body takes over: close your eyes and listen. Lovely sounds. Like singing. Good voice. Lots of variety, up and down. I could go on like this all day.

At three and a half, you've been here forever, and it all hasn't been good, not by a damn sight.

Everything has always been too big. Heavy, awkward to handle. How tired you get! All the wrong size. They get big and dumb and you can't talk to them about anything important. Who cares how they make babies? But you want to watch, and they won't let you. You lay awake and wait and wait and wait while they whisper, loud as sonic booms, "Is he asleep?" Close your eyes and wait some more. Maybe they're afraid I'll laugh at them: they must look silly.

Listen, though, you get smart. You just try not to. They have this special book. Sometimes, though, it's not the book: it's like at the drawer, just now. They're not malicious, just dumb, some of the time.

The damned awful things they do in this book conspiracy, though. The time I had with toilet training; they were going to flush me down the toilet. I thought they would. I really believe they would have. I was scared shitless. But something went wrong, lucky for me, and they didn't, after all. I ought to be grateful to them, I guess, I'm still here. I still don't know why they didn't. They were going to.

There were worse things. The tricks they play on me at night. You wouldn't believe them. I once got so I couldn't sleep at all, just waiting in the night. I had to sleep in the daytime. It's better now. I get more sleep. I asked the other kids at playground; we talk. We make just a few words mean a lot. We know more words than we can use right, so what words we have have to work hard for us. Their parents have special books too.

I'm always afraid they'll do something to my penis. I break out in a sweat when I think about that. That's why I'm so damned afraid at night. One of the reasons.

I used to try to make friends with them, before I got so old. I tried to go get in bed with them, once. They'd fixed up this alarm system; or it came with the book or was part of this course the mailman brings, I think. Oh, it went off with all sorts of sounds and lights flashing, and weird feelings. There I was, trapped, exposed alone on the floor, halfway to their bed, and I just peed all over the carpet.

"Oh, Christ! It's two o'clock in the morning!" That's what he said. Here I was, as scared as anything, standing there, blinking my eyes, and he makes a stupid statement like that.

"Make him feel guilty," she said. "That's what the book says."

"You're a filthy shit!" he screamed at me.

I guess I am. There must be some reason they want to cut my penis off. I heard them say, once, that all your real education takes place before you're four years old: by then your character is established. I think maybe I'll make it. It's still such a long ways off, so long, so long. But maybe I really will make it, even if I'm a nervous wreck.

So I don't feel so good about myself. It could be worse.

There is a place called India. You see it on the newscasts. I was afraid they'd send me there. I don't know why I thought that, but I did. It kept me awake too. I went hungry one day, wouldn't eat at all, just to see if I could take it. I couldn't. They can't either. They die. Several million are starving to death right now. I don't know exactly how many that is. It's more than ten.

But apparently they never intended to send me to India.

Or China.

Or a place called South America.

And people don't starve to death where I live. Except in the slums, and that's different. Whatever the slums are. So at least I'm spared that. It could be worse.

On the newscasts, you see big machines making big piles of people and pee-peeing on them and burning them up. "Why they burn those people, Momma?"

"Hush! It's too awful. They just breed like flies and they can't *feed* themselves."

How do flies breed? What she mean by that? But I think they should let me watch: just to be sure they don't breed like flies do, however that is, so they can continue to feed themselves. I would feed them, though, if it really came to that. I wonder about the Indian children, sometimes. Nobody ever mentions them. Maybe there aren't any.

Flies all fits in, somehow, but it's not too clear to me. Last summer there was really this fly thing. Momma said it was because they couldn't burn people fast enough, and there was a world-wide plague, and I remember how scared they were that we couldn't keep it out. The time everybody had killing flies! It was all over the newscasts.

It went on until it got monotonous. In fact, most newscasts aren't very interesting after a while. They keep changing the places, but there's still this big machine pushing up piles of people and setting them on fire. I like the ones on our space program better. We have a colony on Mars.

We have to have.

For some reason.

Most people go out everyday, all the Poppas, and cheer for this program. I've never seen them do it, but I guess it's like a football game. It's called work. They pay him money for it that Momma writes checks on to pay for credit cards with. They must know what they're doing.

I'm coming along in figuring them out. Every once in a while I think I have it.

I think they have a machine somewhere that makes time, or maybe a press that prints it like a book. They never mention this. Maybe I have to learn how they make electricity, first. They say I'm going to start learning about things like that pretty soon.

And you really have to try to figure the big bastards out. Don't ask me why. You do. You can't do anything about them. They're still going to batter you around. Shaping the personality, it's called. But you have to keep trying, keep hoping. Every once in a great while you can get a conversation going with them. Usually about candy, unfortunately. You learn to like candy, though, and I guess that's something. Sometimes I think it's the most important thing in the whole world.

But if they'd just stop and think every once in a while. If they'd just slow down and talk to you, it might be better. But they don't stop to think. They're always rushing. I give an example. I start up some of the electronic equipment in the basement. We got this electronic dirt remover. I put my bedclothes in it. Sheets, blanket, pillow. Don't you think that wasn't a job! Down two windy flights of stairs with them. Dropping them, picking them up, trying not to make any noise. House quiet. Real early. Everybody asleep.

Off she goes! Beautiful!

It don't stop, though. Like it does for Momma. I hear the bedclothes being torn up. Rip, rip-rip, rip. I better go tell them.

I go into their room. They are still asleep. I tiptoe toward Momma. She maybe won't take it as bad as Poppa.

Bam! I walk into this stupid new fly screen they have on and I forgot about. It shakes hell out of me, and I start to cry. Poppa sets up and screams, "You filthy shit!"

"What time is it?" asks Momma.

I don't understand about all this time thing, but I tell her about the bedclothes.

"My God!"

Stark naked, both of them, down the stairs. They get in each other's way.

I trail after. It's a lot of work, a little boy going down big stairs, trying to hurry. You have to be careful not to fall.

Poppa got it turned off. "That was close. It could have blown up half the house."

"You filthy shit!" Momma screams at me.

"Shut up, Hazel, this is serious. The kid could have killed himself."

I got a long lecture, right there, on how dangerous modern devices are. I wanted them to show me how to operate it right, so I wouldn't do it wrong again. But they were too dumb to do that. No, just leave it *alone!* How can I learn if they won't ever let me do anything? Why did they think I brought the bedclothes down in the first place?

Momma says, "First we got to give you a personality—we got to fix it so you can grow up to be the kind of man you want to be. *Then,* after that, you start going to school to learn things. When you get to be four years old, you start to school to learn things. You're only three and a half!"

Do you know how long you're three and a half? You're three and a half forever. There isn't any time at all. Something has gone wrong with their press, and they don't know it.

"What kind of man I want to be?"

"The country needs scientists," Poppa said. "We take a course from the government called: How to Make Scientists. How to shape personalities who want to understand how things work—who always have to figure things out, who aren't happy unless they're figuring things out. It's a good personality. Don't go fiddling with this electronic gear any more or you'll get killed."

So that's what I'm going to be, a scientist. I don't know what the other choices were, but I guess it's too late anyhow. They might have been worse, at least I like to think that. Like going to India.

We kids at playground, we talk about the big bastards all the time. They used to be like us. Something happened to them that made them forget how to think.

I guess I will too. I get big, like them, I won't remember an
of this, either. Lots of things I can't remember, already. There wa
a time, so long ago I just about can't remember, when Momm
and Poppa loved me. That was in the beginning. But I guess mayb
that's what it said in the book to do, too. It was nicer, then, b
I forget so much. So all this I'll just forget. Because I'm not reall
me yet. They're still making me.

Right now, I think a lot about those people in India. I don
know why I should. I think it would be sensible to set them dow
to a table and feed them. I think that would be a good thing t
do. But I guess when I get interested in learning how things work
won't think that way any more. And I guess I'll just forget all thi

I'm still standing here, crying, by the open drawer that's fille
with this strange world of things. I've finally gotten to her. "Wha
do you *want?*"

It's too late to find out whether there really is candy in there.
always was. She'd never spend all that time to search through ther
with me. It's too late to find out what this thing is for which ther
is no conceivable use. I've been crying so long, I feel hurt by
and I can't stop crying.

"What do you *want?*"

I want to start forgetting. Like what they do to me, sometime
at night, to shape my personality. You wouldn't believe how ba
I want to forget that. And it's such a long time more, such a lon
long, long time. I don't know if I can last, sometimes. I've got t
hurry up and start forgetting. "I want to hurry up and be fou
years old!"


## Afterword:

In "From the Government Printing Office," I have tried to project
future in which the education of children involves striking terror int
their hearts in the hopes of producing more creative individuals. Pe
haps this is not unlike what we have always done, with our frightenir
stories of witches and goblins and evil spirits and threats of hell. In m
view, children are our most important product and should be bett
handled, but in any event one need only listen closely to the speech
children to hear the history of the future.

**Introduction to LAND OF THE GREAT HORSES:**

Look out your window. What do you see? The gang fight on the corner, with the teenie-boppers using churchkeys on each other's faces; the scissors grinder with his multicolored cart and tinkling bells; a pudgy woman in a print dress too short for her fat legs, hoeing her lawn; a three-alarm fire with children trapped on the fifth story; a mad dog attached to the leg of a peddler of Seventh Day Adventist literature; an impending race riot with a representative of RAM on a sound truck. Any or all? It takes no special powers of observation to catalogue the unclassifiable. But now look again. What do you see? What you usually see? An empty street. *Now* catalogue:

Curbstones, without which cars would run up onto front lawns. Mailboxes, without which touch with the world would be diminished. Telephone poles and wires, without which communication would screech to a halt. Gutters, sewers and manholes, without which you would be flooded when it rains. Blacktop, without which the car you own wouldn't last a month on the crushed rock. The breeze, without which, well, a day is diminished. What are these things? They are the obvious. So obvious they become invisible. How many water hydrants and mailboxes did you pass today? None? Hardly. You passed dozens, but you did not see them. They are the incredibly valuable, absolutely necessary, totally ignored staples of a well-run community.

Speculative fiction is a small community. It has its obvious flashy residents. Knight, Sheckley, Sturgeon, Bradbury, Clarke, Vonnegut. We see them and take note of them, and know what they're about. But the community would not run one thousandth as well as it does without the quiet writers, the ones who turn out story after story, not hack work but really excellent stories, time after time. The kind you settle back and think about, after finishing them, saying, "That was a *good* story." And you promptly forget who wrote it. Perhaps later you recall the story. "Oh yeah, remember that one about . . ." and then you wrinkle down and say, "What the hell was the name of the guy who wrote it? He's done a bunch of things, you know, pretty fair writer. . . ."

The problem is a matter of cumulativeness. Each story is an excellence, standing alone. But somehow it never makes a totality, an image of a writer, a career in perspective. This is the sad but obvious thing about R. A. Lafferty's place in speculative fiction.

He is a man of substantiality, whose writing is top-flight. Not merely competent fiction, but genuinely exemplary fiction. He has been writing for—how many years? More than six, but less than fifteen? Something like that. Yet he is seldom mentioned when fans gather to discuss The Writers. Even though he has been anthologized many times, been included in Judith Merril's *Year's Best SF* on several occasions, and the Carr-Wollheim *World's Best* anthology twice, and appeared in almost all the science fiction magazines. He is the invisible man.

It will be rectified here. Raphael Aloysius Lafferty will emerge, will speak, will declare himself, and then you will read another extra-brilliant story by him. And dammit, this time *remember!*

Lafferty speaking: "I am, not necessarily in this order, fifty-one years old, a bachelor, an electrical engineer, a fat man.

"Born in Iowa, came to Oklahoma when I was four years old, and except for four years in the army have been here all my life. Also, one year on a little civil service job in Washington, D.C. The only college I've ever attended was a couple of years in the University of Tulsa's night school division long ago, mostly math and German. I've spent close to thirty years working for electrical jobbers, mostly as buyer and price-quotation man. During WWII I was stationed in Texas, North Carolina, Florida, California, Australia, New Guinea, Morotai (Dutch

East Indies, now Indonesia), and the Philippines. I was a *good* staff sergeant, and at one time I could talk pretty fair *pasar* Malay and Tagalog (of the Philippines).

"What does a man say about himself? Never the important things. I was a heavy drinker for a few years and gave it up about six years ago. This left a gap: when you give up the company of the more interesting drinkers, you give up something of the colorful and fantastic. So I substituted writing science fiction. Something I read in one of the writers' magazines gave me the silly idea that science fiction would be easy to write. It isn't, for me. I wasn't raised on the stuff like most of the writers in this form seem to have been.

"My hobby is language. Any language. I've got at least a thousand dollars in self-teach grammars and readers and dictionaries and Linguaphone and Cortinaphone courses. I've picked up a rough reading knowledge of all the languages of the Latin, German and Slavic families, as well as Irish and Greek; but actually Spanish, French and German are the only ones I read freely with respectable speed. I'm a Catholic of the out-of-season or conservative variety. As to politics, I am the only member of the American Centrist Party, whose tenets I will one day set out in an ironic-Utopia story. I'm a compulsive walker; turn me loose in a strange town and I'll explore every corner of it on foot inside a week. I don't think of myself as a very interesting fellow."

This is the editor again, for a final comment. Lafferty is about as uninteresting as his stories. Which is to say, not at all. As entered for the prosecution's case against R.A.'s contention that he's a neb, the following story, one of my particular favorites in this book.

# ● LAND OF THE GREAT HORSES

## by R. A. Lafferty

*"They came and took our country away from us,"* the people had always said. *But nobody understood them.*

Two Englishmen, Richard Rockwell and Seruno Smith, were rolling in a terrain buggy over the Thar Desert. It was bleak, red country, more rock than sand. It looked as though the top had been stripped off it and the naked underland left uncovered.

They heard thunder and it puzzled them. They looked at each other, the blond Rockwell and the dark Smith. It never thundered in the whole country between New Delhi and Bahawalpur. What would this rainless North India desert have to thunder with?

"Let's ride the ridges here," Rockwell told Smith, and he sent the vehicle into a climb. "It never rains here, but once before I was caught in a draw in a country where it never rained. I nearly drowned."

It thundered again, heavy and rolling, as though to tell them that they were hearing right.

"This draw is named Kuti Tavdavi—Little River," Smith said darkly. "I wonder why."

Then he jerked back as though startled at himself.

"Rockwell, why did I say that? I never saw this draw before. How did a name like that pop into my mind? But it's the low draw that would be a little river if it ever rained in this country. This land can't have significant rain. There's no high place to tip whatever moisture goes over."

"I wonder about that every time I come," said Rockwell, and raised his hand towards the shimmering heights—the Land of the Great Horses, the famous mirage. "If it were really there it would tip the moisture. It would make a lush savanna of all this."

They were mineral explorers doing ground minutiae on promising portions of an aerial survey. The trouble with the Thar was that it had everything—lead, zinc, antimony, copper, tin, bauxite—in barely submarginal amounts. Nowhere would the Thar pay off, but everywhere it would almost pay.

Now it was lightning about the heights of the mirage, and they had never seen that before. It had clouded and lowered. It was thundering in rolling waves, and there is no mirage of sound.

"There is either a very large and very busy bird up there or this is rain," Rockwell said.

And it had begun to rain, softly but steadily. It was pleasant as they chukkered along in the vehicle through the afternoon. Rain in the desert is always like a bonus.

Smith broke into a happy song in one of the Northwest India tongues, a tune with a ribald swing to it, though Rockwell didn't understand the words. It was full of double rhymes and vowel-packed words such as a child might make up.

"How the devil do you know the tongues so well?" Rockwell asked. "I find them difficult, and I have a good linguistic background."

"I didn't have to learn them," Smith said, "I just had to remember them. They all cluster around the *boro jib* itself."

"Around the what? How many of the languages do you know?"

"All of them. The Seven Sisters, they're called: Punjabi, Kashmiri, Gujarati, Marathi, Sindhi, Hindi."

"Your Seven Sisters only number six," Rockwell jibed.

"There's a saying that the seventh sister ran off with a horse trader," Smith said. "But that seventh lass is still encountered here and there around the world."

Often they stopped to survey on foot. The very color of the new rivulets was significant to the mineral men, and this was the first time they had ever seen water flow in that country. They continued on fitfully and slowly, and ate up a few muddy miles.

Rockwell gasped once and nearly fell off the vehicle. He had seen a total stranger riding beside him, and it shook him.

Then he saw that it was Smith as he had always been, and he was dumfounded by the illusion. And, soon, by something else.

"Something is very wrong here," Rockwell said.

"Something is very right here," Smith answered him, and then broke into another song in an India tongue.

"We're lost," Rockwell worried out loud. "We can't see any distance for the rain, but there shouldn't be rising ground here. It isn't mapped."

"Of course it is," Smith sang. "It's the Jalo Char."

"The what? Where did you get a name like that? The map's a blank here, and the country should be."

"Then the map is defective. Man, it's the sweetest valley in the world! It will lead us all the way up. How could the map forget it? How could we all forget it for so long?"

"Smith! What's wrong? You're pie-eyed."

"Everything's right, I tell you. I was reborn just a minute ago. It's a coming home."

"Smith! We're riding through green grass."

"I love it. I could crop it like a horse."

"That cliff, Smith! It shouldn't be that close! It's part of the mir—"

"Why, sir, that is Lolo Trusul."

"But it's not real! It's not on any topography map!"

"Map, sir? I'm a poor *kalo* man who wouldn't know about things like that."

"Smith! You're a qualified cartographer!"

"Does seem that I followed a trade with a name like that. But the cliff is real enough. I climbed it in my boyhood—in my other boyhood. And that yonder, sir, is Drapengoro Rez—the Grassy Mountain. And the high plateau ahead of us which we begin to climb is Diz Boro Grai—the Land of the Great Horses."

Rockwell stopped the terrain buggy and leaped off. Smith followed him in a happy daze.

"Smith, you're wide-eyed crazy!" Rockwell gasped. "And what am I? We're terribly lost somehow. Smith, look at the log chart and the bearings recorder!"

"Log chart, sir? I'm a poor *kalo* man who wouldn't know—"

"Damn you, Smith, you *made* these instruments. If they're correct we're seven hundred feet too high and have been climbing for ten miles into a highland that's supposed to be part of a mirage. These cliffs can't be here. We can't be here. Smith!"

But Seruno Smith had ambled off like a crazy man.

"Smith, where are you trotting off to? Can't you hear me?"

"You call to me, sir?" asked Smith. "And by such a name?"

"Are the two of us as crazy as the country?" Rockwell moaned. "I've worked with you for three years. Isn't your name Smith?"

"Why, yes, sir, I guess it might be englished as Horse-Smith or Black-Smith. But my name is Pettalangro and I'm going home."

And the man who had been Smith started on foot up to the Land of the Great Horses.

"Smith, I'm getting on the buggy and I'm going back," Rockwell shouted. "I'm scared liverless of this country that changes. When a mirage turns solid it's time to quit. Come along now! We'll be back in Bikaner by tomorrow morning. There's a doctor there, and a whisky bar. We need one of them."

"Thank you, sir, but I must go up to my home," Smith sang out. "It was kind of you to give me a ride along the way."

"I'm leaving you, Smith. One crazy man is better than two."

*"Ashava, Sarishan,"* Smith called a parting.

"Smith, unriddle me one last thing," Rockwell called, trying to find a piece of sanity to hold to. "What is the name of the seventh sister?"

"Deep Romany," Smith sang, and he was gone up into the high plateau that had always been a mirage.

In an upper room on Olive Street in St. Louis, Missouri, a half-and-half couple were talking half-and-half.

"The *rez* has *riser*'d," the man said. "I can *sung* it like *brishindo*. Let's *jal*."

"All right," the wife said, "if you're *awa*."

"Hell, I bet I can *riker* plenty *bano* on the *beda* we got here. I'll have *kakko* come *kinna* it *saro*."

"With a little *bachi* we can be *jal*'d by *areat*," said the wife.

*"Nashiva,* woman, *nashiva!"*

"All right," the wife said, and she began to pack their suitcases.

In Camargo in the Chihuahua State of Mexico, a shade-tree mechanic sold his business for a hundred pesos and told his wife to pack up—they were leaving.

"To leave now when business is so good?" she asked.

"I only got one car to fix and I can't fix that," the man said.

"But if you keep it long enough, he will pay you to put it together again even if it isn't fixed. That's what he did last time. And you've a horse to shoe."

"I'm afraid of that horse. It has come back, though. Let's go."

"Are you sure we will be able to find it?"

"Of course I'm not sure. We will go in our wagon and our sick horse will pull it."

"Why will we go in the wagon, when we have a car, of sorts?"

"I don't know why. But we will go in the wagon, and we will nail the old giant horseshoe up on the lintel board."

A carny in Nebraska lifted his head and smelled the air.

"It's come back," he said. "I always knew we'd know. Any other Romanies here?"

"I got a little *rart* in me," said one of his fellows. "This *narvelengero dives* is only a two-bit carnival anyhow. We'll tell the boss to shove it up his *chev* and we'll be gone."

In Tulsa, a used-car dealer named Gypsy Red announced the hottest sale on the row:

"Everything for nothing! I'm leaving. Pick up the papers and drive them off. Nine new heaps and thirty good ones. All free."

"You think we're crazy?" the people asked. "There's a catch."

Red put the papers for all the cars on the ground and put a brick on top of them. He got in the worst car on the lot and drove it off forever.

"All free," he sang out as he drove off. "Pick up the papers and drive the cars away."

They're still there. You think people are crazy to fall for something like that that probably has a catch to it?

In Galveston a barmaid named Margaret was asking merchant seamen how best to get passage to Karachi.

"Why Karachi?" one of them asked her.

"I thought it would be the nearest big port," she said. "It's come back, you know."

"I kind of felt this morning it had come back," he said. "I'm a *chal* myself. Sure, we'll find something going that way."

In thousands of places fawney-men and dukkerin-women, kakki-baskros and hegedusies, clowns and commission men, Counts of Condom and Dukes of Little Egypt *parvel'd* in their chips and got ready to roll.

Men and families made sudden decisions in every country. *Athinganoi* gathered in the hills above Salonika in Greece and were joined by brothers from Serbia and Albania and the Rhodope Hills of Bulgaria. *Zingari* of North Italy gathered around Pavia and began to roll towards Genoa to take ship. *Boemios* of Portugal came down to Porto and Lisbon. *Gitanos* of Andalusia and all southern Spain came to Sanlúcar and Málaga. *Zigeuner* from Thuringia and Hanover thronged to Hamburg to find ocean passage. *Gioboga* and their mixed-blood *Shelta* cousins from every *cnoc* and *coill* of Ireland found boats at Dublin and Limerick and Bantry.

From deeper Europe, *Tsigani* began to travel overland eastward. The people were going from two hundred ports of every continent and over a thousand highroads—many of them long forgotten.

Balauros, Kalo, Manusch, Melelo, Tsigani, Moro, Romani, Flamenco, Sinto, Cicara, the many-named people was traveling in its thousands. The *Romani Rai* was moving.

Two million Gypsies of the world were going home.

At the Institute, Gregory Smirnov was talking to his friends and associates.

"You remember the thesis I presented several years ago," he said, "that, a little over a thousand years ago, Outer Visitors came down to Earth and took a sliver of our Earth away with them. All of you found the proposition comical, but I arrived at my conclusion by isostatic and eustatic analysis carried out minutely. There is no doubt that it happened."

"One of our slivers is missing," said Aloysius Shiplap. "You guessed the sliver taken at about ten thousand square miles area and no more than a mile thick at its greatest. You said you thought they wanted to run this sliver from our Earth through their laboratories as a sample. Do you have something new on our missing sliver?"

"I'm closing the inquiry," Gregory said. "They've brought it back."

It was simple really, *jekvasteskero,* Gypsy-simple. It is the *gadjo,* the non-Gypsies of the world, who give complicated answers to simple things.

"They came and took our country away from us," the Gypsies had always said, and that is what had happened.

The Outer Visitors had run a slip under it, rocked it gently to rid it of nervous fauna, and then taken it away for study. For a marker, they left an immaterial simulacrum of that high country as we ourselves sometimes set name or picture tags to show where an object will be set later. This simulacrum was often seen by humans as a mirage.

The Outer Visitors also set simulacra in the minds of the superior fauna that fled from the moving land. This would be a homing instinct, inhibiting permanent settlement anywhere until the time should come for the resettlement; entwined with this instinct were certain premonitions, fortune-showings, and understandings.

Now the Visitors brought the slice of land back, and its old fauna homed in on it.

"What will the—ah—patronizing smile on my part—Outer Visitors do now, Gregory?" Aloysius Shiplap asked back at the Institute.

"Why, take another sliver of our Earth to study, I suppose, Aloysius," Gregory Smirnov said.

Low-intensity earthquakes rocked the Los Angeles area for three days. The entire area was evacuated of people. Then there was a great whistle blast from the sky as if to say, "All ashore that's going ashore."

Then the surface to some little depth and all its superstructure was taken away. It was gone. And then it was quickly forgotten.

From the TWENTY-SECOND-CENTURY COMPRE-HENSIVE ENCYCLOPEDIA, Vol. 1, page 389—

ANGELENOS. (*See also* Automobile Gypsies and Prune Pickers.) A mixed ethnic group of unknown origin, much given to wandering in automobiles. It is predicted that they will be the last users of this vehicle, and several archaic chrome-burdened models are still produced for their market. These people are not beggars; many of them are of superior intelligence. They often set up in business, usually as real estate dealers, gamblers, confidence men, managers of mail-order diploma mills, and promoters of one sort or other. They seldom remain long in one location.

Their pastimes are curious. They drive for hours and days on old and seldom-used cloverleafs and freeways. It has been said that a majority of the Angelenos are narcotics users, but Harold Freelove (who lived for some months as an Angeleno) has proved this false. What they inhale at their frolics (smog-crocks) is a black smoke of carbon and petroleum waste laced with monoxide. Its purpose is not clear.

The religion of the Angelenos is a mixture of old cults with a very strong eschatological element. The Paradise Motif is represented by reference to a mystic "Sunset Boulevard." The language of the Angelenos is a colorful and racy argot. Their account of their origin is vague:

"They came and took our dizz away from us," they say.

## Afterword:

We are all cousins. I don't believe in reincarnation, but the only system of reincarnation that satisfies justice is that every being should become successively (or sometimes simultaneously) every other being. This would take a few billion lifetimes; the writer with a feel for the Kindred tries to do it in one.

We are all Romanies, as in the parable here, and we have a built-in homing to and remembrance of a woollier and more excellent place, a reality that masquerades as a mirage. Whether the more excellent place is here or heretofore or hereafter, I don't know, or whether it will be our immediate world when it is sufficiently animated; but there is an intuition about it which sometimes passes through the whole community. There is, or there ought to be, these shimmering heights; and they belong to us. Controversy (or polarity) is between ourselves as individuals and as members of the incandescent species, confronted with the eschatological thing. I'd express it more intelligently if I knew how.

But I didn't write the story to point up this notion, but to drop a name. There *is* a Margaret the barmaid—not the one in the story, of course (for we have to abide by the disavowal "Any resemblance to actual persons living or dead is purely coincidental"), but another of the same name—and she is a Romany. "Put my name in a story, just Margaret the barmaid," she told me. "I don't care what, even name a dog that." "But you won't know it," I said, "you don't read anything, and none of the people you run around with do." "I will know it exactly," she said, "when someone else reads it someday, when they come to the name Margaret the barmaid. I know things like that."

Not from me, but from someone who reads it here, Margaret will receive the intuition, and both parties will know it. "Hey, the old bat did it," Margaret will say. I don't know what the reader-sender caught in the middle will say or think.

I am pleased to be a member of this august though sometimes raffish company playing here in this production. It has an air of excellence, and some of it will rub off on me. We are, all of us, Counts of Con-dom and Dukes of Little Egypt.

## Introduction to THE RECOGNITION:

I have this theory. In point of fact I have a barnhouse full of theories, but I've got this *particular* theory about the men who wind up as leaders of movements. It would not surprise me to find out (through the discovery of some new Dead Sea Scrolls perhaps) that allofasudden Jesus turned around (so to speak) on the cross and looked down and said, "How the hell did I get into this?" Did he really think he was going to become the head of a big-deal Movement? Did Gandhi? Did Hitler? Yeah, well, maybe him, but what can you expect from a short ugly plasterer? Did Stokeley Carmichael? Did J. G. Ballard? Oh! *There* we are!

Jim Ballard, who seems to me to write peculiarly Ballardian stories —tales difficult to pin down as to one style or one theme or one approach but all very personally trademarked Ballard—is the acknowledged leader of the "British school of science fiction." I'm sure if you said this to Ballard (who chooses to pronounce it Buh-*lard*), he would stare at you as if you were daft. He certainly doesn't write like the leader of a movement, for a movement generally involves easily cited examples, jingoism, obviousness and a strong dose of predictability. None of these is present in the work of J. G. Ballard.

Among his highly celebrated books are *The Drowned World, The Wind from Nowhere, Terminal Beach, The Voices of Time, The Burning World, Billenium* and *The Crystal World.* None of these contains ideas so revolutionary or arresting that they should comprise a rationale for being a "new movement." Yet *in totality* they present a kind of enriched literacy, a darker yet somehow clearer—perhaps the word is "poignant"—approach to the materials of speculative writing. There is a flavor of surrealism to Ballard's writing. No, it's not that, either. It is, in some ways, *serene,* as oriental philosophy is serene. Resigned yet vital. There appears to be a superimposed reality that covers the underlying pure fantasy of Ballardian conception. Frankly, Ballard's work defies categorization or careful analysis. It is like four-color lithography. The most exquisite Wyeth landscape, when examined more and more minutely, begins to resemble pointillism, and finally nothing but a series of disconnected colored dots. So do Ballard's stories, when subjected to the unfeeling scrutiny of cold analysis, break down into disconnected parts. When read, when assimilated as they stand, they become something greater than the sum of the parts.

One such story is the one you are about to read. It is a prime example of Ballard at his most mysterious, his most compelling. The story says all that need be said about Ballard the writer. As for Ballard the man, the information is as sparse as the stories: he was born in Shanghai, China, in 1930, of English parents; during WWII he was interned in a Japanese prison camp and in 1946 was repatriated to England; he later studied medicine at Cambridge University.

As stated elsewhere in this book about another story, I have no idea whether this is science fiction, or fantasy, or allegory, or cautionary tale. All I know for certain is that it is immensely entertaining, thought-provoking and fits perfectly something Saul Bellow said about the excuse for a story's existence. He said it in 1963:

". . . a story should be interesting, highly interesting, as interesting as possible—inexplicably absorbing. There can be no other justification for any piece of fiction."

# ● THE RECOGNITION

## by J. G. Ballard

On Midsummer's Eve a small circus visited the town in the West
Country where I was spending my holiday. Three days earlier the
large travelling fair which always came to the town in the summer,
equipped with a ferris wheel, merry-go-rounds and dozens of booths
and shooting galleries, had taken up its usual site on the open common
in the centre of the town, and this second arrival was forced to pitch
its camp on the waste ground beyond the warehouses along the
river.

At dusk, when I strolled through the town, the ferris wheel was
revolving above the coloured lights, and people were riding the
carousels and walking arm in arm along the cobbled roads that
surrounded the common. Away from this hubbub of noise the streets
down to the river were almost deserted, and I was glad to walk alone
through the shadows past the boarded shopfronts. Midsummer's Eve
seemed to me a time for reflection as much as for celebration, for
a careful watch on the shifting movements of nature. When I crossed
the river, whose dark water flowed through the town like a gilded
snake, and entered the woods that stretched to one side of the road,
I had the unmistakable sensation that the forest was preparing itself,
and that within its covens even the roots of the trees were sliding
through the soil and testing their sinews.

It was on the way back from this walk, as I crossed the bridge,
that I saw the small itinerant circus arrive at the town. The procession, which approached the bridge by a side road, consisted of no more
than half a dozen wagons, each carrying a high barred cage and
drawn by a pair of careworn horses. At its head a young woman
with a pallid face and bare arms rode on a grey stallion. I leaned
on the balustrade in the centre of the bridge and watched the procession reach the embankment. The young woman hesitated, pulling on
the heavy leather bridle, and looked over her shoulder as the wagons
closed together. They began to ascend the bridge. Although the gra-
dient was slight, the horses seemed barely able to reach the crest,

tottering on their weak legs, and I had ample time to make a first scrutiny of this strange caravan that was later to preoccupy me.

Urging on her tired stallion, the young woman passed me—at least, it seemed to me then that she was young, but her age was so much a matter of her own moods and mine. I was to see her on several occasions—sometimes she would seem little more than a child of twelve, with an unformed chin and staring eyes above the bony cheeks. Later she would appear to be almost middle-aged, the grey hair and skin revealing the angular skull beneath them.

At first, as I watched from the bridge, I guessed her to be about twenty years old, presumably the daughter of the proprietor of this threadbare circus. As she jogged along with one hand on the reins the lights from the distant fairground shone intermittently in her face, disclosing a high-bridged nose and firm mouth. Although by no means beautiful, she had that curious quality of attractiveness that I had often noticed in the women who worked at fairgrounds, an elusive sexuality despite their shabby clothes and surroundings. As she passed she looked down at me, her quiet eyes on some unfelt point within my face.

The six wagons followed her, the horses heaving the heavy cages across the camber. Behind the bars I caught a glimpse of worn straw and a small hutch in the corner, but there was no sign of the animals. I assumed them to be too undernourished to do more than sleep. As the last wagon passed I saw the only other member of the troupe, a dwarf in a leather jacket driving the wooden caravan at the rear.

I walked after them across the bridge, wondering if they were late arrivals at the fair already in progress. But from the way they hesitated at the foot of the bridge, the young woman looking to left and right while the dwarf sat hunched in the shadow of the cage in front of him, it was plain they had no connection whatever with the brilliant ferris wheel and the amusements taking place on the common. Even the horses, standing uncertainly with their heads lowered to avoid the coloured lights, seemed aware of this exclusion.

After a pause they moved off along the narrow road that followed the bank, the wagons rolling from side to side as the wooden wheels slipped on the grass-covered verge. A short distance away was a patch of waste ground that separated the warehouses near the wharves from the terraced cottages below the bridge. A single street lamp on the north side cast a dim light over the cinder surface. By now dusk had settled over the town and seemed to isolate this dingy patch of ground, no longer enlivened in any way by the movement of the river.

The procession headed towards this dark enclosure. The young woman turned her horse off the road and led the wagons across the cinders to the high wall of the first warehouse. Here they stopped, the wagons still in line ahead, the horses obviously glad to be concealed by the darkness. The dwarf jumped down from his perch and trotted round to where the woman was dismounting from the stallion.

At this time I was strolling along the bank a short distance behind them. Something about this odd little troupe intrigued me, though in retrospect it may be that the calm eyes of the young woman as she looked down at me had acted as more of a spur than seemed at the time. Nonetheless, I was puzzled by what seemed the very pointlessness of their existence. Few things are as drab as a down-at-heel circus, but this one was so travel-worn and dejected as to deny them the chance of making any profit whatever. Who were this strange pale-haired woman and her dwarf? Did they imagine that anyone would actually come to this dismal patch of ground by the warehouses to look at their secretive animals? Perhaps they were simply delivering a group of aged creatures to an abattoir specialising in circus animals, and pausing here for the night before moving on.

Yet, as I suspected, the young woman and the dwarf were already moving the wagons into the unmistakable pattern of a circus. The woman dragged at the bridles while the dwarf darted between her feet, switching at the horses' ankles with his leather hat. The docile brutes heaved at their wagons, and within five minutes the cages were arranged in a rough circle. The horses were unshackled from their shafts, and the dwarf, helped by the young woman, led them towards the river where they began cropping quietly at the dark grass.

Within the cages there was a stir of movement, and one or two pale forms shuffled about in the straw. The dwarf scurried up the steps of the caravan and lit a lamp over a stove which I could see in the doorway. He came down with a metal bucket and moved along the cages. He poured a little water into each of the pails and pushed them towards the hutches with a broom.

The woman followed him, but seemed as uninterested as the dwarf in the animals inside the cages. When he put away the bucket she held a ladder for him and he climbed onto the roof of the caravan. He lowered down a bundle of clapboard signs fastened together by a strip of canvas. After untying them the dwarf carried the signs over to the cages. He climbed up the ladder again and began to secure the signs over the bars.

In the dim light from the street lamp I could make out only the faded designs painted years earlier in the traditional style of fair-ground marquees, the floral patterns and cartouches overlaid with lettering of some kind. Moving nearer the cages, I reached the edge of the clearing. The young woman turned and saw me. The dwarf was fixing the last of the signs, and she stood by the ladder, one hand on the shaft, regarding me with an unmoving gaze. Perhaps it was her protective stance as the diminutive figure moved about above her, but she seemed far older than when she had first appeared with her menagerie at the outskirts of the town. In the faint light her hair had become almost grey, and her bare arms seemed lined and work-worn. As I drew closer, passing the first of the cages, she turned to follow me with her eyes, as if trying to take some interest in my arrival on the scene.

At the top of the ladder there was a flurry of movement. Slipping through the dwarf's fingers, the sign toppled from the roof and fell to the ground at the woman's feet. Whirling his short arms and legs, the dwarf leapt down from the ladder. He picked himself off the ground, wobbling about like a top as he regained his balance. He dusted his hat against his boots and put it back on his head, then started up the ladder again.

The woman held his arm. She moved the ladder further along the cage, trying to balance the shafts against the bars.

On an impulse, more or less out of sympathy, I stepped forward. "Can I help you?" I said. "Perhaps I can reach the roof. If you hand me the sign . . ."

The dwarf hesitated, looking at me with his doleful eyes. He seemed prepared to let me help, but stood there with his hat in one hand as if prevented from saying anything to me by an unstated set of circumstances, some division of life as formal and impassable as those of the most rigid castes.

The woman, however, gestured me to the ladder, turning her face away as I settled the shafts against the bars. Through the dim light she watched the horses cropping the grass along the bank.

I climbed the ladder, and then took the sign lifted up to me by the dwarf. I settled it on the roof, weighing it down with two half bricks left there for the purpose, and read the legends painted across the warped panel. As I deciphered the words "marvels" and "spectacular" (obviously the signs bore no relation to the animals within the cages, and had been stolen from another fair or found on some refuse heap) I noticed a sudden movement from the cage below me. There was a burrowing through the straw, and a low, pale-skinned creature retreated into its burrow.

This disturbance of the straw—whether the animal had darted out from fear or in an attempt to warn me off I had no means of telling—had released a strong and obscurely familiar smell. It hung around me as I came down the ladder, muffled but vaguely offensive. I searched the hutch for a glimpse of the animal, but it had scuffled the straw into the door.

The dwarf and the woman nodded to me as I turned from the ladder. There was no hostility in their attitude—the dwarf, if anything, was on the point of thanking me, his mouth moving in a wordless rictus—but for some reason they seemed to feel unable to make any contact with me. The woman was standing with her back to the street lamp, and her face, softened by the darkness, now appeared small and barely formed, like that of an unkempt child.

"You're all ready," I said half jocularly. With something of an effort, I added: "It looks very nice."

I glanced at the cages when they made no comment. One or two of the animals sat at the backs of their hutches, their pale forms indistinct in the faint light. "When do you open?" I asked. "Tomorrow?"

"We're open now," the dwarf said.

"Now?" Not sure whether this was a joke, I started to point at the cages, but the statement had obviously been meant at its face value.

"I see . . . you're open this evening." Searching for something to say—they seemed prepared to stand there indefinitely with me—I went on: "When do you leave?"

"Tomorrow," the woman told me in a low voice. "We have to go in the morning."

As if taking their cue from this, the two of them moved across the small arena, clearing to one side the pieces of newspaper and other refuse. By the time I walked away, baffled by the entire purpose of this pitiful menagerie, they had already finished, and stood waiting between the cages for their first customers. I paused on the bank beside the cropping horses, whose quiet figures seemed as insubstantial as those of the dwarf and their mistress, and wondered what bizarre logic had brought them to the town, when a second fair, almost infinitely larger and gayer, was already in full swing.

At the thought of the animals I recalled the peculiar smell that hung about the cages, vaguely unpleasant but reminiscent of an odour I was certain I knew well. For some reason I was also convinced that this familiar smell was a clue to the strange nature of the circus. Beside me the horses gave off a pleasant scent of bran and sweat. Their downcast heads, lowered to the grass by the water's edge, seemed to hide from me some secret concealed within their luminous eyes.

I walked back towards the centre of the town, relieved to see the illuminated superstructure of the ferris wheel rotating above the rooftops. The roundabouts and amusement arcades, the shooting galleries and the tunnel of love were part of a familiar world. Even the witches and vampires painted over the house of horrors were nightmares from a predictable quarter of the evening sky. By contrast the young woman—or was she young?—and her dwarf were travellers from an unknown country, a vacant realm where nothing had any meaning. It was this absence of intelligible motive that I found so disturbing about them.

I wandered through the crowds below the marquees, and on an impulse decided to ride on the ferris wheel. As I waited my turn with the group of young men and women, the electrified gondolas of the wheel rose high into the evening air, so that all the music and light of the fair seemed to have been scooped from the star-filled sky.

I climbed into my gondola, sharing it with a young woman and her daughter, and a few moments later we were revolving through the brilliant air, the fairground spread below us. During the two or three minutes of the ride I was busy shouting to the young woman and her child as we pointed out to each other familiar landmarks in the town. However, when we stopped and sat at the top of the wheel as the passengers below disembarked, I noticed for the first time the bridge I had crossed earlier that evening. Following the course of the river, I saw the single street lamp that shone over the waste ground near the warehouses where the white-faced woman and the dwarf had set up their rival circus. As our gondola moved forward and began its descent the dim forms of two of the wagons were visible in an interval between the rooftops.

Half an hour later, when the fair began to close, I walked back to the river. Small groups of people were moving arm in arm through the streets, but by the time the warehouses came into sight I was almost alone on the cobbled pavements that wound between the terraced cottages. Then the street lamp appeared, and the circle of wagons beyond it.

To my surprise, a few people were actually visiting the menagerie. I stood in the road below the street lamp and watched the two couples and a third man who were wandering around the cages and trying to identify the animals. Now and then they would go up to the bars and peer through them, and there was a shout of laughter as one of the women pretended to flinch away in alarm. The man with her held a few shreds of straw in his hand and threw them at the door of the hutch, but the animal refused to appear. The group resumed their circuit of the cages, squinting in the dim light.

Meanwhile the dwarf and the woman remained silent to one side. The woman stood by the steps of the caravan, looking out at her patrons as if unconcerned whether they came or not. The dwarf, his bulky hat hiding his face, stood patiently on the other side of the arena, moving his ground as the party of visitors continued their tour. He was not carrying a collection bag or roll of tickets, and it seemed likely, even if only reasonable, that there was no charge for admission.

Something of the peculiar atmosphere, or perhaps their failure to bring the animals from their hutches, seemed to transmit itself to the party of visitors. After trying to read the signs, one of the men began to rattle a stick between the bars of the cages. Then, losing interest abruptly, they made off together without a backward glance at either the woman or the dwarf. As he passed me the man with the stick pulled a face and waved his hand in front of his nose.

I waited until they had gone and then approached the cages. The dwarf appeared to remember me—at least, he made no effort to scuttle away but watched me with his drifting eyes. The woman sat on the steps of the caravan, gazing across the cinders with the expression of a tired and unthinking child.

I glanced into one or two of the cages. There was no sign of the animals, but the smell that had driven off the previous party was certainly pronounced. The familiar pungent odour quickened my nostrils. I walked over to the young woman.

"You've had some visitors," I commented.

"Not many," she replied. "A few have come."

I was about to point out that she could hardly expect a huge attendance if none of the animals in the cages was prepared to make an appearance, but the girl's hangdog look restrained me. The top of her robe revealed a small childlike breast, and it seemed impossible that this pale young woman should have been put in sole charge of such a doomed enterprise. Searching for an excuse that might console her, I said: "It's rather late, there's the other fair . . ." I pointed to the cages. "That smell, too. Perhaps you're used to it, but it might put people off." I forced a smile. "I'm sorry, I don't mean to—"

"I understand," she said matter-of-factly. "It's why we have to leave so soon." She nodded at the dwarf. "We clean them every day."

I was about to ask what animals the cages held—the smell reminded me of the chimpanzee house at the zoo—when there was a commotion from the direction of the bank. A group of sailors, two or three girls among them, came swaying along the towpath. They greeted the sight of the menagerie with boisterous shouts. Linked arm in arm, they made a drunken swerve up the bank, then stamped across the cinders to the cages. The dwarf moved out of their way, and watched from the shadows between two of the wagons, hat in hand.

The sailors pushed over to one of the cages and pressed their faces to the bars, nudging each other in the ribs and whistling in an effort to bring the creature out of its hutch. They moved over to the next cage, pulling at each other in a struggling melee.

One of them shouted at the woman, who sat on the steps of the caravan. "Are you closed, or what? The perisher won't come out of his hole!"

There was a roar of laughter at this. Another of the sailors rattled one of the girls' handbags, and then dug into his pockets.

"Pennies out, lads. Who's got the tickets?"

He spotted the dwarf and tossed the penny towards him. A moment later a dozen coins showered through the air around the dwarf's head. He scuttled about, warding them off with his hat, but made no effort to pick up the coins.

The sailors moved on to the third cage. After a fruitless effort to draw the animal towards them they began to rock the wagon from side to side. Their good humour was beginning to fade. As I left the young woman and strolled past the cages several of the sailors had started to climb up onto the bars.

At this point one of the doors sprang open. As it clanged against the bars the noise fell away. Everyone stepped back, as if expecting some huge striped tiger to spring out at them from its hutch. Two of the sailors moved forward and gingerly reached for the door. As they closed it one of them peered into the cage. Suddenly he leapt up into the doorway. The others shouted at him, but the sailor kicked aside the straw and and stepped across to the hutch.

"It's bloody empty!"

As he shouted this out there was a delighted roar. Slamming the door—curiously enough, the bolt was on the inside—the sailor began to prance around the cage, gibbering like a baboon through the bars. At first I thought he must be mistaken, and looked round at the young woman and the dwarf. Both were watching the sailors but gave no inkling that there was any danger from the animal within. Sure enough, as a second sailor was let into the cage and dragged the hutch over to the bars, I saw that it was unoccupied.

Involuntarily I found myself staring at the young woman. Was this, then, the point of this strange and pathetic menagerie—that there were no animals at all, at least in most of the cages, and that what was being exhibited was simply nothing, merely the cages themselves, the essence of imprisonment with all its ambiguities? Was this a zoo in the abstract, some kind of bizarre comment on the meaning of life? Yet neither the young woman nor the dwarf seemed subtle enough for this, and possibly there was a less farfetched explanation. Perhaps once there had been animals, but these had died out, and the girl and her companion had found that people would still come and gaze at the empty cages, with much the same fascination of visitors to disused cemeteries. After a while they no longer charged any admission, but drifted aimlessly from town to town. . . .

Before I could pursue this train of thought there was a shout behind me. A sailor ran past, brushing my shoulder. The discovery of the empty cage had removed any feelings of restraint, and the sailors were chasing the dwarf among the wagons. At this first hint of violence the woman stood up and disappeared into the caravan, and the poor dwarf was left to fend for himself. One of the sailors tripped him up and snatched the hat off his head as the little figure lay in the dust with his legs in the air.

The sailor in front of me caught the hat and was about to toss it up onto one of the wagon roofs. Stepping forward, I held his arm, but he wrenched himself away. The dwarf had vanished from sight, and another group of the sailors were trying to turn one of the wagons and push it towards the river. Two of them had got among the horses and were lifting the women onto their backs. The grey stallion which had led the procession across the bridge suddenly bolted along the bank. Running after it through the confusion, I heard a warning shout behind me. There was the thud of hooves on the wet turf, and a woman's cry as a horse swerved above me. I was struck on the head and shoulder and knocked heavily to the ground.

It must have been some two hours later that I awoke, lying on a bench beside the bank. Under the night sky the town was silent, and I could hear the faint sounds of a water vole moving along the river and the distant splash of water around the bridge. I sat up and brushed away the dew that had formed on my clothes. Further along the bank the circus wagons stood in the clearing darkness, the dim forms of the horses motionless by the water.

Collecting myself, I decided that after being knocked down by the horse I had been carried to the bench by the sailors and left there to recover when and as soon as I could. Nursing my head and shoulders, I looked around for any sign of the party, but the bank was deserted. Standing up, I slowly walked back towards the circus, in the vague hope that the dwarf might help me home.

Twenty yards away, I saw something move in one of the cages, its white form passing in front of the bars. There was no sign of the dwarf or the young woman, but the wagons had been pushed back into place.

Standing in the centre of the cages, I peered about uncertainly, aware that their occupants had at last emerged from the hutches. The angular grey bodies were indistinct in the darkness, but as familiar as the pungent smell that came from the cages.

A voice shouted behind me, a single obscene word. I turned to find its source, and saw one of the occupants watching me with cold eyes. As I stared he raised his hand and moved the fingers in a perverted gesture.

A second voice called out, followed by a chorus of abusive cat-calls. With an effort, I managed to clear my head, then began a careful walk around the cages, satisfying myself for the last time as to the identity of their tenants. Except for the one at the end, which was empty, the others were occupied. The thin figures stood openly in front of the bars that protected them from me, their pallid faces shining in the dim light. At last I recognised the smell that came from the cages.

As I walked away their derisive voices called after me, and the young woman roused from her bed in the caravan watched quietly from the steps.

## Afterword:

"The Recognition" expresses a cordial distaste for the human race—not inappropriately. The temper of the times seems to be one of self-love, if of a strange sort—Caliban asleep across a mirror stained with vomit. But perhaps the story also illustrates the paradox that the only real freedom is to be found in a prison. Sometimes it is difficult to tell on which side of the bars we are—the real gaps between the bars are the sutures of one's own skull. Originally I toyed with the notion of the narrator entering a cage and joining the circus, but this would have destroyed an important point. The story is not in fact a piece of hard-won misanthropy but a comment on some of the more unusual perspectives that separate us. The most important characters, whose motives are a key to the story, are the young woman and her dwarf. Why do they take this dismal circus on its endless tour?

## Introduction to JUDAS:

Seated at the right hand of God, I was asked, "Give the operable word for John Brunner, the well-known English science fiction novelist." I thought a moment and suggested "urbane." God smiled benignly, but was obviously not satisfied with the initial response. " 'Suave?' " I ventured. God made a tiny *moue* of vexation. " 'Chivalrous? Refined? Cultured? Gracious?' " God gave me one of *those* looks. " 'Charming?' " I said, in a small voice. God broke into a helluva smile. He clapped me on the back with camaraderie. "Excellent, Harlan, *ex*cellent!" he said in his mellow voice.

"Thank you, Mr. Brunner," I replied.

The first time I heard of John Brunner was in 1952. He had one half the magazine known as *Two Complete Science-Adventure Novels* (I *think* that was the title. It's been quite a few years. But I do recall the story on the other half of the magazine was a Poul Anderson epic.) I don't recall the name of the novelette (which they invariably called a "complete novel") but it was published by Fiction House, so it must have been something like "Sex Kings of the Plutonian Pleasure Domes." It was written by Killian Huston Brunner. Ha-*ha,* Brunner, now we gotcha! [And this comment from John Brunner: "Your memory anent the issue of *TCSAB* in which you first saw my name is a trifle astray. It wasn't 1952 but 1953. The other half was Brian Berry's 'Mission to Marakee,' not a Poul Anderson story. The name was—and is—(John) Kilian Houston Brunner (not Killian Huston). And for what it's worth the story was titled 'The Wanton of Argus.'"]

John Brunner was born in 1934, in Oxfordshire, England. He has written the Hugo nominee *The Whole Man,* which was brilliant. In 1940 he found a copy of Wells's *War of the Worlds* in his nursery and was hooked. He has written *The Long Result,* which was almost a total success. In 1943 he started (but did not finish) writing his first s-f story, because he couldn't find enough of the stuff to read. He has written "The Squares of the City," which is a small masterpiece of technique. In 1947 he collected his first rejection slip, and in 1951 sold his first paperback in the United Kingdom. He has written "The Dreaming Earth," which fell apart badly in the last section but was fascinating up to that point. In 1952 he made his first sales to American magazines, and from 1953 to 1955 he was a (drafted without enthusiasm) pilot officer in the RAF. He has written *Wear the Butchers' Medal,* which is a stunning suspense-adventure novel. In 1956 he was a technical abstractor on a magazine edited by "John Christopher" and from 1956 to 1958 was a publishers' editor under Jonathan Burke. He has written *The Space-Time Juggler* and *The Astronauts Must Not Land* and *Castaways' World* and *Listen! The Stars!* and ten others, all for one publisher who slapped the insipid names just listed on books that may not be classics in the field of speculative fiction but are, each and every one, well written, entertaining and worth reading, which makes it a shame they are albatrossed by such hideous titles. But since 1958, when John Brunner got married and turned free lance, he has published over forty books, so he takes the bitter with the sweet.

He has written mainly speculative fiction but his output also includes thrillers and straight novels. He has contributed to almost every magazine in sight, written a great many topical "folk" songs including one recorded by Pete Seeger, and he has managed to visit about fourteen different countries thus far. ("I have the impression that I'm losing ground, though," he writes. "Every time I notch up a new one, another declares its independence and leaves me with just as many still unvisited.")

He lives in Hampstead, London, his favorite place, drives a Daimler

V-8 convertible, and enjoys his work so much it seems to be almost a hobby for him. Brunner's current ambition: to build a villa in Greece and get away from the English winter, which is almost always wet.

The story you are about to read was the third Brunner submission for DANGEROUS VISIONS. Not that either of the first two wouldn't have done marvelously, but there were some minor entanglements. On the first one, called "The Vitanuls," I had the temerity to disagree with John on the manner of presentation of an absolutely brilliant and original concept. I sent him about five single-spaced pages of perceptive, intelligent, pithy comment, outlining rewrite, and with his usual good grace, and with almost a surfeit of *panache,* he wrote me back and told me to get stuffed.

So that took care of *that* one. The stupid bastard doesn't know a new Maxwell Perkins when he sees one. But, great in my magnanimity, I accepted a second submission from Brunner's agent, a wildly hilarious black comedy called "Nobody Axed You," and was ready to send out the check when I was informed, rather sheepishly, by the agent, that there was, uh, one small, er, minor, really insig*nifi*cant, uh, problem with my publishing the story as a brand-new, never-before-in-print original. It had been published in England. But that didn't matter, the agent hastily assured me. After all, it had only been in a British magazine so none of the readers of my anthology could *poss*ibly have seen it. So that took care of *that* one.

A month later Brunner, shamefaced, and having received a cable from the sanitarium where I was under heavy sedation, sent me a story on his own. That story, "Judas," begins on the next page.

You'd love Brunner. He's quiet, but deadly. Like a curare-tipped blow dart in the back of the neck.

## ● JUDAS

### by John Brunner

The Friday evening service was drawing to its close. The rays of the declining spring sun slanted through the polychrome plastic of the windows and lay along the floor of the central aisle like a pool of oil spilt on a wet road. On the polished steel of the altar a silver wheel spun continually, glinting between two ever burning mercury vapour lamps; above it, silhouetted against the darkling eastern sky, there stood a statue of God. The surpliced choir was singing an anthem—"The Word Made Steel"—and the minister sat listening with his hand cupped under his chin, wondering if God had approved of the sermon he had just preached on the Second Coming.

Most of the large congregation was enraptured by the music. Only one man present, at the end of the rearmost row of bare steel pews, fidgeted impatiently, flexing the rubber pad from the forehead rest before him in nervous fingers. He had to keep his hands occupied, or else they kept straying to the bulge in the inside pocket of his plain brown jacket. His watery blue eyes wandered restlessly along the climactic, sweeping lines of the metal temple and shifted away every time they came to the wheel motif which the architect—probably God himself—had incorporated wherever possible.

The anthem closed on a thrilling dissonance and the congregation knelt, their heads against the rubber rests, while the minister pronounced the blessing of the Wheel. The man in brown wasn't really listening, but he caught a few phrases: "May he guide you in your appointed courses . . . serve you as your eternal pivot . . . bring you at last to the peace of the true eternal round . . ."

Then he stood with the rest of them while the choir marched out to the strains of the electronic organ. Directly the minister had disappeared through the vestry door, the worshippers began to shuffle towards the main exits. He alone remained sitting in his pew.

He was not the sort of person one would look at twice. He had sandy hair and a worn, tired face; his teeth were stained and irregular, his clothes fitted badly, and his eyes were a fraction out of focus, as though he needed glasses. Plainly the service had not brought him peace of mind.

Eventually, when everybody else had gone, he stood up and replaced the rubber pad with scrupulous exactitude. For a moment his eyes closed and his lips moved soundlessly; as if this act had endowed him with the courage for a decision, he seemed to draw himself up like a diver poising on a high board. Abruptly he left the pew and walked—soundless on the rubber carpet of the nave—towards the small steel door that bore the single word VESTRY.

Beside it there was a bell. He rang.

Shortly the door was opened by a junior acolyte, a youth in a grey robe woven of metallic links that jingled as he moved, hands in grey shiny gloves, scalp hidden under a smooth steel cap. In a voice made impersonal by careful practice, the acolyte said, "You wish counsel?"

The man in brown nodded, shifting a trifle nervously from foot to foot. Through the doorway were visible many devotional pictures and statues; he dropped his gaze before them.

"What is your name?" the acolyte inquired.

"Karimov," said the man in brown. "Julius Karimov."

He tensed fractionally as he spoke, his eyes fleeting over the acolyte's face in search of any reaction. None showed, and he relaxed on the youth's curt order to wait while he informed the minister.

The moment he was alone, Karimov crossed the vestry and examined a painting on the far wall: Anson's "Immaculate Manufacture," depicting the legendary origin of God—a bolt of lightning from heaven smiting an ingot of pure steel. It was excellently done, of course; the artist's use of electro-luminescent paint for the lightning, in particular, was masterly. But from Karimov it provoked an expression of physical nausea, and after only seconds he had to turn away.

At length the minister entered in the officiating robe which identified him as one of the Eleven closest to God, his headpiece—which during the service had concealed his shaven scalp—discarded, his white, slender hands playing with a jewelled emblem of the Wheel that hung around his neck on a platinum chain. Karimov turned slowly to confront him, right hand slightly raised in a stillborn gesture. It had been a calculated risk to give his real name; he thought that was probably still a secret. But his real face . . .

No, no hint of recognition. The minister merely said in his professionally resonant voice, "What may I do for you, my son?"

The man in brown squared his shoulders and said simply, "I want to talk to God."

With the resigned air of one well used to dealing with requests of that sort, the minister sighed. "God is extremely busy, my son," he murmured. "He has the spiritual welfare of the entire human race to look after. Cannot I help you? Is there a particular problem on which you need advice, or do you seek generalised divine guidance in programming your life?"

Karimov looked at him diffidently and thought: *This man really believes! His faith isn't just pretence for profit, but deep-seated honest trust, and it is more terrifying than everything else that even those who were with me at the beginning should believe!*

He said after a little, "You are kind, Father, but I need more than mere advice. I have"—he seemed to stumble at the word—"prayed much, and sought help from several ministers, and still I have not attained to the peace of the true round. Once, long ago, I had the privilege of seeing God in the steel; I wish to do so again, that's all. I have no doubt, of course, that He will remember me."

There was a long silence, during which the minister's dark eyes remained fixed on Karimov. Finally he said, "Remember you? Oh yes, he will certainly remember you! But *I* remember you too—now!"

His voice shook with uncontrollable fury, and he reached for a bell on the wall.

Strength born of desperation poured through Karimov's scrawny frame. He hurled himself at the minister, striking aside the outstretched arm inches from its goal, bowling the tall man over, seizing the tough chain around his neck, and pulling with every ounce of force he could muster.

The chain bit deep into pale flesh; as if possessed, Karimov tugged and tugged at it, twisted, took a fresh grip and tugged again. The minister's eyes bulged, mouth uttered loathsome formless grunts, fists beat at his attacker's arms—and grew weaker, and ceased.

Karimov drew back, shaking at what he had done, and compelled himself unsteadily to his feet. To the former colleague who now had gone beyond all hope of hearing he muttered his sick apology, then calmed himself with deep breaths and approached the door by which he had not entered the room.

On his throne beneath its wheel-shaped canopy of steel, God sat. His polished limbs gleamed under the muted lights, his head was beautifully designed to suggest a human face without possessing a single human feature—even eyes.

*Blind insensate thing,* thought Karimov as he shut the door behind him. Unconsciously his hand touched what he had in his pocket.

The voice too was more than humanly perfect, a deep pure tone as if an organ spoke. It said, "My son—"

And stopped.

Karimov gave an audible sigh of relief and his nervousness dropped from him like a cloak. He stepped forward casually and sat down in the central one of the eleven chairs arranged in a horseshoe before the throne, while the blank shiny gaze of the robot rested on him and the whole metal frame locked in astonishment.

"Well?" Karimov challenged. "How do you like meeting somebody who doesn't believe in you for a change?"

The robot moved in human fashion, relaxing. Steel fingers linked under his chin while he reconsidered the intruder with interest instead of amazement. The voice rang out afresh.

"So it's you, Black!"

Karimov nodded with a faint smile. "That's what they used to call me in the old days. I used to think it was a silly affectation—assigning the scientists who worked on top-secret projects false names. But it's turned out to have advantages, for me at any rate. I gave my own name of Karimov to your—ah—late apostle outside, and it meant nothing to him. Speaking of real names, by the way: how long is it since anyone addressed you as A-46?"

The robot jerked. "It is sacrilege to apply that term to me!"

"Sacrilege be—bothered. I'll go further and remind you what the A stands for in A-46. Android! An imitation of a man! A sexless insensate assembly of metal parts which I helped to design, and it calls itself God!" Scathing contempt rode the lashing words. "You and your fantasies of Immaculate Manufacture! Blasted by a bolt of heavenly lightning from a chunk of untooled steel! Talk about making men in God's own image—you're the 'God' who was made in man's!"

They had even incorporated the facility of shrugging in their design, Karimov recalled with a start as the robot made use of it.

"Leaving sacrilege on one side for a moment, then," the machine said, "is there any real reason why you should deny that I am God? Why should not the second Incarnation be an Inferration—in imperishable steel? As for your benighted and deluded belief that you created the metal part of me—which is anyway supremely unimportant since the spirit alone is eternal—it's long been said that a prophet is without honour in his own country, and since the Inferration took place near your experimental station . . . Well!"

Karimov laughed. He said, "Well I'm damned! I think you believe it yourself!"

"You are beyond question damned. For a moment I hoped, seeing you enter my throne room, that you'd learned the error of your ways and come to acknowledge my divinity at last. Of my infinite compassion I will give you one final chance to do so before I call my ministers to take you away. Now or never, Black or Karimov or whatever you choose to call yourself: do you repent and believe?"

Karimov wasn't listening. He was staring past the shining machine into nowhere, while his hand caressed the bulge in his pocket. He said in a low voice, "I've plotted years for this moment—twenty years, ever since the day we turned you on and I began to suspect we'd gone wrong. Not till now was there anything I could have done. And in the meantime, while I sweated and hunted for a way to stop you, I've seen the ultimate humiliation of mankind.

"We've been slaves to our tools since the first caveman made the first knife to help him get his supper. After that there was no going back, and we built till our machines were ten million times more powerful than ourselves. We gave ourselves cars when we might have learned to run; we made airplanes when we might have grown wings; and then the inevitable. We made a machine our God."

"And why not?" the robot boomed. "Can you name any single way in which I am not your superior? I am stronger, more intelligent and more durable than a man. I have mental and physical powers that shame comparison. I feel no pain. I am immortal and invulnerable and yet you say I am not God. Why? From perverseness!"

"No," said Karimov with terrible directness. "Because you are mad.

"You were the climax of a decade's work by our team: the dozen most brilliant living cyberneticists. Our dream was to create a mechanical analogue of a human being which could be programmed directly with intelligence drawn from the patterns in our own brains. In that we succeeded—far too well!

"I've had time enough in the past twenty years to work out where we went astray. It was my fault, God help me—the real God, if He exists, not you, you mechanical fraud! Always somewhere at the back of my mind while we were working on you there lurked the thought that to build the machine we had envisaged would be to become as God: to make a creative intelligence, that none save He had yet achieved! That was megalomania, and I'm ashamed, but it *was* in my mind, and from mine it was transferred to yours. No one knew of it; even I was afraid to admit it to myself, for shame is a saving human grace. But you! What could you know of shame, of self-restraint, of empathy and love? Once implanted in your complex of artificial neurones, that mania grew till it knew no bounds, and . . . here you are. Insane with the lust for divine glory! Why else the doctrine of the Word Made Steel, and the image of the Wheel, the mechanical form that does not occur in nature? Why else the trouble you go to to make parallels in your godless existence with that of the greatest Man who ever lived?"

Karimov was still speaking in the same low tones, but his eyes were ablaze with hatred.

"You have no soul and you accuse me of sacrilege. You're a collection of wires and transistors and you call yourself God. Blasphemy! Only a man could be God!"

The robot shifted with a clang of metal limbs and said, "All this is not merely nonsense but a waste of my valuable time. Is that all you came for—to rave at me?"

"No," said Karimov. "I came to kill you."

At long last his hand dipped into the bulging pocket and produced the object there concealed: a curious little weapon, less than six inches long. A short metal tube extended forward from it; backward from the handgrip a flex disappeared inside his coat; under his thumb there was a small red stud.

He said, "It took me twenty years to design and build this. We chose steel for your body that only an atomic bomb could destroy; how, though, could one man walk into your presence with a nuclear weapon on his back? I had to wait until I had a means of cutting your steel as easily as a knife cuts a man's weak flesh. Here it is—and now I can undo the wrong I did to my own species!"

He pressed the stud.

The robot, motionless till that moment as if incapable of believing that anyone could really wish to harm him, jolted upright, turned half around, and stood paralysed as a tiny hole appeared in the metal of his side. Steel began to form little drops around the hole; the surrounding area glowed red, and the drops flowed like water—or blood.

Karimov held the weapon steady, though it scorched his fingers.

Sweat stood out on his forehead. Another half minute, and the damage would be irreparable.

Behind him a door slammed open. He cursed, for his weapon would not work on a man. To the last moment he kept it aimed; then he was seized from behind and pinioned, and the weapon torn from its flex and hurled to the floor and stamped into ruin.

The robot did not move.

The tension of twenty hate-filled years broke and his relief boiled up into hysterical laughter which he fought to quell. When he finally succeeded, he saw that the man who held him was the junior acolyte who had admitted him to the vestry, and that there were other men around, strangers, gazing in utter silence at their God.

"Look at him, look at him!" Karimov crowed. "Your idol was nothing but a robot, and what men make they can destroy. He said he was divine, but he wasn't even invulnerable! I've freed you! Don't you understand? *I've set you free!*"

But the acolyte wasn't paying him any attention. He stared fixedly at the monstrous metal doll, licking his lips, until at last he said in a voice that was neither relieved nor horrified, but only awed, "The Hole in the Side!"

A dream began to die in Karimov's mind. Numb, he watched the other men walk over to the robot and peer into the hole, heard one of them say, "How long to repair the damage?" and the other reply offhandedly, "Oh, three days, I guess!" And it was clear to him what he had done.

Wasn't this a Friday, and in spring? Hadn't he himself known that the robot made careful parallels between his own career and that of the man he parodied? How it had reached the climax: there had been a death, and there would be a resurrection—on the third day. . . .

And the grip of the Word Made Steel would never be broken.

In turn the men made the sign of the Wheel and departed, until one only remained. Stern, he came down from the throne to confront Karimov and address the acolyte who held him in a rigid grasp.

"Who is he, anyway?" the man demanded.

The acolyte gazed at the limp figure slumped on the chair with the weight of all the ages crushing him, and his mouth rounded in an O of comprehension. He said, *"Now* I understand! He calls himself Karimov.

"But his real name must be Iscariot."

**Afterword:**

I don't really know how "Judas" came about, but I suspect it has its roots in the tendency I've noticed in myself as well as in other people to anthropomorphise machinery. I once had a Morgan sports car, a honey of a vehicle with a distinct and rather cranky personality which was about eight years old before I took it over. I swear it hated traffic in the rush hour, and complained bitterly when it was parked unless I'd consoled it for all that overheating and inching along in bottom gear by taking a detour down a stretch of fast road where I could let it out to about fifty or so.

I hope our growing habit of handing over not merely our drudgery but our capacity for making up our minds to our shiny new gadgetry doesn't culminate in literal machine-worship, but just in case it does —there's the story.

## Introduction to TEST TO DESTRUCTION:

I have done so many riffs on who and what Keith Laumer is (not the least of which is a verbose and sententious introduction to his Doubleday collection, *Nine by Laumer*) that, frankly, I don't know what to say that I haven't already said. But . . .

Laumer is a tall, rugged, rather good-looking man, if you admire that kind of cruel mouth and beady little eyes like a marmoset. He has written several volumes of stories about a professional diplomat in the galactic future, a fellow named Retief. It is no mere coincidence that Laumer has been a diplomat, in the U. S. Foreign Service. But the Retief stories are lighthearted, and many readers have failed to take notice (as I pointed out at dreary length in my introduction to his collection) of Laumer's serious work. His many allegories of the world in which we live—stories that take a hard, sometimes distressed look at what we do to each other. His dynachrome stories with their inherent warnings about the age of the computers. His chase-adventures through the Structured Society where the man alone is doomed from the start, yet makes his play because he *is* a man. *These* stories are the real Laumer, and it is a shame he can sell the Retief stuff so easily, because it allows him to coast, allows him to tell extended jokes when he should be grappling with more complex themes, such as the one he offers in the story you are about to read.

Laumer is a singular man. He is a mass of contradictions, a driven talent, a pillar of strength, a man who values and understands ethics and morality on almost a cellular level. It shows up in his work. He is a writer who refuses to ignore reality, even when writing interstellar fantasies. There are basics in the Universe that are immutable to Laumer. I cannot find it in my heart to disagree with him. Love and courage and determination are good; war and laziness and hypocrisy are bad. If I could name a man I have met who seemed to me incorruptible, it would have to be Laumer. (I am cautious about making these value judgments, however. Too often I've raised mere mortals to the pedestal, only to find out they are as strong-and-weak as all other mere mortals, including myself. Laumer may well be an exception.)

Keith's biographical notes are rather interesting. I include them here just as they were submitted, for I think they reflect the truth of what I've just said about him.

"I was born in New York State, lived there until age twelve, then to Florida. Thus, I can see the Civil War from both sides. Perhaps this is at the bottom of my inability to become a true believer in any of the popular causes. (I find that humans can be divided only into two meaningful categories: Decent Humans and Sonsofbitches; both types appear to be evenly distributed among all shapes, colors, sizes and nationalities.)

"In 1943, at age eighteen, I went into the army. Saw Texas, Georgia, Germany, France, Belgium, Holland, Luxembourg, and other strange places. They all seemed to be populated by the same kind of grubby, greedy, lovable/hatable people I had known back home. In 1946, I found myself on the University of Illinois campus, studying architecture. Five years later I had a wife, two tots, and two degrees. Meantime, I had put the final conclusions to my theories about people by having met bastards both black and white, Good Christians and Good Jews. None of them seemed to have a corner on virtue or villainy.

"In 1953, I fooled the authorities by going into the air force as a first lieutenant before they could draft me for WWIII, then imminent. They fooled me instead, by finking out on the war. I spent a year in solitary on a rock in Labrador. In '56, I left the air force to enter the foreign service. Discovered a teeny-weeny preponderance of Sonsofbitches there. I did two years in Burma standing on my ear, and discovered (surprise!) I was a writer. I went back into the air force in 1960, did a tour in London, quit my job in 1965 to become a full-time writer, and I never intend to change jobs again."

He neglects to mention such books as *Embassy, Catastrophe Planet, Envoy to New Worlds, Worlds of the Imperium, Retief's War* and *Earth-blood* (written with Rosel G. Brown). He also neglects to mention he is one of the very few major new talents to emerge in the field of speculative fiction in the past five years. But we can attribute that to Keith's incredible modesty.

Earlier I commented on the serious nature of the best of Laumer's work. What follows, the story "Test to Destruction," is indicative of this seriousness. But Laumer is no mere Edgar Guest of science fiction—a mouther of platitudes—life is real, life is earnest—for he offers us a dangerous vision about the basic nature of man. And it is a comment on his drive to become the compleat storyteller that this tale of morality is couched in the time-honored form of the chase-action-adventure.

# ● TEST TO DESTRUCTION

## by Keith Laumer

### ONE

The late October wind drove icy rain against Mallory's face above his turned-up collar where he stood concealed in the shadows at the mouth of the narrow alley.

"It's ironic, Johnny," the small, grim-faced man beside him muttered. "You—the man who should have been World Premier tonight—skulking in the back streets while Koslo and his bully boys drink champagne in the Executive Palace."

"That's all right, Paul," Mallory said. "Maybe he'll be too busy with his victory celebration to concern himself with me."

"And maybe he won't," the small man said. "He won't rest easy as long as he knows you're alive to oppose him."

"It will only be a few more hours, Paul. By breakfast time Koslo will know his rigged election didn't take."

"But if he takes you first, that's the end, Johnny. Without you the *coup* will collapse like a soap bubble."

"I'm not leaving the city," Mallory said flatly. "Yes, there's a certain risk involved; but you don't bring down a dictator without taking a few chances."

"You didn't have to take this one, meeting Crandall yourself."

"It will help if he sees me, knows I'm in this all the way."

In silence, the two men awaited the arrival of their fellow conspirator.

### TWO

Aboard the interstellar dreadnought cruising half a parsec from Earth, the compound Ree mind surveyed the distant Solar System.

*Radiation on many wave lengths from the third body,* the Perceptor cells directed the impulse to the 6934 units comprising the segmented brain which guided the ship. *Modulations over the forty-ninth through the ninety-first spectra of mentation.*

*A portion of the pattern is characteristic of exocosmic manipulatory intelligence,* the Analyzers extrapolated from the data. *Other indications range in complexity from levels one through twenty-six.*

*This is an anomalous situation,* the Recollectors mused. *It is the essential nature of a Prime Intelligence to destroy all lesser competing mind-forms, just as I/we have systematically annihilated those I/we have encountered on my/our exploration of the Galactic Arm.*

*Before action is taken, clarification of the phenomenon is essential,* the Interpreters pointed out. *Closure to a range not exceeding one radiation/second will be required for extraction and analysis of a representative mind-unit.*

*In this event, the risk level rises to Category Ultimate,* the Analyzers announced dispassionately.

RISK LEVELS NO LONGER APPLY, the powerful thought-impulse of the Egon put an end to the discussion. NOW OUR SHIPS RANGE INTO NEW SPACE, SEEKING EXPANSION ROOM FOR THE GREAT RACE. THE UNALTERABLE COMMAND OF THAT-WHICH-IS-SUPREME REQUIRES THAT MY/OUR PROBE BE PROSECUTED TO THE LIMIT OF REE CAPABILITY, TESTING MY/OUR ABILITY FOR SURVIVAL AND DOMINANCE. THERE CAN BE NO TIMIDITY, NO EXCUSE FOR FAILURE. LET ME/US NOW ASSUME A CLOSE SURVEILLANCE ORBIT!

In utter silence, and at a velocity a fraction of a kilometer below that of light, the Ree dreadnought flashed toward Earth.

### THREE

Mallory tensed as a dark figure appeared a block away under the harsh radiance of a polyarc.

"There's Crandall now," the small man hissed. "I'm glad—" he broke off as the roar of a powerful turbine engine sounded suddenly along the empty avenue. A police car exploded from a side street, rounded the corner amid a shriek of overstressed gyros. The man under the light turned to run—and the vivid blue glare of a SURF-gun winked and stuttered from the car. The burst of slugs caught the runner, slammed him against the brick wall, kicked him from his feet, rolled him, before the crash of the guns reached Mallory's ears.

"My God! They've killed Tony!" the small man blurted. "We've got to get out . . . !"

Mallory took half a dozen steps back into the alley, froze as lights sprang up at the far end. He heard booted feet hit pavement, a hoarse voice that barked a command.

"We're cut off," he snapped. There was a rough wooden door six feet away. He jumped to it, threw his weight against it. It held. He stepped back, kicked it in, shoved his companion ahead of him into a dark room smelling of moldy burlap and rat droppings. Stumbling, groping in the dark, Mallory led the way across a stretch of littered floor, felt along the wall, found a door that hung by one hinge. He pushed past it, was in a passage floored with curled linoleum, visible in the feeble gleam filtered through a fanlight above a massive, barred door. He turned the other way, ran for the smaller door at the far end of the passage. He was ten feet from it when the center panel burst inward in a hail of wood splinters that grazed him, ripped at his coat like raking talons. Behind him, the small man made a choking noise; Mallory whirled in time to see him fall back against the wall and go down, his chest and stomach torn away by the full impact of a thousand rounds from the police SURF-gun.

An arm came through the broached door, groping for the latch. Mallory took a step, seized the wrist, wrenched backward with all his weight, felt the elbow joint shatter. The scream of the injured policeman was drowned in a second burst from the rapid-fire weapon—but Mallory had already leaped, caught the railing of the stair, pulled himself up and over. He took the steps five at a time, passed a landing littered with broken glass and empty bottles, kept going, emerged in a corridor of sagging doors and cobwebs. Feet crashed below, furious voices yelled. Mallory stepped inside the nearest door, stood with his back to the wall beside it. Heavy feet banged on the stairs, paused, came his way. . . .

Mallory tensed, and as the policeman passed the door, he stepped out, brought his hand over and down in a side-handed blow to the base of the neck that had every ounce of power in his shoulders behind it. The man seemed to dive forward, and Mallory leaped, caught the gun before it struck the floor. He took three steps, poured a full magazine into the stair well. As he turned to sprint for the far end of the passage, return fire boomed from below.

A club, swung by a giant, struck him in the side, knocked the breath from his lungs, sent him spinning against the wall. He recovered, ran on; his hand, exploring, found a deep gouge that bled freely. The bullet had barely grazed him.

He reached the door to the service stair, recoiled violently as a dirty gray shape sprang at him with a yowl from the darkness—in the instant before a gun flashed and racketed in the narrow space, shattering plaster dust from the wall above his head. A thickset man in the dark uniform of the Security Police, advancing up the stair at a run, checked momentarily as he saw the gun in Mallory's hands—and before he recovered himself, Mallory had swung the empty weapon, knocked him spinning back down onto the landing. The cat that had saved his life— an immense, battle-scarred Tom—lay on the floor, half its head blown away by the blast it had intercepted. Its lone yellow eye was fixed on him; its claws raked the floor, as, even in death, it advanced to the attack. Mallory jumped over the stricken beast, went up the stairs.

Three flights higher, the stair ended in a loft stacked with bundled newspapers and rotting cartons from which mice scuttled as he approached. There was a single window, opaque with grime. Mallory tossed aside the useless gun, scanned the ceiling for evidence of an escape hatch, saw nothing. His side ached abominably.

Relentless feet sounded beyond the door. Mallory backed to a corner of the room—and again, the deafening shriek of the SURF-gun sounded, and the flimsy door bucked, disintegrated. For a moment there was total silence. Then:

"Walk out with your hands up, Mallory!" a brassy voice snarled. In the gloom, pale flames were licking over the bundled papers, set afire by the torrent of steel-jacketed slugs. Smoke rose, thickened.

"Come out before you fry," the voice called.

"Let's get out of here," another man bawled. "This dump will go up like tinder!"

"Last chance, Mallory!" the first man shouted, and now the flames, feeding on the dry paper, were reaching for the ceiling, roaring as they grew. Mallory went along the wall to the window, ripped aside the torn roller shade, tugged at the sash. It didn't move. He kicked out the glass, threw a leg over the sill, and stepped out onto a rusted fire escape. Five stories down, light puddled on grimy concrete, the white dots of upturned faces—and half a dozen police cars blocking the rain-wet street. He put his back to the railing, looked up. The fire escape extended three, perhaps four stories higher. He threw his arm across his face to shield it from the billowing flames, forced his aching legs to carry him up the iron treads three at a time.

The topmost landing was six feet below an overhanging cornice. Mallory stepped up on the rail, caught the edge of the carved stone trim with both hands, swung himself out. For a moment he dangled, ninety feet above the street; then he pulled himself up, got a knee over the coping, and rolled onto the roof.

Lying flat, he scanned the darkness around him. The level was broken only by a ventilator stack and a shack housing a stair or elevator head.

He reconnoitered, found that the hotel occupied a corner, with a parking lot behind it. On the alley side, the adjoining roof was at a level ten feet lower, separated by a sixteen-foot gap. As Mallory stared across at it, a heavy rumbling shook the deck under his feet: one of the floors of the ancient building, collapsing as the fire ate through its supports.

Smoke was rising all around him now. On the parking lot side, dusky flames soared up thirty feet above him, trailing an inverted cascade of sparks into the wet night sky. He went to the stairhead, found the metal door locked. A rusty ladder was clamped to the side of the structure. He wrenched it free, carried it to the alley side. It took all his strength to force the corroded catches free, pull the ladder out to its full extension. Twenty feet, he estimated. Enough—maybe.

He shoved the end of the ladder out, wrestled it across to rest on the roof below. The flimsy bridge sagged under his weight as he crawled up on it. He moved carefully out, ignoring the swaying of the fragile support. He was six feet from the far roof when he felt the rotten metal crumple under him; with a frantic lunge, he threw himself forward. Only the fact that the roof was at a lower level saved him. He clawed his way over the sheet-metal gutter, hearing shouts ring out below as the ladder crashed to the bricks of the alley.

*A bad break,* he thought. *Now they know where I am. . . .*

There was a heavy trap door set in the roof. He lifted it, descended an iron ladder into darkness, found his way to a corridor, along it to a stair. Faint sounds rose from below. He went down.

At the fourth floor, lights showed below, voices sounded, the clump of feet. He left the stair at the third floor, prowled along a hall, entered an abandoned office. Searchlights in the street below threw oblique shadows across the discolored walls.

He went on, through a connecting door into a room on the alley side. A cold draft, reeking of smoke, blew in through a glassless window. Below, the narrow way appeared to be deserted. Paul's body was gone. The broken ladder lay where it had fallen. It was, he estimated, a twenty-foot drop to the bricks; even if he let himself down to arm's length and dropped, a leg-breaker. . . .

Something moved below him. A uniformed policeman was standing at a spot directly beneath the window, his back against the wall. A wolf smile drew Mallory's face tight. In a single motion, he slid his body out over the sill, chest down, held on for an instant, seeing the startled face below turn upward, the mouth open for a yell—

He dropped; his feet struck the man's back, breaking his fall. He rolled clear, sat up, half dazed. The policeman sprawled on his face, his spine twisted at an awkward angle.

Mallory got to his feet—and almost fell at the stab of pain from his right ankle. Sprained, or broken. His teeth set against the pain, he moved along the wall. Icy rain water, sluicing from the downspout ahead, swirled about his ankles. He slipped, almost went down on the slimy bricks. The lesser darkness of the parking lot behind the building showed ahead. If he could reach it, cross it—then he might still have a chance. He had to succeed—for Monica, for the child, for the future of a world.

Another step, and another. It was as though there were a steel spike through his ankle. The bullet wound in his side was a vast ache that caught at him with every breath. His blood-soaked shirt and pants leg hung against him, icy cold. Ten feet more, and he would make his run for it—

Two men in the black uniforms of the State Security Police stepped out into his path, stood with blast-guns leveled at his chest. Mallory pushed away from the wall, braced himself for the burst of slugs that would end his life. Instead, a beam of light speared out through the misty rain, dazzling his eyes.

"You'll come with us, Mr. Mallory."

### FOUR

*Still no contact,* the Perceptors reported. *The prime-level minds below lack cohesion; they flicker and dart away even as I/we touch them.*

The Initiators made a proposal: *By the use of appropriate harmonics a resonance field can be set up which will reinforce any native mind functioning in an analogous rhythm.*

*I/we find that a pattern of the following character will be most suitable. . . .* A complex symbolism was displayed.

PERSEVERE IN THE FASHION DESCRIBED, the Egon commanded. ALL EXTRANEOUS FUNCTIONS WILL BE DISCONTINUED UNTIL SUCCESS IS ACHIEVED.

With total singleness of purpose, the Ree sensors probed across space from the dark and silent ship, searching for a receptive human mind.

### FIVE

The Interrogation Room was a totally bare cube of white enamel. At its geometric center, under a blinding white glare panel, sat a massive chair constructed of polished steel, casting an ink-black shadow.

A silent minute ticked past; then heels clicked in the corridor. A tall man in a plain, dark military tunic came through the open door, halted, studying his prisoner. His wide, sagging face was as gray and bleak as a tombstone.

"I warned you, Mallory," he said in a deep, growling tone.

"You're making a mistake, Koslo," Mallory said.

"Openly arresting the people's hero, eh?" Koslo curved his wide, gray lips in a death's-head smile. "Don't delude yourself. The malcontents will do nothing without their leader."

"Are you sure you're ready to put your regime to the test so soon?"

"It's that or wait, while your party gains strength. I chose the quicker course. I was never as good at waiting as you, Mallory."

"Well—you'll know by morning."

"That close, eh?" Koslo's heavy-lidded eyes pinched down on glints of light. He grunted. "I'll know many things by morning. You realize that your personal position is hopeless?" His eyes went to the chair.

"In other words, I should sell out to you now in return for—what? Another of your promises?"

"The alternative is the chair," Koslo said flatly.

"You have great confidence in machinery, Koslo—more than in men. That's your great weakness."

Koslo's hand went out, caressing the rectilinear metal of the chair. "This is a scientific apparatus designed to accomplish a specific task with the least possible difficulty to me. It creates conditions within the subject's neural system conducive to total recall, and at the same time amplifies the subvocalizations that accompany all highly cerebral activity. The subject is also rendered amenable to verbal cuing." He paused. "If you resist, it will destroy your mind—but not before you've told me everything: names, locations, dates, organization, operational plans—everything. It will be simpler for us both if you acknowledge the inevitable and tell me freely what I require to know."

"And after you've got the information?"

"You know my regime can't tolerate opposition. The more complete my information, the less bloodshed will be necessary."

Mallory shook his head. "No," he said bluntly.

"Don't be a fool, Mallory! This isn't a test of your manhood!"

"Perhaps it is, Koslo: man against machine."

Koslo's eyes probed at him. He made a quick gesture with one hand. "Strap him in."

Seated in the chair, Mallory felt the cold metal suck the heat from his body. Bands restrained his arms, legs, torso. A wide ring of woven wire and plastic clamped his skull firmly to the formed headrest. Across the room, Fey Koslo watched.

"Ready, Excellency," a technician said.

"Proceed."

Mallory tensed. An unwholesome excitement churned his stomach. He'd heard of the chair, of its power to scour a man's mind clean and leave him a gibbering hulk.

*Only a free society,* he thought, *can produce the technology that makes tyranny possible. . . .*

He watched as a white-smocked technician approached, reached for the control panel. There was only one hope left: if he could fight the power of the machine, drag out the interrogation, delay Koslo until dawn . . .

A needle-studded vise clamped down against Mallory's temples. Instantly his mind was filled with whirling fever images. He felt his throat tighten in an aborted scream. Fingers of pure force struck into his brain, dislodging old memories, ripping open the healed wounds of time. From somewhere, he was aware of a voice, questioning. Words trembled in his throat, yearning to be shouted aloud.

ɪ *I've got to resist!* The thought flashed through his mind and was gone, borne away on a tide of probing impulses that swept through his brain like a millrace. *I've got to hold out . . . long enough . . . to give the others a chance. . . .*

SIX

Aboard the Ree ship, dim lights glowed and winked on the panel that encircled the control center.

*I/we sense a new mind—a transmitter of great power,* the Perceptors announced suddenly. *But the images are confused. I/we sense struggle, resistance. . . .*

IMPOSE CLOSE CONTROL, the Egon ordered. NARROW FOCUS AND EXTRACT A REPRESENTATIVE PERSONALITY FRACTION!

*It is difficult; I/we sense powerful neural currents, at odds with the basic brain rhythms.*

COMBAT THEM!

Again the Ree mind reached out, insinuated itself into the complex field-matrix that was Mallory's mind, and began, painstakingly, to trace out and reinforce its native symmetries, permitting the natural ego-mosaic to emerge, free from distracting counterimpulses.

## SEVEN

The technician's face went chalk-white as Mallory's body went rigid against the restraining bands.

"You fool!" Koslo's voice cut at him like a whipping rod. "If he dies before he talks—"

"He . . . he fights strongly, Excellency." The man's eyes scanned instrument faces. "Alpha through delta rhythms normal, though exaggerated," he muttered. "Metabolic index .99 . . ."

Mallory's body jerked. His eyes opened, shut. His mouth worked.

"Why doesn't he speak?" Koslo barked.

"It may require a few moments, Excellency, to adjust the power flows to ten-point resonance—"

"Then get on with it, man! I risked too much in arresting this man to lose him now!"

## EIGHT

White-hot fingers of pure force lanced from the chair along the neural pathways within Mallory's brain—and met the adamantine resistance of the Ree probe. In the resultant confrontation, Mallory's battered self-awareness was tossed like a leaf in a gale.

*Fight!* The remaining wisp of his conscious intellect gathered itself—

—and was grasped, encapsulated, swept up and away. He was aware of spinning through a whirling fog of white light shot through with flashes and streamers of red, blue, violet. There was a sensation of great forces that pressed at him, flung him to and fro, drew his mind out like a ductile wire until it spanned the Galaxy. The filament grew broad, expanded into a diaphragm that bisected the universe. The plane assumed thickness, swelled out to encompass all space/time. Faint and far away, he sensed the tumultuous coursing of the energies that ravened just beyond the impenetrable membrane of force—

The imprisoning sphere shrank, pressed in, forcing his awareness into needle-sharp focus. He knew, without knowing how he knew, that he was locked in a sealed and airless chamber, constricting, claustrophobic, all sound and sensation cut off. He drew breath to scream—

No breath came. Only a weak pulse of terror, quickly fading, as if damped by an inhibiting hand. Alone in the dark, Mallory waited, every sense tuned, monitoring the surrounding blankness. . . .

NINE

*I/we have him!* The Perceptors pulsed, and fell away. At the center of the chamber, the mind trap pulsed with the flowing energies that confined and controlled the captive brain pattern.

TESTING WILL COMMENCE AT ONCE. The Egon brushed aside the interrogatory impulses from the mind-segments concerned with speculation. INITIAL STIMULI WILL BE APPLIED AND RESULTS NOTED. NOW!

TEN

. . . and was aware of a faint glimmer of light across the room: the outline of a window. He blinked, raised himself on one elbow. Bed-springs creaked under him. He sniffed. An acrid odor of smoke hung in the stifling air. He seemed to be in a cheap hotel room. He had no memory of how he came to be there. He threw back the coarse blanket and felt warped floor boards under his bare feet—

The boards were hot.

He jumped up, went to the door, grasped the knob—and jerked his hand back. The metal had blistered his palm.

He ran to the window, ripped aside the dirt-stiff gauze curtains, snapped open the latch, tugged at the sash. It didn't budge. He stepped back, kicked out the glass. Instantly a coil of smoke whipped in through the broken pane. Using the curtain to protect his hand, he knocked out the shards, swung a leg over the sill, stumbled onto the fire escape. The rusted metal cut at his bare feet. Groping, he made his way down half a dozen steps—and fell back as a sheet of red flame billowed from below.

Over the rail he saw the street, lights puddled on grimy concrete ten stories down, white faces, like pale dots, upturned. A hundred feet away, an extension ladder swayed, approaching another wing of the flaming building, not concerned with him. He was lost, abandoned. Nothing could save him. For forty feet below, the iron ladder was an inferno.

*It would be easier, quicker, to go over the rail, escape the pain, die cleanly,* the thought came into his mind with dreadful clarity.

There was a tinkling crash and a window above blew out. Scalding embers rained down on his back. The iron was hot underfoot. He drew a breath, shielded his face with one arm, and plunged downward through the whipping flames. . . .

He was crawling, falling down the cruel metal treads and risers. The pain across his face, his back, his shoulder, his arm, was like a red-hot iron, applied and forgotten. He caught a glimpse of his arm, flayed, oozing, black-edged. . . .

His hands and feet were no longer his own. He used his knees and elbows, tumbled himself over yet another edge, sliding down to the next landing. The faces were closer now; hands were reaching up. He groped, got to his feet, felt the last section swing down as his weight went on it. His vision was a blur of red. He sensed the blistered skin sloughing from his thighs. A woman screamed.

". . . my God, burned alive and still walking!" a thin voice cawed.

". . . poor devil . . ."

". . . his hands . . . no fingers . . ."

Something rose, smashed at him, a ghostly blow as blackness closed in. . . .

### ELEVEN

*The response of the entity was anomalous,* the Analyzers reported. *Its life tenacity is enormous! Confronted with apparent imminent physical destruction, it chose agony and mutilation merely to extend survival for a brief period.*

*The possibility exists that such a response represents a mere instinctive mechanism of unusual form,* the Analyzers pointed out.

*If so, it might prove dangerous. More data on the point is required.* I/WE WILL RESTIMULATE THE SUBJECT, the Egon ordered. THE PARAMETERS OF THE SURVIVAL DRIVE MUST BE ESTABLISHED WITH PRECISION. RESUME TESTING!

### TWELVE

In the chair, Mallory writhed, went limp.

"Is he . . . ?"

"He's alive, Excellency! But something's wrong! I can't get through to a vocalization level! He's fighting me with some sort of fantasy complex of his own!"

"Bring him out of it!"

"Excellency, I tried. I can't reach him! It's as though he'd tapped the chair's energy sources and were using them to reinforce his own defense mechanism!"

"Override him!"

"I'll try—but his power is fantastic!"

"Then we'll use more power!"

"It's . . . dangerous, Excellency."

"Not more dangerous than failure!"

Grim-faced, the technician reset the panel to step up the energy flows through Mallory's brain.

### THIRTEEN

*The subject stirs!* the Perceptors burst out. *Massive new energies flow in the mind-field! My/our grip loosens . . . !"*

HOLD THE SUBJECT! RESTIMULATE AT ONCE, WITH MAXIMUM EMERGENCY FORCE!

While the captive surged and fought against the restraint, the segmented mind of the alien concentrated its forces, hurled a new stimulus into the roiling captive mind-field.

### FOURTEEN

. . . Hot sun beat down on his back. A light wind ruffled the tall grass growing up the slope where the wounded lion had taken cover. Telltale drops of dark purple blood clinging to the tall stems marked the big cat's route. It would be up there, flattened to the earth under the clump of thorn trees, its yellow eyes narrowed against the agony of the .375 bullet in his chest, waiting, hoping for its tormentor to come to it. . . .

His heart was thudding under the damp khaki shirt. The heavy rifle felt like a toy in his hands—a useless plaything against the primitive fury of the beast. He took a step; his mouth twisted in an ironic grimace. What was he proving? There was no one here to know if he chose to walk back and sit under a tree and take a leisurely swig from his flask, let an hour or two crawl by—while the cat bled to death—and then go in to find the body. He took another step. And now he was walking steadily forward. The breeze was cool on his forehead. His legs felt light, strong. He drew a deep breath, smelled the sweetness of the spring air. Life had never seemed more precious—

There was a deep, asthmatic cough, and the great beast broke from the shadows, yellow fangs bared, muscles pumping under the dun hide, dark blood shining black along the flank—

He planted his feet, brought the gun up, socketed it against his shoulder as the lion charged down the slope. *By the book,* he thought sardonically. *Take him just above the sternum, hold on him until you're sure. . . .* At a hundred feet he fired—just as the animal veered left. The bullet smacked home far back along the ribs. The cat broke stride, recovered. The gun bucked and roared again, and the snarling face exploded in a mask of red—and still the dying carnivore came on. He blinked sweat from his eyes, centered the sights on the point of the shoulder—

The trigger jammed hard. A glance showed him the spent cartridge lodged in the action. He raked at it vainly, standing his ground. At the last instant he stepped aside, and the hurtling monster skidded past him, dead in the dust. And the thought that struck him then was that if Monica had been watching from the car at the foot of the hill she would not have laughed at him this time. . . .

### FIFTEEN

*Again the reaction syndrome is inharmonious with any concept of rationality in my/our experience,* the Recollector cells expressed the paradox with which the captive mind had presented the Ree intelligence. *Here is an entity which clings to personality survival with a ferocity unparalleled—yet faces Category Ultimate risks needlessly, in response to an abstract code of behavioral symmetry.*

*I/we postulate that the personality segment selected does not represent the true Egon-analog of the subject,* the Speculators offered. *It is obviously incomplete, non-viable.*

*Let me/us attempt a selective withdrawal of control over peripheral regions of the mind-field,* the Initiators proposed, *thus permitting greater concentration of stimulus to the central matrix.*

*By matching energies with the captive mind, it will be possible to monitor its rhythms and deduce the key to its total control,* the Calculators determined quickly.

*This course offers the risk of rupturing the matrix and the destruction of the specimen.*

THE RISK MUST BE TAKEN.

With infinite precision, the Ree mind narrowed the scope of its probe, fitting its shape to the contours of Mallory's embattled brain, matching itself in a one-to-one correspondence to the massive energy flows from the Interrogation chair.

*Equilibrium,* the Perceptors reported at last. *However, the balance is precarious.*

*The next test must be designed to expose new aspects of the subject's survival syndrome,* the Analyzers pointed out.

A stimulus pattern was proposed and accepted. Aboard the ship in its sublunar orbit, the Ree mind-beam again lanced out to touch Mallory's receptive brain. . . .

. . . Blackness gave way to misty light. A deep rumbling shook the rocks under his feet. Through the whirling spray he saw the raft, the small figure that clung to it: a child, a little girl perhaps nine years old, crouched on hands and knees, looking toward him.

"Daddy!" A high, thin cry of pure terror. The raft bucked and tossed in the wild current. He took a step, slipped, almost went down on the slimy rocks. The icy water swirled about his knees. A hundred feet downstream, the river curved in a gray metal sheen, over and down, veiled by the mists of its own thunderous descent. He turned, scrambled back up, ran along the bank. There, ahead, a point of rock jutted. Perhaps . . .

The raft bobbed, whirled, fifty feet away. Too far. He saw the pale, small face, the pleading eyes. Fear welled in him, greasy and sickening. Visions of death rose up, of his broken body bobbing below the falls, lying wax-white on a slab, sleeping, powdered and false in a satin-lined box, corrupting in the close darkness under the indifferent sod. . . .

He took a trembling step back.

For an instant a curious sensation of unreality swept over him. He remembered darkness, a sense of utter claustrophobia—and a white room, a face that leaned close. . . .

He blinked—and through the spray of the rapids his eyes met those of the doomed child. Compassion struck him like a club. He grunted, felt the clean white flame of anger at himself, of disgust at his fear. He closed his eyes and leaped far out, struck the water and went under, came up gasping. His strokes took him toward the raft. He felt a heavy blow as the current tossed him against a rock, choked as chopping spray whipped in his face. The thought came that broken ribs didn't matter now, nor air for breathing. Only to reach the raft before it reached the edge, that the small, frightened soul might not go down alone into the great darkness. . . .

His hands clawed the rough wood. He pulled himself up, caught the small body to him as the world dropped away and the thunder rose deafeningly to meet him . . .

"Excellency! I need help!" The technician appealed to the grim-faced dictator. "I'm pouring enough power through his brain to kill two ordinary men—and he still fights back! For a second there, a moment ago, I'd swear he opened his eyes and looked right through me! I can't take the responsibility—"

"Then cut the power, you blundering idiot!"

"I don't dare! the backlash will kill him!"

"He . . . must . . . talk!" Koslo grated. "Hold him! Break him! Or I promise you a slow and terrible death!"

Trembling, the technician adjusted his controls. In the chair, Mallory sat tense, no longer fighting the straps. He looked like a man lost in thought. Perspiration broke from his hairline, trickled down his face.

### SIXTEEN

*Again new currents stir in the captive!* the Perceptors announced in alarm. *The resources of this mind are staggering!*

MATCH IT! the Egon directed.

*My/our power resources are already overextended!* the Calculators interjected.

WITHDRAW ENERGIES FROM ALL PERIPHERAL FUNC-TIONS! LOWER ALL SHIELDING! THE MOMENT OF THE ULTIMATE TEST IS UPON ME/US!

Swiftly the Ree mind complied.

*The captive is held,* the Calculators announced. *But I/we point out that this linkage now presents a channel of vulnerability to assault.*

THE RISK MUST BE TAKEN.

*Even now the mind stirs against my/our control!*

HOLD IT FAST!

Grimly, the Ree mind fought to retain its control of Mallory's brain.

### SEVENTEEN

In one instant, he was not. Then, abruptly, he existed. *Mallory,* he thought. *That symbol represents I/we. . . .*

The alien thought faded. He caught at it, held the symbol. *Mallory*. He remembered the shape of his body, the feel of his skull enclosing his brain, the sensations of light, sound, heat—but here there was no sound, no light. Only the enclosing blackness, impenetrable, eternal, changeless. . . .

But where was here?

He remembered the white room, the harsh voice of Koslo, the steel chair—

And the mighty roar of the waters rushing up at him—

And the reaching talons of a giant cat—

And the searing agony of flames that licked around his body. . . .

But there was no pain now, no discomfort—no sensation of any kind. Was this death, then? At once he rejected the idea as nonsense. *Cogito ergo sum*. I am a prisoner—where?

His senses stirred, questing against emptiness, sensationlessness. He strained outward—and heard sound; voices, pleading, demanding. They grew louder, echoing in the vastness:

". . . talk, damn you! Who are your chief accomplices? What support do you expect from the armed forces? Which of the generals are with you? Armaments . . . ? Organization . . . ? Initial attack points . . . ?"

Blinding static sleeted across the words, filled the universe, grew dim. For an instant Mallory was aware of straps cutting into the tensed muscles of his forearms, the pain of the band clamped around his head, the ache of cramping muscles. . . .

. . . was aware of floating, gravityless, in a sea of winking, flashing energies. Vertigo rose up; frantically he fought for stability in a world of chaos. Through spinning darkness he reached, found a matrix of pure direction, intangible, but, against the background of shifting energy flows, providing an orienting grid. He seized on it, held. . . .

### EIGHTEEN

*Full emergency disengage!* The Receptors blasted the command through all the 6934 units of the Ree mind—and recoiled in shock. *The captive mind clings to the contact! We cannot break free!*

Pulsating with the enormous shock of the prisoner's sudden outlashing, the alien rested for the fractional nanosecond required to reestablish intersegmental balance.

*The power of the enemy, though unprecedentedly great, is not sufficient to broach the integrity of my/our entity-field,* the Analyzers stated, tensely. *But I/we must retreat at once!*

NO! I/WE LACK SUFFICIENT DATA TO JUSTIFY WITH-DRAWAL OF PHASE ONE, the Egon countermanded. HERE IS A MIND RULED BY CONFLICTING DRIVES OF GREAT POWER. WHICH IS PARAMOUNT? THEREIN LIES THE KEY TO ITS DEFEAT.

Precious microseconds passed while the compound mind hastily scanned Mallory's mind for symbols from which to assemble the necessary gestalt-form.

*Ready,* the Integrators announced. *But it must be pointed out that no mind can long survive intact the direct confrontation of antagonistic imperatives. Is the stimulus to be carried to the point of non-retrieval?*

AFFIRMATIVE, the Egon's tone was one of utter finality. TEST TO DESTRUCTION.

### NINETEEN

*Illusions,* Mallory told himself. *I'm being bombarded by illusions.* . . . He sensed the approach of a massive new wave front, descending on him like a breaking Pacific comber. Grimly he clung to his tenuous orientation—But the smashing impact whirled him into darkness.

Far away, a masked inquisitor faced him.

"Pain has availed nothing against you," the muffled voice said. "The threat of death does not move you. And yet there is a way. . . ." A curtain fell aside, and Monica stood there, tall, slim, vibrantly alive, as beautiful as a roe deer. And, beside her, the child.

He said "No!" and started forward, but the chains held him. He watched, helpless, while brutal hands seized the woman, moved casually, intimately, over her body. Other hands gripped the child. He saw the terror on the small face, the fear in her eyes—

Fear that he had seen before. . . .

But of course he had seen her before. The child was his daughter, the precious offspring of himself and the slender female—

Monica, he corrected himself.

—had seen those eyes, through swirling mist, poised above a cataract—

No. That was a dream. A dream in which he had died, violently. And there had been another dream, of facing a wounded lion as it charged down on him—

"You will not be harmed." The Inquisitor's voice seemed to come from a remote distance. "But you will carry with you forever the memory of their living dismemberment. . . ."

With a jerk, his attention returned to the woman and the child. He saw them strip Monica's slender, tawny body. Naked, she stood before them, refusing to cower. But of what use was courage now? The manacles at her wrists were linked to a hook set in the damp stone wall. The glowing iron moved closer to her white flesh. He saw the skin darken and blister. The iron plunged home. She stiffened, screamed. . . .

*A woman screamed.*

*"My God, burned alive,"* a thin voice cawed. *"And still walking!"*

He looked down. There was no wound, no scar. The skin was unbroken. But a fleeting almost-recollection came of crackling flames that seared with a white agony as he drew them into his lungs. . . .

"A dream," he said aloud. "I'm dreaming. I have to wake up!" He closed his eyes and shook his head. . . .

### TWENTY

"He shook his head!" the technician choked. "Excellency, it's impossible—but I swear the man is throwing off the machine's control!"

Koslo brushed the other roughly aside. He seized the control lever, pushed it forward. In the chair, Mallory stiffened. His breathing became hoarse, ragged.

"Excellency, the man will die . . ."

"Let him die! No one defies me with impunity!"

### TWENTY-ONE

*Narrow focus!* the Perceptors flashed the command to the sixty-nine hundred and thirty-four energy-producing segments of the Ree mind. *The contest cannot continue long! Almost we lost the captive then . . . !*

The probe beam narrowed, knifing into the living heart of Mallory's brain, imposing its chosen patterns. . . .

### TWENTY-TWO

. . . the child whimpered as the foot-long blade approached her fragile breast. The gnarled fist holding the knife stroked it almost lovingly across the blue-veined skin. Crimson blood washed down from the shallow wound.

"If you reveal the secrets of the Brotherhood to me, truly your comrades in arms will die," the Inquisitor's faceless voice droned. "But if you stubbornly refuse, your woman and your infant will suffer all that my ingenuity can devise."

He strained against his chains. "I can't tell you," he croaked. "Don't you understand, nothing is worth this horror! Nothing . . ."

*Nothing he could have done would have saved her. She crouched on the raft, doomed. But he could join her—*

But not this time. This time chains of steel kept him from her. He hurled himself against them, and tears blinded his eyes. . . .

*Smoke blinded his eyes. He looked down, saw the faces upturned below. Surely, easy death was preferable to living immolation. But he covered his face with his arms and started down. . . .*

Never betray your trust! the woman's voice rang clear as a trumpet across the narrow dungeon.

*Daddy! the child screamed.*

We can die only once! the woman called.

*The raft plunged downward into boiling chaos. . . .*

"Speak, damn you!" The Inquisitor's voice had taken on a new note. "I want the names, the places! Who are your accomplices? What are your plans? When will the rising begin? What signal are they waiting for? Where . . . ? When . . . ?"

Mallory opened his eyes. Blinding white light, a twisted face that loomed before him goggling.

"Excellency! He's awake! He's broken through. . . ."

"Pour full power to him! Force, man! Force him to speak!"

"I—I'm afraid, Excellency! We're tampering with the mightiest instrument in the universe: a human brain! Who knows what we may be creating—"

Koslo struck the man aside, threw the control lever full against the stop.

### TWENTY-THREE

. . . the darkness burst into a coruscating brilliance that became the outlines of a room. A transparent man whom he recognized as Koslo stood before him. He watched as the dictator turned to him, his face contorted.

"Now talk, damn you!"

His voice had a curious, ghostly quality, as though it represented only one level of reality.

"Yes," Mallory said distinctly. "I'll talk."

"And if you lie—" Koslo jerked an ugly automatic pistol from the pocket of his plain tunic. "I'll put a bullet in your brain myself!"

"My chief associates in the plot," Mallory began, "are . . ." As he spoke, he gently *disengaged* himself—that was the word that came to his mind—from the scene around him. He was aware at one level of his voice speaking on, reeling off the facts for which the other man hungered so nakedly. And he reached out, channeling the power pouring into him from the chair . . . spanning across vast distances compressed now to a dimensionless plane. Delicately, he quested farther, entered a curious, flickering net of living energies. He pressed, found points of weakness, poured in more power—

A circular room leaped into eerie visibility. Ranged around it were lights that winked and glowed. From ranked thousands of cells, white wormforms poked blunt, eyeless heads. . . .

HE IS HERE! the Egon shrieked the warning, and hurled a bolt of pure mind-force along the channel of contact—and met a counterbolt of energy that seared through him, blackened and charred the intricate organic circuitry of his cerebrum, left a smoking pocket in the rank of cells. For a moment Mallory rested, sensing the shock and bewilderment sweeping through the leaderless Ree mind-segments. He felt the automatic death urge that gripped them as the realization reached them that the guiding overpower of the Egon was gone. As he watched, a unit crumpled inward and expired. And another—

"Stop!" Mallory commanded. "I assume control of the mind-complex! Let the segments link in with me!"

Obediently, the will-less fragments of the Ree mind obeyed.

"Change course," Mallory ordered. He gave the necessary instructions, then withdrew along the channel of contact.

### TWENTY-FOUR

"So . . . the great Mallory broke." Koslo rocked on his heels before the captive body of his enemy. He laughed. "You were slow to start, but once begun you sang like a turtledove. I'll give my orders now, and by dawn your futile revolt will be a heap of charred corpses stacked in the plaza as an example to others!" He raised the gun.

"I'm not through yet," Mallory said. "The plot runs deeper than you think, Koslo."

The dictator ran a hand over his gray face. His eyes showed the terrible strain of the last hours.

"Talk, then," he growled. "Talk fast!"

—as he spoke on, Mallory again shifted his primary awareness, settled into resonance with the subjugated Ree intelligence. Through the ship's sensors he saw the white planet swelling ahead. He slowed the vessel, brought it in on a long parabolic course which skimmed the stratosphere. Seventy miles above the Atlantic, he entered a high haze layer, slowed again as he sensed the heating of the hull.

Below the clouds, he sent the ship hurtling across the coast. He dropped to treetop level, scanned the scene through sensitive hull-plates—

For a long moment he studied the landscape below. Then suddenly he understood. . . .

### TWENTY-FIVE

"Why do you smile, Mallory?" Koslo's voice was harsh; the gun pointed at the other's head. "Tell me the joke that makes a man laugh in the condemned seat reserved for traitors."

"You'll know in just a moment—" He broke off as a crashing sound came from beyond the room. The floor shook and trembled, rocking Koslo on his feet. A dull *boom!* echoed. The door burst wide.

"Excellency! The capital is under attack!" the man fell forward, exposing a great wound on his back. Koslo whirled on Mallory—

With a thunderous crash, one side of the room bulged and fell inward. Through the broached wall a glittering torpedo shape appeared, a polished intricacy of burnished metal floating lightly on pencils of blue-white light. The gun in the hand of the dictator came up, crashed deafeningly in the enclosed space. From the prow of the invader, pink light winked. Koslo spun, fell heavily on his face.

The twenty-eight-inch Ree dreadnought came to rest before Mallory. A beam speared out, burned through the chair control panel. The shackles fell away.

*I/we await your/our next command,* the Ree mind spoke soundlessly in the awesome silence.

### TWENTY-SIX

Three months had passed since the referendum which swept John Mallory into office as Premier of the First Planetary Republic. He stood in a room of his spacious apartment in the Executive Palace, frowning at the slender black-haired woman as she spoke earnestly to him:

"John—I'm afraid of that—that infernal machine, eternally hovering, waiting for your orders."

"But why, Monica? That infernal machine, as you call it, was the thing that made a free election possible—and even now it's all that holds Koslo's old organization in check."

"John—" Her hand gripped his arm. "With that—thing—always at your beck and call, you can control anyone, anything on Earth! No opposition can stand before you!"

She looked directly at him. "It isn't right for anyone to have such power, John. Not even you. No human being should be put to such a test!"

His face tightened. "Have I misused it?"

"Not yet. That's why . . ."

"You imply that I will?"

"You're a man, with the failings of a man."

"I propose only what's good for the people of Earth," he said sharply. "Would you have me voluntarily throw away the one weapon that can protect our hard-won freedom?"

"But, John—who are you to be the sole arbiter of what's good for the people of Earth?"

"I'm Chairman of the Republic—"

"You're still human. Stop—while you're still human!"

He studied her face. "You resent my success, don't you? What would you have me do? Resign?"

"I want you to send the machine away—back to wherever it came from."

He laughed shortly. "Are you out of your mind? I haven't begun to extract the technological secrets the Ree ship represents."

"We're not ready for those secrets, John. The race isn't ready. It's already changed you. In the end it can only destroy you as a man."

"Nonsense. I control it utterly. It's like an extension of my own mind—"

"John—please. If not for my sake or your own, for Dian's."

"What's the child got to do with this?"

"She's your daughter. She hardly sees you once a week."

"That's the price she has to pay for being the heir to the greatest man—I mean—damn it, Monica, my responsibilities don't permit me to indulge in all the suburban customs."

"John—" Her voice was a whisper, painful in its intensity. "Send it away."

"No. I won't send it away."

Her face was pale. "Very well, John. As you wish."

"Yes. As I wish."

After she left the room, Mallory stood for a long time staring out through the high window at the tiny craft, hovering in the blue air fifty feet away, silent, ready.

Then: *Ree mind*, he sent out the call. *Probe the apartments of the woman, Monica. I have reason to suspect she plots treason against the state. . . .*

## Afterword:

The process of writing a story is often as enlightening for me as, hopefully, for the reader.

I began this one with the concept of submitting a human being to an ultimate trial in the same way that an engineer will load a beam until it collapses, testing it to destruction. It is in emotional situations that we meet our severest tests: fear, love, anger drive us to our highest efforts. Thus the framework of the story suggested itself.

As the tale evolved, it became apparent that any power setting out to put mankind to the test—as did Koslo and the Ree—places its own fate in the balance.

In the end, Mallory revealed the true strength of man by using the power of his enemies against them. He won not only his freedom and sanity—but also immense new powers over other men.

Not until then did the danger in such total victory become apparent. The ultimate test of man in his ability to master himself.

It is a test which we have so far failed.

## Introduction to CARCINOMA ANGELS:

This is the last introduction to be written, though not the last in the book. Last, because I have put it off time after time. And not because there is a dearth of material to be written about Norman Spinrad, but because there is so much. A leading editor for a hardcover house contends Norman is the hottest young talent to emerge from the field of speculative fiction in years. Another editor, of a magazine, says Norman is an abominable writer (though he buys his work . . . go figure *that*). I think he writes like a lunatic. When he is bad, he is unreadable, which is infrequently. When he is good, he tackles themes and styles only a nut would attempt (knowing in advance the task was impossible) and has the audacity to bring them off in spectacular fashion.

Take for instance his contribution here. It is a funny story about cancer. Now tell me that isn't fresh ground, unbroken by Leacock, Benchley or Thurber.

Spinrad is a product of the Bronx. He's a street kid, with the classic hunger for achievement, status and worldly goods that drives the have-nots to the top. He truly feels there is nothing he can't do, nothing he can't write. He isn't writing *this* novel, or *this* story, he is writing a career, and it pulses out of him in volume after volume. At twenty-six he bids fair to being the first writer of the genre to break out into the bigtime mainstream since Bradbury and Clarke. His drives are worn like a suit of clothes, and they manifest themselves in obvious ways. Let his bank balance sink below a thousand dollars, and he gets twitchy, actually changes disposition like a Jekyll-Hyde, becomes unbearable, driven. Let an idea of purest gold come to him and he paces back and forth, rolls his eyes, scratches his head, stands poised in the center of the room with legs twined around each other like some great redheaded bird ready to go up. He is a creature of emotion, stated in broadest terms. Love will send him driving across a continent. Friendship will plunge him into an emotional maelstrom rather than let someone down. Hate will push him to excesses of language and a killing urge to run other cars off the road. His inquisitiveness sends him where neither angels *nor* fools would tread. His critical faculties are so sharp I have seen him correctly postulate a theory for social behavior that was indicated by only the most casual occurrence. He is gullible. He is cynical. He knows where it's at in terms of his times, and he hasn't the faintest idea when he is being put on. He is truly a wise man, and he is the sheerest buffoon. People do not take him in, yet there have been times when I have seen Norman shucked thoroughly by inept practitioners of the art form. His first novel (*The Solarians,* 1966) is so bad it cannot be read. His third novel (*The Men in the Jungle*) is so brilliant it burns like the surface of the sun.

He was born in New York in 1940, graduating after the usual number of years from the Bronx High School of Science, a "highly overrated think-factory for the production of mad scientists, neurotic adolescent geniuses, bomb-hurling anarchists, and Stokeley Carmichael, who finished a year behind me." He graduated from CCNY in 1961 with the only Bachelor of Science degree in Esoterica ever granted by that institution. (His major consisted of courses such as Japanese Civilization, Asian Literature, Short Story Writing and Geology.)

While in his final term at CCNY, Norman's professor in short-story writing pleaded for stories that *really* pulled out all the stops, much like my request for this book. Norman handed the unsuspecting pedant a story so dirty it *still* hasn't been published. However, the professor was impressed and suggested Norman submit it to *Playboy.* The Bunny-Lovers' Gazette turned it down (though they have since rectified their shortsightedness in matters Spinradian; see "Deathwatch," *Playboy,*

November 1965) but it only took once to get Spinrad into the habit of submitting things he had written to magazines. It seemed so much more advisable than shoving them into the cracks in the walls for insulation. (A simple jump of logic. If the magazine buys the stories, you take the *money* and jam it into the walls for insulation.)

After graduation he went to Mexico where he contracted various nameless diseases and aggravated an old one with a name. In some inexplicable manner this convinced him to become a writer. He returned to New York, wound up living and working in Greenwich Village and put in a stint in the hospital where he *contracted* something called toxic hepatitis, ran temperatures of 106° for five days straight, hallucinating all the while, and held off interns with a bedpan while calling the Pentagon (collect, naturally, he wasn't *that* nuts) and waking a general at 2 A.M., thus getting the idea for his story in this anthology—the interaction between external and internal mythical-subjective universes. Whatever the hell *that* means.

He sold his first story, "The Last of the Romany," in 1962 to *Analog* (thus inciting the rumor that he is a "Campbell writer," which Spinrad denies vehemently everywhere save in the presence of John W. Campbell, editor of *Analog,* at which times all he does is grin fatuously and say, "Yes, John." This is no slur. I know of *no* writer who is a Campbell writer, or even a writer who writes for Campbell [two different things, I assure you], who is not a YesJohn. I have never been a Yes-John. I have also never sold to *Analog*) and aside from a stint in a literary agency and a month as a welfare investigator (having stolen so much from them, he felt it behooved him to make amends by intimidating other poor boys and their tubercular children), he has been a full-time writer ever since. (There are those who say Norman is only a *part*-time writer, being a full-time *noodje!*)

He has had a second paperback novel published—aside from *The Solarians,* which was mentioned deprecatingly already—and *The Men in the Jungle,* both this year. The latter is a truly original experience, a Doubleday book that grew out of a projected short story for this collection and a deep concern with the morality and tactics of Vietnam-style so-called "Wars of National Liberation."

In the works, at this writing, is a new novel titled *Bug Jack Barron,* which Spinrad calls "a synthesis-novel written to satisfy the differing— though not necessarily conflicting—demands of serious mainstream avant-garde yessir boy writing, and science fiction; a coherent 'Nova Express,' in a way." Spinrad gets carried away with his own talent. I have read parts of *Bug Jack Barron*. It is not a synthesis-novel about whachimacallit or avant garde or mainstream or none of that jazz. What *Bug Jack Barron* is, chiefly, is *awful dirty*. It will sell like crazy.

But until your minds can be properly tainted by the full effulgence of Spinrad's foulness, I suggest you pervert yourselves only slightly with "Carcinoma Angels," a funny cancer story.

# ● CARCINOMA ANGELS

## by Norman Spinrad

At the age of nine Harrison Wintergreen first discovered that the world was his oyster when he looked at it sidewise. That was the year when baseball cards were *in*. The kid with the biggest collection of baseball cards was *it*. Harry Wintergreen decided to become *it*.

Harry saved up a dollar and bought one hundred random baseball cards. He was in luck—one of them was the very rare Yogi Berra. In three separate transactions, he traded his other ninety-nine cards for the only other three Yogi Berras in the neighborhood. Harry had reduced his holdings to four cards, but he had cornered the market in Yogi Berra. He forced the price of Yogi Berra up to an exorbitant eighty cards. With the slush fund thus accumulated, he successively cornered the market in Mickey Mantle, Willy Mays and Pee Wee Reese and became the J. P. Morgan of baseball cards.

Harry breezed through high school by the simple expedient of mastering only one subject—the art of taking tests. By his senior year, he could outthink any test writer with his gypsheet tied behind his back and won seven scholarships with foolish ease.

In college Harry discovered girls. Being reasonably good-looking and reasonably facile, he no doubt would've garnered his fair share of conquests in the normal course of events. But this was not the way the mind of Harrison Wintergreen worked.

Harry carefully cultivated a stutter, which he could turn on or off at will. Few girls could resist the lure of a good-looking, well-adjusted guy with a slick line who nevertheless carried with him some secret inner hurt that made him stutter. Many were the girls who tried to delve Harry's secret, while Harry delved *them*.

In his sophomore year Harry grew bored with college and reasoned that the thing to do was to become Filthy Rich. He assiduously studied sex novels for one month, wrote three of them in the next two which he immediately sold at $1000 a throw.

With the $3000 thus garnered, he bought a shiny new convertible. He drove the new car to the Mexican border and across into a notorious border town. He immediately contacted a disreputable shoeshine boy and bought a pound of marijuana. The shoeshine boy of course tipped off the border guards, and when Harry attempted to walk across the bridge to the States they stripped him naked. They found nothing and Harry crossed the border. He had smuggled nothing out of Mexico, and in fact had thrown the marijuana away as soon as he bought it.

However, he had taken advantage of the Mexican embargo on American cars and illegally sold the convertible in Mexico for $15,000.

Harry took his $15,000 to Las Vegas and spent the next six weeks buying people drinks, lending broke gamblers money, acting in general like a fuzzy-cheeked Santa Claus, gaining the confidence of the right drunks and blowing $5000.

At the end of six weeks he had three hot market tips which turned his remaining $10,000 into $40,000 in the next two months.

Harry bought four hundred crated government surplus jeeps in four hundred-jeep lots at $10,000 a lot and immediately sold them to a highly disreputable Central American government for $100,000.

He took the $100,000 and bought a tiny island in the Pacific, so worthless that no government had ever bothered to claim it. He set himself up as an independent government with no taxes and sold twenty one-acre plots to twenty millionaires seeking a tax haven at $100,000 a plot. He unloaded the last plot three weeks before the United States, with UN backing, claimed the island and brought it under the sway of the Internal Revenue Department.

Harry invested a small part of his $2,000,000 and rented a large computer for twelve hours. The computer constructed a betting scheme by which Harry parlayed his $2,000,000 into $20,000,000 by taking various British soccer pools to the tune of $18,000,000.

For $5,000,000 he bought a monstrous chunk of useless desert from an impoverished Arabian sultanate. With another $2,000,000 he created a huge rumor campaign to the effect that this patch of desert was literally floating on oil. With another $3,000,000 he set up a dummy corporation which made like a big oil company and publicly offered to buy his desert for $75,000,000. After some spirited bargaining, a large American oil company was allowed to outbid the dummy and bought a thousand square miles of sand for $100,000,000.

Harrison Wintergreen was, at the age of twenty-five, Filthy Rich by his own standards. He lost his interest in money.

He now decided that he wanted to Do Good. He Did Good. He toppled seven unpleasant Latin American governments and replaced them with six Social Democracies and a Benevolent Dictatorship. He converted a tribe of Borneo headhunters to Rosicrucianism. He set up twelve rest homes for overage whores and organized a birth control program which sterilized twelve million fecund Indian women. He contrived to make another $100,000,000 on the above enterprises.

At the age of thirty Harrison Wintergreen had had it with Do-Gooding. He decided to Leave His Footprints in the Sands of Time. He Left His Footprints in the Sands of Time. He wrote an internationally acclaimed novel about King Farouk. He invented the Wintergreen Filter, a membrane through which fresh water passed freely, but which barred salts. Once set up, a Wintergreen Desalinization Plant could desalinate an unlimited supply of water at a per-gallon cost approaching absolute zero. He painted one painting and was instantly offered $200,000 for it. He donated it to the Museum of Modern Art, gratis. He developed a mutated virus which destroyed syphilis bacteria. Like syphilis, it spread by sexual contact. It was a mild aphrodisiac. Syphilis was wiped out in eighteen months. He bought an island off the coast of California, a five-hundred-foot crag jutting out of the Pacific. He caused it to be carved into a five-hundred-foot statue of Harrison Wintergreen.

At the age of thirty-eight Harrison Wintergreen had Left sufficient Footprints in the Sands of Time. He was bored. He looked around greedily for new worlds to conquer.

This, then, was the man who, at the age of forty, was informed that he had an advanced, well-spread and incurable case of cancer and that he had one year to live.

Wintergreen spent the first month of his last year searching for an existing cure for terminal cancer. He visited laboratories, medical schools, hospitals, clinics, Great Doctors, quacks, people who had miraculously recovered from cancer, faith healers and Little Old Ladies in Tennis Shoes. There was no known cure for terminal cancer, reputable or otherwise. It was as he suspected, as he more or less even hoped. He would have to do it himself.

He proceeded to spend the next month setting things up to do it himself. He caused to be erected in the middle of the Arizona desert an air-conditioned walled villa. The villa had a completely automatic kitchen and enough food for a year. It had a $5,000,000 biological and biochemical laboratory. It had a $3,000,000 microfilmed library which contained every word ever written on the subject of cancer. It had the pharmacy to end all pharmacies: a liberal supply of quite literally every drug that existed—poisons, painkillers, hallucinogens, dandricides, antiseptics, antibiotics, viricides, headache remedies, heroin, quinine, curare, snake oil—everything. The pharmacy cost $20,000,-000.

The villa also contained a one-way radiotelephone, a large stock of basic chemicals, including radioactives, copies of the *Koran,* the Bible, the *Torah,* the *Book of the Dead, Science and Health with Key to the Scriptures,* the *I Ching* and the complete works of Wilhelm Reich and Aldous Huxley. It also contained a very large and ultra-expensive computer. By the time the villa was ready, Wintergreen's petty cash fund was nearly exhausted.

With ten months to do that which the medical world considered impossible, Harrison Wintergreen entered his citadel.

During the first two months he devoured the library, sleeping three hours out of each twenty-four and dosing himself regularly with Benzedrine. The library offered nothing but data. He digested the data and went on to the pharmacy.

During the next month he tried aureomycin, bacitracin, stannous flouride, hexylresorcinol, cortisone, penicillin, hexachlorophine, shark-liver extract and 7312 assorted other miracles of modern medical science, all to no avail. He began to feel pain, which he immediately blotted out and continued to blot out with morphine. Morphine addiction was merely an annoyance.

He tried chemicals, radioactives, viricides, Christian Science, yoga, prayer, enemas, patent medicines, herb tea, witchcraft and yogurt diets. This consumed another month, during which Wintergreen continued to waste away, sleeping less and less and taking more and more Benzedrine and morphine. Nothing worked. He had six months left.

He was on the verge of becoming desperate. He tried a different tack. He sat in a comfortable chair and contemplated his navel for forty-eight consecutive hours.

His meditations produced a severe case of eyestrain and two significant words: "spontaneous remission."

In his two months of research, Wintergreen had come upon numbers of cases where a terminal cancer abruptly reversed itself and the patient, for whom all hope had been abandoned, had been cured. No one ever knew how or why. It could not be predicted, it could not be artificially produced, but it happened nevertheless. For want of an explanation, they called it spontaneous remission. "Remission," meaning cure. "Spontaneous," meaning no one knew what caused it.

Which was not to say that it did not have a cause.

Wintergreen was buoyed; he was even ebullient. He knew that some terminal cancer patients had been cured. Therefore terminal cancer could be cured. Therefore the problem was removed from the realm of the impossible and was now merely the domain of the highly improbable.

And doing the highly improbable was Wintergreen's specialty.

With six months of estimated life left, Wintergreen set jubilantly to work. From his complete cancer library he culled every known case of spontaneous remission. He coded every one of them into the computer—data on the medical histories of the patients, on the treatments employed, on their ages, sexes, religions, races, creeds, colors, national origins, temperaments, marital status, Dun and Bradstreet ratings, neuroses, psychoses and favorite beers. Complete profiles of every human being ever known to have survived terminal cancer were fed into Harrison Wintergreen's computer.

Wintergreen programed the computer to run a complete series of correlations between ten thousand separate and distinct factors and spontaneous remission. If even one factor—age, credit rating, favorite food—*anything* correlated with spontaneous remission, the spontaneity factor would be removed.

Wintergreen had shelled out $100,000,000 for the computer. It was the best damn computer in the world. In two minutes and 7.894

seconds it had performed its task. In one succinct word it gave Wintergreen his answer:

"Negative."

Spontaneous remission did not correlate with *any* external factor. It was still spontaneous; the cause was unknown.

A lesser man would've been crushed. A more conventional man would've been dumbfounded. Harrison Wintergreen was elated.

He had eliminated the entire external universe as a factor in spontaneous remission in one fell swoop. Therefore, in some mysterious way, the human body and/or psyche was capable of curing itself.

Wintergreen set out to explore and conquer his own internal universe. He repaired to the pharmacy and prepared a formidable potation. Into his largest syringe he decanted the following: Novocain; morphine; curare; *vlut,* a rare Central Asian poison which induced temporary blindness; olfactorcain, a top-secret smell-deadener used by skunk farmers; tympanoline, a drug which temporarily deadened the auditory nerves (used primarily by filibustering senators); a large dose of Benzedrine; lysergic acid; psilocybin; mescaline; peyote extract; seven other highly experimental and most illegal hallucinogens; eye of newt and toe of dog.

Wintergreen laid himself out on his most comfortable couch. He swabbed the vein in the pit of his left elbow with alcohol and injected himself with the witch's brew.

His heart pumped. His blood surged, carrying the arcane chemicals to every part of his body. The Novocain blanked out every sensory nerve in his body. The morphine eliminated all sensations of pain. The *vlut* blacked out his vision. The olfactorcain cut off all sense of smell. The tympanoline made him deaf as a traffic court judge. The curare paralyzed him.

Wintergreen was alone in his own body. No external stimuli reached him. He was in a state of total sensory deprivation. The urge to lapse into blessed unconsciousness was irresistible. Wintergreen, strong-willed though he was, could not have remained conscious unaided. But the massive dose of Benzedrine would not let him sleep.

He was awake, aware, alone in the universe of his own body with no external stimuli to occupy himself with.

Then, one and two, and then in combinations like the fists of a good fast heavyweight, the hallucinogens hit.

Wintergreen's sensory organs were blanked out, but the brain centers which received sensory data were still active. It was on these cerebral centers that the tremendous charge of assorted hallucinogens acted. He began to see phantom colors, shapes, things without name or form. He heard eldritch symphonies, ghost echoes, mad howling noises. A million impossible smells roiled through his brain. A thousand false pains and pressures tore at him, as if his whole body had been amputated. The sensory centers of Wintergreen's brain were like a mighty radio receiver tuned to an empty band—filled with meaningless visual, auditory, olfactory and sensual static.

The drugs kept his sense blank. The Benzedrine kept him conscious. Forty years of being Harrison Wintergreen kept him cold and sane.

For an indeterminate period of time he rolled with the punches, groping for the feel of this strange new non-environment. Then gradually, hesitantly at first but with ever growing confidence, Wintergreen reached for control. His mind constructed untrue but useful analogies for actions that were not actions, states of being that were not states of being, sensory data unlike any sensory data received by the human brain. The analogies, constructed in a kind of calculated madness by his subconscious for the brute task of making the incomprehensible palpable, also enabled him to deal with his non-environment as if it were an environment, translating mental changes into analogs of action.

He reached out an analogical hand and tuned a figurative radio, inward, away from the blank wave band of the outside side universe and towards the as yet unused wave band of his own body, the internal universe that was his mind's only possible escape from chaos.

He tuned, adjusted, forced, struggled, felt his mind pressing against an atom-thin interface. He battered against the interface, an analogical translucent membrane between his mind and his internal universe, a membrane that stretched, flexed, bulged inward, thinned . . . and finally broke. Like Alice through the Looking Glass, his analogical body stepped through and stood on the other side.

Harrison Wintergreen was inside his own body.

It was a world of wonder and loathsomeness, of the majestic and the ludicrous. Wintergreen's point of view, which his mind analogized as a body within his true body, was inside a vast network of pulsing arteries, like some monstrous freeway system. The analogy crystallized. It *was* a freeway, and Wintergreen was driving down it. Bloated sacs dumped things into the teeming traffic: hormones, wastes, nutrients. White blood cells careened by him like mad taxicabs. Red corpuscles drove steadily along like stolid burghers. The traffic ebbed and congested like a crosstown rush hour. Wintergreen drove on, searching, searching.

He made a left, cut across three lanes and made a right down toward a lymph node. And then he saw it—a pile of white cells like a twelve-car collision, and speeding towards him a leering motorcyclist.

Black the cycle. Black the riding leathers. Black, dull black, the face of the rider save for two glowing blood-red eyes. And emblazoned across the front and back of the black motorcycle jacket in shining scarlet studs the legend: "Carcinoma Angels."

With a savage whoop, Wintergreen gunned his analogical car down the hypothetical freeway straight for the imaginary cyclist, the cancer cell.

Splat! Pop! Cuush! Wintergreen's car smashed the cycle and the rider exploded in a cloud of fine black dust.

Up and down the freeways of his circulatory system Wintergreen ranged, barreling along arteries, careening down veins, inching through narrow capillaries, seeking the black-clad cyclists, the Carcinoma Angels, grinding them to dust beneath his wheels. . . .

And he found himself in the dark moist wood of his lungs, riding a snow-white analogical horse, an imaginary lance of pure light in his hand. Savage black dragons with blood-red eyes and flickering red tongues slithered from behind the gnarled bolls of great air-sac trees. St. Wintergreen spurred his horse, lowered his lance and impaled monster after hissing monster till at last the holy lung-wood was free of dragons. . . .

He was flying in some vast moist cavern, above him the vague bulks of gigantic organs, below a limitless expanse of shining slimy peritoneal plain.

From behind the cover of his huge beating heart a formation of black fighter planes, bearing the insignia of a scarlet "C" on their wings and fusilages, roared down at him.

Wintergreen gunned his engine and rose to the fray, flying up and over the bandits, blasting them with his machine guns, and one by one and then in bunches they crashed in flames to the peritoneum below. . . .

In a thousand shapes and guises, the black and red things attacked. Black, the color of oblivion, red, the color of blood. Dragons, cyclists, planes, sea things, soldiers, tanks and tigers in blood vessels and lungs and spleen and thorax and bladder—Carcinoma Angels, all.

And Wintergreen fought his analogical battles in an equal number of incarnations, as driver, knight, pilot, diver, soldier, mahout, with a grim and savage glee, littering the battlefields of his body with the black dust of the fallen Carcinoma Angels.

Fought and fought and killed and killed and finally . . .

Finally found himself knee-deep in the sea of his digestive juices lapping against the walls of the dank, moist cave that was his stomach. And scuttling towards him on chitinous legs, a monstrous black crab with blood-red eyes, gross, squat, primeval.

Clicking, chittering, the crab scurried across his stomach towards him. Wintergreen paused, grinned wolfishly, and leaped high in the air, landing with both feet squarely on the hard black carapace.

Like a sun-dried gourd, brittle, dry, hollow, the crab crunched beneath his weight and splintered into a million dusty fragments.

And Wintergreen was alone, at last alone and victorious, the first and last of the Carcinoma Angels now banished and gone and finally defeated.

Harrison Wintergreen, alone in his own body, victorious and once again looking for new worlds to conquer, waiting for the drugs to wear off, waiting to return to the world that always was his oyster.

Waiting and waiting and waiting . . .


Go to the finest sanitarium in the world, and there you will find Harrison Wintergreen, who made himself Filthy Rich, Harrison Wintergreen, who Did Good, Harrison Wintergreen, who Left His Footprints in the Sands of Time, Harrison Wintergreen, catatonic vegetable.

Harrison Wintergreen, who stepped inside his own body to do battle with Carcinoma's Angels, and won.

And can't get out.

**Afterword:**

*Cancer.* Cancer has become a whisper-word, a myth word, a magic word, a dirty word; cancer, you should pardon the expression, is the 20th Century Pox. Prominent Public Personalities, alone, escape from its ravages, as any newspaper obituary column will tell you: "dying after a long, lingering illness," or "passing away from natural causes." Cancer the Crab has even lost his billing in some of the more sensitive Astrological Columns, his piece of the zodiacal pie being pre-empted by "Moon Children"—the powers that be having decided that reminding one-twelfth of the readership that they were born under the sign of cellular madness is bad for the circulation, not to mention the alimentary canal.

So what's with cancer, anyway? (You have now read the word "cancer" six times. Found any suspicious-looking moles yet?) The Gallup Poll shows that seven out of ten Americans prefer tertiary syphilis to cancer. Such unpopularity must be deserved, but why? Just because cancer is your own body devouring itself like a wounded hyena? Simply because cancer is psychosis on a cellular level? Merely because cancer is inexplicable and incurable on the level of objective reality?

Ah, but what about on the level of mythical reality? How else do you expect to fight a myth anyway? Gotta fight Black Magic with White Magic. Couldn't cancer be psychosomatic (a magic word if ever there was one), the physical manifestation of some psychic vampirism? Cancer, after all, is the Ultimate Cannibalism—your body eating itself, cell by cell.

Wouldn't you rather forget about this morbid, unpleasant subject and think about something nicer, like gas ovens or thalidomide or Limited Pre-Emptive Thermonuclear War?

After all, as Henry Miller says in his preface to *The Subterraneans,* *"Cancer! Schmanser!* What's the difference, so long as you're healthy!"

## Introduction to AUTO-DA-FÉ:

It is refreshing to test oneself periodically and find out just how stern is the stuff of which one is composed. Such a test is concluded with this book. The temptation to begin the anthology with A-for-Asimov and end it with Z-for-Zelazny was almost enough to make me twitch with delight. But I have saved the closing spot for "Chip" Delany, for reasons which will be explained in *his* introduction, and moved Roger Zelazny into next-to-closing. The deciding factor was recognition. Delany needs the exposure. Zelazny has ascended to godhood already, and needs no helping hands.

Roger Zelazny is an emaciated, ascetic-looking man of Polish-Irish-Pennsylvania-Dutch origins with a reserved and gentle manner cloaking a sense of humor that might well have been envied by Torquemada. He was born, like the editor of this anthology, in Ohio. In point of fact, very near: Roger comes from Euclid, Ohio. It is a dismal town where once existed an ice cream shop that gave three dips for nine cents, but that was a long time ago. Zelazny's comment on his career prior to becoming a writer goes like this: "Rapidly rose to obscurity in government circles as a claims policy specialist in the Social Security Administration." He attended Western Reserve University and Columbia. God only knows if he won any degrees, and it doesn't matter much. The only writer extant with a more singular approach to the English language is Nabokov. He presently resides in Baltimore with an exceptionally pretty wife named Judy who is far too good for him.

Zelazny, author of such award-winning stories as "He Who Shapes," "A Rose for Ecclesiastes," "And Call Me Conrad" and "The Doors of His Face, the Lamps of His Mouth," has the bad taste to be a glutton for prizes. His novel, *Lord of Light,* will be published soon by Doubleday. At the age of twenty-nine, he has already copped a Hugo and two Nebulas, thus humiliating older, grayer, wiser heads in the field who have worked three times as long, five times as hard, and write one twentieth as well. It is unseemly for one so young.

Which is a strange thing, actually. For there is nothing young about Zelazny's work. His stories are sunk to the knees in maturity and wisdom, in bravura writing that breaks rules most writers only suspect exist. His concepts are fresh, his attacks bold, his resolutions generally trenchant. Thus leading us inexorably to the conclusion that Roger Zelazny is the reincarnation of Geoffrey Chaucer.

Seldom is a writer recognized and lauded so completely in his growth stages (particularly in the sillyass fickle field of science fiction) as Zelazny has been. It is a tribute to his tenacity, his talent and his personal visions of the world that, in any list of the current top writers of speculative fiction, Roger Zelazny's name appears prominently. We can delight in the prospect of many years of fine stories from his typewriter, and as the latest installment, consider the wry comment that follows, a penetrating extrapolation of our "mobile culture."

# • AUTO-DA-FÉ

## by Roger Zelazny

Still do I remember the hot sun upon the sands of the Plaza del Autos, the cries of the soft-drink hawkers, the tiers of humanity stacked across from me on the sunny side of the arena, sunglasses like cavities in their gleaming faces.

Still do I remember the smells and the colors: the reds and the blues and the yellows, the ever present tang of petroleum fumes upon the air.

Still do I remember that day, that day with its sun in the middle of the sky and the sign of Aries, burning in the blooming of the year. I recall the mincing steps of the pumpers, heads thrown back, arms waving, the white dazzles of their teeth framed with smiling lips, cloths like colorful tails protruding from the rear pockets of their coveralls; and the horns—I remember the blare of a thousand horns over the loudspeakers, on and off, off and on, over and over, and again, and then one shimmering, final note, sustained, to break the ear and the heart with its infinite power, its pathos.

Then there was silence.

I see it now as I did on that day so long ago. . . .

He entered the arena, and the cry that went up shook blue heaven upon its pillars of white marble.

"¡Viva! ¡El mechador! ¡Viva! ¡El mechador!"

I remember his face, dark and sad and wise.

Long of jaw and nose was he, and his laughter was as the roaring of the wind, and his movements were as the music of the theramin and the drum. His coveralls were blue and silk and tight and stitched with thread of gold and broidered all about with black braid. His jacket was beaded and there were flashing scales upon his breast, his shoulders, his back.

His lips curled into the smile of a man who has known much glory and has hold upon the power that will bring him into more.

He moved, turning in a circle, not shielding his eyes against the sun.

He was above the sun. He was Manolo Stillete Dos Muertos, the mightiest *mechador* the world had ever seen, black boots upon his feet, pistons in his thighs, fingers with the discretion of micrometers, halo of dark locks about his head and the angel of death in his right arm, there, in the center of the grease-stained circle of truth.

He waved, and a cry went up once more.

"Manolo! Manolo! Dos Muertos! Dos Muertos!"

After two years' absence from the ring, he had chosen this, the anniversary of his death and retirement, to return—for there was gasoline and methyl in his blood and his heart was a burnished pump ringed 'bout with desire and courage. He had died twice within the ring, and twice had the medics restored him. After his second death, he had retired, and some said that it was because he had known fear. This could not be true.

He waved his hand and his name rolled back upon him.

The horns sounded once more: three long blasts.

Then again there was silence, and a pumper wearing red and yellow brought him the cape, removed his jacket.

The tinfoil backing of the cape flashed in the sun as Dos Muertos swirled it.

Then there came the final, beeping notes.

The big door rolled upward and back into the wall.

He draped his cape over his arm and faced the gateway.

The light above was red and from within the darkness there came the sound of an engine.

The light turned yellow, then green, and there was the sound of cautiously engaged gears.

The car moved slowly into the ring, paused, crept forward, paused again.

It was a red Pontiac, its hood stripped away, its engine like a nest of snakes, coiling and engendering behind the circular shimmer of its invisible fan. The wings of its aerial spun round and round, then fixed upon Manolo and his cape.

He had chosen a heavy one for his first, slow on turning, to give him a chance to limber up.

The drums of its brain, which had never before recorded a man, were spinning.

Then the consciousness of its kind swept over it, and it moved forward.

Manolo swirled his cape and kicked its fender as it roared past.

The door of the great garage closed.

When it reached the opposite side of the ring the car stopped, parked.

Cries of disgust, booing and hissing arose from the crowd.

Still the Pontiac remained parked.

Two pumpers, bearing buckets, emerged from behind the fence and threw mud upon its windshield.

It roared then and pursued the nearest, banging into the fence. Then it turned suddenly, sighted Dos Muertos and charged.

His *veronica* transformed him into a statue with a skirt of silver. The enthusiasm of the crowd was mighty.

It turned and charged once more, and I wondered at Manolo's skill, for it would seem that his buttons had scraped cherry paint from the side panels.

Then it paused, spun its wheels, ran in a circle about the ring. The crowd roared as it moved past him and recircled.

Then it stopped again, perhaps fifty feet away.

Manolo turned his back upon it and waved to the crowd.

—Again, the cheering and the calling of his name.

He gestured to someone behind the fence.

A pumper emerged and bore to him, upon a velvet cushion, his chrome-plated monkey wrench.

He turned then again to the Pontiac and strode toward it.

It stood there shivering and he knocked off its radiator cap.

A jet of steaming water shot into the air and the crowd bellowed. Then he struck the front of the radiator and banged upon each fender.

He turned his back upon it again and stood there.

When he heard the engagement of the gears he turned once more, and with one clean pass it was by him, but not before he had banged twice upon the trunk with his wrench.

It moved to the other end of the ring and parked.

Manolo raised his hand to the pumper behind the fence.

The man with the cushion emerged and bore to him the long-handled screwdriver and the short cape. He took the monkey wrench away with him, as well as the long cape.

Another silence came over the Plaza del Autos.

The Pontiac, as if sensing all this, turned once more and blew its horn twice. Then it charged.

There were dark spots upon the sand from where its radiator had leaked water. Its exhaust arose like a ghost behind it. It bore down upon him at a terrible speed.

Dos Muertos raised the cape before him and rested the blade of the screwdriver upon his left forearm.

When it seemed he would surely be run down, his hand shot

forward, so fast the eye could barely follow it, and he stepped to the side as the engine began to cough.

Still the Pontiac continued on with a deadly momentum, turned sharply without braking, rolled over, slid into the fence, and began to burn. Its engine coughed and died.

The Plaza shook with the cheering. They awarded Dos Muertos both headlights and the tailpipe. He held them high and moved in slow promenade about the perimeter of the ring. The horns sounded. A lady threw him a plastic flower and he sent for a pumper to bear her the tailpipe and to ask her to dine with him. The crowd cheered more loudly, for he was known to be a great layer of women, and it was not such an unusual thing in the days of my youth as it is now.

The next was a blue Chevrolet, and he played with it as a child plays with a kitten, tormenting it into striking, then stopping it forever. He received both headlights. The sky had clouded over by then and there was a tentative mumbling of thunder.

The third was a black Jaguar XKE, which calls for the highest skill possible and makes for a very brief moment of truth. There was blood as well as gasoline upon the sand before he dispatched it, for its side mirror extended further than one would think, and there was a red furrow across his rib cage before he had done with it. But he tore out its ignition system with such grace and artistry that the crowd boiled over into the ring, and the guards were called forth to beat them with clubs and herd them with cattle prods back into their seats.

Surely, after all of this, none could say that Dos Muertos had ever known fear.

A cool breeze arose and I bought a soft drink and waited for the last.

His final car sped forth while the light was still yellow. It was a mustard-colored Ford convertible. As it went past him the first time, it blew its horn and turned on its windshield wipers. Everyone cheered, for they could see it had spirit.

Then it came to a dead halt, shifted into reverse, and backed toward him at about forty miles an hour.

He got out of the way, sacrificing grace to expediency, and it braked sharply, shifted into low gear, and sped forward again.

He waved the cape and it was torn from his hands. If he had not thrown himself over backward, he would have been struck.

Then someone cried: "It's out of alignment!"

But he got to his feet, recovered his cape and faced it once more. They still tell of those five passes that followed. Never has there been such a flirting with bumper and grill! Never in all of the Earth has there been such an encounter between *mechador* and machine! The convertible roared like ten centuries of streamlined death, and the spirit of St. Detroit sat in its driver's seat, grinning, while Dos Muertos faced it with his tinfoil cape, cowed it and called for his wrench. It nursed its overheated engine and rolled its windows up and down, up and down, clearing its muffler the while with lavatory noises and much black smoke.

By then it was raining, softly, gently, and the thunder still came about us. I finished my soft drink.

Dos Muertos had never used his monkey wrench on the engine before, only upon the body. But this time he threw it. Some experts say he was aiming at the distributor; others say he was trying to break its fuel pump.

The crowd booed him.

Something gooey was dripping from the Ford onto the sand. The red streak brightened on Manolo's stomach. The rain came down.

He did not look at the crowd. He did not take his eyes from the car. He held out his right hand, palm upward, and waited.

A panting pumper placed the screwdriver in his hand and ran back toward the fence.

Manolo moved to the side and waited.

It leaped at him and he struck.

There was more booing.

He had missed the kill.

No one left, though. The Ford swept around him in a tight circle, smoke now emerging from its engine. Manolo rubbed his arm and picked up the screwdriver and cape he had dropped. There was more booing as he did so.

By the time the car was upon him, flames were leaping forth from its engine.

Now some say that he struck and missed again, going off balance. Others say that he began to strike, grew afraid and drew back. Still others say that, perhaps for an instant, he knew a fatal pity for his spirited adversary, and that this had stayed his hand. I say that the smoke was too thick for any of them to say for certain what had happened.

But it swerved and he fell forward, and he was borne upon that engine, blazing like a god's catafalque, to meet with his third death as they crashed into the fence together and went up in flames.

There was much dispute over the final *corrida,* but what remained of the tailpipe and both headlights were buried with what remained of him, beneath the sands of the Plaza, and there was much weeping among the women he had known. I say that he could not have been afraid or known pity, for his strength was as a river of rockets, his thighs were pistons and the fingers of his hands had the discretion of micrometers; his hair was a black halo and the angel of death rode on his right arm. Such a man, a man who has known truth, is mightier than any machine. Such a man is above anything but the holding of power and the wearing of glory.

Now he is dead though, this one, for the third and final time. He is as dead as all the dead who have ever died before the bumper, under the grill, beneath the wheels. It is well that he cannot rise again, for I say that his final car was his apotheosis, and anything else would be anticlimactic. Once I saw a blade of grass growing up between the metal sheets of the world in a place where they had become loose, and I destroyed it because I felt it must be lonesome. Often have I regretted doing this thing, for I took away the glory of its aloneness. Thus does life the machine, I feel, consider man, sternly, then with regret, and the heavens do weep upon him through eyes that grief has opened in the sky.

All the way home I thought of this thing, and the hoofs of my mount clicked upon the floor of the city as I rode through the rain toward evening, that spring.

## Afterword:

This is the first time I've had a chance to address the readers of one of my stories directly, rather than through the mimesis game we play. While I go along with the notion that a writer should hold a mirror up to reality, I don't necessarily feel that it should be the kind you look into when you shave or tweeze your eyebrows, or both as the case may be. If I'm going to carry a mirror around, holding it up to reality whenever I notice any, I might as well enjoy the burden as much as I can. My means of doing this is to tote around one of those mirrors you used to see in fun houses, back when they still had fun houses. Of course, not anything you reflect looks either as attractive or as grimly visaged as it may stand before the naked eyeball. Sometimes it looks more attractive, or more grimly visaged. You just don't really know, until you've tried the warping glass. And it's awfully hard to hold the slippery thing steady. Blink, and—who knows?—you're two feet tall. Sneeze, and May the Good Lord Smile Upon You. I live in deathly fear of dropping the thing. I don't know what I'd do without it. Carouse more, probably. I love my cold and shiny burden, that's why. And I won't say anything about the preceding story, because if it didn't say everything it was supposed to say all by itself, then that's its own fault and I'm not going to dignify it with any more words. Any error is always attributable to the mirror—either to the way I'm holding it, or to the way you're looking into it—so don't blame me. I just work here. But . . . If anything *does* seem amiss with visions of this sort, keep on looking into the glass and take a couple quick steps backwards. Who knows? Maybe you'll turn into the powder room. . . .

## Introduction to AYE, AND GOMORRAH . . . :

This is the last story in the book. For a very special reason (and not merely because it is the last one to be set in type, smart aleck). It is the end of an adventure and the beginning of a journey. Finis for this anthology and the need to take one last lunge at proving the point the book was intended to prove (in the event, God forbid, all 239,000 words that have gone before have not done the job *more* than adequately); one last firecracker to light the scene. The end. The last one. Maybe a kick in the ass, one to leave them gasping, a knockout.

The beginning of a journey: the career of a new writer. You can be there as the boat sails, to offer the basket of fruit, to throw the confetti, to wave good-by and we've got our eye on you. The big trip into the big world. The trek. But why *this* story, by *this* writer?

Toulouse-Lautrec once said, "One should never meet a man whose work one admires. The man is always so much less than the work." Painfully, almost always this is true. The great novelist turns out to be a whiner. The penetrator of the foibles of man picks his nose in public.

The authority on South Africa has never been beyond Levittown. The writer of swashbuckling adventures is a pathetic little homosexual who still lives with his invalid mother. Oh, Henri the Mad, you were so right. But it is not so with the author of the story I have chosen to close out this attempt at daring.

I have seldom been so impressed with a writer as I was when I first met Samuel R. Delany. To be in the same room with "Chip" Delany is to know you are in the presence of an event about to happen. It isn't his wit, which is considerable, or his intensity, which is like heat lightning, or his erudition, which is whistle-provoking, or his sincerity, which is so real it has shape and substance. It is an indefinable but none-theless commanding impression that this is a young man with great works in him. Thus far, he has written almost nothing but novels, and those for a paperback house praised for its giving newcomers a chance, but damned for the cheapjack look of their presentations. The titles are *The Jewels of Aptor, Captives of the Flame, The Towers of Toron, City of a Thousand Suns, The Ballad of Beta-2, Empire Star* and an incredi-ble little volume called *Babel-17,* which won the 1966 Nebula Award of the Science Fiction Writers of America. Ignore the titles. They are the flushed marketing delusions of editors on whose office walls are tacked reminders to COMPETE! But read the books. They demonstrate a lively, intricate, singular talent in its remarkable growth process. Chip Delany is destined to be one of the truly important writers produced by the field of speculative writing. A kind of writer who will move into other bags and become for the mainstream a Delany-shaped importance like Bradbury or Vonnegut or Sturgeon. The talent is *that* large.

Born April Fool's Day sometime during WWII, Delany grew up in New York's Harlem. Very private, very progressive elementary school education, thence to the Bronx High School of Science, sporadic attend-ance at City College with a term as poetry editor of the *Promethean.* He wrote his first science fiction novel at nineteen. He has worked, in the chinks between novels, as a bookstore clerk, laborer on shrimp boats off the Texas Gulf, folk singer in Greece, and has shuttled be-tween New York City and Istanbul. He is married. He currently resides on the Lower East Side of NYC and is at work on a *huge* science fic-tion novel, *Nova,* which will be published next year by Doubleday. Damned little to know about someone who writes as big as Delany does. But it's all he seems to want to say.

However, his fiction speaks more than eloquently. His novels ap-proach timeworn and shopworn clichés of speculative fiction with a bold and compelling ingenuity. He brings freshness to a field that occasionally slumps into the line of least resistance. This freshness is eminently in evidence in the story you are about to read, in its way one of the best of the thirty-three winners here. It certainly classifies as a "dangerous" vision, and one which both Chip and I felt would have been difficult to market to the established periodicals. Though you may have seen a short story or novelette in print before you see the story that follows, be advised this was Chip Delany's *first* short story. He did nothing but novels before consenting to write a piece for this book. It ranks, for me, as one of the truly memorable solo flights in the history of the genre.

# ● AYE, AND GOMORRAH . . .

## by Samuel R. Delany

And came down in Paris:

Where we raced along the Rue de Médicis with Bo and Lou and Muse inside the fence, Kelly and me outside, making faces through the bars, making noise, making the Luxembourg Gardens roar at two in the morning. Then climbed out, and down to the square in front of St. Sulpice where Bo tried to knock me into the fountain.

At which point Kelly noticed what was going on around us, got an ashcan cover, and ran into the pissoir, banging the walls. Five guys scooted out; even a big pissoir only holds four.

A very blond young man put his hand on my arm and smiled. "Don't you think, Spacer, that you . . . people should leave?"

I looked at his hand on my blue uniform. *"Est-ce que tu es un frelk?"*

His eyebrows rose, then he shook his head. "Une *frelk*," he corrected. "No. I am not. Sadly for me. You look as though you may once have been a man. But now . . ." He smiled. "You have nothing for me now. The police." He nodded across the street where I noticed the gendarmerie for the first time. "They don't bother us. You are strangers, though . . ."

But Muse was already yelling, "Hey, come on! Let's get out of here, huh?" And left. And went up again.

And came down in Houston:

"God damn!" Muse said. "Gemini Flight Control—you mean this is where it all started? Let's get *out* of here, *please!*"

So took a bus out through Pasadena, then the monoline to Galveston, and were going to take it down the Gulf, but Lou found a couple with a pickup truck—

"Glad to give you a ride, Spacers. You people up there on them planets and things, doing all that good work for the government."

—who were going south, them and the baby, so we rode in the back for two hundred and fifty miles of sun and wind.

"You think they're frelks?" Lou asked, elbowing me. "I bet they're frelks. They're just waiting for us give 'em the come-on."

"Cut it out. They're a nice, stupid pair of country kids."

"That don't mean they ain't frelks!"

"You don't trust anybody, do you?"

"No."

And finally a bus again that rattled us through Brownsville and across the border into Matamoros where we staggered down the steps into the dust and the scorched evening with a lot of Mexicans and chickens and Texas Gulf shrimp fishermen—who smelled worst— and *we* shouted the loudest. Forty-three whores—I counted—had turned out for the shrimp fishermen, and by the time we had broken two of the windows in the bus station they were all laughing. The shrimp fishermen said they wouldn't buy us no food but would get us drunk if we wanted, 'cause that was the custom with shrimp fishermen. But we yelled, broke another window; then, while I was lying on my back on the telegraph office steps, singing, a woman with dark lips bent over and put her hands on my cheeks. "You are very sweet." Her rough hair fell forward. "But the men, they are standing around and watching *you*. And that is taking up *time*. Sadly, their time is our money. Spacer, do you not think you . . . people should leave?"

I grabbed her wrist. "*¡Usted!*" I whispered. "*¿Usted es una frelka?*"

"*Frelko in español.*" She smiled and patted the sunburst that hung from my belt buckle. "Sorry. But you have nothing that . . . would be useful to me. It is too bad, for you look like you were once a woman, no? And I like women, too. . . ."

I rolled off the porch.

"Is this a drag, or is this a drag!" Muse was shouting. "Come on! Let's go!"

We managed to get back to Houston before dawn, somehow. And went up.

And came down in Istanbul:

That morning it rained in Istanbul.

At the commissary we drank our tea from pear-shaped glasses, looking out across the Bosphorus. The Princes Islands lay like trash heaps before the prickly city.

"Who knows their way in this town?" Kelly asked.

"Aren't we going around together?" Muse demanded. "I thought we were going around together."

"They held up my check at the purser's office," Kelly explained. "I'm flat broke. I think the purser's got it in for me," and shrugged. "Don't want to, but I'm going to have to hunt up a rich frelk and come on friendly," went back to the tea; *then* noticed how heavy the silence had become. "Aw, come *on,* now! You gape at me like that and I'll bust every bone in that carefully-conditioned-from-puberty body of yours. Hey you!" meaning me. "Don't give me that holier-than-thou gawk like you never went with no frelk!"

It was starting.

"I'm not gawking," I said and got quietly mad.

The longing, the old longing.

Bo laughed to break tensions. "Say, last time I was in Istanbul—about a year before I joined up with this platoon—I remember we were coming out of Taksim Square down Istiqlal. Just past all the cheap movies we found a little passage lined with flowers. Ahead of us were two other spacers. It's a market in there, and farther down they got fish, and then a courtyard with oranges and candy and sea urchins and cabbage. But flowers in front. Anyway, we noticed something funny about the spacers. It wasn't their uniforms: they were perfect. The haircuts: fine. It wasn't till we heard them talking—They were a man and woman dressed up like spacers, trying *to pick up frelks!* Imagine, queer for frelks!"

"Yeah," Lou said. "I seen that before. There were a lot of them in Rio."

"We beat hell out of them two," Bo concluded. "We got them in a side street and went to *town!*"

Muse's tea glass clicked on the counter. "From Taksim down Istiqlal till you get to the flowers? Now why didn't you say that's where the frelks were, huh?" A smile on Kelly's face would have made that okay. There was no smile.

"Hell," Lou said, "nobody ever had to tell me where to look. I go out in the street and frelks smell me coming. I can spot 'em halfway along Piccadilly. Don't they have nothing but tea in this place? Where can you get a drink?"

Bo grinned. "Moslem country, remember? But down at the end of the Flower Passage there're a lot of little bars with green doors and marble counters where you can get a liter of beer for about fifteen cents in lira. And there're all these stands selling deep-fat-fried bugs and pig's gut sandwiches—"

"You ever notice how frelks can put it away? I mean liquor, not . . . pig's guts."

And launched off into a lot of appeasing stories. We ended with the one about the frelk some spacer tried to roll who announced: "There are two things I go for. One is spacers; the other is a good fight. . . ."

But they only allay. They cure nothing. Even Muse knew we would spend the day apart, now.

The rain had stopped, so we took the ferry up the Golden Horn. Kelly straight off asked for Taksim Square and Istiqlal and was directed to a dolmush, which we discovered was a taxicab, only it just goes one place and picks up lots and lots of people on the way. And it's cheap.

Lou headed off over Ataturk Bridge to see the sights of New City. Bo decided to find out what the Dolma Boche really was; and when Muse discovered you could go to Asia for fifteen cents—one lira and fifty krush—well, Muse decided to go to Asia.

I turned through the confusion of traffic at the head of the bridge and up past the gray, dripping walls of Old City, beneath the trolley wires. There are times when yelling and helling won't fill the lack. There are times when you must walk by yourself because it hurts so much to be alone.

I walked up a lot of little streets with wet donkeys and wet camels and women in veils; and down a lot of big streets with buses and trash baskets and men in business suits.

Some people stare at spacers; some people don't. Some people stare or don't stare in a way a spacer gets to recognize within a week after coming out of training school at sixteen. I was walking in the park when I caught her watching. She saw me see and looked away.

I ambled down the wet asphalt. She was standing under the arch of a small, empty mosque shell. As I passed she walked out into the courtyard among the cannons.

"Excuse me."

I stopped.

"Do you know whether or not this is the shrine of St. Irene?" Her English was charmingly accented. "I've left my guidebook home."

"Sorry. I'm a tourist too."

"Oh." She smiled. "I am Greek. I thought you might be Turkish because you are so dark."

"American red Indian." I nodded. Her turn to curtsy.

"I see. I have just started at the university here in Istanbul. Your uniform, it tells me that you are"—and in the pause, all speculations resolved—"a spacer."

I was uncomfortable. "Yeah." I put my hands in my pockets, moved my feet around on the soles of my boots, licked my third from the rear left molar—did all the things you do when you're uncomfortable. *You're so* exciting *when you look like that,* a frelk told me once. "Yeah, I am." I said it too sharply, too loudly, and she jumped a little.

So now she knew I knew she knew I knew, and I wondered how we would play out the Proust bit.

"I'm Turkish," she said. "I'm not Greek. I'm not just starting. I'm a graduate in art history here at the university. These little lies one makes for strangers to protect one's ego . . . why? Sometimes I think my ego is very small."

That's one strategy.

"How far away do you live?" I asked. "And what's the going rate in Turkish lira?" That's another.

"I can't pay you." She pulled her raincoat around her hips. She was very pretty. "I would like to." She shrugged and smiled. "But I am . . . a poor student. Not a rich one. If you want to turn around and walk away, there will be no hard feelings. I shall be sad though."

I stayed on the path. I thought she'd suggest a price after a little while. She didn't.

And *that's* another.

I was asking myself, *What do you want the damn money for anyway?* when a breeze upset water from one of the park's great cypresses.

"I think the whole business is sad." She wiped drops from her face. There had been a break in her voice and for a moment I looked too closely at the water streaks. "I think it's sad that they have to alter you to make you a spacer. If they hadn't, then *we*. . . . If spacers had never been, then we could not be . . . the way we are. Did you start out male or female?"

Another shower. I was looking at the ground and droplets went down my collar.

"Male," I said. "It doesn't matter."

"How old are you? Twenty-three, twenty-four?"

"Twenty-three," I lied. It's reflex. I'm twenty-five, but the younger they think you are, the more they pay you. But I didn't *want* her *damn* money—

"I guessed right then." She nodded. "Most of us are experts on spacers. Do you find that? I suppose we have to be." She looked at me with wide black eyes. At the end of the stare, she blinked rapidly. "You would have been a fine man. But now you are a spacer, building water-conservation units on Mars, programing mining computers on Ganymede, servicing communication relay towers on the moon. The alteration . . ." Frelks are the only people I've ever heard say "the alteration" with so much fascination and regret. "You'd think they'd have found some other solution. They could have found another way than neutering you, turning you into creatures not even androgynous; things that are—"

I put my hand on her shoulder, and she stopped like I'd hit her. She looked to see if anyone was near. Lightly, so lightly then, she raised her hand to mine.

I pulled my hand away. "That are what?"

"They could have found another way." Both hands in her pockets now.

"They could have. Yes. Up beyond the ionosphere, baby, there's too much radiation for those precious gonads to work right anywhere you might want to do something that would keep you there over twenty-four hours, like the moon, or Mars, or the satellites of Jupiter—"

"They could have made protective shields. They could have done more research into biological adjustment—"

"Population Explosion time," I said. "No, they were hunting for any excuse to cut down kids back then—especially deformed ones."

"Ah yes." She nodded. "We're still fighting our way up from the neo-puritan reaction to the sex freedom of the twentieth century."

"It was a fine solution." I grinned and grabbed my crotch. "I'm happy with it." I've never known why that's so much more obscene when a spacer does it.

"Stop it," she snapped, moving away.

"What's the matter?"

"Stop it," she repeated. "Don't do that! You're a child."

"But they choose us from children whose sexual responses are hopelessly retarded at puberty."

"And your childish, violent substitutes for love? I suppose that's one of the things that's attractive. Yes, I know you're a child."

"Yeah? What about frelks?"

She thought awhile. "I think they are the sexually retarded ones they miss. Perhaps it was the right solution. You really don't regret you have no sex?"

"We've got you," I said.

"Yes." She looked down. I glanced to see the expression she was hiding. It was a smile. "You have your glorious, soaring life, *and* you have us." Her face came up. She glowed. "You spin in the sky, the world spins under you, and you step from land to land, while we . . ." She turned her head right, left, and her black hair curled and uncurled on the shoulder of her coat. "We have our dull, circled lives, bound in gravity, *worshiping* you!"

She looked back at me. "Perverted, yes? In love with a bunch of corpses in free fall!" She suddenly hunched her shoulders. "I don't like having a free-fall-sexual-displacement complex."

"That always sounded like too much to say."

She looked away. "I don't like being a frelk. Better?"

"I wouldn't like it either. Be something else."

"You don't choose your perversions. *You* have no perversions at all. *You*'re free of the whole business. I love you for that, spacer. My love starts with the fear of love. Isn't that beautiful? A pervert substitutes something unattainable for 'normal' love: the homosexual, a mirror, the fetishist, a shoe or a watch or a girdle. Those with free-fall-sexual-dis—"

"Frelks."

"Frelks substitute"—she looked at me sharply again—"loose, swinging meat."

"That doesn't offend me."

"I wanted it to."

"Why?"

"You don't have desires. You wouldn't understand."

"Go on."

"I want you because you can't want me. That's the pleasure. If someone really had a sexual reaction to . . . us, we'd be scared away. I wonder how many people there were before there were you, waiting for your creation. We're necrophiles. I'm sure grave robbing has fallen off since you started going up. But you don't understand. . . ." She paused. "If you did, then I wouldn't be scuffing leaves now and trying to think from whom I could borrow sixty lira." She stepped over the knuckles of a root that had cracked the pavement. "And that, incidentally, is the going rate in Istanbul."

I calculated. "Things still get cheaper as you go east."

"You know," and she let her raincoat fall open, "you're different from the others. You at least *want* to know—"

I said, "If I spat on you for every time you'd said that to a spacer, you'd drown."

"Go back to the moon, loose meat." She closed her eyes. "Swing on up to Mars. There are satellites around Jupiter where you might do some good. Go up and come down in some other city."

"Where do you live?"

"You want to come with me?"

"Give me something," I said. "Give me something—it doesn't have to be worth sixty lira. Give me something that you like, anything of yours that means something to you."

"No!"

"Why not?"

"Because I—"

"—don't want to give up part of that ego. None of you frelks do!"

"You really don't understand I just don't want to buy you?"

"You have nothing to buy me with."

"You are a child," she said. "I love you."

We reached the gate of the park. She stopped, and we stood time enough for a breeze to rise and die in the grass. "I . . ." she offered tentatively, pointing without taking her hand from her coat pocket. "I live right down there."

"All right," I said. "Let's go."


A gas main had once exploded along this street, she explained to me, a gushing road of fire as far as the docks, overhot and over-quick. It had been put out within minutes, no building had fallen, but the charred facias glittered. "This is sort of an artist and student quarter." We crossed the cobbles. "Yuri Pasha, number fourteen. In case you're ever in Istanbul again." Her door was covered with black scales, the gutter was thick with garbage.

"A lot of artists and professional people are frelks," I said, trying to be inane.

"So are lots of other people." She walked inside and held the door. "We're just more flamboyant about it."

On the landing there was a portrait of Ataturk. Her room was on the second floor. "Just a moment while I get my key—"

Marsscapes! Moonscapes! On her easel was a six-foot canvas showing the sunrise flaring on a crater's rim! There were copies of the original Observer pictures of the moon pinned to the wall, and pictures of every smooth-faced general in the International Spacer Corps.

On one corner of her desk was a pile of those photo magazines about spacers that you can find in most kiosks all over the world: I've seriously heard people say they were printed for adventurous-minded high school children. They've never seen the Danish ones. She had a few of those too. There was a shelf of art books, art history texts. Above them were six feet of cheap paper-covered space operas: *Sin on Space Station #12, Rocket Rake, Savage Orbit*.

"Arrack?" she asked. "Ouzo or pernod? You've got your choice. But I may pour them all from the same bottle." She set out glasses on the desk, then opened a waist-high cabinet that turned out to be an icebox. She stood up with a tray of lovelies: fruit puddings, Turkish delight, braised meats.

"What's this?"

"Dolmades. Grape leaves filled with rice and pignolias."

"Say it again?"

"Dolmades. Comes from the same Turkish word as 'dolmush.' They both mean 'stuffed.'" She put the tray beside the glasses. "Sit down."

I sat on the studio-couch-that-becomes-bed. Under the brocade I felt the deep, fluid resilience of a glycogel mattress. They've got the idea that it approximates the feeling of free fall. "Comfortable? Would you excuse me for a moment? I have some friends down the hall. I want to see them for a moment." She winked. "They like spacers."

"Are you going to take up a collection for me?" I asked. "Or do you want them to line up outside the door and wait their turn?"

She sucked a breath. "Actually I was going to suggest both." Suddenly she shook her head. "Oh, what do you want!"

"What will you give me? I want something," I said. "That's why I came. I'm lonely. Maybe I want to find out how far it goes. I don't know yet."

"It goes as far as you will. Me? I study, I read, paint, talk with my friends"—she came over to the bed, sat down on the floor— "go to the theater, look at spacers who pass me on the street, till one looks back; I am lonely too." She put her head on my knee. "I want something. But," and after a minute neither of us had moved, "you are not the one who will give it to me."

"You're not going to pay me for it," I countered. "You're not, are you?"

On my knee her head shook. After a while she said, all breath and no voice, "Don't you think you . . . should leave?"

"Okay," I said, and stood up.

She sat back on the hem of her coat. She hadn't taken it off yet. I went to the door.

"Incidentally." She folded her hands in her lap. "There is a place in New City you might find what you're looking for, called the Flower Passage—"

I turned toward her, angry. "The frelk hangout? Look, I don't *need* money! I said *any*thing would do! I don't want—"

She had begun to shake her head, laughing quietly. Now she lay her cheek on the wrinkled place where I had sat. "Do you persist in misunderstanding? It is a spacer hangout. When you leave, I am going to visit my friends and talk about . . . ah, yes, the beautiful one that got away. I thought you might find . . . perhaps someone you know."

With anger, it ended.

"Oh," I said. "Oh, it's a spacer hangout. Yeah. Well, thanks."

And went out. And found the Flower Passage, and Kelly and Lou and Bo and Muse. Kelly was buying beer so we all got drunk, and ate fried fish and fried clams and fried sausage, and Kelly was waving the money around, saying, "You should have seen him! The changes I put that frelk through, you should have *seen* him! Eighty lira is the going rate here, and he gave me a hundred and fifty!" and drank more beer. And went up.

## Afterword:

What goes into an s-f story—this s-f story?

One high old month in Paris, a summer of shrimp fishing on the Texas Gulf, another month spent broke in Istanbul. In still another city I overheard two women at a cocktail party discussing the latest astronaut:

". . . so antiseptic, so inhuman, almost asexual!"

"Oh no! He's perfectly gorgeous!"

Why put all this in an s-f story? I sincerely feel the medium is the best in which to integrate clearly the disparate and technical with the desperate and human.

Someone asked of this particular story, "But what can they *do* with one another?"

At the risk of pulling my punch, let me say that this is basically a horror story. There is nothing they can do. Except go up and down.